THE MODERN LIBRARY
of the World's Best Books

<<<<<<<<<<<<<<<<<<<<<<<<<<<<<<<<<<<<<<<<<

THE COMPLETE WORKS

OF RABELAIS

THE FIVE BOOKS OF

GARGANTUA AND PANTAGRUEL

The publishers will be pleased to send, upon request, an illustrated folder setting forth the purpose and scope of THE MODERN LIBRARY, *and listing each volume in the series. Every reader of books will find titles he has been looking for, handsomely printed, in unabridged editions, and at an unusually low price.*

THE COMPLETE WORKS OF
RABELAIS

THE FIVE BOOKS
OF
Gargantua and Pantagruel
IN THE MODERN TRANSLATION
OF
Jacques Le Clercq

THE MODERN LIBRARY
NEW YORK

The translation used in this edition was made by Jacques Le Clercq for The Limited Editions Club in 1936; it is copyright by The Limited Editions Club, from whom permission has been obtained for its use in this edition.

First Modern Library Giant Edition
1944

THE MODERN LIBRARY

IS PUBLISHED BY

RANDOM HOUSE, INC.

BENNETT A. CERF · DONALD S. KLOPFER · ROBERT K. HAAS

Manufactured in the United States of America

CONTENTS

v

THE *third* BOOK

THE *fifth* BOOK

INTRODUCTION

As if to illustrate the French proverb which tells us that people lend to the rich only, a vast legend has gathered about the figure of François Rabelais.

A legend, in the first place, anecdotal. There is the tale of Gargantua's creator, penniless in Lyons, having himself transported gratuitously to Paris by pretending to have plotted to poison the king. "Le quart d'heure de Rabelais" has passed into the language to designate the moment of paying one's score, or, by extension, any difficult situation. There are hosts of unsupported traditions concerning his youth in Touraine or his student days at Poitiers and at Montpellier. One, for instance, makes Rabelais inaugurate a custom by which newly graduated doctors had to run the gantlet under the thumps and thwacks of their fellows. There is, finally, the death-bed scene, which has him declaring: "Curtain! The farce is finished. I am setting out to seek a vast perhaps!"

A legend, in the second place, polemical. The times of the Renaissance were troublous, politically: international warfare, civil dissension, religious persecution were rife. The year Rabelais published the Third Book of *Gargantua and Pantagruel* (1546), his friend Etienne Dolet, one of the great humanists of the age, was hanged and burned for having published a dialogue, attributed to Plato, which denied the immortality of the human soul. The very year Rabelais died (1553) Calvin burned Servetus, at a Genevese stake, for heresy. As humanist and as satirist, Rabelais fell inevitably between the twin stools of extreme Roman Catholicism and extreme Genevan Protestantism; he attracted the harsh calumny of both bigotry and cant. Thanks to his common sense, he saved his neck (if not his reputation) at the hands of either religious party. Too readily, his works proved a deadly weapon to turn against him; too easy it was, certainly, to identify him with any or all his characters. Thus dour Calvin started the ball rolling, with a written admonition to beware of the rash impiety of certain writers, amongst whom he cited Rabelais by name. These writers were, he declared, "curs who assume the attitudes of comedy in order to enjoy greater freedom to vomit their blasphemies. They revel in banquets and they haunt libertine company where, speaking at pleasure, they leave no stone unturned in destroying all fear of God in the minds of their hearers." Calvin, the Protestant, had personal grounds for hostility; at the other limit of religious creed stood Scaliger, the Catholic, with like individual animus. But even the suave and forceful St. François de Sales, in no wise personally concerned, warned the Roman Catholic flock against "evil books like those of the infamous Rabelais." And but a few years after Rabelais' death, the bibacity of his characters had become so firmly fastened to their author's personality, that the gentle Ronsard, not necessarily in malicious vein, could exclaim:

> *If, from a rotted corpse at rest,*
> *Nature can breed and manifest*
> *New life; if generations can*
> *Rise from corrupted thing or man,*
> *Surely, some vine will grow from out*
> *The paunch and belly of our stout*
> *Friend Rabelais, who never tried*
> *To curb his drinking ere he died.*

In the third instance, the legend founded about the person of Rabelais is inferential, and based upon textual argument. Across the centuries, not a few critics, spurred on by increasing historical knowledge, by increasing research concerning Rabelais himself, and by increasing inclination to read into him what they would wish to find, have vitiated his original intent, the scope of his work and his ultimate performance. Ingeniously, they have built a highly intricate case; ingenuously they have accepted it, where, at mere face value, the intuitions of common sense provided explanation aplenty. Rabelais is broad, all-inclusive; he is the perfect expression of that curiosity, that aspiration and that zest of life we call the Renaissance. His faults themselves prove it. To make of such multitudinous and multifarious energy something exclusively zealot, exclusively satirical, exclusively literary, exclusively pedagogical, or exclusively anything else, is to write oneself down exclusively an ass. "Do I contradict myself?" Walt Whitman inquired of himself. "Very well, then," he answered himself, "I contain multitudes." The miracle of Rabelais is that he handles history, drama, sculpture, architecture, painting, physics, mathematics, chemistry, medicine, astronomy, religion, music, aeronautics, navigation, and God knows what else! Yet —placed in his time, between the relative darkness of the Middle Ages and the relative clarity of French classicism—he is invariably, serenely, ineluctably right, rational, non-contradictory. What saved him is what saved his neck in that age of ferment: those elements he drew from his sound peasant stock, from his love of knowledge, and from his professional experience.

Rabelais was a monk by convenience, a doctor of medicine by instinct and choice, an editor by disinterested zeal, and, finally, a writer, because the medium of literature alone allowed him to express his infinite exuberance.

II

The facts known about Rabelais' life are few indeed: much of the data concerning his early years is putative, and there are wide gaps in his career. Even the date and place of his birth are guesswork. It is supposed that he was born at Chinon, or, hard by, at La Devinière, in the province of Touraine, at some period between 1483 and 1495. The earlier date would seem to make him too old, the later is generally accepted. At all events, he was born within a decade of such revolutionary facts as the discovery of the New World and the establishment of printing presses. Among his close contemporaries were Martin Luther and Ignatius Loyola; while he was yet a child, Louis XI succeeded to the French throne, Henry VII to the English.

Tradition gives us various information, unsupported by documents: his father was an innkeeper or an apothecary of Chinon, with a country house at La Devinière; he had three brothers; he was educated at the Abbey of Seuilly, and later, possibly at the University of Angers, possibly at the convent of La Baumette, near at hand. It is believed he may here have had for schoolfellows the brothers du Bellay and Geoffroi d'Estissac, Bishop of Maillezais, all of whom befriended him later and whom he mentions in his immortal work.

The first record of Rabelais that we possess is his signature on a deed of purchase made by the monks of the Franciscan monastery of

Fontenay-le-Comte. The Franciscan order was notoriously vulgar and unlearned, as compared with the Benedictine; yet it is to be supposed that Rabelais was nevertheless eagerly pursuing his studies. His signature on a document of importance to the religious community would seem to indicate that in 1519 he was of some significance in the abbey, and therefore had taken orders at least five years earlier.

Next, we find him and his fellow-monk and fellow-humanist, Pierre Amy (mentioned in Book III, Chapter X), corresponding with Guillaume Budé, secretary to King François I, and one of the greatest scholars in Europe. At Fontenay, too, Rabelais and Amy frequented a group of jurisconsults and scholars gathered about André Tiraqueau. In the dedicatory epistle to a text Rabelais edited, he describes Tiraqueau as "most learned" and as "the most equitable judge in Poitou"; and he goes out of his way to pay Tiraqueau tribute in the Prologue of Book IV. Tiraqueau was a great anti-feminist; Man vs. Woman was a tradition of medieval debate, sporting or serious; Tiraqueau translated a Latin tract on connubial expediency, dedicating the work to his father-in-law, and, doubtless, the intention, to his wife—a fact interesting in relation to Panurge's quest, which fills three-fifths of Rabelais' masterpiece. He is mentioned also in Book II, Chapter V.

In 1524, through the influence of his friend Geoffroi d'Estissac, Bishop of Maillezais, Rabelais obtained, from the Pope, the somewhat rare permission to transfer from the Franciscan order and Fontenay to the Benedictine and Maillezais, a welcome change affording him the advantages of Benedictine tolerance and scholarship, as well as the bishop's protection. Here he remained some five years.

Before 1530, he left; and he cast off regular for secular garb, a fact proved by his subsequent petition in 1535, to Pope Clement, in which he craved the regularization of his anomalous situation. Possibly during these years he studied at various universities, much as Pantagruel, in his grand tour in Book II. By record, he was at the faculty of medicine at Montpellier in September, 1530; and he graduated bachelor in November, two dates which would support the theory of previous medical studies elsewhere. In the course of that year, as all bachelors, he was required to deliver public lectures; he discoursed upon Galen and Hippocrates. And perhaps he played in the farce of *The Man Who Married a Dumb Wife*, cited in Book III, Chapter XXXIV.

By 1532, Rabelais was in Lyons, then the intellectual capital of France, a populous commercial city, the hyphen between Italy and Europe, the semicolon between Renaissance and Reformation, the lazy colon between a married Luther and a married Pope. With characteristic fougue, Rabelais published several works of medical and scholarly vulgarization, including items by Galen and Hippocrates; produced his first creative work (Book II of the five books of *Gargantua and Pantagruel*) and got himself appointed physician at the Hôtel-Dieu. He also probably produced a son, for there is reference to the death of an infant Théodule, born in Lyons, to François Rabelais.

The next two years—1533 and 1534—proved eventful: The Faculty of Theology of the University of Paris censored *Pantagruel*; Rabelais accompanied Jean du Bellay to Rome as physician-in-ordinary; his father died; he followed du Bellay, now a cardinal, on a second mission Romeward, and offered a petition to the Pope, excusing his assumption of secular garb and removal from Fontenay five years previously (1530). A papal bull, in answer to the petition, permitted him to reënter the Benedictine order (here was security!), and to practise medicine (here were knowledge, action and humanity!). This dispensation, too, enabled him to assume ecclesiastical office and he became canon of St. Maur.

By now, absent from Lyons twice without leave, Rabelais was replaced as physician at the Hôtel-Dieu. In 1537 he proceeded to the degrees of licentiate and doctor of medicine at the University of Montpellier. In 1540, he joined Guillaume du Bellay, now Governor of Piedmont; and, on the voyage homeward, over the Mont Cenis, du Bellay died, in 1543 (cf. Book IV, Chapter XXVII).

The year 1546 marked the publication of Book III, its immediate condemnation by the Sorbonne and a sojourn of Rabelais at Metz. Two years later (1548) the first eleven chapters of the Fourth Book were printed in Lyons; copyright, then a rare privilege, was granted Rabelais by Henri II in 1550, and, in 1552, the complete Fourth Book appeared in Paris, to be immediately proscribed by Parliament at the request of the Faculty of Theology. The following year, Rabelais resigned the curacies of St. Martin de Meudon and St. Christophe de Jambet, which he had received, in 1551, from the du Bellay family. He died three months after.

But the last word was not spoken. After an interval of nine years, there appeared, in 1562, sixteen chapters of what is now Book v, under the title of *Ringing Island by Master François Rabelais*. Two years later, the complete Fifth Book was brought out in Paris, and, in 1567, republished with the other four. Its authenticity has frequently been challenged; there is a burden of evidence either way. It is not unlikely that some portions of it, at least, were edited from notes, or possibly from a first draft, left by Rabelais.

III

Born into that age which, of all ages, possessed the most passionate love of life and knowledge, Rabelais believed intensely in the cultivation of nature, and its enjoyment through every sense and faculty. He is a thoroughgoing realist, interested in life as it is; this realism, moreover, holds the key to his own existence, to his philosophy and to his writings.

To his existence, because, eminently French, he never failed to face facts: this irrepressibly gay, level-headed son of peasants could experience the unnatural rigors of monkhood for over a decade without ever losing his correct judgment and his zest for pleasure. Rabelais at no time abjured the Roman Catholic faith. As hostile to the medieval bigotry of extreme papacy as he was to the new fanaticism of Calvinist cant, he steered, almost miraculously, the middle course of reason.

To his philosophy, because it was concerned solely with actualities, and because it indicated always a reasonable resolution of the problem of life. Rabelais was, after all, no profound thinker, however wide his scholarship; indeed, his ideas are primitive, fundamental and eternal in their simplicity.

To his writings, because those five books, far from being a single work, reflected three decades of constantly changing endeavor in the world, over four centuries ago, yet to-day possess a freshness, a power and an immediacy that are dynamic.

What is the secret of Pantagruelism? It is the theory of life held by your man of the Renaissance: live fully, richly, follow your instincts, find the utmost satisfaction for the body in the pleasures at hand, acquire the utmost delight for the mind in the joys of intellectual curiosity and study. "Do as thou wilt" was the only rule in the house of Thélème; and Rabelais was too confident in the unerring *rightness* of instinct to fancy there lay the slightest danger in doing as one willed. Instinct, with him, thus became a principle of human morality, a principle of human sociability, a principle of science and art. Nature was good; excessive discipline, not to mention the mortifying asceticism of medieval monasticism, was utterly rotten. For the Middle Ages had taught contempt for the body: flagellation of corrupt flesh, and a scholasticism to justify it to the incurious, acquiescent mind. Into this dreary miasma, Rabelais tossed the bombshell of Thélème. He preached the full and free development of every faculty, the rehabilitation of the body, the love of forms; his work was a panegyric of nature, a hymn to life. Is morality menaced? No, he replies in Book I, Chapter LVII, because "men that are free, of gentle birth, well bred and at home in civilized company, possess a natural instinct that inclines them to virtue and saves them from vice. This instinct they name their honor." Was truer, nobler tribute to humanity ever penned?

"What Rabelais has the power of communicating to us," says John Cowper Powys in *Visions and Revisions*, "is the renewal of that physiological energy which alone makes it possible to enjoy this monstrous world . . . Rabelais is the sanest of all the great writers, perhaps the only sane one."

Rabelais believed in God the Creator; he believed, with Christ, in a future life which would repay us for the injustice of our present life. This scoffer, this observer to whom satire was as breath to his nostrils, was capable on occasion of deep, reasonable, realistic piety. The admonitions of Gargantua to Pantagruel (Book II, Chapter VIII): ". . . serve, love and fear God, on Him pin all your thoughts and hopes; by faith, built of charity, cling to Him so closely that never a sin can come between you," might have come from any pulpit in Paris, had the pulpits in Paris cultivated common sense at the time. The conclusion to the chapter on the education given Gargantua by Ponocrates (Book I, Chapter XXIII): "Then they prayed to God the Creator, doing Him worship and confirming their faith in Him, glorifying Him for His immense goodness, vouchsafing thanks for all the mighty past and imploring His divine clemency for all the future," might have been lifted straight out of a religious tract. And, finally, that passage where Pantagruel relates his pitiful tale of the death of heroes, and interprets the death of Pan as that of Christ (Book IV, Chapter XXVIII): " 'For my part,' Pantagruel observed, 'I consider the Pan in question to have been the mighty Saviour of the faithful, who was shamefully put to death in Judæa by the envy and iniquity of the doctors, pontiffs, priests and monks of the Mosaic law. . . . All that we are, all that we live, all that we hope is Himself, in Him, from Him and by Him.' . . . Shortly after, we noticed tears dropping from his eyes, tears fat as ostrich eggs. . . ."

IV

The man, then, was religious in the high sense of the term. But, since he believed in instinct and since "laughter is the essence of mankind," he abandoned himself prodigiously to it, and, mirthfully engaged in a satire which can be qualified only by applying to it a word coined from his own gigantic character, Gargantua. This satire was, ever reasonably, ever realistically, directed against anything that could offend or hinder Rabelais' philosophic conception of liberty. How he assaults your hypocrites (Book II, Chapter XXXIV)! How repeatedly and relentlessly he attacks monasticism! What a ridiculous thing he can make of personal ambition, of militarism and its minions, in the whole episode of the Picrocholine War (Book I, Chapters XXVI-XLIX)! How he reduces to the absurd the abuses of justice in the persons of Bridlegoose, the dicing magistrate (Book III, Chapters XXXIX-XLIII), of the Catchpoles (Book IV, Chapters XII-XVI), and of the even more rapacious Furry Lawcats, with their Archduke Graspall (Book V, Chapters XI-XV)! What a tireless fight against pedantry, be it religious, like the *Decretals* (Book IV, Chapters XLIX-LIV), or academic, like the debate between Thaumastes and Panurge (Book II, Chapters XVIII-XX), or like the catalogue of the library of St. Victor (Book II, Chapter VII) or, especially, like the meeting with a Limousin who spoke spurious French (Book II, Chapter VI). And even assuming Book V to be bogus (which is probably not the case) how Rabelais flays superstition within and without the Mother Church! O laughter, universal, purgative, indestructible, immense!

It is part of Rabelais' infinite genius for reality that almost every single abuse or comicality would prove admirable grist for his mill.

And the secret of his humor? It lies, first, in his making his characters hugely grotesque: from the very first page, the superhuman stature of these good giants will prove rich comic material. Secondly, titanic as they are, able to eat six pilgrims in a salad (Book I, Chapter XXXVIII) or to flood Paris diuretically (Book I, Chapter XVII), God be praised! they rarely accomplish world-moving feats! To be sure, in the First Book, Gargantua wins the Picrocholine War; in the Second, Pantagruel, the Dipsodian. But the other books are no more than a long, gay conversation, in the course of which Rabelais frequently forgets that Pantagruel is really a giant. Thirdly, Rabelais' humor proceeds from his style; it is verbal, consisting in the practical application of a metaphorical expression. Thus Gargantua carries off the bells of Notre Dame (Book I, Chapter XVII), Panurge has a flea in his ear (Book III, Chapter VII); thus, too, the labors of the Royal Abstractors (Book V, Chapter XXII). In the fourth place, Rabelais' humor lies in parody. *Gargantua and Pantagruel* is a burlesque of the medieval adventure romances; of the *Odyssey* and of the *Iliad*, only, however, incidentally: Rabelais had other fish to fry. Fifthly, in the drollery of such incidents as Panurge's quarrel with Dingdong (Book IV, Chapters VI-VIII); sixthly, in such utter impossibilities as have now become realities, as, for instance, the aerial warfare of the Chitterlings (Book IV, Chapter XLI). In the seventh place, Rabelais produced laughter thanks to puns, which are almost untranslatable, plays upon words, endless catalogues of which large portions have become obsolete, and a rich lush use of synonyms. Finally, certain personal allusions—Picrochole is in reality de Ste. Marthe, who had legal difficulties with the local boatmen; Raminagrobis is undoubtedly Melain de St. Gelais, Rabelais' poet friend— must have afforded readers of that day much amusement. But it is dangerous to proceed very far in this direction: Rabelais' vast work is no *roman à clef*. Its catholicity is guarantee that his people possess too many general human characteristics to represent specific individuals of his day.

V

Like all thinking men, especially in an age of discovery and transition, Rabelais was interested in education. His ideas on this subject occupy a very modest portion of the first two volumes of his work;

he relates the education of Gargantua (Book I, Chapter XIV) and
that of Pantagruel (Book II, Chapters V-VIII). His literary method
consists first in sharply satirizing the existing order, the old scholarship routine of the Middle Ages, then in outlining the new humanist
learning. Ponocrates' instruction follows out, step by step, Rabelais'
philosophy: since nature and instinct are good, they should be cultivated to the utmost; since life is enjoyable, the faculties should be
developed and trained to enjoy it to the full. The body is not the
corruption despised by medieval monks, it is the temple of the Holy
Ghost, worshipped by Renaissance men. Accordingly, athletics play
an important part in the program (Book II, Chapter XXIII).

Mentally and intellectually, the plan is encyclopedic; Rabelais
would have Pantagruel become "an abyss of knowledge." No detail
of daily life but serves to teach something useful in the most pleasant
manner. Rabelais' own curiosity, realism and joy pierce through the
text at every line. And finally, the entire system is crowned by
religious faith, in the moving, poetical passages I have cited above.

Is this plan too vast? Is this erudition impossible to achieve? Should
we prefer that of Montaigne, at the end of the Renaissance, the disil-
lusioned dilettante's precepts to prepare the young for a social com-
promise in a sorry, makeshift world? Does Rabelais' idea make his
schoolboy a well-taught compiler, rather than a human being feeling
and experiencing objectively? Does it lack the sense of beauty that
animates the Renaissance poets, does it lack the exquisite tact of
Montaigne?

In fairness to Rabelais, it must be stated that his is a program for
a giant, perhaps less a workable scheme than an ideal to aim at. And,
as such, for all our modernism, we have advanced very little further
in the last four centuries. Again, Rabelais' pupil studies texts and
books; but he also studies the text of nature and the book of life. His
learning derives from things about him; Ponocrates proves more
realistic and one hundredfold more inspiring than Rousseau. If the
enjoyment of art goes by the board, that is a slight loss compared
with the practical results acquired. Montaigne offered us a sceptic
adapting his intelligence to a strangely limited life; Rabelais aimed
to create a man, happy and rich in the satisfaction of his natural instincts. "An abyss of science!" Rabelais' is the higher ideal, and the
closer to a noble tradition which is daily being perverted.

VI

Rabelais the writer must be considered in the light of the French language of his day. Throughout the Renaissance, it was constantly growing and developing; if anything, the faults of sixteenth-century French are due to superabundance rather than to poverty. Halfway through the century a critic declared that spoken French had already changed five or six times in four decades. Thirty years after him, Montaigne complained that in his own lifetime the language had suffered an alteration of fifty per cent.

Rabelais, the first author to observe invariable rules of language in the writing of French prose, deserved Pasquier's praise: "he was the father of our idiom." His was a flexible, supple, abundant style, brilliant with verve and harmony, extraordinarily complex and original; his admirable memory and his bold imagination allowed him the most vertiginous flights of fancy. Into his expression went racy French terms of the soil, the mill, the tavern, the marketplace . . . scholarly terms from ancient philosophy, Renaissance science, jurisprudence, theology, scholastics, medicine . . . terms that were a part of the oral heritage from the Middle Ages . . . phrases borrowed from the Greek, Latin, Hebrew, Arab, English, German, Italian and Basque . . . terms that were provincialisms, popular locutions . . . terms of the arts, crafts, theatre . . . and finally, fantastic terms he himself invented with a robustness and feeling that make James Joyce sound anemic and obscure. . . .

And ever, shot through them, that supreme sense of reality!

Mr. Nock, in his edition of Rabelais, pertinently compares Rabelais' language in its relation to modern French, with Chaucer's in its relation to modern English. True, it has aged considerably. Yet— O consoling thought!—compared with Calvin's, it is rapid, modern and picturesque as the "Normandie"!

VII

It may not be amiss here to say a few words concerning the present translation. There is the standard edition of Urquhart and LeMotteux, published in its collected form early in the eighteenth century. It is, as Mr. Nock observes, one of the masterpieces of world literature. I have had it, in both Mr. Nock's edition and other popular printings, constantly open before me as I worked. Mr. Nock's notes have often proved helpful.

There is a more literal translation, published in 1893 by W. F. Smith, and not easily obtainable, in this country, at least. There is, finally, a translation by Samuel Putnam, published recently in America.

Magnificent as the Urquhart-LeMotteux is, it too, like its original, has in places become obsolete, for all the vigor of its style. It requires annotation, explanation. And it also seemed to me, perhaps rashly, that an idiom closer to modern English and closer to the critical edition of Rabelais, might be employed. In attempting this, I have not consulted either the Smith or Putnam version.

Perhaps rashly, too, I have boldly incorporated into the text, explanations from the footnotes of the Critical French Edition published by Champion, as well as explanations I myself supplied. Is this *lèse-majesté* to the master? I devoutly hope not. Governing myself according to his own golden rule of realism and reason, I have striven especially for interest and readability, trusting that through these the thought and humor of Rabelais might best be communicated.

JACQUES LeCLERCQ

TO MY READERS

Dear friends and readers who may scan these tomes,
Lay by all sense of prejudiced objection,
My pages bring no virus or infection
Across the thresholds of your virtuous homes.
True they can teach you only scant perfection
Save laughter's joys—though I confess I find
No theme more welcome to my heart and mind,
As I observe your melancholy fears,
Your gib-cat airs, your saturnine dejection. . . .
Better to write of laughter than of tears,
For laughter is the essence of mankind.

LIVE HAPPY!

The First Book

THE VERY HORRENDOUS LIFE OF THE GREAT

GARGANTUA

FATHER OF

PANTAGRUEL

Set Down of Yore by
MONSIEUR ALCOFRIBAS
Abstractor of Quintessence

A BOOK FILLED WITH PANTAGRUELISM

THE AUTHOR'S PROLOGUE

HAIL, O most valiant and illustrious drinkers! Your health, my precious pox-ridden comrades! To you alone, I dedicate my writings. Suffer me, therefore, to draw your attention to a dialogue of Plato's called *The Banquet*.

In this work, Alcibiades, praising his master Socrates (undoubtedly the prince of philosophers), happens, among other things, to liken him to sileni.

Sileni, in the days of yore, were small boxes such as you may see nowadays at your apothecary's. They were named for Silenus, foster father to Bacchus. The outside of these boxes bore gay, fantastically painted figures of harpies, satyrs, bridled geese, hares with gigantic horns, saddled ducks, winged goats in flight, harts in harness and many other droll fancies. They were pleasurably devised to inspire just the sort of laughter Silenus, Bacchus' master, inspired.

But inside these sileni, people kept priceless drugs such as balsam of Mecca, ambergris from the sperm whale, amomum from the cardamon, musk from the deer and civet from the civet's arsehole—not to mention various sorts of precious stones, used for medical purposes, and other invaluable possessions.

Well, Alcibiades likened Socrates to these boxes, because, judging by his exterior, you would not have given an onion skin for him. He was ill-shaped, ridiculous in carriage, with a nose like a knife, the gaze of a bull and the face of a fool. His ways stamped him a simpleton, his clothes a bumpkin. Poor in fortune, unlucky when it came to women, hopelessly unfit for all office in the republic, forever laughing, forever drinking neck to neck with his friends, forever hiding his divine knowledge under a mask of mockery. . . .

Yet had you opened this box, you would have found in it all sorts of priceless, celestial drugs: immortal understanding, wondrous virtue, indomitable courage, unparalleled sobriety, unfailing serenity, perfect assurance and a heroic contempt for whatever moves

3

humanity to watch, to bustle, to toil, to sail ships overseas and to engage in warfare.

Alcibiades? Socrates? The sileni? Why all this introductory flourish? Let me explain to you only, O my beloved disciples, and to such other idlers and idiots as read my works. Having noted the flippant titles of certain books of my invention—*Gargantua, Pantagruel, Drownbottle, The Dignity of Codpieces and Trouserflies, Of Peas and Bacon, with Tables and Sauce Material, etc.*—you jump to the conclusion that these tomes are filled with mere jests, vulgarities and buffoonery. Alas! you leap at the outward and visible sign; you swallow the title in a spirit of levity and derision without pausing to make further inquiry. How unseemly to consider so frivolously the works of humankind! Is it you who profess that clothes do not make the man nor robes the monk? Do I quote you when I declare that a fellow most monasterially apparelled may turn out to be a downright infidel whereas another, draped in a Spanish cloak, may possess every virtue on earth except Castilian pride and daring? Well then, you see why you should look beyond my title, open my book and seriously weigh its subject matter. The spice secreted within the box is more precious, far, than its exterior promised. In other words, the topics treated are not so foolish as the title suggested at first hand.

Again, supposing you find enough tomfoolery to live up to the title, must you tarry there, as Ulysses tarried at the song of the sirens? Certainly not. Instead, you should lend a loftier sense to what you first believed written in the exuberance of humor.

Have you ever uncorked a bottle of wine? God help us, do you remember the look on your face?

Or have you ever seen a dog fall on a marrow bone? (The dog, I may add, is, as Plato says in Book II of the *Republic*, the most philosophic beast in the world.) If you have seen my dog, you may recall how intently he scrutinizes his bone, how solicitously he guards it, how fervently he clutches it, how warily he bites his way into it, how passionately he breaks it, how diligently he sucks it. What force moves him to act so, what hope fosters such zealous pains, what recompense does he aspire to? Nothing but a little marrow. (To be sure this little is more toothsome than large quantities of any other meat, for—as Galen testifies in Chapter III of his *Concerning the*

Natural Faculties, and Chapter XI of *Concerning the Uses of the Various Parts of the Human Body*—marrow is the most perfect food elaborated by nature.)

Modelling yourself upon the dog, you should be wise to scent, to feel and to prize these fine, full-flavored volumes. You should be fleet in your pursuit of them, resolute in your attack. Then, by diligent reading and prolonged meditation, you should break the bone of my symbols to suck out the marrow of my meaning—for I make use of allegory as freely as Pythagoras did. As you read, you must confidently expect to become valiant and wise. For here you will find a novel savor, a most abstruse doctrine; here you will learn the deepest mysteries, the most agonizing problems of our religion, our body politic, our economic life.

Do you honestly believe that Homer, penning his *Iliad* or *Odyssey*, ever dreamed of the allegorical patchwork subsequently inflicted upon him by Plutarch, by Heraclides Ponticus, by Eustathius, by Cornutus the Stoic, or by Politian, the Italian who filched his criticism from the lot of them?

If you *do*, you are miles away from my opinion, for *I* hold that Homer no more dreamed of all this allegorical fustian than Ovid in his *Metamorphoses* dreamed of the Gospel. Yet whenever he met folk as witless as himself, a certain Friar Jobbernowl, a true glutton for bacon and misinformation, strove to establish the Christianity of Ovid. Fit lids, that audience, for such a pot, say I, quoting the old saw.

If you agree with the Friar, why refuse the same consideration to my own original mirthful chronicles? Yes, even though I, writing them, gave the matter no more thought than you, who were probably also drinking. I may add that in composing this masterpiece I have not spent or wasted more leisure than is required for my bodily refection—food and drink to you! Is that not the proper time to commit to the page such sublime themes and such profound wisdom? Homer, the paragon of all philologists, knew it perfectly well and Ennius also, the father of the Latin poets, as Horace testifies, though a certain sorry clown has said that his poems smelled more of wine than of oil.

So, too, spoke a third-rate cynic about my books, but a ripe turd to the fellow! Oh, the sweet fragrance of wine! How much more reconciling, smiling and beguiling wine is than oil! Let the world say I spent more on wine than on oil: I shall glory in it, like Demosthenes when they accused him of the opposite. For my part, I consider it honorable and noble to be reputed a sportsman and a wit, for as such I am welcome wherever two or three Pantagruelists are gathered together. Did not a certain surly bore denounce Demosthenes because his *Orations* smelled like a filthy rag in an oil can. Not so, I!

Accordingly, take in perfect part all I write and do; revere the cheese-shaped brain which feeds you this noble flummery; strive diligently to keep me ever jocund.

And now, my hearties, be gay, and gayly read the rest, with ease of body and in the best of kidney! And you, donkey-pizzles, hark!—may a canker rot you!—remember to drink to me gallantly, and I will counter with a toast at once!

I

GARGANTUA: HIS GENEALOGY AND ANTIQUITY

IF you would learn the genealogy and antiquity which produced Gargantua, then I refer you to the lofty *Chronicle of Pantagruel.* Here you will learn in greater detail how giants were born in this world and how Gargantua, father to Pantagruel, descended directly from them. Do not take it amiss if, for the moment, I omit the account here, though the oftener I told the tale, the better it would please your lordships. I make this statement on the authority of Plato, in his *Philebus* and *Gorgias,* and of Flaccus, who declares there that certain topics (ours is undoubtedly among them) improve by repetition.

Would to God every one could be as certain of his pedigree from the days of Noah's celebrated ark down to the present. To my way of thinking, many a man sprung from a race of sham relic-peddlers and journeymen-carriers walks the earth to-day an emperor, king, duke, prince or pope. Similarly, not a few of our sorriest, most miserable tramps are sprung from the blood and lineage of proud kings and emperors. This is due to the unbroken descent of universal monarchy from the Assyrians to the Medes, from the Medes to the Persians, from the Persians to the Macedonians, from the Macedonians to the Romans, from the Romans to the Byzantine Greeks, and, finally, from the Greeks to the French.

What is more, to give you some notion of myself who now address you, I believe I derive my origin from some opulent monarch of olden days. For you never yet clapped eyes upon a man who craved kingship or wealth more passionately than I or longed more fervidly to live sumptuously, to do nothing, to avoid worry, to enrich abundantly both his friends and all other gentlemen of learning and worth. Yet I am consoled as I reflect that I shall be all this in the next world, to a vaster extent even than I dare wish to-day. For your part, if you nourish these or loftier hopes, take comfort in your distress and drink of the best, if you can manage it.

But to return to our sheep, as the Judge said to Pathelin in the farce. Or, to come back to the point at issue! I solemnly declare that by the sovereign gift of Heaven, Gargantua's antiquity and pedigree have been more carefully preserved for us than any save the Messiah's. (Of the latter, I forbear to speak since it lies not in my province and since devils outside the Church and hypocrites within are strenuously opposed to it.)

Gargantua's pedigree was found by Jean Andeau in a meadow he owned at St. Mexme, near the pole-arch below L'Olive as you bear towards the hamlet of Narsay. They were scouring some ditches here when the diggers suddenly struck a tomb, a bronze tomb immeasurably long since it advanced so far into the sluices of the river Vienne that its other end was never found. They opened it where they saw a goblet with the legend HIC BIBITUR or HERE BE DRINKING written in highly obscure Etruscan script. And they found nine flagons, set up as the Gascons do ninepins, in rows of threes. Over the middle pin lay a book—and what a book! At once bulky yet small, big yet little, greasy and gray, mouldy yet fragrant as attar of roses.

Upon its pages lay Gargantua's genealogy, engrossed at length in the cursive penmanship of the Papal Chancelry, not upon paper, nor upon parchment, nor yet upon wax, but on the bark of an elm tree. Unfortunately it was so worn by age that barely three consecutive letters were discernible.

Unworthy though I am, I was summoned. With the invaluable help of a pair of spectacles, I practised that art which, according to Aristotle, makes it possible to read letters unapparent to the naked eye. As you may see, I translated it, pantagruelizing the while. In other words, I drank to my heart's content as I read of Pantagruel's horrendous exploits.

At the end of the book I found a short treatise entitled *Antidoted Flummeries*. Rats and weasels or, to tell the whole truth, various other evil beasts, had nibbled off the beginning. The rest I append below, for the reverence I bear antiquity.

II

ANTIDOTED FLUMMERIES

MARIUS *comes, who overwhelmed the Cimbri, passes,*
Winging his way through air lest dew humect his feet.
When he arrives they fill the cisterns with huge masses
Of yellow butter, which alas! melts in the heat.
Its deluge wets his grandam who can but entreat:
"For God's sake fish him up, My Lords," they heard her shout,
"Behold his muddy shit-streaked beard that once was sweet!
"Or bring a ladder, leastways, so he can climb out."

"Better to lick his slipper," some remark, "than come
"So dearly by his pardons!" Sudden, there approaches
A crafty sneaking knave, new-risen from the scum

That paves the lake where Calvin casts his line for roaches.
"Some of them, Lords, we keep," says he, "despite reproaches!
"The eel hides in his shop, I know he will not budge.
"Look well! you cannot fail to see where he encroaches:
"There! Can't you tell his amice by the greasy smudge."

He settled down to read the chapter when they found
Naught but a pair of horns stripped from a calf now dead.
"The bottom of my mitre feels like icy ground,
"Its chill has rapidly congealed my brain!" he said.
They took a turnip's fragrance to thaw out his head,
And soon he was content to hug a welcome brazier,
Provided they made shafts that might stand in good stead
To hold all crazy folk lest they turn crazier.

Their talk was of St. Patrick's Hole: this set the ball
Rolling . . . Gibraltar next . . . then many an orifice . . .
Could men but seal them up under a scar, withal,
To stop their wracking coughs. All thought it was amiss
To see holes gape as wide and vulgarly as this
With every random wind! Oh, for the brave days when
We shall know how to close each pervious abyss,
Perhaps employing them as hostages to men.

But lately come from Africa, great Hercules
Paused here to skin the raven. Minos, much excited,
Complained: "And why was I unbidden, if you please?
"When every Tom and Dick and Harry was invited.
"More, they expect me now, although supremely slighted,
"To cease delivering them my oysters and my frogs;
"Should he preserve my life, I promise their benighted
"Traffic in distaffs to the devil and his dogs."

Q. B. runs limping up to quell their bitter strife,
Safeguarded by his gentle startlings, on he goes . . .
The sifter, eldest son of Cyclops' brother's wife,
Slew one and all . . . Thereafter, each man blows his nose:
There is no Sodombugger in these parts but knows

The fate of being tossed above the bark-mill here.
Haste thither, lads, at once. Sound the alarum! Those
Who do will reap a harvest greater than last year!

Some time thereafter, Jupiter's immortal bird,
Observing, wagered that the worst must come to pass,
Since all were fighting savagely in deed and word,
He feared lest the empyrean be destroyed, a mass
Of dust and ruin . . . so he preferred to steal, alas!
The flame of heaven and store it where they sell red herring
Than calmly face the foes he purposed to harass
By making them the slaves of Hebrew savants' erring.

Strife yielding soon to Peace, O sweet phenomenon,
Though Athé, heron-thighed goddess of peevishness
Reviled Penthisiléa, once the Amazon
Queen—but a mangy hag, now, peddling watercress.
Each cried: "You grimy collier's slut! You sorceress!
"How dare you smirch the place in which I choose to be!
"You stole the Roman banner, damn your shamelessness!
"You stole that parchment banner wrought so cunningly!"

Juno was out ahunting, a bird perched on her wrist,
Setting a parlous snare, down where the rainbow ended,
Or Athé, noisy termagant, could not have missed
The punishment that had unswervingly descended
On her rash head but now was graciously amended:
Two eggs laid by Persephone were hers at will,
And if once more they caught her brangling, they intended
To tie her up securely on a hawthorn hill.

Seven months thereafter, minus ninety weeks, he came:
The hero who in olden days laid Carthage low.
He asked politely could they tell him what became
Of that inheritance due to him, Scipio?
Let them divide up justly, as the cobblers sew
With equal stitch on either shoe; let them present

A sup of broth as well to those who were not slow,
Though only wretched hacks, to pen his document.

The year will come, marked with a Turkish bow and string,
Five spindles and three bottoms of three types of pot,
In which the backside of a too-uncivil king
Shall in a hermit's frock suffer a hermit's lot.
O pity! Will you let a canting bigot plot
To strip you of so many acres for his sake?
Cease, cease! I know your face, it is not earth-begot,
Devil, I send you back to join your brother snake.

That tragic year done, He that is shall rule alone.
They that have been His friends shall taste sweet quietude,
Good will and harmony shall flourish round His throne,
Where never violence nor outrage dare intrude.
Solace, promised how long ago! how long accrued!
Shall fall on the elect, seated at His right hand.
They who were meek when cast in brutish servitude
Shall ride in royal palfreys through the happy land.

The poor imperfect ways to which our age fell heir
Shall last till Mars is overthrown and fettered fast.
Then shall one come whose soul, noble beyond compare,
Spread grace immeasurable, beauty and gladness. Massed
About him, comrades, lift your hearts up! The repast
Beckons all trusty friends: the man is long since dead
Who dared not for a world return into the past
To live his life again. Lo! all distress is shed!

At last he who was wax, "celui qui fut de cire"
Shall be lodged on the hinge of Jack-upon-the-Clock.
No longer shall men clamor: "Sire!" or Frenchwise: "Cyre!"
Invoking him who shakes his giant-bellied crock.
Ah! could we snatch his sword and massacre the flock
Of vexed perplexities that buzz about us here,
Misfortune would at last have met his stumbling-block
And peace would rule amid good fellowship and cheer.

III

HOW GARGANTUA WAS BORNE ELEVEN MONTHS IN HIS MOTHER'S WOMB

In his day, Grangousier or Greatgullet was a rollicking blade and a superlative toper. With him it was always bottoms-up and no heel taps, for he drank deep as any man on the face of the earth. And he was ever ready to eat salted meat, which serves to rouse the thirst. Thus he was ordinarily well provided with hams from Mainz in Westphalia and Bayonne in Gascony; with oxtongues and chitterlings in season; with salted beef and mustard; with sausages galore— not from Bologna, for he feared the Italian poisoner as a curer of bacon, but from Bigorre, Longaulnay, Brenne and Rouergue, all places nearer home.

Having attained manhood, appropriately enough he married Gargamelle—the name means gullet, also—daughter to the King of the Parpaillos or Butterflies, a jolly hoyden with a pleasing mug. Together the pair often played the two-backed beast, rubbing and grinding their respective bacons together so blithesomely and to such good purpose that she was soon big with a fair son, whom she bore for eleven months.

Does this sound strange? Perhaps. But a woman *can* bear offspring in her belly as long or even longer, especially when that offspring is a masterpiece of nature, destined to accomplish mighty exploits in his due time. Homer, himself, cites the child with which Neptune swelled the nymph Tyro: it was born a whole year after the conception. As Aulus Gellius comments, in Book III of the *Attic Nights*, such gestation was merely in keeping with the Sea God's majesty and assured the child its perfect form. By the same token, Jupiter miraculously protracted the duration of the night he bedded with Alcmena to forty-eight full hours. A shorter period could never have sufficed for the forging of Hercules, who purged the world of its monsters and tyrants.

What I state here, my masters, is confirmed by all the Pantagruelists of antiquity; they establish not only the feasibility of a child being born of woman in the eleventh month but also his legitimacy eleven months after her husband's death. I invoke the authority of Hippocrates, in his book *Concerning Nourishment*; of Pliny the Elder in Chapter v, Book vII of his *Natural History*; of Plautus in his play the *Cistellaria*; of Marcus Varro, who, in his satire *The Testament*, quotes Aristotle to this effect; of Censorinus, in *Concerning the Day of Birth*; of Aristotle, Book vII, Chapters III and Iv of *Concerning the Nature of Animals*; of Aulus Gellius, Book III, Chapter xvI of the *Attic Nights*; of Servius, who, in his commentary of Virgil's *Eclogues*, cites the verse:

Matri longa decem tulerunt fastidia menses

or:

Ten loathsome months these mothers bore their burden

and of a thousand other fools whose number has been increased by the lawyers. (Cf. Justinian's *Pandects* or *Digest*, Law III, Paragraph XIII, Book xxx, Chapter vIII, *De suis et legitimis heredibus, lege intestato* or *Concerning personal and legitimate heirs legally unprovided for by will*; cf. also *Novella* xxxIx, Justinian's *Novels*, which were an unauthorized collection of constitutions subsequent to the lawgiver's *Codex*: *De restitutionibus et ea quae parit in undecimo mense post mortem viri* or *Concerning legal restitution and the female who bears child in the eleventh month following decease of her husband*.)

Furthermore, to the same purpose, the lawyers have scrawled, stamped, sealed and scribbled their bacon-filching Gallus Law (*Digest: De liberis et posthumis heredibus intestuendis vel exheredandis* or *Concerning posthumous children and heirs unprovided for by will or disinherited*) and the Law *De statu hominum: Septimo mense nasci perfectum partum jam receptum est propter auctoritatem doctissimi viri Hippocratis* or *A birth occurring the seventh month following conception is to-day legal and acceptable according to the*

authority of the illustrious scholar Hippocrates (*Digest,* Law XII,
Book I, Chapter LVII) and several other laws that I dare not name at
present. Does this seem involved? I have at least spared you the
jurisprudential transcriptions, which read: *ff. de suis, et legit 1, intestato,* for instance, or *ff. de lib. et posth. 1. sept. ff. de stat. hom.*

Thanks to these learned laws, our virtuous widows may, for two
months after their husbands' demise, freely indulge in games of grip-
crupper with a pig in the poke, heels over head and to their hearts'
content.

As for you, my friends and lusty lads all, should you find any
widows worth lowering your breeches for, I pray you most graciously to mount them, surmount them and bring them home to me.
For, should they bourgeon the third month, the child will fall heir to
the deceased husband and, these ladies' condition being legal and
respectable, they scuttle away, go the whole hog and, *vogue la galère!*
the devil take the hindmost. . . . In brief, they behave like Julia,
daughter of the Emperor Octavian, who never abandoned herself to
her bellybumpers unless she was plump with child, on the principle
that a vessel takes on its pilot only after it has been caulked and laden.
Now if any one upbraids these righteous ladies for suffering themselves to be thus vaginoexcavated on their fullness, when even
the beasts, littering, will not endure their males to masculate, what
will the answer be? Like Populia of yore, according to Macrobius
(*Saturnalia,* Book II), they will reply that those are beasts, precisely,
whereas for their part they are women, skilled and experienced in the
noble joys and the agreeable little quirks of superfetation.

If the devil would not have them potbellied, he must twist the
spigot hard and stop up the bunghole.

IV

HOW GARGAMELLE, BIGSWOLN WITH GARGANTUA, ATE AN ABUNDANCE OF TRIPE

THE occasion and manner of Gargamelle's delivery were as I am about to relate; if you do not believe me, may your vent-peg slip, may your stopper fail your (rectal) organ, your fundament fall and your flue pipe collapse!

This is exactly what happened to Gargamelle, on February third, after dinner. And why? Because she had eaten too abundantly of tripe . . . of that tripe which comes from beeves . . . from beeves which are fatted in their stalls and put to graze in meadows . . . in meadows which bear two crops of grass each year. . . .

Three hundred and sixty-seven thousand and fourteen of these fat beeves had been slaughtered. They were to be salted on Shrove Tuesday so that there would be pressed beef aplenty that spring for the invocation of thirst and its subsequent exorcization by wine.

There was abundance of tripe, as you may imagine, such succulent tripe, too, that every one licked his fingers with glee. But there was a rub—and a four-devil power rub at that! Alas, the tripe could not be kept on hand long or it would spoil—a most disagreeable thought! They therefore decided to guzzle it all down to the last scrap. For fear of leaving any, they summoned all the citizenry of Sinais, Seuilly, La Roche Clermault and Vaugaudry, without forgetting their friends from Coudray-Montpensier and Gué de Vède and other neighbors, all accomplished tosspots, debonair fellows and ha! fine cuedrivers, skilled tailpushers, all!

That dear man Grangousier, mightily pleased at their company, ordered meat by the ton, wine by the thousand gallons. No pains were spared to honor his guests. But he *did* caution his wife to eat sparingly, since she was near her time, and in her condition tripe was not exactly the most suitable diet.

"Whoever eats the skins of these chitterlings," he announced, "is an unparalleled turdchewer!"

Despite his warnings, Gargamelle consumed sixteen quarters, two bushels and six pecks; in cases, barrels and pots. La! the sweet fecality that must have swelled up within her!

After dinner, they all made helter-skelter for La Saussaie, a meadow planted with willow trees. Here, on the soft greensward, they danced so gleefully to the tune of airy flutes and melodious bagpipes that to watch them was a most heavenly pastime.

V

PALAVER OF THE POTULENT

THEN they returned to Grangousier's. Straightway the flagons danced a jig, hams were trotted out, goblets began to fly, carafes to caper and glasses to tinkle.

"Draw my wine, boy!"

"Give me *my* glass!"

"Fill mine up!"

"Water in mine, please."

"I want mine without. So, friend!"

"Polish off that glass, lad: drink up; look sharp now!"

"Produce the evidence: *vin rosé*, bailiff, and let the glass weep from the fullness of its heart!"

"A truce to thirst! Wine is victorious!"

"Ha, shall I ever be rid of the false fever that parches my throat?"

"Upon my word, gammer my darling, I can't feel my way into drinking!"

"You've taken cold, my sweet."

"Ay, so I have, I'm thinking!"

"By the belly of Bacchus! Let's talk about drinking!"

"I only drink at my hours; capricious, I am, like the Pope's mule."

"Pass me that flask shaped like a breviary; I'll drink no other wine; a pious man, I; I'll have breviary wine, ay, like a f-f-fine F-f-franciscan F-f-father S-s-s-superior."

"Which came first: thirst or drinking?"

"Thirst came first. Who would have thought of drinking without being thirsty, in the age of innocence?"

"Drink came first, for *privatio presupponit habitum*, says the law: privation of something presupposes being accustomed to it. A clerk, I. '*Faecundi calices quem non fecere disertum*' Horace put it aptly: the cups of the talkative, but not the eloquent!"

"The age of innocence, you said? We poor innocents drink all too much without being thirsty!"

"You innocents drink without being thirsty? Well, I'm only a miserable sinner, but I'd not drink unless I were dry. Pah! if I'm not thirsty when I drink, I forestall my thirst: I drink to slake the thirst to come! I drink everlastingly: an eternity of drink, a drinking of eternity!"

"A song! A drink! Let us sing a religious chorale!"

"Who will corral wine into my glass!"

"Ho! I'm drinking by proxy it seems: my glass is empty!"

"Do you wet your whistle for the pleasure of being dry later or do you let yourself get parched for the pleasure of wetting your whistle?"

"Bah! I know nothing of theory but when it comes to practice, I'm not so badly off."

"Make haste, boy! My glass!"

"I wet, I dampen, I moisten, I humect my gullet, I drink—and all for fear of dying of aridity!"

"Drink up, you'll never die!"

"Unless I drink, I desiccate; desiccation means death. My soul will fly to seek the moisture of a frog pond, for the soul, says St. Augustine, cannot dwell in a dry place."

"O butlers, O wine stewards, creators of new substantial forms, make of the abstainer that I am a nonpareil drinker!"

"May I be perennially macerated in wine, through these, my sear and sinewy guts!"

"He drinks in vain who does not enjoy it!"

"This potion runs through my veins; my pissing tool shall have none of it!"

"I'd gladly wash the tripe of the calf I dressed this very morning. What calf? My belly. Dressed how? For the table!"

"I have ballasted my stomach choke-full!"

"If the parchment of my writs drank as avidly as I do, no trace of writing would remain upon them. Then, sirs, what bitter wine my creditors would taste when called upon to produce the evidence of my debts!"

"It's your hand makes your nose red . . . you raise it too often to your lips!"

"Ah! how many more beakers shall enter here, ere this one flow out of me!"

"You'll scrape your snout against the bottom if you drink so shallow."

"What are those flagons there for? Decoy birds, *I* say!"

"What is the difference between a bottle and a flagon?"

"A vast difference. The bottle's a spirited man who'll need but light corking to keep him from spilling. The flagon's a spigotted woman who'll need hard screwing to keep her from spitting!"

"Ha! Well said, friend!"

"Our fathers drank lustily and emptied their pots!"

"Well hummed, well bummed: a fine movement of music and bowels. Now let us drink up!"

"This round will wash your guts for you! Have you anything to send to the river? That's where tripe is washed: give this drink your message!"

"I drink no more than a sponge!"

"I drink like a Knight Templar."

"*Spongia,* a sponge, eh? Well, I drink *tamquam sponsus,* like a bridegroom."

"And I *sicut terra sine aqua,* like earth without water."

"Give me a synonym of the word 'ham'!"

"A subpoena served upon thirst; a compulsory instrument in the jurisprudence of drinking. A pulley, too: you use a pulley to get your wine down into the cellar, and ham to get it down into your belly."

"Ho, lad, come here, come here! Another drink! I've not my full complement of cargo! *Respice personam,* respect the person; *pone pro duos,* pour for two! You marvel that I say *duos* for *duobus,* that I, an erudite man, make such an error? Let me tell you that *bus* is obsolete. *Je bus* means I *have* drunk, in the *past*; while our drinking is forever conjugated in the present tense."

"If I could up my limbs as well as I down my liquor, I'd be pacing the ceiling long ago."

> *Drinking made our magnates wealthy.*
> *Drinking makes our bodies healthy!*
> *Thus Bacchus won the giant realm of Ind!*
> *Thus Vasco found that mine of gold, Melinde!*

"A touch of rain allays a lot of wind; long tippling breaks the thunder."

"Would you suck my left ballock if it piddled out such liquor?"

"I always hold it after drinking!"

"Here, boy, a drink, ho! I herewith submit my credentials, certificated by process of law, as a candidate for your favors!"

"Drink up, Will, there's a mugful still!"

"I herewith file a brief of appeal against thirst as abusive. Boy, grant it formally and proceed with the hearing!"

"That last bit of bacon . . . pass it over!"

"In the old days, I used to drink my wine to the last drop. Nowatimes I never leave anything in the glass!"

"Here is tripe worth staking money on and chitterlings you'd do well to stay with. Where do they come from? From the black-streaked dun-colored oxen of this region. For God's sake, friends, let us dispatch this meat to the last frazzle!"

"Drink or you'll see what I'll—"

"No, no, enough!"

"Drink, I beg you!"

"Sparrows won't eat unless you tap their tails; I'll not drink unless you treat me politely."

" '*Lagona edatara*,' say the Basques: bring me a drink, friend. In all my body there's not a hole or warren for thirst to flee to, without this wine ferreting it out!"

"Ha, this draught will whip my thirst up!"

"Ha, this one will drown mine utterly."

"Let us proclaim to the music of flagons and bottles that whoever has lost his thirst need not look for it here. We have voided it out of doors, thanks to prolonged and laxative libations."

"God in His greatness made the Milky Way, we make the winy; God made the comet, we drink its wine!"

"The Saviour's words are on my lips: '*Sitio*, I thirst!' "

"The stone called asbestos is not more unquenchable than my thirst. Give me to drink: am I not your holy father?"

" 'Appetite comes as you eat,' said Bishop Hangest of Le Mans; but thirst vanishes as you drink!"

"Who knows a remedy for thirst?"

"I do! You know how to treat a dog-bite? Well, do exactly the opposite. Always run after a dog and you'll never be bitten; always drink before you're thirsty and you'll never be so!"

"I've caught you: you're asleep. Wake up, man! O steward eternal, keep us from stewing in the juice of sleep. Argus had a hundred eyes to see with; a steward needs a hundred hands, like Briareus, to pour wine indefatigably."

"Let us soak up; to dry thereafter is proud sport!"

"White wine for me, white! Pour up, pour it all out in the devil's name! Pour over here, to the brim: my tongue is peeling!"

"Trink oop, mein frient! Your goot healt', soltchier!"

"Here's to you, mate! Joy and ardor!"

"O *lachryma Christi*, O tears of Christ."

"That wine comes from La Devinière; it's made of the dark grape."

"Oh, what a toothsome little white wine it is!"

"Ay, by my soul it's soft as velvet on the stomach!"

"Ha! that velvet has a rich nap, a smooth texture and a fine finish!"

"Luck to you, comrade!"

"In this game I've done plenty of raising—"

"Your elbow, eh—"

"But I'm several tricks ahead and we'll not lose the hand!"

"*Ex hoc in hoc*: out of my bottle into the mouth. Gentlemen, there is no magic to it: you all saw me! At this job, I'm a past master."

"Ahem, ahem: a massed pastor!"

"Hail to all tosspots! Pity the thirsty!"

"Here, my good lad, fill up my glass. To the top, boy, crown the wine, I pray you!"

"Pour, friend: we'll have my glass red as a cardinal's cape!"

"*Natura abhorret vacuum*—Nature abhors emptiness!"

"Mine is empty: a fly couldn't find a drink in it!"

"Let's drink up like fiddlers, like lords, like Bretons!"

"Polish off this liquor! Come, clean as a whistle!"

"Drink deep, swallow full! Here is a tonic, a sovereign remedy, here is ambrosia!"

VI

THE STRANGE AND WONDERFUL MANNER OF GARGANTUA'S BIRTH

WHILE they were thus engaged in pleasant talk about drinking, Gargamelle began to feel slightly upset in her lower parts. Grangousier immediately rose from the grass and proceeded to comfort her most feelingly. She must now be in travail, he suspected. So he told her to lie down on the grass under the willows and expect shortly to see a pair of new feet next to her own. She must therefore pluck up her courage at the prospect of the babe's arrival; though the pain was somewhat grievous, it would be brief. More, her joy when it was over would banish even the memory of what she had suffered.

"I can prove it to you," he said, "for God, that is our Saviour, says in the *Gospel According to St. John* (Chapter XVI): 'A woman in travail hath sorrow because her hour is come; but as soon as she is delivered of the child, she remembereth no more the anguish.'"

"Ha!" Gargamelle broke in. "You speak nobly. I derive greater pleasure and profit in hearing such thoughts from the Gospel than in listening to the *Life of St. Margaret* or to other like cant prescribed for women in childbearing."

"Courage, girl," Grangousier continued, "all you need is the courage of a sheep! Dispatch this boy and we shall be busy soon making another!"

"Ha," she countered, "it's easy for you men to dismiss it so lightly! Ah, well! by the help of God, I shall strive my utmost, since such is your wish, Grangousier. But would to God it had been cut off you!"

"What?" asked Grangousier.

"Ha," she said, "what an innocent you are! You heard what I said."

"Do you mean my member?" he cried. " 'Sblood! if you wish it, I'll have a knife brought me."

"Oh, never! God forbid! God forgive me, I didn't speak it from my heart, so don't take any notice of what I said. But I shall be having plenty of work to-day, unless God come to my aid, and all because of your member, that you might have pleasure."

"Courage, courage!" he urged. "The worst is over. Once the plow is out of the mire, sit tight and let the four front oxen do the pulling. For my part, I'm off to swill up a few more draughts of wine. Meantime, should any harm befall you, I shall be near by. Halloo through your hands and I shall rush to your side!"

A few moments later she began to groan, lament and cry out. Suddenly crowds of midwives came rushing up from all directions. Feeling and groping her below, they found certain loose shreds of skin, of a rather unsavory odor, which they took to be the child. It was, on the contrary, her fundament which had escaped with the mollification of her right intestine (you call it the bumgut) because she had eaten too much tripe, as I explained above.

Thereupon, a grimy old baggage of the company, who had come from Brisepaille near St. Genou threescore years before, and was reputed to be a great she-physician, administered an astringent. So horrible was this restrictive medicine that it obstructed and contracted the sphincters of Gargamelle's vents and flues, until you could barely have pried them open with your teeth. A truly revolting thought, this, but one suggested by the story of the Devil at St. Martin's Mass noting down the chatter of two trollops and with his teeth stretching the parchment he wrote on, in a vain effort to keep up with them.

As a result of Gargamelle's discomfort, the cotyledons of the placenta of her matrix were enlarged. The child, leaping through the breech and entering the hollow vein, ascended through her diaphragm to a point above her shoulders. Here the vein divides into two; the child accordingly worked his way in a sinistral direction, to issue, finally, through the left ear.

No sooner born, he did not, like other babes, cry: "Whaay! Whaay!" but in a full, loud voice bawled: "Drink, drink, drink!" as though inviting the company to fall to. What is more, he shouted so lustily that he was heard throughout the regions of Beuxe (pronounced "booze") and Bibarois (which in sound evokes bibbers and is how the Gascons pronounce "Vivarais").

Now I suspect that you do not thoroughly believe this strange nativity. If you do not, I care but little, though an honest and sensible man always believes what he is told and what he finds written. Does not Solomon say in *Proverbs* (XIII, 15): "*Innocens credit omni verbo,* the innocent believeth every word," and does not St. Paul (*I Corinthians,* 13) declare: "*Charitas omnia credit,* Charity believeth all."

Why should you not believe what I tell you? Because, you reply, there is no evidence. And I reply in turn that for this very reason you should believe with perfect faith. For the gentlemen of the Sorbonne say that faith is the argument of non-evident truths.

Is anything I have related beyond our law or faith, contrary to our reason, or opposed to Divine Scriptures? For my part, I find nothing in the Holy Bible that stands against it. And if such had been the will of God, would you affirm that He could not accomplish it? Ha, I pray you, do not ambiguembrangle your minds with such vain conceits. I tell you that nothing is impossible to God and, if He but pleased, women would henceforth give birth to their children through the left ear.

Was not Bacchus engendered out of the very thigh of Jupiter? Was not Roquetaillade or Cleftrock ushered into the world through his mother's heel? Did not Croquemouche or Craunchfly first see the light out of his nurse's slipper? Was not Minerva progenerated out of the brain and through the ear of Jupiter? Was not the bark of a myrrh tree brought to bed of Adonis? And did not an eggshell, laid and hatched by Leda, extravasate Castor and Pollux into being?

You would be infinitely more surprised and stunned were I presently to expose to you the entire chapter in which Pliny deals with fantastic and unnatural births, yet I am not nearly so accomplished a liar as he was. Read his *Natural History,* Book VII, Chapter III, yourselves, and do not plague me further with the subject.

VII

HOW GARGANTUA CAME BY HIS NAME AND HOW HE SWILLED DOWN THE WINE

THAT excellent man Grangousier was drinking and making merry with the others, when he heard a horrible tumult. It was his son emerging into the light of this world, bellowing, "Drink, drink, drink!"

At once Grangousier exclaimed: *"Que grand tu as le gousier"* or "What a great gullet you have!" Hearing this, the company declared that the child should indeed be named *"grand tu as"*: Gargantua or Greatgullet. Were these not the first sounds the father had uttered after the child's birth? And was this not an ancient Hebrew custom well worth following? Grangousier assented; Gargamelle was delighted with the idea.

Next, to quiet the babe, they made him drink till his throat almost burst. Then, carrying him to the font, they baptized him, as is the custom among all good Christians.

Shortly after, they appointed seventeen thousand nine hundred and thirteen cows from Pontille and Bréhémont to furnish him with milk in ordinary, for, considering his enormous needs, it was impossible to find a satisfactory nurse in all the country. Nevertheless, certain learned doctors, disciples of Duns Scotus, have affirmed that his own mother suckled him. She could, they say, draw from her breasts two thousand one hundred and three hogsheads and eighteen pints at one time. This seems scarcely probable. Indeed, this point has been condemned by the Sorbonne as mammarily scandalous and reeking with heresy.

Gargantua was thus looked after until he was twenty-two months old. Then, on the advice of the physicians, they began to carry him, and Jean Denyau built a special ox-drawn cart for him. They drove him about in it here, there and everywhere with the greatest pleasure; and a fine sight he was, too, with a great, open face and almost eighteen chins! He cried very little but he beshitted himself at all times. For he was wondrously phlegmatic of bum, as much by natural complexion as from an accidental predisposition, due to exaggerated quaffing of the juices of Septembral mash. Yet he never touched a drop without good reason; for whenever he happened to be out of sorts, vexed, angry or melancholy, if he stamped, wept or shouted, they brought him a drink. This invariably restored his native good humor and at once made him as quiet and happy as before.

One of his governesses told me on oath what a rooted habit this tippling had become. Indeed, the mere clinking of pints and flagons sent him off into the ecstasy of one who tastes the joys of Paradise. Accordingly, in view of this divine character, they used to delight him every morning by making music on glasses with knives, on bottles with their stoppers, and on pots with their lids. At this he would turn gay, thrill with joy, wag his head and rock from side to side, monochording with his fingers and barytoning through his tail.

VIII

HOW THEY ARRAYED GARGANTUA

WHEN he was twenty-two months old, his father ordered clothes for him made in his own livery, which was white and blue. Going to work with a will, the tailors soon cut, sewed and produced his apparel according to the current fashion. From ancient records in the Chamber of Accounts at Montsoreau, I learn that he was arrayed in the following manner:

To make Gargantua one shirt, they cut off nine hundred ells of

Châtellerault linen and two hundred more for the gussets, which were square and placed under the armpits for comfort. His shirt was not pleated, for the pleating of shirts was only discovered later. That was when certain seamstresses, who had broken the point of their needles, turned up their holes and put their tails to work.

For Gargantua's doublet they used eight hundred and thirteen ells of white satin, and for his aglets—the laces that held it together—fifteen hundred and nine and one-half dogs' skins. This was the period when men began to tie their breeches to their doublets and not their doublets to their breeches—the latter habit being contrary to nature, as William of Ockham explained at length in his comment upon the *Exponabilia* of Monsieur Hautechaussade and Master Highbreecham.

Eleven hundred and five and one-third ells of the finest white broadcloth were used for the breeches. They were cut in the form of columns, pinked and grooved behind so as not to overheat his reins: from within the slashes, as much blue damask puffed out as was needful. Note, too, that he had very fine legs, perfectly in proportion to the rest of his body.

The tailoring of Gargantua's codpiece (here was no modern degenerate fly!) required sixteen and one-quarter ells of the same cloth. In shape, it resembled a buttress; it was most gallantly fastened to two handsome golden buckles, caught up by two enamelled clasps. Each had a large emerald, the size of an orange, set in it. As Orpheus points out in his treatise on precious stones, *Liber de Lapidibus*, and Pliny in the last book of his *Natural History*, emeralds exert a highly erective and bracing influence upon the natural member. The gibbosity or bulge of the codpiece stretched out about five and one-half feet; it was jagged and pinked, with flaring blue damask, like the breeches.

Had you seen the delicate embroidery of the gold thread and the priceless network of laces, adorned, by the goldsmith's art, with rare diamonds, rich rubies, precious turquoises, splendid emeralds and choice Persian pearls, what would you have done? Inevitably you would have compared it to some proud cornucopia such as you see on ancient monuments, or such as Rhea gave to the nymphs Adrasta and Ida, nurses to her son Jupiter.

You recall the tale, doubtless. The goat, whose milk nourished the divine infant, happened one day to break one of her horns against a rock. Straightway the nymphs filled it with fruit and flowers to present to Jove, who made of this horn a source of eternal abundance.

Well, Gargantua's codpiece was like that horn: forever lively, succulent and resinous; forever flourishing, pollening and fructifying; full of juice, aflower with pistils and teeming with fruit, in short (but it was never that!), a compendium of delights. May I never meet my God if it was not a brave spectacle to behold! But I reserve the right to deal with it at greater length in a book I have written upon *The Dignity of Codpieces*. One thing, however, I shall disclose: if it was extremely long and extraordinarily expansive, it was also fully stocked and inexhaustible within. Hence it was in no wise comparable to the hypocritical codpieces of a heap of noodles, which are crammed with only wind, to the great prejudice of the female sex.

Gargantua's shoes—calling for four hundred and six ells of dazzling blue velvet—were most stylishly slashed by parallel lines, crossed by uniform cylinders. The soles alone required eleven hundred hides of brown cows, cut like the tail of a codfish.

For his coat, they bespoke eighteen hundred ells of blue velvet, dyed in grain, with elegantly embroidered vine leaves and branches around the border and, in the middle, pint goblets stitched in silver, intermingled with bars of gold and many pearls. The branches, goblets and bars indicated that Gargantua was destined to be a wine-punisher and bottle-flogger of the first . . . water!

Three hundred and one-half ells of silken rep, half blue and half white, unless I err, went to make up Gargantua's belt.

His sword was not of Valencia, nor his dagger from Saragossa, for his father abominated those *hidalgos, borrachos* and *moriscos*— braggarts, sots and Moorish Jew mongrels—as cordially as you hate the devil. No: Gargantua had a noble sword made of wood and a dagger of boiled leather, both as richly painted and gilt as any man could wish.

His purse was fashioned out of the ballock of an elephant, given him by My Lord Pracontal, Proconsul of Africa.

For Gargantua's gown, they employed nine thousand six hundred ells less two-thirds of blue velvet as before. But they decorated it diagonally with such a wealth of gold purling that, seen in proper perspective, it bore that indefinable tint you may observe on the necks of turtledoves. It afforded the eye much pleasure.

His hat used up three hundred and two ells and one-quarter of white velvet. It was wide and round, fitting very close to his head, for his father declared that caps à la Morisco, shaped like pie-crusts, would some day visit ill-fortune upon the shavepates that wore them.

The plume in his hat was a splendid, wide, blue one, plucked from an onocrotal—which we call pelican—in Hircania, that wild vast land in Central Asia. Very proudly, very smartly it swept down over his right ear.

The emblem in his hat? Against a base of gold weighing over forty pounds was an enamel figure very much in keeping. It portrayed a man's body with two heads facing one another, four arms, four feet, a pair of arses and a brace of sexual organs, male and female. Such, according to Plato's *Symposium*, was human nature in its mystical origins. Around the emblem ran a motto in Greek script: Ἀγαπή οὐ ζητεῖ τὰ ἑαυτῆς, Charity seeketh not her own, or more freely, the only virtuous person is one who does good to another whilst profiting himself.

About his neck Gargantua wore a golden chain weighing one hundred and twenty-three hundredweight, two quarter and three pounds. The link between each great berry-shaped bead was a huge, richly engraved green jasper, cut in the form of a dragon with sparks and beams all about him. It was a replica of the necklace worn of yore by Nekhepso, the wizard King of Egypt. This chain reached down to the orifice of his upper belly. All his life long, he was destined, as the Greek physicians well knew, to derive benefit from it, for green jasper has a highly digestive virtue.

The hide of sixteen otters went into Gargantua's gloves, that of three werewolves into their facing, the material being chosen by order of the cabbalistic scholars of the Priory of St. Louand.

Gargantua wore rings, for his father insisted he renew this ancient symbol of nobility. On the forefinger of his left hand, he bore a carbuncle as big as an ostrich egg, handsomely set in gold as pure as that of the Persian coin called seraph. On what is technically called the medical, and, generally, the fourth, finger of the same hand, Gargantua displayed a band wrought most wonderously out of the four metals, without the steel ever impairing the gold, or the silver crushing the copper. This treasure was made by Captain Chappuis and Monsieur Alcofribas, his trusty associate. On the medical finger of Gargantua's right hand hung a spirally shaped ring, with a perfect balas ruby, a pointed diamond and an emerald of Pison, one of the four rivers of the earthly Paradise flowing by Hevilath, where gold came to birth. These stones were of inestimable value, for Hans Carvel, jeweller to the King of Melinde, estimated them at sixty-nine million, eight hundred and ninety-four thousand and eighteen French crowns. The Fuckers or Fuggers, that celebrated family of bankers in Augsburg, concurred in this appraisal.

IX

GARGANTUA'S COLORS AND LIVERY

GARGANTUA'S colors were white and blue, as I have indicated above. By these colors, his father wished to signify that the lad was a heavenly joy to him. White expresses joy, pleasure, delight and rejoicing; blue denotes things celestial.

I realize quite well that, as you read these words, you are laughing at the old toper, for you believe this symbolic use of colors to be crude and extravagant. White, you say, stands for faith, and blue for strength. But without getting excited, losing your temper, flying into a rage or working yourself into a tongue-parched passion—the weather is dangerous—tell me one thing! I shall exercise no compulsion upon you or any one else—I shall merely point to the bottle and trust you will drink with me.

What moves, impels or induces you to believe what you do? Who told you that white means faith, and blue strength?

"A shoddy book," you reply, "sold by peddlers in remote mountain hamlets and by weatherbeaten hawkers God knows where. Its title? *In Praise of Colors.*"

Who wrote it; do you know? Whoever did, had sense enough not to put his name to it. And I cannot tell which I should rather admire: his presumption or his stupidity.

His presumption? Without cause, reason or evidence, he dares to prescribe by his private authority what this color or that shall mean. Such is the practice of tyrants who impose their arbitrary will instead of justice, not of the wise and learned who satisfy their readers by obvious proofs.

His stupidity? The fellow actually believes that the world will interpret its devices according to his inept charlatanry without demanding further demonstration or a more valid argument!

In effect, according to the proverb: "Turd calls to turd," he found some nincompoop leftovers from those rude times when tall bonnets were in fashion. These readers gave his writings some credence. So they carved their mottoes and saws, harnessed their mules, apparelled their pages and quartered their breeches to match their coats-of-arms. They lined their gloves, fringed their bed-curtains, painted their medals, scrolled their emblems, composed songs and—what is worse —visited their impostures and base secret cozenage upon the chastest matrons. Yes, by displaying, without permission, the colors and devices of virtuous women, they actually compromised them.

The same mists of ignorance and error envelop these vainglorious courtiers and miserable punsters who insult ear and eye with their nonsense. Do they wish to represent hope on their crests? They have a *sphere* drawn to illustrate the word *esper*; for *peine*, sorrow, they trace a bird's *pen*; to express *melancholy*, they picture *l'ancolie*, the columbine; a *crescent* moon denotes *increasing* fortune; a breach in a river *bank* signifies *bankrupt*; for *licencié*, a Master of Arts, say, they trace you a *lit sans ciel*, a bed minus its canopy. This mania attains its loftiest limits when a crest bears the Latin word *non* and an *alcret*, which is a piece of armor. Can you guess its meaning? If not, I hasten to point out that an *alcret* is, by definition, a *dur habit* or hard costume. Have you guessed yet? No? Well, this brilliant juxtaposition of the Latin *non* and *dur habit* spells *non durabit*: it will not last! (Let us piously hope this is true!)

These equivokes are so ineffectual, so dull, so crude and so barbarous that we should pin a fox's tail to the coat of the offender and fashion a mask of cow dung for whosoever should attempt this in the realm of France after the renascence of learning.

For like reasons—if reason may be used here rather than folly—I shall have a *panier* or basket painted to attest that I am in *pain*, and a pot of *moutarde* or *mustard* because I am *moult tard* or *much tardy*. Similarly, since a pisspot is sometimes more politely known in French as an *official*, and a bishop is an *official* of the Church, if I am a *bishop*, I shall exhibit a thunder-mug upon my coat-of-arms rather than a *mitre*. Again, the *seat of my breeches* is a harbor full of poops or a vessel full of *farthings*; my *cod piece* is *a fish* swimming in a *sea of urine*; and a dog's *turd* is the *alluring turret* wherein lies the love of my sweetheart.

In the olden days, the sages of Egypt ordered matters better when they wrote in what they called hieroglyphics. No man understood these unless he were familiar with the virtue, property and nature of the things represented. By the same token, all who were conversant could readily decipher these mysterious symbols. Their lore has been dealt with in two volumes in Greek by Orus Apollo the grammarian, and further exposed by Polyphilus in his *Dream of Love*. In France you have a fragment of this science in the device of My Lord Admiral, which he borrowed from Octavian Augustus: a dolphin (signifying speed) upon an anchor (signifying steadfastness), the picture being a symbol of moderation.

But my skiff will adventure no further among these uninviting shoals and shallows: I turn back to call at the haven whence I came. Yet I hope one day to write at greater length upon this subject and to demonstrate—both by philosophical arguments and by time-hallowed authorities—what colors are in nature, how many there are and what every one of them may mean. This, if God preserve my head, for, as my grandam was wont to say, the mould of your cap is your best wine pot.

X

WHAT THE COLORS WHITE AND BLUE SIGNIFY

WHITE, then, signifies joy, solace and gladness—not at random but by unimpeachable authority. You may easily convince yourselves of this if you set aside your prejudices and consent to give ear to what I shall presently expound.

Aristotle proves this. Take two opposites—say, good and evil, virtue and vice, hot and cold, white and black, joy and grief, pleasure and pain, and so on. Couple them so as to make a contrary of one comparison agree reasonably with its fellow in the next comparison. Then inevitably the contrasted contraries to which you have compared them will, in turn, correspond. Thus *virtue* and *vice*, are opposites in one kind; so are *good* and *evil*. Now if one of the contraries of the first kind agrees (like *virtue* and *good*, for we know virtue to be good), then the remaining set of qualities—*vice* and *evil*—will in turn agree, since we know vice to be evil.

Having mastered this logical rule, take one pair of opposites, *joy* and *sorrow*, and couple it with another, *white* and *black*—for they are physically contrary—well then, if *black* signifies *mourning*, then *white* rightly signifies *joy*.

This signification is neither imposed nor instituted by one man. On the contrary, it is admitted by general consent of all men, in accordance with what the philosophers call *jus gentium*, universal law, which rules in all climes.

As you doubtless know, all peoples and nations, whatever their tongues (save the ancient Syracusans and certain other Greeks with contrary souls!), expressed their grief outwardly by wearing black clothes. All mourning therefore was done in black. Any such universal consent is not given without nature supplying certain arguments and reasons which any man may forthwith acknowledge without outside intervention. This we call natural law.

By the same natural token, white has always meant joy, pleasure, solace, gladness and delight. In past ages, the men of Thrace and Crete marked their happy and propitious days by white stones and their sad, inauspicious ones by black.

Is not night mournful, gloomy, melancholy? It is black and obscure for want of light. Does not light bear joy to all the world? Is it not whiter than any other thing on earth? I might, to prove my point, refer you to the book written by the Italian humanist, Laurentius Valla, against the fourteenth-century jurist, Bartolus. But the testimony of the Bible will doubtless content you. It is said in *Matthew*, XVII, that at the Transfiguration of Our Lord *"vestimenta ejus facta sunt alba sicut lux*, his raiment was white as the light." By this luminous whiteness, He wished to convey to His three apostles the idea and figure of eternal joy. Light, it is, gladdens all human beings. You have, in support of this statement, the words of the old woman who, with never a tooth in her head, yet exclaimed: *"Bona Lux!* Light is good!" And in the *Book of Tobit,* Chapter V, we learn that when Tobit, blinded by sparrows "muting warm dung into his eyes," was greeted by Raphael:

"Alas," he answered, "what joy can I know, who may not see the light of Heaven?"

White, too, was the color used by the angels to betoken the joy of the entire universe at the resurrection of Our Saviour (*John*, XX) and at His Ascension (*Acts*, I), whilst vestments of the same hue apparelled the faithful whom St. John the Evangelist saw entering into the blessed and heavenly city of Jerusalem (*Revelation*, Chapters IV and VII).

I urge you further to read the ancient histories, both Greek and Roman. In the latter you will learn that the city of Alba, the earliest pattern of Rome, was not only built on the spot where Aeneas found a white sow among thirty young boars, but also named for the beast.

You will learn, too, that whenever a victorious general was, by senatorial decree, allowed the honors of a triumphal entry into Rome, his chariot was drawn by white horses. In the lesser triumphs—allowed by ovation—white was likewise customary, for the people could not by any other sign or color more clearly express their joy at the hero's homecoming.

In Greek history, you will read how Pericles, the Athenian leader,

ordered those of his soldiers who had drawn white beans by lot to
spend the whole day in joy, comfort and rest, while the others went
into battle. How easily I could cite a thousand further examples and
proofs if this were only the proper place for it!

If you understand the above, you can readily solve a problem considered insoluble by Alexander Aphrodiseus, a contemporary of
Marcus Aurelius. "Why," asks this commentator on Aristotle, "does
a lion, whose mere roar terrifies all animals, fear and respect only the
white rooster?" Because the virtues of the sun are present—as Proclus Diadochus, Platonic philosopher of the fifth century, points out
in his *De Sacrificio et Magia*, *Of Sacrifice and Magic*. The sun is the
organ and receptacle of all terrestrial and sidereal light. Its virtues
are better expressed and symbolized by the white rooster than by the
lion, both because of the rooster's color and because of his essential
attributes. Devils, this authority adds, have often appeared in the
form of lions who suddenly vanished at the sight of a white rooster.

That is why the *Galli*—the French were so named because they are
by nature white as milk, which in Greek is γάλα or *gala*—are pleased
to wear white feathers in their caps. Are they not naturally gay, candid, gracious and popular? Is it surprising therefore to find that their
symbol and sign is the whitest flower on earth: the lily?

Do you ask me how nature would convey joy and gladness to us
through the color white? I reply that it is thus by analogy and con-
formity. For white reflects the rays of the light; it obviously dissolves
the visual spirits, according to Aristotle, in his *Problems*, and other
students of optics. You may best discover the truth of this yourselves
when you pass snow-covered mountains and complain that you cannot see clearly. (Xenophon attests that this happened to his soldiers
and Galen treats of the subject at length in Book x of his *De usu Partium*, *Of the Use of the Parts of the Body*.)

Precisely so the heart. Joy may dilate it and excess of joy actually
make it suffer. Indeed, a frenzy of gladness may so dissolve the vital
spirits that life itself is snuffed out. This destructive excess of joy is
called *perichareia*; Galen discusses it in Book xii, *De Methodo Me-
dendi* or *Of the Method of Healing*; in Book v, *De Locis Affectis*, *Of
the Portions Affected*; and in Book ii, *De Symptomatum Causis*, *Of
the Causes of Symptoms*.

That excessive joy has killed men is attested by witnesses in ancient times: Marcus Tullius Cicero, Book I of the *Tuscan Questions*; Marcus Verrius Flaccus, the Latin grammarian cited by Pliny on unnatural deaths; Aristotle; Livy in his account of what happened after the Battle of Cannae; Pliny in his *Natural History*, Book VII, Chapters XXXII and LIII; Aulus Gellius in his *Attic Nights*, Book III, Chapter XV.

Examples of men who perished of joy include Diagoras of Rhodes, who gave up the ghost when his three sons were crowned victors in the Olympics . . . Chilo, in like circumstances . . . Sophocles and Dionysius, the tyrant of Sicily, when they learned of their triumph in the Tragedy contests . . . Philippides and Philemon, both comic poets, in much the same way . . . Polycrata, when she saw her countrymen of Naxos conquering her abductors and advancing to crown her . . . Philistion, who laughed himself to death . . . M. Juventius Thalva, when he received favorable tidings from the Roman Senate. . . .

Avicenna in Book II of his *De Viribus Cordis, Of the Heart's Strength*, says that saffron so stimulates the heart that, taken to excess, it may cause death through extreme dilation and resolution. This, indeed, applies as much to joy. In this connection, consult Alexander Aphrodiseus, Book I of his *Problems*, Chapter XIX. So much for that!

Enough! I seem to have gone further into this question than I first intended. So I shall strike sail now, referring the rest of this to the book in which I propose to treat of such matters at length. Meanwhile I hasten to add that blue most certainly signifies Heaven and all heavenly things, by the same token and symbols that white signifies joy and pleasure.

XI

OF GARGANTUA'S ADOLES-
CENCE

FROM three to five years of age, Gargantua was, by his father's orders, brought up and instructed in all proper discipline. He spent his time like other small children; namely, in drinking, eating and sleeping; in eating, sleeping and drinking; in sleeping, drinking and eating.

He was forever wallowing in dirt, covering his nose with filth and begriming his face. He wore his shoes down to a frazzle, lay with his mouth gaping to catch heaven knows what, and delighted in chasing butterflies—an infidel tribe over which his father ruled. He used to piddle on his shoes, brown up his shirt-tails, wipe his nose on his sleeve, clear his nostrils into his soup, and dive headlong into the foulest muck at hand. He was wont to drink from his slipper, scratch his belly with a wicker basket and sharpen his teeth on a wooden shoe. When he washed his hands, he did so in his soup; he combed his hair with a drinking cup, fell flat on his rump between two stools, blew hot and cold, cut blocks with a razor and drank while he ate his broth. His bread he consumed without dough; he bit laughing and laughed biting. Often he coughed up, figuratively and literally. Fat? another ounce of wind and he would have exploded. Appreciative? He would piss, full-bladdered, at the sun. Cautious? He used to hide under water for fear of the rain.

Among Gargantua's other pursuits were striking on the iron while it was cold; going woolgathering; shamming Abraham or playing the hypocrite; throwing up his food or flaying the fox, as the saying goes; reciting the monkey's paternoster or letting his teeth chatter like a baboon's. If he had wandered from the point, he invariably followed the Judge's advice to Pathelin, and came back to his sheep ... he turned his hogs to hay or, as some say, took the wrong sow by the ear ... he beat the dog for the lion or thrashed the slave to teach the master a lesson . . . he put the cart before the horse and locked the stable door after the mare was stolen. . . . He did not self-flatteringly scratch himself where he itched, but unexpectedly enough where he did not. He would pump people and bite off more than he could chew, leap before he looked, milk the ram and tickle himself to make himself laugh. A fine trencherman, withal, he plied a tireless knife and fork.

Among his other accomplishments were stealing pigs and giving the feet to God . . . having the magnificat sung at matins and considering it perfectly seasonable . . . eating red cabbage and voiding white beets . . . knowing black from white and spotting a fly in a bowl of milk . . . cooling his heels . . . pouring water into sieves. . . . He would scribble on papers, mess up parchments and save his bacon by taking French leave. He collected hairs from the dog that bit him, tossed the pot, threw up and reckoned without his host. He beat about the bush without stirring the birds; he thought the moon was made of green cheese and bladders were lanterns.

He feathered his nest; had two strings to his bow and two linings to his purse; he would play the ass if he could get a sack of bran out of it and he made a mallet of his fist. With the greatest ease, he caught weasels asleep and washed blackamoors white; and, throwing in his lot with such as believe Rome was not built in a day, he held that some roads led elsewhere.

Gargantua was also inclined to look a gift horse in the mouth . . . tell cock and bull stories . . . throw the helve after the hatchet . . . rob Peter to pay Paul . . . fence in the cuckoo to preserve the summer and keep the moon safe from the wolves . . . hope, if the heavens fell, to catch larks . . . make a virtue of necessity . . . cut his coat according to his cloth . . . split no hairs and care as little for the shaven as for the shorn. . . .

Every morning Gargantua retched, spewed, flayed the fox. He ate out of the same dish as his father's puppies: he would bite their ears, they would scratch his nose, and he blow into their arseholes whilst they licked his chops.

Do you know what else he did, my brave lads? May the drunkard's pip rot your guts if the little lecher wasn't forever groping his nurses upside-down, arsey-turvy, *birdie-girdie, giddy-up, whoah, Hinny*! —and if he wasn't beginning to bring his codpiece into play and turn it to account. Every morning his governesses prinked and dizened it with lovely nosegays and fine silken tassels. Their favorite pastime was to feel and finger his organ, to knead and mould it lovingly as pharmacists handle ointment and salve to make a large, solidified cylindrical suppository. Then they would burst out laughing for joy at the sport as, under their skilled hands, it would prick up its ears.

One called it her darling faucet, another her corking pin, a third her coral branch, a fourth her bungpeg, a fifth her stopgap. Others named it variously their ramrod, their spikebit, their swagdangle, their trunnion, their private hardware because it must be hard where they stocked it, their lever, their borer, their little ruddy sausage, their nutty little booby prize.

"It belongs to me!" one cried.

"No, it's mine!" another protested.

"What about me?" piped up a third. "Shall I have no share in it? By my faith, I'll cut it off then."

"Ha!" said the other. "You would hurt him, Madame, if you cut it off. Do you propose to cut a child's penial utensil? He'd be Master Bobtail, then!"

And so that he might play like other little children they made him a fine whirligig with the wings from a windmill in the Mirebelais region of the Poitou.

XII

OF GARGANTUA'S WOODEN HORSES

So that Gargantua might be a good horseman all his life, they made him a fine large wooden horse, which he put through its paces, making it prance, leap, curvet, at once rear and dance, pace, trot, amble, gallop, cantor, jog and peg. He also made it go the gait of the camel and of the onager or wild ass. Just as monks are accustomed to vary their dalmatics and other vestments according to the holy days, so Gargantua changed the color of his horse's hair from bay-brown to chestnut, dapple-gray, mouse-color, fawn-brown, roan, russet as a cow's hairs, mottled, skewbald, piebald and white.

Gargantua himself made a hunting nag out of a great dray, another horse for daily use out of the beam of a winepress, and a mule with its saddlecloth, for his room, out of a huge oak. Besides these, he had ten or twelve spare mounts and seven post horses, all of which slept at his side.

One day My Lord Breadinbag, Seigneur de Painensac, happened to be visiting Gargantua's father with a great retinue amid much pomp. Other visitors the same day included My Lord Freemeal, Duc de Francrepas, and My Lord Moistwind, Comte de Mouillevent. The house was indeed somewhat small for so many guests; stable room especially was lacking. My Lord Breadinbag's majordomo and his master-of-horse were therefore anxious to learn if there were empty stables elsewhere in the house. Coming upon Gargantua, a mere lad, they asked him privately to show them the stables where the chargers were kept. They were sure the child would readily give away the secret.

Gargantua escorted them up the main stairway of the castle, passing through the second hall into a spacious gallery which led to a great tower. Here, as they climbed still another staircase, the master-of-horse turned to the majordomo:

"This child is deceiving us," he said. "Stables are never at the top of a house."

"You may be mistaken," the other replied. "I know places at Lyons, at La Baumette near Angers, at Chinon and elsewhere, built on the side of a hill with the stables at the top of the house. Possibly there is an entrance further up. But I'll question the child to make sure!" Then: "Where are you taking us, my little lad?" he asked.

"To the stables where I keep my chargers," the child answered. "We are almost there! Just one flight of stairs to climb."

Leading them through still another great hall, he reached his room and, throwing the door open:

"Here are the stables you wanted: here are my jennet, my gelding, my courser and my cob."

Then, beating them on the back with a great cudgel:

"I'll give you this Friesland horse, too," he cried. "I got it from Frankfurt but you shall have it, for it's a nice little nag and never gets tired! With a male goshawk, a half-dozen spaniels and a brace of greyhounds, you can be king of the hares and partridges all winter long."

"By St. John!" they swore. "This lad has gulled us like a pair of monks."

"Ay," said Gargantua, "a pair of monkeys!"

You may imagine whether they had better cause to hang their heads in shame or laugh in amusement. As they were coming downstairs sheepishly, the lad asked:

"Would you like a slobbergag?"

"And what may a slobbergag be?" they inquired.

"It is," he explained, "five turds to make you a muzzle."

"If we are roasted to-day," said the majordomo, "we'll never burn at the fire, for we have been pretty well stuffed, larded, basted and lambasted, I think! O my clever little lad, you have crowned us with straw like a pair of prize kine at a Fair. And I'll live to see you Pope, yet!"

"I expect so," Gargantua agreed. "If I'm *Papa*, the Pope, then you'll be *papilio*, the butterfly or popelet I chase. And your friend here, the Poppet popinjay, will pop his poperies like any pop-eyed hypocrite!"

"Indeed!" the master-of-horse commented.

"Now," Gargantua went on, "guess how many stitches there are to my mother's shirt?"

"Sixteen," said the majordomo.

"That is not gospel truth!" Gargantua objected. "You reckoned the tale complete without thinking how high and gamy behind. You handled the swanpan but what of the stinkpot? You supputed wrongly, both before and behind!"

"When?" asked the master-of-horse.

"When they used your throat as a funnel to draw off the liquid because the bottom burst and let fly!"

" 'Odsbody!" said the majordomo, "we've met with a twaddler! Farewell, Master Tattler, God guard you from harm, for words come tripping dangerously upon your tongue!"

As they ran down under the vault at the foot of the staircase, they let fall the great beam Gargantua had put on their shoulders.

"The devil!" Gargantua exclaimed. "You're sorry horsemen to

let your mounts fail you when most you need them! Had you to
go from here to Cahuzac in Périgord, which would you prefer: to
ride a gosling or lead a sow in leash?"

"I had rather drink," said the master-of-horse.

Whereupon, they joined the company in the common room and
related this new story, causing their hearers to laugh like a swarm
of flies.

XIII

HOW THROUGH THE INVENTION
OF A RUMPSWAB GRANGOUSIER
DISCOVERED GARGANTUA'S
MARVELLOUS INTELLIGENCE

ABOUT the end of the child's fifth year, Grangousier, returning from
the conquest of the Canarrans, paid his son Gargantua a visit. He
was mightily pleased, as such a father might well be on seeing such
a son. Between kisses and embraces, he asked him diverse questions
about childish matters. He drank glass after glass with the lad and
his governesses, carefully examining the latter, among other things,
as to whether they had kept him sweet and clean. Gargantua at once
spoke up. He himself, he said, had taken such pains that there could
not be a cleanlier lad in the length and breadth of the land.

"How is that?" asked Grangousier.

"Through profound and diligent research," Gargantua explained,
"I have invented a means of wiping my bum—it is the most lordly,
excellent and expedient technique ever seen."

"What does it consist in?" Grangousier asked him.

"One moment, and I shall tell you!" Gargantua replied.

"Once I mopped my scut with the velvet scarf of a damozel. It
was pleasurable: the soft material proved voluptuous and gratifying
to my hindsight. Once, too, I used a hood, from the same source and
with the same results. The next time it was her neckerchief; again,
her crimson satin earpieces, but they were bespangled and begilt

with beshitten jewelry that scraped my tailpiece from end to end (St. Anthony's fire roast the bumgut of the decorator and the decorated!).

"I recovered from this, thanks to a page's cap with a plume to it like those the Swiss Guards sport.

"Next, spirting behind a bush, I came upon a March cat (Spring birds are best, runs the rune!) and I put it to excellent advantage though its claws mildly lacerated my perinaeum.

"But I was fit again on the morrow for I employed the gloves of my charming mother; they bore odors of sanctity and scuttling.

"Sage, then, which is capital stuffing for a goose . . . fennel, a fine umbelliferous herb for sauces . . . dill, also yellow and umbelliferous . . . sweet marjoram . . . rose leaves and gourd leaves . . . cabbage, which I define as various kinds of cultivated vegetables with round heart or head . . . beets, vine branches and mallow, that wild and garden plant with hairy stems and leaves and purple flowers . . . mullein, woolly of bud and scarlet to the butt . . . lettuce and spinach leaves . . . all of which was fit for the dusthole and amounted to kicking against the pricks. . . .

"What more? Mercury and purslane, a low succulent herb used in salads, and pickled . . . nettles and comfrey—a tall, rough-leaved ditch plant—from which I caught the bloody Lombardy gripe, but I cured it by applying my codpiece for bum-wad!

"In rapid succession, I utilized sheets, blankets, curtains, cushions, carpets, rugs, mops, napkins, snottingers and barbers' cloths. And I enjoyed it more heartily than the mangiest dog you might rub till Domesday."

"Ay, but tell me," Grangousier put in, "which rumpswab did you find best?"

"I was getting there," Gargantua answered. "You shall know the rub of it soon. Well, I went on with hay, straw, oakum, floss, wool and paper. But:

> *Who uses paper on his filthy bum*
> *Will always find his ballocks lined with scum."*

"Ha! my little rapscallion! you've been wetting your whistle to pipe poetry like that!"

"Ay, surely, my lord and king," the lad answered. "I rhyme my runes till I run with rheum! Listen to what our privy announces to squatters:

> *Come, sit and cack*
> *With lusty back*
> *But leave no wrack*
> *Beside our closet.*
> *Void, spirt and pump*
> *Your turdous rump*
> *But leave no lump*
> *Here for deposit.*
> *He shall know shame*
> *Who misses aim,*
> *St. Anthony's flame*
> *Burn his scut sear,*
> *Who will not swab*
> *His thingumabob*
> *To the last blob*
> *Ere he leave here!*

Would you have more of it?"

"Why, of course," Grangousier assented.

"Well then,'" said Gargantua:

> *"Whilst I was shitting yesterday, I sniffed*
> *The daily tribute that I owe my tail.*
> *Alas! the odors from my penetrail*
> *Proved quite the worst a human ever whiffed.*
> *O had some power but granted me the gift*
> *Of bringing her I waited for (sweet frail!)*
> > *Whilst I was shitting.*
> *I would have rammed and dammed her water-rift,*
> *Engrossed and settled her estate entail,*
> *Whilst she with skilful fingers would avail*
> *To guard my nozzle from the turdous drift,*
> > *Whilst I was shitting.*

Now tell me I know nothing! 'Smother, smother me in the stuff if I made these verses up! No, I heard them recited by this old lady here and I stored them in the budget of my memory."

"Let us get back to the subject!" said Grangousier.

"What: shitting?"

"No, Gargantua: we were speaking of bum wiping."

"Well, will you pay for a puncheon of Breton wine if I score you off?"

"Certainly, my lad."

"There is no need to swab the scut," Gargantua proceeded, "unless it is ordurous. Now it cannot be ordurous unless you have first cacked. Therefore you must cack ere you swab your rump."

"O my splendid little boy, how intelligent you are! I shall very shortly present you as candidate for the degree of Doctor of Philosophy; you are wise beyond your years! Meanwhile, proceed with the scutscouring you told me of, and, by my beard! for one butt you shall have sixty pipes—I refer to that fine old Breton wine, which grows not in Brittany but here in this sweet region of Véron, washed by the Loire and Vienne."

"Next, I wiped myself with a hat," Gargantua resumed. "Then, in turn with a pillow, a slipper, a gamebag and a basket—faugh! what a thorny, unpleasant bumduster! I also used hats, and, in this connection, let me remind you that some hats are smooth, others soft as velure, others shiny as satin, still others crisp as taffeta. But the best of the lot is the beaver for it makes a finished abstersion of the faecal matter.

"I tried a hen, a rooster, a pullet, a hide of calfskin, a hare, a pigeon, a cormorant, a lawyer's briefcase, a woollen hood, a coif and the feathers of a falconer's lure.

"But to conclude: I affirm and maintain that the paragon arsecloth is the neck of a plump downy goose, provided you hold her head between your legs. Take my word of honor on this score and try it for yourself. You will experience a most marvellously pleasant sensation in the region of your scutnozzle, as much because of the fluffy under plumage as because the bird's warmth, tempering the bumgut and the rest of the intestines, actually reaches your heart and brain.

"Do not believe the old women here when they prattle that the felicity of the heroes and demigods in the Elysian Fields lies in their asphodel or ambrosia or nectar. On the contrary, they are happy, to my mind, because they swab their rumps with a goose. Duns Scotus, the learned philosopher, holds the same opinion."

XIV

HOW GARGANTUA WAS TAUGHT LATIN BY A THEOLOGIAN AND SOPHIST

THE excellent Grangousier was rapt with admiration as he listened to his son talking. Truly this lad was marvellously gifted! What a vast intelligence, what cogent understanding! Turning to the governesses:

"Philip, King of Macedon," he declared, "recognized the sound judgment of Alexander, his son, when he saw how skilfully the lad managed his horse. This beast Bucephalus was so fierce and unruly that it threw all its riders. It cracked one man's neck, smashed another's legs, brained a third, and crushed the jawbone of a fourth. No one, then, dared mount it. Alexander happened to be in the hippodrome watching them breaking in and training the horses; he noticed at once that the beast's frenzy came from fright at its own shadow. He therefore made short shrift of vaulting upon its back and heading it towards the sun. There, its shadow falling behind it, he easily mastered it. Philip, by this token, realized the divine insight rooted in his son's intelligence and had him most carefully reared by Aristotle, then the most renowned philosopher in Greece.

"For my part, the brief conversation I have just had with Gargantua in your presence suffices to convince me that his mind is illumined by the divine spark. How else, pray, could he have proved so acute, so subtle, so profound and withal so serene? Give the boy proper schooling, say I, and he will attain a supreme degree of wisdom! Accordingly, I intend to trust him to some scholar who will instruct him to his capacity. What is more, I shall spare no cost."

The name of Master Tubal Holofernes, a great sophist and Doctor of Theology, was proposed to Grangousier. Subsequently this savant taught Gargantua his A B C so thoroughly that he could say it by heart backwards. This took five years and three months. A succession of standard texts followed; the *Facet* (a treatise of puerile moral precepts), the *Ars Grammatica* of Actius Donatus, the fourth-century grammarian; the *Theodolet* (in which Theodulus, Bishop of Syria in the fifth century, exposed in Latin the falsity of mythology and the truth of Holy Scripture) and the *Alanus in Parabolis* (a series of moral quatrains by Alanus of Lille, a thirteenth-century worthy). It took Gargantua thirteen years, six months and two weeks to master these authorities.

It is only fair to add, however, that Gargantua, in the process, learned to write in Gothic characters. (Printing had not yet been invented and the young student had to write out his own texts.)

He had, therefore, to carry in front of him a tremendous writing apparatus that weighed more than seven hundred thousand pounds. The pencase was as large and as tall as the great columns of the Church of St. Martin of Ainay in Lyons; the inkhorn was suspended to it by great iron chains wide enough to hold five cubic yards of merchandise.

Another book, *De Modis Significandi*—a work of speculative grammar by Thomas Aquinas, or Albert of Saxony or probably Duns Scotus—was Gargantua's next reading, together with comments by Hurtebize or Windjammer, by Fasquin or Roadheaver, by Tropditeux or Toomanysuch, by Gualehault or Galahad, by Jean Le Veau or John Calf, by Billonio or Lickspittle, by Brelinguandus or Timeserver, and by a rabble of others. This took more than eighteen years and eleven months, but Gargantua knew the texts so well that at examinations he could recite them by heart backwards. And he could prove to his mother on his fingers' ends that *de modis significandi non erat scientia*, grammar was no science.

Next he read the *Compost* or *Popular Calendar*, and had spent sixteen years and two months at it, when suddenly, in 1420, his tutor died of the pox.

Holofernes' successor was another wheezy old pedant named Master Jobelin Bridé or Jolter Clotpoll, who read him the *Liber De-*

rivationum or *Latin Vocabulary* of Hugutio of Pisa, thirteenth-century Bishop of Ferrara . . . the *Grecism* by Everard de Béthune, a philological lexicon illustrating the Latin words derived from the Greek . . . *De Octo Partibus Orationis* or *Of the Eight Parts of Speech* . . . the *Quid Est?* or *What is it?* a school manual in the form of questions and answers . . . the *Supplementum*, a collection of commentaries . . . the *Mammotreptus*, a monkish or monkeyish commentary on the Psalter and the Saints . . . the *Libellus de Moribus in Mensa Servandis* or *Essay on Manners in Serving at Table*, a rhymed treatise on youthful propriety and morals by Sulpizio de Veroli . . . Seneca's *De Quatuor Virtutibus Cardinalibus* or *Of the Four Cardinal Virtues*, a moral work by Martin de Braga, Bishop of Mondonedo in the sixth century . . . the *Specchio della vera Peni-tenza* or *Mirror of True Penitence* by Jacobo Passaventi, the Floren-tine monk of the sixteenth century—with its inevitable commen-tary! . . . a book of sermons, *Dormi Secure* or *Sleep in Peace*, a collection designed to save the preacher the pains of composing his sermons . . . and finally, other stuff of the same ilk, feather, kidney and broth. . . .

Indeed, Gargantua grew as even as any down ever smoothed, as full of matter as any goose liver ever crammed!

XV

HOW GARGANTUA WAS PUT UNDER OTHER PROFESSORS

AT last his father realized that though Gargantua was studying most industriously and spending all his time at it, he was profiting not at all. Worse, this training had actually made the lad over into a fool, a dunce, a booby and a nincompoop.

One day Grangousier happened to complain of it to Don Philippe des Marais, Viceroy of Papeligosse, a kingdom of Cockaigne. That monarch assured Grangousier that Gargantua would be better off learning nothing than studying books of the sort with pedagogues of that school. Their knowledge, said Don Philippe, was but rubbish, their wisdom flapdoodle; they succeeded merely in bastardizing noble spirits and corrupting the flower of youth.

"Upon my word, I'll prove it!" Don Philippe declared. "Take any lad of to-day with but two years' schooling. If he is not superior to your son in judgment, speech, bearing and personality, then I'm the greatest loggerhead and shallowpate from here to Brenne."

This challenge pleased Grangousier mightily; he at once gave orders that a match of wits take place.

That evening, at supper, Don Philippe brought in a young page of his named Eudemon, which means "the fortunate." The lad hailed from Villegongis near St. Genou in Touraine. He was so neat, so spruce, so handsome and his hair was so beautifully combed that he looked more like an angel than like a man.

Don Philippe turned to Grangousier:

"Do you see this lad? He's not twelve years old. Let us prove, if you will, the difference between the pedantic balderdash of yesterday's wiseacres and the intelligence of our modern boys."

Grangousier was agreeable to such a test and bade the page begin the debate. Whereupon Eudemon, asking leave of the Viceroy, his master, to do so, rose, hat in hand. His face was open and frank, his lips red, his glance confident. Looking at Gargantua with youthful modesty, he proceeded to praise and commend the boy—first for his virtues and good manners, next for his knowledge, thirdly for his nobility, fourthly for his bodily excellences and, in the fifth place, exhorted him most gracefully to reverence his father in all respects, because his father was so careful to have him well brought up. Finally, Eudemon prayed Gargantua to admit him among the least of his bondsmen. He added that the only boon he craved from Heaven, at present, was to serve Gargantua in some agreeable manner. Eudemon accompanied the whole speech with gestures so appropriate, his delivery was so distinct, his voice rang so eloquent, his idiom was so elegant and he couched his phrases in such perfect Latin that he seemed rather a Tiberius Gracchus, a Cicero or an Aemilius Lepidus of old, than a youth of our own day.

Gargantua's only reaction was to burst into tears. He bawled like a sick cow, hung his head and hid his face in his cap, until there was about as much possibility of drawing a word from him as a salvo of farts from the rump of a dead donkey.

This so incensed his father that Grangousier vowed to slay Master Jobelin Clotpoll, but Don Philippe remonstrated with him and, by fair persuasions, soothed his ire. Grangousier thereupon ordered them to pay the pedagogue off and to get him as properly fuddled up as your finest scholar of the Sorbonne. This accomplished, let him go to the devil!

"There is this consolation!" cried Grangousier. "To-day at least, he will not cost his host much if by chance he dies in his cups like an Englishman."

When Master Jobelin Clotpoll had gone away, Grangousier asked Don Philippe's advice about a tutor for Gargantua. They finally decided to appoint Ponocrates, Eudemon's teacher, to the position; auspiciously enough, in Greek the name means "vigorous." And soon, the three were to go to Paris in order to find out what studies young men were at this period pursuing in France.

XVI

HOW GARGANTUA WENT TO PARIS UPON AN ENORMOUS MARE WHICH DESTROYED THE OXFLIES OF THE BEAUCE

IN the same season, Fayolles, fourth king of Numidia, sent Grangousier a mare from Africa. It was the hugest and most enormous mare ever seen, the strangest monster in the world; for Africa, as the saying goes, may always be relied upon to produce something wonderfully new. The beast was as big as six elephants; like Julius Caesar's charger, her feet were cloven into human toes; her ears hung down like those of the goats of Languedoc; and a little horn grew out of one buttock. Save for a few dapple-gray spots as overlay, her coat was the color of burnt sorrel, which shows that she partook of the four elements, earth, water, air and fire. Above all, she had a horrible tail. It was more or less as tall as the tower of St. Mars near Langeais; and just as square, with tufts of hair as tightly spun and woven as the beards on ears of corn.

Do you marvel at this? You have greater cause to marvel at the tails of the rams of Scythia, which weighed more than thirty pounds each, or—if Jean Thenaud speaks truthfully in his *Voyage from Angoulême to Cairo*—at those of the Syrian sheep which are so long and heavy that, to hold them up, the natives have to hitch a small cart to the beast's rump. Ha! my lusty country wenchthumpers, you've no such tails as these!

The mare Fayolles sent Grangousier was brought overseas in three Genoese carracks and a brigantine; she landed at Les Sables d'Olonne in Talmondais.

When Grangousier laid eyes upon her:

"Ah!" he exclaimed. "Here is just what my son needs to bear him to Paris! So now, in God's name, all will go well: Gargantua shall be a great scholar one of these days! Were it not for dumb brutes we should all be scholars!"

Next day, having drunk liberally, as you may imagine, Gargantua set out on his journey, accompanied by his tutor Ponocrates, the young page Eudemon and his train. And, because the weather was serene and temperate, Grangousier had a pair of dun-colored boots made for him. According to Babin and the Chinon cobblers, these are technically known as buskins.

So they travelled along the highway very merrily, living on the fat of the land and making the best of cheer, until a little beyond Orléans they came to a huge forest, about thirty-five leagues long and seventeen wide. Alas! the woods were aswarm with oxflies and hornets of all varieties, so the wretched mares, asses and horses suffered a veritable massacre. But, by means of a trick they never suspected, Gargantua's mare handsomely avenged all the outrages visited upon her kind. For suddenly, when in the heart of the forest the wasps attacked her, she swished her tail and, sweeping all about her, not only felled the stingers but uprooted all the trees. Up and down, right and left, lengthwise and athwart, here and there, over and under, before her and aback, this way and that, she mowed down the woods like so much grass. And this region, which she thus turned into fallow land, has never known tree or wasp since.

Gargantua, delighted by the spectacle, forbore to boast, merely commenting to his followers:

"*Je trouve beau ce!* I find this pleasant!"

Whence this pleasant land has been known as Beauce ever since.

However, when it came to breakfasting, they had to content themselves with their yawns; in memory of which the gentlemen of the Beauce, proverbially poor, still subsist on a diet of yawns and gaping, and find it very nourishing. Indeed, they spit all the better for it.

At last they reached Paris, where Gargantua rested two or three days, making merry with his followers and inquiring about what scholars were then in the city and what wines people drank.

XVII

OF THE TREAT GARGANTUA GAVE THE PARISIANS ON HIS ARRIVAL AND HOW HE CARRIED OFF THE GREAT BELLS OF NOTRE DAME

AFTER a few days' rest, Gargantua went sightseeing. He attracted the attention of all the townsmen because Parisians are such fools, dolts and gulls that a mountebank, a hawker of relics and indulgences, a mule with a bell on its neck or a fiddler on a street corner, collects a greater mob than the most distinguished and authoritative preacher.

They thronged so thick about him that he said in a loud clear voice:

"Upon my word, I think these boobies want me to pay my welcome here and give the Bishop an offertory. Quite right, too! I'll treat them! They'll get their drink! I recognize my obligations and liquidate I shall!—but only *par ris*, for sport!"

Then, smiling, he unfastened his noble codpiece and lugging out his great pleasure-rod, he so fiercely bepissed them that he drowned two hundred and sixty thousand four hundred and eighteen, exclusive of women and children.

By sheer fleetness of foot, a certain number escaped this mighty pissflood, and reaching the top of the Montagne Ste. Geneviève, beyond the University, sweating, coughing, hawking and out of breath, they began to swear and curse, some in anger, others in jest:

—"God's plague and a pox take it! I'll deny God, if . . ."

—" 'Sblood!"

—"Christ, look ye, it's *Mére de* . . . *merde* . . . shit . . . Mother of God!"

—"*Pocapedion!* God's head!" roared a Gascon.

—"*Das dich Gots leyden Schend!*" bellowed a German trooper. "Christ's passion roil you!"

—"*Pote de Christo!*" an Italian voice rang out. "Christ's power!"

—"*Ventre St. Quenet!* . . . By the bellies of all the apostles . . . God's virtue . . . by St. Fiacre of the land of Brie!"

They called upon the renowned saint who cured miraculously such ailments as hemorrhoids and chancres, and who was patron to gardeners and husbandmen; one, doubtless a Scots Guard, invoked St. Andrew; and St. Theobald of Vico, the patron of shoemakers, was duly implored to intercede.

—"*Pasques Dieu!* God's passover!" said one, using an oath consecrated by King Louis XI.

—"*Bonjour Dieu!* God's light!" said another, after the manner of Charles VII.

—"*Le Diable m'emporte!* Devil take me!" said a third, quoting Louis XII.

—"*Foy de Gentilhomme!* My faith as a gentleman!" said a fourth, like Francis I.

—"*Par St. Andouille* . . . by St. Chitterling . . . by St. Godegran stoned to death with apple dumplings . . . by St. Foutin, the fornicators' friend! . . . by St. Vitus and his jig! . . . *Carimari, Carimara, hocus, pocus!* . . . by St. Mamica, the virgin martyr, by our lusty mammical duty to all virgins. . . ."

But, whatever protector each invoked, one and all cried:

"*Nous sommes baignés par ris*, we are drenched *par ris*, for sport."

Accordingly, the city which Strabo (Book IV) calls Leucetia—the name, signifying "whiteness" in Greek, pays a pretty tribute to the thighs of the local ladies—was, ever after Gargantua's exploit, named *par ris* or Paris.

And, since at this new christening every single townsman present swore by all the saints in his parish, the Parisians, who are made up of all nations and all varieties of men, will quite naturally swear at, to or by anything. Indeed they are not a little presumptuous and conceited, whence Joaninus de Barranco in his *Liber de Copiositate Reverentiarum* or *Of the Abundance of Venerable Things* opines that the word *Parisian* comes from the Greek *Parrhesieus*, a bold talker.

His account liquidated, Gargantua considered the great bells in the Towers of Notre Dame and made them ring out most harmoniously. The music suggested to him that they might sound very sweet tinkling on his mare's neck when he sent her back to his father laden with Brie cheese and fresh herring. So he promptly picked up the bells of the Cathedral and carried them home.

Meanwhile, a master beggar or Commander of the Order of St. Anthony came upon his swinish errand. These friars were reputed to cure St. Anthony's fire and to restore ailing pigs that had been placed under the protection of their patron. For this reason, or because they abandoned their original right to let their porkers run free in the streets, they were entitled to donations of ham and bacon. This larded hamster, then, plotted to filch the bells from Gargantua so that he might be heard from afar and make the bacons tremble in the very pantries. However, he very honestly left them behind him, not because they were too precious, but because they were too heavy for him to carry. This friar was not, I may add, the present Commander of the Order at Bourg-en-Bresse who happens to be much too good a friend of mine to behave thus.

The whole city was in an uproar, for Parisians, as you know, are ever prone to insurrection. Indeed, foreigners marvel at the patience of French kings who, faced with troubles arising daily out of the mob's violence, will not justifiedly stamp them out at their source. Would to God I knew the den where these plots and conspiracies were hatched! How speedily I would publish and denounce them in the confraternities of my parish.

You will readily believe that the place where all these people stormed and rioted was the royal Hôtel de Nesle, then the seat of the University Court, but now no longer the site of the Oracle of Lutetia. Here the whole grievance of the stolen bells was discussed and deplored. After extensive argumentation *pro* and *con*, they moved in the finest syllogistic Baraliptonic idiom to empower the oldest and most authoritative member of the faculty to apprize Gargantua of the dreadful damage they suffered through the loss of these bells. Despite certain objections that this mission could be better fulfilled by an orator than by a divine, our Master Janotus de Bragmardo, Doctor of Theology, was delegated.

XVIII

HOW JANOTUS DE BRAGMARDO WAS SENT TO RECOVER THE GREAT BELLS

MASTER JANOTUS, with a haircut like that affected by Julius Caesar, settled the traditional doctoral hood over his cootlike head. Next, he antidoted his stomach against possible contamination, with cakes baked in the most secular ovens, and holy water from his excellently stocked cellar. Then, he proceeded to Gargantua's. Before him crawled three black beadles; behind him he dragged five or six servile and artless Masters of Arts, all of them mildewed and rotten as cheeses.

Ponocrates met them as they entered and was terrified at their motley: he was convinced they must be crazed mummers. He therefore asked one of the artless magisters what this masquerade meant. For answer, he was told they wished to recover the missing bells.

Hearing this, Ponocrates immediately hastened with the news to Gargantua so the latter might have an answer and a plan ready for them. Gargantua, learning what had happened, called aside his tutor

Ponocrates, his steward Philotomus—the name means a lover of carving—his esquire Gymnastes ("teacher of esthetics") and Eudemon. A summary conference was held instanter to plan their reply and subsequent actions. It was unanimously agreed to take the learned doctors to the conservatory or wine room and there make them drink uproariously. Thus this wheezing old dryasdust would be denied the vainglory of supposing the bells had been restored at his request, for, while he tippled, they would summon the Provost of the City, the Rector of the University and the Vicar-General to the Bishop of Paris. To these officers they would hand over the bells ere ever the old sophister had delivered his message. The bells delivered, officers and jokesters would together listen to Janotus' eloquent harangue.

Which is exactly what happened. The authorities arrived, our theologian was ushered into the official meeting, and, having hawked and spluttered, began as follows.

XIX

MASTER JANOTUS' HARANGUE FOR THE RECOVERY OF THE GREAT BELLS

"AHEM, hem, hem! *B'na dies,* Sir, g'day to you, *b'nadies vobis* and g'day to you, gentlemen. It were but right that you should return our bells, for we are in sore need of them! Hem, ahem, ughsh! Many a time we have heretofore refused good money for them from the citizens of London (near Cahors) and of Bordeaux (in the land of Brie). These aspired to purchase our bells for the substantific quality of their elementary complexion which is intronificated in the terrestriality of their quidditative nature to extraneize the tempests and hurricanes that fall upon our vines . . . not our own vines, strictly speaking, but those that lie about us. . . . For, gentles, if we lose the juice of the grape, we lose all, both sense and law.

"If you restore them to us at my request, I shall gain one and one-quarter yards of sausage by it. And a fine pair of breeches, too, which will do my legs a lot of good—or, if I don't, then they'll have broken their promise! No, by God! *Domine*, a pair of breeches is a goodly thing and *vir sapiens non abhorrebit eam*, no, he that is wise will not abhor them. Ha, ha! it's not any sort of man that can come by a pair of breeches. You'll not find them growing on trees, believe me, for *I* know! Consider, *Domine*, O my Lord, that I have spent eighteen long days matagrobilizing this noble speech: *Redite quae sunt Caesari Caesaris et quae sunt Dei, Deo,* Render therefore unto Caesar the things which be Caesar's and unto God the things which be God's. *Ibi jacet lepus*, ay, that's where the hare lies; there's the rub!

"By my faith, *Domine*, by God's body, if you will sup with me *in camera charitatis*, in the guest hall, *nos faciemus bonum cherubin*, we shall make good cheer. *Ego occidi unum porcum*, I have slain a porker, *et ego habet bon vino*, and it's good wine I have, too. But of good wine, man cannot make bad Latin.

"Well then, *de parte Dei, date nobis bellas nostras*, by God, give us back our bells. Look ye, I will give you in the name of the faculty a *Sermones de Utino*, ay, a divine sermon if, *utinam*, would to heaven, you give us back our bells. *Vultis etiam pardonos? Per diem, vos habetis et nihil payabatis.* Do you wish pardons and indulgences into the bargain? By God, you shall have them without paying a penny!

"O Sir, *Domine, restor bellsimus nobis*, give us back our bells! Truly, *est bonum urbis*, it is for the good of the city. Every one here uses them. If your mare enjoys them, so does our faculty *quae comparata est jumentis insipientibus et similis facta est eis, psalmo nescio quo*, our faculty which is comparable to the dumb insensible beasts and fashioned like them, in I forget what psalm. Ay, I have set it down correctly upon my register, *est bonum Achilles*, it is the incontrovertible argument known in scholastics as *Achilles*. So! I prove to you that you must give them up. *Ergo sic argumentor*, thus argue I:

"*Omnis bella bellabilis, in bellerio bellando, bellans bellativo bellare bellantes. Parisius habet bellas. Ergo Gluc.* Every bellable bell, to be belled in the belfry, belling by the bellative, makes the bellers bell bellfully! In Paris there are bells. Q. E. D.

"Ha, ha, ha, that is to the point: it is *in tertio primae*, in *Darii*, ay,

Sir, in the third mode of the first figure of syllogism, in the category called *Darii*—or anyhow you will find it somewhere. By my soul, I have seen the day when I could beat the devil's own tattoo in an argument, but nowadays I simply ramble on deliriously, alas! and henceforth ask nothing but good wine, a good bed, my back to the fire, my belly to the table and a fine dish for my gullet.

"Eh, *Domine*, I beg you, *in nomine patris, Filii et Spiriti Sancti*, in the name of the Father, Son and Holy Ghost, give us back our bells and God rid you of ill and our Lady of Health, *qui vivit et regnat per omna secula secularum, amen*, who liveth and reigneth throughout all eternity, amen! Ahem! hum! ughthasch! gruhemhursch!

"*Verum enim vero, quando quidem, dubio procul, edepol, quoniam, ita certe, meus Deus fidus*, but verily whereas indubitably by Pollux in as much as thus as a matter of course by the God who presideth over good faith, a town without bells is like a blind man without his staff, an ass without a rump or a cow without a clapper. So until you duly restore them to us we shall not stop shouting at you like a blind man who has lost his staff, braying like an ass without a rump and bellowing like a cow that has no bell about its neck.

"A certain Latinist who lived near the hospital once said upon the authority of Nopatus—forgive me! a slip of the tongue! I mean Pontanus, the secular poet—that he wished those bells were made of feathers and their clappers of fox-tails because their chyme, no! their chime produced a colicle—I mean a chronicle—a diarrhoea, no! a diary!—in the bowels of his head when he was trying to compose his carminiformal lines. But *nac petitin petitac, tic, torche, lorgne*, smack, bang, crash, tinkle, tinkle, smash; he was declared a heretic— that's as easily done as making a wax figure!

"More the deponent shall not say. *Valete et plaudite*, hail and applaud our efforts! *Calepinas recensui*, I, Calepinus, I have said my say."

XX

HOW THE THEOLOGIAN CARRIED OFF HIS CLOTH AND WAS ARRAIGNED BEFORE THE SORBONNE

THE theologian had no sooner concluded than Ponocrates and Eude-mon burst into such uproarious peals of mirth that they all but gave up the ghost. Theirs was almost the plight of Roman Crassus who died of laughter when he saw a mule eating thistles and Greek Phile-mon, an ass eating figs prepared for his own dinner. Master Janotus began to laugh too, and all vied in hilarity. Their eyes watered at the violent concussion of the cerebral substance which pressed out these lachrymal humidities and brought them flowing out through the optic nerves. Here was a picture of Democratus heraclitizing and Heraclitus democratizing—your jocund philosopher crying like your pessimist, your malcontent convulsed with merriment.

When their guffaws were spent, Gargantua consulted with his followers as to what to do. Ponocrates proposed that they ply the priceless orator with further drinks since he had afforded them more amusement and jollity than Songecreux, the famous comedian. More, Janotus should be awarded one and one-quarter yards of sausage mentioned in his gleeful harangue, a pair of breeches, three hundred full-size logs of firewood, twenty-five hogsheads of wine, a great bed with three layers of down to the mattress and a deep capacious dish—all of which he had declared necessary for his old age.

This proposal was carried out with the exception of the breeches, for Gargantua did not believe they could readily find a pair suitable to the savant's figure. What fashion, indeed, would become him best? The martingale mode, which provides a drawbridge to the rump for more convenient cacking? Pantaloons, such as Dutch sailors wear, which offer great comfort to the kidneys? Slashed and puffed nether garments such as the Switzers sport to keep the belly warm? Round breeches, with sausage rolls and a seat like a cod's tail, to ventilate the reins?

Considering the difficulty of the problem, Gargantua gave Janotus seven ells of black cloth and three of white for the linings. His porters carried the wood to Janotus' lodgings, the Masters of Arts carried the sausages and vessels while Master Janotus expressed a desire to carry the cloth himself.

One of the Masters of Arts, Jousse Bandouille, objected that it was neither usual nor decent for one of Janotus' high academic standing to do so: he should, rather, depute this task to one of his humbler followers.

"Ha, you mule, you dolt!" Janotus answered. "Your conclusion is not *in modo et figura*, you defy the principles of formal logic. Have you never read our standard textbook? Consult the section *Suppositiones* in the work called *Parva Logicalia*. *Pannus pro quo supponit?* to what object is the cloth related?"

"*Confuse et distributive!*" Bandouille replied. "Its relation is general and particular to no person!"

"I do not ask you, ass, *quo modo supponit, how* it is related but *pro quo, to what object?* The answer, blockhead, is *pro tibiis meis:* to my legs! Therefore, I shall bear the cloth *egomet, sicut suppositum portat adpositum, I myself*, as the substance carries the attribute!"

Whereupon he made off with it as stealthily as Pathelin in the farce.

The cream of the jest was when the wheezy old divine, with utmost confidence, in a full assembly of the Sorbonne, demanded the breeches and sausages promised him by the University. That august body peremptorily denied his claim since he had already been thus repaid by Gargantua, according to information upon the circumstances. Janotus objected that he had received Gargantua's gifts *gratis* and out of pure liberality which in no way released the University from promises made previously. His colleagues replied that he should be content with reason and that he would not get one jot more from the University.

"Reason?" Janotus protested. "We practise none of *that* here! O wretched traitors, you are not worth the room you take! Alas! earth has not spawned creatures more evil than yourselves—that I know well enough. Do not limp before cripples, do not preach to the wise, do not teach your grandmother to suck eggs. Have I not practised wickedness with you? By the spleen and liver of God, I will inform the king of the outrageous abuses that are forged in this inferno by your agency and devising. May I be devoured with leprosy if I do not have you all burned alive like Sodomite buggers, traitors, heretics, fornicators and sworn enemies to God and all the virtues!"

At these words, they drew up an indictment against him; Janotus, for his part, immediately cited them to appear. In sum, the suit was brought into Court and is still pending. From this moment on, the pundits of the Sorbonne vowed they would not remove the filth on their bodies until a definitive verdict was handed down. Janotus and *his* partisans swore they would refrain from blowing their noses.

Because of these vows, the factions have continued dirty and snotty to this day, for the Court has not yet fully considered all the proceedings. A verdict will be given at the Greek kalends or never, for, as you know, these savants accomplish more than nature and go against their own articles.

Do not the Articles of Paris insist that God alone can perform infinite things? Nature, on the other hand, creates nothing immortal: she puts an end and a period to all things by her engendered, for *omnia orta cadunt*, all things rise and fall. . . . But these idlers and pettifoggers make the suits they are concerned in both infinite and immortal. And, in doing so, they justify the words of Chilo, the Lacedemonian, consecrated at Delphos:

"Wretchedness is the handmaiden of lawsuits and suitors are miserable, for they shall reach the end of their lives sooner than the satisfaction of their alleged claims."

XXI

GARGANTUA'S EDUCATION AND SOCIAL LIFE UNDER THE DIRECTION OF HIS PRECEPTORS AT THE SORBONNE

THE first few days having been spent thus and the bells put back in place, the citizens of Paris, in acknowledgment of Gargantua's civility, offered to feed and maintain his mare as long as he wished. Gargantua accepted this courtesy, so the Parisians sent the beast to graze in the Forest of Bière or Fontainebleau. (I do not believe she is still there.)

This accomplished, Gargantua resolved with all his heart to study under the direction of Ponocrates. But the latter, wishing to learn how the lad's former teachers had wasted so much time making a crackbrained, addlepated dunce of him, decided he should do exactly as he had in the past.

Gargantua therefore arranged his schedule so as to awake usually between eight and nine o'clock, rain or shine, dark or daylight, simply because his preceptors had decided this on the strength of the Psalmist's saw: "*Vanum est vobis ante lucem surgere*, it is vain for you to rise up betimes."

Then he wriggled and writhed, wallowing in his bed and tossing about like a parched pea, the better to stimulate his vital spirits. Next, he would dress, according to the season, but he was always happy to don a long, hanging gown of heavy wool lined with fox. Next, he combed out his hair with the comb of Jacques Almain, the Sorbonne theologian, known in English as John Handy—a comb consisting of four fingers and a thumb—for his mentors maintained that to brush one's hair, wash one's face and make oneself clean were, in this world, a pure waste of time.

Next Gargantua dunged, piddled, vomited, belched, broke wind, yawned, spat, coughed, hiccoughed, sneezed and snotted himself as majestically and bountifully as an archdeacon. Next he proceeded to breakfast in order to fortify himself against the morning mist and cold. His menu consisted of splendid fried tripe, choice meats grilled on charcoal, rich hams, succulent roast venison and numerous soups and brews, with toast, cheese, parsley and chopped meat floating on the surface.

Ponocrates objected that he should not eat so soon after rising without having taken any exercise. To which he replied:

"Exercise? Good God, didn't I tumble and jounce in bed six or seven times before I got up? Surely, that is exercise enough? Pope Alexander VI did this on the advice of his Jew physician, Bonnet de Lates, and lived till the day of his death in spite of his enemies. My first masters taught me this habit, for breakfast, they said, gave man a good mind. So they started the day by drinking. It suits me perfectly and I manage to dine the better for it. Master Tubal Holofernes, who was graduated Licentiate in Paris at the head of his class, used to tell me that to hasten was not enough, one must set out betimes. By the same token, the total health of mankind does not consist in drinking down and lapping up, *glub, glub, glub*, like so many ducks, but rather in falling to, early in the morning. *Unde versus;* so runs the rune:

> *Lever matin n'est point bonheur*
> *Boire matin est le meilleur.*

> *To rise betimes is not enough,*
> *To drink at morning, that's the stuff!"*

After an abundant breakfast, Gargantua repaired to church, with, in his train, a varlet bearing a basket. The latter contained a huge breviary swaddled in velvet and weighing about twelve hundred and six pounds including the filth of thumbmarks, dogeared corners, golden clasps and nonpareil parchment. Twenty-six, if not thirty, masses ensued for the benefit of Gargantua and his chaplain. Under his tall hood, this chaplain looked for all the world like a peewit . . . and had very thoroughly antidoted his breath against possible poisons with much syrup of the vine! Chaplain and pupil babbled the mumbo jumbo of the litany, thumbing their rosaries so carefully that not one single bead fell to the ground.

As he left the church, they brought him an oxcart laden with a huge heap of paternosters, chaplets and relics from St. Claude in the Jura, each bigger than a hatblock. Gargantua and his chaplain then strolled in the cloisters, galleries or garden, saying more aves than sixteen hermits.

After, Gargantua would study for a short half-hour, his eyes glued to his book but his mind, to quote Terence's *Eunuch,* woolgathering in the kitchen. Then he proceeded to make water, filling a large urinal to capacity, after which he sat down at table, and, being naturally phlegmatic, began his meal with a few dozen hams, smoked tongues of beef, caviar, sausages and other like forerunners of wine.

Then four servants in turn shovelled mustard into his mouth by the spadeful, thus preparing him to drain a horrific draught of white wine to relieve his kidneys. Then the meal proper began with viands to his liking, according to the season; Gargantua ceasing to eat only when his belly had reached bursting point.

When it came to drinking, he acknowledged neither end nor rule; for, he said, there were no limits and boundaries to swilling until the tosspot felt the cork soles of his shoes swell up a half-foot from the ground.

XXII

GARGANTUA'S GAMES

MUMPING and maundering sepulchrally as he said odd scraps of grace, Gargantua washed his hands in cool wine, chewed on a pig's foot which he wielded like a toothpick and conversed jovially with his people.

Then they spread a green baize cloth over the table and brought up a variety of playing cards, dice and boards for Gargantua's entertainment.

Among the card games were *Flux* or *One Suit Out; Primero,* which calls for a hand with all four suits; *Vole* or *Grand Slam*; *Pille* or *Freebooter*; *Triumph* or *Trumps*, which developed into *Ruff*, then *Whist* and at long last, *Bridge*; *Picardy Spades*; *One Hundred*, a form of *Piquet*; *Epinay* or *Joust*; *Old Maid*; *Fourbi* or *Cheating*; *Ten-up*; *Thirty-one*; *Post and Pair* or *Even and Sequence*; *Three Hundred*; *Low Man Out*; *Condemando* or *Call Your Card*; *Face down-Pay up*; *Unlucky Harry*; *Lansquenet*; *Cuckoo, You're Cuckold*; and *Slap Jack*.

There were other card games, too: *Pillo, Nado, Joco, Foro* or *Scramble, Zero, Game and Out*; *Bride and Groom*; *Pairs*, a game combining the features of *Lansquenet* and *Flux*; *Speculation*; *Giff-Guff* or *Give and Take*; *Sequences*; *Spotted Spaniards*; *Farocco* or *Tarots*, Italian in origin, played with a deck of seventy-eight cards, four numerical suits and twenty-two emblematical cards for trumps; *Tom Noddy's Fool* or *Winner Is Loser*; *Gull*; *Torturer*; *Revy* or *Double the Stakes*; *Glick*, which resembled *Condemando*; and, last but not least, *Honors*.

Besides cards, Gargantua indulged in numerous other amusements. One was the primitive Italian pastime of *Miorra* or *la Mourre* —often facetiously confused with *L'amour*—in which a player raised his hand and extended a certain number of fingers whilst the others guessed whether that number was odd or even. Another was *Fox and Geese*, in which a single chessman attacked and took twelve pawns. A third was *Merelles*, played with tokens on a square board divided by a straight cross and a St. Andrew's cross. A fourth was *Cows*, a form of *Draughts* or *Checkers*; a fifth, *White Lady*, in which a solitary Queen withstood the onslaught of a dozen black chessmen; and a sixth, called *Renette* or *Queen*, was somewhat similar.

Dice figured conspicuously in the program, with *Mumchance*— in which seven and its multiples alone scored—*Three Dice* and various forms of *Backgammon*, such as *Tables, Knick Knock* or *Kettle Noddy, In the Lurch, Add Six, Tric-Trac, Four Squares* and *Piles*. Further games calling for dice, counters or boards were *Deny Thy Saviour*; *Forzato* or *Galley Slave*; *Dames*, which is *Draughts* or *Checkers*; and *Baboo*.

Another variety of amusements included *Primus Secundus*, which resembled *Tiddlywinks*; *Mark Knife*, which consisted in tossing a coin as close as possible to a blade buried in the table; *Keys,* like the above save for the use of keys instead of coins; *Shovel Board,* in which three counters or coins were slid over a smooth board; *Odd or Even,* in which the players must guess the number of coins in a closed fist; *Cross and Pile,* sometimes called *Heads or Tails; Knuckle- bones; Jacks;* and *Ground Billiards* or *Croquet. Hunt the Slipper* aroused much merriment, especially when the victim's back, auspi- ciously turned, was belabored with an old shoe; *Hoot Owl, Hare and Hounds* and *Follow My Leader* were so popular. Additional chil- dren's games were *Pick Up,* in which the players run a race punc- tuated by stones or other objects they must gather, then throw or kick forward; *Magpies,* a hopping contest; *Shrovetide Ox,* based on the quaint custom of decorating an ox and parading him through the streets to the sound of music on the Thursday before Easter; *Screech Owl; Horns,* with appropriate pantomime; *Dare You to Laugh,* in which two children hold one another's chin, make faces and say: "Pinch you, pinch you, don't laugh or cry!" There were various tricks of fun based upon tickling and poking: *Prickle Me, Tickle Me; Unshoeing the Ass,* with the soles of the feet the object of attack; *Cocksess* or *Giddy up, Mule;* and *Whippetty, Hinny*—the last three being species of donkey-shines!

Popular, too, were *Down I Sit,* which is sometimes known as *Musi- cal Chairs* or *Going to Jerusalem; Beardibus Goldibus,* in which sev- eral players, pretending to raise a golden beard on the chin of a blindfold victim, daub his face with ordure; *Bastard Cherry; Draw the Spit,* apparently a game with a catch in it as one child, bending forward passes his fingers between his legs to his comrade and, as the latter pulls hard, poops in his face; *Lend Me Your Bag,* perhaps a singing game with a series of rhymes answering the question "What shall I put in it?" or a practical joke, in which case the reader may guess what was put in the bag of the candid soul who complied. They likewise played *Ramballock,* so called because the ball used was covered with the hide of a ram's testicle; *Wall Ball,* in which one player hit another with a ball bouncing off a wall; *Marseilles Figs; Mousqueto* or *Musketoon,* in which the players run round a mound of flowers; *Thieves and Archers; Flaying the Fox,* a game whose title we have seen elsewhere in the sense of vomiting after too generous potation; *Coasting* or rolling down a slope on a log; *Jostle and Fall* or *Grapple My Lady*, whose main feature consisted in tripping up an opponent; and *Buy My Barley*, a game of *Forfeits*.

Blow the Coal was an engaging pastime on a winter's night. A live coal hung from the ceiling by a pin on the end of a long thread; the players kneeled or squatted in a circle, the coal dangling on a level with their faces. They had then to try to blow it against some one of their number who warded it off, similarly, with all his breath. *Hide and Seek* proved invariably a great success, as did *Quick Judge, Dead Judge*, and *Oven and Iron*, in which the players extend their index fingers on the knee of one who represents the oven and who tries to seize them as they touch him. *Quails* and *Humpback Senator* are two games unknown to-day; *Find the Saint* was probably a form of *Hide and Seek*, and *Pinch and Laugh not*, a form of *Dare You to Laugh*, which we have mentioned above. *Pear Tree*, in which the players stood on their heads or hands; *Thwack and Thump*, wherein the players kicked each other in the rear, and *Triori*, a Breton jig, all had their devotees.

Gargantua and his friends jumped through hoops and played such games as *Sow to Your Pen*, driving a ball into a hole or pocket; and *Belly to Belly*, also called *Topsy-Turvy World*, where one child stands on his hands and another, standing normally, wraps his arms about him: thus locked, they topple over on to the back of a third child who is crouched on all fours. The result is a sort of human see-saw.

They went in for *Cubes* and for *Top Rod*, which consisted in crossing two small rods, each player thrusting his own upward in turn, the winner being the one on top in the end. The game was played on a table or flat ground. *Horseshoe and Quoits; I'm in*, a ball and racquet game; *Fucker* or *Squirrel*, where the players must blow through their noses to extinguish a lighted torch; *Tenpins, Ninepins* and *Skittles*, all forms of bowling; *Vireton* or *Veer and Turn*, a game played with arrows; *Fly to Rome*, where a twig pointed at both ends is sent flying in the air by a rap with a staff; *Crunchcrap*, a game like *Beardibus Goldibus* mentioned above; *Angenart;* and *Short Bowling*, a game played on a special green, were often indulged in.

There were further contests in *Volant* which has become *Badminton;* in *Shrivel up*, which may have been a form of *Hide and Seek*, or

Leap Frog or again something quite different; in *Smashpot,* where the players tossed a pot to each other and the player who muffed the catch lost; in *My Wish Is—*, a sport the scope of which you will have to guess, and in *Twirl and Whirl.* This last sport is relatively complicated but still played in the country. Across two stones you lay a somewhat short stick called the pirouette, which, with the help of a staff, you shoot off at your opponent who must, in return, propel it against your staff between the twin stones.

The list includes many more diversions, such as *Spillikins* or *Spelicans,* played with splinters of wood or bone; *Short Staff,* a kind of *Tug of War; Whirligig,* comparable to *Vireton,* cited above; *Hide and Seek; Pickett* or *Off You fly,* a form of *Fly to Rome,* cited above; *Blanks,* a form of lottery, where, with a pin, you open a book at a certain page, most of the pages being blank, though a few bear lucky numbers; and *Catch the Ferret,* in which the players pass an object among each other to elude the pursuer.

There were various forms of *Marbles: Boss Out* or *Hit and Span,* also known as the *Going to School Game,* because, being progressive, it helps the players along the road; *Fortifications* or *Pyramids* where you aim at a heap of marbles; *Plum Pudding* or *Picking the Plums,* where you shoot at marbles in a row; *Ring Taw* and *Nine Holes.*

Tops, also, were made use of as, for instance, the *Bull Roarer,* which made a humming, booming noise; the *Trump,* the *Snorting Monk* and the *Thunderwolf.* There was *Nonpluss,* a game of which we know nothing. And *Soulle,* a Breton term for a bladder filled with bran or a wooden ball, which was thrown into the air by one of the players and which the others tried to hit as far as possible with a special sort of stick. Three sports unknown to us were *Shuttlers,* *Smackscut* and *Broom. St. Cosme, I Come to Adore Thee* found its host of victims, as you may imagine when I tell you the rules. A player, seated on a milestone, represents the saint; the others advance in turn to present him with some ridiculous object, whilst he, for his part, makes the most outlandish faces in an effort to make the successive worshippers laugh. Later, this sport served to fool the credulous, who were blindfolded and, after a laying-on of hands, found their faces thoroughly begrimed. *Brown Beetle* was played on all fours; *Caught You Napping* pretty much in any position. In the appropriate season *Soft and Fair Passeth Lent* was much indulged in: the point here was to say these words to one's fellows on Ash Wednesday before they did.

Certain exercises required greater skill, such as the *Forked Oak,* where they had to stand on their hands with their legs spread, and *Stoop Horse,* a kind of *Leap Frog. Wolf's Tail* was simply the modern French *A la Queue leu leu,* where children follow one another single file like wolves, each stepping in the tracks of the one ahead. *Farthin' Face* had nothing to do with a coin but was rather what happened when two lads, locked in an embrace top against bottom, rolled down a slope, the head of each between the other's legs, with somewhat draughty results. *My Lance, Sir Knight* went further still, as the child climbed another's back and ordered his squire to give him the weapon, which of course was a stick covered with excrement. Often they swung on a *Grandelle* which is a swing made by two branches joined end to end or they played *Thirteeners.* The latter game owes its origin to the practice of covering a dozen sheaves of corn with a thirteenth which serves as a hat to keep them dry; in practice it consists of a dozen players standing in pairs one in front of the other whilst a thirteenth takes his place as third man behind any one given pair. He is at once pursued by a fourteenth who runs around the ring and he can escape only by getting between one pair. This forces the player who had become Number Three of the trio to escape in his turn. Such players as are caught become pursuers. Then there were *Birch,* a game we know nothing of; and *Mouche* or *Fly,* where one player, chosen by lot, plays the fly and the others whack at him as though to drive him off; and *Dilly, Dilly, Darling,* which may have been a form of *Ox Foot,* described later, or again simply the old smacking sport of *Hot Hand.*

Question and Answer created hilarity when a certain number of players formed a circle and each whispered a question to his neighbor on the right and an answer to that of his neighbor on the left and, the round done, he paired off question and answer. *Nine Hands* was probably the same as *Ox Foot:* the players placed their hands on top of one another, the first counting one, the second two and so forth until nine, when the ninth seizes some one's hand, crying: "Nine hands, nine hands! Here Ox Foot Stands!" *Chapifou* or *Crazyhead* was simply another name for *Blind Man's Buff* and *Fallen Bridge* was no more and no less than the game we call *London Bridge*. *Bridle Noddy* was a variety of *Blind Man's Buff* also; *Crow* consisted in hopping on one leg over figures traced on the ground and with one's foot pushing a quoit into each empty space without touching the lines; *Biff and Smack* was a kind of *Battledore*; and *Blind Man's Buff* we have already mentioned under other titles. *Mirrely-Muffely* is quite unknown to-day; doubtless the game derived its name from some childish formula; *Informer* is also unknown to us but *Toad* must have consisted in hopping, like *Crow*, or in playing on all fours, like *Brown Beetle*.

They played at *Cross*, the ancestor of *Hockey*, *Golf* and *Polo*; at *Pump the Bucket*, unknown to us by that name, and at *Cup and Ball*; at *Kings and Queens*; at *Trades*, where one side must guess the trade the other side acts out in pantomime; at *Heads-up*, in which the player must guess whether the pins in his opponent's fists are all laid head to head or no; at *Cherry Pips*; at *Uneasy Death*; at *Croquinoto* or *Flicks and Fillips*, where the tendon between the nostrils came in for some harsh treatment; at *Wash Your Headpiece, Lady*, and at *Sieve*, where two players stand with clenched hands pushing one another in turn as though driving flour through a strainer.

Sowing Oats was accompanied by appropriate song as they sowed, cut, bound and thrashed; *Briffo* or *Glutton* had its adepts, as did *Windmill*, where they held one another's hands, put the soles of one foot together and whirled dizzily about. *Defendo* consisted in counting pieces of bread laid out in a line as certain words were recited and taking that piece, large or small, upon which the title word fell. They turned *Handsprings* and played *Riding the Wild Mare*, where a victim was seized by his hands and feet and landed onto the ground on his rump; they also enjoyed *Plow*, which probably consisted in dragging some one vigorously along to plow up the ground and therefore resembled *Dead Beast*; *Hoot Owl*, where the players imitate the cries of birds and the owl is always first to be chosen; *Wild Sweepings*, *Dead Beast* and *Climb the Ladder*. The latter is to-day a favorite pastime for children. One closes his fist against his knee, sticking up his thumb, over which the other closes *his* fist and so on, the players each reciting the words of the title as their hands rise ever higher.

Among other entertainments were *Dead Hog*; *Pickled Arse*; *Scissors Cut Paper*, and *Odd Man*, a very ancient game referred to above as *Thirteeners; Burning Bush,* where they leaped either over a flaming thicket or over a line of people representing one, and *Hurdle the Brushwood; Cross Tag; I Spy; Penny, Penny, Arse Purse; Buzzard's Nest; Fig,* which apparently had something to do with a gesture of contempt, and *Petarrado,* which describes a sound of rectal scorn made with the mouth; *Pound out the Mustard; Cambo* and *Relapse,* both unknown to us; *Picando,* a game of darts; *Knock Pate,* which is a species of *Leap Frog; Rook; Crane* and a series of games with blows, taps or flicks, such as *Slap Neck, Nosardo, Swallowsmacks* and *Filliping.*

When they had played, striven, and agreeably passed their time, drinking was somewhat in order and each man accounted for about eleven bumpers. Then, immediately after, Gargantua would stretch out on a comfortable bench or a deep, soft bed, and sleep blissfully for two or three hours.

On awakening, he would wag his ears a little whilst they brought him fresh wine and he fell to, better than ever. In vain Ponocrates remonstrated that to drink immediately upon waking was unhealthy.

"Such is the true life of the Holy Fathers," he would reply. "My sleep is naturally salty; it is sleeping puts these great hams of flesh upon me."

Next he would begin to study a little and resume his paternosters; to dispatch them more roundly, he would ride an old mule that had served nine kings. Or with a deal of monkeychatter and head wagging, he might go to look at some rabbit caught in a trap. On his way back, he would drop in at the kitchen to see what roast was on the spit. To be sure, he dined very handsomely and often enjoyed inviting some tosspot of his neighbors whom he matched, draught for draught, old or young.

Among his retinue were My Lords of Fou, of Gourville, of Grignault and of Marigny. After supper they brought out many splendid wooden gospels—that is to say, many game boards that opened out like holy books—for play at *One, Two, Three* or, to finish up, *Everything Goes.* Or they might go to visit the young maids of thereabouts, organizing many a banquet, collation and postcollation in their honor. Then, without interruption, they slept a good eight hours into the morning.

XXIII

HOW PONOCRATES GAVE GAR GANTUA SUCH INSTRUCTION THAT NOT AN HOUR OF THE DAY WAS WASTED

WHEN Ponocrates saw Gargantua's vicious mode of life, he determined to bring him up otherwise. But for the first few days he bore with him, for he realized that nature cannot endure sudden and violent changes.

To begin his work the better, Ponocrates requested a learned physician of the times, Master Theodore—the name means "God-given" —to examine Gargantua thoroughly with a view to steering him on the right course. The scholar purged Gargantua canonically with Anticyrian hellebore, an herb indicated for cerebral disorders and insanity, thus cleansing his brain of its unnatural, perverse condition. Ponocrates, by the same aperient means, made the lad forget all he had learned under his former teachers, just as Timotheus of old treated pupils who had already studied under other musicians. Timotheus, incidentally, used to charge this class of students double!

For Gargantua's further edification, Ponocrates made him mingle among learned men whose company fired him with a desire to emulate them, to study more profitably and to make his mark. Next, Ponocrates so arranged the lad's schedule that not a moment of the day was wasted; all his time was spent in the pursuit of learning and honest knowledge.

By this new dispensation, Gargantua awoke at about four in the morning. While the servants massaged him, he would listen to some page of Holy Scripture, read aloud in clear tones and pronounced with fitting respect for the text. A young page, a native of Basché, near Chinon, was appointed reader, as his name, Anagnostes, shows. According to the purpose and argument of this lesson, Gargantua frequently turned to worship, adore, pray and reverence Almighty

God, Whose majesty and wondrous wisdom were made manifest in the reading.

Next, he would repair to secret places to make excretion of his natural digestions; here his tutor repeated what had been read, expounding its more obscure and difficult features. Returning to the house, they would study the heavens. Was it the same sky they had observed the night before? Into what signs was the sun entering that day? and the moon?

After this astronomical survey, Gargantua was dressed, combed, curled, trimmed and perfumed, and, while this was being done, he heard the lessons of the day before. Then, having recited them by heart, he would argue certain practical, human and utilitarian cases based upon the principles enunciated. This part of the program sometimes took two or three hours, though usually he had exhausted it by the time he was fully clad.

Then, for three good hours, he was read or lectured to, after which they went to the Tennis Court at the Grande Bracque in the Place de l'Estrapade or to the playing fields.

On the way, they discussed various aspects of the subject previously treated. Then they would play tennis, handball and three-cornered catch, exercising their bodies as vigorously as they had exercised their minds before.

All their play was free for they left off when they pleased, which was usually when they had sweated a good bit or were otherwise tired. They were thoroughly wiped and rubbed down, after which they changed their shirts and walked quietly home to see if dinner were ready. As they waited, they would go over certain points they had retained of the lectures.

Meanwhile My Lord Appetite put in an appearance and they sat down most opportunely to table.

At the beginning of the meal, they listened to the reading of some agreeable chronicle of chivalry in ancient times, until Gargantua gave the signal for wine to be served. Then, if they wished, the reading went on or they could talk merrily together. Often they discussed the virtues, property, efficacy and nature of what was served at table: bread, wine, water, salt, meat, fish, fruit, herbs, roots and their preparation. Thus Gargantua soon knew all the relevant passages in Pliny's *Natural History* . . . in the grammarian Athenæus'

Deipnosophistes or *The Banquet of the Sages,* which treats of flowers, fruits and their various uses . . . in Dioscorides' famous medical treatise, the bible of apothecaries . . . in the *Vocabularium* by Julius Pollux, a grammarian and sophist of Marcus Aurelius' day, who wrote of hunting and fishing . . . in Galen's numerous dissertations upon alimentation . . . in the works of Porphyrius, the third-century Greek author of a *Treatise upon Abstinence from Meat* . . . in Oppian's two poems, *Cynegetica* which deals with venery and *Halieutica* with angling . . . in *Of Healthy Diet* by Polybius of Cos, disciple and son-in-law of Hippocrates . . . in Heliodorus of Emesa, Syrian Bishop of Tricca and a celebrated novelist of the fourth century . . . in Aristotle's essays on natural history . . . in the Greek works upon animals by Claudius Ælianus, a Roman contemporary of Heliogobalus . . . and in various other tomes. . . . Often for surer authority as they argued, they would have the book in question brought to the table. Gargantua so thoroughly and cogently learned and assimilated all he heard that no physician of his times knew one-half so much as he.

They discussed the lessons they had learned that morning and topped their meal off with quiddany, a sort of quince marmalade and an excellent digestive. After which Gargantua picked his teeth with a fragment of mastic, washed his hands and daubed his eyes with cool clear water, and, instead of saying grace, sang the glory of God in noble hymns, composed in praise of divine bounty and munificence.

Presently cards were brought them and they played, not for the sake of the pastime itself but to learn a thousand new tricks and inventions all based on arithmetic.

Thus Gargantua developed a keen enthusiasm for mathematics, spending his leisure after dinner and supper every evening as pleasantly as once he had, dicing and gaming. As a result, he knew so much about its theory and practice that Cuthbert Tunstal, Bishop of Durham and secretary to King Henry VIII, a voluminous writer on the subject, confessed that, beside Gargantua, he knew no more about arithmetic than he did about Old High Gothic. Nor was it arithmetic alone our hero learned, but also such sister sciences as geometry, astronomy and music.

Now the digestion of foods is a most important matter. There is the first stage which occurs in the stomach, where the viands are changed into chyle; the second, in the liver, where the chyle is transformed into blood; the third, in the habit of the body, where the blood is finally converted into the substance of each part. So, whilst Gargantua awaited the first stage of digestion, they made a thousand delightful instruments, drew geometrical figures and even applied the principles of astronomy.

After, they amused themselves singing a five-part score or improvising on a theme chosen at random. As for musical instruments, Gargantua learned to play the lute, the spinet, the harp, the nineholed transverse or German flute, the viol and the sackbut or trombone.

Having spent an hour thus and completed his digestion, he discharged his natural excrements and then settled down again to work three hours or more at his principal study. Either he revised the morning reading, or proceeded in the text at hand or practised penmanship in the most carefully formed characters of modern Roman and ancient Gothic script.

Next, they went out with a young gentleman of Touraine, the esquire Gymnastes, who instructed Gargantua in the art of horsemanship. Having changed his clothes, he proceeded to mount a fiery Italian charger, a Flemish dray horse, a Spanish jennet, an Arab thoroughbred and a hackney. These he would put vigorously through their paces, letting them "career" or gallop a short distance at full speed, making them leap high in the air, jump ditches, clear stiles, and turn short in a ring both to the right and to the left. Next he wielded but did not break his lance, for it is arrant stupidity to boast: "I have broken ten lances in a tilt or fight." A wretched carpenter can do the same. On the contrary, the whole glory of such combat lies in besting ten enemies with one and the same lance. So with strong, stiff, steel-tipped lance, Gargantua would force the outer door of some house, pierce an adversary's armor, beat down a tree, pick up a ring, carry off a cuirassier saddle, a hauberk or a gauntlet. And he performed these feats armed cap-à-pie.

In the technique of parading his horse with prances and flourishes to a fanfare of trumpets—the ceremonial of knights as they enter the lists—he had no equal. As for the divers terms of the equine vocabulary from *giddy-up* and *cluck* to *whoa* and *grrr*, no horseman could hold a candle to him. Indeed Cesare Fieschi, the celebrated jockey of Ferrara, was a mere monkey in comparison.

He learned, too, to leap hastily and with singular dexterity from one horse to another without setting foot to the ground (the nags were circus horses or, to be technical, "desultories"). Further, lance in hand, he could leap on horseback from either side without stirrups and rule the beast at will without a bridle, for such accomplishments are highly useful in military engagements.

Another day he would practise wielding the battle-axe, which he managed so skilfully, in the nimblest thrusts, the most powerful lunges and the vast encircling sweeps of the art, that he passed knight-at-arms in the field and at all tests. Sometimes unarmed, sometimes carrying a buckler or a rolled cape of mail over his arm or a small shield over his wrist, Gargantua brandished the pike, plied the double-edged, two-handed sword, the bastard claymore used by archers, the Spanish rapier, the dagger and the poniard.

He hunted, too: stag, roebuck, bear, fallow deer, wild boar, hare, partridge, pheasant and otter . . . he played at ball, ever ready with well-aimed foot or powerful fist to send the great sphere whizzing through the air . . . he learned to wrestle and to run. . . . As for jumping, he did not go in for the various forms of running jumps, such as the three-steps-and-a-leap, the hop-step-and-jump or the German high-jump. As Gymnastes pointed out, these were quite useless in warfare. Instead, he practised the standing jumps. Starting from scratch, he could in one leap top a hedge, clear a ditch, mount six paces upon a wall and thus reach a window-ledge one lance's height from the ground.

Gargantua could swim in the deepest water, breaststroke, back and sidestroke, using his whole body or his feet alone. He could cross the breadth of the Seine or the Loire at Montsoreau, dragging his cloak along in his teeth and holding a book high and dry over the waters—thus renewing the exploit with which Plutarch credits Julius Cæsar during the Alexandrian War. Then, using one hand only, he could, with a single great pull, climb into a boat, whence a moment later he would dive headlong into the water again, sound its utmost depths, touch bottom, explore the hollows of rocks and plunge into any pits and abysses he fancied. He would turn the boat about, managing it perfectly, bringing it swiftly or slowly upstream or down and arresting its course at a milldam. He could guide it with one hand while he plied hard about him with a great oar; he could run up a sail, hoist himself up a mast by the shrouds, dance along the yards, operate the compass, tackle the bowlines to sail close to the wind and steer the helm.

His water sports done, he would dash full speed up a mountain, then down quite as fast. He climbed trees like a cat, hopping from one to the next like a squirrel and pulling down great boughs—like the celebrated Milo of Crotona who, Pausanias tells us, met his death devoured by wolves, his hands caught in the cleft of an oak he had sought to split. With two well-steeled daggers and a pair of well-tried mason's punches, he could scurry up the side of a house like a rat, then leap down again, from roof to ground, so expertly that he landed without hurt. Gargantua also cast the dart, threw the iron bar, put the stone, tossed the boar-spear, hurled the javelin, shied the halberd. He drew the bow to breaking point; he could shoulder a harquebuss—a great siege piece weighing fifty pounds—and fire it off like a crossbow. He could set a huge cannon on its carriage, hit buttmarks and other targets for horizontal shooting, or, point-blank, bring down papgays (stuffed figures of parrots on poles), clay pigeons and other verticle marks, facing them on a level or upwards, or downwards or sidewise. Like the ancient Parthians, he could even hit them as he retreated.

They would tie a cable to a high tower and let it dangle to the ground. Gargantua hoisted himself up with both hands, then slipped down again as evenly, surely and plumb as a man running along a flat meadow. Or they would set a great pole across two trees for Gargantua to hang from by his hands. He moved along the pole from tree to tree so swiftly, without setting foot on *terra firma*, that a man, running on the ground below, could not have caught him. To expand his chest and exercise his lungs, he would roar like all the devils in hell. Once indeed, I heard him call Eudemon across all Paris, from the Porte St. Victor, the gate by the University, all the way to Montmartre, a village on a hill two miles beyond the walls of the city. Stentor, who cried louder than forty men, displayed no such vocal power, even at the siege of Troy.

To develop his sinews, they made him two great pigs of lead, each weighing eight hundred and five tons. These pigs (called salmons in France because the metal is shaped like this fish) Gargantua named *alteres*, an ancient Greek term for the weights used to give jumpers their initial spring—our modern dumb-bells. Taking one in each hand, Gargantua then performed an inimitable feat. He would raise them high above his head and, never turning a hair, stock-still as a statue, hold them aloft for three-quarters of an hour. He played at Barriers or Tug-of-War with the stoutest champions. When his turn came he took root so firmly as to defy the sturdiest to budge him. Nor was it thus alone he emulated Milo of Crotona. Like the ancient athlete, he could hold a pomegranate so fast in his hand that none could wrest it from him, yet so adroitly that he did not crush it.

Having spent his time in such manly sports, he had himself washed, rubbed down and given a change of clothes. Then he returned home at a leisurely pace, passing through some meadow or grassy space to examine the trees and plants. These he would compare with what the authorities wrote of them in their books: among the Ancients, Theophrastus, the successor of Aristotle and teacher of Menander . . . or Palladius, whose poem *De re rustica* was translated by Pietro Marini . . . or Dioscorides Pedanius, the Greek physician of the first century . . . or Pliny or Nicander or Aemilius Macer, the Roman, or Galen himself. . . . Gargantua and his companions picked specimens by the handful and took them home to a young page named Rhizotome or Rootcutter, who watched over them and the various small mattocks, pickaxes, hooks, hoes, pruning-knives, shears and other botanical instruments.

At home, whilst the servants prepared dinner, our young men repeated certain passages of what had been read. Then they sat down to table. Here I would have you note that their dinner was simple and frugal; they ate no more than necessary to quiet the baying of the belly. Supper, on the contrary, was a large and copious meal; they ate what they needed for their sustenance and nourishment. Such indeed is the true system prescribed by the art of sound, self-respecting physicians though a rabble of dunderhead quacks, wrangling eternally in the claptrap routine of the Arab nostrum shop of Avicenna, recommend the exact opposite. During supper, they continued the lesson given at dinner as long as they saw fit; the rest of the meal was spent in earnest and profitable discussion.

Having said grace, they applied their voices to sing tunefully or they played upon harmonious instruments. Or they amused themselves with such minor pastimes as cards, dice cups and dice afforded. Sometimes they tarried here enjoying themselves and making merry until bedtime; they would visit learned men or such as had travelled in foreign lands. Well into the night, before retiring, they would go to the most exposed spot in the house, whence they examined the face of the sky, noting the comets, if any were visible, and the various figures, positions, aspects, oppositions and conjunctions of the heavenly bodies.

According to the Pythagorean system, Gargantua would, with his tutor, recapitulate briefly all that he had read, seen, learned, done and assimilated in the course of the day.

Then they prayed to God the Creator, doing Him worship and confirming their faith in Him, glorifying Him for His immense goodness, vouchsafing thanks for all the mighty past and imploring His divine clemency for all the future.

And so they retired to rest.

XXIV

HOW GARGANTUA SPENT HIS TIME IN RAINY WEATHER

IN intemperate or rainy weather, things went on much the same as usual before dinner except that Gargantua had a fine bright fire lighted to correct the inclemency of the air. But after dinner, instead of gymnastics, they stayed indoors and, by way of apotherapy or exercise amused themselves by bundling hay, splitting logs, sawing wood and threshing sheaves in the barn. Then they studied the arts of painting and sculpture. Or they revived the ancient Roman game of *Tali*, dicing as the Italian humanist Nicolaus Leonicus Thomaeus wrote of it in his dialogue *Sannutus, Of the Game of Dice,* and as our good friend Janus Lascaris, librarian to our sovereign king, plays at the game. In their sport, they reviewed such passages of ancient authors as mention or quote some metaphor drawn from this play.

In much the same way, they might go to watch workmen forging metals or casting pieces of ordnance. Or they might visit the lapidaries, goldsmiths and cutters of precious stones in their ateliers, the alchemists in their laboratories, the coiners at the mint, the tapestry-workers, velvet-workers and weavers at their looms, the watch-makers, looking-glass framers, printers, lutemakers, dyers and other such artisans in their workshops. Wherever they went, they would distribute gratuities, invariably investigating and learning the various inventions and industry of the trade.

Or they might attend public lectures, official convocations, oratorical performances, speeches, pleadings by eloquent attorneys and sermons by evangelical preachers—that is, such priests as wished to restore Christianity to the primitive tradition of the Gospel. Gargantua also frequented fencing halls and tested his skill at all weapons against the masters, proving to them by experience that he knew as much as they and, indeed, even more.

Instead of herborizing, they would inspect the shops of druggists, herbalists and apothecaries, studiously examining the sundry fruits, roots, leaves, gums, seeds and exotic unguents and learning how they could be diluted or adulterated. He viewed jugglers, mountebanks and medicasters—who sold Venice treacle, a cure for all ills—carefully observing their tricks and gestures, their agile capers and smooth oratory. His favorites were those from Chauny in Picardy who are born jabberers and the readiest expounders of mealy-mouthed flimflam concerning their ability to weave ropes of sand, extract sunbeams from cucumbers and milk a he-goat into a sieve.

Returning home to supper, they would eat more sparingly than on fine days. Their meats would, by the same token, be more desiccative and extenuating so as to counteract the humidity communicated to their bodies by the necessary contiguity of the atmosphere and to nullify what harm might arise from lack of their customary exercise.

Such was Gargantua's program and so he continued from day to day, benefiting as you would expect a young man of his age and intelligence to benefit under such a system faithfully applied. To be sure, the whole thing may have seemed incredibly difficult to him at the outset, but it soon proved so light, so easy and so pleasant as to appear more like a king's pastime than the study of a schoolboy.

However, Ponocrates was careful to supply relaxation from this violent bodily and mental tension. Once a month, on some very bright serene day, they would clear out of town early in the morning, bound for the near-by villages of Gentilly, Boulogne, Montrouge, Pont-de-Charenton, Vanves or St. Cloud. There they spent the whole day enjoying themselves to their heart's content, sporting and merrymaking, drinking toast for proffered toast, playing, singing, dancing, tumbling about or loafing in some fair meadow, turning sparrows out of their nests, bagging quail and fishing for frogs and crayfish.

But though this holiday was free of books and reading, it was not spent unprofitably. Lying in the green meadow, they usually recited certain delightful lines from Virgil's *Georgics*, from Hesiod's *Works and Days* or from Politian's *Husbandry*. Or they broached some savory epigram in Latin, then turned it into a French roundelay or ballade.

In their feasting, they would sometimes separate the twin elements, isolating the wine and the water in their drink by pouring the latter into a cup of ivy-wood, as Cato teaches in his *De re rustica*, and Pliny elsewhere. Then they would wash the wine in a basin full of water and draw it out with a funnel, as pure as ever. And they pumped the water with a syphon from one glass to another, manufacturing several sorts of automatic or self-operating devices.

XXV

HOW GREAT STRIFE AROSE BETWEEN GARGANTUA'S COUNTRYMEN AND THE LERNÉ BAKERS AND HOW FIERCE WARS RESULTED

IT was early autumn, the vintage season, when the shepherds of the land guard their vines against marauding starlings.

Just then the bakers of Lerné happened to pass down the highway, bound for Tours, with ten or twelve horseloads of their succulent merchandise.

Our shepherds courteously asked to buy a few cakes at the current market price against cash. You would have done the same, for Lerné cakes are excellent breakfast fare—especially with grapes. And grapes of all sorts, too: Blackboy, Figsavor, Muscat, Goatbody and, best of all, Crapman, a luscious specimen that will turn out a turd long as a scythe. (Addicts of Crapman, hoping to eventuate, often beshit themselves and are accordingly known as vintage prophets.)

The bakers not only turned a deaf ear to our shepherds' request but, worse, insulted them outrageously. Apparently our men were waifs, snaggleteeth, red-headed Judases, wastrels and shitabeds; they were stinkers and fly-by-night smoothsters—idlers, too, yet nicksters—belly-busters, proudsters, badsters, clots, sharpers, puts, scabbard-dragglers and sweets. (The latter mild epithet applies to one whose fly is lined with silk and satire.) Jokesmiths, they were, yet lazy, riffraff oaves, louts, wompsters, tonies, wonglers, fops and rattletooth almsters, and, for occupation, they herded petrified turds and shepherded stillicidious excrement. Such was the harvest of defamatory epithets our herders reaped and, hard upon it, the flat statement that they were unfit to taste dainty pastry. Let them be satisfied with coarse bread or hard-loaf.

To which insults one of the shepherds, an honest, personable young man named Forgier, replied calmly as follows:

"Since when have you calves grown the horns of bulls to become so arrogant? Tell me: didn't you always sell us your cakes? And now you refuse to! It isn't neighborly of you. Do we do the same when you come here to purchase our fine corn that *makes* your cakes and your buns? What's more, we would have given you some of our grapes into the bargain. 'Smother, smother me in shit if you'll not be repenting of it, likely, when some fine day you have to call upon us. Then we'll do the like to you and don't forget it."

Marquet, ranking officer in the Bakers' Guild, answered:

"You're rearing your cocks' crests very high this morning, I think; you must have eaten a deal of millet. Step up, step up, my lad, and I'll give you all the cake you can handle."

And, as Forgier, believing the other was about to produce some of his cakes, in all candor drew a crown out of his girdle, Marquet whipped him so fiercely across the legs as to raise large welts. Marquet sought to flee; Forgier roaring help and murder, threw his great club at him. It struck Marquet on the frontal jointure, under the temporal artery at the right side; he fell from his mare, more dead than alive.

Meanwhile the farmers who were knocking down nuts near by ran up with their great poles and proceeded to lay on the bakers like threshers on green rye. Other herders and shepherdesses, hearing Forgier's cry, came on with their slings and catapults, peppering the bakers so hard and so fast that it seemed like hail. Finally they caught up with them and took four or five dozen cakes. But they paid the customary price for them, throwing in one hundred shelled nuts and three basketfuls of sweet white grapes. The bakers helped Marquet back on his mare—he was seriously injured—and returned to Lerné without going further along the road to Parilly. As they retreated, they heaped dire threats upon the herders, shepherds and farmers of Seuilly and Sinais.

The bakers gone, our shepherds and shepherdesses feasted on their cakes and fine grapes, danced to the sound of pipes and laughed at these fine proud bakers who had met with evil because they had made the sign of the cross with the wrong hand that morning. And they

bathed Forgier's legs so carefully in the juice of dog-grape that he
was speedily cured.

XXVI

HOW THE MEN OF LERNÉ, ACTING ON ORDERS FROM PICROCHOLE, THEIR KING, FELL UPON GARGANTUA'S SHEPHERDS UNAWARES

THE bakers, returning to Lerné, did not pause to eat or drink but
made straight for the palace. Here, in the presence of Picrochole the
Peevish, third king of that name, they set forth their grievance. Producing their broken baskets, their crumpled caps, their torn clothes,
their empty paniers and, to cap the climax, a terribly wounded Marquet, they accused Grangousier's shepherds and farmers of these
wrongs, specifying that the highway beyond Seuilly was the scene
of operations.

Without stopping to consider the circumstances, Picrochole flew
into a mad rage. He called the First Ban and Second Ban, summon-
ing both immediate and distant vassals; upon pain of hanging, every
citizen must appear under arms in the great square in front of the
castle at noon.

To make assurance doubly sure, he had the drum beaten all
over town; then, while dinner was being prepared, he had his artillery mounted, his colors and royal standard displayed and a quantity
of equipment and supplies put in readiness.

During dinner, he gave his officers their various commissions: My
Lord Trepelu or Shagrag was put in command of the vanguard
which numbered sixteen thousand and fourteen harquebusiers and
thirty-five thousand and eleven foot, the latter volunteers and un-
paid. My Lord of Touquedillon Tickledingus and Touchfaucet, Mas-

ter-of-Horse, was given the artillery, numbering nine hundred and fourteen pieces. There were heavy pieces, each weighing seven thousand pounds and requiring thirty-five horses to drag it . . . basilisks that could throw stone shot of two hundred pounds . . . long-muzzled serpentines, weighing one hundred and fifty pounds and firing lead . . . culverins, slender and thin as the snakes they were named for . . . bombards, falcons, passevolans and spiroles. . . . My Lord Duke Raquedenier of Farthingscraper commanded the rearguard while the King and the princes of the blood were in the main army.

Thus hastily organized, before setting out, they sent three hundred light horse under Captain Suckwind Engoulevent to reconnoitre and look for possible ambush. A diligent search on their part revealed a country, peaceful and silent, without the slightest hint of public assembly. Receiving this report, Picrochole ordered each unit to speed under its colors. So they took to the road without order or discipline, breaking out of rank, spoiling and ravaging every hamlet on their way, sparing neither rich nor poor, consecrated nor lay ground. They drove away oxen and cows, steers, calves and heifers; sheep, lambs and ewes; goats and kids; hens, capons and pullets; goslings, ganders and geese; pigs, sows and hogs . . . they knocked down the nuts, spoiled the vines, carried off the stalks and stripped the trees of their fruit. No one resisted them as they threw everything into utter disorder; on the contrary, to a man, Grangousier's subjects threw themselves on Picrochole's mercy. Could they not act more humanely? After all, since time out of mind, these peoples had been good friendly neighbors; they had committed no excess or outrage to warrant such sudden molestation, and God Himself would swiftly punish the invaders' barbarity.

The latter, for sole reply, stated that they would teach Grangousier's men to eat cakes.

XXVII

HOW A MONK OF SEUILLY SAVED THE ABBEY CLOSE FROM BEING RAVAGED BY THE ENEMY

THIEVING, pillaging, robbing and plundering along the way, they finally reached Seuilly, where they stripped both men and women of all they possessed. Nothing was too heavy to carry off, nothing too hot to handle, nothing unworthy of capture. Though the plague was raging in town at the time, they broke in everywhere, spreading ruin and destruction as they went. Curiously enough, not one of them fell ill; whereas the curates, vicars, preachers, physicians, surgeons and apothecaries who went to visit, dress, heal, preach and administer to the sick, had all died of infection. Yet these cursed robbers and murderers never took ill. Why was that, gentlemen, I ask, and urge you to give the matter thought!

The town ransacked, they proceeded to the abbey amid a horrible din. Finding it closed and the approach cut off, they split into two groups: the main body marched to the Gué de Vède, whilst seven companies of infantry and two hundred lancers remained to break down the walls of the close and lay waste the vineyards.

The monks, poor devils! did not know what saint to turn to. In their dilemma, they took a chance and had the bells rung *ad capitula capitulantes, All voters to the Chapter House,* the signal for general assembly. Here they decided to march in solemn procession to a ceremony spiked with brave fine prayers, chants and litanies against *hostium insidias,* the ambush of the enemy. To these, they made appropriately noble responses *pro pace,* in favor of peace.

At the time, the abbey included a monk called Friar John of the Funnels, a youthful, gay, wide-awake, good-humored and skilful lad. Tall, slim, with a wide mouth and a great nose, bold, venturesome, deliberate, Friar John was a crack patterer of psalms; he could polish off a mass or get through a vigil in record time. In brief, here was a true monk if ever there was one since the monking world started monkeying in monkeries. Withal, when it came to the breviary, a clerk to the teeth!

Hearing the enemy's tumult in the vineyard, Friar John went out to discover what they were up to. To his horror he found them gathering the grapes upon which the monks depended for all their next year's supply of wine. Hastening back to the choir of the church, he found his colleagues struck all of a heap like so many ducks in a thunder storm. They were singing: *Inininim, pennenenenenne, tumnenumninimi, coconenononini, rumnenummum*, which in the breviary reads *Impetum inimicorum ne timueritis—Fear not the onslaught of your foes!*

"Bravo, bravo: Well shit, well sung!" mocked Friar John. "But in God's name, why not sing: *Baskets farewell for vintage is over?* The devil take me if those bastards are not in our vineyard, hacking away at vines and grapes so thoroughly that for the next four years we can use our close for cacking. By God's body and the belly of St. James, what will we poor devils have to drink in the meanwhile? Lord God, *da mihi potum*, give me a flagon of wine."

The prior roared:

"What is this drunkard doing here? How dare he interrupt the divine service? Take him off to prison!"

"One moment," Friar John protested. "What about the wine service? Let's not disturb that, for you yourself, My Lord Prior, like to drink of the best. As does any good man, I may add. No person of parts ever hated good liquor; that's a monastical maxim. By God, these responses you're chanting are certainly out of season." He drew a deep breath. "Why are our devotions so short in time of harvest and vintage, so long at Advent and in winter? The late Friar Macé Pelosse, of sainted memory, was a true zealot of our religion or the devil can have my soul! Well I remember his answer to that question: 'So we might make our wine in the autumn,' said he, 'and whiff it up in winter.'

"Hark ye, my masters, all ye who love good wine. God's body, do ye follow me. Let St. Anthony's fire burn me to a cinder if those who daren't defend their vines taste one drop of the liquor! No, no, no: why the devil should they? St. Thomas à Becket was willing to die for the clergy; wouldn't I too be canonized if ill befell me? But it won't: I refuse to die. If anybody dies, *I'll* do the killing."

So saying, he took off his long robes and seized the staff of the cross, which was made of the heart of a sorb apple tree. The length of a lance, rounded to fit snugly in the hollow of a large hand, it was covered here and there with fleur-de-lys almost all erased by frequent handling. Over his fine tunic, he draped his cowl like a scarf across his breast, and, wielding the staff of the cross, he fell furiously upon the enemy. The latter were without leader, ensign, drummer or bugler. The ensigns had laid their standards against the walls, the drummers knocked out one head of each drum to use it for a grape basket, the buglers were staggering under heavy branches of grapes. Accordingly, when Friar John of the Funnels swooped down upon them unawares and hacked away so lustily, they fell on all sides like so many nine-pins. Thwack to the right, thwack to the left, Friar John struck in the old-fashioned style of fencing; thwack, thwack, he felled them like so many hogs. He brained some, smashed the legs and arms of others, broke a neck here, cracked a rib there. He flattened a nose or knocked an eye out, crushed a jaw or sent thirty-two teeth rattling down a bloody gullet. Some had their shoulderblades dislocated, others their thighs lammed to pulp, others their hips wrenched, others their arms battered beyond recognition. Let a wretched fellow seek hiding amid the densest vines and Friar John ripped him up the back, gutting him like a cur. Let another take to his heels and Friar John split his head at the lambdoid suture. Let a third scramble up a tree and Friar John impaled him by the fundament.

"Ho, Friar John, ho, friend, I surrender!" cried an old acquaintance.

"What else *can* you do?" Friar John retorted. Then, with a sledgehammer blow: "You can surrender your soul, too, to all the devils of hell."

Where a man had the temerity to offer resistance, Friar John gave an exhibition of muscular competence as he bashed in the rashling's chest, exposing heart and lungs. Thumping others under the ribs, he mauled their stomachs so severely that they died at once. A whack on the navel and what enemy tripe came spurting forth!

A lash at the testicles and out flew their bumguts. Undoubtedly, here was the most horrible spectacle ever seen upon earth.

Some called upon Ste. Barbe, others upon St. George; "Ste. Nitouche, touch me not," cried the sham-Abrahams. The air was filled with appeals to Our Lady of Cunault in Anjou, Our Lady of Loretta, Our Lady of Good Tidings by Marseilles, Our Lady of Lenou and Our Lady of Rivière on the Vienne. Some vowed pilgrimages to St. James at Compostella, others to the holy shroud at Chambéry. (Unfortunately the latter was burned up three months later so not a shred remained.) Still others offered vows to famous shrines such as those of St. Cadouin in the Dordogne where the shroud of Jesus was preserved, of St. John at Angély, of St. Eutropius at Saintes in the Charente, of St. Martin at Candes, of St. Clouaud at Sinays. The relics of Javarzay and a myriad other good saintlets and hagiolings found votaries aplenty. Some died silent, others lived shouting; some died speaking, others spoke as they died. Still others yelled: "Confession, confession! *Confiteor!* . . . *Miserere!* . . . *In manus!*"

So loud were the cries of the wounded that My Lord Prior and all his monks came crowding out of the abbey. Seeing all the victims in the vineyard they at once administered confession *in extremis*. While the veteran priests were thus busied, the younger monklings rushed up to Friar John of the Funnels and asked him how they could help.

"By cutting their throats," he said, pointing to his victims on the ground.

Laying their great cowls on the trellises, the little monkeys throttled and dispatched all those Friar John had struck down. Can you guess what instruments they used? Those fine little edge-tools children use hereabouts to scoop the kernel out of ripe walnuts.

Meanwhile, staff of the cross in hand, Friar John of the Funnels advanced into the breach the enemy had made. A few monklets seized the abandoned standards and pennants, carrying them off to their rooms to make garters of them. As those who had made confession sought to get away through the gap, Friar John laid them low, crying:

"These have confessed, these are repentant, these have won pardon. Off they go to Paradise on a road straight as a sickle, sheer as a ram's horn."

Thus it was that Friar John's prowess annihilated the entire host that entered the vineyards. The enemy losses rose to thirteen thousand six hundred and twenty-two, exclusive, of course, of women and children.

Maugis the hermit, celebrated in the *Tale of the Four Sons of Aymon*, never acquitted himself more heroically against the Saracens with his pilgrim's crook than Friar John of the Funnels against the pillaging cake-bakers with the staff of the cross.

XXVIII

HOW PICROCHOLE STORMED LA ROCHE CLERMAULT AND HOW GRANGOUSIER RELUCTANTLY AND REGRETFULLY WENT TO WAR

WHILE Friar John was skirmishing against the invaders of the close, Picrochole hastily crossed the ford at Vède and attacked La Roche Clermault, meeting with no resistance whatever. Because it was already night, he resolved to take up quarters there with his army, and rest from the effects of his furious choler.

In the morning he stormed and captured the bulwarks and castle, fortified the latter and provided it with all the munitions he could requisition. As the place was strong both by art, by nature and by its admirable situation, he considered it a capital base of defense to retreat to, where he assailed from any other quarter.

Let us leave him there and return to our good Gargantua and that fine old man, Grangousier, his sire. The former was in Paris, diligently absorbing the best learning, and developing his body in athletic recreation. The latter sat toasting his genitals before a great, clear, roaring fire after supper, watching the chestnuts roasting. With the charred end of the stick used for poking the logs, he was drawing figures in the ashes on the hearth whilst he told his wife and companions fine old stories of bygone days.

Suddenly a shepherd named Pillot, who kept the vines, arrived with tidings of Picrochole, King of Lerné. Grangousier learned of the pillage and devastation of his lands, of the wholesale barbarities committed everywhere save at Seuilly Close, which Friar John of the Funnels had so nobly saved, and of Picrochole's stay at La Roche Clermault.

"Alas, alas!" Grangousier cried. "What news is this, good people? Am I dreaming or is it true? Picrochole, my old friend, my contemporary, my fellow-countryman, my ally; Picrochole has turned against me! What urges him to do so, what has he against me, who advised him to attack me? O God, O my blessed Saviour, grant me Thy Help; inspire me and counsel me for I know not what to do. Have I ever given Picrochole cause to be angry, or damaged his people or laid his land waste? I protest, I swear solemnly before my God that I have never done so. Surely then, He will look favorably upon me?

"On the contrary, I have invariably come to Picrochole's help; whenever I could be of use to him, I have helped him with men, money, influence and advice. He must be possessed of a devil to outrage me thus. O Blessed God, Thou knowest my heart since nothing can be hidden from Thine eye. If Picrochole has lost his reason and Thou hast sent him to me to be cured, grant me the power and knowledge to bring him back under the yoke of Thy will.

"Oh, oh, oh, good people, dear friends and loyal servants, you will have to give me all your help in this dreadful crisis. Woe is me! In my old age, all I wished for was rest; all my life the one thing I worked for was peace. But now I realize I must put armor over my aged, weary, feeble shoulders, I must seize lance and mace with trembling hand to succor and protect my unhappy people. Reason dictates this course, since it is by the fruit of their labor and the sweat of their brow that I and my children and household are kept alive!

"Nevertheless, I shall go to war only after I have exhausted every attempt at peace. That I am determined upon!"

Grangousier then summoned his council and laid the matter before them. They decided to send a prudent legate to Picrochole to inquire why the King of Lerné had suddenly broken the peace and invaded lands over which none but Grangousier had the flimsiest title. They also resolved to summon Gargantua and his followers to the defense of the land if it were necessary. Grangousier agreed with the council and endorsed their resolutions, dispatching Basque, his lackey, to Paris with the following letter.

XXIX

THE TENOR OF THE LETTER GRANGOUSIER WROTE TO GARGANTUA

THE *enthusiasm with which you pursue your studies would prevent me from breaking in upon your philosophic repose had not the friends and allies I always trusted disappointed me in my old age. But since destiny wills that I be disturbed by those I most relied on, I must perforce call you back to defend the people and possessions entrusted to you by right of nature. For, just as arms are unavailing abroad if there be no counsel at home, so study and consultation are futile unless they be applied fittingly and in good season.*

I intend to appease rather than provoke, to defend rather than assault; I do not seek to conquer new lands but rather to preserve my faithful subjects and hereditary dominions, which Picrochole has invaded without rhyme or reason, and which he oppresses day by day with a fury intolerable to freeborn spirits.

I consider it my duty to assuage his tyrannical anger; I have offered him all I thought might satisfy him; several times I have dispatched friendly envoys to find out how and by whom he considered himself outraged. But his only answer has been this declaration of war and the claim that he sought to put order in my land. Hence I concluded that the Eternal Master had abandoned him to the government of his own will and sense. And how shall these be anything

*but evil unless the grace of God continually guides them? I believe
the Divine Power has sent him here under such grievous auspices
so that I might bring him back to his senses.*

*Accordingly, my dear son, as soon as you receive this letter, come
home as speedily as ever you can; haste not only to the defense of
your father (which is mere filial duty) but also to that of your
people, whom reason orders you to protect and to preserve. This
must take place with the least bloodshed possible and, if we can
manage it, by means of expedience, policy and strategy, for we must
save all our souls and send them happily back to their homes.*

*My dearest son, the peace of Jesus Christ our Redeemer be upon
you. My cordial greetings to Ponocrates, Gymnastes and Eudemon.*

Your father,

The twentieth day of September.   GRANGOUSIER

XXX

HOW ULRICH GALLET WAS
DISPATCHED TO PICROCHOLE

THE letter dictated and signed, Grangousier sent his chancellor Ulrich Gallet to Picrochole to inform the latter of what had been decreed. Gallet was a discreet and sagacious man whose judgment and
tact Grangousier had already tried on several critical occasions.

Old Gallet set out at once, crossed the ford at Vède and asked the
miller about Picrochole. The miller replied that Picrochole's soldiers
had robbed him of his last cock and hen, that they occupied La Roche
Clermault and that he, Gallet, would do well to go no further because Picrochole's fierce scouts were scouring the land. Gallet readily
believed the miller and put up that night at the mill.

Next morning he went with a bugler to the castle gate and asked
the guards to admit him into the king's presence for an audience
that was of concern to His Majesty.

Informed of this, Picrochole refused to allow the gates to be opened. Instead, from the ramparts, he shouted to the ambassador: "What news have you? What do you want?"

Gallet replied as follows.

XXXI

GALLET'S ADDRESS TO PICROCHOLE

"No juster cause for grief can exist among men than when they receive hurt and damage from those they might justly expect to show them courtesy and good will. In the past, many a people, reduced to such a calamity without cause or reason, have considered that indignity utterly intolerable and have proved so at the price of their very lives. When they have been unable to find remedy by force or otherwise, they have preferred to forfeit the breath of existence.

"Accordingly it is natural that King Grangousier, my master, is much displeased at your outrageous invasion. How can he help but be amazed? You and your subjects have perpetrated a series of unparalleled excesses upon King Grangousier's people and lands; you have omitted no sample of inhumanity. How then could my master fail to lament your barbarity when he is wounded in the profound affection he bears his people—a people who venerate him more deeply than any mortal upon earth?

"However, considering all right and wrong, King Grangousier particularly deplores the fact that you and yours committed these offenses. Time out of mind, you and your ancestors have been bound to him and his by the most sacred pact of alliance and friendship. This covenant has been so devoutly observed, so inviolably maintained down to this very day that not only King Grangousier and his people but even the heathen nations of Poitou, Brittany, Maine, the Canaries and Isabella in the New World have not dared impair it. Truly, they would have considered it easier to drag down the firmament and set the depths of hell above the clouds than venture to break our alliance. Ay, in their enterprises they have so sedulously respected our league that they never dreamed of provoking, annoying or molesting one power for fear of the other. More, this hallowed amity has reached so far that few nations inhabiting the continents and islands of this universe did not aspire to be received into our league. They were, in point of fact, most eager to be admitted upon such terms as you yourselves were pleased to impose, for they prized our confederation as highly as their own territories and possessions. Thus there was never within memory of man a ruler or realm so proud or rash as to dare attack not your own lands but even those of your confederates. Indeed, if they impulsively presumed to meditate aggression against the weakest member of our republic, they speedily desisted at the mere mention of the name and title of its allies.

"What madness possesses you? What fury drives you to shatter our alliance, to transgress all law, to trample friendship in the dust? Why do you make hostile invasion upon my master's lands when neither he nor his have in any wise provoked, wronged or damaged you? Where are faith and law? What of reason and humanity? Where is your fear of God?

"Do you believe your outrages are hidden from the Eternal Spirit, from that sovereign God Who judges all our undertakings? If so, you err, for all things shall be brought before His throne.

"Have the stars in their course or the hand of destiny moved to abolish your peace and leisure? For all things have their period and appointed end: having reached their peak, they cannot long people this eminence and must perforce crumble at their foundation. Such is the end of those who cannot temper their fortune and prosperity with reason and moderation.

"Since you are thus bewitched and since both joy and rest must be denied you, why should you choose to fall upon my king, the very agent of your greatness? If your own house was doomed, why should its ruins fall upon the hearths of those who were its principal adornment? The whole thing is so unreasonable, so contrary to good sense as to defy all human understanding. No stranger will credit it until the outcome proves that all we hold sacred and holy abandons such as break away from God and Reason to woo their own depraved inclinations.

"Have we in any way wronged your subjects or done damage to your lands? Have we favored your enemies or looked askance upon your name or honor? Have we ever failed to come to your help? No, a thousand times no! Well, then, if the Evil Spirit has led you into temptation, inspiring you with the delusion that we have done anything unworthy of our ancient friendship, you should have first investigated the whole matter. Then, learning the truth, you should have advised us: we would have acted to your satisfaction. But (O Eternal God!) what do you purpose, Picrochole? Would you, like a perfidious tyrant, ravage my master's realm? Do you suppose him too cowardly and base to oppose you? Do you consider him so ill-provided with men, money, counsel and military competence as to tolerate your iniquitous attack?

"Withdraw from here forthwith and let to-morrow's sun go down upon you in your own dominion; take care you do no violence on your homeward way and pay one thousand golden bezants to my lord and master for the harm you did his country. You may acquit yourself of half that sum to-morrow, leaving the other half for the ides of May. But you must leave as hostages the Dukes of Tournemoule, Basdefesses, Menuail, the Prince of Gratelles and the Vicomte de Morpiaille, or, as we know them, My Lords Twiddle-mussle, Lowbuttock, Smalltittle, Scratchballock and Diddlesnoop."

XXXII

HOW GRANGOUSIER, INTENT ON PEACE, RESTORED THE CAKES

Good old Gallet thereupon held his peace. But Picrochole, for all answer to his harangue, simply shouted:

"Come and fetch them, come and fetch them, they have great soft ballocks, they'll knead you some cakes!"

Whereupon Gallet returned to his master. He found the old king on his knees, bareheaded, crouching in a small corner of his study and praying God that He be pleased to assuage the fury of Picrochole without forceful suasion. Seeing Gallet:

"Ha, friend!" he exclaimed. "What news do you bring me?"

"All is chaos," the legate lamented. "Picrochole is insane, our God has abandoned him."

"True, true, but what reason does he give for his excesses?"

"None," said Gallet. "All he did was shout angrily about cakes. Can any one have harmed his cake-bakers?"

Grangousier was pensive.

"I must go thoroughly into the matter before I decide what to do," he said.

Investigation revealed that some cakes had been forcibly seized from Picrochole's men and that Marquet had been knocked on the head. But the cakes had been paid for, and Marquet had been the aggressor. The council decided that since Marquet had lashed Forgier with his whip, Forgier was perfectly justified in defending himself. Nevertheless, Grangousier announced that since it was only a question of a few cakes, he would attempt to conciliate Picrochole rather than go to war. Having ascertained that only four or five dozen cakes had been taken, Grangousier had five cartloads baked that very night. One cartload, he insisted, must be made of the best butter, yolks of eggs, saffron and spices; it was to go to Marquet, together with seven hundred and three thousand gold coins for damages and medical attention. Further, he settled upon Marquet and his heirs in perpetual freehold the farm of La Pomardière in the commune of Seuilly. Gallet, who was appointed to conduct negotiations, made his little band stop on the way at a willow brake to gather boughs of cane and reed; the drivers laid them on their carts, each driver holding one in his hand. Gallet did likewise. Thus Picrochole would realize they sought only peace and had come to buy it.

At the castle gate, they asked to speak to Picrochole on Grangousier's behalf. That monarch denied them admittance or audience, sending word that he was busy. They might, he added, convey their errand to Captain Tickledingus, Lord of Touquedillon and Touchfaucet, who was on the ramparts laying down a battery of cannon. Goodman Gallet addressed him:

"My Lord, to cut short all cause for conflict and remove all occasion for you to remain outside our holy alliance, we herewith return to you the cakes that gave rise to the controversy. Our countrymen took five dozen and paid very fairly for them: but we desire peace so earnestly that we are bringing you five cartloads. One is for Marquet, who has the deepest grievance. What is more, to give him complete satisfaction, we are adding seven hundred thousand and three gold coins stamped with the effigy of Philip of Macedon. I am instructed to deliver these to him for the damages he may claim to have suffered, together with the deed in perpetuity to the farm of La Pomardière in fee simple for him and his people, free of all duty, levy or tax. Here is the document. In the name of God, let us live henceforward in peace; deliver up this place to which, on your own statement, you have no right, and let us be friends as heretofore."

Captain Tickledingus Touchfaucet repeated the entire speech to Picrochole, spurring him on to apoplectic anger:

"These louts have good reason to be afraid: by Heaven, Grangousier is beshitting himself with terror, poor drinker! His business is to drain flagons, not to wage war. I say we keep his cakes and his money, speedily fortify this place and pursue our fortune. Do they think you're a nincompoop to serve you up those wretched cakes? You see what has happened: they despise you because of the courtesy and familiarity you have always shown them. Anoint a serf and he will whip you; whip a serf, he will anoint you!"

"All right, all right!" Picrochole roared. "By St. James, they shall have what they deserve. Do just as you suggested!"

"There's one more piece of advice I should like to give Your Majesty," Captain Tickledingus Touchfaucet continued. "We're rather poorly supplied with victuals. If ever Grangousier laid siege to us, I and my men could have all our teeth pulled but three, yet still exhaust our provisions all too soon."

"We'll have plenty to eat, man. After all, did we come to guzzle or fight?"

"To fight, of course. But from the paunch comes the dance; where famine rules, strength is scattered."

"Talk, talk, talk!" Picrochole grumbled. "Take what they've brought and shut up."

So Captain Tickledingus Touchfaucet seized the money, the cakes, the oxen and carts, dismissing the messengers with a warning that they would never approach so near again, for a reason to be vouchsafed them on the morrow. Thus Gallet and the mission returned to Grangousier, related everything and, dispelling the last hope of peace, prepared their master for a fierce and brutal war.

XXXIII

HOW CERTAIN ADVISERS OF PICROCHOLE LED HIM INTO EXTREME PERIL BY THEIR RASH COUNSEL

THE cakes were unloaded and the Duke of Smalltittle, Count Swashbuckler and Captain Krapp reported to their sovereign:

"Sire, this day we proclaim you the most valorous and knightly prince that ever was since the death of Alexander of Macedon."

"Put your hats on, my lords, let us not stand upon ceremony."

"Gramercy, gramercy, Sire, we but do homage." They bowed low. "Here is what we propose. Your Majesty will leave a captain here in charge of a garrison strong enough to hold the fort. Both its natural position and the fortifications you have devised make it eminently safe. We suggest you then divide your army in half, as you alone know how. One party falls upon Grangousier and his men, routing them at the very outset and thus obtaining money for you, since the churl is rolling in wealth. A churl, we say, for what *noble* prince ever had a farthing? To hoard money is the act of a churl and a simpleton.

"Meanwhile, the other part of Your Majesty's forces will bear upon Aunis, Saintonge, Angoumois and Gascony, then march to Périgord, Médoc and the Landes, occupying towns, castles and fortresses without the least resistance. Reaching the southernmost shore, you will seize all the shipping in the harbors of Bayonne, St. Jean-de-Luz and Fontarrabia. Coasting along Galicia and Portugal, you will pillage every seaport all the way to Lisbon, where you will find all the reënforcements due a conqueror. Woosh! God help us, and Spain will yield, since Spaniards are a race of loafers. Passing the Straits of the Sibyl which are called Gibraltar, Your Majesty will pause to erect a pair of pillars more magnificent than those of Hercules, to stand as an eternal memorial to your name. These straits thenceforth shall be known of men as the Picrocholinal Sea. Once the Picrocholinal Sea is crossed, what do you find? Why, Khair-ed-Din, the Barbarossa of Algiers, delivering himself to you in ignominious servitude."

"I shall treat him fairly," Picrochole put in.

"Certainly, to be sure," they agreed, "so but he be baptized. This done, you will proceed to conquer the kingdoms of Tunisia, Hippos or Bizerta, Bomina or Bône, Corona or Cyrene, all Barbary in brief. Obviously the next step is to annex Majorca, Minorca, Sardinia, Corsica and all the other islands in Genoan and Balearic waters. Moving to the left, you conquer all Gallia Narbonensis, Provence, the land of the Allobroges and Helvetians, Genoa, Florence, Lucca and, by God, Rome! Pity My Lord the Pope, already he shivers in his mules!"

"By the soles of the Apostles, I shall never kiss his slipper!" Picrochole cried.

"Italy occupied, you have Naples, Calabria, Apulia, Sicily all ransacked, not to mention Malta. Those ridiculous knights of Jerusalem that used to live in Rhodes will need more than Maltese Crosses to withstand King Picrochole. Let them but try; we would soon find out what stuff these Maltese cats are made of. By God, I'd give a fortune to see the color of their piss!"

"I wouldn't at all mind going to Loretta," Picrochole commented.

"No, no, Your Majesty, we'll take Loretta on the way home! Next you seize Crete, Cyprus, Rhodes and the Cyclades Islands, then swoop down upon Morea. No sooner said than done: Morea is Picrochole's! By St. Ninnyhammer, God help Jerusalem: the wretched Egyptian Sultan stands no earthly chance against you!"

"That's where I shall have Solomon's temple built," observed Picrochole.

"No, no," they objected. "Not so fast. We can do that on the way home. Your Majesty is too hasty in enterprise. Remember Octavius Augustus: *Festina lente,* slowly does it!" Before you erect Solomon's temple, Your Majesty simply must see Asia Minor, Caria, Lycia, Pamphilia, Cilicia, Lydia, Phrygia, Mysia, Bithynia, Carazia or Sardis, the Lydian capital; Satalia or Adalia, as some call it, Samagaria, Kastamuni, Luga, Savasteia—in brief all the lands up to the Euphrates."

"Shall we see Babylon and Mount Sinai?"

"That is unnecessary just now," they told him. "Is it not enough to have crossed the Caspian, taken the twin Armenias in our stride, and shot like lightning through the three Arabias?"

"Two Armenias?"

"Ay, Sire, the greater and the lesser!"

"Three Arabias?"

"Ay, Sire, the desert, the fertile and the stony regions."

"God help us!" cried Picrochole. "We are undone. Fools, abject fools to venture here!"

"What do you mean?" his counsellors demanded.

"In heaven's name, what shall we drink in the desert?" Picrochole wailed. "Didn't the Emperor Julian's entire army perish of thirst in the desert?"

"That was the Emperor Julian," they told him. "Our case is quite different: we have already provided for everything. Fourteen huge craft speed across the Syriac Sea laden with the choicest vintages in the world. I see them sailing into Jaffa. There, twenty-two thousand camels and sixteen hundred elephants await them. (You remember, you captured them at Sidjilmassa, in the Oasis of Tafilelt, when you entered Libya.) Besides, there's the whole caravan of pilgrims that goes yearly from Cairo to Mahomet's tomb at Mecca. Surely, that will be wine enough!"

"Quite so," said Picrochole, "but we shall not drink it fresh!"

"Small fry drink fresh," they objected. "But a conqueror, a hero who lays claim to the empire of the universe, cannot always have things as he wills them. Thank God you and your army have reached the Tigris safe and sound!"

Picrochole scratched his head.

"One thing bothers me," he said at length.

"What is that, Sire?"

"I'm wondering what the other part of my army is doing meanwhile."

"They're wasting no time," he was informed. "We shall meet them anon. Already they have conquered Brittany and Normandy,

Flanders, Hainault, Brabant, Artois, Holland and Zeeland. Over the Rhine they go, dancing a jig on the bellies of the slain Swiss and German mercenaries. A detachment conquers Luxemburg, Lorraine, Champagne and Savoy; at Lyons they meet your forces returning home, fresh from their naval conquests in the Mediterranean. They rally in Bohemia after sacking Swabia, Württemberg, Bavaria, Austria, Moravia and Styria. Bravely they march against Lübeck, Norway, Sweden, Denmark, Gothland, Greenland and the Hanseatic towns up to the Frozen Sea. Now they capture the Orkneys, subdue Scotland, England, Ireland; now, sailing across the Sandy Sea to the Sarmates, they conquer and reduce Prussia, Poland, Lithuania, Russia, Wallachia, Transylvania, Hungary, Bulgaria and Turkey. Ha! they are masters of Constantinople!"

"Let us join them posthaste," Picrochole urged, "for I will be Emperor of Trebizond as well. Shall we not slaughter all these dogs, Turks, Mahomedans and the rest?"

"What the devil won't we do to them?" they agreed. "Your Majesty shall give their lands and possessions to your faithful followers."

"That is only reasonable and fair. You three may have Carmania, Syria and all Palestine."

"Syria! How kind of Your Majesty. A thousand thanks, Sire, and may God ever prosper you."

Now among those present was a seasoned veteran named Prudent Echephron. Hearing this talk, he remarked:

"I greatly fear this project is of one piece with the tale of the milkpot. The cobbler who owned it, dreamed a way of enriching himself when crash! the pot fell, broke into a thousand fragments and where was our cobbler's dinner? What do you expect from these vast conquests? To what end all this toil and travel?"

"When we return, we will rest at leisure."

"Suppose you never return?" Echephron put in. "That is a long and perilous journey you propose. Would we not do better to rest now rather than expose ourselves to all these risks!"

"Bah!" grumbled Swashbuckler. "The fellow's a milksop. By God, let us go hide in a chimney corner and spend the rest of our lives and leisure stringing pearls with the ladies or knitting like Sardanapalus. 'Nothing ventured, nothing gained—not even a horse or mule,' says Solomon."

"But in the *Dialogues* Marcoul gives Solomon an answer," Eche-phron insisted. "And that answer is: 'Venture too much and you will lose both horse and mule!'"

"Enough," Picrochole interrupted, "go ahead. All I'm afraid of is those cursed troops of Grangousier's. What if they attack us from the rear when we're in Mesopotamia? What then?"

"We can cope with that!" Captain Krapp boasted. "A nice little mission sent to Muscovy will put four hundred and fifty thousand crack troops into the field in double-quick time.

"If Your Majesty appoints me your Lieutenant-General, I'll kill a feather for its birds. Behold, I roar, I grit my teeth, I fall upon the host, I strike, I capture, I slay and I deny my Saviour!"

"Forward," screamed Picrochole. "Make haste, all! Let him that loves me follow in my train!"

XXXIV

HOW GARGANTUA FORSOOK THE CITY OF PARIS TO SUCCOR HIS COUNTRY AND HOW GYMNASTES AFFRONTED THE ENEMY

MEANWHILE Gargantua, having immediately on receipt of his father's letter left Paris on his great mare, was by now almost home. Already, near Chinon, he had crossed the Nuns' Bridge, so called because the toll collected went to the Convent of Fontevrault. Ponocrates, Gymnastes and Eudemon had taken post horses to follow him; the bulk of his retinue succeeded by even journeys, bringing all his books and philosophic instruments.

When Gargantua reached Parilly, a farmer of Gouguet's told him how Picrochole had seized La Roche Clermault and dispatched Captain Tripefart Tripet at the head of a large army to occupy the woods of Vède and Vaugaudry. Already the enemy had actually reached the winepress at Billouard, near Chinon; the excesses and ravages they committed in the region were beyond belief. This frightened Gargantua: he was at a loss what to say or do. But Ponocrates suggested they go to the Lord of Vauguyon, ever a friend and ally of theirs, who could advise them better in their trouble. They did this at once and found him very willing to assist them. They ought, he said, to send one of his followers to reconnoitre the countryside and ascertain the enemy's strength and position. This accomplished, they could take counsel and proceed as circumstances warranted. Gymnastes offered to go, but they decided that he had best take along some one who knew the roads, détours and rivers thereabouts. My Lord of Vauguyon deputed Prelinguand, his equerry. Together they fearlessly investigated all the neighborhood. Gargantua, in the meantime, took a little refreshment himself and had his men do likewise; he also had them feed his mare seventy-four quarters and three bushels of oats. Gymnastes and his companions rode so far that at last they met the enemy forces, scattered and in disorder, pillaging and plundering on every side. Seeing him from afar, a host of them rushed at him, bent on robbery.

"I am a poor devil, my masters!" he cried. "Have mercy upon me, I beseech you. I still have a few crowns; let us drink them up for they are *aurum potabile*, liquid gold. As for my horse, we'll sell him so I can pay a round of welcome. After, let me join up with you, for you never saw my match at finding, stealing, larding, roasting and preparing a hen—yes, by God, and at dismembering and guzzling it. For my welcome, I drink to all good fellows."

Unscrewing his leather flask, Gymnastes then drank very handsomely, without putting his nose into it. The rogues watched him, opening their snouts a foot wide and sticking their tongues out like greyhounds, as they waited their turn to drink. But Captain Tripefart Tripet, their leader, rushed up.

"Here, Captain, drink her down!" cried Gymnastes, offering the bottle. "I've tasted it for you: it's wine of La Faye Monjault."

"What?" growled Tripet. "This wag is pulling our legs! Who the devil are you?"

"Only a poor devil, sir!"

"Well, if you're only a poor devil, we'll let you go, for all poor devils pass everywhere without tax or toll. But most poor devils are not so handsomely mounted. I shall therefore request you to dismount, My Lord Devil, and give me that stallion of yours. If he carries me ill, Master Devil, it is *you* I shall ride, for I dearly love the idea of a devil like you carrying me off."

XXXV

HOW GYMNASTES NEATLY DISPATCHED CAPTAIN TRIPET AND OTHER SOLDIERS OF PICROCHOLE'S

AT these words, some of Picrochole's men grew frightened, and, believing he might well be a devil disguised, made the sign of the cross hand over fist. One of them, Goodjohn Bonjean, a captain of militia, drew his psalter out of his codpiece and shouted the formula of exorcism:

"*Hagios ho Theos*, God is Holy. If you be God, then speak; if the other spirit, avaunt!"

But Gymnastes did not budge. Whereupon, some of the soldiers who had witnessed the scene, moved away.

Observing this, Gymnastes made as if to dismount, but, poising himself on the near side, suddenly swung most adroitly in the stirrup, shifted his feet and, sword in hand, leapt into the air, landing with heels joined upon the saddle, his back to the horse's head. Then:

"Watch me fly ballocking back!" he cried.

Then, in the same position, he gambolled on one foot and, turning to the left, brought himself back to his original stance without swerving a hair's breadth.

"Ha," cried Captain Tripet. "I wouldn't do this now and I know why!"

"Shit, I failed that time!" Gymnastes growled. "Watch me undo this turn."

With amazing strength and agility, turning to the right, he made the same gambol. Next, he set his right thumb on the hind bow of the saddle, and, poised on its nerves and muscles, he raised his body upward and whirled about three times. Instead of a fourth whirl, he reversed completely, without touching anything, bringing himself down between the horse's ears. There he executed the same feat as before but this time poised on his left thumb. In this posture he did the trick called the millwheel. Then, clapping his right hand flat upon the middle of his saddle, he swung up with a jolt that landed him on the crupper, seated sidewise like a gentlewoman. This done, with perfect ease he slung his right leg over and sat as one who rides behind the saddle.

"I had better get between the bows of the saddle!" he cried.

Whereupon, poised on both thumbs on the crupper before him, he suddenly turned arse over head in the air to land in a perfect seat in the middle of the saddle. Once again, with a somersault, he sprang aloft, ending with both heels together between the bows, where he did more than a hundred turns, his arms out crosswise and shouting:

"I rage, devils, I rage, I rage. Hold me, devils, hold me, hold!"

Seeing him vaulting, the rascals said in great amazement:

"God's Mother, it is a goblin or devil in disguise. *Ab hoste maligno, libera nos, Domine*, O Lord, deliver us from the evil foe."

And they took to their heels with the look of curs that have stolen chickens.

Gymnastes, perceiving his advantage, dismounted, drew his sword and charged down upon the nearest, tumbling them to the ground in heaps, maimed, wounded and slain. Not one offered the slightest resistance. Thanks not only to his wonderful acrobatics, but also to Captain Tripet's epithet "poor devil," they all believed Gymnastes to be a starved fiend. Tripet alone moved treacherously, from behind, and would have split Gymnastes' head with his broadsword; but Gymnastes wore a stout helmet and so felt only the weight of the blow. Suddenly, veering around, he dealt Tripet a flying thrust, and, as Tripet raised his arm to parry it, ran him through the middle. With that one lunge, Gymnastes sliced the fellow's stomach, colon and half his liver. As Tripet fell to the ground, his intestines gushed out. They would have filled say about four tureensful of soup. And his soul mingled with the mess.

Gymnastes then withdrew from the field. Did not wisdom demand that great hazards should not be pushed too far, that knights should not exhaust their good fortune? Leaping upon his horse, he spurred the beast forward and, with Prelinguand at his side, sped homeward to La Vauguyon.

XXXVI

HOW GARGANTUA DEMOLISHED THE CASTLE AT THE GUÉ DE VÈDE AND HOW THEY CROSSED THE FORD

IMMEDIATELY upon arrival, Gymnastes reported the enemy's strength and condition, giving an account of the stratagem by which, single-handed, he had accounted for the whole mob. The fellows, he said, were mere marauders, pillagers and brigands, ignorant of all military discipline. Gymnastes therefore advised Gargantua and his army to take boldly to the field where he could slaughter the enemy like so many beasts.

Accompanied as we have told, Gargantua mounted his great mare and advanced resolutely. Along his way, he found a tall elm known thereabouts as St. Martin's tree, because the saint had planted a pilgrim's staff on that spot in the days of yore.

"Here is what I want," cried Gargantua. "This tree will serve me both for staff and lance."

Without the slightest effort, he uprooted it, plucked off the boughs and trimmed it to his fancy. Meanwhile his mare, pissing to relieve her belly, made such abundant water that it inundated the countryside within a radius of seven leagues. The yellow angry flood, rolling into the ford of Vède, so swelled its waters that all the enemy forces (save those by the hills on the left) were drowned amid scenes of excruciating horror.

At the woods of Vède, Eudemon informed Gargantua that remnants of the enemy still occupied the castle.

"Are you there or are you not?" Gargantua bellowed. "If you are, don't stay; if you aren't, I've nothing to say."

Suddenly a ruffian gunner in the fort fired a cannon ball at him, striking him violently on the right temple. Yet Gargantua was no more hurt than if it had been a grape seed. Indeed, he believed it was.

"What is this?" he commented. "Why are you tossing grape seeds at us? That vintage will cost you dear!"

Picrochole's men, busy pillaging the castle, heard the reports. Rushing to the towers and fortresses, they fired their harquebusses and falconets, wasting nine thousand and twenty-five shots, all aimed at his head. So thick fell the projectiles that Gargantua turned to Ponocrates:

"Gad, my dear fellow, these flies are blinding me; give me a branch off one of those willows to chase them off."

For he actually believed these stones and cannon balls to be but gadflies. When Ponocrates explained that what he considered flies was, on the contrary, heavy ammunition fired from the castle, Gargantua swung his huge tree down upon the latter. With a few hearty blows, he razed the towers, levelled the castle and tumbled everything to the ground. The entire garrison was of course crushed, battered and pounded flat.

Reaching the Mill Bridge, they found the ford so thick with corpses that the mill was choked up, for those drowned by the mare's urinal deluge dammed up the waters. Now their problem was to cross the barrier of cadavers.

"Devils have crossed," Gymnastes cried. "Why shouldn't I?"

"The devils crossed to bear away the souls of the damned!"

"By St. Ninnypoop," cried Ponocrates, "it logically follows that Gymnastes shall do so."

"True, true, or I'll stick in the way."

Giving his horse the spur, Gymnastes cleared the ford without the beast shying at the corpses, for its master had taught it to fear neither the bodies nor the souls of the dead. This was, indeed, quite in keeping with the teachings of Ælian in his *De Natura Animalium*. To accustom a horse to dead bodies, says Ælian, it is wrong to kill their grooms, as Diomedes killed the Thracians. It is just as wrong to place slain enemies at a horse's feet, as Ulysses did, according to Homer. No—the proper procedure is to place a scarecrow in the horse's hay and walk the beast over the dummy at feeding time.

His three companions followed without mishap except in Eudemon's case. The latter's horse sank knee-deep in the belly of a monstrous fat churl who lay drowned there, face up. Eudemon could not draw his beast out and stood stuck fast, until Gargantua with the tip of his staff whisked the rest of the villain's entrails into the water. Only then could the horse pull up his foot. And—a remarkable case in the annals of veterinary art!—that horse was cured of a ringbone by mere contact with the burst guts of the deceased clodhopper.

XXXVII

HOW GARGANTUA, COMBING HIS HAIR, PRODUCED AN ARSENAL OF ARTILLERY

HAVING crossed the Vède, they soon reached Grangousier's castle, where the old man had been impatiently awaiting them. It was a delirious reunion, accompanied by the most fervent embraces; never were happier people seen on earth. Indeed the *Supplementum Supplementi Chronicorum* or *Commentary on the Commentary of the Chronicles* states that Gargamelle died there of sheer joy. For my part, I know nothing about it and care less for her or for any other female.

The truth is as follows: While changing his clothes, Gargantua ran through his hair a thousand-foot comb, with teeth made of solid elephant tusks. At every rake he gave, more than seven cannon balls, which had stuck there since the battle at Vède, fell crashing to the ground. Seeing this, Grangousier leaped to the conclusion they were lice.

"Upon my word, son, why have you brought us verminhawks from the Collège de Montaigu? I did not know you had taken up your residence there."

Ponocrates spoke up.

"Do you suppose, My Lord, that I placed him in the lousy college called Montaigu. Why, I had as lief quarter him among the riffraff at St. Innocent's graveyard, for all the cruelty and villainy I have observed there. Moorish and Tartar galleyslaves, murderers in the depths of dungeons, indeed the veriest curs in your stables are better treated than the luckless students in that so-called institution of learning. If I were King of Paris, the devil take me if I would not set the place afire, burning both Principal and Professors for allowing such inhumanity to go on under their eyes."

Then, picking up a bullet:

"These are cannon balls traitorously fired at your son Gargantua a few hours ago as he passed by the woods of Vède. But he rewarded the enemy handsomely: they perished to a man under the ruins of the castle, like the Philistines by Samson's trick and like those whom the Tower of Siloam crushed, in *Luke* XIII. The cowards! Let us pursue them, say I, whilst luck is with us, for time is now all forelock; neglect to seize it and he vanishes. Alas! once he has passed, you notice how bald he is behind, you know he never will return again!"

"No," Grangousier replied, "not now. For I mean to regale you this evening with a great feast of welcome."

Thereupon supper was prepared and in honor of the special occasion, they added to the regular menu sixteen oxen, three heifers, thirty-two calves, sixty-three young kids, ninety-five wethers, three hundred milch-sows soaked in sweet wine, elevenscore partridges, seven hundred woodcocks, four hundred capons from Loudun and Cornouailles in Brittany, six thousand pullets and as many pigeons again, six hundred crammed hens, fourteen hundred young hares, three hundred and three bustards and one thousand and seven fat capons. As for venison, all they could obtain was eleven wild boars sent by the Abbot of Turpenay, eighteen fallow deer presented by My Lord of Grandmont and sevenscore pheasants from My Lord of Les Essards. In addition, there were dozens of ringdoves and riverfowl, ducks, drakes, bitterns, curlews, plovers, francolins, sheldrakes, Poitou woodcocks, lapwings, shovellers, herons, moorhens, storks, orange flamingos, cranes, geese, ptarmigans, turkey hens, prepared with quantities of soups, broths, sauces and stew.

Beyond all doubt, here were victuals aplenty, cooked to a turn by Grangousier's cooks Wolfsauce, Hotchpot and Lickjuice. The stewards, Jockbottle, Guzzletun and Clearglass, kept their beakers brimful with wine.

XXXVIII

HOW GARGANTUA ATE SIX PILGRIMS IN A SALAD

WE must now relate what happened to six pilgrims who were returning from St. Sebastien-d'Aigne, near Nantes. Afraid of the enemy, they sought shelter that night in the garden, crouched among the cabbage, lettuce and peas.

Gargantua, being somewhat thirsty, asked for some lettuce salad. When they told him the lettuce in that garden was the greatest and finest in the land (some heads were tall as plum trees or walnut trees) he determined to pick it himself. Plucking what he thought good, he also carried off in the hollow of his hand the six pilgrims, who were too terrified to cough, let alone to speak.

While Gargantua was washing the heads of lettuce in the fountain, the pilgrims plucked up their courage and held a whispered consultation.

"What can we do?"

"We're drowning in all this lettuce!"

"Dare we speak?"

"If we speak, he'll kill us for spies."

Amid their deliberations, Gargantua put them with the lettuce in a bowl of Grangousier's large as the tun at the Abbey of Cîteaux, in Burgundy, a fine huge cask reputed to hold three hundred hogsheads. Then he doused the leaves (and pilgrims) with salt, vinegar and oil, and, for refreshment before supper, began to eat. He had already swallowed five pilgrims and the sixth lay under a leaf, completely invisible save for his staff, when Grangousier pointed to the latter.

"Look, Gargantua, that's a snail's horn. Don't eat it!"

"Why not? Snails are good this month."

Picking up staff and pilgrim, he swallowed them neat, then drank a terrific draught of red Burgundy while awaiting his supper.

The pilgrims thus devoured crept out of his gullet as best they could, avoiding the millstones of his teeth. They believed they had been cast into the pit of the lowest dungeon in a prison. When Gargantua downed his wine, they all but drowned; the crimson torrent almost swept them down again into the abyss of his belly. However, leaping on their staffs as the Mont St. Michel pilgrims do, they found shelter in the chinks between his teeth. Unhappily one of them, sounding the lay of the land with his staff to ascertain its safety, struck hard into the cavity of a sore tooth and hit the mandibulary nerve. Gargantua screamed with pain, then, for relief, reached for his toothpick. Strolling out towards the great walnut tree in the garden, he proceeded to dislodge our six gentlemen pilgrims. He jerked one out by the legs, another by the shoulders, a third by his scrip, a fourth by his pouch, a fifth by his neckerchief and the last, the poor devil who had hurt him, he pulled out by the codpiece. This turned out to be a piece of great good fortune for the pilgrim, since Gargantua in the process broke a chancre that had been torturing him since they left Ancenis on the Loire.

The pilgrims, thus dislodged, scurried away, at top speed. Gargantua's toothache subsided, just as Eudemon announced dinner.

"Very well," said Gargantua. "I shall piss away my misfortune."

Which he proceeded to do so copiously that the pilgrims' road was washed away and they were forced to wade through this vast,

foamy salt lake. Skirting a small wood, all but Fournillier were
swept off their feet into a trap set for wolves. But they finally
escaped, thanks to the industry of Fournillier, who broke all the
snares and ropes. Free once again, they spent the rest of the night
in a hut near Le Coudray, where they drew comfort in their misfortune from the words of one of their number, Lasdaller or Dogweary, who reminded them that this adventure had been foretold
by the prophet David in his *Psalms*.

Cum exergerent homines in nos, forte vivos deglutissent nos,
then had they swallowed us up when their wrath was kindled
against us (in other words, when we were eaten in salad with salt,
oil and vinegar) . . . *cum irascaretur furore eorum in tuos forsi-*
tan aqua absorbuisset nos, then the waters had overwhelmed us,
the stream gone over our soul (that was when he took the deep
draught of wine) . . . *forsitan pertransisset anima nostra aquam*
intolerabilem, then the proud waters had gone over our soul (that
was when he took the piss!) . . . *Benedictus Dominus qui non*
dedit in captionem dentibus eorum, blessed be the Lord who hath
not given us as a prey to their teeth (alas, the mandibulary nerve
we struck!) . . . *Anima nostra sicut passer erepta est de laqueo*
venantium, our soul is escaped as a bird out of the snare of the
fowlers (when we fell into the trap!) . . . *laqueus contritus est*
a Fournillier et nos liberati sumus, the snare is broken by Fournil-
lier and we are escaped . . . *Adjutorum nostrum, etc.; Our help*
is in the name of the Lord, etc.

XXXIX

OF THE MONK'S BANQUETING
WITH GARGANTUA AND OF
HIS JOVIAL TABLE TALK

AFTER they had been at table a while and guzzled the preliminary
dishes, Grangousier began to explain the cause of the war between
him and Picrochole. Presently relating how bravely Friar John of

the Funnels had triumphed in the defense of the abbey close, the old man vaunted the monk's prowesses above those of Camillus, Scipio, Pompey, Cæsar and Themistocles. Gargantua at once wished to meet him and ask his advice as to future engagements.

Unanimously they decided to send Gargantua's steward after him and soon the beaming friar arrived astride Grangousier's mule, the staff of the cross in hand. His advent was the signal for a myriad handshakes, embraces and greetings.

"Ha, Friar John, bless you, my friend!"

"God be with you, Friar John, my well-beloved cousin!"

"Friar John of the Funnels, in the devil's name, let me embrace you."

"My turn now: here, Friar John, let *me* hug you to my bosom!"

"Here, you cod, let me wring you till you're limber!"

"I'll crush him till his ballocks burst!"

Friar John of the Funnels, radiant, joked here, laughed there, the most courteous and gracious man on earth.

"Ho, there, a stool, boy!" Gargantua cried. "Come, Friar John, sit here beside me at this end."

"A thousand thanks since such is your good pleasure," the monk answered. Then: "Fill my glass, lad, fill away: it's good for my liver. Give me some to gargle, too."

"*Deposita cappa*, remove thy cope," said Gymnastes. "Friar, let us tear off that cowl of yours."

"Ho, my dear gentleman, by God! there's a chapter in *Statutis Ordinis*, the *Statutes of the Order*, that forbids it."

"Crap for the *Statutes* and shit for the *Order*," Gargantua bawled. "That wretched cowl is weighing your shoulders down. Toss it off, Friar!"

"Leave it to me, friend," said the monk. "For by God! I drink the better for it; I like the feel of it upon my body. What, I ask you, would happen if I left it off? The pages, God bless them, would make garters of it, as happened to me once at Coulaines, hard by Chinon. Worse, I would lose my appetite. . . . On the other hand, if I sit down at table with my frock on, then by Christ! I'll drink to you and your horse and God help the company! I've had dinner already; but I'll eat now none the less heartily, for my stomach is hollow as St. Benedict's boot, that fine winecask at Bologna. . . . Bologna? Praise God, my gut is open wide as a lawyer's briefcase. I'll swallow any fish save tench; I'm partial, too, to a partridge wing and the thighs of a virgin novice. Oh no! it's a sad end to be buried with a tall erection, wondering all about life. . . . Incidentally, our prior is not averse to white capon meat."

"Not like the foxes," Gargantua said. "They carry off capon, hen and pullet but never eat the white."

"And why?" asked Friar John.

"Because," Gymnastes explained, "they have no cooks that know their business. Confound it! meat that is not decently cooked, invariably stays red. How then to find white meat? The red simply proves a lack of cooking—save for crawfish and lobster that you cook red as a cardinal's hat."

"That's right," the monk agreed. "Consider the abbey nurse or the abbey porter: neither's thoroughly boiled because his eyes are crimson. Here's a portion of hare that is good for the gout! Speaking of nothing, why are the thighs of maidens always cool?"

"The answer," said Gargantua, "cannot be found in Aristotle, Alexander, Aphrodiseus or Plutarch."

"Three answers," cried Friar John of the Funnels, "all three based upon the natural freshening of a given place. *First*, because water runs all over it; *second*, because it is a black, shaded, tenebrous precinct on which no sun has even shone; *third*, because it is continuously ventilated by breezes fresh from the windhole, the shirt, and best of all, the codpiece. And lustily!

"Ay, boy, some liquor here. A-a-a-a-a-h! praise God who gives us such good wine! I swear to God that had I lived in the days of Jesus Christ, I should have stopped those Jews from leading him to the Mount of Olives. Devil take me if I failed to hamstring My Lords the Apostles who fled so cravenly after a fine supper, leaving their good master in the lurch. Worse than poison I abominate the man who runs away when the occasion calls for swordplay.

"Alas, would I were King of France for four or fivescore years. By God, I would castrate those wretched runaways from the battlefield of Pavia, plague and pox pucker them! Why did they not prefer dying to leaving their dear prince stranded? As though it were not nobler and more honorable to die fighting gamely than to live, thanks to ignominious flight? . . . We're not likely to eat many goslings this year; therefore, my lad, give me some of that roast pig. *Diavolo*, there is no more wine: *germinavit radix Jesse*, there has come forth a rod out of the stem of Jesse. I renounce life, I perish of thirst.

"Ha, this wine is not of the worst. . . . What vintage did you drink in Paris, My Lord Gargantua? I yield to the Evil One if I didn't keep open house in Paris for all comers over a period of six consecutive months. Do you know Friar Claude Gallongulp at St. Denis? Ah, there's a good egg of a man! But I cannot imagine what bee inhabits his bonnet: the fellow has done nothing but study since God knows when. For my part, I study not at all; in our abbey we avoid learning for fear of the mumps. Our late abbot always said it was a monstrous thing to see a learned monk. By God, My Lord Friend, *magis magnos clericos non sunt magis magnos sapientes*, the greatest clerks are not the cleverest, and that is that. . . .

"Dear me, you never saw so many hares as there are this year, but try and find a single gosling or falcon! My Lord of La Bellonnière promised me a shrike but he wrote me a while ago that the beast was pursy. As for the partridges, just watch them multiply: they'll be about our ears this winter. I take no pleasure in still-hunting, tunnelling, trapping and snaring; nine times out of ten it gives me the rheum. Unless I can rush around and dash about, I'm a fish out of water. True, when I leap hedges and clear briars, my hood may end over the windmill and my robe leave its nape on the bushes.

"Just lately, I found a marvellous greyhound: I commit him to Satan if a single hare gives him the slip. A lackey was taking him to My Lord Scanthunt de Maulevrier when I stole the beast. Was I right?"

"No, Friar John, no," said Gymnastes, "by all the demons that haunt this earth, you were wrong."

"Very well," said the monk. "A health to these devils so long as they live! God's life, what could this gout-ridden skinflint do with so splendid a dog! By the body of God, that dryballs prefers a yoke of oxen."

"Dear me, Friar John, did I hear you swear?" asked Ponocrates

"If I swear," the monk replied, "I do so but to adorn my language. For what are oaths save colorful figures of Ciceronian rhetoric?"

XL

WHY MONKS ARE PARIAHS AND WHY SOME HAVE BIGGER NOSES THAN OTHERS

"By my faith as a Christian," said Eudemon, "I wonder and marvel as I consider this friar's excellence. God bless the honest fellow, for he delights us all! How then can you explain that any decent company excludes monks? Why are they considered death's heads? Why do we drive them from our midst as bees drive drones far from their hives? Recall old Maro's *Georgics*:

> *Ignavum fucos pecus a praesipibus arcent*
> *Drive in the drones, lazy herd, from the field.*"

Gargantua interposed:

"Frock and cowl obviously attract opprobrium, insult and malediction as surely as the wind Cecias, from the northeast, attracts the clouds. My Lords Aristotle, Pliny, Gellius and Erasmus vouch for my climatology. Do you know the peremptory reason why humanity eschews monks? I'll tell you: it's because they eat the turds of the world, or, if you prefer, because they batten upon the sins of the people. That is pretty disgusting! Can you wonder, therefore, that they are banished to the privies—or, as they call them, convents and monasteries? Are we wrong to cut them off from our polite intercourse? If so, then let us place our lavatories next to our dining rooms.

"Take the ape. Can you explain why a monkey is invariably scoffed at and teased? Well then, you understand why monks are invariably given wide room by old and young. The monkey does not watch the house like a dog, draw the plow like the ox, yield milk like the cow or give wool like the sheep, nor, let me add, bear burdens like the horse. What, pray, does he do? He spills shit over everything and befouls it: there lies the reason for the mockery and beatings we allot him.

"By the same token, take a monk, I mean a lazy, timeserving monklet. He does not plow like the peasant, defend his country like the soldier, heal the sick like the doctor, preach and elevate like the teacher, nor, let me add, handle essential commodities like the merchant. Very good: there lies the reason for the hatred and revulsion we allot him!"

"One moment!" Grangousier broke in. "Monks pray to God on our behalf!"

"Right!" Gargantua conceded. "They make life hideous everywhere with their eternal jangling of bells!"

"But a mass, a matin, a vesper well rung are already half said," Friar John protested.

"They mumble a quantity of litanies and psalms which they do not begin to understand. Automatically and without the slightest comprehension, they say countless paternosters, interlarded with interminable aves. I call that flouting God, not worshipping Him. I will go further. So help me God, if they pray for us, do you know why? Because they're terrified of losing their white bread and savory stews. All true Christians of all classes and conditions always and everywhere send up their prayers to the Creator; the Holy Spirit intercedes on their behalf and God is gracious to them. Now Friar John of the Funnels is just such a Christian; therefore we welcome him in our midst and prize him. Is he a bigot or dissenter? No—Friar John is downright, straightforward, happy, merry, and good company. He works hard, defends the oppressed, comforts the afflicted, succors the ailing and guards the abbey's close."

"I do more," said the monk. "Let me tell you. While we are dispatching our matins and memorial masses in the choir, I am also busy making crossbow strings, polishing arrows, cleaning weapons, lacing nets and snares to catch rabbits. By God, I am not idle one second of the livelong day. . . . But ho there! fill my glass, pour on! And pass me some fruit. Cheers! here are chestnuts from Estroc near Fontenay and a brisk new wine to wash them down with. Bottoms up, lads, and that liquor will make your bums produce an Oratorio. You are not yet half-shot; by God! like a horse in heat, I drink at all fords."

"Suppose, my dear Friar," Gymnastes ventured, "you wipe the snot dangling from your nostrils?"

"Pooh!" the monk countered. "Must I drown because there's water over my mouth? A thousand times no. *Quare? quia?* wherefore and how? Water drips out, granted: but have you seen any go in? And why not? Because, my friends, wine acts as antidote. A man with winter boots of that leather can fish for oysters with impunity: no water will leak *in!*"

"Why has Friar John of the Funnels such a beautiful nose?" Gargantua asked the company.

"Because God wills it so," Grangousier explained. "God moulds us like a potter his vessels in such shape and to such an end as please His divine judgment."

"Because," Ponocrates explained, "Friar John was among the first to reach the Nose Market. He therefore chose the biggest and the most handsome."

"Pooh!" cried the monk, "go further into it. True monastical philosophy can prove the point. My nose is large because my wet-nurse had billowy soft milkers; when she gave me suck, my nostrils sank into them as into butter. Hard bubs make pug-nosed children. But la, la! *ad formam nasi cognoscitur . . . ad te levavi,* by their noses shall ye know them . . . unto Thee lift I up mine noselike erection. . . .

"I loathe sweet things; jam is for others. Page, bring me liquor now and food, to boot."

XLI

HOW THE MONK PUT GARGANTUA TO SLEEP AND OF HIS HOURS AND BREVIARIES

SUPPER finished, they discussed the business in hand. It was decided to sally forth at about midnight to ascertain the movements of the enemy. Meanwhile, they might rest to be in better trim. Gargantua, however, could not sleep, no matter how he lay. Observing this:

"I never sleep so well as during a sermon or prayers," Friar John of the Funnels remarked. "I earnestly advise you to try my system. Let us both say the seven penitential psalms: we'll soon find out if you can sleep or not."

Gargantua, delighted with the idea, launched into the first of them; by the time they had reached *Beati quorum* . . . or *Blessed are the* . . . they were both sound asleep. Yet the monk, accustomed to the routine of the cloister, did not fail to awake shortly before midnight. What then should he do but rout out the others by singing at the top of his lungs:

> *The morning sun shines down on us*
> *From the bright noonday skies.*
> *Wake up and labor, Lazarus*
> *Up, lazybones, arise.*

When all were roused, he addressed them as follows:

"Gentlemen, according to a common saying, we begin matins with a gasp of phlegm, supper with a gulp of wine. I now propose the contrary. Let us now begin matins with a stiff drink and compete in hawking to-night."

"To drink so soon after sleep is contrary to all medical science,"

Gargantua objected. "First we must clear our bellies of superfluity and excrement."

"My arse to your quacks!" growled Friar John. "A hundred devils trample me down if old drunkards do not outnumber old doctors. I have made a covenant with my appetite: it goes to bed when I do (I attend to that daytimes) and it rises when I do. What, are our bodies falcons? Very well, then: you purge your fowl till you're blue in the face, I'll 'draw' mine with a ball of feathers to make it gag. My drawer, ho!"

"Your drawer?" Gargantua asked. "What do you mean?"

"My breviary!"

"Your breviary?"

"Ay, this fine psalter-shaped flagon filled with distilled wisdom. Do falconers fail to 'draw' their hawks with a hen's leg before feeding them? How else, pray, could they purge the beasties' brains of phlegm and whet their appetites? Even so, by taking this joyous little breviary in the morning, I clear my lungs and so am ready to drink!"

"How do you say these fine prayers?" Gargantua asked him.

"Catch as catch can," Friar John replied. "Three psalms, three lessons, like in Lent. The minimum, what? And sometimes nothing at all, if the spirit so moves. Why should I tie myself down to hours and sacraments? They were created for man, not *he* for *them*. I treat my devotions as I do my stirrup straps, lengthening or shortening them when I think good:

> *Brevis oratio penetrat cœlos*
> *Longa potatio evacuat scyphos.*
>
> *The shortest prayers go quickest to the sky,*
> *The longest draughts drain the decanter dry.*

I forget, what major prophet said this?"

"Upon my word, I haven't the faintest idea!" Ponocrates cried. "But I do know this, you blessed little ballock-bearer, you're worth the weight of your pendicula in gold!"

"Just like yourself!" the friar agreed. "But *venite apotemus, O come let us drink to Him!*"

Grilled meats of all sorts, soups, sauces and stews were produced
and the good monk drank his fill. Several of them imitated him;
others abstained. Then they prepared their armor and weapons,
insisting, much to Friar John's disgust, that he do likewise. (All
he wanted was his frock and the staff of the cross.) He inclined to
their desires, however, was armed cap-à-pie, provided with a fine
broad sabre and mounted on a good native steed. Beside him rode
Gargantua, Ponocrates, Gymnastes, Eudemon and twenty-five of
Grangousier's most daring knights, armed to the teeth, lance in
hand, mounted like St. George, but each with a gunner on the
back of his horse.

XLII

HOW THE MONK EXHORTED HIS COMPANIONS AND HOW HE DANGLED FROM A WALNUT TREE

THUS our noble champions set forth on their adventures, determined to know how to behave and what to guard against on the
day of the grim, horrific battle. Friar John of the Funnels exhorted them, saying:

"Banish all doubt and fear, children, for I shall bring you out
safely. God and St. Benedict go with us! God's death, if my
strength matched my courage, I would pluck the lot of them like
so many ducks. I myself fear nothing save artillery: however, I
know a certain prayer which will preserve a man against all gun
and cannon fire. The subsexton of our abbey taught it to me. The
only trouble is that it will do me no good because I've no faith in it.
But my staff of the cross, that is something else again: it will work
wonders. Only ducks dive at the first sign of danger. By God, if
I catch a single one of you ducking, devil take me if I don't make
him monk in my stead and wrap him up in my frock. That's a
capital cure for cowardice. Have you ever heard of My Lord of

Meurles and his greyhounds? The best was hopeless in the fields, so My Lord put a frock about his neck. By the Almighty's body, that hound never let hare or fox escape him; better still, he laid all the bitches in the country. And without the frock, he had been weak-reined, or, as the *Decretals* have it *frigidos et maleficiatos*, frigid and impotent through witchcraft."

As the monk angrily gave vent to these sentiments, heading for the willow grove, he passed under a walnut tree and caught his visor on a great branch. Nevertheless he spurred his horse savagely. The latter, a high-strung, ticklish beast, bounded forward. Friar John, seeking to disengage his visor from the bough, let go his bridle and so was left hanging by one hand to the tree while his horse escaped from under him. There the monk dangled, bawling for help, invoking murder and protesting treason.

Eudemon first noticed him and called Gargantua:

"My Lord, come and see Absalom hanging!"

Gargantua considered Friar John's position and expression; then he corrected:

"Not Absalom, for he hung by his hair. This monk is bald; he dangles by his ears."

"Help me, in the devil's name!" Friar John expostulated. "This is no time to gossip! You're no Decretalist preachers! Let them behold their fellow in mortal danger and forbear to help him; let them prefer, on pain of three-forked excommunication, to shrive him and put his conscience in the state of grace. By God, next time I see a man drowning in the river, I shall not lend a helping hand, no, I shall preach a fine, long sermon *de contemptu mundi et fuga seculi*, concerning scorn of the world and flight from its vanities. When he's dead as a doornail, I'll go and fish him out."

"Don't move, my sweet chuck!" cried Gymnastes. "I'll come and pull you down, for you're a charming little *monachus*:

> *Monachus in claustro*
> *Non valet ova dua;*
> *Sed quando est extra*
> *Valet bene triginta.*

> *A monk in his cloister*
> *Is not worth one oyster,*

Being lazy and dirty;
But just let him roister
Outside—he's worth thirty!

I've seen more than five hundred men strung to trees, but I never yet saw one who dangled so gracefully. If I thought I could match your technique, I'd gladly swing all my life."

"Haven't you done preaching?" Friar John demanded. "Help me in God's name, since you will not in the devil's. By the holy frock I wear, you shall repent *tempore et loco praelibatis*, in good time and place."

Gymnastes dismounted, climbed the tree, braced the monk up under one armpit and unfastened his visor from the branch. Friar John then fell to the ground, shortly followed by his rescuer. No sooner on *terra firma* than the monk tossed off all his armor, flinging piece after piece about the field. Then, with but his frock and the staff of the cross, he remounted the horse Eudemon had recaptured, and they moved merrily along toward the willow grove.

XLIII

HOW GARGANTUA MET PICROCHOLE'S SCOUTS AND HOW THE MONK SLEW CAPTAIN DRAWFORTH AND THEN WAS TAKEN PRISONER BY THE ENEMY

HEARING from the survivors how they had been routed and Captain Tripet untriped, Picrochole trembled with rage. The cursed devils to fall upon his men! A council was held all night long. At last Hâtiveau Rashcalf and My Lord Tickledingus Touchfaucet, summing up the unanimous sentiments of the assembly, declared that Picrochole could defeat all the devils in hell, if these so much as showed their noses. Without believing this wholesale, the monarch none the less did not question its truth.

He therefore sent a force of sixteen thousand light horse, under Count Windsucker Drawforth, on a skirmishing expedition. All were well sprinkled with holy water, invested with the blessing of St. Gregory and given stoles about their necks to dispel the Evil Spirit, for, as is well known, Gregorian water and stoles put the most vicious demons to flight. They rode forward to the outskirts of La Vauguyon and La Maladerie—the leper house at St. Lazare, by the Nuns' Bridge, south of Chinon—without coming upon a mortal soul; whereupon they changed their course and in the shepherd's hut near Le Coudray, they found the five pilgrims. Despite their pious victims' explanations, denials and prayers, they scoffed at them, bound them fast and carried them away towards Seuilly, where Gargantua heard them.

"Enemy troops, my friends!" cried Gargantua. "They outnumber us ten to one. Shall we have at them or no!"

"What the devil else should we do?" Friar John of the Funnels replied indignantly. "Do you judge men by their numbers or by bravery and daring?" Then: "Charge, devils, charge!" he roared. "Up, devils, charge them!"

Hearing his cry, the enemy, believing that real devils were about to attack them, took to their heels. Drawforth alone stood his ground, settled his lance on its rest and let Friar John have it full in the chest. But, as the iron hit the monk's miraculous frock, it was blunted and shattered, as a small wax candle struck against an anvil. Down came the staff of the cross, between Drawforth's neck and shoulders, square on the scapula. The blow fell so vigorously that Drawforth lost consciousness and toppled down at his horse's feet. Seeing his stole:

"These men are but priests," cried the friar. "A priest is but the embryo of a monk. By St. John, I am a proper monk: I'll kill them like flies."

Galloping after the enemy, he soon overtook their rearguard and, striking every which way, mowed them down like barley. Gymnastes then asked Gargantua: should they follow up?

"Not at all," Gargantua replied. "True military discipline forbids you to make the enemy desperate. That only revives his spent courage and increases his strength. The only salvation left to disconsolate and exhausted soldiers is to be denied all hope of salvation. How many victories have been wrenched out of the victors' hands because they lost control, sought wholesale carnage and destruction to the last man? Rather open all possible ways and roads to the enemy; build them bridges of silver as avenues of escape."

"Yes, but they have the monk!"

"Oh, they have, eh?" cried Gargantua. "Then on my honor, they shall rue it dearly. But to leave no loophole open, let us not retreat yet. We must wait here in silence. I think I already know our enemy's strategy: they proceed by chance, not by intelligent plan."

Whilst they lay hidden among the walnut trees, Friar John of the Funnels was after the foe, charging all he overtook and giving no quarter. Presently he met a horseman carrying one of the wretched pilgrims behind him. He was about to settle him, when:

"Ho, My Lord Prior, ho, my friend, Master Prior, save me, I implore you."

Hearing this, the enemy horsemen turned back to discover that a monk, single-handed, was creating all this havoc. At once they loaded him with blows as heavily as you load an ass with wood. But his skin was so tough that he felt nothing, even when they struck his cowl.

Having taken him prisoner, they handed him over to two archers, and, seeing no one else, supposed Gargantua's forces fled. They therefore rode off at full speed towards the walnut grove.

Gargantua, hearing the neighing and hoofbeats of the horses, said to his followers:

"Friends, I hear the enemy approaching; I can already see those in the van. Let us rally here and hold fast: we can withstand their charge to our honor and their loss!"

XLIV

HOW THE MONK GOT RID OF HIS GUARDS AND HOW PICROCHOLE'S VANGUARD WAS DEFEATED

THE monk, seeing them rush off in disorder, guessed they were about to set upon Gargantua and grieved sorely at his inability to fly to their aid. Examining the two archers who guarded him, he noted that they kept looking regretfully toward the valley their fellows were crossing. Doubtless they, too, longed to be taking their share of booty. The monk reasoned:

"These louts know nothing of warfare. They haven't demanded my parole or taken my sword from me."

Whipping it out in a trice, he brought it down upon the archer on his right. The blow severed the jugular veins and the parotid arteries and the throat to the uvula, split the thyroid glands and, hacking further, opened the spinal marrow between the second and third vertebrae. The first archer fell dead at his feet.

Then the monk, reining his horse to the left, ran upon the other. Seeing that his fellow was dead and that the monk held the advantage, the second archer shouted:

"Ha, My Lord Prior, I surrender. Quarter, dear Lord Prior, my beloved friend!"

"Ho, My Lord Posterior, surrender you do!" the monk retorted. "You shall get yours, My Lord Posterior, on the backside!"

"Oh, My Lord Prior, sweet and gentle Lord Prior, may God make you an abbot!"

"By the cloth, I wear, I'll make you a cardinal! Good God, are you trying to offer ransom to a religious? I shall cut you a fine blood-red cardinal's hat in one minute!"

"My Lord Prior, dear My Lord Prior," the archer shrieked. "My Lord Abbot-to-be, My Lord future-Cardinal, dear My Lord

Everything! Oh, no, no, no, no! My Lord Prior, my dear, kind, good, noble, sweet Prior, I deliver myself up to you."

"And I deliver you to all the devils."

"Quarter! quarter!"

"I'll quarter you!"

With one blow, Friar John struck off his head, cleaving his skull at the temple bones, lifting the two parietal bones—*ossa bregmatis*—together with the suture uniting them—*commissura sagittalis*—and a great portion of the coronal or frontal bone. The two *meninges* or cerebral membranes were cut in two; the two posterior ventricles or cavities of the brain were heavily slashed. The top of the fellow's head hung by the skin down his back like a doctoral bonnet, round, black without and red within. He, too, fell stone dead to the ground.

Then Friar John spurred his horse down the road the enemy had taken. They had, meanwhile, met Gargantua on the highway and sustained terrific casualties, thanks to Gargantua and his great tree, Gymnastes, Ponocrates, Eudemon and the rest. Have you ever seen a horsefly sting a mule in the arsehole? The wretched beast scampers right and left, heedless of where it goes, throwing its load on the ground, breaking its bridle and reins, taking no time to rest or breathe, unaware of what worries it since it can see nothing. So then ran Picrochole's hosts, rushing in mad haste and utter disarray . . . frightened out of their wits as if death had risen in person before them . . . fleeing without visible cause . . . pursued by a panic terror of their own imagining. . . .

Friar John of the Funnels, seeing their only thought was to escape, dismounted. Scaling a great rock by the roadside, he swung his broadsword indefatigably right and left, laying so many low that the blade snapped in two. This, he decided, was a sign that he had killed enough of them; the others should be spared to bear tidings of their rout to Picrochole.

Jumping down from his rock, he gathered the battle-axes of the dead; then returning to his point of vantage, watched the fugitives wallowing among the corpses. As they passed, he confiscated their pikes, swords, lances and other arms. When those who bore the pilgrims rode by, he forced them to dismount and give their horses to their prisoners, whom he kept with him against the hedge. As for My Lord Touquedillon Tickledingus of Touch-faucet, Friar John kept him captive.

XLV

HOW THE MONK BROUGHT BACK THE PILGRIMS AND HOW GRANGOUSIER TALKED TO THEM MOST WISELY

THE fight over, Gargantua and his followers turned homeward; at daybreak they found Grangousier in bed, praying for their safety and victory. Seeing them unhurt, he embraced them affectionately and asked after the monk. Gargantua answered him that the monk was doubtless with the enemy.

"Then they shall rue it!" cried Grangousier, and, as we know, rue it they did. (To-day in France "to give a man the monk" is still a popular saying; it means to give him something to worry about.)

Then Grangousier ordered a hearty breakfast prepared for them. When it was ready, they called Gargantua, but he was so sad at the monk's disappearance that he refused food or drink.

Suddenly a loud cry rose from the outer court.

"Wine, ho! fresh wine, Gymnastes, my friend. Bring me fresh wine!"

Gymnastes hurried out to find Friar John standing there with five pilgrims and Captain Tickledingus, his prisoner. Gargantua ran out to meet him, too. None but gave the monk the heartiest welcome; then Grangousier received him and questioned him about his adventures. Friar John explained how he had been captured, how he had got rid of the archers, how he had wrought bloody murder on the highway, how he had rescued the pilgrims; and how he had seized My Lord of Touquedillon Tickledingus and Touchfaucet. Then they all sat down to banquet merrily together.

Grangousier turned to the pilgrims. From where had they come, he asked, and where were they bound for?

Lasdaller or Dogweary acted as spokesman. They were all, he explained, from the neighborhood of Châteauroux in Brenne, west of Berry.

"My Lord, I hail from St. Genou, this man from Paluau, this man from Onzay, this man from Argy and the last man there, from Villebrenin. We were all returning by small stages from St. Sebastian, near Nantes."

"And what," Grangousier asked, "were you doing at St. Sebastian?"

"We went to offer the saint our vows against the plague!"

"Alas! poor wretched men!" Grangousier moaned. "Do you believe the plague comes from St. Sebastian?"

"Of course: our preachers tell us so!"

"False prophets only could spawn such imposture. What blasphemy, O God, to liken Your saints and holy men to those devils who do but hurt mankind! Apollo, Homer tells us, sent a plague down on the Greeks; other poets tell us of a rabble of Vejoves and other maleficent gods. Even so, some doddering hypocrites at Sinais had the temerity to preach that St. Anthony sent the fire into men's legs, St. Eutropius gave them dropsy, St. Gildas made them mad, St. Genou wished the gout on them. O Lord, and why? Shall I tell you? Because we honor the first by giving his name to erysipelas; because *Eutrope* sounds like *hydrope*; because St. Gildas is the patron of *gilles* or fools; because *genou* means knee!

"Well, I punished him so exemplarily (though he denounced me as a heretic) that no humbug has shown his smug face in my country since. Indeed, I marvel that your monarch allows the preaching of such scandalous doctrine; for it is worthier of punishment than the magic arts or other deviltry that spread the plague over this land. The plague kills only the body; such imposters poison the very soul."

"Where are you from, poor man?" Friar John broke in resolutely.

"From St. Genou."

"And how," asked the monk, "is your abbot, Tranchelion Gulligut, that true toper? How are the dear monks faring? God's body, may I roast in hell if they're not ramming your wives' pleasure-vents while you gad about, pilgrimizing."

"Bah!" sighed Dogweary. "I'm not afraid for mine. No man seeing her by daylight would ever break his neck to spend the night with her."

"That's incompatible, it holds no water, the cap won't fit. (I refer to your words, not to the vents!) Were your wife uglier than Proserpine, by God, she'd find herself jerkthumped as long as there was a monk within a thousand miles. Good carpenters use every kind of timber. The pox riddle me if you don't all find your wives pregnant on your return. The very shadow of an abbey spire is fecund!"

"Like the waters of the Nile," Gargantua agreed, "if we believe Strabo and Pliny, Book VII, Chapter III. The former says the Nile is so prolific that Egyptian women brought forth their brats four at a time. Pliny puts it at the more conservative figure of three!"

"Go your ways, poor man," Grangousier said compassionately. "Go your ways in the name of God the Creator, and may He guide you forever. Henceforth do not be so ready to undertake these idle and unprofitable journeys. Look after your families, work each at his trade, educate your children and live by the teachings of that good apostle, Paul. Do this and you will earn the protection of God, His Angels and His Saints; nor is there plague or evil that can possibly assail you!"

Gargantua then took them to the hall for refreshment, but the pilgrims only sighed, saying:

"Blessed the country with such a man for king! We are more edified and convinced by the few words he spoke to us than by all the sermons ever preached in our city."

"That," answered Gargantua, "is what Plato says in Book v of the *Republic*: commonwealths will be happy only when rulers philosophize or philosophers rule."

Then he had their pouches filled with provisions, their bottles with wine and he gave each a horse to ease the journey and some money to live on.

XLVI

OF THE HUMANE TREATMENT GIVEN THE PRISONER TICKLEDINGUS BY GRANGOUSIER

CAPTAIN MY LORD TICKLEDINGUS TOUCHFAUCET was ushered into Grangousier's presence and questioned concerning Picrochole's enterprises. What, Grangousier asked, did Picrochole intend to gain by this prodigious turmoil? To which Lord Tickledingus replied that his master's purpose and destiny were to conquer the whole country in return for the injury done his bakers.

"The undertaking is too great," said Grangousier. "All or nothing ends in nothing; gripe much, hold naught. The day of conquering kingdoms to your Christian neighbor's loss is long since past. To imitate the ancient Herculeses, Alexanders, Hannibals, Scipios, Cæsars and that ilk is contrary to the profession of the Gospel. Does not Christ enjoin us each to preserve, rule, keep and administer his own lands and possessions? Does He not forbid us to make hostile invasion upon others? Is it not true that what the Saracens and Barbarians once called prowess, we term wickedness and brigandry? Picrochole had done better to stay within his frontiers, governing his land like a true king, than to intrude on mine and plunder it. For, by wise rule, he would have enlarged his boundaries; by robbing me, he will meet his destruction.

"Go your way in God's name; do what is right; point out the errors you recognize to your monarch. And never advise him on matters to your personal advantage, for the common downfall entails private ruin. As for your ransom, I let you go scot free: your arms and horse also will be returned. It is only fitting I do this since we are neighbors and former friends. As Plato points out in Book v of the *Republic*, our difference is not war but sedition. If by some misfortune the Greeks took up arms against one another, the philosopher termed it sedition and advised the utmost moderation. Of course, you may *call* it war. But how superficial! Does it reach the depths of our hearts? No—for neither of us is outraged in his house. The whole problem is one of repairing some petty harm done by our people—I mean both ours and yours. Such harm you ought to have overlooked, even though you knew it had been done, for quarrelsome people were better dismissed than despised. Especially since I offered to give them satisfaction according to the damage suffered.

"God will be just judge of our variance. I can but implore Him to cut my life short or annihilate my possessions in my very sight ere I or any subject of mine offend Him."

Grangousier called Friar John of the Funnels:

"Friar John, my friend, did you capture Captain Tickledingus here?"

"Sire," replied the monk, "he is present, he has attained the age of discretion and I should prefer he tell you than I."

"My Lord," said Tickledingus, "indeed he captured me and I freely constitute myself his prisoner."

"Did you set his ransom, Friar John?"

"No, My Lord: I care nothing about that."

"How much do you want for his capture?"

"Nothing, nothing: it's no concern of mine."

Grangousier ordered his treasurer to count out seventy-two thousand saluts, minted in Paris under the English kings, and to pay them to Friar John as ransom for Tickledingus. Then the latter was served a collation and, well dined and well wined, asked whether he preferred to stay with Grangousier or return to Picrochole.

"I will follow your advice, My Lord."

"Well, then, return to your king and God be with you!"

Grangousier presented him with a sword and a necklace. The former was a blade forged at Vienne in Dauphiny, with a golden scabbard ornamented by vignettes of the most delicate engraving. The latter, golden also, weighed three hundred and ten thousand pounds and, with the gems that garnished it, was worth sixty thousand ducats. In addition, Grangousier added a personal cash bounty of ten thousand crowns. For escort, Gargantua gave him thirty men-at-arms and six-score archers, under Gymnastes, with orders to accompany him to the very gates of La Roche Clermault, if necessary.

Tickledingus gone, the monk gave back the ransom money to Grangousier:

"Sire, now is no time to make such gifts. Wait till this war is over. Who knows what may turn up? Remember that war waged without good store of money is but a patchwork thing. Coin is the sinews of war!"

"Very well," said Grangousier, "this war ended, I shall reward you handsomely and all others who have served me well."

XLVII

HOW GRANGOUSIER SENT FOR HIS TROOPS AND HOW TICKLEDINGUS, HAVING SLAIN RASHCALF, WAS IN TURN SLAIN BY ORDER OF PICROCHOLE

ABOUT this time, the men of Bessé, of Vieux Marché, of Bourg St. Jacques, of Trainneau, of Parilly, of Rivière, of Les Roches St. Paul, of Le Vaubreton, of Pontille, of Le Bréhémont, of Pont-du-Clain, of Cravant, of Grandmont, of Les Bourdes, of La Villeaumaire, of Huymes, of Ligré, of Hussé, of St. Louant, of Panzoust, of Les Coudreaux, of Véron, of Coulaines, of Chouzé, of Varennes, of Bourgueil, of L'Ile Bourbon, of Le Croulay, of Narsay, of Candes, of Montsoreau and other places near by, sent ambassadors. They had learned, they said, of the wrongs done him by Picrochole; in the name of their old alliance, they offered all their support, in troops, funds and supplies.

The money amounted to seventy-four million, two and one-half crowns of pure gold. The troops numbered fifteen thousand men-at-arms, thirty-two thousand light horse, eighty-nine thousand gunners, one hundred and forty thousand mercenaries, forty-seven thousand pioneers, all paid and victualled for six months and four days.

There were eleven thousand two hundred light cannon, heavy cannon, basilisks and culverins.

Thanking them heartily, Grangousier neither wholly accepted nor rejected the offer. He would, he declared, wage war in such a way as to avoid bothering so many good men and true. For the time being, he called out only the troops normally garrisoned at La Devinière, Chavigny-en-Vallée, Gravot near Bourgueil and Le Quinquenais, north of Chinon. These came to two thousand five hundred men-at-arms, sixty-six thousand foot, twenty-six thousand gunners, twenty-two thousand pioneers, six thousand light horse. There were also two hundred heavy pieces of ordnance. These men were so well organized —so efficiently supported by quartermasters, commissaries, smiths, farriers, armorers and other service-of-supply forces—so well armed, trained in discipline and coöperation—so well drilled and inured to fatigue—so swift to move, so strong to strike and so prudent in their adventures that they resembled rather the works of an organ or the machinery of a clock than a body of human beings.

Immediately upon returning, Tickledingus had reported to Picrochole on what he had seen and done. He ended by earnestly advising his master to come to terms with Grangousier, whom he knew by personal experience to be the best man in the world. It was, he went on, both unreasonable and profitless for Picrochole to molest neighbors that had never done him aught but good. Most important of all, if Picrochole ever did manage to emerge from this business, it would be to his dire misfortune, for Gargantua was strong enough to defeat him easily. Poor Tickledingus had barely finished when Rashcalf shouted,

"Woe is that prince whose servants are as easily corrupted as I know Tickledingus to be! Behold what a change of heart! Why, he would gladly have joined our enemies, betrayed us and borne arms against us, had Grangousier been willing to retain him. But just as virtue is patent to all, friends or enemies, so wickedness is soon discovered. Ay, though the enemy make use of the latter, they nevertheless hold it in abomination."

At this, Tickledingus, out of patience, drew his sword and ran Rashcalf through just under the left nipple, killing him instantly. As he pulled back the blade, he said boldly:

"Thus perish all who blame a faithful servant."

Picrochole, seeing Tickledingus' handsome Vienne sword and its richly ornamented scabbard, flew into a furious rage.

"Were you given this weapon," he demanded, "to murder my beloved friend Rashcalf in cold blood under my very eyes?"

Without pausing for an answer, he ordered his archers to rend Tickledingus limb from limb, which they did so savagely that rivers of blood flowed over wall and floor. Then Picrochole had Rashcalf's body buried with due solemnity and Tickledingus' tossed over the walls into the ditch.

News of this barbarity having spread among the troops, not a few began to murmur against Picrochole. Whereupon My Lord Grippeminaud Skinflint advised his master:

"My Lord, I dare not prophesy the end of this adventure. But I can see that the morale of your troops is far from promising. They consider themselves poorly equipped and ill-supplied. Already three or four sallies have diminished their numbers. Worse, your enemies are receiving great reënforcements and vast supplies. If ever they besiege us, I see nothing but our total ruin!"

"Shit, shit!" roared Picrochole. "You are like the Melun eels: you cry before you are skinned. Just let the enemy advance, we'll show them!"

XLVIII

HOW GARGANTUA ATTACKED PICROCHOLE AT LA ROCHE CLERMAULT AND ROUTED HIS ARMY

GARGANTUA was placed in charge of the entire army. His father, remaining in his castle, exhorted them with noble words, promising great rewards for special feats of prowess. Gargantua first got his army across the ford at Vède: thanks to boats and quickly erected bridges, they were over in a trice. Then, considering the situation of the town, which was built on a strategic height, he spent that night with his council, formulating a plan of action.

"My Lord," said Gymnastes, "the French temperament is such that we are good only at the first rush. Then we are fiercer than the devils in hell. But break our spirit by delay and we become softer than women. My advice is to let your troops catch their breath and take some refreshment, then strike at once!"

The advice was considered good: Gargantua therefore marshalled his army in line, with the reserves and auxiliaries occupying the left. Friar John of the Funnels, with six companies of foot and two hundred horse, hastily crossed the marsh and scaled the hill of Le Puy, coming out on the highway from La Roche Clermault to Loudun. Meanwhile, the attack began; Picrochole's men were at a loss whether to sally and join battle or sit tight within the walls. Picrochole, however, made a furious sortie with a band of Household Cavalry; he was welcomed by a hail of cannon from Gargantua's batteries on the hill. Gargantua's infantry then retreated into the valley to give their own gunners a free field. Picrochole's garrison defended itself as best it could, but their shots passed over without inflicting the slightest hurt. A few of Picrochole's horse, which had survived our artillery, now fell fiercely upon our ranks but in vain. All were allowed to come within our ranks and there promptly struck down. Their fellows, seeing this, sought to retreat; but Friar John had cut them off. Whereupon they took to flight amid the greatest confusion.

A few of the monk's troops wished to chase the runaways, but Friar John held them back. He realized that by breaking ranks in the heat of pursuit, they would be at the mercy of the garrison, if the latter chose to charge. Having waited a spell without any sign of the enemy appearing, the monk sent Duke Prudent Phrontistes to Gargantua, advising the latter to occupy the hill to the left and thus cut off Picrochole's retreat on that side. Gargantua at once complied, dispatching four brigades under Sebastes the Honored. They no sooner reached the summit than they met Picrochole face to face. The latter's forces at once scattered and Sebastes' followers charged them bravely. Unfortunately, however, Sebastes and his men suffered great losses from the garrison gunners, who harassed them from the walls with bow and gun. Observing this, Gargantua sped to their help, training his artillery fire so densely upon that portion of the walls that troops were mustered thither from every other part of the garrison.

Friar John immediately realized that the side he was besieging now lay unguarded. He moved swiftly up with a few followers to the town walls. He was well aware that a surprise attack inspires more terror than the most powerful onslaught. So he made no sound until all his men had scaled the walls except two hundred horse whom he posted behind him for emergencies. When they were all drawn up, they burst into the most horrible shouting, slew the guard at the gate, proceeded without resistance to open it wide to their cavalry. Together, infantry and horse dashed toward the east gate, where the tumult raged and, closing upon the defenders from the rear, overthrew their forces. The garrison, besieged on all sides in a town occupied by Friar John, surrendered, begging for mercy. The monk disarmed them, cleared the churches of every staff of the cross within, sent his prisoners there and posted guards at the doors. Then, flinging open the east gate, he rushed to Gargantua's help.

Picrochole, seeing a mass of soldiers sallying from the town, believed them to be reënforcements from the garrison. Rashly pressing even further forward, he was about to make a desperate charge to regain La Roche Clermault, when the monk appeared.

"Friar John, my friend, Friar John, you are come in the nick of time!" Gargantua cried.

Picrochole and his men, seeing all was lost, took to their heels in all directions. Gargantua pursued them beyond Vaugaudry, massacring them all the way. Then he sounded the retreat.

XLIX

HOW PICROCHOLE IN HIS FLIGHT MET WITH SERIOUS MISFORTUNE AND WHAT GARGANTUA DID AFTER THE BATTLE

PICROCHOLE was speeding in desperate flight toward L'Ile Bouchard when, on the Rivière road, his horse stumbled and fell. Flying into a temper, he drew his sword and in a fury killed the beast. Then, finding no one who could remount him, he was about to take an ass from the mill near by. But the miller's men fell upon him, belabored him with blows and stripped him of his clothes, leaving him only an old serge smock to cover his nakedness.

Thus apparelled, the choleric wretch went away. Crossing the water at Port Huault, he met an old witch to whom he unfolded the tale of his misfortunes. She assured him his kingdom would be restored to him at Tib's Eve, at the Greek kalends or at the coming of the dodo birds and cocklicranes.

No one knows what has become of him. However, I did hear that he is now a common stevedore at Lyons, quite as waspish as ever, and constantly complaining to who will listen about Tib, the Greeks, the dodo and the cocklicranes. When these matters are settled, doubtless he hopes to be reëstablished in his kingdom.

After the retreat, Gargantua's first step was to call the muster roll. Only a few of his men had perished in the battle: some foot-soldiers from Captain Audacious Tolmere's company. Ponocrates, too, figured on the list of wounded, with a musket shot through the doublet. Next, Gargantua had them refreshed in company units, ordering his own treasurer to defray the cost. Next, he gave strict orders that no outrage should be committed in the town since it was now his. After their meal, the troops were summoned to the public square in front of the castle and paid six months' wages. Finally, Gargantua assembled all that remained of Picrochole's forces and, before the prince and captains of his court, addressed them as follows.

L

GARGANTUA'S ADDRESS TO THE VANQUISHED

"Our fathers and forefathers before them, time out of mind, believed that, having won a victory, they could find no nobler memorial of triumph than one inspired by magnanimity. Accordingly, they did not raise monuments of architecture on lands conquered by force but monuments of affection in hearts conciliated by generosity. For they deemed the eloquent memory their mercy earned of living men, more precious and more enduring than mute inscriptions upon dead arches, columns and pyramids—these being the sport of tempests and the object of universal envy.

"You cannot but remember what mansuetude they showed the Bretons on the dismantling of Parthenay and after the Battle of St. Aubin-du-Cormier. You have heard and marvelled how splendidly they treated those barbarians from Hispaniola who had plundered, ravaged and decimated our maritime borders of Olonne and Talmandais.

"On another occasion, all heaven rang with the praises and gratulations offered up by your forefathers and yourselves. That was when King Alpharbal of Canarra, not content with his fortune, furiously invaded the land of Aunis and practised fell piracy throughout the Armoric Islands and the adjacent regions of Brittany. In a fierce naval battle, my father, Grangousier—God guard him and protect him!—defeated King Alpharbal and took him captive. What happened?

"Here I might say that other sovereigns—indeed even such as arrogate to themselves the title 'Catholic'—other sovereigns, I say, would have dealt harshly with him, flung him into prison and held

him for an exorbitant ransom. What did my father do? He treated
Alpharbal with courtesy and respect, lodged him in his own palace,
and (O height of loving-kindness!) sent him back under safe conduct, laden with gifts, favors and tokens of friendship.

"With what result? With this result: Alpharbal returned to his
kingdom, assembled all the princes and states of his realm, told them
of the humanity he found in us and begged them to deliberate. It was
his hope, he added, that all the world might be vouchsafed an example of their honest graciousness to us in return for our gracious
honesty towards them. They thereupon unanimously decreed to offer
us their entire lands, dominions and kingdoms to dispose of at our
pleasure. King Alpharbal in person suddenly landed on our shores
with nine thousand and thirty-eight great cargo vessels bearing not
only the treasures of his royal house and dynasty but of practically
the whole empire. For, when he embarked, the crowds thronged
about his ships, tossing into them all they held precious: gold, silver,
rings, jewels, spices, drugs, aromatics, parrots, pelicans, monkeys,
civets, genets and porcupines. Nor was he accounted a good mother's
son who failed to cast in his treasure.

"Immediately upon landing, King Alpharbal wished to fling himself on the ground and kiss my father's feet. The salutation was
deemed degrading and intolerable: my father raised him up and embraced him as a brother. Alpharbal offered him his presents; they
were refused as being excessive. Voluntarily, he gave himself and his
posterity into perpetual bondage; the offer was rejected because it
seemed inequitable. By a decree of state, with a deed of conveyance
duly signed, certified and sealed, he offered all his lands, territories
and possessions; my father took the document and tossed it in the
fire. At length my father was moved to tears of pity and admiration
for the Canarrans' simplicity, for their good will. In the most tactful
words, he minimized the courtesy he had done them. It was not
worth a fig, a button, a wisp of straw. If he had shown them the
slightest favor, it was because he was in duty bound. But Alpharbal
exaggerated it all the more.

"What does all this prove?

"By a ransom, we might have extorted about twenty times one
hundred thousand crowns, holding his eldest sons as hostages. Instead, they made themselves perpetual tributaries and undertook of

their own accord to pay us yearly two million in gold at twenty-four carats fine. The first year they paid the entire sum; the second, of their own free will, twenty-three hundred thousand crowns; the third, twenty-six hundred thousand; the fourth, three millions. Now, year in, year out, their tribute increases in such proportions that soon we shall have to forbid them to bring us any more. Such is the nature of gratitude. Time which mines and corrupts all other things on earth unfailingly increases and augments men's benefactions. A generous deed done to a man of reason grows constantly by human appreciation and remembrance.

"For my own part, I am unwilling to degenerate in any wise from the hereditary decency of my fathers. I therefore hereby absolve, deliver and set you unconditionally free as heretofore. What is more, as you pass by the gate, you shall each receive three months' wages to enable you to return to your homes and families. And I have arranged for an escort of six hundred cavalry and eight thousand foot, under my equerry, Alexander, to protect you from possible molestation at the hands of my peasantry.

"Go, now, and God be with you.

"I have but one regret: that Picrochole is absent. I would have made him understand that I engaged in this war against my will, without hope of increasing my possessions or renown. But since he has mysteriously vanished, I wish his kingdom to remain intact for his son. The lad is young—not yet five years old, I believe—therefore he shall be governed and educated by the oldest princes and most learned men of the land. And because a realm bereft of a king and administered by regents inevitably crumbles unless the latters' covetousness and avarice are checked, I will and ordain that Ponocrates be supreme over these governors. He shall have all the authority requisite thereto; he shall attend the child assiduously until such time as he recognize him able to govern himself. Then Ponocrates shall resign.

"I believe that an exaggerated tendency to forgive wrongdoers encourages them but to begin their mischief anew. I know that Moses, the meekest man of his day, severely punished such Israelites as rebelled. I recall what Cicero said of Cæsar: 'His fortune was sovereign and his virtue supreme because he could and would spare and forgive.' Yet Cæsar none the less dealt rigorously with mutiny.

"Governed by these examples, I order you before you leave to deliver up: first, that fine specimen, Marquet, whose arrant boastfulness was the initial cause of all this warfare; secondly, his fellow bakers, who neglected immediately to curb his senseless temerity; and
thirdly, all such of Picrochole's counsellors, captains, officers and domestics as pushed, incited, or advised him to sally forth from his
kingdom and thus harry us."

LI

HOW THE VICTORIOUS GAR-
GANTUANS WERE REWARDED
AFTER THE BATTLE

WHEN Gargantua had finished his speech, all the troublemakers were
delivered to him save two cake-bakers and My Lords Swashbuckler,
Smalltittle and Krapp. The bakers had been killed in action; the captains had shown a clean pair of heels six hours before the battle.
Without pausing to catch their breath or to glance backward, one
had scurried off as far as the Agnello Pass in the Alps, the other to the
valley of Vire in Normandy, the third to Logrono, a Spanish city on
the border of Navarre. The worst harm Gargantua did the hostages
was to make them work the screw-presses in the printing house he
had newly installed. The fallen, he had honorably buried in the valley
of Noirottes and at the camp of Brûlevieille. The wounded, he had
transferred for treatment in his vast Nosocome or hospital. Then he
turned his attention to the damage done to the town and its inhabitants, paying the people indemnities upon their own sworn estimates.
Finally, he built and garrisoned a fort for their better protection in
future emergencies.

At his departure, he thanked all his soldiers most graciously and
sent them back to their posts for the winter, except for certain crack
units which had particularly distinguished themselves, and for the
various commanding officers. These marched back with him to Grangousier.

Seeing them return, the dear old man was indescribably moved. Immediately he ordered the most magnificent, abundant and delicious feast ever seen on earth since the days of King Ahasueras, when the latter entertained his officers for one hundred and eighty-seven days, his men for seven.

When they arose from the board, Grangousier gave them all the plate that graced it, weighing wholly eighteen hundred thousand and fourteen bezants of gold. It included great antique vessels, huge pots, monster basins, gigantic cups, beakers, goblets, candelabra, baskets, gravy boats, dishes, boxes, platters and other such vessels, the whole of massive gold with stones, enamelling and workmanship even more valuable than the gold itself. Out of his own coffers he had each man given twelve hundred thousand crowns in cash. Besides this, Grangousier gave to each in perpetuity (unless he died without heirs) the castle and lands he preferred.

To Ponocrates, the vigorous, he gave La Roche Clermault; to Gymnastes, the teacher of esthetics, Le Courday; to Eudemon, the fortunate, Montpensier; to Tolmere, the audacious, Le Riveau. Ithyboles, the upright, received Montsoreau; Acamas, the tireless, Candes; Chironactes, the busyhanded, Varennes; Sebastes, the honored, Gravol. Finally Le Quinquenais went to Alexander, protector of men; Ligré to Sophrones, the wise.

LII

HOW GARGANTUA HAD THE ABBEY OF THÉLÈME BUILT FOR THE MONK

THERE remained only the monk to provide for. Gargantua offered him the Abbey of Seuilly: he refused. What about the Benedictine abbeys of Bourgueil or St. Florent, among the richest in France: he might have either or both? Again, the offer met with a flat refusal: Friar John of the Funnels answered peremptorily that he did not seek the charge or government of monks.

"For," he explained, "how shall I govern others when I cannot possibly govern myself?" There was a pause. "But—" he hesitated. "But if you believe I have given and can give you good service, let me found an abbey after my own heart."

The notion delighted Gargantua: he forthwith offered his estate of Thélème, by the Loire, two leagues away from Port Huault. Thélème in Greek means free will, an auspicious name for Friar John's abbey. Here indeed he could institute a religious order contrary to all others.

"First," said Gargantua, "you must not build a wall around it, for all other abbeys are solidly enclosed."

"Quite so," agreed the monk, "for where there are *mures*, walls, before, and *mures*, walls, behind, we have *murmures*, murmurs of envy and plotting."

Now in certain monasteries it is a rule that if any women enter (I mean honest and chaste ones) the ground they tread upon must be swept over. Therefore it was decreed that if a monk or nun should by any chance enter Thélème, every place that religious passed through should be thoroughly disinfected.

Similarly because all monasteries and convents on earth are compassed, limited and regulated by hours, at Thélème no clock or dial of any sort should be tolerated. On the contrary, their time here would be governed by what occasions and opportunities might arise. As Gargantua sagaciously commented:

"I can conceive of no greater waste of time than to count the hours. What good comes of it? To order your life by the toll of a bell instead of by reason or common sense is the veriest piece of asininity imaginable."

By the same token, they established the qualifications for entrance into their order. Was it not true that at present women took the veil only if they were wall-eyed, lame, hunchbacked, ill-favored, misshapen, half-witted, unreasonable or somewhat damaged? That only such men entered monasteries as were cankered, ill-bred idiots or plain nuisances?

("Incidentally," said Friar John, "if the woman is neither fair nor good, of what use is the cloth?")

"Let the clot hump her," Gargantua replied.

"I said 'cloth' not 'clot.'"

"Well, what's the answer?"

"To cover her face or her arse with!")

Accordingly, they decided to admit into the new order only such women as were beautiful, shapely, pleasing of form and nature, and such men as were handsome, athletic and personable.

Again, because men entered the convents of this world only by guile and stealth, it was decreed that no women would be in Thélème unless men were there also, and vice-versa.

Moreover, since both men in monasteries and women in convents were forced after their year of noviciate to stay there perpetually, Gargantua and Friar John decided that the Thélèmites, men or women, might come and go whenever they saw fit.

Further, since the religious usually made the triple vow of chastity, poverty and obedience, at Thélème all had full leave to marry honestly, to enjoy wealth and to live in perfect freedom.

As for the age of initiation, they stipulated that women were admissible between the ages of ten and fifteen, men between twelve and eighteen.

LIII

HOW THE ABBEY OF THÉLÈME WAS BUILT AND ENDOWED

To build and furnish the abbey, Gargantua paid in cash twenty-seven hundred thousand eight hundred and thirty-one crowns in current coin of the realm, fresh from the mint, with a sheep on the obverse and the king's head on the reverse. He undertook to pay yearly, until the project was completed, sixteen hundred and sixty-nine thousand crowns, with the sum on the obverse, and as many again with the seven stars, the whole to be levied upon custom receipts.

For the foundation and maintenance of Thélème, he settled in perpetuity twenty-three hundred and sixty-nine thousand, five hundred and fourteen nobles (a coin stamped by the English kings with the rose of York), free of all tax, burden or fealty, payable yearly at the abbey gate. These privileges were all corroborated by letters patent.

The building was hexagonal; in each corner rose a great, circular tower, each identical, sixty yards in diameter. To the north, the river Loire flowed past the first tower which was named *Arctice* or Northern. East of it rose *Calaer* which means "situated in the balmy air"; then, successively, *Anatole* or Eastern; *Mesembrine* or Southern; *Hesperia* or Occidental; and the last, *Cryere* or Glacial. The distance between each tower was three hundred and twelve yards. The building was throughout six storeys high, counting the underground cellar for one. The ground floor was vaulted like a basket handle; the others, covered with Flanders mistletoe, jutting out like brackets and pendants. The roof, of finest slate, was lined with lead and bore little figures of mannikins and animals well assorted and gilt. The gutters jutted out from the walls between the casement arches; they were painted diagonally gold and blue down to the ground, where they ended in pipes which carried the water into the river below.

This building was a hundred times more magnificent than Bonnivet, Chambord or Chantilly. There were nine thousand three hundred and thirty-two suites, each with a salon, a study, a dressing room, an oratory and an exit into a great hall. In the wing between each tower was a winding stairway. The steps, grouped in units of twelve between each landing, were of porphyry, of Numidian stone, of serpentine marble; they were twenty-two feet long and three fingers thick. At each landing, two splendid round antique archways admitted the light and led to an open loggia of the same dimensions. The stairway, rising to the roof, ended in a pavilion; on either side lay a great hall which in turn led to the apartments.

The wing between the towers called *Arctice* and *Cryere* contained rich libraries of Greek, Latin, Hebrew, French, Italian and Spanish volumes, grouped in their respective sections. In the centre rose a marvellous winding ramp conceived in such ample proportions that six soldiers with their lances at rest could ride up it abreast to the top of the palace. Its entry, outside the house, was an archway six fathoms wide.

Between *Anatole* and *Mesembrine* were spacious galleries with murals representing heroic feats of olden times, scenes from history and pictures of the earth. Here again were a stairway and gate as described upon the river side. On this gate, couched in great antique letters, ran the following legend.

LIV

INSCRIPTION ENGRAVED ON THE MAIN GATE AT THÉLÈME

HERE *enter not, smug hypocrites or holy loons,*
Bigots, sham-Abrahams, impostors of the cloth,
Mealy-mouthed humbugs, holier-than-thou baboons,
Lip-service lubbers, smell-feast picaroons.
Else had we to admit the Goth and Ostrogoth
Precursors of the ape and others of that broth.
Hence, sneaks and mischief-makers, colporteurs of lies,
Be off to other parts to sell your merchandise.

> *Being foul you would befowl*
> *Man, woman, beast or fowl.*
> *The vileness of your ways*
> *Would sully my sweet lays,*
> *Owls—And your own black cowl,*
> *Being foul, you would befoul.*

Here enter not, defenders of dishonest pleas,
Clerks, barristers, attorneys who make freemen slaves,
Canon Law pettifoggers, censors, Pharisees,
Judges, assessors, arbitrators, referees
Who blithely doom good people to untimely graves,
The gibbet is your destination, legal knaves!
Be off: indict the rope if you should find it short,
Here there is no abuse; we do not need your court.

> *Tangle, wrangle, brangle*
> *We loathe, from any angle.*
> *Our aim is joy and sport,*

Time's swift, youth's fleet, life's short.
You, go and disentangle
Tangle, wrangle, brangle!

Here enter not, curmudgeon, loan shark, muckworm, hunks,
Bloodsucking usurer, extortioner, pennystint, . . .
Hence, lawsuit-chasing crimps, greedy as starving punks
Tracking a patron; lickgolds, hiding cash in trunks,
Harpyclaws, crunchfists, jaundiced zealots of the mint,
Your crackling, sallow palms are itching. Skin a flint!
Heap up your hoard, O scrub-faced curs, heap up afresh,
And as you grudge and gripe and screw, God rot your flesh!

Those grim and grisly faces
Bear all the ravaged traces
Of hidebound avarice;
We cannot stomach this.
Banish from all blithe places
Those grim and grisly faces.

Here enter not, you churls, sour boors, invidious fools,
Old, jealous brabblers, scolds, neither by night nor day,
Nor grumblers, soreheads, sulkers, badgers bred in schools
Of hate; nor ghosts of malaperts; nor firebrands' ghouls
From Rhineland, Greece or Rome, fiercer than wolves at bay;
Nor you, riddled with pox, your face a Milky Way
Of scars not stars; nor you, clapstricken to the bone:
Enjoy your shameless crusts and blemishes alone.

Honor, praise and pleasure
Are here in goodly measure:
Health reigns supreme because
We follow Nature's laws.
Ours is a triple treasure:
Honor, praise and pleasure.

But enter here thrice welcome, men of goodly parts,
Gallants and noble gentlemen, thrice welcome be!

Here you will find an abbey after your own hearts,
Where living is esteemed the highest of the arts.
Come in your tens and hundreds, come in thousands, we
Shall clasp you to our bosoms in fond amity:
Come wise, come proud, come gay, come courteous, come mellow,
Come true sophisticate, come worldling, come, good fellow!

> Comrades, companions, friends,
> Assemble from the ends
> Of earth in this fair place
> Where all is mirth and grace.
> Felicity here blends
> Comrades, companions, friends.

Here enter, all ye loyal scholars who expound
Novel interpretations of the Holy Writ.
Here is a fort and refuge; from this favored ground
You may confound the error that is elsewhere found,
You may found a profound new faith instead of it,
Sweeping away false teachings, bit by fallacious bit.
Come unto us and make your cogent meanings heard:
Destroy the foes of God and of his Holy Word.

> The Holy Word of God
> Shall never be downtrod
> Here in this holy place,
> If all deem reason grace,
> And use for staff and rod
> The Holy Word of God.

Here enter, ladies fair of eminent degree,
Come soon with starry eyes, lips smiling, comely face,
Flowers of loveliness, angels of harmony,
Resplendent, proud yet of the rarest modesty,
Sprightly of flesh, lithe-waisted and compact of grace,
Here is your home. A gallant lord designed this place
For you, that beauty, charm and virtue might find room
Deliciously to breathe, exquisitely to bloom.

Who makes a priceless gift
Wins pardon without shrift.
Donor, recipient
Alike find rich content.
To him your voices lift
Who makes a priceless gift.

LV

HOW THE MONKS AND NUNS LIVED AT THÉLÈME

IN the middle of the lower court stood a magnificent alabaster fountain, surmounted by the Three Graces holding cornucopias and spouting water through their breasts, mouths, ears, eyes and other orifices. The buildings above this court stood upon great pillars of chalcedony and porphyry, forming classical arches about lengthy wide galleries adorned with paintings and trophies of various animals: the horns of bucks, unicorns and hippopotami, elephants' tusks and sundry other curiosities.

The ladies' quarters ran from *Arctice* all the way to the *Mesembrine* Gate; the rest of the abbey was reserved for men. In front of this part, between the outer two towers, lay the recreational facilities: the tilting yard, the riding school, the theatre and the natatorium which included wonderful swimming pools on three different levels, with every sort of equipment and myrtle water aplenty.

Near the river was the fine pleasure garden, with, in the middle, a maze. Tennis courts and football fields spread out between the next two towers. Close to *Cryere*, an orchard offered a mass of fruit trees laid out in quincunxes, with, at its end, a sizy park abounding in venison.

The space between the third pair of towers was reserved for the shooting ranges: here were targets and butts for harquebuss, long bow and crossbow. The servants' quarters, one storey high, were situated outside *Hesperia*. Beyond was the falconry, managed by expert falconers and hawk trainers and annually supplied by the Cretans, Venetians and Sarmatian Poles with all manner of birds. There were priceless eagles for hunting hares, foxes and cranes. There were gerfalcons, goshawks, sakers for hunting wild geese, herons and bitterns. There were falcons, lanners, sparhawks and merlins for hunting larks and partridges. Other birds there were, too, in great quantities, so well trained that when they flew afield for their own sport they never failed to catch every bird they encountered. . . . The venery with its hounds and beagles stood a little further along towards the park.

All the halls, apartments and chambers were richly hung with tapestries varying with the season; the floors were covered with green cloth, the beds all embroidered. Each rear chamber boasted a pierglass set in a heavy gold frame adorned with pearls. Near the exits of the ladies' halls were the perfumers and hairdressers who ministered to the gentlemen before the latter visited the ladies. These attendants furnished the ladies' rooms with rose water, orange-flower water and angelica, supplying a precious small atomizer to give forth the most exquisite aromatic perfumes.

LVI

HOW THE MONKS AND NUNS OF THÉLÈME WERE APPARELLED

WHEN first the abbey was founded, the ladies dressed according to their taste and pleasure. Subsequently of their own free will they modified their costume as follows.

They wore hose, of scarlet or kermes-red, reaching some three inches above the knee, the edge being exquisitely embroidered or slashed. Their garters, which matched their bracelets, came both a whit over and under the knee. Their shoes, pumps and slippers were of red, violet or crimson velvet and jagged as a lobster's claws.

Over their slips, they put on a tight tunic of pure silk camlet, and over that a taffeta farthingale or petticoat, red, white, beige, gray or of any other color. Above this farthingale went a skirt of silver taffeta, with fine gold embroidery and delicate cross-stitch work. According to the temperature, the season or the ladies' whim, these skirts might be satin, damask or velvet and, in color, orange, green, cendré, blue, canary yellow, scarlet, crimson or white, or of cloth-of-gold, cloth-of-silver, or any other choice material variously embroidered, stitched, brocaded or spangled according to the occasion for which they were worn.

Their gowns, or over-garments, were also governed by timely considerations. They might be cloth-of-gold with silver embossing or red satin with gold brocade or taffeta, white, blue, black or tawny. Or they might be silk rep, silk camlet, velvet, cloth-of-silver, cloth-of-gold or satin variously figured with gold and silver thread.

In summer, instead of these gowns, they wore lovely light smocks made of the same material, or capes, Moorish-fashion, with hoods to protect and shade their faces from the sun. These Moresco capes were of violet velvet, having raised gold stitching over silver purl or gold piping and cording, with small Indian pearls at their ends. And ever a gay colored plume, the color of their sleeves, bravely garnished with gold! In winter, their gowns were of taffeta in all the colors mentioned above, but lined with lynx, weasel, Calabrian marten, sable and other rare fur. Their beads, rings, chains and necklaces were of precious stones: carbuncles, rubies, balas rubies, diamonds, sapphires, emeralds, turquoises, garnets, agates, beryls and priceless pearls.

Their headgear also varied with the season. In winter, it was in the French fashion with a cap over the temples covered by a velvet hood with hanging veil. In spring it was in the Spanish, with laces and veils. In summer it was in the Tuscan, the hair elaborately entwined with gold chains and jewels. On Sundays and holidays, however, they followed the French mode which is more seemly and modest.

The men, too, dressed according to their personal taste. Their hose were of light wool or serge cloth, white, black, scarlet or kermes-red. Their velvet breeches were of the same hue or almost; they were embroidered or slashed to their taste. The doublet was of cloth-of-gold, cloth-of-silver, velvet, satin or damask, embroidered, panelled or slashed on one model, the points silk to match and the ornaments of fine enamelled gold.

Their cloaks and jerkins were of cloth-of-gold, cloth-of-silver, gold tissue or velvet, purfled or brocaded at pleasure; their over-garments were every whit as costly as the ladies'. Their girdles were silk, matching their doublets. Each wore on his side a handsome sword with gilt hilt and pommel; the scabbard velvet, matching his breeches, and the ferrule a wondrous example of the goldsmith's art. So too the dagger. Their caps were of black velvet, trimmed with jewels and rings and buttons of gold, with a white plume set in jauntily and parted by many rows of spangles from which hung splendent emeralds and various other stones.

Such was the sympathy between the gallants and their ladies that they matched one another's costumes every day. And in order to be sure of it, certain gentlemen were appointed to report every morning to the youths what garments their ladies planned to wear on that occasion. All here was done for the pleasure of the fair.

Handsome though the clothes were and rich the accoutrements, lads or girls wasted no time in dressing. The wardrobe masters had everything ready before their gentlemen arose and the maids were so nimble that in a trice their mistresses were apparelled from head to toe.

To facilitate matters, over a distance of half-a-league, a row of light, well-appointed cottages housed the goldsmiths, lapidaries, embroiderers, tailors, gold drawers, velvet weavers, tapestry makers and upholsterers. Here each worked at his trade, and all for the jolly friars and comely nuns of the new abbey. They received materials and stuffs from My Lord Nausiclete, famous for his ships, as the name indicates. Each year brought them seven vessels from the Pearl and Cannibal Islands or Antilles, laden with ingots of gold, raw silk, pearls and precious stones.

If pearls through age tended to lose their lustre, the jewellers, following the method of Avicenna, fed them to the roosters, and they regained their native sparkle.

LVII

HOW THOSE OF THÉLÈME WERE GOVERNED IN THEIR MANNER OF LIVING

THEIR whole life was ordered not by law, statute or rule, but according to their free will and pleasure. They arose when they pleased. They ate, drank, worked and slept when the spirit moved them. No one awoke them, forced food or drink upon them or *made* them do anything else. Gargantua's plan called for perfect liberty. The only rule of the house was:

DO AS THOU WILT

because men that are free, of gentle birth, well-bred and at home in civilized company possess a natural instinct that inclines them to virtue and saves them from vice. This instinct they name their honor. Sometimes they may be depressed or enslaved by subjection or constraint; for we all long for forbidden fruit and covet what is denied us. But they usually apply the fine forces that tend to virtue in such a way as to shake off the yoke of servitude.

The Thélèmites, thanks to their liberty, knew the virtues of emulation. All wished to do what they saw pleased one of their number. Let some lad or maid say "Let us drink" and all of them drank, "Let us play" and all of them played, "Let us frolic in the fields" and all of them frolicked. When falconry or hawking were in order, the ladies sat high upon their saddles on fine nags, a sparhawk, lanner or merlin on one daintily gloved wrist, while the men bore other kinds of hawks.

They were so well-bred that none, man or woman, but could read, write, sing, play several instruments, speak five or six languages and readily compose verse and prose in any of them. Never had earth known knights so proud, so gallant, so adroit on horseback and on foot, so athletic, so lively, so well-trained in arms as these. Never were ladies seen so dainty, so comely, so winsome, so deft at handwork and needlework, so skilful in feminine arts, so frank and so free as these.

Thus when the time came for a man to leave the abbey (either at his parents' request or for some other reason) he took with him one of the ladies—the particular one who had chosen him for her knight— and they were married. And though they had lived in devotion and friendship at Thélème, their marriage relations proved even more tender and agreeable. Indeed to the end of their lives they loved one another as they had on the day of their wedding. . . .

I must not forget to give you a riddle engraved on a copper plate and discovered in the foundations of the abbey. It ran as follows.

LVIII

A PROPHETICAL RIDDLE DISCOVERED IN THE FOUNDATIONS OF THE ABBEY OF THÉLÈME

POOR *humans here below who look for happiness,*
Lift up your hearts in cheer, give heed to my address.
Suppose it is allowed to champion the conviction
That, through the bodies lodged in Heaven's jurisdiction,
The mortal mind may soar above the common mass
To cite events before they have been brought to pass—
Suppose through the support of some divine decree
We can possess such knowledge of what is to be
That we may judge with perfect equilibrium
The destiny and course of years that are to come—
Then I asseverate to all who care to hear
That not subsequent to the winter of this year,
(And possibly before) there shall appear a race
Much different from ours, here in this very place.
It shall consist of men who, bored with indolence,
And tired of lethargy, will boldly venture hence,

Suborning folk of every calibre and station
To sow dissension and to foster altercation—
Whoever entertains or credits their advice
(Whatever the result and at whatever price)
Shall find himself embroiled in bitter public rout.
Friend shall contend with friend, close kinsmen shall fall out,
Arrogant sons shall rise up overnight, abroach
To join their fathers' foes, fearless of all reproach
Exalted lords and lieges of the loftiest order
Shall find their vassals storming them at every border,
The principles of honor and respect thus banished,
All sense of fitness, all distinction will have vanished.
"Each in due turn must scale the heights," they will maintain,
"But each in turn must likewise plumb the depths again."
On this point there shall be such wrangling to and fro,
Such fierce commotion and such an imbroglio
That the supreme recorder of our woes and wonders,
History's Muse herself, shall fail to match its thunders.
Spurred on by youthful zest, hosts of brave men shall lay
Too great faith in their fervor, know one fleeting day,
Then perish in their prime: for once he has begun,
No mortal shall agree to leave this work undone.
They shall fill earth with din of marching men, and heaven
With a horrendous tumult fit to wake the seven
Sleepers . . . they shall make tumult till both just and base
Without distinction merge in chaos and disgrace.
Ay, one and all shall bow to doctrines and to rules
Set by a herd of ignoramuses and fools,
The dullest lout of whom shall be Lord Justice. . . . 'Sblood!
We face a perilous and deleterious flood!
A deluge, truly, and I use the word with reason,
Since these calamities shall still remain in season
Till earth entire be drowned, from coast to distant coast,
By a vast, liquid wave. Even the hindermost
And meekest shall be caught fighting and shall be drowned.
And rightly so because mankind shall not have found
In his pugnacious heart indulgence for the least
Mercy towards his friend, the inoffensive beast.

How many wretched animals seized by the scut
Have been deprived by man of sinew, bowel and gut
Not for due sacrifice to the high gods but merely
For the base human needs man cherishes too dearly.
I leave you to imagine how the universe
Will fare as things go steadily from bad to worse
And what repose our globe terrestrial shall taste!
The happiest shall be those who refuse to waste
Or to misuse its benefits; they shall possess
The better part of it and with extreme finesse
They shall in divers ways strive ardently to master
And prison it in such a way that all disaster
Shall fall upon the man who brought it on. And worst
Amid the tragic fate with which all earth is cursed,
The shining sun ere it complete its daily round
And settle in the west, shall cast a more profound
Glooom than eclipses, even, or natural nights produce—
This globe shall lose its freedom, it shall lose the use
And favor of the light the lofty heavens released:
Ay, earth shall be a wilderness, to say the least.
Yet long before this final ruin and desolation
Will come a fearful quake, in force and in duration
More vehement than when Jove rolled Mount Ætna on
The head of sad Typhœus, Titan's fearless son,
With shocks more sudden than those which shook Inarimé
(The island which we know as Ischia to-day)
When poor Typhœus, struggling, writhed so violently
That he dislodged high hills and flung them in the sea. . . .
Thus in a few short hours, this globe shall be reduced
To ruin; it shall have changed so oft that they who used
To hold it shall surrender it to other men.
The time will be propitious and welcome then
To end this too long and too strenuous exercise,
For the great waters which you heard of shall arise
And make each man look promptly for the best retreat.
Yet, ere they part, they shall experience the heat
Of a huge flame that rises steadily to burn
The waters up and terminate the whole concern!

These accidents achieved, it now remains to tell
That the elect shall be refreshed and very well
Rewarded with earth's goods and Heaven's manna which
Will make them satisfied and prosperous and rich.
At last, the others shall be stripped, and with good reason,
So that when the great work shall finish, in due season,
Each meets his destined fate: for so the pact was cast,
And worthiest of praise who battles to the last.

When this inscription had been read through, Gargantua heaved a cavernous sigh and, addressing the bystanders:

"It is not to-day alone that persecution hounds those who believe in the Gospel. Happy indeed the man who will not be scandalized! Happy the man who, refusing to be hindered or misled by carnal instincts, aims constantly at that joy God foretold through His only begotton Son!"

"What do you think this riddle means?" the monk asked.

"What else can it refer to but the maintenance and progress of the divine truth?" Gargantua answered.

"By St. Goderan," the monk cried, "that is not my explanation. The style is that of Merlin the prophet. Make the gravest allegories and interpretations you wish, muse upon it, you and every one else, as long as you like. For *my* part I see nothing but the obscurely worded description of a game of tennis.

"The suborners of men are the makers of matches who are usually friends. . . . After the two services, the man in the upper end of the court goes out and the other comes in. . . . They believe the first who says the ball was over or under the line. . . . The waters are simply the players' sweat. . . . The strings of the rackets are made of the guts of sheep or goats. . . . The globe is the tennis ball. . . . After the game, the players refresh themselves before a clear fire and change their shirts. . . . Then they banquet amid great cheer, the winners more merrily than the losers.

"And so, more power to them!"

The Second Book

PANTAGRUEL

KING OF THE DIPSODES
RESTORED TO HIS TRUE NATURE TOGETHER WITH
HIS DEEDS AND HORRENDOUS FEATS

Set Down by the Late
MONSIEUR ALCOFRIBAS
Abstractor of Quintessence

DIZAIN

Inscribed by Master Hugues Salel
to the author of this book.

If writers who both teach and entertain
Are cherished by humanity, then you,
Being wise and gay, must certainly obtain
The lofty mead of praise that is your due.
Could it be otherwise, when you pursue
Progress behind your quips and repartees,
Laughing, like a Democritus, at ease,
To fend the good and to impugn the base?
Give us more books, then: your reward for these,
If not on earth, lies in a higher place.

LONG LIVE ALL GOOD PANTAGRUELISTS!

THE AUTHOR'S PROLOGUE

O MOST illustrious and most valorous champions, gentlemen and all others who delight in honest entertainment and wit, I address this book to you. You have read and digested the *Mighty and Inestimable Chronicles of the Huge Giant Gargantua*. Like true believers, you have taken them upon faith as you do the texts of the Holy Gospel. Indeed, having run out of gallant speeches, you have often spent hours at a time relating lengthy stories culled from these *Chronicles* to a rapt audience of noble dames and matrons of high degree. On this count, then, you deserve vast praise and sempiternal memory.

I intend each and every reader to lay aside his business, to abandon his trade, to relinquish his profession, and to concentrate wholly upon my work. Rapt and absorbed, all might then learn these tales by heart, so that if ever the art of printing perished and books failed, these tales might be handed down, like mystic religious lore, through our children to posterity! Is there not greater profit in them than a rabble of critics would have you believe? And what critics! Scabby-faced windbags, who understand these droll anecdotes even less than Raclet, the silver-tongued Professor of Law at Dôle, understands the *Institutes* of Justinian.

I have known a number of proud and powerful lords who delighted in hunting huge beasts, or in flying hawks after wild ducks. Suppose, in the course of their sport, they failed to track down the deer when the huntsmen headed him off. Or suppose the falcon refused to soar in pursuit when the prey whirred away amid a tumult of wings. These lords were quite naturally incensed. But do you know what comfort they found in their disappointment? Do you know how they cheated their boredom? By relating the priceless exploits of the said Gargantua.

Others upon this planet (here is no cock-and-bull story!), being chronic sufferers from toothache, vainly spent all their wordly fortune upon physicians. In the end, these found no more expedient remedy than to lay the *Chronicles* between two pieces of warm linen, apply them to the painful spot and, adding a little quackshit powder, use them as a poultice.

What shall I say of those wretched devils plagued by pox and gout? How often they have appeared before us saturated with quicksilver ointment, salves and grease. Their faces shone like a larder keyhole . . . their teeth danced in their heads like the keyboard of an organ or spinet under the fingers of a maestro . . . they foamed at the gullet like a boar at bay in the toils of a pack of bloodhounds. . . . What did they do in this crisis? Their sole consolation was to have somebody read them a few pages of this book.

Some, experiencing no manifest relief at this reading, delivered themselves up to fivescore giant casks of devils, just as women in travail do when the *Life of St. Margaret* is read to them.

Is this nothing? Then find me a book in any language, in any branch of art or science, that possesses such virtues, properties and prerogatives. Find it, I say, and I will buy you a pint of tripes! No, gentlemen, no, none such exists. My book is peerless, incomparable, nonpareil, and—I maintain it in the teeth of hellfire—unique! If any one contradicts me, let him be herewith denounced as a false prophet, a champion of predestination, a poisoner and seducer of the people.

To be sure, you can find certain occult properties in some works of high timber such as *Fessepinte* or *Whip Pot, Orlando Furioso, Robert the Devil, Fierabras the Saracen Giant, William the Fearless, Huon of Bordeaux, Mandeville the Traveller* and *Matabrune*. But they are not to be mentioned in the same breath with the work we speak of. Has not the whole world been forced by infallible experience to recognize the tremendous advantages and benefits to be derived from the *Gargantuan Chronicles?* Within two months the printers sold more copies of this work than they will sell Bibles for nine years to come.

Desiring, therefore, to entertain you further, I subscribe myself your humble servant, and herewith offer you another volume of identical stamp. Identical? It is, if anything, a little more worthy of faith and respect than its predecessor. Do you believe, unless you wilfully court error, that I speak of my book as the Jews speak of the Mosaic Law? I was born under a different planet: it has never occurred to me to lie or to make false representation. I speak like

St. John in the Apocalypse: "*Quod vidimus testamur*, we relate what we have seen." Or rather I quote his words like some lusty Thurifer (should I say Turdifer?) of the Martyr Lovers, or some Terrifying Torrefier of the affections. Ay, *quod vidimus, testamur*: I speak to you of the horrendous and frightful feats and prowesses of Pantagruel, whose flunkey I have been from infancy until now, when I come, by his leave, to visit my native cow-country, and to ascertain if any of my relatives are alive.

However, before I conclude this prologue, I hereby deliver myself up body and soul, belly and bowels, to a hundred thousand basketfuls of raving devils, if I have lied so much as once throughout this work. By the same token, may St. Anthony sear you with his erysipelatous fire . . . may Mahomet's disease whirl you in its epileptic jitters . . . may the festers, ulcers and chancres of every purulent pox infect, scathe, mangle and rend you, entering your bumgut as tenuously as mercurialized cow's hair . . . and may you vanish into an abyss of brimstone and fire, like Sodom and Gomorrah, if you do not believe implicitly what I am about to relate in the present *Chronicles.* . . .

DIZAIN

Newly Composed in Praise of the Author's Wit.

Couched in the dizain form or virelay,
A century of songs, a chiliad,
Capped with the brave rhymes of Marot, and clad
In the proud verbal dress of St. Gelais,
Produced most gallantly without delay
In the sweet presence of the Oread,
Dryad and Sylphid hosts—to all these add
Bales of ballades by subtle Pont-Alais,
These still could not suffice to hymn the glad,
The sapient and the gentle Rabelais.

I

OF THE ORIGIN AND ANTIQUITY OF THE GREAT PANTAGRUEL

It will not be amiss, since we have the leisure, to acquaint you with the primeval origin of our good Pantagruel. I know that all good historiographers have handled their chronicles thus, not only Arabs, Barbarians and Latins, but also Greeks and Gentiles (great drinkers these!) and finally writers of Holy Scripture like St. Luke and St. Matthew. You must therefore remember that I speak of the beginning of the world, of long ages since, of more than forty times forty nights ago, to reckon as the Druids did.

A little while after Cain slew his brother Abel, the earth, imbued with the blood of the just, was one year extremely fertile in all fruits. Medlars were particularly plentiful and large, just three to the bushel. So that year was recorded in the memory of men as the year of the great medlars.

That year, too, the Greek kalends first figured in the almanacs, March coincided with Lent, it was mid-August in May. The week famed in the *Annals*, the week of the three Thursdays, fell in October—or September, to exclude all possibility of error, since I am bound to remain scrupulously accurate. Three Thursdays it had, because of the irregular bissextile. The sun swerved a little towards the left, like a debtor ducking the bailiffs. The moon shifted about five fathoms off her course. The firmament called Aplanes (the heaven of fixed stars surrounding the seven heavens of planets) showed distinct signs of trepidation. As a result, the middle Pleïad abandoned her fellows and declined toward the equinox. The star called Spica, in the constellation of the Virgin, moved over to the neighboring constellation of the Balance or Libra. Dreadful events these, matters too hard for astrologians to set their teeth in, even if the latter could have reached so high.

You may be certain that every one ate most heartily of these medlars, which were beautiful to see and delicious to taste.

Now you recall Noah, that holy man to whom we are so eternally grateful for planting the vine whence we obtain that nectarian, delicious, precious, heavenly, joyful and deific liquor known as bibbage. Noah drank of it and he was mocked, for he was unaware of its great powers and virtues. Even so, now in the year of the medlars, men and women enjoyed eating that fat juicy fruit. But many and divers accidents befell them. Alas! one and all suffered a most terrible swelling in their bodies, though not each in the same place.

Some swelled in the belly, their paunches sticking out in front of them like great tuns. Of these it is written *Ventrem omnipotentem*: honest ventripotent men, these, and merry blades. St. Paunchard, St. Fatgulch and Mardigras are of their company.

Others swelled at the shoulders, growing so hunchbacked that they were called Montifers or Hummock-bearers. You still see some of these of either sex in various stations of life; Æsop, whose noble words and deeds you have in writings, was of that ilk.

The expansion of others occurred lengthwise in that member we call the husbandman of nature. This appendage of joy grew amazingly long, stout, fat, muscular and crested in the old fashion; its crest, in point of fact, rose on the least provocation. It was crested, too, in the new fashion; its bearer was prominent and certainly had a handle to his name. Men used their tools as girdles, winding them five or six times around their waists. If you could have seen these fellows with their members full cocked or spooming along with a fair wind behind them, you would have sworn they were knights with their lances settled on their rests, about to run at the ring, or tilt at quintain. Of these, the race is utterly spent and lost, as the women tell you when they continually lament:

There aren't any more great gyratory diddly-whackers,
Elongated, diathermal, bumgut-tickling kidney-crackers, etc. etc.

You know the rest of the song.

Others incrassated so enormously in the ballocks that the organic trio filled a large hogshead. From these come the nuts of Lorraine which never fit snug into a codpiece but draggle down to the bottom of the breeches.

Others grew in the legs: they looked like cranes or flamingos or people walking on stilts. Others grew in the feet, and snotty school-boys called them Spondees because there were two long feet.

In others, the nose stretched so far that it looked like the beak of an alembic, all bediapered and bespangled with pimples, pullulant and bepurpled with nobs, enamelled, buttoned and embroidered with gules and crimson. Of such are Canon Panzoult or Potgut, and Piedeboys or Woodenfoot, the physician of Angers. Few of this race cared for broths and brews of herb or plant; all were devotees of the septembral juice. Publius Ovidius Naso and the poet Ovid were two sprung from that race, as were all those of whom it is written: *the Noes have it*!

Others put forth greater ears to such lengths that the right would have supplied material for a doublet, a pair of breeches and a jacket, while the left availed to bury its owner as in a Spanish cloak. This race, they say, still exists in Bourbonnais; such ears are known as Bourbons.

Others, finally, grew in length of body. Of these came the giants; of them Pantagruel.

And the first was Chalbroth, who begat Sarabroth, who begat Faribroth, who begat Hurtali, a brave eater of pottage who reigned in the time of the flood. He sat on the roof of the Ark and Noah passed food to him through a trapdoor.

Hurtali begat Nembroth, who begat Atlas, whose shoulders kept the skies from falling. And Atlas begat Goliath, who begat Eryx, inventor of the game of Tippling, who begat Titus. And Titus begat Badeloury, who killed seven cows that he might eat of their livers; and Badeloury begat Eryon, who begat Polyphemus, who begat Cacus, who begat Etion, the first man ever afflicted with the pox, and that for failing to drink fresh in summer or closing his mouth when he slept, as Bartachin the Italian commentator on the *Pandect* testifies.

Cacus begat Enceladus, who begat Ceus, who begat Typhœus, who begat Aloeus, who begat Othus, who begat Aegeon. Aegeon begat Briareus, who had a hundred hands; who begat Porphyrio, who begat Adamastor, who begat Anteus, who begat Agatho, who begat Porus, against whom Alexander the Great waged war.

And Porus begat Aranthas, who begat Gabbara. Gabbara, the tallest man under the Emperor Claudius, was nine feet nine; he invented the drinking of toasts and begat Goliath of Secundilla, who lived in the reign of Augustus and was ten feet three. He in turn begat Offot, terribly well-nosed for drinking at the barrelhead; who begat Artachaeus, who begat Oromedon, who begat Gemmagog, the inventor of Poland shoes, which are open on the foot and tied over the instep with a latchet.

From him sprang Sisyphus, who begat the Titans, of whom Hercules was born, who begat Enay, the most skilful man that ever was known at extracting fleshworms from under his fingernails.

And Enay begat Fierabras, vanquished by Oliver, a peer of France and Roland's comrade in arms. Fierabras begat Morgan, the first in the world to wear spectacles when he diced and the hero celebrated by Pulci in *Il Morgante Maggiore*; Morgan begat Fracassus, celebrated by Merlin Coccaius, the monk Teofilo Folengo, learned author of *Opus Macaronicum*. Of Fracassus was born Ferragus; who begat Hapmouche or Swallowfly, the first to dry tongues in the chimney, for hitherto people had salted them, as they now salt hams.

And Hapmouche begat Bolivorax, who begat Longis, who begat Gayoffo, whose ballocks were poplar and his rod service wood; he begat Mâchefain or Crunchneat, who begat Brûlefer or Ironburner, who begat Engoulevent the Windsucker, who begat Galehault, the inventor of flagons.

The last begat Mirelangaut, who begat Gallaffre, who begat Falourdin, who begat Roboast, who begat Sortibrant of Coïmbra in Portugal, who begat Brûlant, the Fire Eater of Mommiré; who begat Bruyer that was overcome by Ogier the Dane, a peer of France. Bruyer begat Maubrun of Aigremalée, a Saracen, who begat Foutanon or Donkeyphucker, who begat Haquelebac or Brangleferry, who begat Graincock or Vitdegrain, who begat Grangousier, who begat Gargantua, who begat the noble Pantagruel, my master.

I know that as you read this passage, you will retain a learned doubt. Quite rightly, too. How can this account possibly be true, you will argue, when the entire universe perished at the flood save

Noah and seven others in the ark? (Hurtali, mentioned above, is not cited among the latter.)

Your point is, of course, reasonable and obvious; but my answer will satisfy you, or I am an idiot. Since I was not alive at the time, I can tell you nothing on my own authority; I shall therefore cite the Massorets, a learned group of commentators. Good ballocking lads, these, and fine Hebrew bagpipers, who assert that Hurtali was certainly never inside Noah's ark. How indeed could he have got in? He was much too big! Well, he straddled it, one leg to the right, one to the left, like a child riding a hobby-horse, or like the soldier they call the great bull of Berne. (He, it was, sounded the attack on the bull's horn; in the battle of Marignano he sought to spike the enemy's guns and perished, sprawled over a great mortar. A pretty mount, undoubtedly, an easy, pleasant ambler!)

Hurtali, perched in this posture, was responsible for the salvation of the Ark—after God, that is! For with his legs, he gave it the necessary balance, and with his feet, he turned it whichever way he wished, like a ship's rudder. Those within sent him up victuals aplenty through a trapdoor; they were grateful for the service he did them. And sometimes they conversed as the philosopher Icaromenippus did with Jupiter, when, according to Lucian, he merely gazed at the trapdoors through which the prayers of men reached the ear of the Almighty.

Have you understood all this perfectly clearly? Then drink a good deep draught without water. Now if you don't believe me—

"*No, truly I do not,*" *quoth she,* to cite a popular song—
Then all the worse for you.

II

OF THE NATIVITY OF THE MOST REDOUBTABLE PANTAGRUEL

At the age of four hundred fourscore and forty-four years, Gargantua begat his son Pantagruel upon his wife named Badebec, daughter to the king of the dimly-seen Amaurotes in Utopia. She died in the throes of childbirth. Alas! Pantagruel was so extraordinarily large and heavy that he could not possibly come to light without suffocating his mother.

If you would fully understand how he came to be christened Pantagruel, you must remember that a terrible drought raged that year throughout the land of Africa. For thirty-six months, three weeks, four days, thirteen hours and even longer, there was no drop of rain. And the sun blazed so fiercely that the whole earth was parched.

Even in the days of Elijah, the soil was no drier, for now no tree on earth bore leaf or flower. The grass had no verdure; rivers and springs ran dry; the luckless fishes, abandoned by their element, crawled on solid earth, crying and screaming most horribly. Birds fell from the air for want of moisture; wolves, foxes, harts, wild boars, fallow deer, hares, rabbits, weasels, martens, badgers and other beasts were found dead in the fields, their mouths agape.

As for the men, their state was very piteous. You should have seen them with their tongues dangling like a hound's after a run of six hours. Not a few threw themselves into the wells. Others lay under a cow's belly to enjoy the shade—these it is whom Homer calls *Alibantes*, the desiccated. The whole country was at a standstill. The strenuous efforts of mortals against the vehemence of this drought was a horrible spectacle. It was hard enough, God knows, to save the holy water in the churches from being wasted; but My Lords the Cardinals and our Holy Father laid down such strict rules that no man dared take more than a lick of it. In the churches, scores of parched, unhappy wretches followed the priest who distributed it, their jaws yawning for one tiny driblet. Like the rich man in *Luke*, who cried for Lazarus to dip his fingers in water, they were tormented by a flame, and would not suffer the slightest drop to be wasted. Ah! thrice happy that year the man who had a cool, well-plenished wine cellar underground!

In discussing the question: "Why is sea water salty?" the philosopher Aristotle, after Empedocles, supplies the following reason. When Phœbus gave the reins of his luminous chariot to Phaëton, his son, the latter, unskilled in the art of driving, was incapable of following the ecliptic lines between the two tropics of the sun's sphere. Accordingly, he strayed from the appointed path and came so close to earth that he dried up all the countries under his course. He also burnished that great portion of heaven which philosophers call *Via Lactea* or the Milky Way, and good drinkers St. James' Way, since it is the starry line that guides pilgrims to Santiago de Compostella. (On the other hand, poets declare that it is here Juno's milk dropped while she was suckling Hercules.)

Earth at that time was so excessively heated that it broke into an enormous sweat which ran over the sea, making the latter salty, since all sweat is salt. If you do not admit this last statement, then taste of your own sweat. Or savor the perspiration of your pox-stricken friends when they are put in sweatboxes for treatment. It is all one to me.

Practically the same thing happened the year I am speaking of. On a certain Friday, all the people were intent upon their devotions. A noble procession was in progress with plenty of litanies and fine preachings. Supplications arose toward Almighty God beseeching Him to cast His eye of mercy upon them in their affliction. Suddenly they clearly saw some great drops of water stand out upon the ground, exactly as from a person sweating copiously.

The wretched populace began to rejoice as though here were a great blessing. Some declared that, since the air lacked all moisture, earth was supplying the deficiency. Other scientists asseverated that it was a shower of the Antipodes, as described by Seneca in *Quaestiones Naturales*, Book IV, where he treats of the Nile's source, attributing its floods to distant rains washed underground into the river. But they were thoroughly deceived. For, the procession done, when each sought to gather up this dew and drink it up by the bowlful, they found it was only pickle, far saltier than the saltiest water of the sea.

Another great mishap befell Gargantua that week. A dungchafing lout, bearing two great bags of salt and a hambone in his game-pouch, walked into poor Gargantua's mouth as the giant lay snoring. The clod spilled a quantity of salt in Gargantua's throat. Gargantua, crazy with a thirst he could not slake, angrily snapped his mouth shut. He gnashed his teeth fiercely; they ground like mill-stones. Later the rascal told me he was so terrified you could have stopped up his nose with a bale of hay. He fell flat on his face like a dead man, dropping the two saltbags that had tormented Gargantua. They were at once swallowed up and entombed.

My rogue vowed vengeance. Thrusting his hand in his game-pouch, he drew out a great hambone, highly salted, still covered with hair, and twenty-eight inches long. Ragefully he rammed it down Gargantua's throat. The giant, drier than ever, felt the pig's hair tickling his belly and, willy-nilly, spewed up all he had. Eighteen tumbrils could not have drawn away the rich nauseous yield. My dungchafer, hidden in the cavity of one of his teeth, was forced to take French leave in such pitiful condition that all who saw him were horrified. Gargantua, looking down, noticed this jackpudding whirling about in a great puddle.

"Here is some worm that sought to sting me in the belly," he mused, happy to have expelled him from his body.

Because he was born that very day, his father called him Panta-gruel or All-Athirst, a name derived from the Greek *panta* meaning all, and the Hagarene or Saracen *gruel* meaning athirst. Gargantua inferred thereby that at his son's birth the entire universe was wholly parched. Prophetically, too, he realized that some day Pantagruel would become Supreme Lord of the Thirsty, a fact indicated even more surely by a further portent.

For while his mother Badebec was bringing him forth and the midwives stood by ready to receive him, there first issued from her belly seventy-eight salt-vendors, each leading a salt-laden mule by the halter. They were followed by nine dromedaries, bearing hams and smoked oxtongues; seven camels bearing chitterlings; twenty-five cartloads of leeks, garlic, onions and chives. This terrified some midwives, but others said:

"Here is good provision! As it is, we drink but lazily, instead of vigorously. This must be a good omen, since these victuals are spurs to bibbing wine!"

As they were tattling away, out pops Pantagruel, hairy as a bear! At which, prophetically, one of them exclaimed:

"God help us, he is born hair and all, straight from the arse of Satan in flight. He will do terrible wonders. If he lives, he will grow to a lusty age!"

Of Pantagruel's race are those who drink so heavily in the evening that they must rise at night to drink again, quenching the coals of fire and blistering thirst in their throats. This form of thirst is called Pantagruel, in memory of the giant.

III

OF GARGANTUA'S GRIEF AT THE DEMISE OF HIS WIFE BADEBEC

At Pantagruel's birth, none was more amazed and perplexed than his father Gargantua. On one hand, he saw his wife Badebec dead, on the other, his son Pantagruel, large as life and much noisier. He was at a complete loss what to say or do. A terrible doubt racked his brain: should he weep over the death of his wife or rejoice over the birth of his son? On either hand, sophistical arguments arose to choke him. He could frame them capitally *in modo et figura*, according to the modes and figures of the syllogism in formal logic. But he could not resolve them. So there he was, fretting like a mouse caught in a trap, or a kite snared in a gin.

"Shall I weep?" he cried. "Ay! . . . And why? Because my dear wife is dead! She was the most *this* and the most *that* who ever lived! I shall never see her again, I shall never know her like, I have suffered an irreparable loss! O God! what have I done to Thee to be thus punished? Why didst Thou not snatch me away before her, when to live without her is but to languish! Ah, Badebec, my darling, my love, my sweetheart, my dainty follicle (yet in area it was a good five and a half acres!), my tender mistress, my codpiece darling, my favorite pump, my dearest slipper, never shall I see you again! Alas, poor Pantagruel, you have lost your blessed mother, your indulgent nurse, your beloved lady! Ha, false Death, how outrageously evil to rob me of one that should by rights have been immortal. . . ."

As he spoke, he cried like a cow. But suddenly, struck by the thought of Pantagruel, he began to laugh like a calf.

"Ha, my little son!" he said, "my ballocky darling, my adorable fartlet, how lusty you are! How grateful I am to God for granting me a son so handsome, so sprightly, so gay and so spirited! Ho, ho, ho, ho, how happy I am! Let us drink, ho! and put away our melancholy! Bring out the best wine, rinse the glasses, lay the table, drive out those dogs, poke up this fire, light the candles, close that door there, cut the bread in sippets for our pottage, send away these beggar folk but give them anything they ask for! You, there, hold my gown! I shall strip to my doublet to entertain the gossips better!"

As he said this, he heard the priests chanting litanies and mementos as they bore his wife off to burial. All his glee suddenly evaporated; he was transported to the opposite extreme of emotion.

"Lord God," said Gargantua, "must I cry myself blind? This is the torment of hell! I am no longer young, I grow old, the weather is dangerous: I might easily fall ill of a fever. Already I am beside myself. Upon my faith as a gentleman, it were better I weep less and drink more. My wife is dead; well then, by God—*da jurandi veniam*, excuse my language—my tears will not resurrect her. It is well with her . . . she is in Paradise at least, if no higher . . . she is praying to God for us . . . she is happy, beyond the reach of our miseries and calamities. . . . The same fate stares us all in the face. God help the survivor, I must think of finding me another wife.

"But here is what *you* must do—" He turned to the midwives. "Midwives, sages-femmes! (Where are they, good people, I cannot see them? Who ever saw a *femme* who was really *sage*!) Go, go to my wife's funeral whilst I stay here holding my son, for I feel somewhat out of sorts and dare not expose myself to sickness. Down a good drink first, too! You will be all the better for it, I assure you."

Doing as they were bid, they attended Badebec's funeral, while poor Gargantua remained at home, composing the following epitaph to be engraved upon her tombstone:

Here lies sweet Badebec, snatched in the middle
Of bearing child. What a metathesis!
Her face was like the carving on a fiddle,
Her body Spanish and her belly Swiss,
Pray God if she wrought anything amiss,
He pardon her and she be sanctified.
Here lies her body that expired, I wis,
The very year and day wherein she died.

I V

OF PANTAGRUEL'S CHILDHOOD

IN the ancient historiographers and poets, I find many cases of extraordinary childbirth. They would be too long to repeat, so if you are interested, I simply refer you to Chapter VII of Pliny's *Natural History*: *De Prodigiosis Partubus* or *Of Prodigious Births*.

Be that as it may, you have certainly never heard of any birth so wonderful as Pantagruel's. Indeed, his growth in stature and strength, during his brief sojourn in his mother's belly, almost defies belief.

Hercules, who slew two serpents in his crib, was small beer compared to Pantagruel, for the serpents were tiny and weak, whereas Pantagruel, while still in the cradle, accomplished feats of the most terrific kidney.

I shall not here dwell upon how at each of his meals he lapped up the milk of forty-six hundred cows . . . how, to make a skillet to boil his pap in, all the braziers of Saumur in Anjou, of Villedieu in Normandy, of Bramont in Lorraine, were set to work day and night . . . how, to serve him this pap, they used a colossal cup. . . . You may still see that cup in Bourges in front of the palace of the Duc de Berry: it is called the Giant's Bowl and filled with wine once a year for the poor. As an infant, Pantagruel had such long powerful teeth that he bit a great piece off the edge, as plainly appears to-day.

One morning when they brought in a cow to give him suck (history tells us he never had any other nurse) he worked one of his arms free from the swaddling bands that prisoned him. Seizing the cow below the hamstring, he chewed up two of her teats and half her belly, including liver and kidneys. He would have devoured her whole, had she not bellowed as if a pack of starving wolves had their fangs in her legs—at which horrible tumult, crowds of people rushed into the nursery and led her away. But they did not do a thorough job, for the babe still held on to the quarter he had seized and gulped down its meat as effortlessly as you would dispatch a sausage. When they sought to take the bone away, he swallowed it whole, as a cormorant bolts down a small fish. Though still unable to speak, he mumbled "Goo, goo, goo!" to convey his appreciation and eager acceptance of another.

After this scene, his attendants bound him with great cables like those manufactured at Tain on the Rhône for the transport of salt to Lyons and Vienne, or like those holding the pride of the French Navy, the *Grande Française*, in the port of Le Havre de Grâce in Normandy.

One day a huge bear Gargantua had raised, escaped from his cage and began licking Pantagruel's face. (His nurses had failed to wipe his chops thoroughly.) The babe snapped off his chains as easily as Samson broke the bonds of the Philistines and, if you please, picked up My Lord Bear, tore him to pieces like a chicken and swallowed him in one fine hot mouthful!

Gargantua grew alarmed; he feared the babe would come to grief. So he had four great iron chains forged and bound him to as many arched props fastened to his cradle. Of these chains, one is now at La Rochelle; they draw it up at night, between the great towers of Chaîne and St. Nicolas, to close the harbor. Another is at Lyons, stretched across the Saône from the Abbey of Ainay to the Porte St. Georges. A third is at Angers, where it controls navigation on the Maine. The fourth was carried off by the devils to bind Lucifer when he ran amuck because of a colic caused by eating a bailiff's soul fricassée for breakfast. On this score you may credit what Nicolas de Lyra, the Italian biblical scholar, has to say on the passage in the *Psalter* which begins: "*Et Og regem Basan*, And *Og*, King of Bashan. . . ." Here Og, though still tiny, was so hardy and tough that they had to secure him in his cradle with iron fetters.

For a while Pantagruel remained tranquil and at peace, unable to break his bonds since he could not even swing his arms.

But not for long. On a great holiday, his father was sumptuously entertaining all the princes of his court. The members of the household were naturally too busy serving the banquet to bother about poor Pantagruel, who was left behind *a reculorum*, like a poop! What do you suppose he did?

What he did, my friends? Listen!

With his arms, he strove to break the chains. In vain: they were too strong. So he stamped his feet so furiously that he knocked out the bottom end of his cradle, a great square seven-span beam. Having got his feet out, he edged down until his soles touched the ground. Then, with tremendous force, he rose to his feet and strode off, the cradle bound to his back. He looked for all the world like a tortoise crawling up a well or a five-hundred-ton galleon advancing on end.

Thus disguised, he burst into the banquet hall, terrifying the company. But, as his arms were bound, he could reach for no food. So, with great effort, he bent over to lap up a choice morsel with the flat of his tongue. His father realized that they had neglected to feed him, and, having consulted his guests, ordered the chains removed. The physicians intervened. If Pantagruel were kept in his cradle any longer, they averred, he would suffer all his life from gallstones.

The babe unchained, they made him sit down. He proceeded to eat his fill. Then with one blow of his fist, he struck savagely at his cradle, smashing it into more than five hundred thousand pieces. And he swore he would never lie in it again.

V

THE NOBLE PANTAGRUEL'S
ADOLESCENCE

PANTAGRUEL grew and developed visibly from day to day, which naturally delighted his father. While he was still a tiny mite, his father had a crossbow made for him to shoot at small birds. It is still preserved in the great tower at Bourges; they call it the crossbow of Chantelle, because it was made in the famous arsenal there.

Desiring the lad to study during his formative years, Gargantua sent him to Poitiers, where he profited greatly. It was here he noticed how heavy time hung on the students' hands, pitied them for it, and determined to remedy the situation. So one fine day he picked up a great stone off a ledge of rocks called Passelourdin and, though it was two thousand yards square and fourteen feet thick, easily set it on four pillars in the middle of a field. Thus, when the university students wanted something to do, they could spend their time climbing on top of it, banquet there abundantly upon flagons of wine, hams and pasties, and carve their names upon it with a knife.

To-day, this stone is known as La Pierre Levée, the Lifted Stone. In memory of Pantagruel's feat, no student can register at the University of Poitiers without first drinking in the mystic fountain of Croûtelle, going to Passelourdin and scaling the Lifted Stone.

Reading the noble *Chronicles* of his ancestors, Pantagruel discovered that Geoffroi de Lusignan, known as Geoffrey with the Great Tooth, his stepmother's daughter-in-law's uncle's son-in-law's aunt's eldest sister's cousin-in-law's grandfather, was buried at Maillezais, the abbey he had destroyed and later rebuilt. Accordingly, like a dutiful relative, Pantagruel took a day off to call on Ardillon, the noble abbot; then, passing through Sansay, Celles, Coulonges and Fontenay-le-Comte (where he saluted the learned Tiraqueau), he reached Maillezais and duly visited the sepulchre of Geoffrey with the Great Tooth.

It frightened him not a little to see his ancestor portrayed there as a furious warrior, his fierce broadsword half-drawn. When Pantagruel asked the reason for this savage depiction, the canons of the place merely quoted Horace: "*Pictoribus atque poetis, etc.*, poets and painters are entitled to depict whatever they like according to their own fancy." But Pantagruel was not satisfied with their answer.

"He is not presented thus without cause," he replied. "I suspect some wrong was done him at his death. Some wrong, I may add, which he looks to his kindred to avenge. I shall inquire further into the matter and do what is right."

Instead of returning to Poitiers, he decided to inspect the other universities of France. Proceeding to La Rochelle, he embarked for Bordeaux, where he found no great activity except for some stevedores playing chuckfarthing on the strand.

From Bordeaux he went to Toulouse, where he learned to dance very gracefully and to ply the two-handed sword, a tradition among the students of this university. But he did not tarry long when he saw that they burned their professors alive like red herrings.

"God forbid that I should die thus!" he cried. "For I am naturally dry enough already, without heating myself further."

Next, he journeyed to Montpellier, where he found some excellent Mirevaux wines and jovial company. He thought of studying medicine here but decided the profession was too troublesome and morbid. Besides, physicians smelled hellishly of enemas. He was, however, anxious to study law. But the faculty, in the way of jurists, consisted of three scrofulous mephitics and a bold coot. So he left the city.

Less than three hours later, he had crossed the famous Roman aqueduct called the Pont du Gard and reached the amphitheatre of Nîmes, a feat seemingly divine rather than human.

Thence he went to Avignon, where, within three days, he fell in love, for the local women are great thigh-squeezers, it being Papal territory. Seeing this, his tutor, Epistemon the Learned, took him to Valence in Dauphiné. Here he saw scant activity, but observed that the town bullies used to beat the scholars. This infuriated Pantagruel; accordingly, one fine Sunday morning, he took appropriate action. The populace was dancing on the square. A student sought to join in—an impertinence these lubbers would not countenance. Observing this, Pantagruel chased the whole crowd to the edge of the

Rhône and would have drowned them, had they not burrowed into the earth like moles and lain in hiding a good two miles under the river. The hole down which they escaped may still be seen there to-day.

Leaving Valence, in three hops and a jump, Pantagruel was in Angers, where he settled comfortably and would have remained but for the plague. So he went to Bourges, where he studied long and to great advantage under the Faculty of Law. He would sometimes remark that law books were like a fair robe of gold, priceless and dazzling, but edged with excrement.

"For," he added, "no books on earth are so rich, so beautiful, so decorative as the texts of the Roman *Pandects*. But their border—the marginal glosses by medieval commentators like Accursius—is lousy, foul and villainous as a hundred tubs of shit!"

From Bourges, Pantagruel migrated to Orléans, where he found many a swaggering scholar to celebrate his arrival. The students here were much given to tennis; Pantagruel learned fast, and in an incredibly short time became a champion. Sometimes they would take him to the islands, the waterfront district of Orléans, to play Poussavant, which some call Push-it-in, and others, Bowling. And, fearful lest he strain his eyes, Pantagruel took good care not to study too hard. In point of fact, he did nothing. Had not a professor of his often declared in public that ophthalmia was harmful to the eyes?

One day a fellow-student of his received the degree of Master of Laws. His learning would have fit in a nutshell, but he danced beautifully and played a fine game of tennis. Pantagruel wrote the following lampoon in honor of the Masters of Laws of the University of Orléans:

> *One tennis ball in pocket and*
> *One tennis racket in your hand.*
> *One solitary law to coddle*
> *In the desert of your noddle,*
> *One pair of heels to dance with. . . . Good!*
> *You qualify to wear the hood*
> *Of Legum Magister, and are*
> *Forthwith admitted to the Bar.*

VI

HOW PANTAGRUEL MET A LIMOUSIN WHO SPOKE SPURIOUS FRENCH

ONE evening after supper—I cannot say exactly when—Pantagruel was strolling with some friends near the north gate of Orléans, by the road to Paris. Here he met a neat young student walking down the road. After they had bowed to one another, Pantagruel asked:

"Well, friend, where are you coming from at this time of day?"

The scholar replied:

"From the alme, inclyte and celebrate academy which is vocitated Lucetia."

"What on earth does he mean?" Pantagruel asked one of his men.

"He means: 'From Paris!'"

"So you come from Paris, eh?" Pantagruel resumed. "And how do you gentlemen students spend your time in Paris?"

The scholar replied:

"We transfretate the Sequana at the dilucul and crepuscul; we deambulate by the compites and quadrives of the metropolis; we despume the Latin verbocination and, like verisimilary amorabonds, we captate the benevolence of the omnijugal, omniform and omnigeneous muliebrine sex. At certain diecules, we invisitate upon the lupanars and, amid a venerean ecstasis, we inculcate our virilia into the most antipodean recesses of the pudenda of these supremely amicable meretricules. Then we proceed to pabulate in the mercantile taberna of the *Fir Cone*, the *Castle*, the *Magdalen and the Mule*, upon rare vervicina spatula performinated with petrosil. If by misfortune, there be rarity or penury of numismatical in our marsupia, or if we be exhausted of ferrugine metal, to pay, we demit our codexes and we oppignerate our vestments while we prestolate the Tabellaries who are to come from our patriotic Lares and Penates."

"What the devil is this jargon?" cried Pantagruel. "By God, I think you must be some sort of heretic."

(There was no interpreter here to tell Pantagruel that what the fellow meant was this: "We cross the Seine at dawn and dusk; we walk through the thoroughfares and crossroads of the city; we rake up Latin to speak and, as true lusty fellows, we win the favors of women. Occasionally we go to brothels and, hot with love, push our cods into the depths of these friendly little harlots' cunnies. Then, in the taverns of the *Fir Cone*, the *Castle*, the *Magdalen and the Mule*, we eat shoulders of mutton garnished with parsley; should we have little money in our purses or be out of cash, we settle the bill by pledging our books and pawning our clothes while awaiting remittances from home.")

So then, Pantagruel having taxed the Limousin student with heresy:

"Nay, my Lord," he replied, "for libentissimally as soon as it illucesces a minutule fragment of the day, I demigrate to some one of those so well architected ecclesiastical abodes. There, irrorigating myself with sweet lustral water, I rattle off little slices of some missic precation of our sacrificula. Submurmurating my horary precules, I elave and absterge my anima of its nocturnal inquinations; I revere the Olympicoles; I latrially venerate the supernal astripotent; I dilige and redame my proxims; I observe the Decalogical precepts and, according to the facultatule of my vires, I do not discede from them one unguicule. However it is veriform that since Mammona does not supergurgitate anything in my loculas, I am somewhat rare and tardigrade in supererogating the eleemosynaries to these indigents who hostially queritate their stipend."

(Poor Pantagruel! He could not know the fellow meant: "For when day breaks I withdraw to a well-built church, and there, sprinkling myself with holy water, I mumble a few words of the mass. While saying my prayers, I wash and cleanse my soul of the pollution of the night; I worship the high gods; I adore the master of the spheres; I love and cherish my neighbors; I follow the Ten Commandments and, within the measure of my power, I do not deviate a nail's breadth from these teachings. It is certain that because the Goddess of Wealth puts nothing in my purse, I very rarely give alms to the beggars who seek money from door to door.")

So, hearing the Limousin's mad flow of words:

"Midden and dung!" Pantagruel roared. "What does this lunatic mean? I think he is forging some diabolic tongue and laying a spell of witchcraft upon us."

To which one of his followers replied:

"Doubtless, My Lord, this rascal is trying to imitate the language of the Parisians. But all he is doing is to flay the Latin tongue, under the impression that he is using the noble style of Pindar. He fancies himself no end of an orator in French because he disdains our usual mode of speech."

"Is that true?" Pantagruel asked the scholar.

"Ah, My Lord!" the scholar replied, "my genius is not natively adept to what this flagitious nebulon manifests, as he excoriates the cuticle of our vernacular Gallic. On the contrary, I applicate my scruples viceversally and with the auxiliary of both sails and oars— *veles et rames*—I effortize to locupletate it with Latinicome redundance."

(All of which simply meant: "My genius is not naturally apt to grasp what this worthless vagabond says as he accuses me of flaying the skin of our French vernacular. On the contrary, I devote all my attention and make every possible effort to endow it with a Latin richness.")

"By God," Pantagruel growled, "I'll teach you how to speak. But come here, first, and tell me where you hail from?"

"The primeval origin of my aves and ataves," said the scholar, "was indigenous to the Lemovican regions where requiesces the cadaver of the hagiotate St. Martial."

(Which being interpreted meant: "My ancestors were born in the Limousin where St. Martial is buried.")

"I understand you perfectly," Pantagruel roared. "It all boils itself down to the fact that you're a Limousin trying to play the Parisian. Come here, my lad, and I'll curry your hair for you."

Seizing him by the throat:

"You're a flayer of Latin, eh? By St. John, I'll make you flay the fox—or vomit, ay, since you don't understand French. Unless I flay you alive!"

The wretched Limousin at once changed his tune.

"Eh but lawd gen'leman! Ho, Sint Martiaw, ho, cum to me help! Ooh, ho, leave me but be, and do ye not tech me!"

To which Pantagruel answered:

"Now you are speaking naturally."

So he let him go, for the unhappy Limousin had completely be-fouled his breeches, which were cut like a codfish tail, with a slash and not full-bottomed. At which Pantagruel cried:

"By St. Alipentin, what a civet, what a stew! The devil take this turnip-fed bumpkin. Phew! he whiffs to high heaven!"

And Pantagruel fled. But the scholar was thoroughly impressed by Pantagruel's throat-squeezing influence. He declared ever after that Pantagruel held him by the gullet. And he repented throughout his life, until some years later he died the death of Roland—from thirst! Thus the law of divine vengeance vindicated the instructions of Favorinus, the philosopher, in Aulus Gellius' *Attic Nights* where we are warned to speak the common idiom and where Octavius Augustus urges us to steer clear of unusual words even as mariners avoid reefs at sea.

VII

HOW PANTAGRUEL CAME TO PARIS AND OF THE EXCELLENT BOOKS IN THE LIBRARY OF ST. VICTOR

AFTER Pantagruel had studied profitably at Orléans, he determined to visit the great University of Paris. But before leaving he was told that there was a huge bell buried at St. Aignan by Orléans. It had been there over two hundred and fourteen years, for it was so big that every device they had, failed to unearth it. And they neglected nothing: Vitruvius' *De Architectura*, Alberti the Florentine's *De Re Edificatoria*, Euclid, Theon of Smyrna, Archimedes, and Hero of Alexandria's *De Ingeniis* were all consulted and applied. But to no avail.

Accordingly, Pantagruel gladly granted the humble request of the citizenry that he replace the bell in the tower built for it. When they led him to the spot where it lay buried, he proceeded to lift it out of the ground with his little finger as easily as you would a hawk's bell. But before putting it in the belfry, he carried it through the streets and, shaking his hand, made music for the people. They were delighted, but unfortunately, a great disaster resulted.

As Pantagruel bore it ringing through the streets, all the good Orléans wine turned and soured. Yet the people failed to notice this until the following evening, when they were so dry from having drunk these turned wines that they spat white as Malta cotton.

"We've got the Pantagruel," they said: "our throats ache and are salted."

After this exploit Pantagruel proceeded to Paris with his retinue. At his entrance the whole city turned out to greet him, for the Parisians are notoriously idle and rebellious oaves by nature, by the key of B-flat or B-sharp or any other key you pitch. They stared at him in great amazement, and in terror, too, lest he carry away the Law Courts and place them elsewhere in some land *a remotis* or abroad, as his father had carried away the bells of Notre Dame to tie them to his mare's neck.

After Pantagruel had stayed there a little while, and with diligence and profit studied the seven liberal arts—Grammar, Logic, Rhetoric, Arithmetic, Geometry, Music and Astronomy—he declared it was a good town to live in, but not to die in. And why? Because the beggars of St. Innocent's graveyard use dead men's bones to toast their rumps at night; they pick the exhumed bones off the open attic to use for kindling. Another feature of Paris that appealed to Pantagruel was the magnificent library of the Abbey of St. Victor, where he discovered certain admirable books. The list follows:

Bigua Salutis, The Tumbril of Salvation . . . *Bragueta Juris*, The Codpiece of the Law . . . *Pantofla Decretorum*, The Slippers of the Decretals . . . *Malagranata Vitiorum*, The Pomegranate of Vice . . . *Ars Theologiae*, the Arse of Theology . . . The Preacher's Dinglescrew by Turlupin . . . The Lush Ballock of Heroes . . . The Henbane of Bishops . . . *Marmotretus: De Baboonis et Chimpanzibus, cum commento Dorbellis*, Concerning Baboons and Chimpanzees, by Monkeyshiner, with a commentary by Nicolas des Orbeaux, a Franciscan teacher of Poitiers . . . *Decretum universitatis Parisiensis super gorgi asitate muliercularum ad placitum*, Decree of the University of Paris on the Elegance of Women in the Matter of

Vestment . . . The Apparition of St. Gertrude to a Pregnant Nun at the Convent of Poissy . . . *Ortruinum: Ars honeste petandi in societate*, The Gentle Art of Farting in Company, by Hardouin de Grätz, a theologian of Cologne . . . The Mustard Pot of Penitence . . . The Buskins of Patience . . . *Formicarium artium*, Of the Antlike Arts . . . *De brodiorum usu et honestate chopinandi*, Of the Use of Cups and Honest Swigging, by Sylvester de Priero, a Jacobin friar . . . The Cuckold in Court . . . The Notaries' Frail . . . The Marriage Package . . . The Crucible of Contemplation . . . The Fiddle Faddle of the Law . . . The Goad of Wine . . . The Spur of Cheese . . . *Decrotatorium scholarium*, Of Scholarly Dungchafers . . . *Tartaretus: De modo cacandi*, A Treatise on Crapping by Pierre Tartaret, a Scotch professor at the Sorbonne.

The Windbags of Rome . . . *Bricot: De differentiis soupparum*, Of the Differences in Soups by Father Bricot, a priest of Notre Dame . . . The Dregs of Discipline, with Appendix, Tailpieces and Closebreeches . . . Humility, an Old Shoe . . . The Tripe Merchant of Pious Thought . . . The Cauldron of Magnanimity . . . The Tangle-ballocking of Confessors . . . The Knuckle Rapping of Curates . . . *Reverendi patris fratris Lubini provincialis Bavardiae, de croquendis Lardonibus libri tres*, On Guzzling Bacon, in three volumes, by the Reverend Father Brother Gutcrammer, a Bavarian citizen . . . *Pasquilli doctoris marmorei, de capreolis cum chardoneta comedendis tempori papali ab Ecclesia interdicto*, Of Eating Goatmeat with Thistles, in the Papal Time, forbidden by the Church . . . The Invention of the Holy Cross, a play for six characters, impersonated by six wily clerks . . . The Spectacles of Roming Pilgrims . . . *Majoris, De modo faciendi boudinos*, Concerning the Making of Blood Sausage by John Mayr, Professor of the Collège de Montaigu . . . The Prelates' Bagpipe . . . *Beda: De optimate triparum*, Of the Excellence of Tripe by Noël Béda, Principal of the Collège de Montaigu . . . The Complaint of the Lawyers on the Reformation of Gratuities . . . Attorneys and Furred Cats . . . Of Bacon and Peas, with Tables and Sauce Material . . . The Percentage on Indulgences . . . *Aristotelis: libri novem de modo dicendi horas canonicas*, Nine Books on how to tell the Canonical Hours, by Aristotle. . . .

Praeclarissimi juris utriusque doctoris Magistri Pilloti Requede-

nari: De bobelidanis glossae Accursianae baguenandis petitio enucidi-luculidissima. A most Sapisagacisavantesque Inquiry into the Fiddle Faddle of the Amphibobiguous Gloss of Accursius by Master Saltcone Pennycroaker, Most Illustrious Doctor of Laws . . . *Stratagemata Francharchieri de Baignolet*, The Dodges of the Militiaman of Bagnolet . . . *Franctopinus: De re militari, cum figuris Tevoti*, Of Military Science, by Clodbumpkinus, with Figures by Tivvot . . . *De use et utilitate escorchandi equos et equas, authore M. Nostro de Quebecu*, Of the Habit and Usefulness of Flaying Horses and Mares by our learned Master de Quebec . . . The Cheek of Country Stewards . . . *M. N. Rostocostojambedanesse: De mustarda post prandium servienda, libri quatuordecim apostilati per M. Vaurrillonis*, Concerning the Serving of Mustard after Meals, in Fourteen Books, by our Learned Master Rusticockpiddleshankcrapwallopper, with a Commentary by Vorilonge, a Franciscan critic of Scotus and Peter Lombard . . . The Ballock-Thrusting of Promoters . . . *Jabolenus: De cosmographia purgatori*, Of the Cosmography of Purgatory by Jiabolo . . . *Quaestio subtillissima, utrum Chimera in vacuo bombinans possit comedere secundas intentiones, et fuit debatuta per decem hebdomadas in concilio Constantiensi*, The Most Subtile Question as to whether the Chimera, Fartwhooshing in the Void, may Eat its Second Intentions, Debated for Ten Weeks at the Council of Constance . . . The Grinding of Advocates . . . *Barbouillamenta Scoti*, The Scribblerot of Duns Scotus. . . .

The Scragglescraping of Cardinals . . . *De Calcaribus removendis decades undecim per M. Albericum de Rosata*, Of the Removing of Spurs during Eleven Decades by our learned Master Albericus de Rosata, jurisconsult of Bergerac . . . *Ejusdem, de castrametandis crinibus, libri tres*, Of Splitting Hairs, in Three Books, by the Same Author . . . The Entrance of Antoine de Lève into the Territories of Brazil . . . *Marforii bacalarii cubantis Romae: De pelendis mascarendisque cardinalium mulis*, Of the Peeling and Chewing of the Mules of Cardinals . . . The Same Author's Apology against those who allege that the Pope's Mule eats at its own Hours . . . *Prognosticatio quae incipit "Sylvii Triquebille," balata per M. N. Songecrusyou*, The Prophesy which begins "O Sylvan Trickball" interpreted by our learned Master Songecreux Hollowthought, the Famous Mummer. . . .

Boudarini episcopi: De emulgentiarum profectibus eneades no-
vem, cum privilegio papali ad triennium et postea non, Bishop Sulk-
sausage Boudarini's Nine Ænead Books on the Benefits of Emulsions
. . . The Papshit of Virgins . . . The Bald Arse of Widows . . .
The Headgear of Monks . . . The Brummagem of Celestine Friars
. . . The Toll of Beggarliness . . . The Chattering Teeth of Louts
. . . The Shovels of Theologues . . . The Mouthpiece of Masters
of Arts . . . Occam's Shavepate Clerklings . . . *Magistri N.*
Fripesaulcetis: De grabellatonibus horrarum canonicarum lib. quad-
raginta, Of the Crapifications of Canonic Horrors in Forty Books by
our learned Master Lickstewpanus . . . *Cullebutatorium confra-*
triarium, incerto authore, Of the Arseyturvytumblers in the Brotherhoods, Author Unknown . . . The Rasher of Gluttons . . . The
Randiscrewishness of Spaniards, Supercockcuntified by Friar Inigo
. . . The Crackslattern of Verminous Beggars. . . .

Poiltronismus rerum italicarum authore magistro Bruslefer, The
Hairsnaggle of Italian Affairs, by Master Ironburn . . . *R. Lullius:*
de Batisfolagiis principum, Of the Skullduggeries of Princes, by R.
Lullius, an alchemist and philosopher . . . *Calibistratorium caf-*
fardiae, authore M. Jacobo Hocstraten haereticometra, The Cackle-
boozing of the Cockroach by Master Jacob Hochstraten, Prior of the
Dominicans of Cologne . . . *Chault-Couillons: De magistro nos-*
trandorum magistro nostratorumque beuvetis lib. octo gualantissimi,
On the Master of Antidoting and those Antidoted by Means of
Drinks, in Eight Joyous Books by Burns-Ballocks . . . The Farta-
dillos Scriveners, Copyists, Scribes of Bulls, Abbreviators, Reporters,
Registrars and Notaries, Compiled by Regis . . . A Perpetual Al-
manac for the Gouty and Venereals . . . *Manieres ramonandi four-*
nellos per M. Eccium, The Cleaning of Flues by Master Eccins or
John Eck . . . The Sabre of Merchants . . . The Pleasures of
Monastic Life . . . The Confusion of Hypocrites . . . The History of Hobgoblins . . . The Roguery of Militiamen . . . The
Fibs of Commissaries . . . The Hoards of Treasurers . . . *Badina-*
torium sorboniformium sophistarum, Of the Numbskullery of the
Sorbonne Pedagogues . . . *Antipericatametaanaparbeugedamphi-*
cribrationes merdicantium, Antipericatametaanaparcircumvolutio-
rectumgustpoops of the Coprofied. . . .

The Snail of Rhymesters . . . The Forward Thrust Windpiece of

Alchemists . . . The Gimmypleas of Alms Collectors, Rambucti-
pursified by Friar Moneypry . . . The Shackles of Religion . . .
The Racket of Swaggerers . . . The Prop of Old Age . . . The
Muzzle of Nobility . . . The Ape's Paternoster . . . The Crickets
and Tinklebells of Devotion . . . The Pot of the Seasonal Fasts
. . . The Mortar of Public Life . . . The Trouserflies of Nudists . . .
The Flaps of Hermits . . . The Hoods of Penitentiary Friars
. . . The Smacksmock of the Knocking Friars . . . *Lourdaudus:
De Vita et honestate braguardorum*, Of the Life and Honesty of
Scrougephuckers, by Blockheadodus . . . *Cyrippii Sorbonici mor-
alisationes per M. Lupoldum*, The Moral Reflections of Tirralirra-
peepee, a Doctor of the Sorbonne, by Master Loopholed . . . The
Bells of Travellers . . . The Bibblings of Tippling Bishops . . .
Tarraballationes doctorum coloniensium adversus Reuchlin, The
Paroxypothers of the Doctors of Cologne against Reuchlin in regard
to Pfefferkorn, a converted Jew who sought to Deprive the Hebrews
of their Books . . . The Cymbals of Ladies . . . The Shitsters'
Farthingale . . . *Virevoustatorum nacquettorum per F. Pedebil-
letis*, The Fillybustertwiddlery of Knockers by Friar Poopballite
. . . The Patchwork of Stout Hearts . . . The Mummery of Jack
o'Lanterns and Robin Goodfellows . . . *Gerson: De auferibilitate
Papae ab Ecclesia*, Of the Removability of the Pope by the Church,
by Gerson . . . The Catalogue of Nominated and Graduated Persons . . . *Jo. Dytebrodii: De terribiliditate excommunicationum,
libellus acephalos*, Of the Terribility of Excommunication, a work
without Title, by Joseph Diddlesnuff . . . *Ingeniositas invocandi
diabolos et diabolas per M. Guinguolfum*, Ingenius Ways of Invoking He-Devils and She-Devils by Master Gincuddygolfer . . . The
Hotchpot of the Perpetually Begging Friars . . . The Morris Dance
of Heretics . . . The Whinnyings of Cajetan . . . *Moillegroin,
doctoris cherubici: De origine Papelutarum et Torticollorum ritibus,
libri septem*, Of the Origin of the Rites of Popicults and Necktwist-
ers in Seven Books by the Cherubic Doctor, Marrowgrain . . .
Seventy-nine highly Fat Breviaries . . . The Nightmares of the
Five Mendicant Orders . . . The Skinnery of the Humbuggers,
Extracts from the Yellow Boot, incornifistibulated in the *Summa
Angelica* . . . The Ravisher in Cases of Conscience . . . The Potgut of Judges . . . The Donkeypizzler of Abbots . . . *Sutoris,*

adversus quedam qui vocaverat cum fripponnatorem et quod frip-
ponnatores non sunt damnati ab Ecclesia, Cobbler or Pierre Cordon-
nier, a Doctor of the Sorbonne, against Whoever Consorted with
Scoundrels and why Scoundrels are not damned by the Church . . .
Cacatorium medicorum, Of the Medical Dungers . . . The Chim-
ney Sweep of Astrology . . . The Fields of Enemas by S. C. or Sym-
phorien Champier, a Doctor of Lyons . . . The Poopdrawer of
Apothecaries . . . The Arsekisser of Surgery . . . *Justinianus:*
De cagotis tollendis, Of the Toleration of Bigots, by Justinian . . .
Antidotarium animae, The Souls of Antidoters . . . *Merlinus Coc-*
cais, De patria diabolorum, Of the Devil's Country by Folengo or
Merlin Coccais. . . .

Some of the books in this library were already printed. The rest
are now in the press in this noble city of Tübingen, the home of pub-
lishing.

VIII

HOW PANTAGRUEL IN PARIS RECEIVED A LETTER FROM HIS FATHER GARGANTUA

As you may suppose, Pantagruel studied very hard and profited
much by his study, for his intelligence was naturally active and his
memory as full as twelve casks of olives. While in Paris, he received
the following letter from his father:

My beloved son,
Among the gifts, graces and prerogatives with which our sovereign
Creator, God Almighty, blessed and enriched humanity from the
beginning, there is one that I deem supreme. By its means, though we
be mortal, we can yet achieve a sort of immortality; through it, we
may, in the course of our transitory lives, yet perpetuate our name
and race.
To be sure, what we gain by a progeny born of lawful wedlock

*cannot make up for what we lost through the sin of our first parents.
Adam and Eve disobeyed the commandments of the Lord their God:
mortality was their punishment. By death the magnificent mould in
which Man was fashioned vanished into the dust of oblivion.*

*However, thanks to seminal propagation, what a man loses his
children revive and, where they fail, their children prevail. So it has
gone, and so it shall be, from generation to generation, until the Day
of Judgment, when Christ shall restore to God the Father His kingdom pacified, secured and cleansed of all sin. Then all generation and
corruption shall cease, for the elements will have completed their
continuous transmutations. The peace humanity has craved so anx-
iously will have been attained; all things will have been reduced to
their appointed end and period.*

*I therefore have reason to give thanks to God, my Saviour, for
having granted me the joy of beholding my old age blossom anew in
your youth. When, by His pleasure, which rules and orders everything, my soul must abandon this human habitation, I shall not believe I am dying utterly, but rather passing from one place to another. For in you my visible image will continue to live on earth; by
you, I shall go on frequenting honorable men and true friends, as I
was wont to do.*

*My associations have not been without sin, I confess. We all trans-
gress and must continually beseech God to forgive us our trespasses.
But they have been without reproach in the eyes of men.*

*That is why if, beside my bodily image, my soul did not likewise
shine in you, you would not be accounted worthy of guarding the
precious immortality of my name. In that case, the least part of me
(my body) would endure. Scant satisfaction, that, when the best
part (my soul, which should keep my name blessed among men) had
degenerated and been bastardized. I say this not through any doubt
as to your virtue, which I have already often tested, but to encourage you to go on doing ever better and profiting by your constant
improvement.*

*My purpose is not so much to keep you absolutely on your present
virtuous course as to make you rejoice that you have kept and are
keeping on it. I seek to quicken your heart with resolutions for the
future. To help you make and carry these out, remember that I have
spared nothing. I have helped you as though my sole treasure on earth*

were once in my lifetime to see you well-bred and accomplished in honesty and valor as well as in knowledge and civility. Ay, I have longed to leave you after my death as a mirror of your father's personality. The reflection may not prove perfect in practice, but certainly I could not more studiously wish for its perfection.

My late father Grangousier, of blessed memory, made every effort that I might achieve mental, moral and technical excellence. The fruit of my studies and labors matched, indeed surpassed, his dearest wish. But you can realize that conditions were not as favorable to learning as they are to-day. Nor had I such gifted teachers as you. We were still in the dark ages; we still walked in the shadow of the dark clouds of ignorance; we suffered the calamitous consequences of the destruction of good literature by the Goths. Now, by God's grace, light and dignity have been restored to letters, and I have lived to see it. Indeed, I have watched such a revolution in learning that I, not erroneously reputed in my manhood the leading scholar of the century, would find it difficult to enter the bottom class in a grammar school.

I tell you all this not through boastfulness, though in writing to you I might be proud with impunity. Does not Marcus Tullius authorize it in his book OF OLD AGE, *and Plutarch in* HOW A MAN MAY PRAISE HIMSELF WITHOUT ENVY? *Both authors recognize that such pride is useful in fostering the spirit of emulation. No—I do it simply to give you a proof of my love and affection.*

To-day, the old sciences are revived, knowledge is systematized, discipline reëstablished. The learned languages are restored: Greek, without which a man would be ashamed to consider himself educated; Hebrew, Chaldean and Latin. Printing is now in use, an art so accurate and elegant that it betrays the divine inspiration of its discovery, which I have lived to witness. Alas! Conversely, I was not spared the horror of such diabolic works as gunpowder and artillery.

To-day, the world is full of learned men, brilliant teachers and vast libraries: I do not believe that the ages of Plato, Cicero or Papinian afforded such facilities for culture. From now on, it is unthinkable to come before the public or move in polite circles without having worshipped at Minerva's shrine. Why, the robbers, hangmen, adventurers and jockeys of to-day are infinitely better educated than the doctors and preachers of my time. More, even women and girls aspire

to the glory, the heavenly manna of learning. Thus, at my advanced
age, I have been forced to take up Greek. Not that I had despised it,
like Cato; I never had the opportunity to learn it. Now I delight in
reading Plutarch's MORALS, *Plato's noble* DIALOGUES, *the* MONU-
MENTS *of Pausanias and the* ANTIQUITIES *of Athenæus, as I await the*
hour when it shall please God, my Creator, to call me back to His
bosom.

That is why, my dear son, I urge you to spend your youth making
the most of your studies and developing your moral sense. You are in
Paris, which abounds in noble men upon whom to pattern yourself;
you have Epistemon, an admirable tutor, who can inspire you by
direct oral teaching. But I demand more of you. I insist you learn
languages perfectly! Greek first, as old Quintilian prescribes; then
Latin; then Hebrew for the sake of the Holy Scripture; then Chaldee
and Arabic, too. Model your Greek style on Plato, your Latin on
Cicero. Let no history slip your memory; cultivate cosmography, for
you will find its texts helpful.

As for the liberal arts of geometry, arithmetic and music, I gave
you a taste of them when you were a little lad of five or six. Proceed
further in them yourself, learning as much as you can. Be sure to
master all the rules of astronomy; but dismiss astrology and the di-
vinatory art of Lullius as but vanity and imposture. Of civil law, I
would have you know the texts of the Code by heart, then compare
them with philosophy.

A knowledge of nature is indispensable; devote yourself to this
study with unflagging curiosity. Let there be no sea, river or fountain
but you know the fish that dwell in it. Be familiar with all the shrubs,
bushes and trees in forest or orchard, all the plants, herbs and flowers
that grow on the ground, all the birds of the air, all the metals in the
bowels of earth, all the precious stones in the orient and the south. In
a word, be well informed in everything that concerns the physical
world we live in.

Then carefully consult the works of Greek, Arabian and Latin
physicians, without slighting the Jewish doctors, Talmudists and
Cabbalists. By frequent exercises in dissection, acquire a perfect
knowledge of that other world, which is man.

Devote a few hours a day to the study of Holy Writ. Take up the
New Testament and the Epistles in Greek; then, the Old Testament

*in Hebrew. Strive to make your mind an inexhaustible storehouse of
knowledge. For you are growing to manhood now: soon you will
have to give up your studious repose to lead a life of action. You will
have to learn to bear arms, to achieve knighthood, so as to defend my
house and help our allies frustrate the attacks of evildoers.*

*Further, I wish you soon to test what profit you have gained from
your education. This you can best do by public discussion and debate
on all subjects against all comers, and by frequenting learned men
both in Paris and elsewhere.*

*But remember this. As Solomon says, wisdom entereth not into a
malicious soul, and science without conscience spells but destruction
of the spirit. Therefore serve, love and fear God, on Him pin all your
thoughts and hopes; by faith built of charity, cling to Him so closely
that never a sin come between you. Hold the abuses of the world in
just suspicion. Set not your heart upon vanity, for this life is a transitory thing, but the Word of God endureth forever. Be serviceable to
your neighbor, love him as you do yourself. Honor your teachers.
Shun the company of all men you would not wish to resemble; receive not in vain the favors God has bestowed upon you.*

*When you realize that you have acquired all the knowledge Paris
has to offer, come back so I may see you and give you my blessing before I die.*

My son, the peace and grace of Our Lord be with you. Amen.

Your father,
GARGANTUA

From Utopia, the seventeenth day of September.

Having read this letter, Pantagruel, greatly encouraged, strove
more ardently than ever to profit in his work. Had you seen him
studying vigorously, practically and tirelessly, you would have compared his spirit moving among his books to flames blazing through a
bonfire of dry branches.

IX

HOW PANTAGRUEL MET PANURGE WHOM HE LOVED ALL HIS LIFE

ONE day Pantagruel was walking in the country towards the Abbey of St. Antoine, conversing and philosophizing with his servants and some students. Suddenly he met a man of fine stature and handsome mien, but severely wounded in several places, and so tattered that he must have been fighting a pack of mastiffs. His clothes were as ragged as a Norman apple-picker's.

Seeing him from afar:

"Do you see that fellow coming from the Charenton bridge?" Pantagruel asked his companions. "Upon my word, he is poor only in fortune; his face bespeaks a rich and noble family. Doubtless the misadventures that invariably beset too-curious people have reduced him to his present misery."

When the fellow drew close, Pantagruel addressed him.

"Stop, friend, I beg you, and answer a few questions," he said. "I assure you you'll have no cause to regret it. The calamity that has befallen you moves me to pity; I am eager to help you however I can. Tell us, friend: who are you? Where are you going? What do you wish? And what is your name?"

The fellow answered:

"*Juncker, Gott geb euch glück unnd hail. Zuvor, Lieber Juncker, ich las euch wissen das da ir mich von fragt, ist ein arm unnd erbarmglich ding, unnd wer vil darvon zu sagen, welches euch verdruslich zu hoeren, unnd mir zu erzelen wer, viewol die Poeten unnd Orators vorzeiten haben gesagt in iren Sprüchen unnd Sentenzen, das die Gedechtnus des Ellends unnd Armuot vorlangs erlitten ist ain grosser Lust.*"

(He spoke in German, saying: "Young gentleman, God prosper you and bring you joy. But first, my dear young gentleman, I must inform you that what you seek to know is a wretched and pitiful thing. It would make an endless story. And it would prove no pleasanter for you to hear than for me to tell, though the poets and orators of ancient times have stated in maxim and adage that the remembrance of sorrows endured is a great joy.")

"My friend," said Pantagruel, "I cannot understand this gibberish. If you expect us to understand, then speak another tongue."

The stranger replied:

"*Al barildim gotfano dech min brin alabo dordin falbroth ringuam albaras. Nin porth zadikim almucathin milko prin al elmim enthoth dal heben ensouim: kuthim al dum alkatim nim broth dechoth porth min michais im endoth, pruch dal maisoulum hol moth dansrilrim lupaldas im voldemoth. Nin hur diavosth mnarbotim dal gousch palfrapin duch im scoth pruch galeth dal Chinon min foulchrich al conin butathen doth dal prim.*"

(The words sounded vaguely like Arab, but it was a fantastic jargon he spoke. His hearers could make out only a single place-name: Chinon.)

"Can you make head or tail of it?" Pantagruel appealed to the others.

"I think it is the language of the Antipodes," Epistemon ventured. "But it's such a jawbreaker not even the devil himself would dare twist his tongue to it."

"My friend," said Pantagruel, "the walls may understand you, if they have ears to hear. But not one man jack among us can follow a syllable."

The stranger sighed. Then:

"*Signor mio: voi videte par exempio che la cornamusa non suona mai s'ella non ha il ventre pieno,*" he went on. "*Cosi io parimente non vi saperei contare le mie fortune, se prima il tribulato ventre non a la solita refettione, alquale è adviso che le mani et li denti abbui perso il loro ordine naturale et del tuto annichillati.*"

(A person conversant with Italian would have gathered: "My Lord, you know, for example, that no bagpipe ever makes a sound without a full belly. By the same token, I couldn't possibly tell you my adventures unless my tormented stomach first received its usual refreshment. To my paunch, it appears as though my hands and teeth had lost their natural functions and were utterly annihilated.")

"We're no better off than before," Epistemon grumbled.

The stranger continued:

"Lord geft tholb be sua virtiuss be Intelligence ass yi Body schal biss be naturall relvtht, tholb suld of me pety have, for Natur hass ulss equaly maide; bot Fortune sum exaltit hess, and oyis deprevit. Non ye less viois mou virtius deprevit and virtius men descrevis; for anen ye lad end, iss non good."

(This was Scots English. Its purport: "My Lord, if your generosity of spirit is as lofty as your body is by nature, you will have pity on me. For Nature hath created us equal, but Fortune hath exalted some, and others she hath brought low. Nevertheless, though virtue be often beggarly and the upright scorned, yet till the hour of death, no man may boast that he is good.")

"Floored again," cried Pantagruel. Panurge immediately resumed:

"Jona andie, guaussa goussy etan behar da erremedio, beharde, versela ysser lan da. Anbates, otoyyes nausu, eyn essassu gourr ay proposian ordine den. Non yssena bayta fascheria egabe, genherassy badia sadassu noura assia. Aran Rondovan gualde eydassu nay dessuna. Estou oussyc eguinan soury hin, er darstura eguy harm, Genicoa plasar vadu."

(A bastard Basque, this. Most Gascon lackeys could have told Pantagruel it meant: "Great Lord, all things have their remedy: if unapparent, then we must sweat to find it. I implore you therefore to let me know clearly if my suggestion is in order. If you see no inconvenience, then give me my fill. Once you have done that, ask me what you will: I shall not fail you. Please God, I speak the truth from the depths of my heart.")

"Are you there, Genoica?" mocked Eudemon. "My God!!!"

"By St. Ninnyhammer," cried Carpalim, Gargantua's valet. "May your bum burst if I didn't almost get the drift of it."

"Prug frest strinst," the stranger continued, *"sorgdmand strochdt drhds pag brleland* Gravot, Chavigny, La Pomardière, *rusth pkallhdracg* La Devinière près Nays, Seuilly. *Halmuch monach drupp delmeupplistrincq drlnd dodelb up drent loch minc stzrinquald* de vins der Cordelis hur jocst-stzampenards."

Again, in this mad balderdash, all they made out was the place-names Gravot, Chavigny, La Pomardière, La Devinière, Nays, Seuilly and the word "wines."

"Do you speak Christian, my friend," Epistemon asked, "or Gipsy language, Welsh or Czech?"

"No," said another, "that's Lantern Language, spoken in the Isles of Nowhere."

The stranger changed his tack:

"Herre, ie en spreeke anders gheen taele, dan kersten taele; my dunct nochtans, al en seg icu met een woordt, mynen noot verklaert ghenonch wat ie begeere; gheeft my uyt bermherticheyt yet waer vn ic ghevoct magh zunch."

(Translated from the Dutch this meant: "Sir, I speak no tongue that is not Christian. Yet I should think that, without my saying a word, my rags betray clearly enough what it is I wish. In human charity, give me something to revive me!")

"It's all of one piece," Pantagruel grumbled. "And about as clear as mud."

"Seignor, de tanto hablar yo soy cansado. Por que suplico a Vostra Reverentia que mire a los preceptos evangeliques, para que ellos movant vostra Reverentia a lo que as de conscientia, y, si ellos non bastarent para mover Vostra Reverentia a piedad, suplico que mire a la piedad natural, la qual yo creo que la movra, como es de razon, y con esto non digo mas."

(The Spanish means: "My Lord, I am tired from so much speaking. So I beg your Reverence to consider the precepts of the Gospel, so that they may move your Reverence to fulfill the demands of conscience. If they do not suffice to move your Reverence to pity, then I implore you to consider natural compassion, which I think must reasonably do so. On this head, I shall say no more.")

"By God, I've no doubt you can speak a score of languages fluently," said Pantagruel. "But tell us what you want in some language we can understand."

"Myn Herre," the stranger said, *"endog jeg med ingen tunge talede, lygesom boeen, ocg uskielig creatuer; myne kledebon och myne legoms magerhed uudviser allyguevel klarlig huvad tyng meg meest behoff girered, som aer sandeligh mad och drycke: hwarfor forbarme teg omsyder ofvermeg, oc befael at gyffue meg nogeth, aff huglket jeg kand styremyne groeendes maghe, lygeruüss son mand Cerbero en soppe forsetthr: Soa shal tue loeffve lenge och lyksaligth."*

(Translating the Danish: "Sir, even if like a babe or beast I spoke no language whatever, my clothing and my emaciated body should plainly show what I need: food and drink. Have pity on me then and order them to give me something to master my baying belly, even as sops are tossed to Cerberus. Do this and you will live long and happy."

"I think," Epistemon said, "that is how the Goths spoke. Were God willing we would all speak thus—through our tailpieces!"

"*Adoni, scolom techa,*" the stranger cried. "*Im ischar harob hal hebdeca bemeherah thithen li kikar lehem, chancathub: Laah al Adonai cho nen ral.*"

(In Hebrew: "Sir, the peace of God be upon you. If you wish to do good to your servitor, give me a loaf of bread at once, for it is written: 'He that hath pity upon the poor lendeth to the Lord.' ")

"Ha!" cried Epistemon. "This time I understand. That's Hebrew, well turned and rhetorically pronounced."

The wag resumed:

"*Despota tinyn panagathe, doiti sy mi uc artodotis? Horas gar limo analiscomenon eme athlios. Ce en to metaxy eme uc eleis udamos, zetis de par emu ha u chre, ce homos philologi pamdes homologusi tote logus te ce rhemeta peritta hyrparchin, opote pragma afto pasi delon esti. Entha gar anancei monon logi isin, hina pragmata, hon peri amphibitumen, me prosphoros epithenete.*"

(In Greek: "Excellent master, why do you give me no bread? You see me miserable and perishing of hunger, yet instead of coming to my aid, you ask me irrelevant questions. Nevertheless, all intelligent people agree unanimously that discourse and words are superfluous when the facts are patent to all. The only words needful here are those you should speak to give me what we are arguing about.")

"Good Lord! That's Greek!" cried Carpalim. "I've heard it spoken before. How do you know it? Have you ever lived in Greece?"

The stranger, for only answer, said:

"*Agonou dont oussoys vou denaguez algarou, nou den farou zam-ist vous mariston ulbrou, fousquez vous brol, tam bredaguez mou-preton den goul houst, daguez daguez nou croupys fost bardounno-flist nou grou. Agou paston tol nalprissys hourtou los ecbatonous prou dhouquys brol panygou den bascrou noudous caguons goul-fren goul oust troppassou.*"

"I believe I understand him," said Pantagruel. "Either that language is my native Utopian or it is much like it in sound."

But as he sought to address him, the stranger interrupted:

"Jam toties vos per Sacra perque Deos Deasque omnis obtestatus sum ut, si qua vos pietas permovet, egestatem meam solaremini, nec hilum proficio clamans et ejulans. Sinite, quaeso, sinite, viri impii, Quo me fata vocant abire, nec ultra vanis vestris interpellationibus obtundatis, memores veteris illius adagii, quo Venter famelicus auriculis carere dicitur."

(Which Latin meant: "Already, by all I hold sacred, by the gods and goddesses above, I have repeatedly implored you to allay my suffering, if pity can move you. But I have gained nothing by my prayers and supplications. Leave me, therefore, I pray you, O impious men; let me go whither destiny calls. Cease wearying me with your vain questions and remember the ancient adage: 'The empty belly hath no ears to hear.' ")

"By God, friend, can't you speak French?" Pantagruel demanded.

"Why of course, I can speak French very well," the stranger answered. "It is my natural language, praise God, my mother-tongue, for I was born and brought up in Touraine, the garden of France."

"Then tell us what is your name," Pantagruel urged, "and explain where you have come from. By my faith, I've already taken such a liking to you that if you incline to my wishes, you shall never budge out of my company. God's truth, you and I shall make a pair of friends to match Æneas and Achates."

"My Lord, my true and proper Christian name is Panurge. I have just returned from Turkey whither I was taken prisoner after the disaster at Mytilene. I shall be only too pleased to tell you of my adventures, which are more wonderful than those of Ulysses. But you are pleased to attach me to your person; I heartily accept the offer and swear never to leave you, should you go to all the devils in hell. I shall therefore have more leisure at another time to give an account of myself. For the moment, I most urgently need to feed. My teeth are sharp, my belly empty, my throat dry and my appetite a devouring flame. All is ready if you will but give the word. To see me fall to, would be a feast for the eyes. For God's sake, order me some food."

Pantagruel bade them take him home and provide him with vic-

tuals aplenty. Panurge ate abundantly that evening, went to bed
with the chickens, and slept until the morrow at dinner time. Thus
the interval from bed to board was but three steps and a jump.

X

HOW PANTAGRUEL SETTLED AN EXTRAORDINARILY INVOLVED CONTROVERSY SO EQUITABLY THAT HIS JUDGMENT WAS REPUTED MORE MARVELLOUS THAN SOLOMON'S

REMEMBERING the advice in his father's letter, Pantagruel determined to put his knowledge to the test. So, according to custom, he
advertised the subjects he wished to debate, nailing, at all the crossroads of the city, his nine thousand seven hundred and seventy-four
theses. These dealt with the gravest doubts and most recondite
subtleties of science.

Considering it the lowest faculty, he began with the Faculty of
Arts, in the Rue de Feurre or Straw Street, so called for the straw
upon which the students sat. Here he contended with all the professors, lecturers and orators, turning them arseyturvy. Then he
tackled the savants of the Theological Faculty at the Sorbonne,
opposing all the divines from four o'clock in the morning to six at
night, with only two hours off for meals and rest. After all, he did
not wish to prevent these learned Sorbonvivants from drinking at
their favorite taverns.

Most of the lords of the royal court, the Lords Justices, Chancellors, Counsellors, officers of the Treasury, secretaries, attorneys and
other jurists, as well as the sheriffs, physicians and professors of canon
law, attended these debates. The majority of these scholars took the

floor, but Pantagruel bested their sophistical and fallacious arguments, exposing them as so many robed, hooded and bewigged mooncalves.

Rumors of Pantagruel's phenomenal knowledge began to spread. Even the old sluts, washerwomen, vendors of roasts, knifegrinders and procuresses marvelled, and pointed him out as he passed. At which he was mightily pleased, like Demosthenes, the prince of orators, when an old hag cried: "There goes the great man!"

Now at the time, there was a lawsuit pending in court between two great noblemen: My Lord Kissarse, plaintiff, party of the first part, and My Lord Bumfondle, defendant.

Their controversy was so involved and jurisprudentially abstruse that the highest court in the land found it about as clear as Old High German. The king, intervening, assembled the four greatest and wisest tribunals in France, the Privy Council and the principal university professors, not only French, but Englishmen and Italians, like Jason Maïnus of Padua, Philippus Decius of Pisa (Peter of the Granite-heads) and a rabble of judicial rabbinists.

For more than forty-six weeks they struggled with the problem, but could find no way out of its tortuous obscurities. Brought to a complete standstill, they bemerded themselves horribly, out of sheer exasperation. At length one of them, Du Douhet, the most learned, experienced and practical of the lot, found a solution. Pointing out how their minds had become besotted and philogrobolized:

"Gentlemen," he said, "we have been here many weeks, wasting both time and money. This case is a muddy stream in which we welter, unable to touch bottom or reach land. The harder we work at it, the less we understand about it—which is a cause for shame and a burden upon our consciences. To my mind, if we keep on at this rate, we will emerge dishonored and ridiculous.

"Now I have a plan. You have doubtless heard of a mighty person named Lord Pantagruel. As a result of the theses he defended in public against all comers, he has been recognized as the most profound scholar of the times. I suggest we invite him here and lay the whole matter before him. If he does not settle it, then no man on earth can!"

The counsellors and doctors willingly agreed. They summoned Pantagruel on the spot, apprised him of the difficulty, begged him to go over the whole case and report upon it in whatever legal form he wished. They would begin, they said, by giving him all the briefs and records of the suit, which in bulk and weight would have taxed four castrated asses. But Pantagruel objected:

"Gentlemen, gentlemen, are the two principals in the case still living?"

"Certainly, My Lord!"

"Then what the devil's the use of all this scribblescrabble fools-cap?" he bawled. "Wouldn't it be better to hear their variance face to face, from their own lips? Instead of all this flapdoodle monkey-writing? Why, those mountains of documents are a compendium of chicanery, ruses and frauds, based on Copola's handbook on how to evade the law. Pure subversions of equity, that's what all this is!

"I am convinced that you, and all those who have touched this case, have supplied as much *pro* and *contra* as you could. No doubt it was once perfectly clear and fit to try. But you have obfuscated it by all manner of nonsensical complications, based upon such inept opinions as you found in Accursius, in Peter Baldus of Ubaldis, in Hippolytus of Ferrara, in Bartolus of Bologna (my God! they called him 'the lantern of the law'!); in Paul de Castro, the Italian professor; in Panormitamus or Nicolas Tedesco, the canon law expert; in Bertachin of the Consistory, in Alexander Tartagno; in Curtius, counsellor to the Marquis of Montferrat; in Imola of Bologna.

"Ay, you have buried the issue under the dung of a thousand old mastiffs who never grasped the simplest law of the *Pandects*, of blockheads and tithe-calves, of dolts lacking the rudiments that make it possible to begin to understand the law. Did they know Greek and Latin? Certainly not? Well, what did they know? Merely the Gothic and Barbarian tongues. Yet Ulpian tells us in his *Liber de Origine Juris, Of the Origin of Law,* that our code came from the Greeks. Isn't it full of Greek words and sentences? From the Greek, then, it was translated into Latin, into the purest, most admirable style conceivable in that language. And, as I say this, I do not forget Sallust, Varro, Cicero, Seneca, Livy or Quintillian. How then could these old dullards appreciate the text of the laws when they never clapped eyes on a decent Latin book? Their style suffices to prove it: it is the style of chimney sweeps, cooks and scullions, not jurists.

"Besides, the law grew up out of the field of moral and natural philosophy. Then how could these idiots construe it when by God! they studied less philosophy than the average mule? The humanities, a knowledge of antiquity, history? In these subjects your dotards were about as well equipped as a toad is with feathers. Yet, without these, law is unintelligible, as I intend to prove more fully in a future work.

"Very well, then: if you want me to handle this suit, first burn up all this trash. Then summon the two parties before me. When I have heard them, I shall give you my opinion without pretence or reservation."

In all congregations, there are more fools than intelligent men; and, as Livy, speaking of the Carthaginians, points out, the majority prevails. Many jurists therefore disapproved of Pantagruel's plan. But Du Douhet fought them tooth and nail. Pantagruel, he asserted, was quite right; these records, bills of inquest, exceptions, appeals, counterappeals, replications, demurrers, rebutters, rejoinders, surrebutters, surrejoinders and other like deviltries were but tricks to prolong lawsuits and foil justice. The devil, he warned, would carry them all off to hell if they did not proceed according to the precepts of philosophical and evangelical justice.

In the end, the papers were burned and the two lords cited to appear before the Court. As they did so:

"Are you the parties in this suit?" Pantagruel asked them.

"Yes, My Lord."

"Which of you is the plaintiff?" he asked.

"I am," said My Lord Kissarse.

"Go ahead, my friend, tell me your grievance, point by point. And the truth, too, for, God's body! if I catch you in a lie, I'll sever your head from your shoulders to prove that Truth is sacred in law. Take care neither to exaggerate nor minimize any point as you present your case. Proceed."

XI

HOW MY LORDS KISSARSE AND BUMFONDLE PLEADED WITHOUT BENEFIT OF COUNSEL BEFORE PANTAGRUEL

KISSARSE began as follows:

"My Lord, the truth is that a good woman of my house was taking her eggs to market—"

"Let us not stand on ceremony, Kissarse: put on your hat."

"Gramercy, My Lord," said Kissarse, "but to my case.

"*Whereas* there passed between the twin tropics the sum of three-pence towards the zenith . . . and *whereas* the Riphaean Mountains had that year suffered a great sterility of paste and imitation stone . . . and *whereas* this was due to a warfare of fiddlefaddle seditiously fomented between the tripegabblers and the Accursian maunder-mongers . . . and *whereas* the cause of the contention was the re-bellion of the Switzers, who had assembled to the number of three, six, nine and ten . . . and *whereas* they did this to get presents on New Year's Day, at the season when soup is served to oxen and the keys of the coal cellar given to country wenches so they may feed the dogs plenty of oats. . . .

"Well, My Lord, all night long they kept their hands on the pot, dispatching Bulls on horseback and Bulls on foot to keep the ships in harbor, because the tailors insisted on making stolen tatters into

> *A peashooter to shoot a pea*
> *Across the Oceanic Sea*

which at the moment was pregnant with a potful of cabbage, accord-ing to the opinion handed down by the manufacturers of hay-bun-dles. On the contrary, the physicians maintained that the urine re-vealed no positive traces

In the pacing of the bustard
That he ate his hash with mustard.

"Unless My Lords of the Court please to hand down a decision in B-flat enjoining the pox to forego grappling the cauldron-makers and strolling about thus during the divine service . . . in so much as the jobbernowls had already long begun dancing the Breton jig on the diapason:

One foot in the fire,
Keeping time with the fiddle,
Your hands in the pyre
And your head in the middle

as goodman Ragot, king of the beggars, was wont to proclaim. . . .

"Ay, gentlemen, I pause to observe that God rules all things according to His will, and against the pricks, a carter flattened his whip, and broke it. That was when the shanty was returned, when Master Anitus des Cressonnières, Lord of the Watercress Plots, was graduated Licentiate in all competences, as the canons say. Heavy, dullard, logerheaded timber, say I. But what makes Lent so high, by St. Fiacre of Brie, is exactly this:

It never comes Pentecost
But to my grievous cost

yet

Joy before, grief behind,
A small rain stills a raging wind.

"Now *whereas* we realize that the sergeant did not point-blank place the point so high above the blank that the Clerk of the Court failed to lick his fingers orbicularly . . . and *whereas* these fingers were bristling with goosefeathers . . . *therefore* we see manifestly that they fail, unless, considering things in their proper perspective, they look towards the place in the chimney where hangs the sign of forty reptile-power wine, the snakes being necessary to twenty basic quinquennials. . . .

"However, who would not let fly the bird before the cheesecake rather than discover it after, when memory is often lost, as a man puts on his shoes awry? Anyhow, God guard Thibaut Mitaine from all danger!"

"Gently, friend, gently," Pantagruel interrupted. "Speak slowly. Don't lose your temper. I understand your point; proceed."

"People are quite right," My Lord Kissarse resumed, "when they claim that advice should be forthcoming repeatedly. After all, fore-warned is forearmed. Well, My Lord, the old egg-woman I was tell-ing you about, was in the midst of her prayers, *Ave* this, *Ave* that and *Gaudi nos*! How then, by God's might! could she cover herself with a cloak of counterfeit shame against the prerogatives and privi-leges of the University without angelically bathing her parts, cover-ing one with a seven of diamonds and piercing the fellow with the point of the blade in the nearest place where they sell the old rags Flemish painters use when they neatly square the circle by clapping horseshoes on grasshoppers? Indeed, I must confess I am amazed the world does not lay, considering what a noble and pleasurable thing it is to hatch."

Here My Lord Bumfondle sought to interrupt. Pantagruel rose:

"By St. Anthony's gut, are you supposed to speak without per-mission? Here I sit sweating away, trying to judge fairly of the point at issue, and you get up to nettle me! Peace, in the devil's name, peace: you shall speak your bellyful when this man has done. Go on, Kissarse, and take your time."

"My Lord," said Kissarse, "*whereas*

> *The Sanction Pragmatic*
> *Was very phlegmatic*
> *Towards this rheumatic*
> *Stigmatic fanatic*

making no mention whatever of the question . . . and *whereas* His Holiness the Pope gave each and every man leave to break wind at his ease, so long as the materials of solid color are not striped, how-ever tragic the poverty of the world . . . providing only that men refrain from making the sign of the cross with the left hand . . . and *whereas* the good woman previously mentioned began to pour

out the soup by the faith of her rich-ballocked goldfishes . . . and
whereas ruffians ruffed and the rainbow was newly forged in Milan
to bring forth larks . . . *therefore* my good old woman was perfectly justified in exhausting her sciatica by virtue of the solemn
protestation of the testiculose fishes who were·indispensable for the
better construction of old boots. . . .

"However, Jean le Veau, or Honest John Calf, her first-cousin,
shaken about by a log of printed letters, earnestly advised her not
to dare wash the flummery in lye, ere she set the paper on fire. Was
he right? He was, My Lord, so much so, that *Pillo, Nado, Joco, Foro,
Scramble, Zero, Game and Out*:

> *Non de ponte vadit*
> *Qui cum sapienta cadit*
>
> *Who falls adroitly in the water*
> *Is not marked for death or slaughter*

especially since My Lords of the Treasury were far from concurring
in the summation of the German flutes out of which they framed
those *Spectacles for Princes* by Jean Meschinot, newly printed at
Antwerp. There, gentlemen, is what a false return of writ can do;
that, gentlemen, is how the world believes the adverse party. But,
in sacer verbo dotis, I mean *in verbo sacerdotis*, on a priest's word, the
contrary is exact.

"However, desiring to obey the king's pleasure, I armed myself
cap-à-pie and re-soled my belly to go to find out how my vintagers
had pinked their tall hats, the better to ram the rod and bury the
mutton dirk. Now *whereas* the times were somewhat parlous because
of the county fairs . . . and *whereas* not a few militiamen had been
dismissed from parade despite the height of the chimneys, the size
of Friend Baudichon's quittors, and the surface of his malanders
. . . and *whereas* consequently it was a splendid year for shellfish
in the Artois, which brought good luck to the club-bearers because
people ate dodo-birds and cocklicranes without plucking them—
and ate till their bellies were fit to burst. . . .

"*Therefore,* if, as I wished, each had as fair a voice, we could play
a faster game of tennis and the little trickeries employed in ety-

mologizing slippers would flow more easily into the river Seine to serve as perpetual bridges like the Pont-aux-Meuniers. This is just as decreed of yore by the King of Canarra which act is duly registered in the archives of the Clerk of this Court.

"*Therefore*, My Lord, I most humbly request that by virtue of your office, your Lordship pronounce and publish reasonable judgment upon the case with costs, damages and interest."

"Have you anything else to say, my friend?"

"No, My Lord: I have said the essential, I have told the *tu autem*, and upon my word of honor, I have not altered a single word."

"Your turn then, My Lord Bumfondle," said Pantagruel. "Say what you like and be brief. But do not omit anything you may think revelant to the issue."

XII

HOW MY LORD BUMFONDLE PLEADED BEFORE PANTAGRUEL

My Lord Bumfondle then addressed the Court:

"My Lord and gentlemen, if the iniquity of men were as plainly visible in a categorical judgment as flies are in milk, the world—four oxen!—would not be devoured by rats. Many an ear, too, on this earth would not have been so treacherously gnawed. Now, though everything my adversary has said is perfectly true, in so far as the letter and history of the *factum* are concerned, yet nevertheless the most subtle trickeries, dodges and chicane lie between the lines.

"I eat my stew with the best, ay, and never a harmful thought or word in my mind. Must I then tolerate people coming to pester, irk and wherret my brain, friggling and screwing away as they sing the old jingle:

Who drinks while eating stew, 'tis said
Will neither see nor hear when dead.

"By the Holy Virgin, when on the field of battle the blows dealt
with the brotherhood's sanctified bread fell fast, how many great
captains have we seen straining their utmost to swang-dangle, to
play the lute, to make music with their tails and to jiggle about on
the platform, shod with dainty slippers slashed like the beard of a
crayfish? Alas! the world to-day is utterly unbound by bales of
Leicester linen: one takes to debauchery, another hides his mug from
the blasts of winter, a third does the same as the first, and so do Numbers Five, Four and Two. Therefore, unless it please the Court to
take some orderly action in this matter, the gleaning this season will
be as disastrous as when it made or will make goblets.

"Let a wretched man go to the public baths to illumine his snout
with cowpat or to purchase a pair of winter boots, what happens?
The sergeants or soldiers of the watch, passing by, receive the
decoctions of an enema or the faecal matter of a bedpan on their
heads. Is that a reason for clipping coins and frying wooden dishes?
Sometimes we think of one thing, but God does another, and when
the sun has set, all beasts are in the shade. Let me never be believed
again if I fail to prove this conclusively through frank and worthy
witnesses.

"In the year thirty-six, I bought a German bobtail, tall and short,
of pretty good wool and dyed in the grain, so the goldsmiths assured
me, though the notary slipped some etceteras in. I am not enough of
a scholar to snatch the moon with my teeth. But as for the tub of
butter where they sealed the volcanic instruments, rumor ran rife
that salted beef helped one find wine at midnight without a candle,
even were it hidden at the bottom of a collier's sack, and your collier
equipped with horse-armor and thigh-pieces required for frying a
head of mutton properly. The proverb bears that out: It is pleasant to
see black cows in burned wood at the climax of coition.

"I laid the matter before the clerks, begging these gentlemen to
examine it. They concluded in *frisemorum*, according to the modes
in the first figure of the syllogism, that nothing can compare with
mowing in summer in a cellar provided with pen and ink, with paper
and penknives from Lyons on the Rhône, tittuppy-tattuppy. It
surely must be obvious that, the moment armor smells of garlic, rust
eats it to the very liver? Besides, they do nothing but wrangle and
brangle among themselves, inciting the wrynecks and headtwisters

as they skim over the postprandial nap. That, I insist, is what makes salt so dear.

"Gentlemen, pray do not believe that *whereas* the old woman covered her hind pocket with birdlime to offer it as a souvenir to the best-hung sergeant . . . and *whereas* the tripe, entrails and pluck described a complete revolution in the usurers' purses . . . *therefore*, the best means to preserve one from cannibals was (1) to take a string of onions, (2) to knit it to three hundred turnips and scraps of chitterlings of the best alloy the alchemists possess, (3) to strike hard, (4) to burn the slippers to ashes, mufflety-duffety with fine beet sauce, and (5) to hide in a small molehill without failing to save the bacon.

"*Whereas* the dice are unwilling to turn up anything but double ace, double threes or ace up, and you must settle the queen in the corner of the bed, cunticudgelling her prickety-split, holus-bolus, drinking bottoms-up and living in suspense without fishing frogs in all the rarest buskins . . . and *whereas* the little moulting goslings are amusing themselves playing at the wagtail game of Fouquet (Fucker or Squirrel), while waiting to beat the metal and heat the wax for the slobberers of salvation . . . and *whereas*, admittedly the four oxen mentioned above were somewhat short in memory, though to tell the whole truth they feared neither cormorant nor Savoy duck . . . and *whereas* the good people of my land were transported with hope . . . and *whereas* they declared: 'These children will become skilled in the science of algorism and numbers, it will be a rubric in the law books!' . . . *therefore* we cannot fail to catch the wolf if we make our hedges taller than the mill which the plaintiff mentioned.

"Now the great devil was angered thereby and beset the Germans backwards as they played the devil, tippling, '*Bi Got, Her, trink, trink*: by God, sir, drink, drink!' And I was astounded to see how the astrologers eschew it in their astrolabes and their almucantaraths, considering that these circles parallel to the horizon mark a two-spot in my favor. For there is no truth in the street-cry: 'Farm-chickens for sale on the Petit-Pont near Notre Dame.' In point of fact, they were as high-crested as marsh-peewits, if in truth they sacrifice their reddle to the ink fresh-spilled from capitals or slanting letters. But for my part, I care not so but the headband of the book breed no worms. Let us assume that when the buckhounds were copulating, the puppies had blown their horns for the kill before the notary had registered the act cabbalistically. Does it follow (unless the Court be pleased to reverse its judgment) that six acres of meadowland of the greatest width make three gallons of fine ink without blowing into the basin? Remember that, at King Charles' funeral, wool was obtainable in the open market for six pieces per fleece, and I mean pieces of wool, on my woolgathering oath.

"*Whereas* I ordinarily notice in all good houses that when they go birdhunting with decoys, they give the chimney three sweeps of the broom and put their names upon record . . . and *whereas*, if it be too hot, people do nothing but stretch their kidneys and blow through their bumvents, whirrberry-whortlechuck:

> *The letter finished off, at once*
> *They gave the cows back to the dunce.*

"My Lords, a similar decision was handed down, double or quits, in the year seventeen, because of the evil government of Louzefougerousse, I humbly request the Court be pleased to give it due consideration.

"*Tunc*, My Lord, *quid juris pro minoribus*; what judgment for the least? *Whereas* I do not pretend that a man may not equitably and judicially dispossess men who swig holy water as who might swallow a weaver's shuttle . . . and *whereas* suppositories are made of them for those who refuse to resign . . . and *whereas* they accept only tit for tat, ell for tell, hocus for pocus . . . also *whereas* the common application of the Salic Law commits the first incendiary who flays the cow as it blows its nose in a full concert of music, without pitching the note of the cobblers' stitches . . . and *whereas* this same law condemns said incendiary in times of swollen bellies to sublimate the penury of his member with moss gathered while people stand shivering at midnight mass to strappado these Anjou wines which gambol neck to neck and leg to leg in the Breton fashion. . . .

"*Therefore*, I do conclude as before in claiming costs, damages and interest."

When My Lord Bumfondle had finished, Pantagruel asked Kissarse:

"Have you any comment to make?"

"No, My Lord, I have spoken already and told the whole truth. So I now pray you humbly for God's sake to put an end to our suit, since we are here at great cost."

XIII

HOW PANTAGRUEL DELIVERED JUDGMENT ON THE DIFFERENCE BETWEEN THE TWO LORDS

PANTAGRUEL then rose, assembled all the magistrates, counsellors and doctors and said:

"Well, gentlemen, you have heard their difference *vivae vocis oraculo*, by the oracle of the living voice. What do you think of it?"

"We have heard all plainly," they replied, "but the devil take us if we understood one word. We therefore unanimously implore you to condescend to deliver judgment however you see fit. Convinced beforehand that it will be suitable, we ratify it *ex nunc prout ex tunc*, in prospect and retrospect."

"Very good, gentlemen," said Pantagruel, "since you wish it, I will do so. But I must confess I find the case less difficult than you pretend. Your paragraph *Cato*, the laws *Gallus*, *Frater*, *Quinque pedum*, *Vinum*, *St. Dominus*, *Mater*, *Mulier bona*, *Si quis*, *Pompinus*, *Fundi*, *Emptor*, *Praetor*, *Venditor*—especially those concerning brothers, five feet, wine, a good woman, the purchaser and the vendor—seem to me far more intricate."

Then he took a turn or two around the room, apparently lost in profound meditation; as he labored, he groaned like an ass that is too tightly strapped. What a responsibility to pass judgment, scrupulous of the plea of one party without favoring the other! Returning to his seat, he delivered the following decision.

"Having seen, heard and carefully weighed the difference existing between My Lords Kissarse and Bumfondle, the Court has come to the following decision:

"*Whereas* the flittermouse bat in horripilation declined gallantly from the summer solstice, to beflower, perfume and woo the fiddle-faddles which checkmated the pawn by the nefarious vexations of the lucifugal nicticoraces which are inquiline in the Roman climate of a crucifix on horseback with an ape stretching a crossbow behind him, *therefore* plaintiff was within his rights when he caulked and stopped up the galleon your old woman was pumping with wind, one foot shod and the other bare, reimbursing the sum, low and stiff in his conscience, with as many bladder nuts as there are hairs in the eighteen cows, *plus* many for the embroiderer.

"Plaintiff is likewise innocent of the case privileged from the dogglebastardies he was presumed to have incurred because he could not jocundly excrete, through a decision handed down by a pair of gloves perfumed with arseoptera and fartiola by the light of the Mirabeau candle, made of nuts and with a hempen wick. Slacking the bowline with the brazen bullets, wherewith the scullion pastrycooks by way of protestation baked his vegetables interlarded with dormouse and attached them to hawk's bells made of Hungarian lace which his brother-in-law is remembered to have worn in a basket near by, bordered with *gules*, displaying three chevrons, belabored with canvas at the angular dunghole from which you fire at the clay pigeon with the ballockscourer.

"But insomuch as he charges the defendant with being a botcher, a cheese-eater and a tarrer of mummies, which in the course of swagglescrewing was found false, as said defendant plainly demonstrated, the Court sentences plaintiff to surrender to defendant three porringers of curds, cemented, preinconballifused and gaudipiddled as the custom of the country provides, these to be payable at mid-August in May. However, said defendant shall be bound to furnish said plaintiff with the hay and stubble necessary for stopping up the caltrops of his throat, impissocrapigated with finely gravelled capes of high mettle. So let them be friends as heretofore without costs and for cause."

This sentence having been pronounced, the contesting parties withdrew, both satisfied with the judgment. An incredible thing, truly, for since the deluge, no two parties at law have ever been discovered who were content with the definitive decision. Nor will such a phenomenon occur again before thirteen jubilees hereafter.

As for the scholars and juriconsults, they were rapt with ecstasy for three long hours; admiration for Pantagruel's superhuman wisdom in solving this terrific problem left them petrified. And they would still be there had not somebody supplied quantities of rose water and vinegar to bring them back to their senses.

For which, praise God everywhere, Amen!

XIV

HOW PANURGE TOLD OF HIS ESCAPE FROM THE TURKS

PANTAGRUEL's judgment was at once printed, filed in the archives of the law and widely distributed among the eager public. People almost everywhere began comparing Pantagruel with Solomon.

"Solomon," they said, "restored the child to its own mother as much by a lucky guess as anything else. He never gave proof of such marvels of sagacity as our good Pantagruel, for whose presence in this land, praise God!"

They were determined to make him Lord Chief Justice and Master of the Rolls, but he refused graciously.

"These offices," he explained, "require too much slavery of their holders. Again, given the corruption of men, very few such officers win salvation and then only at immense pains. If the benches in heaven vacated by Lucifer, and the fallen angels are not filled by people of another sort, then we shall have no Judgment Day within thirty-seven jubilees, and Nicolas de Cusa, the Franciscan, will be disappointed in his conjecture that the world will end at the thirty-fourth. Remember, I have given you fair warning. . . . Of course, if you have any hogsheads of good wine, I shall be very glad to accept them as a present."

So they sent him the best wine in town which he drank with relish. Panurge entered into its consumption valiantly, for he was dry as a salted herring, and slunk about like a sick cat. In the midst of one of

Panurge's deep draughts of red wine, somebody taxed him with his potulence:

"Steady on there, friend, you're bibbing like a lunatic."

"Look at me!" Panurge urged. "Devil take you if you see one of those Paris tricklepalates who sip no more than a dicky bird and only then if you rap them on the tail like a sparrow. God help me, mate, if I could rise up as fast as I swallow down, I would long ago have been above the sphere of the moon with My Lord Empedocles, who was hoisted thither by the eruption of Ætna. But I can't tell what's the matter. This wine is strong and delicious, yet the more I drink, the thirstier I get. I think the mere shadow of My Lord Pantagruel engenders thirst even as the moon produces catarrhs."

At these words, the company burst into laughter. Pantagruel turned around:

"What's the joke, Panurge?"

"My Lord," the other explained, "I was telling them how unlucky those fiendish Turks are never to drink a drop of wine. Were there no other prohibition in Mahomet's Koran, that one alone would keep me from under his law."

"Tell us how you escaped from the Turks," Pantagruel suggested.

"Very well, My Lord," said Panurge. "And by God! I shall not breathe the wraith of a lie!"

"Go on, then."

"Well, My Lord, those lewd Turks larded me up like a rabbit (I was so thin my flesh would otherwise have provided a poor grade of meat), ran a spit through me and were grilling me alive. As I roasted, I recommended myself to the Divine Grace. Remembering good St. Lawrence, I kept hoping that God would deliver me from this torment. As a matter of fact, that is exactly what happened—and in a very strange manner, to be sure!

"Whilst I was thus committing myself with all my heart to the Almighty, crying: 'Lord God, help me, Lord God, save me! Lord God, save thy son from this torture visited upon him by these heathen dogs because he sought to uphold Thy Law against them,' suddenly my turnspit fell asleep through the Divine Will or through that of some beneficent Mercury such as brought Argus to slumber for all his hundred eyes.

"When I saw he had ceased turning the broach, I hazarded a glance at him and perceived he was sound asleep. With my teeth, I seized a firebrand by the unburned end and tossed it into my roaster's lap. Then I seized another and tossed it as best I could under my roaster's cot, which stood near the chimney and bore his straw pallet. Immediately the straw caught on fire; the flames spread to the bed, and, from the bed, to the loft, which was panelled with fir. The cream of the jest was that the firebrand I tossed into my master turnspit's lap burned all his penis and was attacking his testicles. But the fellow was so caked with filth that he felt nothing until daybreak. Adaze, he rose, tottered across the room and from the window bawled: '*Dal baroth! dal baroth!*' which is their heathen way of saying 'Fire! Fire!'

"Then he returned to cut the cords about my hands. He was just breaking those about my feet when someone appeared. It was the master, who had been strolling past his house with several other pashas and mustaphas when he heard the alarm and smelled the smoke. He rushed up to save what he could and to carry off his jewels.

"Arriving upon the scene, he forthwith drew the broach on which I was spitted and killed my roaster then and there for his want of vigilance or some other reason. The spit penetrated a little above the navel, towards the right flank, piercing the third lobe of the liver, slanting upwards through the diaphragm into the pericardium, to emerge at the shoulders between the joints of the backbone and the left shoulderblade.

"I must confess that as the pasha drew the spit from my body, I fell down on the andirons and hurt myself somewhat. But not very seriously because the lardons basted about me broke the fall. The pasha, seeing his house irremediably burned and everything lost, committed himself whole to all the devils, calling as many as nine times upon Grilgoth, Asteroth, Rapallus and Scribblescrew. I was pretty frightened, for if all these demons appeared to carry off this madman, they would probably carry me off as well. 'I'm half roasted already,' I said to myself. 'This cursed bacon basted about me will be my ruin!' For Satan's minions are notoriously partial to lardons, as is proved by Jamblicus, the neo-Platonist, and Murmel, the Münster professor. But I crossed myself, crying: '*Hagios, Athanatos, ho theos!* God is holy and immortal.' Nor did any one appear.

"Thereupon my rascally pasha wished to turn my spit upon him·

self, and indeed placed it against his breast, pushing as hard as he could. But it was not pointed enough to sink in. So I rose and said to him: 'Master Buggerino, you'll never kill yourself like that. All you'll do is wound yourself and languish the rest of your life, suffering in the hands of physicians. I'll tell you what: if you like, *I'll* kill you. Outright, too: you'll not feel a thing. You can trust me: I've killed a heap of others and they were never the worse off for it, either.'

" 'Ah, my friend, please do that. If you will, I shall give you my purse. Here you are, take it. There are six hundred seraphs in it and some rubies, and some flawless diamonds.' "

"What happened to the money?" Epistemon asked. "Where are the treasures?"

"By St. John!" Panurge answered, "they must be dizzy, if they're still in circulation.

Mais où sont les neiges d'antan?

Where are the snows of yesteryear?

Such was the greatest worry of François Villon, the Parisian poet."

"Get on, I beg you!" Pantagruel put in. "We want to hear how you settled your pasha."

"On my word as an honorable man, I do not lie in the slightest particular. Well, I tied the pasha with some scurvy half-burned rags; I bound his hands and feet roughly with my own cords. Ha, he couldn't move! So I ran my spit through his throat . . . fastened its ends to two great hooks on which they hung their halberds . . . and left him dangling there, while I stirred up the fire beneath him. . . . God's truth, I dried Milord like a herring in a chimney.

"Then, taking his purse and a small javelin from the hooks I just mentioned, I made hot-foot out of the place. God knows how I could feel anything in the roast shoulder of mutton upon my person!

"I found the street full of people fighting the fire with buckets of water. Seeing me half-roasted, they naturally took and threw all their water upon me. It was gloriously refreshing. They even offered me food, but I could not eat much, as they served only water, according to their custom. They did me no other harm except one nasty little knob-breasted Turklet who was furtively chewing away at my lardons. I gave him such a sharp rap on the fingers with my javelin that he did not begin again. Then a young Corinthian girl brought me a pot of preserved fruit, Myrobalan emblics, they were. I recall she stared at my poor organ, which looked flea-bitten and bedraggled and was so limp, after its roasting, that it reached only to my knees. I must in all fairness add that this roasting completely cured me of a sciatica I had been subject to for more than seven years. My turnspit had left me on that side when he fell asleep.

"While the crowd was looking after me, the fire kept raging. More than two thousand houses were ablaze. One of my Turks noticed this and: 'By the Prophet's belly,' he cried, 'the whole city is flaming and we waste our time here!' To a man, they sped to their own houses whilst I made for the city gates. At length, standing on a hillock in the country, I turned back, like Lot's wife, to see the whole city burning like Sodom and Gomorrah. I was so delighted I almost opened the rear sluices for joy. But God punished me severely for it."

"How was that?" asked Pantagruel.

"As I watched this fire, I was beside myself with happiness. I kept jesting and making mock. 'Ha, poor lice!' I jeered. 'Ha, poor mice! it's a sorry winter you'll have of it, with your ricks ablaze.' Suddenly six hundred—no, more than six, indeed more than thirteen hundred and eleven dogs appeared on the horizon. One and all, great and small, every cur in town had joined the exodus. Sniffing my half-roasted flesh, they swooped down upon me, and would have devoured me on the spot if my good angel had not inspired me with a sovereign remedy against toothache."

"Toothache?" said Pantagruel. "Why toothache? Were you not cured of your rheums?"

"By the Easter sun!" cried Panurge. "What greater toothache than when a pack of hounds bury their fangs in your legs? Luckily I remembered my lardons and threw them to the dogs. In a trice they were pouncing down upon them, crowding, jostling and scrimmaging in a vast savage turmoil. I let them fight it out as I made my escape, exulting, safe, thanks to roasting, for which God bless grilled meats."

XV

HOW PANURGE PRESCRIBED A HIGHLY ORIGINAL WAY TO BUILD THE WALLS OF PARIS

ONE day for relaxation from his studies, Pantagruel was strolling in the suburbs towards St. Marcel; his objective was the Gobelins where there were famed dye-works, marvellous tapestry manufactories and an excellent *bordello*. Panurge was of the company, with the inevitable bottle and slice of meat under his gown. They were, he said, his bodyguard; it never occurred to him to go anywhere without them. He refused to wear a sword. When Pantagruel offered him one, he replied that it would but heat his spleen.

"But if you were attacked," Epistemon objected, "how could you defend yourself?"

"With the toe of my boot," he replied, "so long as thrusts were forbidden."

On their way homeward, Panurge considered the walls of Paris and observed derisively to Pantagruel:

"What wonderful walls! How solidly built and splendidly fortified! An ideal fence to keep moulting geese from straying. By my beard, they're utterly unfit for a city like this; a cow with one fart could lay low more than six fathoms of them."

"Do you know what Agesilaus said?" Pantagruel answered. "They asked him why the great city of Lacedæmon was not girded with walls. Pointing to the citizens, expert in military discipline, strong and so admirably equipped: 'These are the walls of the city!' he said. He meant that cities need no stouter or safer walls than the valor of their citizens. Even so, Paris is secure enough in the courage of its warlike population not to worry about building more walls. Besides, even if they wished to do as Strasbourg, Orléans or Ferrara, they couldn't. It would cost too much!"

"Perhaps," Panurge conceded. "But still, an exterior of stone is pretty useful to oppose to the enemy, if only as a sort of challenge. As for the enormous expense you mention, I could teach the city fathers a marvellous new way to erect fortifications cheaply. I would too, if they gave me my reward in wine."

"How?" asked Pantagruel.

"If I tell you, you must promise not to repeat it. Do you agree?"

"Ay."

"All right, then: look here! I've observed that the pleasure-twats of women in this part of the world are much cheaper than stones. Therefore, the walls should be built of twats, symmetrically and according to the rules of architecture, the largest to go in front. Next, on a downward slope like the back of an ass, the medium-sized, and last of all, the least and smallest. These should all be made to dovetail and interlace, diamond-shape, like the great tower of Bourges, with as many horny joy-dinguses, which now reside in claustral codpieces.

"What devil could possibly overthrow these walls; what metal on earth could stand up as well against punishment? Let the culverins try and brush up against them and by God, before you knew it, they would distill the blessed fruit of the great pox, light and thin as rain. God help any one who touches them, by all the devils! What is more, no lightning could strike them. Why? Because they are consecrated. Indeed, I can see but one drawback to the whole plan."

"Ho, ho, ho, ha, ha, ha!" roared Pantagruel. "What drawback?"

"The flies," Panurge disclosed. "They're extraordinarily partial to such surroundings. They would soon make them their headquarters and cover them with their ordure, here, there and everywhere, until the work was ruined and dishonored." There was a pause. Then: "By God, I've just thought of a remedy. Our walls must be wiped out and cleared of flies with foxtails, or good strong donkey-pizzles from Provence. Incidentally, on the way to supper, I'll give you a fine example from Friar Lubin Wittol's *Liber de Compotationibus mendicantium*, a work on the compotations of the Mendicant Friars.

"In the days when beasts still had the power of speech (it wasn't the day before yesterday), a poor lion was strolling in the forest of Fontainebleau, saying his own private devotions. Thus intent, he walked under a tree on which a churl of a charcoal-burner had climbed to cut down wood. Seeing the lion, the man hurled his axe at him, inflicting a deep leg wound. Whereupon the lion limped away, wandering through the forest in search of aid. As luck would have it, he met a carpenter who was glad to examine his wound, clean it as best he could and fill it up with moss. And he told the lion to wipe his wound well so no flies cack in it whilst he, the carpenter, went in search of a certain medicinal herb called carpenter's weed.

"The lion, healed, walked on through the forest until he met a sempiternal old hag, gathering wood. Terrified at the sight of him, she fell down backwards, in such a way that the wind blew up her gown, skirt and shirt above her shoulders. The lion, pitying her, ran up to see if he could help her. Standing above her, surveying her jorum, he cried: 'Poor woman, how did you get such a wound?' As he spoke, he spied a fox and called him: 'Ho, halloo, whsht, czz! Come here—and for cause!'

"As the fox arrived, Leo said: 'Friend Tod, somebody has dealt this poor old woman the most inhuman wound between the thighs. There is a manifest solution of continuity. Look how big the gash is, it runs from scut to navel; why, it must be at least forty-four inches long. It was done with a hatchet, I suspect, and quite recently, too. We must be careful to let no flies settle on it. Wipe it, then, my friend, wipe away, I beg you, inside and out. You've a fine, long, bushy tail; brush away at the wound, Friend Tod, brush away, I implore you. Meanwhile I'll go off to fetch some moss to fill it. We must all help one another, God wills it so. Therefore, sweep and brush, Brother Fox, you must keep this wound clean as a whistle or the poor thing will suffer. Swab and scour, friend, wipe and brush for all you are worth: God has provided you with a rich tail, long and proportionally thick. Then fall to, friend, and never weary of the task. The best brushers are the briskest, they brush broadly and breathlessly with their bristles brushing on and on brushfully, brushing the breach and bramble bravely clean of flies! Mop and swab, my ballocky beadle, my bouncing bully, I'll not be gone long.'

"The lion then set off in search of moss, but from afar, just before disappearing, he shouted further encouragement: 'Brush away, friend, until it's clean as a hound's tooth. Brush, rebrush and superbrush and never regret your brotherly brushing. By God, my gamesome gossip, I shall have you appointed Brusher and Wiper-in-ordinary to Queen Marie or to King Pedro of Castile.'

"The wretched fox wiped up and down, across and back, inside and out; but the false old hag fizzled and farted and funked like a thousand devils. Poor Tod was most uncomfortable; he did not know which way to turn to avoid the odor of the old baggage's hindblasts. As she shifted about, he noticed another orifice, somewhat more remote and less extensive than the one he swept. This, he ascertained, was the seat of the noxious and poisonous air.

"Presently Leo returned with enough moss to make at least thirty bales. As he stuffed it into the wound with a staff he picked up for the purpose, he exclaimed with amazement: 'Devil take it, this wound is deep; it will hold more than two cartloads of moss. Ah, well! God's will be done.' As he kept pounding it in, the fox intervened. 'Friend Leo,' he said, 'please don't put *all* the moss in. Keep some, I implore you. Because there's another little hole further back; it stinks like five hundred devils. I'm almost choking; it's pestiferous beyond all imagining!'

"That," Panurge concluded, "is how we should guard the walls of Paris from the onslaught of flies, allowing wages to official wipers and brushers."

But Pantagruel seemed less interested in this theory than in the observation which had prompted it.

"How do you know," he asked, "that the privy parts of women are so cheap? Paris includes many virtuous, honest, chaste women besides the virgins."

"*Et ubi prenus?*" said Panurge. "I tell you my opinion, based upon personal experience and concrete fact. I do not brag when I say I have friggle-riddled four hundred and seventeen women since I came here nine days ago. But this very morning I met a man carrying a double bag like Æsop's—you recall, the back pocket was for his faults, the front for the faults of others. My fellow, however, carried two girls in his, one before and one behind, both of them two or three years old at the most. He demanded alms; I replied I had more cods than cash. Then I asked him if the two girls were virgins.

" 'Brother,' he answered, 'I have been carrying them around for two years. The one in front is constantly under my eye; I believe her to be a virgin, though I would not put my hand in the fire to prove it. As for the one behind, I can say nothing about it.' "

"By heaven, you're a merry companion!" said Pantagruel. "I will have you clad in my livery."

So Panurge was bravely apparelled according to the prevailing fashion, except that he insisted on a codpiece three feet long and cut square instead of round. It was done, and provided a gallant spectacle. He would often remark that people had not yet appreciated the emolument and utility of wearing huge flies, but time would some day teach them, since time uncovered everything.

"God preserve the good fellow whose long codpiece has saved his life!" he would add. "God preserve him whose long codpiece has netted him one hundred and sixty thousand and nine crowns in a single day! God preserve him whose long codpiece has saved a city from dying of starvation. And by God, give me a little leisure and I shall write a book called *Of the Commodity of Long Codpieces*."

Indeed, he did produce a fat volume with appropriate figures; but it has not been printed yet, so far as I know.

XVI

OF THE CHARACTER AND CONDITION OF PANURGE

PANURGE was then about thirty-five years old and as fine to gild as a dagger of lead. Of medium height, neither too tall nor too short, he had an aquiline nose, shaped like the handle of a razor. He cut a very gallant figure though he was a trifle lewd by nature, and subject to a disease at that time called impecunitis, an incomparable malady.

Yet when he needed money, he knew thirty-three methods of acquiring it, the most ordinary and honorable of which was filching. He was a quarrelsome fellow, a sharper, a toper, a roisterer and a profligate, if ever there was one in the city of Paris. In every other respect, he was the best fellow in the world.

He was constantly plotting against the sergeants and the watch. Sometimes he assembled three or four sportsmen, plied them with drink until they were boozy as Knights Templars, then took them up the hill to Ste. Geneviève or near the Collège de Navarre. Placing his sword on the pavement and his ear to his sword, he waited till he heard the blade shake—an infallible sign that the watch was not far off. Then he and his companions took a dung cart and rolled it down hill. Ere it was halfway down, they had fled in the opposite direction, for in less than two days Panurge knew every street and alley in Paris as well as his postprandial grace: *Deus det nobis pacem suam*, God grant us His peace.

Another time he laid down a train of gunpowder where the watch was due to pass. Just as the troop debouched, he set fire to it, vastly delighted in observing how gracefully they took to their heels, in mortal terror that St. Anthony's fire had caught them by the legs.

The luckless Masters of Arts and theologians he persecuted more than any other class of men. When he met one, he never failed to do him some harm, either slipping a turd into his hood or pinning little foxtails or hares' ears to his back.

One day when all the theologians had been summoned to the Sorbonne to examine the articles of the faith, he made a tart of garlic, asafoetida, galbanum, castoreum and steaming excrement, which he steeped and tempered in the corrupt manner of chancres and pockbiles. Very early in the morning he so theologically greased and anointed the lattices and grates of the trellised gallery of the Hall of Records that not even the devil himself had dared stay there. The worthy pedagogues pewked in public as abundantly as though they had flayed the fox. Ten or twelve died of the plague, fourteen contracted leprosy, eight came down with pestiferous ulcers, and more than twenty-eight caught the pox. But Panurge was jubilant.

Usually he carried a whip under his gown with which he mercilessly belabored such pages as he met bearing wine for their masters, in order to speed them on their way.

In his coat he had more than twenty-six little pockets and pouches which were always full. One held a pair of loaded dice and a small knife like a glover's awl to cut purses with. Another, verjuice to throw in the eyes of those who annoyed him. A third, burrs, penned with gosling or capon feathers, to stick on to the robes and bonnets of honest people. He often gave married men a fine pair of horns which they bore through the city sometimes all their lives long. To the back of the women's hoods, he liked to affix various knickknacks shaped like the sexual organ of man.

Another pocket held a lot of little packages filled with fleas and lice which he recruited from the tramps at St. Innocent's graveyard and cast with small sticks or quills down the backs of the smartest gentlewomen he could find. He did this even in church, for he never sat up in the choir, preferring to stand in the nave among the women during mass, vespers or sermon. Another pocket held a large supply of bent nails with which he would couple men and women together where they sat. This was particularly amusing when the victims wore gowns of costly sarsenet taffeta, because they ripped them to shreds as they sought to separate. Still another pocket held a squib with tinder, flints, matches, vesuvians, sulphur and other combustibles. Another, two or three burning-glasses with which he tortured and disconcerted men and women at church. For he said there was only an antistrophe between *femme folle à la messe* and *molle à la fesse* or working a cunning stunt and a stunning cunt. Another pouch held needles, threads and pins for all manner of minor deviltries.

Once at the door of the Great Hall in the Palais de Justice, Panurge saw a Cordelier father getting ready to say mass before the proceedings of the day. Immediately he ran up to help the holy man don his vestments and, in the process, managed to sew his alb to his robe and shirt. Then, as the magistrates arrived for mass, Panurge withdrew. Mass done, as he reached the formula *Ite, missa est*, the wretched friar tried to take off his alb. But, at the same time, off came the robe and shirt solidly sewn to it. Our Cordelier, thus stripped to the shoulders, revealed his dangledingus to all the world—and it was no small crosier, as you may imagine. The harder he tugged, the more he exposed himself. So much so, indeed, that one of the counsellors cried:

"What is the matter? Is this good friar making an offering of his tail for us to kiss? No, by heaven, let St. Anthony's fire kiss it for us!"

From then on, an ordinance forbade the poor good fathers to disrobe before the world, the vestry-room being indicated as the only fit place for this. They were especially warned against doing so in the presence of women, lest it tempt the latter to sin through longing.

When people wondered why the fathers were genitally so well-equipped, Panurge solved the problem.

"What makes the ears of asses so long?" he asked, and answering his own question: "Their dams put no caps on their ears. Alliacus, Chancellor of the University and Chaplain to Charles VI, proves this in his *Suppositiones*. Similarly, what makes the whangletools of our holy fathers hang so low? Well, they never wear dark breeches, so their lusty organs, dangling down at liberty like a horse given head, knock against their knees like women's beads. Why are they correspondingly large? Because, with all this waggling to and fro, the humors of the body sink down into these parts. Do not the legists point out that continual agitation and continual motion are the cause of attraction?"

Another of Panurge's pouches held stone-alum, an itching-powder which he poured down the backs of those he considered the proudest and most stately ladies. Some would at once strip off their clothes then and there before the public . . . others danced like cats on hot coals or a drumstick on a tabor . . . others again rushed madly into the street and he at their heels. . . . Those inclined to disrobe, he assisted by sheltering them under his cape, as any courteous and gallant gentleman would have done.

In another pocket he had a small leather bottle full of old oil. If he saw a man or woman in a handsome costume, he would grease and stain it in the most conspicuous places. His technique here was an art. Pretending to admire the material, he would finger it.

"Rare cloth, this, sir," or "Fine satin, upon my word!" or "Oh, what lovely taffeta, Madame!" he would exclaim. "God give you all your noble heart desires. You have a new suit, My Lord! And you a new dress, My Lady. Well, you know the saying: New clothes, new friends. God give you joy in them!"

As he spoke, his hands passed lightly over the shoulders and a long ugly smear remained

> *So indelible a spot*
> *Stamped on body, soul and fame*
> *That the devil could not blot*
> *Out its testament of shame.*

As he took his leave of the ladies, he would say:

"Madame, take care not to fall. You've a huge filthy hole out of sight in front of you, there!"

In another pocket he kept euphorbium, very finely pulverized and spread over a dainty handkerchief he had stolen from a pretty salesgirl in the Galleries of the Sainte-Chapelle, hard by the law courts and frequented by the gallants of the day. (He filched it while removing from between her breasts a louse he had dropped there.)

When he happened to be in gentle company, he would steer the conversation on to the subject of lace and lingerie. Then, thrusting his hands into some lady's bosom:

"Glorious work, this. Is it Flanders or Hainault?"

Then, drawing his handkerchief:

"Just look at this kerchief, Madame. Would you say it was Frontignan or Fontarabia?"

Shaking it hard under her nose, he would make her sneeze for hours at a time. Then he would fart like a dray horse.

"Tut, tut," the lady would say. "Are you whiffling, Panurge?"

"No, Madame," he would reply gallantly, "I am merely tuning my tail to the plain song you make with your nose."

Panurge was never without pincers, a picklock, a pelican, a jimmy, a crook or other tools against which no chest or door could avail. Finally, in another pocket he kept a whole battery of small goblets which he worked with amazing skill, for his fingers were nimble and adroit as those of Minerva or Arachne. He had indeed once been an itinerant quack, barking antidotes for poison. When he presented a sum of money and asked for change, the changer had to be spry as Argus to catch Panurge spiriting away five, six or seven coins at a time, visibly, openly, manifestly, without lesion or hurt, whilst all the changer noticed was a slight draught.

XVII

HOW PANURGE WON INDULGENCES, HOW HE MARRIED OFF VARIOUS OLD WOMEN, AND HOW HE FOUGHT SEVERAL LAWSUITS IN PARIS

ONE day I found Panurge silent and sullen. Suspecting he was penniless, I said:

"Panurge, I can see by your face that you are sick. I know your trouble: you've a flux in your purse. Don't worry, old fellow. Like Pathelin I've still:

> *Four coins of one kind, five of the other*
> *Changelings, bereft of both father and*
> *mother.*

Do you need them? They're yours to acquire as readily as the pox."

"A turd for money!" he exclaimed. "I'll be rolling in wealth some day. For I've a philosopher's stone which draws money out of men's purses as surely as a magnet draws steel. By the way, how about coming along to gain a few pardons?"

"I'm no great hand at pardons in this world," I said. "And I'm not so sure I shall be in the next. But let us go, in God's name, for one pardon, if it costs no more than one penny."

"Fine! You lend me a penny at interest," said Panurge.

"No, no, I'll give it to you gladly."

"*Grates vobis dominos*, thank you, My Lord!"

We began with St. Gervais where I stopped at the first box, gave my alms, received my pardon and cried quits. (I am easily satisfied in such matters.) I was saying a few prayers to St. Bridget before the image of Christ when I noticed Panurge stopping at every box and always handing money to the pardoners.

From St. Gervais we proceeded successively to Notre Dame, to St. Jean, to St. Antoine and to all the other churches that had cashier's desks for trading in pardons. I myself acquired no more, but Panurge kissed the relics at every box and everywhere paid the piper (I mean the pardoner!). To be brief, on our way home he stood me to a drink at the Taverne du Château, and there showed me ten or twelve of his little pouches, cram-full of cash. I crossed myself.

"Where on earth did you find all that money in so short a time?" I asked.

"Where else but in the collection plates?" he answered. "When I gave them my first penny, I laid it down so neatly that it looked like three-pence. So with one hand, I took up three, six, ninepence, indeed, a shilling or even two; while with the other, I raked in as much again. So it went, in all the churches we visited."

"But Panurge, you've damned yourself for a sacrilegious thief."

"I suppose it seems so to you. But *I* don't look at it like that: I consider this money a gift from the pardoners. When they presented the relics to me, did they say '*Centuplium accipies!*' or not? Does that mean that for one penny I shall have one hundred, or not? *Accipies* is the future: it means thou shalt have. Well, the Hebrews always used the future tense to denote the imperative as in the law *Dominum Deum tuum adorabis et illi soli servies; diliges præmium tuum et sic de aliis*, Thou shalt adore thy God and serve Him only; thou shalt take thy reward, and thy fellows, likewise. Thus when the pardoner says '*Centuplium accipies*, thou shalt have one hundred' he means '*Centuplium accipe*, have a hundred.' Rabbi Kimchi, the learned Jew of Narbonne, and Rabbi Aben Ezra, the celebrated Spaniard, both expound this principle *et ibi Bartolus*, Bartolo too!

"What's more, Pope Sixtus IV granted me a yearly pension of fifteen hundred francs from his ecclesiastical revenues and treasure when I cured him of a chancrous swelling. It had tortured him so cruelly he feared he would remain a cripple for the rest of his days. Thus I am paying myself my due out of the ecclesiastical treasure with my own hands, since others will not.

"Ha, my good friend," Panurge went on, "you would be dumbfounded if I told you how nicely I feathered my nest during the Mytilene Crusade. Why, I netted more than six thousand florins cash!"

"What ever has become of them?" I asked incredulously. "You haven't a sou to your name now."

"They went where they came from," he told me. "They simply changed hands. But I used up a good three thousand marrying off women. Not girls, you understand, they come all too easily by a husband. No, I married off ancient hags, horrible old sempiternal trots without a tooth in their heads.

"I figured it this way: 'These superannuated harridans spent their youth to advantage, thigh-squeezing and buttock-clenching with their arses cocked for all comers,' I said. 'In the course of time, no one would have traffic with them any more. Well, by God, I intend to treat them to one more branglebump before they die.'

"So I gave one a dowry of one hundred florins, another one hundred and twenty, a third three hundred, briefly, a sum always proportional to their degree of infamy, horror and repulsion. There were others who had to be still more heavily endowed or even the devil himself would have forborne to scrobiculate them. Then I sought out some strapping hodcarrier or some thumping colossus of a stevedore and performed the marriage myself.

"But before showing him his hag, I flashed the money before him, saying: 'This is yours, lad, if you'll undertake to pull off one good tailrasping bumswink.' Poor devils, they gaped like old mules. So I made careful preparations, served them a fine meal with the best of wine and heady spices to put the old witches in rut and heat. In the end, they buckled to, like all good Christian souls. When the belles were too horribly ugly and mouldering, I had them put their heads in a sack to hide their faces. . . .

"I have also lost a good deal of money in lawsuits."

"What lawsuits can *you* have had?" I asked. "You own no house or lands."

"True, but I had suits aplenty. Inspired by the devil, the ladies of this city invented a sort of high-mounted neckpiece, closed in front and slit behind; it covered their breasts so completely that a wretched man couldn't slip his hands under for love or money. You can imagine how their poor, contemplative lovers grieved. Well, one fine Tuesday, I presented a petition to the Court making myself a party against these ladies. I established the great interest I laid claim to in the matter, and I protested that, by the same process, I would have the fly of my trousers sewn over my bum unless the Court acted immediately.

"The ladies for their part, formed an association for their common defense, drew up their *fundamenta* (I mean basic arguments, of course) and appointed an attorney to represent them. However, I pursued them so vigorously that a decree of the Court abolished these horse-collars unless they were also openable in front. But it cost me a pile of money.

"I had another lawsuit, too. A very nasty business it was. This time I attacked Master Fiefaugh, the city dung-farmer and scavenger. I petitioned the Court that neither he nor his deputies be allowed to mull over the *Pipes of Pan* or the mountains of *Sentences* by night, but, on the contrary, they should peruse these in broad daylight in the schools of the Sorbonne and in the presence of the theologians. I was condemned to costs through the mistaking of some minor clause in the sergeant's evidence.

"Another time I complained to the Court against the mules of the magistrates, counsellors and other officers of the Palais de Justice. I sought to obtain that, when they left these mules to champ on their bridles in the lower courtyard, the beasts be given bibs. Thus they would not cover the pavement with their drivelling and slobbering, and the pages of the Palais might play dice or *Deny Thy God* without dirtying the knees of their breeches. I won a fine decree, but it cost a tidy sum.

"Apropos, guess how much I have to pay for the little banquets I give the pages every day?"

"Banquets? I didn't know you gave them banquets?"

"My poor friend, you get no fun at all out of life!" he sighed. "But I—well, I get more than the king himself. If only you joined me, we could raise a thousand devils!"

"No, no," I protested, "by St. Adauras, I will not. Some day or other, you will be hanged!"

"And you buried! Which is the more honorable, air or earth? Ha, you old dullard, didn't Christ hang aloft?"

"Hm!"

"To get back to my story. As these pages are banqueting, I keep their masters' mules. And I invariably cut the stirrup-leather of one or two mules on the mounting side so it hangs by a thread. When

some great puffbelly of a counsellor takes a swing to mount, he falls
flat as a hog, affording the spectators much more than a hundred
francs' worth of amusement. But I laugh even more as I think how
the minute they reach home they thrash Master Page like green rye.
That amply compensates me for what it costs me to banquet them."

In conclusion, as I said before, Panurge knew thirty-three methods
of acquiring money. But he knew two hundred and fourteen methods of spending it, exclusive of wetting the yawning gulf that spread
below his nostrils.

XVIII

HOW A GREAT SCHOLAR OF ENGLAND SOUGHT TO ARGUE AGAINST PANTAGRUEL AND HOW HE WAS OVERCOME BY PANURGE

ABOUT the same time, an illustrious savant, Thaumastes (the name
signifies a worker of wonders), hearing rumors of Pantagruel's reputation for incomparable knowledge, came from England to meet him
and prove whether his celebrity were justified. Reaching Paris, he
called on Pantagruel at the Hôtel St. Denis. (Situated at the corner
of the Rue St. André-des-Arts and the Rue des Grands-Augustins,
it later became a hostel for students of the Benedictine order.)

Pantagruel was, at the moment, strolling in the garden, philosophizing as the Peripatetics used to do. Seeing his enormous height, the
Englishman trembled with fear; then, recovering his wits, he bowed
courteously and said:

"My Lord, Plato, the prince of philosophers, says: 'Verily if the
image of knowledge and wisdom were corporeal and visible to mortal
eye, it would stir up the admiration of all the world.' Surely this must
be so when the mere rumor of knowledge, scattered in the air, can
haply reach the ears of those men we call philosophers because they

are curious and studious of wisdom? Surely this must be so when, reaching their ears, that mere rumor does not suffer them to sleep or rest in peace, but inspires and fires them to haste towards that mortal in whom Wisdom has established her temple and uttered her oracles. All this has been clearly demonstrated by many examples in the past. The Queen of Sheba came from the furthest borders of the East, from the Persian Sea, to observe the order of Solomon's house and to hear his wisdom. Anacharsis travelled from distant Scythia all the way to Athens to visit Solon. Pythagoras sought out the prophets of Memphis. Plato journeyed to Egypt to interview the magicians and to Tarentum to meet Archytas. Apollonius of Tyana journeyed to the remote Mount Caucasus, tarried among the Scythians, the Massagetes, the Indians, sailed down the great river Pison to reach the land of the Brahmans where he conversed with Hiarches and continued to Babylon, Chaldea, Media, Assyria, Parthia, Syria, Phoenicia, Arabia, Palestine, Alexandria, and even Ethiopia where he consulted the Gymnosophists. Livy, too, is a case in point. Not a few studious persons came from various points in France and Spain to see, hear and question him.

"I dare not include myself among these lofty souls. . . . But I will admit that I am studious and a lover, not of letters only, but of lettered people also. When I heard reports of your wisdom, I left my country, my home, my kinfolk and my friends; I came hither, reckoning as nothing the length of the journey, the discomforts of the sea, the strangeness of this land. I had but one purpose: to see you and confer with you about certain problems in philosophy, geomancy, and occult science about which I am doubtful and cannot find satisfaction. If you can resolve them, I will deliver myself to you as a slave, together with my posterity. (This is the most valuable gift I have at my disposal.) My problems I shall draw up in writing and communicate to all the learned men in town. As soon as this is done, we can discuss them publicly.

"But I would wish us to conduct our argument in a particular way. Let us not proceed *pro* and *contra* like the crackpate theologians. Let us not proceed after the manner of the Academics, by declamation, which is an exercise of oratory rather than debate. Let us not proceed by numbers, as Pythagoras did or as Pico della Mirandola wished to do at Rome. I would prefer to discuss by signs alone,

without speaking a word, for alas! these subjects are too profound
for human words to explain them to my satisfaction. To this effect,
may it please My Lord to be in the great Hall of Navarre to-morrow
morning at seven o'clock."

When he was done, Pantagruel answered civilly:

"Sir, what favors God has given me I could not refuse to share
with any man on earth. No good but comes from Him and He is
pleased to have it increased among men worthy and fit to receive the
heavenly manna of pure knowledge. Because I recognize that you
hold the first rank among such, I am ready, at any hour you wish, to
accede to the best of my poor ability to any request you make.

"Naturally I shall learn more from you than you from me. However, you ask that we confer together concerning your doubts; you
wish us to seek a solution by plunging into that inexhaustible well at
the bottom of which, says Heracles, the truth lies hidden. I commend
the mode of disputation you propose; I welcome signs rather than
words, for I am convinced we shall understand one another thoroughly. Nor shall we be annoyed by the hand-clapping of those
theological blockheads at every conclusive point of an argument.

"Tomorrow, therefore, I shall appear without fail at the appointed place at seven o'clock in the morning. Finally, I must beg
that there be no strife or tumult, since we seek neither honors nor applause but the truth only."

"My Lord," Thaumastes answered, "God keep you ever in His
grace. I thank your highness and magnificence most heartily for
deigning to abase itself to my mediocrity. So, farewell until to-
morrow."

Readers, as you peruse this page, do not believe that any two human beings were ever more elevated or transported in thought than
Thaumastes and Pantagruel that night. In fact Thaumastes confided
to the porter of the Hôtel de Cluny, where, as a distinguished foreign
visitor, he lodged, that never before in his life had he been so dry.

"I much fear Pantagruel has me by the throat!" he said. "Ay, I've
got the Pantagruel! Tell them to bring me wine to drink, I beg you,
and let me have some fresh water to gargle my palate."

Pantagruel, for his part, escaped into the loftiest realms of speculation, spending the whole night conning the Venerable Bede's *Of
Numbers and Signs*, which treats of the expression of thought by

manual movements . . . Plotinus' *Of the Unrelatable*, dealing with neo-Platonic metaphysics . . . Proclus' *Of Sacrifice and Magic* . . . Artemidorus Daldianus' *The Interpretation of Dreams*, which is the source of all modern manuals of fortune telling . . . Anaxagoras' *Of Signs* . . . Dinarius' *Of the Ineffable* . . . the works of Philistion . . . Hipponax's *On the Things that must be passed over in Silence* and a vast quantity of other works. . . .

At last Panurge remonstrated with him:

"Put away all this rubbish, My Lord, and go to bed. I can see you're so excited and wrought up that you'll take some sudden fever from this excess of thinking. Follow my advice: first, drink down twenty-five or thirty hearty draughts of wine; then go to bed and sleep your head off. To-morrow morning, I'll tackle Master Englishman, and if I don't drive him *ad metam non loqui*, to the limits of speech, you can call me an idiot."

"But he's extraordinarily learned, Panurge. How can you answer him?"

"Leave it to me!" Panurge answered. "Is any man as learned as the devils?"

"Certainly not, save by the special grace of God."

"Well, every time I've debated with the devils," Panurge declared, "I've floored them and turned them scut over head. Don't you worry: I'll have that Englishman evacuating vinegar before the public."

Panurge then spent the night tippling and staking the last point on his breeches at *Primus et Secundus*, a game like Tiddlywinks and *Vergette* or Top Rod. But he did not fail to escort his master to the appointed place in ample time.

You may be sure the hall was filled, for neither great nor small in Paris but thought:

"That devil of a Pantagruel confounded and overthrew all the jobbernowl theologians, the addlepated Sorbonne theorists! But he's met his match now: that Englishman's a devil of a fellow! We shall see what we shall see!"

When all were assembled, Thaumastes stood waiting for Pantagruel and Panurge; as the three entered the hall, the professors, Masters of Arts and students burst into applause according to their absurd custom. Pantagruel, in a voice loud as the report of a double cannon, shouted:

"Peace, peace, in the devil's name. Peace, by God, you rascals, or if you go on bothering me, I'll cut your heads from your shoulders!"

At which they sat there, struck of a heap and blinking like owls. Had they swallowed fifteen pounds of feathers, they would not have dared cough. The mere sound of his voice so parched their throats that their tongues hung a half-foot out of their mugs. It was as though Pantagruel had salted their throats.

Panurge then addressed the Englishman:

"Sir, have you come here to dispute contentiously the propositions you put forward, or to learn the truth?"

"Sir," Thaumastes replied, "one thing alone brings me here: my longing to discover the truth about matters that have puzzled me my whole life long. To the problems I now proffer, I never yet found a satisfactory solution in book or scholar. As for contentiously disputing anything, I will not do it. It is a wretched waste of time which I abandon to those sottish sophisters, sorbillants, sorbonagres, sorbonigenes, sorbonicoles, sorboniforms, sorbonisecs, niborcisants, sorbonisants, saniborsants, sorbonnets, sorbonzes and sorbondsmen who, in their discussions, seek not the truth but only contradiction and debate."

"Sir," said Panurge, "I am but a humble disciple of Pantagruel, my master. Yet if I can give you satisfaction on all these points, it would be a slight upon my master's eminence to trouble him therewith, would it not? It is fitter, therefore, that he take the chair and sit as judge and moderator of our theses, and, furthermore, give you satisfaction on those particulars in which I fail to measure up to your expectations."

"That will be perfectly satisfactory," Thaumastes agreed. "Proceed, sir."

Here I must beg you to note that Panurge had affixed to the end of his elongated codpiece a rich tuft of red, white, green and blue silk. He had also put a fat orange in his pocket.

XIX

HOW PANURGE NONPLUSSED THE ENGLISHMAN WHO ARGUED BY SIGNS

THE audience watched breathlessly.

The Englishman raised one hand, then the other, clinching his fingertips together to form the figure we of the Chinon country call the hen's arse. Next, he clapped the nails of one hand over the other four times. Next, he opened out his palms and smacked them sonorously together once. Linking his hands again in the figure described above, he struck twice; then, opening them out again, four times. This done, he joined his hands in an attitude of prayer.

Panurge suddenly shot his right hand up into the air . . . placed his thumb in his nostril . . . held the four fingers extended parallel from the point of his nose . . . closed his left eye completely . . . and winked with the right in such a way as to mark a deep depression of lid and lash. . . . Then he manoeuvred correspondingly with his left hand, there being an interval of about a cubit and a half between hands. Then, in the same position, he lowered one hand after the other to the ground. Finally he flung both out as though aiming straight at the Englishman's nose.

"But if Mercury—" the Englishman cried.

"Mum's the word!" Panurge objected.

The Englishman raised an open left hand, made a fist, placed his thumb on the point of his nose. Then he quickly raised his right hand, open too, to bring it down and link his left little finger with his right thumb, moving the other fingers slowly through the air. He then repeated the operation, the right hand doing what the left hand had done, and conversely.

Panurge betrayed not the slightest astonishment. Drawing out his thrice-great codpiece with his left hand, he picked out of it with his right a stump of a white oxrib and two similarly shaped bits of wood, one ebony, the other red Brazil wood. Holding them between his fingers, he clicked them together like castanets or like the clappers with which the lepers in the Breton colonies warn people of their approach. Panurge's rendering, however, was both more harmonious and finished than the lepers'. Bending his tongue back against the roof of his mouth, he began chirruping most merrily, his eyes fastened upon the Englishman.

The theologians, physicians and surgeons were convinced that Panurge meant the Englishman was riddled with leprosy. The counsellors, jurisconsults and decretalists were certain he sought to convey that leprosy possessed some mysterious form of human felicity, as Our Lord had once maintained.

The Englishman, nothing daunted, held his hands aloft, closing the three major fingers in his fist and passed his thumbs through index and middle finger. He paused a moment, then presented this figure for Panurge's inspection. Then he joined his hands so that thumbs and little fingers met.

Panurge, without uttering a word, put the nail of his left forefinger to that of his left thumb, forming a buckle-shaped hollow. Closing all the fingers of his right—save the index—in his fist, he held that index stiffly forward and kept pushing it vigorously into the buckle described above and pulling it as vigorously out, with quick, deep, staccato thrusts. Next, he extended his right index and middle finger, stretching them as far apart as he could and directing them accusingly at Thaumastes. After, he placed his left thumb on the corner of his left eye, spreading his hand like the wing of a bird or like the fin of a fish, moving it most gracefully this way and that. He repeated the gesture, conversely, with his right hand.

Thaumastes grew pale . . . trembled. . . . With a quavering right hand, he struck his middle finger against the muscle of the palm, a little above the thumb. Then he placed his right index finger into the buckle so made, but he thrust it under, not over, as Panurge had done.

Panurge then clapped his hands and blew into his palm. This done, he once more brought his right index into the buckle-shaped orifice made by his left, with the same jiggling in and out as before. Then he thrust out his chin and stared at Thaumastes.

The audience, which knew nothing about all these signs, at

least understood quite clearly that Panurge was asking Thaumastes: "What do you mean by that?"

In effect, Thaumastes began to sweat like a horse. Great beads of perspiration stood out on his wan brow. He looked like a man wonderfully, strangely rapt in august contemplation. Recovering his presence of mind, he put all the nails of his left against those of his right, opening his fingers in semicircles and holding his hands as high as he possibly could.

With lightning speed, Panurge set his right thumb under his jaw and his little finger in the buckle of his left hand. Holding this stance, he made his teeth rattle together very melodiously, the upper against the lower.

Thaumastes, though exhausted, rose panting. But, in rising, he let a great fart—a waiter's fart, for the stew followed. And he piddled strong vinegar. The fellow stank like all the devils of hell. A moment after, the audience began holding their noses, for Thaumastes was bemucking himself with sheer anguish.

All the same, he raised his right hand, bringing the tips of its fingers together. And laid his left flat on his chest.

Panurge replied by pulling out his long codpiece with its multicolored tuft, stretching it about a cubit and a half, then holding it in the air with his left hand. With his right, he seized his orange, tossed it up in the air seven times, and, at the seventh, hid it in his right fist. Here he held it motionless, then began shaking it before Thaumastes. The latter, his cheeks puffed out like a bagpiper's, blew as though he were inflating a pig's bladder. So Panurge placed one finger on his left hand in his anus, while he sucked in the air with the sound a man makes when he eats oysters in the shell or when he sips soup. Next, he opened his mouth a little and clapped his right hand down on it, making a resonant, loud sound that seemed to emerge from the depths of the diaphragm up through his windpipe. He repeated this noise sixteen times.

Thaumastes kept blowing like a goose. So Panurge put his right forefinger into his mouth, pressed it very hard against the oral muscles and drew it back sharply, making a noise like a child shooting off a pop-gun. He did this nine times in succession.

"Gentlemen, gentlemen, the great secret!" Thaumastes shouted. "He's up to the elbows in it!"

And he drew a dagger which he held point down. Panurge, in turn, pulled out his long codpiece and shook it violently against his thighs. Then he placed his hands in the form of a comb and laid them on his head, pulling his tongue out as far as possible and rolling his eyes like a dying goat.

"Ah, I understand," cried Thaumastes. "But what?"

So saying he pressed the handle of his dagger against his chest and the flat of his hand against its point, turning the tips of his fingers inward.

Panurge bowed his head to the left, buried his middle finger in his right ear and raised his thumb . . . crossed his arms over his breast and coughed five times in succession. . . . At the fifth cough, he stamped his right foot on the ground, raised his left arm, and, closing his fist, held the thumb against his forehead, striking his breast six times with his right hand.

As though not yet utterly satisfied, Thaumastes put his left thumb to the tip of his nose, closing the other fingers in his fist. Panurge put his two forefingers on either side of his mouth, drew it out as far as he could, exposing all his teeth; with his thumbs, he lowered his pupils. It was, the audience agreed, a most unpleasant sight.

XX

HOW THAUMASTES PRO- CLAIMED THE VIRTUES AND KNOWLEDGE OF PANURGE

THAUMASTES rose. Doffing his doctoral bonnet, he thanked Panurge under his breath, then in a loud voice addressed the audience:

"Gentlemen, this is a fitting time to cite the words of the Gospel: '*Et ecce plusquam Salomon hic*, And behold, a greater than Solomon is here!' Ay, gentlemen, you have in your midst a nonpareil treasure. I refer to Monsieur Pantagruel. Rumor of his fame drew me out of the depths of England to journey hither and confer with him upon certain insoluble problems—of magic, alchemy, cabbalistics, geomancy, astrology and philosophy—problems that would give me no peace. Well, sirs, now I resent his reputation, because it has proved, as it were, jealous of him: it reports only one thousandth part of what is really his.

"You have watched his mere disciple give me satisfaction and, indeed, tell me more than I had asked for. Better, he indicated and solved further inestimable doubts for me. Again, I swear he discovered, for my benefit, the true source, well and abyss of the encyclopedia of learning. And he did so incomparably. Truly, I never dreamed I could find a human being capable of grasping the rudiments of Monsieur Panurge's reasoning—I refer to our discussion by signs, when not one word, indeed not a half-word, passed our lips. But I intend at a future time to put our theses and solutions in writing so that none dare suspect it was a hoax or a piece of tomfoolery. And I shall print my findings so that all may learn as I learned.

"Imagine what the master could have done when the disciple has achieved such an eminent feat. For *non est discipulus super magistrum*, the disciple is not above his master. At all events, God be praised and magnified forever! And you, gentlemen of the audience, I thank you from the depths of my heart for the honor you have done us. May the Lord repay you for it eternally!"

Pantagruel in turn thanked the spectators, and took Thaumastes off to dinner with him. You may be certain they drank at top speed as all good Christians on All Souls' Day, ay, with belly unbuttoned, as the phrase goes—for in those days they fastened their bellies with buttons as we now fasten the collars of our doublets. On they bibbed and caroused, till they had not the foggiest notion of whether they were coming or going. Blessed Lady! how they spliced the main brace! And the flagons trotting every which way, and they bawling:

"Page, draw, wine ho!"

"Pour, by the devil, pour."

"Here, boy! wine for me!"

"Wine, wine. . . ."

Never a one of the company but consumed at least twenty-five or thirty hogsheads. Do you know how? *Sicut terra sine aqua*, like earth without water, for the weather was hot. Besides, they were very dry.

As for the theses propounded by Thaumastes and the meaning of the signs exchanged, I would gladly explain them. But I am told

Thaumastes has written and published in London a voluminous tome
in which he exhausts the subject, omitting not the minutest detail.
For the nonce, I therefore take no note of the matter.

XXI

HOW PANURGE FELL IN LOVE
WITH A PARISIENNE OF
HIGH DEGREE

As a result of his debate with the English scholar, Panurge had acquired quite a reputation in Paris. The activity of his codpiece was
proportionally greater, and, to that effect, he had it pinked and
slashed with ornate embroidery, after the Roman fashion. His praises
became a topic of general conversation. There was even a song written to celebrate his exploits; the little children sang it as they went
to fetch mustard. Best of all, he was made welcome in the most elegant circles. But it went to his head; he actually had the presumption
to beleaguer one of the great ladies of the city.

Scorning the rigmarole of prefaces and preliminaries dear to such
languishing, dreamy lovers as never touch meat in Lent, Panurge
popped the question outright.

"Madame," he told this lofty lady, "it would prove beneficent to
the commonwealth, pleasurable to your person, honorable to your
progeny and necessary to me that I cover you for the propagation
of my race. You may take my word for this, Madame; experience
will prove it to you conclusively."

The lady, indignant, thrust him a thousand leagues away.

"You crazy knave, how dare you talk like that? Who do you think
I am? Get out of here at once and never let me lay eyes upon you
again. For two pins, I'd have your arms and legs sawed off!"

"Madame," he protested, "I would not care two pins if my arms
and legs were sawed off, providing you and I had first fought a merry
bout of spermary-snuggery. For," he showed her his long codpiece,
"here is Master Johnny Inigo, a master instrumentalist who begs to

fiddle and thrum, sweep the *viola d'amore*, play the manichord, tweedle the gittern, strike the lyre, beat the drum, wind the horn and grind the organ until you feel his music throbbing in the marrow of your bones. A wily gallant, Master Johnny: he will not fail to find all the cranks, winches, wedges, pullies, nippers, clutches, teeth, springs and rigging stored in your delicate cockpit. You'll be needing no scouring or brushing up after *him*."

"Go to, scoundrel, and away! One more word out of you and I'll shout for help; I'll have my servants beat you to death."

"No, Madame," Panurge protested. "You are not as cruel as you pretend. You cannot be or else your face is a living lie. Let earth soar upward into the firmament, let high heaven sink into the bottomless pit, let the whole concert of nature be annihilated ere your beauty and grace secrete one drop of gall or malice. They say that it is virtually impossible for man:

> *To find in women beauty unallied*
> *With arrogance or cruelty or pride*

but that holds only for vulgar beauties. Your own is so priceless, so unique, so heavenly that I vow Nature has bestowed it on you as a paragon to prove what she can do when she cares to muster all her power and science. Everything in you is honey, sugar, celestial manna. To you Paris should have awarded the golden apple, not to Venus or Juno or Minerva. For Juno possessed no such nobility, Minerva no such wisdom, Venus no such comeliness.

"O ye heavenly gods and goddesses! how happy the man whom you allow to kiss and fondle you, to cosset, nuzzle and cockle you, to thrust his prolific engine of pleasure into the pod of your quivering quim. By God, I am that man, I plainly feel it. Already she loves me her bellyful I swear; ay, Panurge is predestined to it by the nixies and fairies. Let us lose no time: come, slap-dash, helter-skelter, holus-bolus, to horse and fair riding, tantivy, hoicks!"

Whereupon he sought to embrace her; but she moved towards the window as if to call for help, so Panurge made off hastily. Yet ere retreating:

"Madame," he said, "wait for me here; I'll call your friends, don't bother!"

And he withdrew, unfeased and no less cheerful despite the rebuff.

Next day, as she arrived at church, Panurge stood waiting at the door, offered her holy water, bowed deep as she passed, then kneeled familiarly beside her:

"Madame," he declared, "you must know how madly in love with you I am. Why, I can neither piddle nor cack for love of you! I don't know how *you* feel, but, Madame, suppose I took ill from it, wouldn't you be responsible?"

"Go away, I don't care anything about it. Leave me alone to my prayers."

"One moment!" Panurge begged. "Please equivocate on '*à Beaumont le Viconte*?' or on 'Runt and Codger are fellow-muckers!' "

"I don't know what you mean!"

"Quite easy! '*A beau con le vit monte*,' 'Cunt and Rodger are mellow fuckers!' Now, pray to God that He grant whatever your noble heart desires. And oh, Madame, I beg you: give me those beads a moment."

"Here you are, stop bothering me."

She was about to take off her rosary—it was of cestrin wood with gold ornamentation—when Panurge promptly drew one of his knives and neatly cut it. Before carrying it off to pawn:

"Would you like my knife?" he asked.

"No, certainly not!"

"It's yours to grind or sheathe, Madame, body and soul, bag and baggage, tripe and guts."

But the lady was worried over the loss of her beads, so many implements to help her keep her countenance in church:

"This chattering scoundrel must be some eccentric foreigner," she mused. "He will never return my rosary. What will my dear husband say? He'll be furious! But I'll tell him a sneak thief cut it off me at church. He must believe me: I've still the end fastened on my girdle."

After dinner, Panurge went to call on her with, in his sleeve, a purse full of tokens specially struck for use in the law courts.

"Which of us is the better lover, Madame, you or I?"

"For my part I cannot hate you," she said magnanimously. "God commands us to love our neighbors."

"Aren't you in love with me?"

"I've told you repeatedly not to talk to me like that!" she insisted.

"If you mention it again, I'll show you I'm not to be trifled with. Go away, I tell you. But give me back my rosary; my husband might ask me for it."

"Give you back your rosary? No, by heaven, I shall do nothing of the sort. But I'll tell you what I *will* do: I'll gladly give you another. Would you like one in beautifully enamelled gold with beads shaped like great pendulous knockers? Or like loveknots or ingots, heavy in the hand? Or ebony or broad zircons or square-cut garnets with mountings of rare turquoises, or costly topazes or priceless sapphires or precious rubies set with glittering diamonds of twenty-eight facets? No, no, that is a trumpery gift. I know of a marvellous rosary: it's made of exquisite emeralds with a mounting of speckled gray amber; at the buckle there's a Persian pearl fat as an orange . . . and the bauble costs but a paltry five-and-twenty thousand ducats. I will make you a present of it; I've heaps of cash!"

He made his tokens ring as though they were genuine, authentic golden crowns with the shining sun of France stamped upon them.

"Do you fancy a piece of violet or crimson velure, dyed in grain, or a piece of scarlet or brocaded satin? Is it your pleasure to accept chains, brooches, tiaras or rings? You have but to say the word: fifty thousand is a trifle!"

His offer made her mouth water. Yet she stood her ground.

"No, thank you, I want nothing to do with you."

"By God, I certainly want to do something with *you*! What I want will cost you nothing; you'll be out nothing when you've given it. Look, Madame," and he showed her his long codpiece. "Here is Master Johnny Scramblecunney who craves lodging."

He was about to strike root there, when she started to cry out, though none too loud. The mask of courtesy fell from Panurge's face.

"So you won't let me have a little harmless fun, eh? Not even a morsel for me, eh? A bucket of turds to you! you don't deserve the honor or pleasure of it. But by God! I'll make the dogs ride you!"

With which he beat a hasty retreat in dread of blows. (He was by nature fearful of them.)

XXII

HOW PANURGE PLAYED A NONE TOO PLEASANT TRICK ON THE PARISIENNE OF HIGH DEGREE

NEXT day was Corpus Christi, a feast on which the ladies of Paris put on their stateliest apparel. Panurge's charmer was decked out in a rich gown of crimson velvet, with a skirt of costly white velure.

The day before, Panurge scoured the town for a bitch in heat. Having found one, he tied his belt around her neck and took her home. All that day and through the night, he fed her abundantly; in the morning he killed her, plucked out that part the Greek geomancians know, cut it as fine as he could, tucked it away in one of his innumerable pockets and went to the church. He was sure his lady would soon arrive to take part in the procession always held on that day.

When she entered, Panurge bowed courteously, offered her some holy water and, shortly after she had finished her petty devotions, sat down on the bench beside her. As she looked up, he passed her a paper on which he had written the following rondeau:

> *Sweet lady, once, once only I expressed*
> *My admiration; you denied my quest,*
> *You drove me irremediably away*
> *Although I never harmed you (welladay!)*
> *In act or word or libel or the rest. . . .*
> *Granted my wooing stirred no answering zest,*
> *You could have been more honest, and confessed:*
> *"I do not wish it, friend. Leave me, I pray!"*
> > *Sweet lady, once,*
> *Once more and never again I shall protest*
> *Ere love's flame utterly consume my breast,*

One boon alone I languish for: to lay
My peacock, shoveller, cockerel, popinjay
Deep in the shelter of your downy nest.
Sweet lady, once!

While she was unfolding the paper to see what was inside, Panurge deftly sprinkled his drug all over her, spilling it impartially in the folds of her sleeves and skirt.

"Madame," he said before taking his leave, "a lover's life is not always a bed of roses. In my case I can only hope the anguished nights, the sorrows and tribulation I undergo for love of you will be deducted from my trials in purgatory. At least pray God He give me patience to bear my affliction."

Panurge had scarcely spoken when all the dogs in the church, attracted by the odor of the drug, scurried over to the lady. Big and little, large and small, one and all came up, sniffed, raised their legs, cocked their members and let fly on her dress. It was the most horrible sight imaginable.

Panurge pretended to chase them off, then bowed and retired to watch the sport from the vantage point of a chapel. Those wretched curs were squirting all over her clothes. One huge greyhound placed a paw on her shoulder to aim at her head . . . other dogs pumped in her sleeves . . . still others drenched her backside, while the puppies piddled in her shoes. . . . The women close to her sought to keep the beasts off, but with scant success. Meanwhile, holding his sides, Panurge, between guffaws of laughter, told certain lords who were next to him:

"I think that lady's in heat. Or some wolfhound covered her recently."

Seeing the dogs crowded as thick about her as about a bitch in heat, he ran off to fetch Pantagruel. On the way, he stopped to kick every dog he met, crying:

"To church with you! To your genuflexions! Follow the odor of sanctity! Be off and join your fellows at the urinarian baptism! Forward, by all the devils, be off, devil take you!"

"Master," he said breathlessly to Pantagruel, "please come and see all the dogs of the country gathered about the loveliest lady in town, and every one of them agog to scrounge her!"

Pantagruel, delighted at the novelty of it, accompanied Panurge back to church and enjoyed the fun immensely. By the time the procession began, matters had reached a crisis. There were more than six hundred thousand and fourteen dogs thronging about her and finding one thousand and one means of harassing her. Whichever way she turned, the newcomers followed the scent, dogged her heels and flooded whatever spot her dress touched. The only course left her was to go home. As she fled through the streets, every one stopped to watch the dogs leaping high as her neck, turning her elegant toilette into a very toilet, as she ran on, helpless and steaming. It was impossible to give them the slip, the trail was too pungent. So they followed her to her residence.

While she hid in her room and her chambermaids burst into laughter behind politely raised aprons, all the dogs within a radius of a half-league came rushing up and showered so hard against the gate as to form a stream in which ducks might very well have swum. To-day this same current, now called the creek of Bièvre, flows through the grounds of the Abbey of St. Victor and past the Gobelin dye-works. Materials steeped in its waters turn a rare scarlet thanks to some special virtue of these pissdogs, as our learned Master Doribus recently pointed out in a brilliant sermon. God help us, a mill could have ground corn there, though not so much as the famous Bazacle in Toulouse on the Garonne.

XXIII

HOW NEWS CAME THAT THE DIPSODES WERE INVADING THE LAND OF THE AMAUROTES, HOW PANTAGRUEL LEFT PARIS, AND WHY LEAGUES ARE SO SHORT IN FRANCE

A LITTLE while after, Pantagruel learned that, like Ogier the Dane and King Arthur of the Round Table, his father Gargantua had been translated to Fairyland by Morgan the Fay. News of this translation having spread, the Dipsodes had marched over the border, invaded a large portion of Utopia and were now besieging the great city of the Amaurotes. Pantagruel, realizing that speed was essential, did not stop to take leave of anyone, but sped posthaste to Rouen. With him went Panurge, Epistemon, Eusthenes and Carpalim.

As they hastened along the road, it occurred to Pantagruel that the leagues in France proper, as compared with lands like Normandy, Burgundy or Provence, were extraordinarily short. When he asked Panurge the reason for it, the latter told him a story which the monk Marotus du Lac relates in his *Acts of the Kings of Canarra*.

In the days of yore, apparently, space was not reckoned in leagues, miles, furlongs or parasangs. It was King Pharamond the Merovingian who inaugurated this reform in the following manner.

Choosing one hundred handsome, lusty, muscular Parisian youths and one hundred buxom Picardy wenches, he had them well nourished and entertained for a week. Then, assembling them, he paired off one wench with each lad, provided them with plenty of money for their expenses, and dispatched them to fivescore picked places in Europe. Wherever the lads stopped to larrup the wenches, they were told to lay down a stone, which would mark off a distance of one league.

Very gaily they set out on their errand of business and pleasure. At first, while they were still sprightly and fresh, they straddled and strummed at every other field. That is why the leagues around Paris are so short. But after they had gone a long way and the poor devils were exhausted, there was almost no oil left in their lamps, so they scut-scuffled less often, content (I speak of the men) with one paltry, fly-bitten brabble per day. That is why the leagues in Brittany, in Gascony, in Germany and elsewhere, are so long.

"Various historians give other reasons," Panurge concluded. "But I find this one the most convincing."

In which Pantagruel heartily concurred.

From Rouen, they hurried to Honfleur, where they embarked. As they caulked their ship and awaited a favorable wind, Pantagruel received a letter from a lady in Paris whom he had kept for a long time. The letter was addressed on the outside:

To the best cherished by the fair
To the least loyal of the brave
P. N. T. G. R. L.

XXIV

OF THE LETTER A MESSENGER BROUGHT TO PANTAGRUEL FROM A LADY IN PARIS AND THE EXPLANATION OF A PHRASE ENGRAVED ON A GOLDEN RING

PANTAGRUEL, much surprised at the inscription, asked the messenger who had sent the letter. Opening it, he found nothing whatever inside save a golden ring with a square flat-topped diamond. Panurge opined that, though the paper was blank, it had probably been written upon with invisible ink. So he proceeded to hold it close to the fire to see if the lady had used a solution of sal ammoniac steeped in water. Next he dipped it in water to see if she had used sugar of tithymales, a species of euphorbium. Next, suspecting it might be the juice of a white onion, he held it against a candle. Successively, he tested it for the lye of a fig tree by rubbing one part of it with oil of nuts . . . for the blood of a venomous toad by applying the milk of a woman suckling her firstborn daughter . . . for the dew found in *pomae Alicacabutae* or winter cherries, by rubbing one corner with the ashes of a swallow's nest . . . for the gall of a raven by applying earwax . . . for the acrid milk of a spurge by soaking it in vinegar . . . for whalesperm or ambergris by greasing it with the lard of a bat . . . for alum of lead by passing it evenly across a basin of cold water and very abruptly drawing it out. . . .

Completely baffled, he summoned the messenger:

"My friend, did the lady who sent you here give you a staff to bring too?"

When the varlet gave a negative answer, Panurge wanted to have his head shaved to find out if the lady had written her message with whortleberry juice on his scalp. But noticing how long his hair was, Panurge abandoned the idea. Obviously hair could not grow to such length in so short a time.

"God's belly, master, I'm stumped!" he told Pantagruel. "I've used most of the methods recommended by Master Francesco de Nianto, the Tuscan, an authority on how to decipher invisible letters, by Zoroaster in *Of Undistinguishable Letters*, by Calphurnius Bassus in *Concerning Illegible Script*. All I can think of is the ring: let's have a look at that."

Examining it carefully, they found a Hebrew inscription engraved within: *Lamah sabacthani*, which, Epistemon informed them, meant, "Why hast thou forsaken me?"

Suddenly Panurge uttered a cry of triumph.

"I understand the whole business," he said. "See that diamond? It is a false one. The lady's a punster: for '*diamant faux*' read '*dis, amant faux*.' Her message is: 'Say, false lover, why hast thou forsaken me?'"

Pantagruel, much depressed, recalled how he had neglected to bid the lady farewell, and would willingly have returned to Paris to make his peace with her. But Epistemon cited Æneas' separation from Dido, and a maxim from Heraclides of Tarentum to the effect that, when the ship rides at anchor and departure is urgent, we must cut the cable rather than waste time untying it. To deliver his native place from the danger threatening it, Epistemon concluded, should be Pantagruel's sole concern.

An hour later a northwester rose; hoisting sail, they put out for the open sea. Within a few days they passed Porto-Santo, in the archipelago of the Madeiras, and went ashore in the Canary Islands. Then they set sail again, proceeding past Capo Blanco, a promontory on the west coast of Africa, Senegal, Capo Verde, the river Gambia, Sagres, a cape on the Liberian coast, Melli, a land in the same region, and the Cape of Good Hope. They paused a little while at Malinda, a city of Zanzibar where Vasco de Gama had tarried, then sped past Meden, Uti, Uden, Nihil, Nichts and Niente to Gelasim or Risibilis, coasted the Isles of the Fairies and rounded the Kingdom of Achory. At last they put in at a Utopian port three leagues from the city of the Amaurotes.

After they had landed and rested somewhat, Pantagruel said:

"My friends, the city is fairly near. Before we go further, it would be advisable to plan our movements instead of consulting after the fact, like the Athenians. Are you resolved to live and die with me?"

"Ay, Lord," they cried to a man. "You may rely on us as surely as on your own fingers."

"One point worries me: I haven't the foggiest notion of the besieging army's strength or organization. If only I had some information on the subject, I should set off with greater assurance. Let us put our heads together and devise a means of finding this out."

"We'll find out," they said in one voice. "You wait here. We'll have that information before sundown."

"As for me," said Panurge the crafty, "I will undertake to elude the guards, slip past the watch, enter their camp, feast off their tables, rummage their women, inspect their artillery, search the captains' tents and hobnob with the soldiers, without anyone noticing me. The devil himself could not identify me, for I am of the lineage of Zopirus, who, cutting off nose and ears, passed himself off among the Babylonians as a deserter mutilated by his master Darius."

"As for me," said Epistemon the learned, "I know all the stratagems and ruses of the brave captains of old, all the tricks and subtleties of military science. I will undertake to go among them, and even were I discovered, to escape by making them believe anything I like. For I am of the race of Sinon the Greek, who persuaded the Trojans to bring the wooden horse into their city."

"As for me," said Eusthenes the stalwart, "I will undertake to cross their trenches despite guards and sentries, to tread upon their bellies, to break their arms and twist their legs, were they strong as the devils of hell. For I am of the race of Hercules, a brawny colossus!"

"As for me," said Carpalim the fleet, "I will undertake to get in if ever a bird can. I am so nimble and swift that I shall have crossed their trenches and passed through their camp before they catch sight of me. I fear no shot or arrow or horse, however speedy, were it that Pegasus, sprung from the blood of the Medusa when Lord Perseus beheaded her, or that wooden steed which, like a bird, transported the dwarf Pacolet magically through the air. I will undertake to dance over the ears of corn and tread the grass in the meadows without silk or blade bowing a nail's breadth. For I am of the race of Camilla, the Amazon who did likewise."

XXV

HOW PANTAGRUEL'S COMRADES, PANURGE, CARPALIM, EUSTHENES AND EPISTEMON, CUNNINGLY DISCOMFITED SIX HUNDRED AND SIXTY KNIGHTS

As Carpalim spoke, they saw six hundred and sixty light horse advancing toward the harbor to ascertain what vessel had just put in. They rode at top speed, evidently intending to capture Pantagruel and his men.

"My friends," Pantagruel ordered, "get back to the ship. Here come the enemy. Were they ten times as strong, I would crush them like flies. Meanwhile, be off and amuse yourselves watching."

"No, My Lord," Panurge objected. "There's no point in your doing this. On the contrary, _you_ retire on board with the others; I will handle them by myself. Look sharp, there's no time to waste."

"Panurge is right," the others cried. "You go, My Lord; we'll stay and help Panurge. You'll see what we can do."

"Very well, but if you get the worst of it, I shall not fail you."

Panurge took the stout ship's cables, tied one end of them to the capstan on the orlop deck, laid them along the ground in two great circles and said to Epistemon:

"Get on board at once. When I give you the word, turn the orlop capstan for all you're worth and gather in the cables."

To Eusthenes and Carpalim:

"You two wait here. Offer yourselves freely to the enemy. Do whatever they tell you and pretend to surrender. But mind you don't stand inside these ropes! Whatever you do, stay clear of them."

Jumping on board, he seized a bundle of straw and a barrel of gunpowder, strewed the explosive within the circles formed by the cables, and stood by with a lighted brand.

Suddenly the knights came riding up with such fury that the foremost actually crashed against the ship, and, the bank being extremely slippery, fell, horse and rider, to the number of forty-four. The others, behind, concluded that their leaders had met with resistance. But Panurge cried:

"I fear you are hurt, gentlemen. Forgive us, it is not our fault. Salt water is always rather slippery. We submit ourselves to your good pleasure."

Eusthenes and Carpalim spoke likewise, as did Epistemon, shouting from the orlop deck. Panurge edged off. Observing that all the enemy were within the cables, and that his companions had backed away to make room for the knights, who were crowding about the vessel, Panurge suddenly shouted to Epistemon:

"Heave away, lad, heave ho!"

Epistemon at once wound the capstan; the cables, tangled in the horses' legs, tripped them up; horses and men tumbled to the ground. The latter drew their swords, seeking to sever the cables, but Panurge set fire to the train of powder he had laid and the wretched enemy burned like damned souls in hell. Out of all the horses and men, only two living creatures escaped: one knight and his Turkish courser. They had dodged the cable when Carpalim saw them, but he scurried after them, overtaking them within a hundred yards. In one leap he was on the horse's crupper; in a trice he had flung his arms about the rider from behind. And so he brought him back to the ship.

Pantagruel was overjoyed at the victory. He praised his friends' ingenuity in the most lavish terms, making them rest after their exertion, feasted them abundantly and gave them ample tipple, which they consumed lying on their bellies. Their prisoner sat familiarly in their company, but the poor devil was ill at ease, fearing lest Pantagruel devour him whole. Certainly Pantagruel could have made one mouthful of him, for his throat was wide enough to down the fellow like a sweetmeat. Truly, on Pantagruel's tongue the prisoner would have loomed as conspicuous as a grain of millet seed in the mouth of an ass.

XXVI

HOW PANTAGRUEL AND HIS COMPANIONS, WEARY OF SALTED MEAT, FEASTED UPON VENISON THAT CARPALIM HAD HUNTED

WHILE they were eating and drinking, Carpalim said:

"By the belly of St. Quenet, shall we never eat venison? That salted meat parches my throat. I'll go fetch the haunch of one of those horses we burned; it should be pretty well roasted."

Rising to do so, he caught sight of a great healthy roebuck which had emerged from its covert, attracted, I suppose, by Panurge's bonfire. Carpalim, like a bolt from a crossbow, shot after the beast and clapped his hands on its horns. But between leaving the group and catching the deer, he bagged much game besides. With his hands he plucked out of the air four large bustards, twenty-six gray partridges, thirty-two red ones, sixteen pheasants, nine woodcocks, nineteen herons and thirty-two ringdoves. With his feet, he killed ten or twelve rabbits and hares (both leverets and aged conies), eighteen landrails in pairs, fifteen young boars, two badgers and three fat foxes.

Striking the buck's head with his sword, he killed it and, as he brought it back to his friends, he picked up the hares, rails and boars. From afar they could hear him shouting:

"Panurge, my friend, vinegar, vinegar!"

Our blessed Pantagruel supposed Carpalim was sick at his stomach and ordered them to fetch it. But Panurge immediately realized

there was hare in the offing and drew his master's attention to Carpalim, advancing with a roebuck necklace and a girdle of rabbits.

Invoking the nine Muses, Epistemon fashioned nine splendid antique wooden spits; Eusthenes helped skin the game; Panurge laid
two cuirassier saddles down to serve as andirons. Promoting their
prisoner to the rank of cook, they had their venison roasted by the
fire in which the enemy burned. Then they doused their food with
vinegar and fell to with a vengeance, guzzling like so many famished
devils. To see them wolf down their food was a triumphant spectacle.

"Would to God you all had two pairs of church bells hanging on
your chins," Pantagruel said, laughing. "And I the great bells of
Rennes, Poitiers, Tours and Cambrai. By heaven! we would boom
out a fine carillon to the wagging of our chops."

Panurge was practical:

"We had better consider the business in hand and plan how to beat
the enemy," he advised.

"Quite right!" Pantagruel approved. Then, turning to the prisoner:

"Tell us the truth, friend, the plain unvarnished truth. And not
the tiniest lie unless you crave to be flayed alive. Remember: I am the
one who likes to eat little children. How is your army organized?
How many men? What effectives?"

"My Lord, here is the whole truth. There are three hundred giants,
all clad in stone armor and all wonderfully tall, though not so tall as
you. Except one, named Loupgarou or Werewolf, who is armed cap-
à-pie with the Cyclops' anvils. Then we have one hundred and sixty-
three thousand infantry armed with the hides of hobgoblins, all exceptionally strong and valiant . . . eleven thousand four hundred
men-at-arms . . . three thousand six hundred double cannon . . .
harquebusiers innumerable . . . ninety-four thousand pioneers
. . . and one hundred and fifty thousand harlots, beautiful as goddesses."

"Those are for me!" Panurge commented.

"Some of these women are Amazons," the cook went on. "Others
hail from Lyons, Paris, Touraine, Anjou, Poitou, Normandy and
Germany. We have, I make bold to say, harlots of all tongues and
countries."

"So," said Pantagruel. "But tell me: what about your king?"

"His Majesty is there in person, My Lord. He is called Anarchus, King of the Dipsodes—which means the thirsty people. Indeed, you never saw men so parched and eager to tipple. His Majesty's tent is guarded by the giants."

"That will do," said Pantagruel. Then, to the others: "Well, friends, are you ready to go with me?"

"God confound the man who leaves you!" Panurge answered. "The truth is, I've found a way to serve the lot of them up to you dead as mutton. Not one hamstring will slip the devil's grasp. There is only one point that worries me."

"What?"

"This," Panurge answered. "How can I manage to whorljorum all the strumpets there this very afternoon and have:

> *Not one trollop hidden*
> *Not one trull escaped*
> *That I have not ridden*
> *Rodgered or raped.*"

"Ha, ha, ha," Pantagruel roared.

"Devil take those chasms if I don't plumb a brace of them," cried Carpalim.

"What about me?" Eusthenes demanded. "I've not been wound up since we left Rouen: at least not hard enough to raise my needle above ten or eleven o'clock. What's more, it's in high feather now and stiff as a poker."

"Right," said Panurge, "you shall have the plumpest and sturdiest of them."

"What!" Epistemon shouted. "Is everybody going riding while I must lead the ass? Devil take the man who tries that on me. We will obey the law of warfare: *Qui potest capere, capiat*, let who can, capture!"

"No, no, no," said Panurge, "tie your ass to a hook and ride like every one else."

Good Pantagruel laughed at all this, then remarked:

"You are reckoning without your host. I'm much afraid that ere dark you'll be in no condition to ride the two-legged mare or wield your lances. You'll probably be more like mules ridden by the enemy and belabored with their pikes."

"Bah!" said Epistemon, "I'll bring them for you to roast, boil, fry or make paste of. They're not so many as Xerxes' army, which numbered thirty hundred thousand combatants, if you believe Herodotus and Trogus Pompeius. Yet Themistocles with a handful of men trounced them royally. For God's sake, don't worry about us."

"Holy 'Smother! smother me wholly in midden if I don't dust off the men with my codpiece, while St. Sweephole, who dwells within, scours the women's vesicles."

"Forward then, lads," cried Pantagruel. "Let us be on our way."

XXVII

HOW PANTAGRUEL SET UP A TROPHY TO COMMEMORATE THEIR PROWESS, HOW PANURGE SET UP ANOTHER TO COMMEMORATE THE HARES, HOW PANTAGRUEL, FARTING, ENGENDERED LITTLE MEN, AND POOPING, LITTLE WOMEN, FINALLY HOW PANURGE BROKE A LARGE STAFF WITH TWO GLASSES

"Ere we leave here," said Pantagruel, "to commemorate your exploits, I wish to erect a fine trophy on this spot."

Very joyfully, singing country ballades as they worked, they set up a huge post. On it they hung a cuirassier saddle, the armored headpiece of a steed, bridle-bosses, stirrup-leathers, spurs, a coat of mail, a steel-tempered corselet, a battle-axe, a sabre, a gauntlet, a mace, arm-covers, leg-guards and a gorget with all the other equipment required for a triumphal arch or trophy. Then, to perpetuate their exploit, Pantagruel wrote the following paean:

> Nonpareil skill and valor without peer
> Hallowed this spot when four brave champions rose
> With wisdom for their only fighting-gear,
> Like Fabius or a pair of Scipios,
> To vanquish five-and-fifty dozen foes.
> (Those ruffians, roasting, crackled like dry gorse!)
> Learn this, kings, lords, drunkards, magnificoes:
> Intelligence must triumph over force.

> > We humans all
> > Know victories fall
> > But at the nod
> > Of One Whose thrall
> > Man is. . . . We call
> > This power: God!

> Let tyrants storm, rogues rage and bullies brawl,
> We know he conquers who is bravely shod
> In faith, and clad with hope; though he be small,
> His hand is armed with the Almighty's rod.

Whilst Pantagruel was inscribing the above verses, Panurge took a large stake, dug it into the ground, split it at the top and crowned it with the horns of the roebuck. Along it he hung the roebuck's hide and right forefoot, the ears of three leverets, the chine of a rabbit, the jaws of a hare, the wings of two bustards, the feet of four ring-doves, a bottle of vinegar, a horn they kept salt in, one of their wooden spits, a larding stick, a battered kettle riddled with holes, a pan to mix sauce in, an earthen salt cellar and a goblet of glazed pottery from the famed manufactories of Beauvais. Then, in imitation of Pantagruel's verses and trophy, he wrote as follows:

> Four gormandizing bottle-floggers here
> Sat on their arses, redder than the rose,
> Worshipping Bacchus with the best of cheer,

Drinking like carps or Papal nuncios.
Here, too, the paragon of all the roes,
Well-sacrificed at fires of crackling horse
And sizzling knight, proved sweet to tongue and nose
With salt and vinegar to speed his course.

> *We bibbers bawl*
> *Across the hall*
> *Unless our nod*
> *Produces tall*
> *Cups to forestall*
> *Drouth in the pod.*

Hail, meat! Praise, sauce! And long live wine, withal!
Tumbrils of shit for the abstemious clod!
Septembral juices grace our bacchanal
To fill the paunch and elevate the cod.

Then Pantagruel said:

"Come, lads, let us be gone! We've spent too much time over our food, remember that the greatest banqueters rarely prove the bravest fighters. There is no shade like that of flying banners, no smoke like that of horses' panting and sweating, no music like that of clanking armor."

Epistemon smiled:

"There is no shade," he said, "like that of a kitchen ceiling, no smoke like that of venison pies, no music like the ringing of goblets."

"There is no shade," Panurge put in, "like that of a pair of curtains, no smoke like that of a woman's breasts, no music like the clattering of ballocks."

Then he rose, gave a poop, a leap and a whistle, shouting joyously: "Long live Pantagruel!"

Pantagruel sought to imitate him. Unfortunately his blast shook the earth for nine leagues around. Out of all this tumult and corrupted air he begat over fifty-three thousand little men, dwarfs of the most repulsive appearance. Pooping again, he engendered as many little stoop-shouldered women, like those you see in various places, who never grow save downwards like cows' tails or roundwise like Limousin radishes.

"Well, well," cried Panurge, "how fertile your farts are! By God, here are fine farts of men and rare poops of women! Let us marry them off together and beget wasps!"

Pantagruel did as he suggested and called the breed Pigmies. He sent them off to live on an island near by where ever since they have increased mightily. The cranes wage continual war upon them, but they defend themselves heroically, for these little bits of men (called turd-handles in Scotland) are exceptionally choleric. The physical reason for this is that their hearts lie very close to their evacuations.

Panurge then took two tumblers of equal size, filled them with water to the brim, and set them on stools more than five feet apart. Taking the staff of a javelin five and one-half feet long, he laid it on the glasses so the ends of the staff just touched the brims of the glasses. Picking up a stake, he said to his companions:

"Look, my masters, look how easily we will overcome our enemies. Just as I break this staff on these glasses without smashing or even cracking them—more, without even spilling a drop of water—so we shall break the heads of the Dipsodes without any one of us suffering wound or scratch."

They stared at him incredulously.

"One moment!" he cried. "Here, Eusthenes, just to prove there is no witchcraft in this, you take this stake and hit that staff as hard as ever you can."

Eusthenes did so. The staff snapped in two; not a drop fell from the glasses. Panurge said:

"I know a great many more such tricks. Let us therefore march boldly into battle."

XXVIII

HOW PANTAGRUEL CON-QUERED THE DIPSODES AND GIANTS IN AN EXTRAOR-DINARY MANNER

AFTER all this talk, Pantagruel addressed the prisoner.

"Go back to your king," he said. "Tell him all you have seen to-day and bid him prepare to entertain me at noon to-morrow. For as soon as my galleys arrive—which will be to-morrow at the latest—I will prove to him, to the tune of eighteen hundred thousand soldiers and seven thousand giants taller than myself, that he was insane to invade my native land."

The prisoner begged that he might become Pantagruel's slave, to fight by the giant's side against his own compatriots if, by the grace of God, Pantagruel were willing. But Pantagruel ordered him away at once.

Just before he left, however, Pantagruel gave him a jar filled with euphorbium, mixed with spurge flax and brandy into a sort of syrup. He was to bring this to King Anarchus with a message to the effect that if His Majesty could take one ounce without drinking immediately after, then he might await Pantagruel without fear.

The prisoner implored Pantagruel on bended knees to take pity upon him in the hour of battle.

"When you have told your king everything," Pantagruel advised, "I won't tell you like a prig 'God helps those who help themselves.' Exactly the opposite is true: the devil cracks their necks. No, what I say is: place all your faith in God, He will not abandon you. I myself, powerful as you see, command vast companies of men-at-arms; yet I trust not in my strength or skill but only in the Almighty. Ay, God is my protector nor will He ever forsake such as offer Him their thoughts and hopes."

The prisoner then begged Pantagruel not to ransom him excessively. Pantagruel at once replied that he had no intention of robbing or ransoming men; on the contrary, he aimed to enrich and free them.

"Go in the peace of the living God and never keep evil company lest misfortune fall upon you."

The prisoner gone, Pantagruel explained to his companions:

"I told him we had an army on the seas with which to attack to-morrow solely to put the fear of God into them. If they expect a vast host, they will spend the night in preparations. I intend to fall upon them soon, about the hour of the first sleep."

Now let us leave Pantagruel and his companions for a moment and turn to King Anarchus and his army.

The prisoner arrived, obtained audience immediately and reported how a colossal giant named Pantagruel had vanquished and cruelly roasted six hundred and fifty-nine knights, leaving only himself to bring back tidings of them. Further, the giant had charged him to bid His Majesty prepare to receive an attack on the morrow towards noon. There was, too, a jar of syrup with specific instructions as to its use.

King Anarchus barely swallowed one spoonful when a terrific burning seared his mouth, ulcerated his uvula and peeled the whole surface of his tongue. No remedy offered him seemed to bring the slightest relief save incessant drinking; the moment he took the cup from his lips, his tongue scorched. So they kept pouring wine down his throat through a funnel.

His captains, pashas, and bodyguard, observing this, wished to test the virtues of the syrup on themselves. As in their monarch's case, they found cause to rue it.

Crazed with pain, they began to drink so wildly that ere long the entire camp learned how the prisoner had returned, how there was to be an attack on the morrow and how king, captains and body-guard were preparing for it by drinking like madmen. Whereupon the whole host began to booze, guzzle and swill until in the end they fell into a dead sleep, grunting and snoring like hogs, pell-mell, over the camp.

Let us leave them in this piteous condition to return to our excel-lent Pantagruel and relate his exploits that night.

Leaving the trophies, he picked up the ship's mast for a staff, placed eighteen thousand gallons of Anjou and Rouen white wine in its top, filled the dinghy with salt and, tying it to his girdle, carried it as easily as lansquenets their baskets of provisions. Then they set forth. But as they neared the enemy encampment, Panurge spoke up:

"Master, if you want to do the proper thing, you'll haul that wine down from the mast-top so we can drink like Breton fiddlers."

Pantagruel complied with alacrity and they imbibed so gallantly that the whole eighteen thousand gallons vanished, except a few wretched lees to serve for vinegar and a leather Touraine bottle which Panurge filled up for himself. He called it his *vade mecum*. To crown such hearty bibacity, Panurge gave Pantagruel a fiendish drug made up of lithontripton (an electuary which dissolves gallstones in the bladder), nephrocatarticon (a kidney purge), and quince marmalade mixed with Spanish fly and other diuretics.

"Get into the city, Carpalim," Pantagruel ordered. "Scale the walls like a rat, as you alone can do. Tell our friends there to make a sortie and fall upon the enemy as fiercely as they can. Then light a torch, go back to the enemy's camp and set it on fire, tents, pavilions and the rest of it. This done, as you retire, shout at the top of your lungs: that voice of yours is far more terrifying than Stentor's, even though he was heard by the Trojans above the tumult of battle."

"Very well, sir. But wouldn't it be a good idea to spike their guns?"

"No, no," Pantagruel answered. "Just blow up their powder."

Carpalim carried out his orders to the letter. All the fighting men sallied from the city. . . . Carpalim set fire to tents and pavilions . . . then he passed unnoticed over the sleepers (they were drunk and snoring, too!) . . . then, finding their ammunition dump, he fired it as well. . . . A highly dangerous job, for it ignited so suddenly that Carpalim narrowly escaped being blown up. Only his extraordinary agility (no shot from a crossbow could have overtaken him) saved him from roasting like a pig.

Once out of their trenches, he gave a bloodcurdling shriek that sounded as though all the devils of hell were unleashed. This deafening clamor awakened the enemy, but do you know in what state? The louts were as dazed as the monks at the first peal to matins—the rub-ballock they call it in the Luçon country.

Meanwhile Pantagruel scattered the salt from his dinghy into their gaping mouths in such quantities that the poor wretches barked like foxes.

"Oh, oh, Pantagruel, Pantagruel," they hawked. "Why do you add further heat to the firebrands in our throats?"

Suddenly Panurge's drugs began to take effect and Pantagruel felt an imperious need of draining his bladder. So he voided on their camp so freely and torrentially as to drown them all and flood the countryside ten leagues around. We know from history that had his father Gargantua's great mare been present and likewise disposed to piss, the resultant deluge would have made Deucalion's flood seem like a drop in the bucket. A mare of the first water, Gargantua's; it couldn't relieve itself without making another Rhône or Danube.

The soldiers sallying from the city saw the whole thing.

"The enemy have been hacked to bits," they exulted. "See the blood run!"

But they were mistaken. What they believed in the glow from the burning camp and the dim moonlight to be the blood of slaughtered enemies was but the wine from our giant's bladder.

The enemy now awakened thoroughly to see their camp blazing on one hand and Pantagruel's urinal inundation on the other. They were, so to speak, between the fiery devil and the deep Red Sea. Some vowed the end of the world was at hand, bearing out the prophecy that the last judgment would be by fire. Others were certain they were being persecuted by the sea-gods Neptune, Proteus, Triton and others. Certainly the waters flowing over them were salty.

Oh, who on earth were able fitly to relate how Pantagruel demeaned himself against the threescore giants? O my Muse, O Calliope, mother of epic song, and thou, Thalia, with thy comic lyre, inspire me in this hour, restore my powers to me, for here is the *pons asinorum* of logic, here is the stumbling block: how shall I sing the horrible battle that ensued?

Would to God I had at my disposal just one bottle of the best wine you readers of this veracious narrative ever drank!

XXIX

HOW PANTAGRUEL DISCOM-FITED THE THREE HUNDRED GIANTS IN STONY ARMOR AND THEIR LEADER WERE-WOLF

THE giants, seeing their camp flooded, carried their king, Anarchus, out of the fort on their backs just as Æneas bore his father, Anchises, from the conflagration of Troy. Observing them, Panurge remarked to his master:

"My Lord, look at those giants coming out there. Lay on with your mast lustily in the old fighting style: now is the time to show them the honest stuff you're made of. We'll not fail you either; I myself will kill a crowd of them outright. David killed Goliath easily, didn't he? And David was only a little snot; I'm worth twelve of him. All right then, I'll kill a dozen giants. And that great lecher Eusthenes is stronger than four oxen; he'll give them what for. Be of good courage, then; lay on with point and edge."

"Courage?" cried Pantagruel. "I've more than fifty Franks' worth! But *ne Hercules quidem adversus duos*, Hercules never fought against two."

"Shit, shoddy and shibboleth!" Panurge exclaimed. "Are you comparing yourself to Hercules? By God, you've more grit in your teeth and common scents in your tail than ever he had in body and soul. A man is as good as he thinks he is."

While they spoke, Werewolf and his giants drew up. As he saw that Pantagruel was practically alone, Werewolf was carried away with temerity and presumption: Pantagruel to him was as good as killed. Turning to his fellow-giants:

"Back, you wenchers of the nether lands, back I say! By Mahomet, if a single one of you tries to fight these fellows, I'll torture him to death. This is my own private battle; you shall have good sport watching us."

The giants, King Anarchus, Panurge and his companions withdrew to where the Dipsodes kept their flagons. Panurge, pretending he had the pox, twisted his mouth, crooked his fingers and said raucously:

"My good friends, let me deny God if we are here to make war. Give us some food too, so we may all eat together whilst our masters are fighting."

King Anarchus and his giants invited them to fall to, and, as they ate, Panurge told them anecdotes from Turpin's *Chronicles*, various miracles of St. Nicholas, selections from *Mother Goose* and other tall stories.

Out in the field, Werewolf was advancing, armed with a mace weighing one million eighty-six thousand six hundred and twenty-four pounds. It was made of the finest Calibes steel, with, at its end, thirteen pointed diamonds, the smallest of which was as great as the large bell of Notre Dame in Paris. (In the strict interests of truth, I hasten to suggest that it might possibly have been a mite smaller—say by the breadth of a fingernail, or, to be scrupulously exact, of the back of one of those blades used to cut off the ears of malefactors.) More, it was enchanted: it could never break, but shattered anything that touched it.

As Werewolf swaggered up, Pantagruel lifted his eyes to heaven, commended himself to His Maker with all his soul and made the following vow:

"Lord God, Who hast always been my preserver and protector, behold the peril that now encompasses me. Nothing brings me here save the natural will Thou grantest men to defend themselves, their wives and children, their country and their homes, when Thine own cause (which is the Faith) is not attacked. In Thine own cause Thou hast forbidden us to bear arms; Thou needest no coadjutor but only that we profess the Catholic faith and obey Thy Holy Word. Being almighty, Thou wilt take into Thy hands a defense strong beyond our conceiving. For Thou hast angels in millions of million legions, the least of whom can slay all mortal men and turn heaven and earth about at pleasure, as Sennacherib's mighty hosts discovered to their loss.

"O Lord, my hope and trust lie in Thee alone. If then it please Thee to succor me in the hour of peril, I do offer up a vow. In Utopia and in all lands over which I may hold power and sway, I will cause Thy holy gospel to be purely, simply and entirely preached. And I will blot out the abuses of a rabble of ranters, popemongers and false prophets who, by human fabrications and depraved subterfuges, have poisoned the world we live in."

Then there was heard a voice from heaven, saying: "*Hoc fac et vinces*, do this and thou shalt conquer."

Seeing Werewolf approach with jaws agape, Pantagruel advanced boldly, crying his loudest: "You shall die, villain, you shall die," intending by his horrible noise to terrify the enemy, a practice of the ancient Lacedæmonians.

Then from the dinghy on his belt, he threw more than eighteen kegs and four bushels of salt into his foe's mouth, throat, and eyes. Maddened by this attack, Werewolf sought to bash his brains out with his mace. But Pantagruel was nimble—he had always had a quick foot and a sharp eye—and dodged the blow by stepping backward. He had not time, however, to pull the dinghy at his girdle clear. Alas, it broke into four thousand and eighty-six smithereens as the rest of the salt spilled on to the ground.

So Pantagruel swung his arm lustily and, with flawless technique, drove the end of his mast home to a spot a little above his antagonist's breast. Then, slashing through to the left, he struck him between neck and shoulders. Next, advancing his right foot, he rammed his mast into Werewolf's genitals, which broke its top and smashed the three or four remaining kegs of wine. Seeing the red flow, Werewolf thought Pantagruel had pinked his bladder and drawn urine.

Not content with this, Pantagruel would have dealt him a side swipe, but Werewolf raised his mace, took one step forward and brought it crashing down with all his might. The thump was so fierce that, but for God's help, our excellent Pantagruel would have been split from the crown of his head to the bottom of his guts. But, thanks to his agility, the blow glanced a little to the right. The mace first cleaved an enormous rock, from which it raised a flame of more than nine thousand and six tons. Then it buried itself in more than sixty-three feet of earth.

As Werewolf strained to pull up the mace caught between rock and earth, Pantagruel put in a thwack that should have severed his head from his shoulders. Unfortunately, his mast grazed the handle of the mace, which, as we said, was enchanted. In a thrice the mast snapped about six inches above Pantagruel's hands. He stood there, like a duck in thunder.

"Alas! Panurge, where are you?" he cried.

Panurge warned King Anarchus and the giants:

"By God, they'll hurt each other if you don't interfere!"

But the giants were happy as larks. Carpalim then sought to come to his master's aid. A giant roared:

"By Goulfarin, the gormandizing nephew of Mahomet, if you so much as budge, I'll clap you into the bottom of my breeches as a suppository. For my belly's a pit of constipation, and I can only cack by grinding my teeth."

Bereft of a staff, Pantagruel took up the very end of the mast and struck at the giant with might and main. But he hurt him about as severely as you would an anvil with a fillip of the fingers.

Werewolf, meanwhile, drew his mace out of the ground and sought to beat Pantagruel with it. But the latter was very quick on his feet, avoiding every blow.

"Ha, villain!" Werewolf bragged as he saw Pantagruel on the defensive. "Now I shall make mincemeat of you, ay, to teach you not to make wretched men thirsty."

But Pantagruel dealt Werewolf such a vicious kick in the belly, that he fell backward, his heels over his head; then he proceeded to drag him tailscraping the length of a bowshot. Werewolf screamed, "Mahomet! Mahomet! Mahomet!" as the blood spurted from his mouth. Hearing his cry, the giants rose to a man. But Panurge cautioned:

"Gentlemen, take my word for it, don't go out there. My master has gone mad; he's walloping right and left and every other way, without looking where he hits. You'll rue it if you go, My Lords Giants."

But when they realized Pantagruel was without a staff they ignored Panurge's warning.

Seeing them advance, Pantagruel picked up Werewolf by the feet and wielded his body like a pike. As Werewolf wore armor, he made a capital weapon; Pantagruel wrought havoc upon those stone-clad

giants, battering them down as a mason does a wall. Never an opponent stepped up but Pantagruel felled him amid a deafening tumult
as his stony armor crumbled to dust. It reminded me of the great butter tower of the Cathedral of Bourges—not the one built recently
with money given for indulgences to eat butter in Lent—but its predecessor, which melted in the sun.

In the meantime, Panurge, Carpalim and Eusthenes were busy
cutting the throats of those laid low, so that not a single giant survived to tell the tale. As for Pantagruel, he looked like a mower who
with his scythe (Werewolf himself) cut down the meadow grass
(My Lords the Giants).

But this exercise cost Werewolf his head. That was when Pantagruel crushed a certain Riflandouille. Unlike his comrades with but
soft Touraine stone and sandstone, this giant was armed to the teeth
with huge flints. A chip off his armor flew up, caught Epistemon in
the throat and sliced his head clean off.

The giants all dead, Pantagruel flung Werewolf as hard as he
could into the city. The giant landed on his belly in the middle of the
main square; in one fell swoop he crushed a singed tomcat, a
drenched kitten, a pooping duck and a bridled goose.

XXX

HOW PANURGE INGENIOUSLY HEALED A DECAPITATED EPISTEMON WHO BROUGHT BACK TIDINGS OF THE DEAD AND THE DAMNED

THIS titanic victory achieved, Pantagruel retired to the flagons and
summoned his companions. All of them turned out to be safe and
sound except Eusthenes—his face had been scratched a little by one
of the giants whose throat he cut—and Epistemon, tragically killed.
Pantagruel was so depressed that he would have committed suicide,
but Panurge urged:

"For God's sake, My Lord, wait a moment. We will go look for him among the dead and give you a full report."

Searching the field, they found Epistemon dead as a doornail, his bloody head in his hands.

"Ah, fell death!" Eusthenes lamented. "Thou hast robbed us of the most perfect of men."

At which, Pantagruel arose in the profoundest sorrow ever beheld on earth, and whispered gloomily to Panurge:

"Alas, my friend, your omen of the glasses and staff was all too deceptive!"

"Don't waste your tears, lads," Panurge replied. "He is still warm. I'll cure him for you and make him as sound as ever he was."

Lifting Epistemon's head, he pressed it against his codpiece to keep it warm. Eusthenes and Carpalim bore the body from the field; they dared not hope he would recover, but they wished Pantagruel to see him in death. Again Panurge comforted them:

"If I do not cure him, then I hope to lose my own head—which is a fool's wager! Leave off crying, friends, and give me a hand here."

Panurge straightway cleaned Epistemon's neck and head very thoroughly with white wine, infused them with crapocatholicon which he always carried in one of his pockets, then anointed them with a mysterious salve, fitting head to body, sinew to sinew and joint to joint, so that he should not be wry-necked. (Panurge nursed a deadly hatred of wry-necked people!)

This done he sewed the head to the neck with some fifteen or sixteen stitches to prevent its falling off again, and greased it with an unguent he called resuscitative.

Suddenly Epistemon began to breathe, then he opened his eyes, yawned, sneezed. . . . Finally he let a great household fart.

"He's healed now all right!" Panurge exclaimed, giving him a glass of strong white wine with a slice of sugared toast. And healed he was, though for the next three weeks very hoarse and sorely afflicted with a dry cough he could dispel only by drinking.

Epistemon started to speak. He had seen the devils, he told them, he had spoken familiarly with Lucifer, he had had a rollicking time in hell and in the Elysian Fields. The devils, he testified, were such excellent fellows and jovial company that he regretted Panurge's recalling him back to life so soon.

"I enjoyed seeing them immensely."

"How so?" Pantagruel asked.

"They are not so badly treated as you suppose," Epistemon explained. "The only thing is that their conditions are changed very curiously. I saw Alexander the Great, for instance. Do you know what he does?"

They had not the faintest notion.

"Well, he earns the barest living by darning old hose. Xerxes is a crier of mustard, Romulus a saltmaker; Numa Pompilius, the royal Roman lawgiver, is a nailsmith; Tarquin, a porter; Piso, the successor of Galba, a peasant clod; Sulla, a boatman.

"Mighty Cyrus, who captured Babylon and delivered the Jews, is a cowherd . . . Themistocles, who saved Greece from the Persian invaders at Salamis, is by trade a glazier . . . Epaminondas, the Theban champion, is a framer of mirrors. . . . Brutus and Cassius are land-surveyors, Demosthenes tends the vines, Cicero kindles fires, while Fabius Cunctator is the swiftest threader of paternosters and rosaries in all hell. Do you remember Artaxerxes Mnemon of the phenomenal memory? O shades of the retreating ten thousand Greeks, Artaxerxes, if you please, makes ropes for a living! Æneas is a jolly miller, Achilles a scrofulous beggar, Agamemnon (peace be to Iphigenia!) is a lickplatter scullion, Ulysses a hay-mower, wise Nestor a forester.

"What is Darius who vanquished India, conquered Thrace, led Macedonia into bondage, only to fall in turn at Marathon? Darius is a scavenger, a coprofer, a farmer of turds and snapper-up of unconsidered dung.

"Ancus Martius, grandson of Numa and founder of fair Ostia, is a ship's trimmer . . . Camillus, who saved Rome from the Gauls, is a sabot-maker . . . Marcellus, the enemy of Carthage, shells beans. . . . Where is Drusus, the first Roman to reach the Danube? Where Scipio Africanus, who vanquished Hannibal? Where Hasdrubal, founder of Carthagena and lone negotiator of treaties? Drusus is a wax-chandler, Scipio cries lye in a wooden shoe, Hasdrubal manufactures lanterns. And you, Hannibal, who crossed Spain, Gaul, the very Alps in their height, you, Priam, you, Sir Lancelot of the Lake? One sells eggs, the other old rags, the third is a flayer of dead horse flesh.

"As for the Knights of the Round Table, they manage the scantest of penny-pinching existences by rowing My Lords the Devils across the rivers of hell, cruising down the Cocytus, Styx, Phlegeton, Acheron, and Lethe. For the devils occasionally like aquatic pastimes and hire these knights as one might hire boatmen at Lyons, or gondoliers in Venice. For pay, they get a flick on the nose; in the evening they are given a crust of mouldy bread.

"The twelve peers of France? They are in hell too, but they do nothing I saw. I was told they supported themselves by submitting to raps, strokes, smacks and punches on the teeth.

"Once Trajan increased the Roman population, discomfited the Dacians, blazed a trail across the Persian Gulf . . . once Antoninus built the noble wall they call Graham's Dyke and gave just laws to the people . . . once Commodus, the cruel son of a divine philosopher, ruled with a hand of iron . . . once Pertinax wore the purple . . . once Lucullus dined with Lucullus . . . once Justinian gave the code, annexed Africa and bedded with the lovely Theodora. . . . Now Trajan fishes for frogs, Antoninus is a flunkey, Commodus a collier, Lucullus a manufacturer of fripperies, Justinian a toymaker.

"Hector is now a chef's panscraper, Achilles bundles hay; Cambyses, who drove the Egyptians before him, is a muleteer.

"The other Artaxerxes, called the longhanded because his right was longer than his left, a lofty ruler and son to Xerxes, is a scummer of pots. Nero is a street-fiddler and Fierabras, hero of French song, Nero's valet. But the master has to submit to a thousand indignities, eating coarse black bread and drinking sour wine while the lackey feeds and bibs of the choicest. Pompey and Julius Cæsar are ship's caulkers.

"Valentine and Orson, the brothers who were parted and, thanks to a bear's teats, brought together again, are attendants in the public bathhouse of hell, where they clean out bathtubs and massage scurvy old stinkpots . . . Giglan and Gawain, heroes of Breton epics, are miserable swine-herds . . . Geoffrey with the Great Tooth, Lord of Vouvant and Mervent, ravager of Maillezais, peddles matches . . . Godefroy de Bouillon, crusader extraordinary, Defender of the Holy Sepulchre and Sovereign of Jerusalem, makes hoods and capes. . . .

"Time was when Jason, raised by a centaur, led the adventurers on the quest of the Golden Fleece, wed Medea and ascrobiculated

Creusa; that very Jason now makes bracelets at a bench side by side with Baldwin of Flanders, quondam King of Jerusalem and Emperor of Constantinople, Cruel Pedro of Castile, the Justiciary, and assassin, hawks indulgences; Morgan is a brewer.

"Of yore Huon, a paladin of Charlemagne, slew the emperor's nephew and was sent to beard the Turk and wed his daughter; Oberon helped him with fivescore thousand warriors, he slew the giant Agrapard, defended his chastity against all temptation and in the end, married fair Esclarmonde. To-day he rots in hell, nailing hoops to barrels.

"Pyrrhus put terror into Roman hearts with his huge elephants and won the day at Asculum; but little it profits him to-day as he washes dirty stew-pans . . . Antiochus the Great gained mastery of India, Palestine and Asia Minor, but it is forgotten as he diligently sweeps his sooty chimneys . . . Romulus ekes out his living as a saltmaker by repairing falderals . . . Octavian, whose existence some deem fabulous, is there in flesh and bone, scraping parchments . . . and Nerva, the sagacious emperor who obtained an apotheosis, alternates with Charlemagne policing the woodland. . . .

"John of Paris, hero of chivalry, is a greaser of boots; conversely King Arthur of Britain is an ungreaser of round hats. As for Bethis of Britain, called Perceforest, who walked through the Enchanted Wood, I saw him staggering under a great load and suppose his job is carrying logs.

"Popes, popes!" Epistemon suddenly shouted. "I saw a pisspotful of popes!

"Do you recall Pope Julius II, my friends? Eight bishoprics beside the archiepiscopal see of Avignon, he had, when he was still a shaveling turdlet. He set them all fighting like hornets in Italy, Venetians, French and Germans and the rest. And in his spare time, laid the foundation stone of St. Peter's. You remember that shocking beard he grew long after all Christendom had given up the fashion? Well, lads, you'll be glad to learn that Pope Julius makes his way by crying meat pies. That great buggerish beard round his chin has been shaved and his hair grows wild elsewhere.

"Do you recall Pope Boniface VIII, who fought our Philip the Fair and instituted the swindle of the jubilees? Well, lads, you'll be glad to learn he scours out old pots.

"Do you recall Pope Nicholas III? And Pope Alexander VI, who battled desperately in the Old World and settled the destinies of the New? The former, I may inform you, is a paper-maker, the latter a rat-catcher.

"Do you recall Pope Sixtus IV? They called him the father of Christendom, possibly because he resisted all the efforts made by the Italian rulers to secure peace, or because he helped his enemy the King of Naples trounce the rascally Turk. He feathered the nests of his brood, the nepotist, even though they tell he could not personally bear the sight of money! And he was the second founder of the Vatican Library. Well, old Sixtus has a very fine position in hell salving and anointing the luckless venereals—"

"What!" exclaimed Pantagruel. "Do they have the pox in hell?"

"Of course," Epistemon informed him. "I never saw so many pox-bloods in my life. There must be over a hundred million. You see, those who never caught it in this world contract it in the other!"

"God's body! I'm safe!" cried Panurge. "I've been all the way to the hole of Gibraltar and the utmost bounds of the Pillars of Hercules, and I've gathered of the ripest, too!"

"There are two more popes I must pop at you. Pope Calixtus III, the old dodderer who preached a crusade no one would go to, is a specialist in hairdressing: he is barber and trimmer of women's *sine qua non*. And Pope Urban VI, who began the schism, cheated on the jubilees, and fell off his mule to die, now exercises the profession of dishwasher.

"Let me see, who else was there? Oh, yes: Ogier the Dane, Charlemagne's champion to whom Morgan the Fay promised immortality at Avalon, polishes armor and shines harnesses . . . King Tigranus of Armenia, friend of Mithridates and conqueror of Mesopotamia, lines roofs and mends leaky ceilings . . . as does Pepin the Short, first Carolingian king . . . while Galen the Reformer, the restorer of chivalry in the decadence following Roncevaux, catches moles at so much a head . . . and the four sons of Aymon, doughty outlaws famed in French story, are toothpullers in hell."

"Are there no women?" asked Eusthenes.

"Certainly!" Epistemon answered. "Melusine who built Lusignan for her husband and vanished when he saw one of the weekly transformations of her thighs into the tail of a serpent, Melusine is a kitchen mopsy. Accordingly, I dismiss as superstition the story that she returns to shriek whenever a Lusignan is about to die.

"Then I saw Matabrune, who is a laundress, and Cleopatra, a crier of onions. Helen conducts a bureau for chambermaids and is, to all intents, a procuress. Semiramis, proud builder of Babylon and loveliest of women, was not turned into a dove, as legend asserts. She is, on the contrary, entrusted with the delousing of beggars. Dido hawks mushrooms through the streets. Penthesilea, daughter of Mars, Queen of the Amazons and ally of the Trojans, is a watercress huckster. Lucrece, whom Sextus tarradiddled, thereby causing the establishment of the Roman republic, keeps an alehouse. Hortensia, famed for her oratory, now operates a spinning-wheel, while Livia, wife of Augustus and mother of Tiberius, scrapes verdigris from copper plates to use in dyes."

It was the rule in hell, Epistemon explained, that all who had been great lords and ladies on earth were condemned to struggle for the most ignoble, precarious and miserable livelihood below. On the contrary, philosophers and such as had been needy on this planet became puissant lords in the inferno. Epistemon went on to give examples.

"I saw Diogenes," he said, "enjoying the most magnificent luxury. He wore a rich purple robe and held a sceptre in his right hand. When Alexander the Great failed to patch Diogenes' breeches, he abused him until the ex-monarch trembled with fury. And Diogenes never failed to beat him for his incompetence.

"I saw Epictetus, too, most gallantly garbed in the French fashion. He was sitting under a cool pleasant arbor with a bevy of comely ladies. Here every one frolicked, drank, danced and made merry. He was rolling in money: I almost had a sunstroke looking at old Sol engraved on Epictetus' golden crowns. I read his motto, inscribed over the lattice of the arbor:

> *Saulter, dancer, faire les tours,*
> *Et boire vin blanc et vermeil,*
> *Et ne faire rien tous les jours,*
> *Que compter escuz au soleil.*
>
> *We frolic and dance, make music and song,*
> *White wine or red, we drink by the tun,*

With nothing to do the whole day long
But count our coin in the warm summer sun.

"When Epictetus saw me, he graciously invited me to join him, which I did with the greatest pleasure. We tippled and bibbed in the most approved theological fashion. Suddenly Cyrus came shuffling up, begging Epictetus in Mercury's name to give him a penny to buy a few onions from Cleopatra for his supper.

" 'No, no, when I give alms, I don't give pennies. Here, varlet, here is a crown for you. And be an honest man.'

"Cyrus was overjoyed at his windfall. But the other rascally kings in hell, Alexander, Darius and that rabble, picked his pockets the same night.

"I saw Master Pierre Pathelin who was treasurer to Rhadamanthus, one of the three judges of hell. Pope Julius was hawking his meat pies and Pathelin was trying to bargain him down.

" 'How much a dozen, churl?'

" 'Threepence, if you please, My Lord.'

" 'No, thief!' cried Pathelin. 'Three thwacks of the cudgel! Put them down there, churl, and fetch some more.'

"The unhappy pope beat a lachrymose retreat. Arriving at his employer's, he blubbered how he had been robbed of his wares. For his pains, he got such a drubbing that his skin wouldn't have served to make bagpipes of.

"I saw the master poet, Jean Le Maire de Belges, impersonating a pope and making all the luckless popes and kings below kiss his feet. With great pomp and circumstance he gave them his benediction:

" 'Get indulgences, rogues, gain pardons: they are going cheap. I absolve you of bread and stew; you may dispense with the hope of ever amounting to a straw.'

"Then he called Caillette and Triboulet, jesters to Louis XII and François I.

" 'My Lords Cardinals,' he said, 'give each of them the apostolic bull.'

"His order was carried out forthwith. The bull, however, was not an edict but a great pizzle to thwack their backs with.

"I also met Master François Villon, engaged in conversation with Xerxes.

" 'What does this mustard sell for, lout?'

" 'A penny, My Lord.'

" 'Pox take you for a swindler. It's worth no more than a farthing; you're profiteering, you scoundrel.'

"And he voided into the bucket just as mustard-vendors do in Paris.

"I saw the Franc-Archier de Baignolet, that swaggering militia-man, acting as an inquisitor of heretics. He came upon Perceforest relieving his bladder against what must have been a hospital wall, for, as with us, St. Anthony's Flames were painted upon it. At once our friend denounced the fellow, and would have burned him then and there had not Morgan appeared and for *proficiat* or visitation-present, together with other odd fees, given him nine hogsheads of beer. . . ."

Pantagruel was most enthusiastic about Epistemon's long report.

"Splendid, splendid!" he cried. "But keep the rest of these fine tales for a rainy afternoon. However, there is one thing I must ask. How do they treat the usurers in hell?"

"They were all scouring the gutters for rusty pins and old nails, just like the beggars here. But a hundredweight of this ironware won't buy a crust of bread. At that, it's hard to dispose of. The un-happy misers therefore often went over three weeks without one scrap of bread. Yet day and night they toiled, waiting for a windfall. And they reckon this labor of misery as nothing for they are too cursedly busy trying to earn one scurvy penny at the end of the year."

"Thank you, Epistemon," said Pantagruel. "Now, lads, let us fall to. Food up, drink ho! bottoms up, lads; this month marks the height of the bibbing season."

Out came the flagons, up came the Dipsodes' provisions, though poor King Anarchus found scant grounds for rejoicing.

"What job could we give King Anarchus now," Panurge asked, "to fit him for his profession in hell?"

"I hadn't thought!" said Pantagruel. "An excellent idea, Pan-urge." He seemed to reflect a moment. "I'll tell you: you can have him. I give him to you; make what you like of him."

"Gramercy, My Lord," said Panurge, "this present brooks no re-fusal. And I prize it the more because you are the donor."

XXXI

HOW PANTAGRUEL ENTERED INTO THE CITY OF THE AMAUROTES AND HOW, THANKS TO PANURGE, KING ANARCHUS BECAME A BRIDEGROOM AND A HAWKER OF GREENSAUCE

AFTER this stupendous victory, Pantagruel sent Carpalim to the Amaurotes with tidings that King Anarchus had been captured and the enemy defeated. The inhabitants flocked out to meet Pantagruel, accompanying him, in orderly array and with great pomp, back to the city. Huge bonfires were lighted, long tables set up in the streets and spread with the best victuals the country afforded. Their celebration was so hearty it seemed as though the Golden Age were come again.

Pantagruel assembled the senate and addressed them as follows: "Let us strike, gentlemen, while the iron is hot. Before we celebrate any further, I intend to attack the Dipsodes and occupy their kingdom. Let such of you as wish to join me prepare to leave to-morrow after drinking: my departure is set for that hour. Not that I need any help, mind you; Dipsody is as good as conquered. But I have noticed that this city is so overcrowded that a man has barely room to turn around in the streets, let alone swing a cat.

"To-morrow, then, I will lead the volunteers into Dipsody and establish them there as a colony, bestowing the entire country upon them. Many of you have been there; I need not tell you it is the richest, most fruitful and pleasantest country on earth. Let such as wish to come be ready to-morrow."

Pantagruel's proclamation having been published throughout the city, on the morrow, at the hour appointed, upwards of eighteen hundred and fifty-six thousand and eleven inhabitants (exclusive of women and children) assembled on the square before the palace. As they marched off to Dipsody, they were as admirably disciplined as the children of Israel departing out of Egypt to pass over the Red Sea.

But before going on to chronicle this expedition, I must relate how Panurge treated King Anarchus.

Remembering what Epistemon had told of the treatment accorded and the trades allotted in the Elysian Fields to kings and millionaires, Panurge felt no compunction about his prisoner. One day, therefore, he apparelled his ex-Majesty in a smart doublet of the roughest canvas, slashed like an Albanian's headgear, and fine ballooning trousers, like a Dutch sailor's pantaloons. He gave him no shoes, however, for, he said, they would only ruin his sight. But on Anarchus' head, he clapped a little plum-blue bonnet with a great capon feather in it. (Perhaps I err: I seem to recall there were two feathers.) Finally, he wound a girdle about him, remarking how well it became him, since the colors were *pers* (blue gray) and *vert* (green), and their wearer *pervers*, a perverse fellow.

Thus accoutred, he brought him into Pantagruel's presence and asked:

"My Lord, do you know this freak?"

"Certainly not, Panurge."

"He is Anarchus, King and *monarchus* of his own vile carcass. I intend to make a decent man of him. The trouble with these cursed kings here is that they are stupid calves. All they ever plan or do is to visit misery upon their unfortunate subjects and trouble the whole world with war for their own detestable pleasure. Now I'm going to give this fellow here a job: he shall mix ginger and verjuice into a sauce and hawk it through the streets. A greensauce crier: that's the stuff! Go ahead, man; let me hear you shout: 'Sorce for sile, gre-e-e-e-n sorce for s-i-i-l-e!'"

Which the ill-starred devil attempted to do.

"Too low, much too low!" Panurge scolded. Then, pulling His Majesty by the ear:

"Sing higher, louse. Pitch it in G-major, so: *la, ré, do, do*! You've a good throat and lusty lungs. The luckiest thing that ever happened to you was to lose your throne!"

Naturally Pantagruel was vastly entertained, for I dare say Anarchus was the funniest puppet that ever danced from the end of a staff, and Panurge the most original joker. And so it was Anarchus became an accomplished crier of greensauce.

Two days later, Panurge married him off to an aged harlot and himself superintended the wedding. They consumed enormous quantities of juicy sheep's-heads, succulent pig's fry with mustard and fragrant tripe stew with garlic. Panurge sent five horseloads to Pantagruel; our good giant ate up every scrap. They washed the food down with white wine and Poitou cider. For dance music, Panurge hired a blind man with a hurdy-gurdy. Then, dinner over, he took them to the palace to present them to Pantagruel. Pointing to the bride:

"There's a bride who'll not crack or explode!" he said.

"Why's that?" Pantagruel asked.

"Because she's pretty well slit already."

"What do you mean by that?"

"Haven't you ever roasted chestnuts in the fire?" Panurge asked. "Put them in whole, and they crack, explode, pop, fart like mad. But slit them and they won't make a sound. Well, this bride is too thoroughly slit below to crack, explode or anything else."

Pantagruel gave them a little cottage in a humble quarter and a stone mortar to pound out their sauce. Here they settled and carried on their little business, Anarchus becoming the prettiest little crier of greensauce in all Utopia.

Recently, however, I heard that Madame beats the poor devil like a carpet and he, the oaf! is too stupid to dare defend himself.

XXXII

HOW PANTAGRUEL COVERED A WHOLE ARMY WITH HIS TONGUE AND WHAT THE AUTHOR SAW IN HIS MOUTH

PANTAGRUEL's progress through Dipsody was one continuous triumph, the inhabitants greeting him joyfully and surrendering on the spot. Of their own accord, the citizens would come out to meet him bearing the keys of the city he was approaching. The Almyrodes or Dirtyones alone sought to resist, replying to his heralds that they would surrender only on the best terms.

"What better terms could we have been on than sitting together with my hand on the pot and their glasses in their fists?" Pantagruel grumbled. "Oh, well, come along, let us go sock them."

So he drew up his army in battle formation, and they proceeded against the enemy. As they were passing by extensive meadowlands, suddenly they were caught by a heavy rain, which made them shiver, worry, and crowd together. Pantagruel bade their captains assure them it was nothing serious. Could he not see over the top of the clouds? He could, he did and all he made out up there was a little dew. At all events, let them draw up in close order and he would shelter them. So they formed a serried line and Pantagruel, putting out his tongue, covered them as a hen covers her chicks.

Meanwhile, I, who am simply reporting cold fact, had sought cover under a burdock leaf almost as large as the arch of the Montrible Bridge. When I saw Pantagruel's men in their snug refuge, I decided to join them. But they were too numerous; there was no room for me. After all, a foot is a foot and not thirteen inches, as the saying goes. The best I could do, therefore, was to climb on to Pantagruel's tongue and make for his mouth, which I finally reached after a two leagues' journey.

But O gods and goddesses of high heaven, what did I behold? May Jupiter confound me with his three-pronged lightning if I lie!

I walked in there as people walk into the church of St. Sophia at Constantinople. And I saw tall rocks looming up like the mountains of Scandinavia (his teeth, I fancy) . . . endless green fields . . . extensive forests . . . massive cities, fortified, and no less populous than Lyons or Poitiers. . . .

The first person I met was a goodman planting cabbages. Amazed, I asked:

"What are you doing here, friend?"

"Planting cabbages!"

"Why? How?"

"Faith, sir, we can't all sport ballocks as heavy as mortars and we can't all be rich. *I* earn *my* living planting cabbages *here* and selling them in market in the city yonder."

"Good Lord, is this a new world?"

"No, no, there's nothing new about this place. Though they do say there is a world beyond here somewhere—a new world too—with a sun and a moon in it and all sorts of fine jobs for a man. Maybe so, maybe not. At any rate, *this* is the *old* world!"

"Really?" I pondered the question a moment. Then: "This city where you sell your cabbages—what do they call it?"

"It's called Aspharage; the citizens are good Christians and friendly souls. They will give you a rousing welcome."

On his recommendation, I decided to go. On my way, I came upon a man lying in wait for pigeons.

"Good morning, friend. Those pigeons you get—where do they come from?"

"From the other world."

I concluded that when Pantagruel yawned, the pigeons, believing his throat to be a dovecote, doubtless flew in in flocks. Presently I reached the city which I found to be picturesque, strongly fortified and prosperous in appearance. At the gate, the sentries stopped me for my pass. Amazed, I cried:

"What is the matter, gentlemen? Is there an epidemic of the plague?"

"My Lord!" they groaned. "We've had so many deaths hereabouts that the tumbrils drive through incessantly."

"Hereabouts, you say? Where?"

They told me the plague was raging in Larynx and Pharynx, large and bustling cities like Rouen and Nantes. It was due, apparently, to a noxious, malodorous and infectious exhalation which had been rising out of the abyss for some time now. Within seven days, more than twenty-two hundred and seventy-six thousand and sixteen people had perished. As I thought back, reckoning the dates, I realized that it was the unsavory breath emanating from Pantagruel's belly, since he had eaten the garlic-strewn stews that illustrated King Anarchus' wedding.

Leaving hastily, I passed among the rocks of his teeth and kept walking until I got to the top of one. Here I found the fairest pleasure resort in the world, with large tennis courts, spacious galleries, sweet meadows, plentiful vines and an infinity of pretty houses, built Italian-fashion in the midst of delightful verdure. Here I spent a good four months and never fared better in my life.

Then I went down by the back teeth towards the jaws, but I was robbed by footpads in a great forest near the ears. Coming down again, I stopped at a small village the name of which I have forgotten. Here I did even better than before; I actually managed to make a little money to live on. Do you know how? By sleeping.

I am not lying: in this extraordinary place, the inhabitants hire people to sleep and pay them five or six sous a day. Heavy snorers get as much as seven and a half.

I told the senators how I had been robbed in the valley. They explained that the folk in those parts were lowlifes and by nature inclined to brigandry. From which I concluded, just as we have countries Cisalpine and Transalpine, they have countries Cidentine and Tradentine. But it is better living on this side because the air is purer.

I began to appreciate the truth of the axiom *Not half the world knows how the other half lives*. Imagine: no one has yet described this country though it includes more than twenty-five populous kingdoms, vast stretches of desert and a great arm of the sea. But I have written a voluminous book upon the subject. The title is *History of the Gorgians*. I named them so because they live in the throat of my master Pantagruel.

At last I returned via the beard, cast myself on his shoulders and

thence made my way to *terra firma*. I fell right in front of him. Seeing me:

"Where the devil have you been, Alcofribas?" he asked.

"In your throat, sir."

"How long, may I ask?"

"Ever since you set out against the Almyrodes."

"That was six months ago," he said. "And how did you live?"

"Handsomely, I thank you."

"What did you find to eat?"

"Plenty."

"To drink?"

"My Lord, I ate and drank just as you did, for I took my toll of
the daintiest morsels and most toothsome wines that passed through
your throat."

"Indeed, indeed. . . . But where did you cack?"

"Down your throat, My Lord."

"Ha, ha, what a wag you are!" he roared. "Well, since you left,
with God's help we conquered all of Dipsody. I will give you the
domain of Salmagundi for your part."

"I thank you, My Lord, you reward me beyond my deserts."

XXXIII

HOW PANTAGRUEL FELL ILL
AND HOW HE WAS CURED

SHORTLY after, Pantagruel was taken ill. He suffered so severely
from stomach trouble that he could neither eat nor drink. As afflic-
tions never come singly, something else rose to torment him more
cruelly than you can possibly imagine. What happened was this: a
stroke of misfortune caused the pale-yellow fluid secreted by his
kidneys, stored in his bladder and discharged by his urethra, to burn
like the geysers of hell.

Fortunately, his physicians treated him with great skill, and
thanks to various lenitives and diuretics, he voided his ailment and
urine simultaneously.

The latter was so hot that it has not cooled off yet. According to the course it took, you can still find it in France and Italy in so-called watering-places or thermal springs. Such spas are Luchon in the Pyrenées and Cauterets, near by . . . Dax in Gascony . . . Balaruc near Montpellier . . . Néris in Bourbonnais . . . Bourbonne-Lancy in Burgundy. . . . Jets of Pantagruel's penial flood landed in Italy at Appona, St. Peter in Padua, St. Helena, Casanova, St. Bartolomeo, and, in the county of Bologna, at Porretta, and in a thousand other places.

That a horde of foolish scientists and physicians waste their time arguing about the origin of these boiling springs is, to me, an amazing phenomenon. Some vow it is borax, others, alum. Still others champion the cause of saltpetre. Tommyrot, all of it. They would do far better to rub their scuts with thistles than consume their energy discussing a matter they know nothing about. The answer is crystal clear. The only possible conclusion is that these watering-places are hot because they came from water made by Pantagruel when a slight misadventure caused that water to flow hot.

To cure his principal ailment, he took the following purgative: four hundredweights of scammony from Colophon near Ephesus, one hundred and thirty-eight cartloads of casaia, eleven thousand nine hundred pounds of rhubarb, not to mention other incredible pharmaceutical hotchpots. After lengthy consultations, his physicians determined that whatever was disturbing his stomach must be removed. To this effect, engineers built seventeen huge copper globes as tall as Virgil's obelisk in Rome, each fitted with trapdoors opening or closing automatically.

A servant went into one of these globes with a lantern and a lighted torch; Pantagruel swallowed it as you would a small pill. Three brawny peasants, armed with picks, climbed into each of five more globes; other stalwart varlets with huge shovels filled an additional three. The rest were manned by hosts of lumbermen with enormous baskets, and all went down Pantagruel's gullet like so many pills.

Once in his belly, they released the springs and emerged through the trapdoors, the lantern-bearer in the van. Doggedly they forged ahead more than half a league through a gulf of corruption more fulsome and putrid than Mephitis, goddess of Sulphur . . . more

fetid than the marshes of Camerina, mentioned by Virgil . . . more
putrid than the rank lake of Sorbona, cited by Strabo. . . . Had
they not thoroughly antidoted their hearts, their stomachs and the
winepots we call noddles, they would have been asphyxiated by these
nauseous fumes. Oh, what perfumes, what evaporations to copro-
contaminate and scatoscandalize the pretty little snouts of adoles-
cent punks!

Groping and sounding their way through the stench, these heroes
approached the fæcal matter and the corrupt humors, finally discovering a heap of ordure. The picks struck valiantly to break it loose,
the shovels did double duty filling the baskets. When the pit was
thoroughly scoured, the men reëntered their globes, closing the trapdoors behind them.

Pantagruel then forced himself to vomit, and thus brought them
back to earth very easily. Rising, they made no more show in his
throat than a fart in yours. As they emerged from their globes, they
looked for all the world like the Greeks leaping out from the Trojan
horse.

Thus Pantagruel was cured and restored to his usual good health
and spirits.

XXXIV

THE CONCLUSION OF THIS
BOOK AND THE AUTHOR'S
APOLOGY

GENTLEMEN, you have now heard the beginning of the horrendous
story of My Lord and Master Pantagruel. I will leave off here because
my head aches a little and I realize that the registers of my brain are
somewhat blurred by this septembral mash. (As you well know, new
wine is heady!)

But I promise you the continuation next spring at the time of the
Frankfort Fair. In it you will read how Panurge was married and
cuckolded within a week . . . how Pantagruel found the philoso-

pher's stone . . . how once found, it should be used . . . how Pantagruel crossed the Caspian Mountains between Armenia and Media . . . how he navigated the Atlantic Ocean . . . how he vanquished the Cannibals and conquered the Isles of Perlas in the West Indies . . . how he married the daughter of Prester John, King of India . . . how he fought against the devils, burned five chambers of hell, sacked the great black apartment, tossed Persephone into the fire and drubbed Lucifer, breaking four of his teeth and the horn in his scut . . . how he visited the regions of the moon to ascertain if it were whole or if women bore three-quarters of it in their heads. . . . Ay, you shall learn a thousand other authentic and very humorous facts, brave things, truly, gospel texts set down in French.

Good night, gentles all. *Perdonate mi*, as the Italians say; forgive me and do not dwell so long upon my faults that you forget your own.

Do I hear you saying: "Master, it scarcely seems sensible of you to be writing such jocose twaddle!" My reply is that you are no more sensible to waste your time reading it.

But if you do so as a gay pastime—which was the spirit in which I wrote—then you and I are less reprehensible than a rabble of unruly monks, critters and hypocritters, sophists and double-fists, humbugs and other bugs, and all folk of the same water and kidney who skulk under religious robes the better to gull the world. For they seek to persuade ordinary people that they are intent solely upon contemplation, devotion, fasts, maceration of their sensualities—and that merely to sustain the petty fragility of their humanity! Whereas, quite to the contrary, they were roistering, and God knows how they roister! As Juvenal has it: "*Et Curios simulant sed bacchanalia vivant*, they play the austere Curius yet revel in bacchanalian orgies." You may read the record of their dissipation in great letters of illuminated script upon their florid snouts and their pendulous bellies unless they perfume themselves with sulphur.

As for their studies, they read only Pantagrueline books, not so much to pass the time merrily as to hurt some one mischievously. How so? By fouling and befouling, by twiddling their dry fingers and fingering their dry twiddlers, by twisting wry necks, by bumming, arsing and ballocking, by devilscutting, in a word by calumniating. Rapt in this task, they are like nothing so much as the brutish village clods who in the cherry season stir up the ordures of little children to find kernels to sell to druggists for pomander oil.

Flee these rascals at sight, hate and abhor them as I do myself, and, by my faith, you will be the better for it. Would you be good Pantagruelists? That is, would you live peaceful, happy, healthy and forever content? Then never trust in people who peep through holes, especially through the opening of a monk's hood.

HERE END THE CHRONICLES OF PANTAGRUEL, KING OF THE DIPSODES, RESTORED TO THEIR TRUE NATURE, TOGETHER WITH HIS DEEDS AND HORRENDOUS FEATS, SET DOWN BY THE LATE MONSIEUR ALCOFRIBAS, ABSTRACTOR OF QUINTESSENCE.

The Third Book

THE HEROIC SAYINGS AND DEEDS OF THE EXCELLENT

PANTAGRUEL

Set Down by

MASTER FRANÇOIS RABELAIS
Doctor of Medicine

THE ABOVE AUTHOR BEGS HIS BENEVOLENT READERS TO REFRAIN

FROM LAUGHING UNTIL THE SEVENTY-EIGHTH BOOK

DIZAIN
FRANÇOIS RABELAIS

To the soul of the QUEEN OF NAVARRE

You have, O royal Soul, without regret,
Fled softly from your mortal habitation
(Your comely body which was ever set
On doing your will here in its earthly station).
In heaven, your element, your inchoation,
You are content. . . . Yet let a kindly fate
Restore you to our midst, compassionate,
Making your eyes to range, your thoughts to dwell
On this, which is the third book to relate
The Joyous Feasts of Good Pantagruel.

THE AUTHOR'S PROLOGUE

GOOD people, most illustrious topers and you, thrice-precious gouty gentlemen, I wonder if you ever saw Diogenes, the Cynic philosopher? If you did, then you certainly had a sharp pair of eyes in your head, or I am lost to all intelligence and logic. Light is beautiful! The sparkle of wine . . . no, I err: the twinkling of doubloons . . . no, no, I meant the light of day. . . . (At last, I make myself clear!)

I base this observation on the case of the blind man so renowned in the Bible. Asked by the Almighty to choose whatever he pleased, he was content to beg for the mere gift of sight.

You are no longer young, my friends; you are equipped to philosophize metaphysically in vinous matters, to be enrolled at once in the Bacchic council. Here, wining, as you swill, you may ween what you will of the substance, color, odor, quality, superiority, propriety, faculty, virtue, effect and dignity of our blessed, much-desired liquor.

If you never saw Diogenes (as I am prepared to believe), at least you have heard speak of him. For a good many years now, the air of earth and the reaches of heaven have echoed with the fame and memory of his name. Besides, unless I err, you are all of Phrygian blood, since it was Francus, Hector's son, who founded your fatherland. To be sure, you have not as many golden crowns as Midas; but you certainly possess an indefinable something that was his. A quality indeed, which the ancient Persians prized most highly in their spies . . . a faculty the Emperor Antoninus Caracalla specially exacted of his confidential servants . . . a gift which gave the Rohan serpentine its surname. In brief, my lusty comrades, you have fine ears!

If, however, you never heard speak of Diogenes, I should like to tell you a story about him. It will flavor your wine (drink up, lads) and improve your minds (do listen carefully!). First, though, lest your naïveté abuse you like the heathens', I must inform you that in his day Diogenes was a rare philosopher, and the most rollicking blade in the world. Had he a few shortcomings? Well, so have you, so have we all, since none but God is perfect. Nevertheless, Alexander the Great, though educated and advised by Aristotle himself, vowed that, were he not Alexander, he would have liked to be Diogenes of Sinope.

When Philip, King of Macedon, undertook to besiege and destroy Corinth, the Corinthians were warned by their spies that a vast hostile army was advancing against them. They were, naturally, terrified. Immediately, they strained every nerve preparing to resist him, each man being assigned his individual duty and responsibility. Some brought stores into the fort, contributing cattle, corn, wine, fruit, victuals and sundry foodstuffs. Others fortified the walls of the city, raised bastions, squared outworks, dug trenches, laid counter-mines, filled wicker cylinders with earth for purposes of engineering and defense, set up platforms, cleared the casemates in the fortresses and barricaded the passages outside the walls in front of the ramparts. Others erected cavaliers, or fortifications, looming up behind the inner lines; others repaired the outer walls, plastered the ramparts, lengthened the gunpits, banked up the parapets, secured the loopholes, relined the vents, fastened the portcullises and herses, posted sentries and sent out patrols. None but was actively on the watch, none but did his bit.

Some polished corselets, varnished backplates and breastplates, cleaned headpieces, coats and jackets of mail, sallets or round light helmets, hauberks, legpieces, armguards, shields, bucklers, gauntlets, greaves, spurs and various pieces of armor. Some worked on bows, slings, crossbows, pellets, catapults, grenades, firebrands, scorpions, ballistas and other engines calculated to stop the enemy's helepolides or moving siegetowers. Some sharpened longhandled weapons such as staves, pikes, halberds, hooks, lances, adzes, battle-axes, spears, clubs, javelins, maces, darts and truncheons, or handweapons such as scimitars, cutlasses, sabres, rapiers, daggers, poignards, stilettos, short broadswords, dirks, knives, arrows and the like. No man but exercised his own weapon, couched his private lance, drew his personal bilbo. No woman, however staid or aged, but furbished up her tackle, polished her fittings and lay in arms, ready to buckle conclusions at the drop of a hat. (You know the Corinthian women enjoyed a great reputation for going clapperclaw to loggerheads and coming very much up to scratch in a brabble!)

Diogenes, seeing them so warm at work while he was unassigned to duty by the magistrates, watched them very seriously for several days without uttering a word. Then, suddenly, as though driven by a martial urge, he slung his cloak over his shoulder; pulled up his shirtsleeves to the elbow like an applepicker; gave a friend his wallet, his books, his writing tablets, and left town for Craneum, a hilly promontory near by. There, on a level space, he brought the tub which served him for a house and a shelter against the fury of the elements; there, furiously, amid a great straining of arms, he wheeled and whirled it about, shoving it here, pushing it there . . . pulling it one way, tugging it the other . . . tumbling it one side up, then overturning it again . . . shifting, thrusting, driving, jostling and hustling it every which way . . . now impelling it to the left, now hurtling it to the right, jogging it here, butting it there . . . beating, slamming, dashing, banging and kicking it . . . sending it crashing downhill from the heights of Craneum into the valley, then rolling it up again, like a new Sisyphus with his legendary stone. . . . Indeed, Diogenes so belabored it that he all but knocked out its bottom.

One of his friends, noticing the philosopher's activity, inquired why he was thus exerting his body, taxing his mind and tormenting his tub. To which the philosopher replied that, since the republic had employed him in no office, he was forced to create his own activities. For he refused to be idle or lazy whilst a whole people was earnestly at work.

By the same token, though I am out of danger, I am not unmoved by what is happening about me. Shall I be accused of inertia when, throughout this most noble kingdom of France, on either side of the mountains, men are doing double duty, to fortify and defend their native land or to repel the foe and attack them in turn? They are doing this under such perfect direction, in such flawless order, that the frontiers of our land will be magnificently extended and our people assured of a well-earned rest. Again, they are doing this so admirably that I almost agree with good Heraclitus when he states that war is the parent of all good things. One might almost suppose, as our fathers did, that our French word *bel* was derived from the

Latin *bellum*, as though nobility and beauty came from war. Only the mouldiest patchers of rusty Latin would have you believe that this is not the fact. For has not war disclosed all manner of benefits and wonders? Has it not abolished evil and ugliness? Why could Solomon, a sagacious and peaceful monarch, find no more perfect expression for the ineffable glory of divine wisdom than the phrase "terrible as an army with banners"?

Alas! I have been considered by my compatriots as unfit to join them in an offensive capacity; nor am I employed in a defensive, though I would gladly have lugged hods, shelled pods, dug sods or broken clods. I would deem it very disgraceful indeed to stand aside as but an idle spectator whilst so many valiant and eloquent heroes perform soul-stirring rôles in the magnificent epic spectacle all Europe watches to-day. Disgraceful, I repeat, not to contribute to the great cause this nothing which is my all. Tell me what honor falls to such as merely look on, liberal with their eyes but niggardly with their efforts . . . hoarding their money . . . scratching their scalps like louts and oaves . . . gasping at flies like tithe calves . . . wagging their ears like Arcadian asses at the melody of the musicians, and, with expressionless mien, approving of the performance . . . ?

Having made my choice, I considered it neither unprofitable nor offensive to set into motion my Diogenic tub, the lone thing I salvaged out of my shipwreck upon Misfortune Shoals.

But now I have it rolling, what shall I do with it? Have you any suggestions? By the turnuppy, cockuppy virgin that tucks up her gown, I haven't the faintest idea how to proceed. Wait a moment, I pray, while I swallow a deep draught of this bottle here, my one and only Helicon (sweet mountain of the Muses in Bœotia!), my caballine fountain (fair Hippocrene, sprung splashing from the heel of Pegasus!), my sole enthusiasm! Drinking thus, I meditate, I discourse, I resolve, I conclude. The epilogue dispatched, I laugh, I write, I compose, I drink again. Did not Ennius, drinking, write and, writing, drink? Did not Æschylus (if Plutarch's *Symposiacs* deserve credence) quaff while composing and, quaffing, compose? Homer never wrote on an empty stomach; Cato never set pen to paper until he had wet his whistle. I bring these examples to your notice to prove that I follow the rule of better and more praiseworthy men. The lesson they teach still holds good and keeps fresh, as though entering into the rarefied state dear to the alchemists—for which praise God, the good God Sabaoth, Lord of Hosts, eternally! If, by the same token, you decide to take a deep draught, or two small ones, I shall not object so you but breathe a sigh of thanks to the Creator.

Though my luck and destiny are such as I told you (it is not granted to all men to enter or live in Corinth), I am resolved to engage in some sort of helpful activity. Yes, I am determined to be of service to these or those.

Amongst the pioneers and garrison laborers, I shall act like Laomedon, Neptune and Apollo, who built the walls of Troy at Jupiter's command, or like Renaud de Montauban, who, as penance in his old age, was set to work on the walls of the Cathedral of Cologne. I shall help the masons, I shall set the pot to boiling for them and, the meal done, I'll play my bagpipe till the mellow tones raise yellow stones. So, Amphion, son of Zeus and Antiope, strummed the lyre Mercury gave him and, at its sound, the stones arose of themselves to build the mighty city of Thebes.

For the combatants, I intend to tap a third barrel of a liquor you would fully appreciate, had not dishonest printers adulterated and vitiated the two preceding. From the vintage of our frivolous pastimes, I vow to draw for them a gallant third, and, later, a jocund quart of Pantagruelian sentences, which I give you leave to call Diogenical. Since I may not be the fellow-soldier of our brave warriors, I shall be their excellent butler, ready to comfort them to the best of my poor ability and with the best of my rich wine, when they return from the alarms of war. I shall also be the tireless singer of their praises and prowesses; nor shall I fail unless March fails to fall in Lent, which the cunning lecher will take care not to do.

At this point, I recall reading how one day Ptolemy, son of Lagus, publicly presented to the Egyptians, among other spoil and booty, a Bactrian or two-humped camel from Asia. It was jet black. He had it led into the arena by a curiously complexioned slave, half-black, half-white, not horizontally divided in colors (like the female votary of Venus seen by Apollonius of Tyana) but vertically. As such a phenomenon had never before been beheld in Egypt, Ptolemy hoped by the originality of the exhibit to win the love of his people.

What happened? Well, they first saw the camel and were terrified; then they saw the man and were indignant. Some jeered; others inveighed against what they considered a detestable monster spawned by a freak of nature. In brief, he botched an opportunity to entertain the Egyptians and thereby increase their natural affection for him; he learned that they preferred the beautiful, the harmonious, the perfect, to the grotesque and the abnormal. So he took such a dislike to camel and slave that, through negligence or lack of attention, both died very shortly after.

This example keeps me on tenterhooks between fear and hope. What if instead of the delight I strive to create, I should meet with disgust from my readers? What if my treasure be but coals; my gold, dross? What if I throw the antic dice and, instead of Venus and a pair of sixes, I turn up the dog-faced boy and two aces? What if I annoy instead of please? What if I turn out to be like that rooster of Euclio's celebrated by Plautus in his *Aulularia* or *Pot of Gold*. Celebrated by others, too; by Ausonius, for example in his *Gryphus*, a poem he pretended to have unearthed in the rubbish of a library, just as Euclio's rooster turned up the treasure. You recall the tale: the wretched fowl had its throat cut for its trouble in discovering the gold. Suppose this occurred in my case, would there not be cause for anger? It did occur before and might easily again.

But, by Hercules, it shall not. For in my readers I discern the same specific force that our ancestors called Pantagruelism. Thanks to this personal property, they cannot misunderstand anything born of a good, free and loyal heart. How often have I seen them prodigal of kindliness, indulgent towards the paltry efforts of the entertainer!

Having settled this point, I return to my tub. Come, lads, have at this excellent wine! Fall to, comrades, drink it up by the bowlful. Of course, if it does not seem good to you, then by all means leave it. I am not one of those importunate sots who by taunt, force or intimidation, make their guests to bib, tope and swig—and, worse, rebib, supertope and hyperswig! No, no—all good drinkers, all honest gout-ridden gentles and all thirst-stricken souls come to my barrel. But they do not partake of it against their will.

If the wine tickle their palates and satisfy their worshipful worships, then they imbibe freely, frankly, resolutely, without paying and welcome, too, according to my decree. And never fear that the wine run short, as it did at the wedding feast at Cana in Galilee. As much as you draw forth at the tap, I shall drain in at the bung, so our barrel will prove inexhaustible, lively at the source and of perpetual flow. Such was the nectar in Tantalus' cup, which the Brahman sages represented figuratively; such was the Iberian mountain of salt so highly vaunted by Cato; such the golden bough sacred to the underground goddess which Virgil sings of so sublimely. Ay, my barrel is a veritable cornucopia of merriment and mockery. Even if, at times, it may seem to you to be drained to the lees, it is not wholly dry. As in Pandora's jug (erroneously reported to be a box), hope lingers in its depths. Unlike the sieves through which the Danaïdes strained water in hell for having killed their husbands, it is not lined with despair.

I shall take the stand of the poet Lucilius when, fearing Strabo's criticism of his Greek, he announced that he wrote for the bilingual Tarentines and Calabrians of Cosenza who, speaking both Latin and Greek, were critics of neither. To avoid all misinterpretation, I serve fair warning that I have tapped my barrel only for honest fellows, drinkers of the first vintage, consumers of the first edition, gouty blades of the highest degree. Giftmongers, bribetakers, parasites of the law courts will find game aplenty in the pouches holding their briefs and in the wind up their tails. That is fair hunting for them; here is no prey to their liking.

As for you, pettifoggers and scribblers, I beg you not to address me —I beg it in the name of the four thighs that engendered you, and out of respect for the vivifying coupling-rod which then linked them. As for holier-than-thou hypocrites, I would suffer them still less gladly, even though they be finished tosspots, hardshell crusties of the pox, afflicted with an unquenchable thirst and an inexhaustible hunger. Why will I not tolerate them? Because the goodness they display is no more and no less than the evil we daily pray God to deliver us from; because, though they play Lazarus at the rich man's table, we know old apes cannot make pretty faces.

Back, curs, to heel! Out of my way, back from the barrel, out of the sunlight, you scum of the devil! Away, hypocrites and sham-Abrahams! How dare you come here, arsing and parsing, mumbling for my wine and then bepiddling my barrel? Look out! here is the staff Diogenes willed to be laid beside him after death so he might exterminate such deadly larvae and gravelice as yourself. To your flocks, mastiffs; fly hence, buzzards, by all the devils of hell!

What! You are still here! By God, for my part, if I stomach you, let me surrender my share of Paradise—yes, my share of Papimany, the Pope's temporal possessions!—Grrrrrrr! Grrrrr! Kssssss! Kssss! Away, away with them! Are they not yet gone?

May you never contrive a shit without first being lambasted with stirrup-straps . . . may you never squeeze out a piddle without being previously strappadoed . . . and may you never know bodily heat save that induced by the cudgel!

I

HOW PANTAGRUEL TRANS-PORTED A COLONY OF UTO-PIANS INTO DIPSODY

HAVING subdued Dipsody, a land sparsely inhabited and partly wilderness, Pantagruel decided to colonize, cultivate and improve it. He therefore transported 9876543210 Utopians, exclusive of women and children. Among them were craftsmen of all trades and professors of all liberal sciences.

You know, of course, that the Utopians have always multiplied like rabbits; I need go no further into this. For, since time immemorial, the gentlemen of that land have possessed genitals of extraordinary fecundity. As for the ladies, their matrices have always been so inordinately ample, glutinous, tenaciously retentive and architectonically cellulated, that every nine months produced at least seven children of either sex to grace each marriage. The Utopians thus imitated the Jews in Egypt, if Nicholas de Lyra is not delirious in his biblical commentary.

Despite this, the overpopulation of Utopia was not Pantagruel's primary reason for establishing a colony in Dipsody. Nor did he do so because of the fertility of Dipsody soil, the salubrity of its climate, or the commodities of the country. On the contrary, Pantagruel's policy was extremely far-sighted. He wanted, above all, to hold a rebellious people to duty and obedience by grafting on to them his most ancient and loyal subjects. Time out of mind, the Utopians had known, acknowledged, recognized, and served no lord but himself. At birth, together with their mothers' milk, they imbibed the sweetness and light of his government; as they grew up, they developed and mellowed therein. They would far sooner have abandoned their lives than swerved from the innate and natural obedience they owed their prince. Obviously, such loyalty could stand the test of all migration, dissemination and transportation. Furthermore, not only would these colonists produce children of like temper, but they could be relied on to influence and maintain the newly-annexed peoples in the same fealty and discipline.

This theory of Pantagruel's worked admirably; he was disappointed in no respect. If, before their transplantation, the Utopians had been appreciative and dutiful, the Dipsodes, after a few days' association, became even more so. This was due to a certain indefinable inherent fervor that all humans nourish when they undertake any task they enjoy. Their sole complaint—and they called the heavens and the gods to witness—was that the fame of good Pantagruel had not reached them sooner.

Here I draw the attention of my bibbing readers to a point of statesmanship. Certain despotic spirits, to their shame and loss, promulgate violence. What an error! On the contrary, in order to instill and maintain obedience in a newly-conquered people, the one thing a monarch must avoid is pillaging, harrying, vexing, oppressing, and tyrannizing them. The rod of iron will not work; woe to the conqueror who swallows a nation in his maw—a demovorous king, as Achilles called Agamemnon when they quarrelled at the siege of Troy. But I will not quote the writers of antiquity to prove my point; I need but call to your minds what your fathers and yourselves, if not too young, have seen with your own eyes. Conquered nations are newborn babes; as such they must be given suck, they must be rocked, fondled and amused. Like newly-planted trees, they must be supported, propped up, and protected from all tempests, injuries and calamities. Like convalescents from lengthy illnesses, they must be nursed, coddled and cherished. Do this and they will be convinced that never a king or prince in Christendom seeks fewer enemies and more friends.

Thus Osiris the Great, King of Egypt, conquered the whole earth, not by force of arms, but by easing the people of their troubles. He taught them how to live well, he gave them a chance to prosper honestly, he granted them decent laws, he showed them mercy and kindness. As a result, he was known throughout the world as the great King Energetes or the Benefactor, thus·fulfilling the prophecy given by Almighty Jupiter to Pamyla, a woman of Thebes.

Similarly, Hesiod, in his hierarchy, places the good demons—you may call them angels or genii as you will—as intercessors and mediators between gods and men, inferior to the former, superior to the latter. Through their hands pass the riches and benefits of heaven; they are therefore continually doing us good and preserving us from evil. Hesiod calls them kings because always to do good and never harm is a wholly royal act.

Because Alexander of Macedon followed this principle, he became emperor of the universe. Of such, too, was Hercules, who possessed the whole continent. He relieved humanity of monsters, oppression, exactions and tyranny . . . he treated men with tact and feeling . . . he maintained them justly and equitably . . . he inaugurated a benevolent policy . . . he framed judicious laws suited to the particularity of individual countries . . . he supplied what was lacking . . . he abolished what was superfluous . . . invariably he rubbed the slate clean, with a sempiternal oblivion of past offences.

Such, too, was the amnesty declared by the Athenians when the prowess and industry of Thrasybulus overthrew the thirty and ten tyrants, and banished them alone. Such, too, the clemency of Cicero, and, later, of the Emperor Aurelian in Rome.

It is the filtres, potions and allure of affection that assure a lasting peace to a land painfully subdued. No conqueror, be he king, prince or philosopher, can reign more auspiciously than by crowning his valor with justice. That valor was manifest in his victory; that justice will appear when, through good will and sympathy towards his subjects, he grants laws, publishes ordinances, establishes religions, and respects the rights of all men. As the noble poet Virgil writes of Octavian Augustus:

> *A conqueror who gives laws to willing states*
> *And thus attempts his way to heaven. . . .*

Hence Homer in his *Iliad* calls good princes and great kings κοσμήτορα, or ornaments, of the people.

Numa Pompilius, the second king of the Romans, followed the same rule. A just, politic and philosophical sovereign, he ordered that nothing that had died be sacrificed at the festival called Terminales, in honor of the god Termes. Thereby, he proved that the limits and frontiers of kingdoms should be guarded and governed peacefully, amicably and satisfactorily without pillage or bloodshed. Whoever does otherwise will not only lose his gains. He will also earn the shameful reproach of having made them wrongfully and unjustly, since it is ill-gotten gains that fall to ruin. Further, even supposing he enjoy them peacefully all his own life, if they fall away from his heirs, that opprobrium and ignominy will still cling to his memory, cursing him for an iniquitous despot. As the Latin proverb has it: Of ill-gotten gains the enjoyment cometh not to the third inheritor.

I beg you also to note another point, O precious legatees, grantees and vavasours of gout. Unlike Charlemagne who out of one devil made two, when he transported the Saxons into Flanders and the Flemish into Saxony, Pantagruel made two angels out of one. Charlemagne, unable to subject the Saxons of his empire, and ever fearful of open rebellion if he should be drawn into Spain or some other remote region, made the Saxons emigrate to Flanders, a land whose subjects obeyed him naturally. The loyalty of the Flemings and Hainaulters, subjects of long standing, he could trust, even though they had been transplanted into a foreign land. Alas, what happened was that the Saxons persisted in their earliest obstinacy and rebellion, while the transplanted Flemings became imbued with Saxon stubbornness and pugnacity.

II

HOW PANURGE WAS MADE LORD OF SALMAGUNDI IN DIPSODY, AND HOW HE SQUANDERED HIS MONEY BEFORE IT CAME IN

WHILE Pantagruel was establishing a sound government in Dipsody, he assigned to Panurge the lordship of Salmagundi. The annual income from this domain rose to 6789106789 gold royals of assured rent, plus the variable revenue of cockchafers and snailshells, which, taking one year with another, amounted to a good 2435768 or 2435769 French crowns, gold. In a good season, with bold cockchafers and snailshells in demand, it might rise as high as 1234554321 Turkish seraphs. But that was not, however, every year.

The new lord governed his estate so wisely and prudently that, in less than a fortnight, he had squandered his assured and varying incomes for the next three years.

The money did not go, as you might suppose, to a worthy cause such as founding monasteries, building churches, erecting colleges, establishing hospitals, or casting his bacon to the dogs. No, My Lord Panurge ran through his fortune in a thousand gay banquets and convivial entertainments, in keeping open house for all comers, all good company, jolly lads, pretty maids and comely wenches. He felled whole forests of trees, burning the logs for what their cinders would fetch, obtaining loans in advance, purchasing at a high price, selling cheap, counting his chickens before they were hatched, and eating his corn, as it were, ere it grew on the stalk.

Apprised of the state of affairs, Pantagruel was neither offended, grieved nor sorry. Was he not, as I told you once, and repeat again, the best little great good fellow that ever buckled on a sword? He took everything in good part, viewed every action in the most favorable light, was never in the least worried or shocked. To allow anything to upset or vex him, he believed, was tantamount to flying the divine coop of his reason. He knew well that everything heaven covers and earth bears, in all dimensions of height, depth, length and breadth, does not warrant our troubling our equanimity or perplexing our spirit.

Pantagruel merely took Panurge aside and gently pointed out that, if he continued on his extravagant course, he, Pantagruel, could not possibly (or only with the greatest difficulty) make Panurge rich.

"Rich!" Panurge gasped. "Is that what you intended? Did you actually undertake to enrich me in this world? Good heavens, My Lord, in the name of God and all good men, aim rather at living the merriest possible life. Let no other purpose or care pass the sacrosanct portals of your celestial cerebellum! May no cloud of sullen thought, no shadow of grim misfortune ever darken the serene pastures of your heavenly soul! Instead, live gay, merry, full of joy, and I shall be only too rich in watching you!"

Panurge went on to show how every one cried thrift and economy, when not one man in a million knew the meaning of the words. On the contrary, Pantagruel should imitate Panurge. The very behavior Pantagruel blamed as vicious was modelled upon that of the University and Parliament of Paris, the cradles of pantheology and justice. Whoever doubted this—more, whoever failed implicitly to believe it in every detail—was an out-and-out heretic. Did they not in a single day gobble up their bishop (or the revenue of the bishopric, it was all one!)? This occurred on the day he took his seat; if he protested, he risked being lapidated on the spot.

"What you call extravagance, My Lord, has also been considered a virtue sprung of the four cardinal virtues: prudence, justice, fortitude, temperance. Let me prove this to you.

"First, prudence. Is it not wise to borrow in anticipation or spend beforehand, when you cannot tell what may happen? Who shall certify that the world will last another three years? And suppose it does, what man dare promise he will live that long? As Seneca says:

> *What man knows God's will well enough to say*
> *To-morrow he shall live like yesterday?*

"Second, justice, both commutative (which maintains the relation of equality between purchase and price), and distributive (which gives to each according to his merits). Commutatively, by buying dear—on credit, mark you—and selling cheap—on a cash basis. Need I quote Cato's *Husbandry*: 'The father of a family must be a perpetual seller.' Such being the case, how can he help but get rich, if he has enough to keep on selling? Distributively, by nourishing good (I emphasize the word: good) and well-bred lads, whom Fortune has shipwrecked without provision upon the shoals of appetite, just as it cast Ulysses upon the Phæcian rock. Not lads alone, either, but also good young maids—and please to note both adjectives, for, according to Hippocrates, youth is impatient of hunger, especially when lively, spirited, brisk, stirring and lusty. What is more, these wenches joyfully devote themselves to the pleasure of honest men; being both Platonists and Ciceronians, they realize they were born into this world not for their own sakes, but to offer their persons partly to their country, partly to their friends.

"Third, fortitude. By imitating Milo of Crotona, the celebrated Greek lumberjack, what do I accomplish? Laying these dark forests low, I clear the lairs of wolves, the dens of wild boars, the holes of foxes, the strongholds of brigands and murderers, the workshops of counterfeiters, the refuges of heretics. What do I make of them? Fine airy clearings, plain level ground where, to the sound of oboe and flute, my people prepare their seats for the Day of Judgment.

"And fourth, temperance. By eating my corn when it is still but grass, I resemble the hermit who lives upon salads and roots; I triumph over sensual appetites; I abandon the delicacies of life to the ailing and crippled. Thus, too, I save a lot of money which would go to highly-paid agricultors . . . to reapers in harvest time, who drink deep and without water . . . to gleaners, who must be served cakes after working . . . to winnowers, who leave no leek, garlic or onion in the garden, if we are to believe Thestylis, the maid in Virgil who prepared the harvesters' meals . . . to millers, who are almost invariably thieves . . . and to bakers, who are little better. . . . I suppose you don't call that saving! And I haven't even mentioned the mischief done by field-mice, the upkeep of barns, the havoc wrought by mites and weevils."

The four cardinal virtues disposed of, Panurge went on to praise unripe corn as a marvellous base for greensauce, which was easy to cook and to digest. And what results that sauce produced! It refreshed the brain, exhilarated the animal spirits, rejoiced the sight, stimulated the appetite, tickled the palate, and pleased the tongue . . . it strengthened the heart, cleared the complexion, developed the muscles, tempered the blood, and eased the diaphragm . . . it cooled the liver, flushed the spleen, relieved the kidneys, fortified the joints of the back, cleaned out the urethra, dilated the spermatic vessels, and jacked up the cremasters or testicle-strings . . . it purged the bladder, swelled the genitals, righted the foreskin, hardened the gland and rectified the penis . . . finally, it set the belly in apple-pie order, so a man could belch, fart, poop, piddle, shit, sneeze, sob, cough, throw up, yawn, puff, inhale, exhale, snore, snort, sweat and wangle the ferrule to his heart's content. . . . In a word, it possessed a thousand advantages.

"I quite understand," Pantagruel exclaimed, "you infer that mean-spirited people cannot spend so much money in so short a time."

Panurge was silent.

"You're not the first to uphold that heresy," Pantagruel continued. "Nero, for instance, admired, above all men, his uncle Caligula, because the latter, in a few days, was ingenious enough to dissipate the totality of what Tiberius left him."

Panurge, Pantagruel protested, had not observed the sumptuary laws of the Romans concerning banqueting—the laws called *Orchia, Fanuia, Didia, Licinia, Cornelia, Lepidiana, Antia*. He had also flown in the face of the Corinthian laws, which punished severely any man spending more than one year's income. He had offered up the sacrifice of *Protervia*, which to the Romans was like the paschal lamb to the Jews when everything edible was consumed, the remainder thrown into the fire, and nothing left for the morrow.

"I am justified," Pantagruel concluded, "in saying of you what Cato said of Albidius. The latter had wasted his fortune, until there remained nothing but one small house; so he burned it, the better to say: '*Consummatum est, it is finished.*'

"The same holds true of St. Thomas Aquinas and the lamprey!"

Panurge gathered Pantagruel's meaning as he recalled the famous story. St. Thomas, dining with King Louis IX, was so absorbed in composing the concluding lines of a hymn, that he ate the whole of the fish served for His Majesty. Having done so, "*Consummatum est!*" he cried. The guest believed he was applying the last words of Jesus not to the conclusion of his hymn, but to the lamprey he had finished.

III

PANURGE IN PRAISE OF DEBTORS AND CREDITORS

"BUT," Pantagruel objected, "when will you be out of debt?"

"At the Greek kalends," Panurge replied. "In the sweet never-never, when all the world is content and each man is his own heir. I pray God keep me in debt because, otherwise, I could not find a soul to lend me a sou. Leave no leaven overnight and where will you find dough in the morning?"

Pantagruel made no answer.

"But stay in debt," Panurge pursued, "and your creditors will pray God to grant you a long, happy, prosperous life. Does your name occur in a conversation, at once they will shower you with praise—praise that will win you new creditors. And creditor number one is perfectly right, since he is repaid at the cost of those who follow him. Rob Peter to pay Paul, it is all one to Paul.

"Take the Gauls of old: their druidic laws sentenced slaves to be burned on their masters' funeral pyres. Naturally, then, the terrified servants implored their gods to spare the masters as long as possible. Teutates, the Gallic Mercury, and Dis, their Pluto, god of wealth, were constantly beset with invocations. You can also imagine how carefully those servants watched over their masters and served them.

"You may well believe that a man's creditors will pray God even more fervently that he live, since his death means the loss of their money. As you know, such folks had rather lose their right arms than a purse, their lives than their loans. The usurers of Landerousse offer an example; they hanged themselves when, thanks to good weather, the price of wheat and wine fell.

"By God, the more I think of it, the flatter you leave me when you hold my debts and creditors against me. Why, by my mere status as debtor, I considered myself important, respected and feared. Do not all philosophers agree that nothing can be made out of nothing? Well, I had nothing, not even the most basic matter, yet I created and manufactured something.

"What did I create? A splendid body of creditors. I maintain most earnestly (short of trial by fire or burning at the stake) that creditors are priceless creatures. Whereas those beast-brutes who refuse to lend are the spawn of the foul fiend of hell.

"What did I manufacture? Debts, debts, O rare and hallowed things, debts, I say, exceeding the total permutations and combinations of the vowels and consonants in the alphabet. Old Xenocrates the Academic calculated these to be over one hundred million. Ay, my friend, judge the perfection of a debtor by the multiplicity of his creditors and you will never go wrong in practical arithmetic!"

Panurge expatiated upon his delight at awakening every morning to see his creditors thronging about him. Such humble, serviceable, reverential fellows! Did Panurge look more favorably upon a particular one, the scoundrel forthwith believed his score settled. The idiot congratulated himself on being the first paid off; he took Panurge's smile for twinkling cash! To Panurge, it always seemed as though he were enacting a part in the most elaborate passion play of the century. On every side he found candidates for his favors, body-guards, greeters, saluters, supporters and champions interminable.

Panurge vowed that the perfection of heroism, as dreamed by Hesiod, must surely be the maximum of debts. In this study, he himself had already fallen a degree or two. All humans aspired and tended to this goal, but few reached it for "strait is the gate," competition was fierce: every one nowadays strove fervidly, fiercely to discover fresh creditors, to incur new debts. Yet it did not lie in the power of every one to be a debtor; the conferring of creditor rank called for highly individual talents.

And now, here was Pantagruel seeking to deprive Panurge of this exquisite, suave joy . . . trying to deprive Panurge of creditors. . . .

"Worse still, My Lord Pantagruel, may St. Babolino take my babbling soul if I did not believe debts to be a sort of link and stepping-stone between earth and heaven . . . a unique tonic for the human species . . . an indispensable factor in the existence of the human family . . . in a word, that illimitable human soul which, according to the Academics, quickens the universe. . . .

"To prove this, imagine, without bias, the idea and form of a world without creditor or debtor. If you like, take but one thirtieth of the worlds Metrodorus, Epicurus' disciple, declares infinite, or one seventy-eighth of the hundred and eighty-six computed by Petronius of Hymera, the Pythagorean. A world without debts? Why, the very stars would be stopped in their course, the cosmos would crumble to dust."

Jupiter, Panurge asserted, would cease feeling obligated to benevolent Saturn, dispossess him of his sphere, and, with his Homeric chain, suspend all intercommunication. Gods, heaven, demons, genii, heroes, fiends, earth, sea and the various elements would tumble to bits. Saturn would join Mars and visit strife upon the entire world. Mercury, meanwhile, refusing to be subjected to the other planets, would cease to serve as their Camillus, to use the Latin term for messenger. Why, indeed, when he owed them nothing? Venus, for her part, would be venerable no longer, since she had done nothing for which to be venerated. The moon would remain bloody and obscure, for why should the sun impart his light, since he owed nothing either to her or, worse, to earth! The stars would exert no auspicious influence, since earth ceased imparting to them that food without which (according to Heraclitus, the Stoics and Cicero) they cannot live.

Similarly, there would be no symbolization, alteration or transmutation of the various elements, since none borrowing anything, none would feel obligated. Earth would not become water, water would not turn into air, air would make no fire, fire would afford no heat to earth. The world would produce only monsters, titans, giants; no rain would fall; no light shine; no wind blow; the seasons would not exist. Lucifer, breaking his bonds, would emerge from the depths of hell with a horde of furies, fiends and horned devils, to drive out from heaven all the gods of both the greatest and smallest nations.

"Were there no give and take," Panurge cried, "we would be a pack of snarling curs . . . an aggregation as harmonious as the University of Paris, with a Rector eligible by how many national factions? . . . as a catch-as-catch-can comparable to the most harrowing devil's interlude in a medieval miracle play!"

No human being would succor his fellow. Cry "Help!" "Fire!" "I'm drowning!" "Murder!" and where look to rescue? Why should a victim expect a rescuing arm when none owed him anything? His ruin, his destruction, his decease were of no import to such as his prosperity, success and life never affected. This world, Panurge insisted, was based upon mutual help and succor. Where, then, short of assistance, except faith, hope and charity? Rather, look for distrust, suspicion and rancor with their baleful train of misery and evil. Pandora's bottle (others call it her box!) might as well be emptied (or gutted!).

"Your average man would have to fear his fellow worse than the proverbial wolf. Wolf, did I say. No, werewolf, hell's fiend. . . . He would become a Lychaon, King of Arcady, changed to a wolf by Jupiter for violating the laws of hospitality . . . or a Bellerophon, who sought to scale Olympus on Pegasus' back and was therefore turned by Jupiter into an eternal wanderer . . . or a Nebuchadnezzar, King of the Jews, who ended as a pasturing beast . . . a brigand, assassin, poisoner, miscreant, evil-thinker and evildoer, like Ishmael, whose hand was set against every man's . . . or Metabus, Virgil's outcast from men . . . or Timon of Athens, renowned misanthrope. . . . As easy to feed fish in air, or to pasture deer in the caves of the ocean, as to imagine a debtless universe. God help a beggarly world whence free exchange was banished!

"Take this universe," Panurge concluded, "and reduce it to the other little world, which is man. Grievous and abandoned as is the former, how thoroughly concordant will you find the latter? Your head will deny its eyes the light to direct your hands and feet; your feet will not condescend to hold up your body; your hands will forget to coöperate. Your heart will balk at moving the pulse, your lungs will tire of playing bellows for you, your liver refuse to produce blood.

"Your bladder? Unwilling to combine forces with the rest of your system, your wretched bladder will cry quits with your kidneys and thus abolish urine. Your brain, faced with such anarchy, will run amuck, deprive your nerves of sensation, your muscles of motion. In brief, without exchange, barter or loan, you would find as untidy a mess as Agrippa exposed to the Romans, when he begged them to consider what would happen if the belly rebelled against its fellow members.

"Were Æsculapius himself the patient, the whole system would not only perish but perish soon. Very soon the body would petrify, and the rebellious soul follow the money I had spent to pay my debts, into the land of the thousand devils."

IV

PANURGE IN PRAISE OF DEBTORS AND CREDITORS (CONTINUATION)

"On the other hand," Panurge went on, "just imagine another world, where all men borrowed and all lent, all were debtors and creditors. Oh, what a harmony would attend the regular motions of the heavens! I think I can hear it as plainly as Plato when, beholding a siren upon each of the eight circles of the planetary system, he listened to the music of the spheres. What a perfect symphony among the elements! How Nature would delight in her works and productions: Ceres, laden with corn, Bacchus with wine, Flora with blossoms, Pomona with fruits, and Juno, throning it in the ethereal heights, a model of serenity, health and pleasure. I am lost in this lofty contemplation.

"Among humans, all would be peace, love, concord, loyalty, repose, banquets, feasting, joy, gladness, with gold, silver, money, chains, rings and like treasures passing from hand to hand. Never lawsuits, war or argument; no usurer, glutton, miser or hardhearted refuser. By the living God, it would be the golden age of Saturn's rule, the true picture of Olympus, where all forces vanish under the absolute government of a triumphant charity."

All men, Panurge exposed, would be virtuous, beautiful and just.

O happy world inhabited by happy, thrice-happy, fourfold happy people! Panurge really believed he was even now among them.

"I vow that if this glorious world had a pope pullulating with cardinals and associates in his sacred college, in a very few years you would find more wonderful and miraculous saints, more collects read to their glory, more vows offered up, more pilgrims' staves, more votaries' banners, and more candles than in the nine bishoprics of Brittany, the cradle of minor hagiology. As you see, I except St. Ives, for that Breton saint has been adopted by the lawyers as their patron.

"Remember, I beg you, the *Farce of Master Pierre Pathelin.*

"The noble Master Pierre, wishing to deify and extol to the third heavens the father of Master Guillaume Jousseaume, the draper, could find no praise higher than:

> *How graciously the dear man loaned*
> *What goods and merchandise he owned*
> *To all who wished. . . .*

That, truly, was nobly spoken!"

Were this reasoning applied to the microcosm, or little world, that is man, we would find its members lending, borrowing and owing— in brief, living according to natural law, since man was created solely to that end. Even the harmony of celestial bodies could not match such organization. Did not the Creator fashion the body as a host for the soul and for life? Life was blood, blood the seat of the soul; a single activity engrossed humankind: to make blood continually. In this manufacturing process, all the members of the organism played their appointed parts; such was their hierarchy that each invariably lent to the other, each being both debtor and creditor. The stuff and matter Nature found suitable for the production of blood—i.e. bread and wine—included all manner of nourishment. The *Langue Goth* or Gothic tongue—here Panurge corrected himself, explaining that he meant the *Langue d'Oc* or southern French —proved this fact in the term *companage*, which described all food put on the table and more, all household expenses incurred, save bread and wine. To gather, prepare and cook up these, our hands moved, our feet supported and transported the entire mechanism, our eyes led the way. In the maw of the belly, the intestine supplied a little bitter humor called melancholy or black bile; this generated the appetite, which warned when to set the food in the oven. The tongue tested that food, the teeth chewed it, the belly received it, digested it and turned it into chyme. The mesenteric veins sucked out the best of it, leaving behind the excrement, which was expulsed through special conduits. Then the veins bore it to the liver which, through a new transformation, turned it into blood.

"Can you imagine," Panurge thrilled, "what joy fills these good officers and servants when they behold the rivulet of ruddy gold which is their sole restorative? Such gladness is not even felt by alchemists when, after lengthy experiment, vast study and much expense, they perceive their precious metals being transmuted in their furnaces.

"Then each member applies itself, trying once again to purify and to refine this treasure. From the blood, the kidneys, through the emulgent or renal veins, draw that water you call urine, which they speed through the urethra, downwards into a perfectly-appointed receptacle, the bladder, to be voided by the latter in good time.

"From the blood, the spleen draws the lower part, the dregs you call the melancholy or black bile, while the superfluous choler, or yellow bile, is drained by the bottle of the gall or gallbladder, to be transmitted to still another workshop, where it is even better refined. I mean the heart. Here, by diastolic and systolic movements—by contraction and relaxation—the blood is subtilized and inflamed, brought to perfection in the right ventricle, and shot out through the veins."

Panurge, developing his theme, showed how each unit of the human frame—feet, hands, eyes and all the rest—attracted the blood to itself and fed upon it according to its need, by which process such as had previously been creditors became debtors. The heart, in its right ventricle, which is the hottest point in the body, so depurated the blood that we call the fluid obtained "spiritual"; this immaculate blood then sped through the arteries to all parts of the human mechanism to warm or to cool off the coarser blood in other veins. The lungs never ceased to fan it with their lobes and bellows. Grateful for this service, through the arterial vein, the heart fed its richest blood. At last the blood was so clarified and refined in what is called the *rete mirabile*—a wondrous arterial network—as to produce the animal spirits, thanks to which man possessed the power to think, speak, judge, resolve, deliberate, ratiocinate and remember.

"By God's might!" Panurge exclaimed. "I drown, I perish, I am spirited away as I consider the depths of this world of lenders and borrowers. Ah, what a divine thing, lending; what a heroic virtue, owing!"

Nor was this all. The interdependent universe was so beautifully organized that, the problem of nutrition perfected, it went on to lend to those unborn—a loan, by means of which it sought to perpetuate and multiply itself in its own image: children.

"To this end, each particular elects and pares off the most precious elements of its food to dispatch them downward into vessels and receptacles most suitably contrived by nature. These elements flow down long circuits and flexuosities into the genitories; receive a competent form; find chambers designed, in both male and female, for the preservation and perpetuation of humankind. And all of it is done by loans and debts, a fact proved by the phrase 'the obligations of wedlock.'

"Let any contribuent refuse to lend and nature visits grievous vexation upon his members, fury upon his senses; the lender, on the contrary, receives a set reward, which is pleasure, mirth and delight."

V

CONCERNING PANTAGRUEL'S HATRED OF DEBTORS AND CREDITORS

"I SEE your point," said Pantagruel, "and you argue it well. You are indeed a fine speaker. But prattle and preach till Domesday, patrocinate till Pentecost—when you're done, to your amazement, you'll *not* find me contracting debts. 'Owe no man any thing,' says Paul to the Romans, 'but to love one another.'

"I must confess, your graphides and dyaptoses—or, to explain obsolete terms of rhetoric, your descriptions and figures—please me mightily. Yet I defy you to send back a shameless, importunate borrower to a town already wise to his ways. Let him enter and the citizens are more terrified than the Ephesians at the plague. You remember the story in Apollonius of Tyana. They called the latter in as physician to combat the pestilence; he gathered them about an old man in rags, whom he invited them to stone to death. They refused, amazed. Then, when he insisted, they crushed the fellow under a heap of stones. When the débris was cleared, what did they find? The carcass of a mad dog, great as a lion.

"Again, I agree with the Persians who hold that lying, as a vice, comes second only to owing. Understand me, however: I don't mean to infer a man must never lend or borrow. None is so rich but he sometimes owes, none so poor but he sometimes can lend. In this connection, I recall the advice Plato gives us in his *Laws*. Never let your neighbors draw any water out of your well, unless they have first dug in their own ground. Good honest spadework will help them strike that potter's clay we call ceramite, where they will find a spring or stream of water; for this clay, being fat, strong, firm and close in substance, retains its humidity, resists leakage or evaporation. Only after your neighbor has dug for his own, let him have your water."

It was a great shame, Pantagruel concluded, to be borrowing right and left on all occasions, instead of going to work and earning one's own living. The only suitable time to borrow and lend was when the worker, despite his labor, failed to make a profit, or when a person suddenly lost all his wordly possessions.

"And so, no more of the subject. Henceforth, don't run up debts, Panurge. As for the past, I absolve you!"

"The least I should, and the most I can do, is to thank you heartily," said Panurge. "If gratitude is proportionate to the benefactor's affection, then my thanks are infinite and sempiternal. The love you bear me spontaneously, through no merit of mine, is beyond all reckoning: it transcends weight, number, measure; it is endless and everlasting. Indeed, to appraise it by the criteria of your generosity or of the recipient's content, would be to underestimate it cruelly. You have done me much good: more than my condition or merit warrants, I must confess. Yet not so much as you believe in the present circumstances. What gripes, itches and pains me is this: henceforth, being out of debt, what countenance can I keep? Believe me, for the first few months, I shall cut a dreadful figure, I fear, for I was never brought up nor accustomed to that mode of life.

"Besides, you know the saying. 'That makes it quits!' Never a man pooped a zephyr in this zephyr-pooping universe, but he uttered those words. Henceforward, no fart will flower in all Salmagundi but its fragrance will be directed at my nostrils. Alas, my days are numbered, I plainly see; I recommend to you the making of my epitaph, for I shall die asphyxiated. And some day, if the usual remedies fail to raise wind in old women suffering from chronic colic, physicians will prescribe mummy oil from my gust-ridden, odoriferous body. Let them take but a sniffle, they will blast like a hurricane.

"That is why I implore you to leave me a few hundred debts, just as Miles d'Illiers, Bishop of Chartres, implored King Louis XI to leave him a few lawsuits to plead for the exercise of his mind. They can have all my cockchafers and snailshells, if only they do not subtract anything from the principal sums I owe."

"Let us drop the subject," said Pantagruel. "I have already suggested we do so."

VI

WHY NEWLY MARRIED MEN WERE EXEMPTED FROM GOING TO WAR

"By the way," asked Panurge, "what law exempted from warfare, during the first year, all those who planted a new vineyard, built a new house or got married?"

"The Mosaic Law," said Pantagruel, "in *Deuteronomy*."

"Why those newly wed?" Panurge inquired. "The vine planters, I am too old to bother about: I bear their ills blithely. As for those fine new builders of dead stone, they do not figure in my book of life. I build with the live stone that is man."

The purpose of this law, according to Pantagruel, was to allow newly wedded couples to enjoy their love to the full, to produce offspring, and to propagate heirs. Thus, if they were killed in battle the second year, their names and coats-of-arms might be carried on by their children. Further, considering the age at which they married in those days, one year was enough to prove the wives sterile or fecund. After the husbands' decease, the widows might then be better assorted for a second marriage, the fecund going to such men as sought to multiply, the sterile to such as, desiring no children, chose their mates for their virtues, grace, sociability and domestic qualities.

Panurge objected that the preachers of Varennes, near Chinon, decried second marriages as odious and foolish.

"Poor fellows!" cried Pantagruel. "Second marriages burn them like the four-day fever."

"True," said Panurge, "and Friar Enguainant Sheatheblade is a case in point. Preaching at Parilly against second marriages, he swore he would deliver himself up to the first devil out of hell, if he had not rather puncture a hundred maidenheads than crankle one single widow. I consider your point well taken indeed. But—"

But Panurge, it appeared, had another objection. What would Pantagruel say if the exemption from warfare were granted the newly wedded on quite different grounds? During that first year, the grooms would probably (in all equity and reason) enter so thoroughly into their fresh-won possessions, grinding their organs so gleefully, that their spermatic vessels would be drained dry. These lads, then, having become feeble, emasculated, nervous and pithless, would shirk battle, ducking away amid the baggage trains, instead of striving among the warriors and champions, where Bellona reared her head and the thwacks fell fast. How could they strike rude blows under the banner of Mars when their lustiest cudgelling had been done behind the curtains of his sweetheart Venus?

Proof of this existed to-day, among other ancient traditions, in all good households. After a few days, they invariably sent the grooms off to visit their uncles, thus separating them from their brides, and giving them a chance to rest and revive before returning to the fray. This happened even if they had no uncles—or aunts, for that matter.

"Similarly after the battle of the Hornbrows," said Panurge, "our master King Hullabaloo did not cashier us—I mean Quailpiper and myself—but sent us home to rest in our own houses. (He is still looking for his.)

"When I was a small boy, my grandfather's godmother used to tell me:

> *Save to believers, prayers are prattle,*
> *Paternosters bric-a-brac,*
> *Better one tyro going to battle*
> *Than two old soldiers coming back.*

"This merely goes to confirm my opinion that the vintners could not have eaten many of the grapes or drunk much of the wine of their labors during the first year. And that the builders did not move into their newly erected dwellings very soon, for fear of suffocation. Does not Galen in his *Of the Use of the Parts of the Body*, in Book II, *Of the Difficulty of Breathing*, learnedly advise against living in freshly-whitewashed rooms?

"I did not ask this question of you save in causal course and in seasonable reason, so I pray you take no offence," Panurge concluded.

VII

HOW PANURGE, WITH A FLEA IN HIS EAR, GAVE UP WEARING HIS MAGNIFICENT CODPIECE

NEXT day, Panurge had his right ear pierced with an awl, as the Jewish slaves used to do, and a light ring of damascened gold attached to the lobe. A flea was set in the bezel of the ring. For your further information, since it is a splendid thing always to be thoroughly informed, I may add that the flea was black. Its cost, when carefully computed, amounted to no more per quarter than the marriage of a Hyrcanian tigress or a Caspian virago: 600000 maravedis or Spanish pence. When he made this vast outlay and was out of debt, he was annoyed at his extravagance; thereafter, like any tyrant or lawyer, he bore it by the sweat and blood of his subjects and clients.

Taking four ells of coarse brown cloth, he draped the material about him like a long closed coat, threw away his breeches and tied a pair of spectacles to his cap. As he appeared thus apparelled before Pantagruel, the latter found the disguise bizarre; he also missed Panurge's magnificent and ostentatious codpiece. Where, he asked in wonder, was this ultimate anchor of Panurge's hope, this last refuge in a tempest of misfortunes? What did this new masquerade signify?

"I've a flea in my ear," Panurge replied. "I want to get married."

"Bravo! I'm delighted to hear it," said Pantagruel. "But, upon my word, I wouldn't bank upon it. Lovers don't usually leave off their breeches, let their shirts hang down to their knees and wear coarse cloth cloaks. Persons of worth and quality do not wear dirty brown fustian of that sort!"

In the past, a few heretics and sectarians had appeared so accoutred; many accused them of trickery, of imposture, of seeking by this affectation to mislead the common people. Pantagruel, however, would not blame them or suggest sinister motives. Did not every man abound in his own sense and fancy, particularly in the strange, the bizarre and the inconsequential? It did not necessarily follow that these eccentricities were essentially good or bad. They were born of our hearts and souls, the forge of all good and evil; they proved good if that forge were good and ruled by custom, evil if perverted by the devil's malice.

"Such innovations offend me only in their sensationalism," he concluded, "and in their flouting of current usage."

"That color," Panurge replied, "I quite properly consider a prop à propos! This cloth is at once the brown bays about my brow, and the brown baize over which I shall sit, administering my affairs. Since for once I'm out of debt, you'll never see a more unpleasant man than myself, if God help me not!

"Take a look at my goggles! Why, from ten feet away, I look like some famous Franciscan intellectual, some silver-tongued divine. I really think next year I'll preach the Crusade again, God keep my vesicles snug in their scrim!"

Did Pantagruel see that coarse brown fabric draped about Panurge? Well, let him realize it contained an occult property known but to very few people. Only this morning Panurge had taken it on, yet already he was mad with lust, high-wrought, over-reaching, in a towering passion, blazing to caper like hell's maroonest devil over a compliant wife, with never fear of clapraps or poxknocks. Oh, what a fine provider in his *cache*, what a stout husbandman of his territory, what a stiff coxswain on his own vessel he would be! After death, they would burn him upon a pyre of honor, preserve his ashes as those of the most exemplary aranger of ends' meetings imaginable, the most perfect featherer of a nest.

By God's body, Panurge wore the coarse cloth with which desks were lined, but certainly no Lord High Treasurer would bend over it to cross the *f* of *fous* and make them into the *f* of francs.

"Behold me fore and aft!" Panurge exulted. "Admire this Roman toga, a hallowed garb of peace. I copied it from Trajan's Column, from the triumphal arch of Septimus Severus. I am weary of war, of armor, of coats-of-mail; my shoulders are bruised from the bearing of armament. Let the harness of war yield to the toga of concord, at least for next year, if I am married, as you proved yesterday by Mosiac law.

"As for my breeches, my great-aunt Laurentia long ago told me they were designed solely for the codpiece. I believe this as implicitly as I believe gay old Galen, when in his eighth—or is it his ninth?— book, he tells us the head was designed for the eyes. Surely, otherwise, Nature would have put that head in an elbow or knee? But she meant the eyes to discern objects from afar. Therefore, she placed them at the top of the body, as on the end of a pole. So lights are placed in tall towers, on the tops of rocks, to direct navigators.

"Accordingly, I would like a short while, a year at least, to rest from warfare, or, put otherwise, to get married. That is why I have given up wearing a codpiece and, as a natural consequence, breeches. Is not the codpiece the principal article of a warrior's armor?

"So," Panurge concluded, "short of trial by fire, I maintain that the Turks are pretty poorly equipped, since their laws forbid them to wear codpieces."

VIII

CONCERNING THE SUPREMACY OF THE CODPIECE AS ARMORED PROTECTION

"I SEE," said Pantagruel. "For you, the codpiece is the first piece of military armor. That is a novel, somewhat paradoxical theory. After all, the spurs come first for two reasons: one, because new-dubbed knights are given them before any other piece: two, because you can't put them on after you've already donned a leg-guard."

"Nevertheless, I stand my ground," said Panurge. "And rightly, by God! Take Nature. Having created plants, trees, shrubs, grasses and zoöphytes, she determined to prolong and perpetuate them throughout all successive ages, so that, though the individuals might perish, the species would endure. She therefore most curiously armed their sperm and seed for just such perpetuity. She covered and equipped them with admirable mechanisms of sheaths, pouches, shells, nuclei, chalices, husks, pods, down, bark, couches, prickles. Strong and beautiful, these serve them as natural codpieces. This is quite apparent in peas, beans, kidney beans, nuts, peaches, cotton, watermelons, bitter gourds, corn, poppies, lemons, chestnuts and, generally, in all plants whose sperm and semen are obviously more covered, protected and armed than any other portion of them.

"In regard to man, however, Nature acted otherwise. Man was created naked, tender, frail, unprovided with offensive or defensive arms. He was born in that state of innocence which was the first golden age. He was designed as a living being, not as a plant—a living being, I say, devised for peace, not war; brought forth for the incomparable enjoyment of all fruits and vegetables, for peaceful dominion over all beasts upon earth."

Panurge developed his theme. Though born for peace, men began to heap malice upon malice, and the iron age of Jupiter succeeded the golden age of Saturn. Then earth began to furnish the vegetable kingdom with nettles, thistles, thorns and similar elements rebellious to humankind. By the same token, following a fatal law, almost all the animals broke away from his rule, conspiring tacitly to serve or obey him no longer, to resist in every possible way, indeed to hurt him as much as they could. Man determined to maintain his original mastery and enjoyment; again, there were certain beasts he could not do without. He therefore had, necessarily, to put on arms.

"By holy St. Goostache!" cried Pantagruel. "Since the last rains, you've become a mighty fizzleoffer—I mean philosopher."

"Consider how Nature inspired man to arm himself," Panurge continued, "and what part of his body he first clapped armor on. It was, by God's might, the ballock:

> When man had sheathed Priapus John
> With his two precious hangers-on,
> He knew the job was fitly done."

Moses, Panurge pursued, the great Hebrew captain and philosopher, affirmed that he armed himself with a stout and gallant codpiece most skilfully contrived out of fig-leaves, these, by their solidity, indentations, frizzling, gloss, size, color, odor, and other characteristics proved capital covering and protection for man's whangdoodle.

With, however, one exception: the terrific knockers of Lorraine, which dangle down like huge plummets at the very bottom of their owner's hose, fractious to the discipline of high stately codpieces. As an example of such, Panurge cited the noble Viardière, who, at a Valentine Festival or Feast of Fools in Nancy, won the title of Valentine or King Fool. Panurge saw him preparing to look his smartest on that May Day: the fellow had his pendicula spread out over the table like a Spanish cloak and was assiduously scraping away at his scrotum.

Because of the codpiece's importance, henceforward, whoever wished to speak correctly, when he bid a militiaman godspeed on his way to the wars, should not, as in the popular farce, stroke the fellow's head, urging:

> Look out for that winepot, Tevot, my lad

but, rather his knockers, saying:

> Look out for that milkpot, Tevot, my lad.

Surely, this must be obvious, by all the devils of hell, since, when a man's head was cut off, only the victim perished; whereas, with the loss of ballocks, all human nature would perish?

"Gay old Galen makes the same point in his Book I, *Of Sperm*, where he roundly avers that to possess no heart would be a lesser evil than to be destitute of genitories. For, in the latter, as in a sacred repository, rests the vital germ of mankind's existence. So that, for less than one hundred francs, I would readily believe these are the very stones by which Deucalion and Pyrrha restored humankind after its destruction in the famous deluge sung by the poets. This, too, moved valiant Justinian to write in his Book IV, *Of Bearing Bigots*, the phrase: *Summum bonum in braguibus* and *bragetis*, the supreme virtue in trousers and codpieces.

"This and other reasons likewise inspired My Lord of Merville one day, when he was trying on a new suit of armor, before following his king to battle. His old half-rusted gear was useless now, because in the last few years the skin of his belly had moved far away from his kidneys. Seeing that he was covering the staff of love and bundle of marriage with merely coat-of-mail, his wife considered he took but scant care of them. Meditating at length thereon, she decided he had much better shield and armor them behind a huge tilting-helmet which lay idle in his closet. It is of her they sing in the third book of the *Lacrimocrappia*, *A Handbook for Virgins*:

> Her lord, bound for the wars, was fully armed,
> Yet she observed his codpiece stood exposed.
> "Protect what I love best, lest it be harmed,"
> She wept, "I would not have it indisposed."
> And was the counsel wrong, your ladyships?
> I hold her mortal fear advised her well,
> To save the joint at which she smacked her lips,
> The clapper that made music in her bell.

"Cease therefore to be surprised, My Lord Pantagruel, at my new accoutrement."

IX

HOW PANURGE CONSULTED PANTAGRUEL ON THE ADVIS-ABILITY OF HIS GETTING MARRIED

As Pantagruel vouchsafed no reply, Panurge heaved a cavernous sigh and continued:

"My Lord, you have heard me say I am determined to get married, unless, by some misfortune, all available orifices are closed, bunged and sealed. In the name of the love you have long borne me, I beg you to give me your advice."

"Well," Pantagruel replied, "since you have set your heart upon it, made up your mind and cast the die, there's no use discussing it further. The time is ripe for action."

"Action, ay—but I desire action only upon your counsel and advice."

"I counsel and advise you to go ahead!" said Pantagruel, picking up Panurge's last word each time he replied to the other's argument.

"But if you knew it were better I remain as I am, without venturing on new paths, then I would prefer not to get married."

"Very well, then, prefer not to get married!"

"But good heavens! do you expect me to spend my whole life lonely and alone, bereft of conjugal company? Remember *Ecclesiastes: Vae soli*, woe to him who stands alone! Bachelordom tastes no such joys as does your married couple."

"Couple away then; marry, get married!"

"But suppose my wife made me a cuckold. (As you know, cuckolds are a drug on the market!) What then? Why, I should fly off the handle! I like cuckolds well enough; they are quite proper fellows and very good company, too. But I'd rather die than be one of them. Wedlock may be one sweet song, but I don't relish being the cuckold in the refrain!"

"Refrain from wedlock then," Pantagruel answered, "for Seneca's axiom, 'Others will serve you as you served them,' is true without exception."

"Without exception, you say?"

"Seneca says 'without exception,' " Pantagruel replied.

"Ho, ho!" said Panurge. "By my pet devil, does Seneca mean in this world or the next? Verily, I can no more do without a woman than a blind man without his staff; my gimlet must drill or I could not live. This being so, had I not better associate myself with some decent honest woman than go on changing day after day, perpetually risking being clapped in prison or prisoned in clap? Not to mention a thorough drubbing! I must confess, I have never had much good of married women, with all due respect to friend husband."

"Friend, husband it, then, by God!" Pantagruel advised.

"But," Panurge objected, "what if, by God's will, I happened to marry a respectable woman and she beat me? I would be a miniature Job not to go mad with rage. They say these respectable matrons are often headstrong. Their vinegar is strong, too: you know the proverb: Good housewife, good vinegar! I would go her one better and batter her gewgaws—I mean her arms, legs, head, lungs, liver and bile; I would tatter her gowns so thoroughly with a tattoo of the cudgel that the Lord High Devil himself would await her damned soul at the gates of hell. I could do very well without such embroilments this year; indeed, I never relished a fierce hand-to-hand engagement."

"Engagement forgo and wedlock avoid!" Pantagruel declared.

"But consider my situation," Panurge protested. "I am free of debts and unmarried. I hasten to add unhappily free of debts, for were I otherwise, my creditors would be only too chary of my paternity. Now, however, without creditor or wife, I have none to worry about me or bear me that great love men call conjugal. Were I to fall ill, I would be very poorly looked after. The sage has said: 'Great is the misery of the sick where there be no woman beside him.' I mean of course an honest woman, a *materfamilias* in holy wedlock. I've seen this clearly proved by popes, nuncios, cardinals, bishops, abbots, priors, priests and monks. You may be sure that is an arrangement to which you will never bind me!"

"Bind yourself then in the holy bonds of wedlock, in God's name," Pantagruel admonished.

"But," Panurge countered, "suppose I fell ill and could not fulfill the duties of marriage? Suppose my wife, impatient at my languor, gave herself to another man, not only failing to help me in my need, but also mocking me in my disaster? Worse, suppose she stole from me, as I have often observed wives stealing from indisposed husbands? Why, it would be enough to drive me crazy with grief, to set me running through the fields in my shift."

"Shift not then your condition," Pantagruel warned. "But remain a bachelor."

"All right," agreed Panurge. "But look here! How else could I have legitimate sons and daughters? How else perpetuate my name and arms? How else bequeath my goods and possessions? (For some day, have no doubt, I shall have vast ones and, moreover, will reimburse great sums to inheritances I have encumbered.) For I wish offspring, with whom I may make merry when otherwise I should be glum. I wish to be doing just as I see Gargantua, your debonair and benign father doing, with you. I wish to be like all decent folk in their own domestic and private lives. For, being free of debt yet not married, I fear you would give me but gibes instead of consolation in my misadventure."

"Adventure, then, in the name of God and be married," said Pantagruel.

X

HOW PANTAGRUEL SHOWED PANURGE THE DIFFICULTIES OF GIVING ADVICE ABOUT GETTING MARRIED, AND HOW DRAWING BY LOT FROM HOMER AND VIRGIL BORE HIM OUT

"Unless I err," said Panurge, "your advice reminds me of the Master Facing Bothways' song: the question is the answer. Moreover, it is full of sarcasm, raillery and paradoxical iteration. One statement annuls the other; I can't tell which to credit."

"Naturally! Your questions are so full of ifs and buts that I cannot base an argument, let alone determine an answer. There must be a point to them somewhere, but it lies buried under a heap of casual considerations, dependent wholly upon the fatal will of heaven.

"How many people to-day are so lucky that their marriages shine like the reflection and expression of paradisial joys! How many others, again, are more unhappy in their mating than even the most miserable devils that tempt the hermits of the Egyptian deserts or the monks of Montserrat in Catalonia! You must run your chance, shut your eyes, bow your head before the charge; you must kiss the ground as a mark of submission to the divine will, just as the Swiss and German mercenaries, the Spaniards and the Gascons do, ere they go into battle. Commend yourself to God, then, since you have decided to try your luck. This is the only assurance I can possibly give you."

Panurge made no reply. Pantagruel, suddenly inspired, proceeded:

"I'll tell you what to do, if you see fit. Bring me the works of Virgil. Three times we will open the book at a certain page and, according to the numbers of lines agreed upon, we will ascertain your fate as a future husband. Many a man has hit upon his destiny by drawing by lot from Homer!"

Pantagruel then proceeded to list instances in point. First Socrates, in prison, hearing someone recite these lines about Achilles in the ninth book of the *Iliad*:

> *I shall arrive, without undue delay,*
>
> Ἤματί κεν τριτάτῳ Φθίην ἐρίβωλον ἱκοίμην;
>
> *In rich and fertile Phthia, the third day*

and assuring Æschines of his own death three days after. (Plato in his *Crito*, Cicero in his first book *De Divinatione*, and Diogenes Laertius in his *Lives of the Philosophers*, all bore witness to the truth of this story.)

Next, Opilius Macrinus. Desiring to know whether he would one day become emperor, he found the answer by lot, in the eighth book of the *Iliad*:

Ὦγέρον, ἦ μάλα δή σε νέοι τείρουσι μαχηταί,
Ση δὲ βίη λέλυται, χαλεπὸν δέ σέ γῆρας ὀπάζει;

Dotard, to younger warriors you must yield,
Infirm old age will drive you from the field.

True enough, the old man, having sat on the throne a bare fourteen months, was driven out and killed by the younger, more powerful Heliogabalus.

Then there was Brutus. Seeking to discover the outcome of the battle of Pharsalus (in which he was doomed to die), he came upon this statement, concerning Patroclus, in the sixteenth book of the *Iliad*:

Ἀλλά με μοιρ᾽ ὀλοὴ καὶ Λητοῦς ἔκτανεν υἱός;

Woe! I am shot! My fortune is undone
By traitorous Fate and by Latona's son.

Accordingly, *Apollo* was chosen as watchword that day.

Drawing from Virgil had revealed extraordinarily weighty matters, including the award of the Roman Empire. Did not Alexander Severus open the sixth book of the *Æneid*, to read:

Tu regere imperio populos, Romane, memento

Learn, Roman, what the future holds in store:
A day will dawn with you as emperor

and find the prophecy fulfilled in a year?

So, too, with Hadrian. Doubtful about Trajan's feelings towards him, he opened the *Æneid*, at the same book, to read:

Quis procul ille autem ramis insignis olivae
Sacra ferens? nosco crines, incanaque menta
Regis Romani.

Who is it that I spy from far, who bears
Green olive boughs in noblest offering?
By his white hair and the proud garb he wears,
I know him for the hallowed Roman king.

Shortly after, Hadrian was adopted by Trajan and succeeded him on the imperial throne.

To Claudius, that excellent ruler, the sixth book of the *Æneid* declared:

> *Tertia dum Latio regnantem viderit æstas,*

> *When the third summer of his reign was come*
> *As sovereign on the throne of Latium*

and, in effect, he did not reign three years.

The same Claudius inquired about his brother Quintilius, whom he wished to install as co-ruler, and, in the same book of the *Æneid*, in a passage relating to Marcellus, nephew of Augustus, learned that:

> *Ostendent terris hunc tantum fata.*

> *The Fates alone, in whom all things have birth*
> *Will mark the course he is to tread on earth.*

Exactly seventeen days after his appointment, Quintilius was killed.

Gordian the younger had a like experience. And Claudius Albinus, anxious to divine the future, also turned up the sixth book of Virgil, to be informed that:

> *Hic rem Romanam magno turbante tumultu,*
> *Sistet; eques sternet Pœnos, Gallumque rebellem.*

> *Menaced with tumult and confusion, lo,*
> *This knight, defending Roma's ancient walls*
> *Shall rise to save the nation, overthrow*
> *The Punic host and quell the rebel Gauls.*

Again, the Emperor D. Claudius, Aurelian's predecessor, curious about his posterity, turned up these lines, in the first book of the *Æneid*:

> *Hic ego nec metas rerum, nec tempora pono.*

> *I prophesy long life for these nor lay*
> *Limit or bound to their success to-day.*

Finally, my friend Friar Pierre Amy, eager to know if he would elude the hobgoblins' ambush and save his Greek texts from confiscation by his Franciscan colleagues, found the answer in Book III of the *Æneid*:

> *Heu fuge crudeles terras, fuge litus avarum!*
>
> *Flee this ungrateful soil, this cruel shore,*
> *Seek out a land that honors knowledge more.*

which inspired him to skip free of their toils.

"It would be tedious to recount the adventures befalling thousands of others, who learned their fates by opening the works of various poets at a certain page," Pantagruel concluded. "At the same time, however, I do not wish to imply that such a test is infallible. I would hate to see you, for instance, disappointed."

XI

HOW PANTAGRUEL PROVED THAT TESTING ONE'S FORTUNE BY DICE WAS UNLAWFUL

"You could accomplish your purpose more quickly," Panurge suggested, "by throwing dice."

"No," Pantagruel replied. "That test is deceptive, unlawful and scandalous. Do not put your trust in it. That cursed volume *The Pastime of Dice*, written by Lorenzo de Spirito da Perugia, was long ago invented by the foul fiend in Achaia, in a town called Boura. (I hereby remind you that *bourre* in French means trash.)

"Your Greek would stop before the statue of Bouraic Hercules, invoke the god, pick four dice out of the heap at the statue's foot, and throw them on a table with figures engraved upon it. Many a simple soul erred there and fell headlong into the toils of Satan. To-day, the same thing still goes on in various places. Why, my father Gargantua forbade the practice throughout his dominions: he had the oracle-boards burned, and he stamped out the nuisance as a dangerous plague."

Moreover, what Pantagruel said of dice also held good of the Latin *tali*, rounded on two sides and marked on only four; they were no less an abuse. Nor would he accept the argument of Tiberius' lucky throw when, having consulted the oracle of Geryon near Padua, he was told to throw golden *tali* into the fountain of Aponus and, obeying, learned his fate. The *tali* were still to be seen at the bottom of the fountain, to be sure; yet the procedure was but a bait, by which Lucifer drew ingenuous souls to eternal perdition.

Nevertheless, to give Panurge satisfaction, Pantagruel was perfectly willing for him to roll three dice on the table before them. The score he threw would be the number of the line on the page they opened.

"Have you any dice about you, Panurge?"

"A whole bagful. My *vade mecum*! I'd be fined for not wearing such insignia. Merlin Coccais—our old friend Folengo—exposes this to us in the second book of *De patria diabolorum, Of the Devil's Country*. As you know, the volume is in the Library of St. Victor. The day I'm without dice, Old Nick would *vade mecum* pretty thoroughly and pin the insignia of his prongs on my backside."

Panurge chose three dice, rolled them on the table and produced a five, a six and a five.

"Sixteen, that makes," said Panurge. "Let us take the sixteenth line on the page I open the book at. I fancy the number; I trust we will have luck. And," he added, "let the devil knock me over like a bowl crashing into so many ninepins . . . let him mow me down like a cannonball shooting through a battalion of foot . . . let me be damned to hell, if sixteen isn't my score at shuttlecock on my wedding night."

"I've not the slightest doubt that's true," Pantagruel replied. "But you need not have made such a horrible vow. Your first service will be a fault: score—love fifteen. In the morning, when you come off your roost, you'll serve once more. Score—sixteen!"

"So that's your idea of the thing, eh? Let me tell you the valiant champion that stands sentry over my abdomen never failed to snap smartly to attention. I'm a demon server; have you ever seen me fail to make my point? No, never, at no period, even! I'm advantage in;

I'm set; I'm balls to you. Whusht! see me wield my racket. Ask my partner about how I play the game."

Pantagruel sent for a copy of Virgil; but before opening it, Panurge confessed:

"My heart is like a pair of mittens. Mittens worn by guests as they applaud bride and groom at a wedding . . . mittens regaining their shape when you've taken your hands off them . . . mittens tossed into the air triumphantly! . . . My heart throbs like a donkey's pizzle! Feel my pulse; gauge the tremor of this artery in my left arm. Its high frequency would suggest a candidate being put through his paces at the Sorbonne. Before going any further, don't you think we had better invoke Hercules of Boura, or the Tenites, those goddesses said by Pomponius Festius to throne it in the chambers of judgment?"

"Neither Hercules nor the Tenites," said Pantagruel. "Just open that book!"

XII

HOW PANTAGRUEL CONSULTED VIRGIL AS TO PANURGE'S MARITAL DESTINY

PANURGE opened the book bravely. The sixteenth verse on the page flashed its message:

Nec Deus hunc mensa, Dea nec dignata cubili est.

"He shall not grace my board," the great God said;
The Goddess: "I won't have him in my bed."

"Humph!" observed Pantagruel. "That's not exactly what you would call a favorable answer. It plainly means your wife will be a strumpet, you a cuckold."

The goddess unfavorable to Panurge, he explained, was none other than Minerva, a most fearsome virgin, a powerful, fulminant deity who abominated all cuckolds, joyboys, adulterers and adulteresses. The god, of course, was Jupiter, storming and thundering out of heaven.

According to the teachings of the ancient Etrurians, *manubies*, as they called Vulcan's darts and thunderbolts, belonged only to Minerva and to the father from whose head she was sprung. That goddess proved this clearly enough when she burned the Grecian ships of Ajax Oïleus. No deity on Olympus, other than Minerva and Jove, was allowed to dispatch thunderbolts; accordingly, they were the most feared by humans.

This truth, said Pantagruel, was borne out by the profoundest mysteries of mythology. When the giants dared wage war against the gods, the latter at first scorned them: the titans, they declared, were fit to battle only against the gods' varlets. But when the giants began piling Pelion on Ossa; when Olympus itself began to shake, as they prepared to pile it on the other mountains, the gods grew thoroughly frightened. Jupiter called a general meeting, where the gods unanimously voted to defend themselves valiantly. Having often seen battles lost because of the women accompanying the armies, they determined to banish all the celestial trollops. They therefore changed them into weasels, polecats, bats, shrewmice and like beasts, and drove them into Egypt and along the Nile. Minerva alone was kept in heaven so she might coöperate with Jupiter in discharging thunder. Indeed, they prized her as goddess of arts and battle, of counsel and dispatch, a deity armed from birth, and dreaded in heaven, in the air, by land and by sea.

"God's belly!" Panurge swore. "Do you imply I am the Vulcan whom Virgil saw banished from Jupiter's table and Minerva's bed? Vulcan, the patron of cuckolds because his wife Venus slept with Mars? Pooh! I'm not lame, nor a smith, nor a forger, like him. To be sure, my wife will probably be as beautiful and beguiling as his Venus; but she'll not be a whore like Venus, nor I a cuckold like Vulcan. Why, the poor limping churl had the gods decree in solemn assembly that he was a cuckold!"

Vulcan being what he was, Panurge declared that Virgil's verse should be interpreted very differently. In point of fact, it prophesied that Panurge's wife would be honest, virtuous and chaste, instead of warlike, vicious, headsprung and headstrong. No dashing Jupiter would rise to rival Panurge, or stoop to dip his finger in Panurge's pie, if they should happen to sit at table together.

"Consider Jupiter!" Panurge stormed. "Consider his feats and prowesses! The fellow was the most ruffianly emissionary ever whoredained, the most blaring trumpeter that ever strumpeted, a randier bandier than the wildest boar. Is Agathocles of Babylon a creditable witness? Well then, Jupiter was more lickerish than a goat! Besides, he was suckled by a sow in the Dictean caves of Crete. (Others claim it was Amalthea, daughter of Melisseus, King of Crete, who fed him goat's milk. In gratitude for this, he broke off one of the goat's horns and gave it to her, its possessor always receiving in abundance everything desired.)

"By the devils of hell—or the virtues of Acheron, I suppose I should say—that horny Jupiter friggled in a single day one-third of the world, its men and beasts, its rivers and mountains. I refer to Europa! In memory of the colossal piece of friggling, Jupiter was henceforth portrayed by the Ammonites as a ram ramming, with horn erect."

Anyhow, Panurge knew how to guard against this hornjacking Jack Horner. After all, what was Jupiter's record? He had assumed Amphitryon's shape in order to visit the latter's wife at night and taradiddle a Hercules upon her . . . he had, by his music, put Argus to sleep, for all the latter's hundred spectacles, in order to ramboodle the Io, whom Argus was supposed to guard . . . he had turned himself into a golden rain to enter Danae's room, eluding Acrisius, her father, and, by strumming her to the tune of a Perseus nine months later, he had fulfilled the prophecy that Acrisius would die at the hand of his grandson, an eventuality against which Acrisius had imprisoned Danae . . . he had impregnated Antiope with two lads, who killed Lycus, the Theban, her uncle, for unrudimenting her when still a minor . . . he had bilked Agenor and bulked his daughter Europa . . . he had cullied the river god Asopus and cunnied his daughter Aegina . . . he had changed Lychaon, King of Arcadia, into a wolf, in order to ravish his daughter Callisto . . . he had beguiled Corytus of Tuscany and Atlas, respectively the husband and father of Electra, to beget Dardanus of his pleasure with her.

Panurge, for his part, defied Jupiter since he, Panurge, was no

idiot Amphitryon, no ninny Argus, no craven Acrisius, no dreamy
Lycus, no dotard Agenor, no phlegmatic Asopus, no lupine Lychaon,
no loutish Corytus, no broadbacked Atlas. Time after time, Jupiter
might turn himself into a swan, as he did to seduce Leda . . . into a
bull, as he did to ravish Europa . . . into a satyr, as when he gam-
moned Antiope . . . into a rain of gold, as for Danae . . . into a
cuckoo, as when he deflowered Juno, his sister . . . into an eagle, as
when he plucked up Ganymede . . . into a ram or into a dove, as he
did when amorous of the Achaian virgin, Phthia . . . into a flame
or a snake or even a flea . . . into Epicurean atoms or, to be more
philosophodoctoral, into what, in scholastics, is called second intentions—the conception of the conception of an object. . . .

"I'll collar him," Panurge vowed. "Ay, I'll scotch the brangler.
And do you know what I'll do to him? What Saturn did to his father
Cœlus, what Rhea did to Atys, what both Seneca and Lactantius
foretold I would do: I'll cut the fellow's knockers off so close that
never a hair will stand to tell the tail.

"You remember how since Pope Joan was Holy Father, the cardinals have insisted on a testicular examination of candidates. Well, I
warrant you Jupiter will never be Pope, for *testiculos non habet*,
he'll have no boulders."

"Steady, lad," urged Pantagruel, "steady! Open the book a second
time!"

Obediently, Panurge turned up the line:

Membra quatit, gelidusque coït formidine sanguis.

His bones and joints quake with vexatious pains.
Fear numbs his heart, panic congeals his veins.

"Humph!" Pantagruel commented. "This means she will beat
you, back and belly."

"Not at all!" Panurge protested. "Virgil refers to me. He says I
shall rend her like a tiger, if she annoys me. Staff Officer Long John
will do the job. And failing a stout cudgel to poke her with, the devil
swallow me if I don't gobble her up as Cambles, King of Lydia, gobbled up his wife."

"Yes, yes, you are very brave," Pantagruel declared. "Even Hercules would not dare face you in this fury. Have you ever played cards: trictrac, for instance?"

"Ay," said Panurge, surprised.

"Do you know what a *Jan* is?"

"Certainly: a throw which loses or wins a point."

"How much do you score by it?"

"It's worth two," Panurge replied.

"All right, then: you know quite well Hercules never undertook to fight against two!"

"Hold!" Panurge cried with sudden alarm. "*Jan* means something else, too!"

"What?"

"A wittol, a complaisant cuckold!"

"Oh yes," Pantagruel agreed. "But I was thinking of games played over a board on a table, not over a bawd in a bed."

"Thanks," said Panurge, somewhat mollified.

For his third attempt, Panurge bared the line:

Fœmineo prædæ et spoliorum ardebat amore.

He was afire to rob, after the fashion
Of women. Theft consumed him like a passion.

"Humph!" said Pantagruel. "This means she will steal from you. Well, my lad, you're well set for the future, judging by these three lines: you will be a cuckold, you will be beaten and you will be robbed."

"Nonsense!" Panurge protested. "This line means that my wife will love me with all her heart. Juvenal, the satirist, did not lie when he said a woman passionately in love sometimes enjoyed stealing from her lover. But what did she steal? A glove, a spangle, a trifling bauble, just to give him the trouble of looking for it. By the same token, the little disagreements and petty differences that crop up between husband and wife merely serve their love as diversions and stimuli. You know how knifegrinders hammer their whetstones, the better to sharpen their blades. I consider these three lines of Virgil as highly auspicious. If not, I register a protest."

"No protest is possible against a judgment handed down by lot or fate. Our most ancient jurists establish this. See Baldus, the four-teenth-century jurisconsult; read the last chapter of his *De Legibus*."

"Hm!"

"Why is this so?" Pantagruel concluded. "Because fate acknowl-edges no superior with whom to register a protest. In the present in-stance, the pupil may not be restored to his right in full, as Baldus states clearly in *Digest* IV, *Title* IV, *Paragraph 7*."

XIII

HOW PANTAGRUEL ADVISED PANURGE TO FORETELL BY DREAMS THE SUCCESS OR FAILURE OF HIS MARRIAGE

"SINCE we cannot seem to agree on the authority of Virgil," said Pantagruel, "I suggest we try some other form of divination."

"What form?"

"An ancient, authentic and efficacious form. I refer to dreams."

"Dreams?"

"Certainly. Consider the authorities: Hippocrates in his book *Peri Enuption* or *Of Dreams* . . . Plato in the ninth book of his *Repub-lic* . . . Plotinus; Iamblicus, also a Platonist; Synesius of Cyrene, Bishop of Ptolemais, a fifth-century philosopher and chief authority of Cornelius Agrippa . . . Aristotle, Xenophon, and Galen, in his *Of Muscular Movement* . . . Plutarch, on the dubiety of autumnal dreaming . . . Artemidorus of Daldis . . . Herophilus, the Bithynian, who was the first to dissect the human body . . . Quin-tus of Smyrna, the fourth-century Greek poet, called Calaber, be-cause his works were recently discovered in Calabria . . . Theocri-tus . . . Pliny in his *Natural History* . . . Athenæus and a host of others. All these authors describe the conditions in which the soul, dreaming, may foresee what is to come."

Surely Pantagruel need not go into detail to prove this; Panurge could recognize its validity by a very familiar example. When a babe has been cleaned, suckled and laid to rest, it falls into a slumber. Whereupon its nurse may be dismissed from the cradle, her presence being unnecessary, and sent to amuse herself as best she may. Just so when, its digestion completed, the body slept, the mind could absent itself and, until the body awakened again, could enjoy itself, revisiting its native land of heaven.

"There," Pantagruel explained, "the soul receives signal intimation of its divine origin; there it contemplates an infinite intellectual sphere, whose centre is everywhere, whose circumference is in no one particular place in the universe. This sphere is God, according to Hermes Trismegistus, the second-century neo-Platonist. There nothing unknown or unforeseen occurs to the soul, nothing passes into oblivion, nothing is lost; all time is the present, as the soul observes not only what has gone by, but also what is to come. Bringing back an account of this to the body, it acts through the latter's organs and senses, it divulges its tidings to humankind, it is therefore termed a soothsayer and prophet."

Truth to tell, the soul was seldom able to recount its adventures in the full force and immediacy with which it had experienced them, because of the frailty and imperfections of the corporeal senses. Exactly so the moon, deriving its light from the sun, could not communicate that light so purely, brightly, hotly and intensely as it had received it. To interpret dreams, a deft, wise, sagacious, rational and expert medium was necessary. The Greeks dubbed that medium onirocritical (able to read dreams) and oniropolic (treating of dreams).

Thus Heraclitus stated that dreams neither revealed nor concealed anything. They simply supplied us with an indication of what might happen favorably or unfavorably to ourselves or our friends. Holy Scripture and profane letters offered many cases in point; a thousand things happened both to the subject and object of dreams.

The citizens of Atlantis, and those who dwelled on the island of Thasos, in the Cyclades, were actually denied the power of dreaming. According to Herodotus, Cleon of Daulia never dreamed a dream; nor did Thrasymedes; nor, finally, in our own day, did learned Villanovanus, the Frenchman—I mean Simon de Neuville, who was born a Hainaulter.

"To-morrow, my dear Panurge, when Aurora's rose-tipped fingers part the curtains of the night, dream deeply in the joy of dawn. But, to qualify for this visitation, first do away with all human passion, be it fear, hatred, hope or love."

As authority for his advice, Pantagruel cited Proteus, the mighty soothsayer of old. He could turn himself into fire or water, into the shape of tiger, dragon or into any other apparition. Yet before the gift of prophecy was granted him, he had to resume his own form. So man must quell and appease the most divine portion of his being— *nous*, the Greeks call it; *mens* the Latins—ere the holy gift of prophecy be granted him. Any base, human passion must not occupy and distract the soul.

"I'm all for it!" Panurge piped up. "Dream ho! Must I eat or fast the night before? I've good reason to ask, for when I fail to eat abundantly, my sleep is troubled, I'm in a brown study—brown as my tongue and empty as my belly!"

Pantagruel looked him over.

"I think," he said judicially, "considering your physique and constitution, you had better fast. Or almost. Amphiaraus, Apollo's son, was a celebrated medium. He insisted that whoever hoped to receive his oracles in dreams should eat nothing (and drink no wine!) three days before. In your case, Panurge, we will not apply so strict a diet."

A man stuffed with food and crapulous with wine did not seem to Pantagruel to be necessarily prepared to receive mystical tidings. At the same time, a man who had starved himself to death was no better prepared for intimations from heaven.

"Doubtless you recall how my father Gargantua—all honor to him!—used to tell us about hermits, fasters and self-torturers. Their writings, he said, were as pithless and stale as their sallow, brittle bodies. How can the mind function when the body is sick? Have not philosophers and physicians established the science of flesh and spirit! Animal spirits find their birth, exercise and health in the blood of the veins. This blood is strained and purified to perfection, in what is vulgarly called *rete admirabile*—the net wonderful—which lies at the base of the brain, under the ventricles."

Pantagruel also told how Gargantua, his father, had provided a splendid example in the person of a certain philosopher. This man believed he would be better able to meditate, write and produce, if he could flee the madding crowd. Accordingly, he sought a retreat in the forest. Everywhere about him, dogs barked, wolves howled, lions roared, horses neighed, elephants trumpeted, snakes hissed, asses brayed, grasshoppers chirped and pittered, turtle doves billed and cooed. In brief, he would have found greater calm amid the tumult of the fair at Niort or Fontenay.

A hungry man, Pantagruel thought, was no more comfortable. His belly rumbled, his sight dazzled, his veins sucked up their proper substance from the flesh-producing members. From below, they drew out the vagrant spirits which stimulated every part; they defied and betrayed their nurse and host, the whole body. It was as if, in falconry, whenever a bird on the wrist sought to soar into the air, the leather thongs about it pulled it back.

"My father Gargantua quoted Homer, father of all science, who tells how the Greeks ceased mourning Patroclus, Achilles' friend, only when they were too hungry to produce tears out of their bellies. Their bodies exhausted by long fasting could not supply the necessary force to lament."

Moderation was the cardinal virtue: Panurge should observe it in this instance. Pantagruel recommended for Panurge's supper a menu without hare or any other meat. He must abstain too from eating beans, octopus (called polyp by some), cabbage or any other food calculated to disturb or burden his animal spirits. Even as a mirror could not reflect objects set before it when its bright surface was clouded by breath or mist, so the dreaming spirit received the impression of forms it divined, only when the body was free from the fumes and vapors of food. Such was the indissoluble sympathy binding body and soul.

"I'll tell you what to eat, Panurge," Pantagruel continued. "Some good Sabine and Bergamo pears, a Golden Pippin apple, a few Touraine plums and some cherries from my orchard at Thélème. To be sure, certain Peripatetic philosophers have asserted that, since men eat more fruit in autumn than at any other season, their dreams become ambiguous, doubtful and untrustworthy. The mystic prophets and poets of old, too, taught us that our vain, deceptive dreams lay hidden under the leaves on the ground, because in autumn the leaves fall from the trees. No, Panurge, you need not fear for your dreams. The natural effervescence that abounds in new fruits is distilled and absorbed into the animal parts with extraordinary rapidity, much as must ferments into wine. This effervescence then will have expired, and been assimilated in your body long before you dream. As for liquids, you shall drink the clear water of my fountain."

"These are pretty difficult conditions," Panurge confessed. "Yet I consent, whatever the cost or result. And I serve fair warning that I shall breakfast at the earliest moment to-morrow morning after my dreaming. Further, I commend myself to Homer's twin portals of dreams; to Morpheus, god of slumber; to Phantasus, god of appearances; and to Icelon and Phobetor, twin gods of fright. If they succor me in my need, I shall raise in their honor a handsome altar, covered with softest down. Were this Laconia instead of Touraine, were I in Ino's temple between Œtyle and Thalamis, Ino would long ago have banished my perplexity by granting me the brightest, sweetest dreams."

Withal, there was still something on Panurge's mind.

"Wouldn't it be a good idea to put a few twigs of laurel under my pillow?"

"Quite unnecessary," Pantagruel told him. "That is a superstition and a delusion. I know that Serapion of Ascalon, in his treatise on dreams; Antiphon of Athens, Socrates' contemporary, in his *Of Dream Crises*; Philochorus, the polygrapher, four hundred years before our era; Artemon of Miletus; and Fulgentius Plantiades, fifth-century Bishop of Carthage, in the *Mythologicum*, all wrote at length on the subject. Superstition, all of it. And the same goes for the left shoulder of a crocodile or chameleon, with all due respect to old Democritus . . . for the *eumetrides* or Bactrian stones, which must be placed on the head at night . . . for the fossil shell called ammonite, a golden gem which the Ethiopians know as the horn of Ammon, because it is shaped like a ram's horn and esteemed in honor of Jupiter Ammon. Let the Ethiopians believe that those who carry ammonite dream divine oracles."

Panurge looked somewhat discouraged.

"As a matter of fact," Pantagruel resumed, "Homer and Virgil wrote much the same thing about the twin portals of dreams, to which you commended yourself. The first is of ivory. Through it pass all confused, ambiguous and unintelligible dreams. For, however slender ivory is, it is impossible to see through; its density and opacity prevent the animal spirits from radiating out of the eye and the im-

corner; you shall be King Horn and I shall drink to the Horn of Horn; I'll make a spoon of one horn, a foghorn of the other. Let Dr. de Hornibus preach; I'll take the collection plate around the parish."

"Not at all!" Panurge replied. "My dream means just this: when I marry, all sorts of prosperity will grow about me; I shall enjoy the horn of plenty. You claim mine will be satyr's horns: so much the better. *Amen, amen, fiat, fiat, ad differentiam papae; so be it, be it so, let it be so and, as the Pope does not say, let it so be!* My joyrod will always be primed and tireless, like my fellow-satyrs', a condition that all men desire but few obtain from heaven. Therefore I shall never be a cuckold; for the sole reason and *sine qua non* of cuckoldry lies in a limber dingus. What makes poor rascals beg? A house without the wherewithal to fill their pokes. What makes wolves emerge from the woods? Lack of meat. What makes women trollops? You can grasp what I mean. . . ."

Panurge appealed to the authority of lawyers, judges, counsellors, advocates, juries and professional talesmen—or should he say tailsmen? He appealed to the greatest commentators of the clause *De frigidis et maleficiatis, Of those rendered frigid and impotent through sorcery*, in the *Decretals*. With all due respect to his friends' views, Panurge considered they shot wide of the mark when they attributed his horns to cuckoldry. Diana wore horns in a noble crescent upon her head: did that constitute her a cuckold? How, in God's name, could she be a cuckold when she never married? Panurge implored his friends to be more accurate lest she make them horns like those she made Actaeon, who, surprising her at her bath, was changed into a stag and devoured by his own hounds.

Genial Bacchus wore horns; so did Pan, and Jupiter of Ammon and how many others? Were they cuckold? If Jupiter was, then, inevitably, according to the figure called metalepsis or transposition, Juno must inevitably have been a whore. The principle was the same as that involved when you called a child a bastard or whoreson in his parents' presence; it was plainly, if tacitly, accusing the father of being a cuckold, the mother a punk.

"No: let us be more exact," Panurge concluded. "First, the horns my wife gave me were horns of plenty; abundance of good things rose all about me, I assure you. Secondly, I shall be as joyful as a wedding tabor, forever rolling and rumbling, rub-a-dub-dubbing, humming, bumming and thundering. Third, my wife will be winsome and blithe as a pet madge owl. Whoever does not think so:

> *Well,*
> *Let him hang or go to hell*
> *Carol, Christmas chimes: Noël.*"

Here Pantagruel took exception. He could not but compare Panurge's last statement with his first. The comparison was revealing. In the beginning, Panurge was delighted with his dream; in the end, he awoke, to quote his own words, "perplexed, annoyed and full of rage."

"Certainly!" Panurge put in. "I had not supped the night before!"

"Alas!" cried Pantagruel, "everything will go to rack and ruin, I plainly foresee. For you must know that any slumber, interrupted with a start and leaving the sleeper 'perplexed, annoyed and full of rage,' either signifies or presages evil."

How did Panurge's awakening signify evil? It proved a cacoëthal or morbid condition in the centre of the body, a malign, latent, hidden pestilence within. During sleep—which, according to the laws of medicine, invariably strengthened the powers of digestion —this diseased matter declared itself, and began to move towards the outer area of the body. Such an unfortunate stirring immediately woke up the sleeper, warning him, by a sharp pain risen in the heart, to attend to himself and seek relief. Various proverbs proved this. We were told to let sleeping dogs lie. We were warned against stirring up a hornet's nest and fishing in troubled waters. What happened to the Sicilians when, against Apollo's oracle, they sought to dry up the malaria-infested bog of Camarina? Their enemies marched over it and plundered the city. *Ne moveas Camarinam*, ran the rune: leave well enough alone.

How did Panurge's awakening presage evil? By giving him to understand, in the midst of his somnial divination, that some misfortune was being prepared for early realization.

History furnished us with examples galore. There was Hecuba who experienced a horrible dream; there was Eurydice, Orpheus' wife. Their dreams done, they both awakened with a start of terror, so Ennius, the Latin poet tells us. Shortly thereafter, Hecuba was to see Priam, her husband, and all their children, massacred, their homes laid waste. Shortly thereafter, Eurydice perished miserably.

Again, Æneas, dreaming he was speaking to dead Hector, awoke with a start: that very night Troy was sacked and burned. On another occasion, dreaming he beheld his Penates and familiar gods, he awoke with a start; next day, he almost lost his life in a tempest at sea. Then there was Turnus, also. Urged by a fantastic apparition of the infernal fury to engage in a bloody war against Æneas, he awoke with a start, "perplexed, annoyed and full of rage." Some time later, after suffering defeat and desolation, he was to die by Æneas' hand. These were only a few among thousands of instances.

Speaking of Æneas, let us not forget Fabius Pictor, the father of Roman history, who certifies that Æneas never undertook anything —indeed, nothing ever befell him—without it appearing previously to him in some somnial divination.

There were as many reasons for this as there were examples. For if sleep and repose were a specially beneficent gift from the gods, as philosophers averred and as the poet Virgil put it:

> *It was the hour when god-sent sleep falls on*
> *Tired humans like a benediction,*

then that gift could not properly end amid perplexity, annoyance and rage, unless it portended some signal misfortune. Otherwise, repose would be a molestation, and the divine gift a scourge sent by the devils our foes. Panurge knew the Greek saying: ἐχθρῶν ἄδωρα δῶρα, gifts from foes are never gifts.

Pantagruel summed up his argument:

"Here is the thing in a nutshell. The father of a family sits down to a meal on a groaning board. He feels in the pink of condition; his appetite is excellent. Suddenly he rises with a start, 'perplexed, annoyed and full of rage.' Anyone observing him would be amazed at his conduct. But why does he behave thus? Well, he has just heard his grooms shout: 'Fire!'; his maids shriek: 'Stop thief!'; and his children bawl: 'Murder!' So he must needs leave his food there and rush up to bring aid.

"Another thing: I remember how the Cabbalists, those noted

Jewish scholars, and the Massoreths, those Hebrew commentators of sacred script, show how to differentiate between the apparitions of angels and devils. (As you know, Satan frequently appears as an angel of light.) They declare that when the benign, consoling spirit appears to man, it first terrifies him, but finally comforts him, leaving him satisfied and content. But the malign, seductive spirit first delights him; then, after, it leaves him 'perplexed, annoyed and full of rage.' "

XV

HOW PANURGE MADE EXCUSES AND SET FORTH THE MONASTIC MYSTERY CONCERNING PICKLED BEEF

"GOD save such as see, yet do not hear. I see you plain as a pike-staff; but I haven't the faintest notion of what you said. The hungry belly hath no ears to hear: you know the old saw! By God, my belly roars with a fury of hunger. I have performed too gruelling a task: it will need a master juggler to gull me into forfeiting my supper this year, for the sake of a lot of silly dreams. No supper, by all the devils, a pox cripple me if I do it again. Come along, Friar John, let us breakfast. If I have fed well, if my belly has had its ration of oats and hay, I might possibly, in a great emergency, do without dinner. But not without supper, no! Pox take me if being supperless isn't a mighty error, a crime against Nature!"

Panurge then developed his thesis. Nature created the day as a period in which man went about his business, plied his trade and did his job. That he might perform this function more favorably, she furnished him with a candle—the bright sweet light of the sun. As evening drew near, she took it away from him, implying tacitly, but as vividly as though she spoke:

"Well done, children, you are honest folk; you have labored enough. Night cometh: you must now put away your labor and seek refreshment in good bread, good wine, good food. Amuse yourselves a little; then go to bed and rest, so you may be fresh and keen as ever for your work to-morrow."

Falconers worked on the same principle. They did not at once fly their birds on a full stomach; they allowed them to digest on the perch. The worthy pope who instituted the custom of fasting was well aware of this great truth. The faithful should fast, he ruled, until three o'clock in the afternoon; the rest of the day they were free to feed.

In ancient times, few people dined at noon except monks and canons. Churchmen really had no other occupation: every day was a feast day to them, and they observed most diligently the claustral proverb *de missa ad mensam*, from mass to mess. The moment divine service was over, they adjourned to the refectory. Settling down to table, did they defer eating for anyone or anything? Certainly not: they fell to without further ceremony—a habit which gave rise to the expression "to wait for the abbot" or to eat while waiting for somebody. Under those circumstances, they would have "waited for the abbot" all day long.

Of old, then, no one dined at noon except a few idlers and wastrels; everyone supped at night. The word *cœna* or supper means "the meal common to all."

"You know that quite well, Friar John," Panurge wound up. "Come, friend, in the name of all the devils, come along. My stomach, in its ill-starred hunger, bays like a dog: let us toss some bread down its maw as the sibyl did to quell Cerberus, the watchdog of hell. You're the product of a monastery: you like choice bits to eat at ungodly hours; I myself prefer the big game our hounds run down and a huge cut of the plowman, put through nine lessons."

"I catch your meaning!" cried Friar John. "You got your metaphor out of the cloister kettle. By plowman you mean the ox who plowed and labored; by 'put through nine lessons' you mean 'cooked to perfection.'"

Friar John went on to show how, in his day, the holy religious fathers obeyed a certain ancient cabbalistic institution, unwritten, but handed down through the ages. Following its tenets, arising for matins, they performed various important preambles ere entering church. They would dung in the dungeries, urinate in the urinals, spit in the spittoons, cough most melodiously in the cougheries and idle in the idleries, in order to bring nothing indecent with them to the divine services. These preambles accomplished, they would repair zealously to the holy chapel (which, in their jargon, meant the abbey kitchen) to make certain the beef be put on the stove for the breakfast of the religious brothers of Our Lord. Often, they kindled the fire under the pot themselves.

Nowadays, their matins consisted of nine lessons, so they got up betimes to dispatch them the quicker. The earlier they rose, the sharper their appetites, and the quicker their lipservice, so that, eventually, matins consisted of from one to three lessons only. By this ancient tradition, then, the earlier they rose, the sooner the beef was on the fire; the quicker this happened, the longer it boiled, the tenderer it was, the less it taxed their teeth, the more it pleased the palate, the less it weighed on the stomach and the better it fed the excellent fathers. Which was the sole end and intention of the founders, seeing that men do not eat to live but live to eat, owning, in this world, no thing but their lives.

Having unburdened himself of this tirade:

"Come, Panurge, let us breakfast," the friar urged.

"This time I *have* heard, my plushcod friar," cried Panurge. "And I've understood you, my conventual, my cabbalistic, my capital cockahoop. Capital, did I say? I release sum, interest and charges, retaining only the costs, because you have so eruditely commented on the mysterious doctrine of kitchen and convent. Come along, Carpalim. Friar John, you are as close to me as my money-belt; come, my blessed bellyband. I wish you good day, My Fair Lords. I have dreamed enough to drink. Let us go!"

Panurge had not finished, when Epistemon cried:

"To conceive, understand, know and foretell the misfortunes of others is no strange or unusual quality among humans. But what a rare thing to foretell, know, understand and conceive one's own misfortunes! How sagaciously Æsop spoke in his *Apologues*! You remember: he said that every man born to this earth wore a bag around his neck. In the fore part of the bag lay the faults and misfortunes of others, forever exposed to his sight and knowledge; in the hind part his own, forever hidden and obscure, unless he be one whom the stars favored at birth."

XVI

HOW PANTAGRUEL ADVISED PANURGE TO CONSULT THE SIBYL OF PANZOULT

SOME time later, Pantagruel sent for Panurge and told him:

"The deep love I bear you, hallowed by a succession of time, now prompts me to plan for your welfare and profit. Listen to my plan. I am told that there is a very famous sibyl at Panzoult, near Le Croulay, here in Touraine. She has the gift of foretelling all things to come. Take Epistemon with you, go to her and find out what she has to tell you."

"If she's a sibyl, well and good," said Epistemon. "But what if she were some pythoness or sorceress like the Canidia and Sagana, that Horace describes in his *Epodes*? I say this because her native town enjoys the evil reputation of harboring more witches than ever infested Thessaly. I'm not keen on going there. The thing is forbidden by the law of Moses: 'There shall not be found among you anyone that useth divination, or an enchanter, or a witch.'"

"We are not Jews," Pantagruel answered. "Nor has the woman been legally proved to be a witch. Let us sift and weigh all these minute details when you have come back. How do we know she isn't an eleventh sibyl, a second Cassandra? Even if she is neither, nor merits the name, what harm is there in consulting her about your problem? Especially since she is said to know more than is customary in her sex and in her country. Knowledge never harmed a man, whether he learned from grot, pot, sot, slot, or snot."

Pantagruel then reminded them how Alexander the Great, after his victory over Darius at Arbela, refused repeatedly, in his satraps' presence, to receive a rascal that begged for an audience. Later, time after time he repented—in vain. To be sure, he proved victorious in Persia. Yet he was very far removed from Macedonia, his hereditary kingdom: obstacles of vast distances, huge rivers, endless deserts and enormous mountains lay between them. Then Alexander bitterly regretted being unable to discover the slightest means of obtaining news from the homeland. His perplexity and worry were extreme. In his absence his country might be invaded, his kingdom overthrown, a new monarch enthroned and a foreign colony planted, long before he got word of it.

At this stage, a Sidonian merchant, a canny, sensible man, but poor and shabby, appeared before Alexander. He announced with insistence that he had found means by which, within a space of five days, Alexander could get news of his Indian victories home, and, in turn, hear from Egypt and Macedonia. Alexander considered the proposal so improbable that he refused to receive, let alone hear the merchant. Yet what would he have lost by allowing the fellow to speak? What hurt or damage would he have incurred by learning what the fellow had contrived?

"It seems to me," Pantagruel concluded, "that Nature had reasons for giving us open ears whereas other organs—the tongue, the eyes and so forth—are protected by gates and enclosures. I suppose she hoped that, day long, night long, we might use our ears to listen and, listening, learn. Is not hearing the fittest of all our senses when it comes to taking in knowledge of arts and sciences? Who knows but the Sidonian messenger was an angel—that is a messenger from God —just as Raphael, appearing before Tobias, showed him how to catch the fish that sought to devour him, and to cure his father Tobit's blindness with its gall."

"You are right," Epistemon conceded. "But you will never convince me that it is profitable for a man to marry on a woman's advice —especially such a woman, from such a home!"

Panurge disagreed violently:

"For my part, I find women the best counsellors, especially old women. Thanks to their advice, every day I produce one or two extra evacuations of the bowels. My dear fellow, they are perfect pointers, capital hunting bitches; they are as sententious as the rubrics of the law."

A *sage femme*, Panurge explained, was a midwife, but the epithet *sage* meant wise; it had been granted to woman because she was wise and skilful in her ways. For his part, he felt inclined to call them *présage femmes*, because they could, through divine knowledge, presage and foretell accurately everything to come. At other times, he called them not *mannettes*, which meant sluts, but *monettes*, for the monitions they give like Roman Juno, goddess of monitions, whose temple was a mint. Ah, what salutary and profitable advice was theirs! Panurge quoted Pythagoras on the score of woman's divine prescience. He recalled how Socrates compared himself to a *sage femme*, or midwife, because he delivered the pregnant minds of men, as she the pregnant wombs of women. He cited Empedocles. Nor did he forget our learned Master Ortuinus (Hardouin de Grätz) who, spurning his correspondent's suggestion that he find an old woman, proceeded to fructify the servant-girl of a bookseller friend.

"Furthermore," Panurge said, "I praise to high heaven the ancient custom of the Germans. They revered old women; they prized them 'after the shekel of the sanctuary,' to use a biblical phrase. Wisely following their counsel, they prospered exceedingly. Witness aged Aurinia and good mother Vellede, whom they worshipped in Vespasian's day. You may take my word for it, they are sablesmooth sayers—I mean sibylsmooth sayers. Let us be off, God help us; let us be off, in God's name. Farewell, Friar John; look after my codpiece, for you know I wear it no longer."

"Well," Epistemon said. "I will follow you. But I give you solemn warning, if I catch her using charms or witchcraft in her answers, I'll leave you at her gate—and not one step further shall I venture!"

XVII

HOW PANURGE SPOKE TO THE SIBYL OF PANZOULT

THEY were three days on the road. The third day, they caught sight of the seeress' house under a tall, spreading chestnut tree on the top of a hill. They made their way without difficulty into a poorly built, ill-furnished and smoky thatched cottage.

"Ah, well," Epistemon sighed. "Heraclitus Skoteinos, as tenebrous and obscurantist a philosopher as our Duns Scotus, was not at a loss when he entered a similar hovel. Turning to his disciples and pupils, he told them the gods resided there as happily as in a palace of delights. Do you remember Hecate, the Attic hag who befriended Theseus in his youth, and whom he showered with honors after her death? I'm sure she lived in just such a lair. So, too, did Hyræus or Œnopion, who acted as host to Jupiter, Neptune and Mercury, a grateful trio. A wet night and a wet party: they liquidated their debt by forging Orion. And how did they forge Orion? By pissing on the hide of the bull Hyræus sacrificed to them, and covering the soaked hide with earth."

The hag crouched in one corner of the hearth.

"A true sibyl," was Epistemon's comment. "Just the type Homer described as τῇ καμίνοι, when he compared Ulysses to an old hag in the chimney corner."

Grim she was, indeed: of sinister aspect, ill-clad, emaciated, toothless, blear-eyed, bent over double, almost exanimate. She was, at the moment, brewing her dinner: cabbage soup, with a rasher of yellowish bacon, and the traditional hollow porkbone that serves to flavor how many such messes how many times!

"God's truth!" Epistemon exclaimed. "We have made a botch of it. She will never answer us: we failed to bring the golden bough, which the Sibyl of Cumæ insisted Æneas bring, if he hoped to enter the kingdom of Proserpine."

"I have made ample provision," Panurge replied. "In this pouch of mine, I've a golden bough, if you will, but rounded in the shape of a ring. And I've some fine ringing golden coins beside it."

So saying, Panurge bowed deeply to the sibyl and presented her six tongues of smoked beef . . . a great butter pot, full of couscous, an Arab dish, consisting of granulated flour steamed over broth . . . a bumgut-shaped flagon, full of good tipple . . . a ramscod purse, stuffed with newly minted coins. . . . Finally, with a still more ceremonious salutation, Panurge slipped over her middle finger a handsome gold ring, with a priceless toadstone, from Beuxes, in the Vienne country, richly inset. Then, briefly but pertinently, he told her why he had come, begging her most civilly to give him her advice and predictions in view of his projected marriage.

For a while, the hag maintained a thoughtful silence, grinding her teeth sulkily. Presently, she sat on the edge of a box, picked up three ancient spindles, turning and twisting them variously between her fingers. Then, she tested their points, retained the sharpest, and tossed the two others under a large mortar. Next, she picked up a pair of skeinwinders, which she twirled exactly nine times; the ninth turn given, she leaned back to watch them whirring around, never moving until they had come to a standstill.

Having removed one of her wooden shoes, she proceeded to drape her apron over her head (much as a priest his amice before mass), fastening it under her throat with an old spotted cloth. Under this improvised hood, she tossed off a deep draught of the flagon Panurge had brought her, took three coins from the ramscod purse he had given her, and put them into as many walnut shells. These she tossed into a great pot in which she saved feathers for mattresses. Sweeping the chimney out thrice with her broom, she threw a half-bundle of heather and a branch of dry laurel on to the fire. In utter silence, she watched them burn: though the flames rose, there was neither crackle nor pop. Suddenly she screamed, muttering, between clenched teeth, some barbarous incantation that fell weirdly on the ear.

Panurge turned to Epistemon:

"By the power of God, I'm all atremble; I swear I am bewitched. That is no Christian language she's speaking! Look! she's four yards taller than before she put that apron over her head. What does she mean by grinding her jaws, wriggling her shoulders, and making her lips chatter like a monkey dismembering a lobster? My ears are ringing: here is Proserpine, the wife of Lucifer, raising the roof of Hades with her clamor; any minute the hordes of hell will break loose. For God's sake, let us flee the horrible beasts. By His own snake, I die of fright, for I was never a friend of devils; they vex me and play evil tricks. Come, lad, let us abscond! Farewell, my good woman; grammercy for your favors. I'll not get married, no; I'll do without, as I used to!"

With which, Panurge shot away. But the hag, spindle in hand, cut off his retreat. Leading the way to an old sycamore in the little garden behind her hovel, she shook the tree three times. Eight leaves fell to the ground. Like the Sibyl of Cumæ, with the point of her spindle, she scratched a legend upon each and, tossing them to the wind:

"Go get them, if you care to; find them if you can; they bear, written upon them, the destiny of your marriage."

So saying, she withdrew into her den, but, ere she vanished, she pirouetted on the doorsill, yanked her dress, petticoat and skirt up to the armpits, and exhibited her scut.

"God's ways are deep!" cried Panurge. "I'm damned if that's not the Sibyl's Hole, of which Virgil speaks with such terror."

Ere he finished speaking, the hag slammed the door and bolted it. (She was never seen again!)

Epistemon and Panurge dashed after the eight leaves; the wind scattered them amid the underbrush in the valley; it was not without difficulty they caught them.

Laying them end to end, they read:

> *She'll bleed you, cup*
> *You—to your rue!* . . .
>
> *She'll breed, she'll pup,*
> *But not through you* . . .
>
> *She'll suck, she'll sup*
> *Your better end* . . .
>
> *She'll trim you up—*
> *(Not wholly, friend!)*

XVIII

OF THE DIFFERENT MEANING PANTAGRUEL AND PANURGE GATHERED FROM THE SIBYL'S ORACLE

CARRYING the leaves carefully in the proper order, Epistemon and Panurge returned to Pantagruel's court. They were half pleased, half vexed: pleased at heading homeward; vexed at the rough stony road they must travel. To Pantagruel, they gave a complete account of their journey and of the sibyl; then they showed him the syca-more leaves with the verses minutely scrawled upon them.

"A fine pickle you're in," Pantagruel sighed, after reading the leaves attentively. "The sibyl's testimony clearly bears out what we learned from Virgil and from your own dreams. Your wife will disgrace and cuckold you; abandoning herself to others, she will become pregnant through another's good offices. What's more, she will filch a good part of your possessions. Finally, she will beat you, pluck your skin, and bruise some member of your body."

Panurge writhed.

"You seem to handle an oracle as familiarly as a swine does pearls. Forgive my somewhat vigorous simile; but that sticks in my gizzard! Listen to my side of it; you will realize that the truth is diametrically opposed to your interpretation."

Panurge explained the hag's message as follows:

"The bean is not visible until it is husked; just so, Panurge's vir-tues and perfections could not shine forth unless he were married."

Pantagruel grunted; Panurge appealed to him:

"How many times," Panurge asked, "have I heard you say that public office and civic duty show what a man has under his hat and under his belt? Put him in a position of authority, and you will soon learn his worth; leave him to lead his private existence, and he is as manifest to you as a bean in its husk. So much for Item One. Otherwise, you might as well argue that a man's decency and honor depended on a whore's tail."

As for the second article of the sibyl's message, Panurge acknowl-edged his wife's pregnancy. Therein lay the prime felicity of mar-riage. Pregnant, yes but not pregnant with Panurge. God help us, how could she be? No—she would be pregnant with a fine little lad manufactured by Panurge. Why, right here and now, Panurge loved the little shaver to distraction. Heaven bless the angelic, wee calf! Let the world visit its fiercest vexations upon Panurge, at the mere glimpse of his babe, babbling and prattling its gibberish, they would fall off him, like water off a duck's back. God bless the old trot! Panurge earnestly desired to settle a pension upon her from his Salmagundi revenue: not the variable income of an idiot, working on commission, but the regular, dependable trust-fund that delights your capitalist's heart.

If Pantagruel's argument were right, then Panurge's wife would bear him, Panurge, in her womb; she would give him birth so people might say:

"Panurge is born twice, like Bacchus, who first was conceived by mortal Semele, and again sprang out of Jupiter's thigh. Panurge is reborn as was Hippolytus, first by the Amazon and, after his horses trampled him to death, again by Diana . . . as was Proteus, the Egyptian god, first by Thetis, and again by the mother of Apollonius, the philosopher of Tyana . . . as were the two Palici, whose mother, the nymph Thalia, was hidden underground by Jupiter until, her delivery forthcoming, Jove caused earth to open, and the twins to emerge at Simaethos in Sicily. Panurge's wife was bigswoln with him; in Panurge are reënacted a reduplication and a rebirth."

"*Bis repetita placent*," says Horace, repetition is welcome! This would be good news to the ancient Megarians who believed in palintocy or reproduction to the second degree! It would also delight Democritus, the champion of palingenesis or renascence. No—the thing was unthinkable and Panurge begged Pantagruel never to mention it again.

"So much for Item Two," Panurge persisted. "Now let us take up the third statement of the sibyl. My wife, she said, shall suck my better end. All the better, say I; that will raise my spirits, make me perk up, cockahoop! Don't you see the sibyl meant good old *fellatio*? My better end is my uniterminal, intercrural asparagus stalk. I hereby vow and promise to keep it succulent, with good measure pressed down and running over. It shall not suckle her in vain; she'll not look for oats in the nosebag I clap over her pretty snout, nor for negus in my ballocky bumper.

"According to your allegorical exposition of this passage, to suck me dry means to rob and despoil me. I applaud the argument, I delight in the allegory, but not in the sense you take it. Probably your sincere affection for me inspires these adverse and refractory thoughts: do not the learned assure us that love is a fearsome thing and true love is never without misgiving? But, if you ask me my opinion, I believe—"

"You believe what?" Pantagruel challenged.

"I believe," said Panurge, "that in your inmost heart you consider the larceny, here presaged, in the same sense as the Greek and Latin authors. Such pilfering applies to the luscious fruits of amorous dalliance, which Venus insists be secretly palmed, filched and purloined."

"How so?"

"How so, you ask? Because I maintain, with all due respect to more authoritative opinion, that this particular form of snapdragon pleases the Cyprian goddess more, when enjoyed slyly and surreptitiously between two doors, than when practised blatantly in the broad light of day. (You recall how Diogenes the cynic declared that if it was not evil for a man to lie with his wife, then it was not evil for him to do so in public.) Cytherea delights in this ravishment when relished on a pair of steps, under the bushes, behind curtains or against a few propped logs. She disapproves of its perfunctory performance under a stately canopy, between rich cloth-of-gold curtains, at stated intervals—with a crimson velvet swatter and an ostrich-plume fan, stroking a fly from all angles, whilst Madame picks her teeth with a straw plucked out of the mattress.

"If my interpretation is wrong, My Lord Pantagruel," Panurge cleared his throat, "then, according to you, she would ransack me by labial extirpation—much as you gulp an oyster, or better as the women of Cilicia snap cochineal seeds out of the evergreen oak, squeezing them sedulously in their mouths. Dioscorides is my authority in this instance.

"I trust you will not mind my suggesting that here you err. A thief does not lap up, he snatches . . . he does not coax, he grabs . . . he does not swallow, he snorts, whoofs and plays catch-as-catch-can . . . (light-fingered gentry on slippery feet!)."

As for the sibyl's fourth point, Panurge could easily dispose of it. She had said that his wife would "trim him up" or flay him, "but not wholly." Pantagruel took this to mean that she would subject Panurge to assault and battery. That was plain as a pikestaff, clear as the way to parish church, obvious as the noonday sun. If only Pantagruel would rise above base earthly things, and contemplate loftily the marvels of nature! In this particular instance, moreover, Pantagruel should blame himself for the errors he had committed in expounding perversely the prophecies of the holy sibyl. Panurge was willing, for the sake of argument, to assume—without allowing its truth—that his wife, inspired by the devil, might wish and attempt to play him an ill turn, to disgrace him, to cuckold him to the cack-hole, to rob and to assault him. But, the assumption made, did it follow that her will and effort must succeed?

"I say this," Panurge elaborated, "on the authority of universal theology; I was told it by Friar Tailwaggle some years ago . . . a Monday, I recall . . . we were eating a bushel of blood-sausages . . . and, unless I err, it was raining . . . God bless him and grant him joy!"

Panurge continued his exposition. At the beginning of the world, or somewhat later, women conspired to flay men alive; they swore by God's holy blood to do so. And why? Because men had sought to dominate them in every respect. But alas for the vain undertakings of woman, alas for the brittleness of the sex feminine! She began to flay man—or peel him, as Catullus says—by the most delectable member, the nervous, cavernous pole. Six thousand years or more had elapsed, yet, at the present writing, she had got no further than the head in her flaying. In the teeth of this, the Jews themselves snipped off their own heads circumcisionally, preferring to be dubbed shavetail and bobtail than to suffer women to flay them as other races do. Indeed, the converted Spanish Moors and Jews underwent a further operation of preputial reconstruction to conceal their racial origin.

"According to this feminine agreement," Panurge wound up, "my wife will most certainly flay me, if I'm not already well flayed enough. I consent to this, radically, upright and downright, substantially; the long and short of it are hers. But she shall not flay me wholly—no, never wholly, my friend!"

Epistemon interrupted:

"But, Panurge, you've said nothing about her sharp, blood-curdling scream when she and both of us saw the laurel branch burn without crackle or pop? That, as you know, is an evil omen, a token of disaster. Propertius and Tibullus; Porphyrius, the subtle neo-Platonist; Eustathius, Archbishop of Thessalonica and twelfth-century commentator of Homer's *Iliad*; and how many others bear this out?"

"Stuff and nonsense!" Panurge replied. "Your authorities were fools as poets, dunderheads as philosophers: they were as crammed with balderdash as their fine doctrine."

XIX

HOW PANTAGRUEL PRAISED THE COUNSEL OF DEAF-MUTES

For a long while, Pantagruel held his peace. He seemed rapt in thought. Presently:

"The evil spirit misleads you, Panurge," he declared, "but listen to me. I have read that in times past the best and surest oracles were not uttered by word of mouth or by writing. Very often, even men reputed to be the most learned and intelligent of their age, were deceived as much by ambiguities, obscurities and equivokes as by laconism. Thus Apollo, god of divination, was surnamed the indirect.

"No, the truest and most creditable oracles were delivered by sign and gesture. Heraclitus vouches for it. So Jupiter decreed in Ammon; so too Apollo in Assyria, if we are to believe the poet Lucian. That is why the Assyrians invariably pictured Apollo with the sedate clothes and gray beard of an old man, not naked, young and clean-shaven as the Greeks saw him."

Basing his suggestion on such authorities, Pantagruel believed that Panurge had best abandon words for signs, and seek counsel of one denied the gift of speech.

"Quite so!" Panurge agreed.

"But," Pantagruel qualified the suggestion, "your oracle should be a deaf-mute by birth. What mute could be more natural and sincere than one who has never heard?"

"I don't understand," Panurge objected. "If you maintain no man ever spoke without having heard others do so, I will bring you to admit logically a most paradoxical, abhorrent proposition. But enough! You do not believe Herodotus, I suppose? Do you remember his account of the two children King Psammeticus of Egypt kept in retreat and perpetual silence? Eventually, they cried *Becus!*—which, in Phrygian, means *bread*."

"Not at all," Pantagruel argued. "I believe it a gross error to say there is such a thing as a natural language. Speech is created by arbi-

trary institutions, by national agreement; words, in the technical
sense, mean no more in themselves than what their earliest users intended they should. Is my statement gratuitous? Certainly not.
Bartolus, the Italian jurisconsult, tells us of a contemporary of his,
Messire Nello de Gabrielis, who by accident became deaf. Well, it
didn't prevent him from understanding any Italian dialect, spoken
even in a whisper. He could do so by observing the speakers' gestures, and reading their lips."

Further, Pantagruel begged to quote the erudite and polished
author who related the visit to Rome, in Nero's day, of Tyridates,
King of Armenia. To create an eternal bond of friendship, the
Roman senate and people received this monarch with the utmost
cordiality and pomp: there was no sight or rarity in the city he was
not shown. When Tyridates left, the emperor showered him with
gifts; more, he begged Tyridates to choose the thing that had most
pleased him. Rome, he added, bound itself to grant whatsoever the
royal visitor desired.

"Do you know what Tyridates asked for?" Pantagruel said. "A
mummer, ay, a mountebank. Tyridates, seeing him, had not understood a word he spoke; but he had been convinced by his signs and
gestures. The monarch explained that his empire included peoples
of various language; usually, interpreters were required, but this
Roman pantaloon would do to interpret Tyridates' thought to one
and all. The fellow was such an excellent mime that his very fingertips seemed to speak an unmistakable idiom."

Panurge, however, should choose a natural deaf-mute, whose sign
language would prove inherently natural instead of affected and
feigned. The only point to settle was: should this deaf-and-dumb
oracle be a man or woman?

"I would prefer a woman," said Panurge, "were it not for two
things."

"What?"

"What two things?"

Panurge examined his questioners:

"First," he said deliberately, "whatever women see, they never
think, imagine or conceive it save in terms of the stout, stiff-standing
deities Ithyphallos and Penis Erectus. No gesture, sign or move you
make in their presence but they ascribe it to the incorporate move-

ment of dangletwat. Obviously then, with woman interpreting our every act as an invitation to cunnytrundle, we men would be frequently deceived."

Panurge could cite a case in point: the event occurred in Rome two hundred years after the founding of the city. A young gentleman, strolling on Mount Celion (one of the seven hills of Rome, today St. John Lateran) chanced to meet a lady named Verona, a deafmute from birth. Unaware of her deafness, with the voluble gestures of your Italian, he asked her what senators she had met in her walk. Not hearing what he said, she took his gestures literally to express the request any young man naturally makes to a woman. (I may add here that signs, when it comes to lovemaking, prove infinitely more attractive, speedy and efficacious than words.) Thus by pantomime, Verona drew the gentleman to her house; advised him that the game pleased her no end. And finally, without a word being exchanged, a fine bout of spasms and throes resulted.

"My second objection to consulting female deaf-mutes," said Panurge, "is that they would not answer at all: they would merely fall backwards in wordless intimation that they accepted our tacit demands. Or if they did make countersigns, these would prove so foolish and absurd that we could not help divining the gamut of their thought, from f to g, as in f——g."

Here again Panurge supplied an anecdote in corroboration. At Brignoles, in Provence, a nun called Soeur Fessue or Sister Fatrump was impregnated by a young lay brother, Friar Plummet. Her pregnancy known, she was summoned by the abbess before the whole convent, and accused of incest. But she excused herself: she had not consented; on the contrary, Friar Plummet had interpenetrated by force and violence.

"You wicked girl!" the abbess replied. "Didn't it happen in the dormitory?"

Sister Fatrump acknowledged this.

"Well, you should have shouted; we would have come to your help."

"But, Mother," the nun whined, "I didn't dare shout in the dormitory, because the rules say the dormitory must be a place of eternal silence!"

"Very well, you wicked child," said the abbess. "You could at least have signalled to your neighbors."

"But I did signal as vigorously as I could; only nobody helped me."

"How did you signal?"

"I flapped my buttocks with all my might!"

"Oh, you evil child!" the abbess wailed. "Why did not you come to me at once and make a regular complaint? Had this horrible thing happened to me, I should have done just that to establish my innocence."

"I knew," Sister Fatrump declared, "that, if I was struck by sudden death, I would be in a state of sin and in danger of eternal damnation, unless I made confession. So before Friar Plummet left the room, I made confession to him; for penance, he commanded me not to tell anyone about it. To reveal such a confession, he said, would have been too grievous an offence to God and the angels. It might have brought flames from heaven to burn the nunnery and to send us, one and all, to the bottomless pit with Korah, Dathan and Abiram, who were swallowed up by the earth for revolting against Moses."

Pantagruel gazed at Panurge.

"Jest as you will," he said, "but you cannot make me laugh. I know that all monkdom and nunhood had rather smash God's commandments to bits, than disregard the minutest of their provincial statutes. Take a man, then, Panurge. Nazdecabre—you know, Goatsnose—he seems suitable: he was born deaf and dumb."

XX

HOW GOATSNOSE ANSWERED PANURGE IN THE LANGUAGE OF SIGNS

GOATSNOSE, duly summoned, arrived on the morrow. Panurge at once gave him a fatted calf, half a hog, eighty gallons of wine, a load of corn and thirty francs. Then he led him before Pantagruel and the gentlemen of the bedchamber.

The debate in sign language began.

First, Panurge yawned cavernously and, while yawning, repeatedly made the figure of the Greek letter T or *Tau* with his right thumb. Raising his eyes to heaven, he proceeded to roll them around in his head, like a she-goat giving birth to a still-born kid. Meanwhile, he sighed, cleared his throat, coughed. Next, pointing to the place where, before his marital urge, he used to wear a codpiece, he drew out his mutton dagger, made a fist around it, and smacked it against his thighs with a melodious clacking. Next, he bowed his left knee, bent forward, and crossed his arms over his breast.

Goatsnose surveyed him curiously. Then he raised his left hand in the air, hid three fingers under his palm, but held up thumb and index, nail to nail.

"That sign means marriage," cried Pantagruel. "Just as in numerology, according to the Pythagoreans, the number 30 symbolized marriage. Panurge will be married!"

"Thanks very much!" said Panurge, turning towards Goatsnose. "Thanks, my little majordomo, my blessed convict boss, my catchpole friend, my sweet bumbailiff, my cuntstable!"

Goatsnose raised his left hand, spreading out his five fingers fanwise.

"Ho!" cried Pantagruel. "Here he explains more fully, by the symbol 5, that you will be married. Indeed, not only will you become affianced, betrothed and wedded, but you will cohabit long before the ceremony. Pythagoras declared the quinary a nuptial figure. Why? Because it is composed of a ternary (the first odd and superfluous group) and a binary (the first even number). The trio stands for man, the duo for woman: their sum stands for male and female accouplement. On wedding nights, the ancient Romans used to light five waxen tapers; the richest were not allowed to light more, the poorest less. The heathens, moreover, invoked marital felicity of five gods, or of one god beneficent in five respects. Such deities were the nuptial Jove; Juno, presiding over the feast; Venus, the spirit of beautiful; Pitho, deity of persuasion and fair speech; Diana, who favored childbearing."

"O charming Goatsnose!" cried Panurge. "I shall give him a farm near Cinais and a windmill near Mirebeau!"

Suddenly the deaf-mute sneezed violently, and jerked his whole frame to the left.

"What in the name of God is that?" Pantagruel cried. "This sign is not in your favor, Panurge; it means that your marriage will be ill-starred and unfortunate. According to Terpsion's doctrine in Plutarch, this sneezing is the Socratic demon. A sneeze to the right signifies that you may boldly and confidently pursue your undertaking: each step, from beginning to end, will prove auspicious. A sneeze to the left signifies the exact opposite."

"You always see things from the worst possible angle," Panurge grumbled. "You're as obstructive as the slave Davus in Terence. I don't believe a word of what you say: indeed, I never knew your wretched old Terpsion, save as a hopeless imposter."

"But Cicero also wrote something to the same effect in his second book *Of Divinations*," Pantagruel persisted.

Panurge, ignoring him, wheeled around upon Goatsnose and began an elaborate series of signs. First, he turned back his eyelids, twisted his jaws from right to left, and stuck his tongue halfway out of his mouth. Next, he opened wide his left hand, save for the middle finger, which he stuck downward, perpendicular to his palm and, in this position, settled on the place his codpiece had once decorated. Closing his right hand save for a protruding thumb, he brought the latter backward under his right armpit, and settled it above his buttocks, on what the Arabs called *al Katim*, and we, the sacrum or pelvis. Next, he did the same trick nine times, alternately changing hands. Finally, he brought his eyelids, jaws and tongue back to their normal positions, and squinted at Goatsnose, his lips quivering like a monkey's when it shells a nut, or a hare's when it munches oats off the stalk.   At which Goatsnose raised his right hand, spread it wide, slipped its thumb, up to the first joint, between the third joints of the middle and ring fingers. He locked the latter fast around the thumb, closed his other fingers, save for the index and little finger, which he stretched out straight. Holding his hand in this pose, he laid it over Panurge's navel; then, moving the thumb constantly, he balanced his hand on index and little finger as on a pair of legs. Little by little, he walked it, so to speak, successively over Panurge's belly, stomach, chest and neck. Drawing his ever-quivering thumb under, then over Panurge's chin, he placed it inside his victim's mouth, then rubbed the luckless fellow's nose with it and, reaching the eyes, made as though to gouge them out.

Panurge annoyed, tried to retreat, but Goatsnose followed him up, ever stroking him with the trembling thumb, now on his eyes, now on his forehead, and ultimately over the tip and edges of his cap. At length, Panurge lost his temper:

"By God, master fool, if you don't leave me alone, I shall thrash you within an inch of your life. Just keep on annoying me and see if my hand won't make your face look as though you were wearing a mask!"

"But the fellow is deaf!" Friar John observed. "He can't hear what you're saying to him, my ballocking blade! Make gestures to show you mean a rap on the snout!"

"What the devil is this buzzard trying to prove!" Panurge grumbled. "Curse all such Tom Noddies! He's poked my eyes till they look and feel like poached eggs with tomato sauce. By God (*da jurandi*, if I may swear!) I'll buffet the clod: I'll treat him to bumpers of assorted punches, with plenty of power in them!"

And, reproducing labially the breaking of wind, Panurge backed away.

But Goatsnose intercepted him forcibly, and made a new sign. This time, he lowered his right arm as far towards his right knee as he could . . . thrust his thumb between his index and middle finger . . . brought his left hand under his right elbow, and began to massage the latter . . . worked this hand along the whole forearm . . . lowered it again, and kept up the gesture, now raising it, now lowering it, but always exhibiting it to Panurge. . . .

Panurge, furious, lifted his hand to strike the deaf-mute; but he checked himself out of respect for Pantagruel.

"If the mere signs anger you," Pantagruel commented, "what will you do when the things signified happen to you? All truths agree and are one: this deaf-mute merely states, as best he can, that you will be married, cuckold, beaten and robbed."

"The marriage I concede," Panurge declared. "But I deny the rest. And I beg you to believe this: so far as women or horses go, no man ever knew such good fortune as lies in store for me!"

XXI

HOW PANURGE SOUGHT COUNSEL OF AN OLD FRENCH POET NAMED RAMINAGROBIS

PANTAGRUEL spoke:

"I never dreamed I could possibly meet a man as wilful and obstinate as you are, Panurge. However, to clear your doubts, I propose to leave no stone unturned. Listen to my plan."

Swans, Pantagruel explained, were sacred to Apollo; they sang only at the point of death. This was especially true of the swans in the Meander, a Phrygian stream. (Pantagruel cited this last detail only because Ælian, the honey-tongued Roman who preferred Greek letters, and Alexander Myndius, the Carian philosopher, stated that they had elsewhere seen swans die without singing ere they died.) The swan's song, then, was a certain presage of imminent death, since no swan perished without having chanted its farewell.

The same held good of poets, too. Were not poets under the protection of the divine Apollo? As they drew near their end, usually they became prophets, and, inspired by the god, sang of future things.

Further, Pantagruel had often heard that any aged, decrepit and moribund man possessed a clear gift of prophecy. Aristophanes, in some comedy or other, called old people sibyls:

The sibyl fills the oldster's thoughts.

So we ourselves, looking out from land at a shipload of sailors and passengers, kept silence, as we prayed for their safe landing. Then, as they sailed into the haven, we cheered and congratulated them.

So, too, according to Plato, the angels, heroes and good demons. As they watched men nearing death—a sure, salutary, tranquil and peaceful haven, free from all earthly tumults and tempests—they greeted and consoled them, conversed with them, and already initiated them into the art of divination.

Pantagruel refused to heap up examples from the ancients: Isaac, knowing his death to be at hand . . . Jacob, foretelling the destiny of his twelve sons . . . Patroclus, reading Hector's fate, and Hector, Achilles' . . . Polynestor, divining the lot of Agamemnon and Hecuba . . . the man of Rhodes—celebrated by Posidonius—who picked out six contemporaries of his, and anticipated their deaths in the order in which these occurred . . . Calanus, mounting the scaffold, assuring Alexander they would meet soon, and Alexander perishing a few days later. . . . Many other examples occurred to Pantagruel. There was Orodes, mortally wounded by Mezentius and warning him of a like fate; there were hosts of others.

Pantagruel would quote only one case.

"That wise and gallant knight, Guillaume du Bellay, Lord of Langey in Touraine, died as he was crossing Mont Tarare, in the Lyonnais mountain range. It was on January tenth, in his climacteric or critical year, since he was sixty-three—a product of seven by nine and hence significant. (The year was 1543, by our way of reckoning.) The last three or four hours of his life he spent, tranquil and serene, conversing with us about all manner of things. Some of these, we have seen fulfilled; others we are still awaiting. At the time, these phophecies seemed wild and absurd, since we could discover no possible sign or symptom of them."

"Ah!" Panurge sighed.

"At Villeaumaire, in the Chinon forest," Pantagruel continued, "I know a man called Raminagrobis. He is very old, indeed, and he is a poet. (His second wife was Mistress Broadsow Syphthroat, who bore him two daughters, Gono and Rhea.) I have heard that he is at death's door."

"Well?" Panurge asked.

"Well," Pantagruel echoed, "you had better scuttle off there, fast as you can! Go to his bedside, listen to his song. You may perhaps obtain what you wish; perhaps, through him, Apollo will settle your problem."

"Yes, yes, by all means!" Panurge cried. "Come along, Epistemon; let us go at once. If only he doesn't die before we get there! Are you with us, Friar John?"

"I don't mind at all," the monk said. "In fact, I'll come gladly, for love of you, my ballocking pizzlepusher: you warm the very cockles of my heart!"

So they set out at once.

Reaching the good old man's house, they found him in the agony of death; yet his bearing was cheerful, his expression open, his glance clear. With a bow, Panurge slipped his gift—a gold ring with a great, brilliant oriental sapphire enchased in its bezel—over the middle finger of his left hand. Then, imitating Socrates, whose last words, spoken to Crito, were: "I owe a cock to Æsculapius; remember to pay the debt!" Panurge offered Raminagrobis one. No sooner set on the bed, the beast reared its crest joyfully, shook out its plumage and crowed lustily.

"I beg you," Panurge said courteously, "to give us your opinion on my intended marriage."

Having ordered pen, paper and ink, the old man wrote the following poem:

> *Take her or not! Take her or not!*
> *If so you do, the better so!*
> *Failing, your strenuous labors go*
> *To help another fill the slot.*
> *Speed, gallop; draw your rein in, trot;*
> *Recoil, thrust forward; ebb and flow:*
> > *Take her or not!*
> *Fast like a saint; swill like a sot,*
> *Break barriers reared long years ago;*
> *Raise up what was long since laid low,*
> *Wish life or death to be her lot—*
> > *Take her or not!*

Handing them the paper, Raminagrobis said:

"Go, lads; God in heaven protect you! And do not bother me with this or any other business whatever. To-day, the last day of May and of my life, I have with the greatest of pains driven from my house a rabble of evil, shameless and pestilent beasts. They were black, they were striped, they were buff, they were white, they were ashen, they were speckled."

(Could Raminagrobis have been referring to the begging friars?)

"They would not suffer me to die in peace," the old poet murmured.

"By insidious pricking, by harpylike clutching, by waspish stinging, compounded in the workshop of God knows what insatiable devil, they drew me out of the sweet contemplation wherein I was seeing, touching and enjoying the blessings God has prepared for his elect in the future, immortal life. Steer away from their course; do not resemble them. Disturb me no more, I pray, and take your leave in silence."

XXII

PANURGE'S PLEA IN DEFENSE OF THE BEGGING FRIARS

As they left Raminagrobis' room, Panurge started back, as though gripped by a mortal fear:

"By the power of the Almighty!" he cried, "if that man isn't an out-and-out heretic, then I surrender my soul to the devil. He slanders the good Franciscan and Dominican friars, the very hemispheres of the Christian world. These, by their gyronomic circumbilivaginations, function as two celivagous filopendula which poise homocentrically the entire autonomatic metagrabolism of a Roman church already embranglefuddled by the farrago of error and the hotchpotch of heresy."

(Panurge meant that as surely as the shadow circles the sundial, so these Franciscans and Dominicans went about rounds quite as all-embracing and described about centres quite as hot. The two orders were heaven-sent pendula to balance over the same centre a church suffering from brain-fag, dislocation, mental derangement, apostasy and irreligion.)

"What, by all the devils, did those poor devils of Capuchins and Minims do to Raminagrobis?" Panurge demanded. "Aren't they wretched enough as it is? They may not eat meat, so they stuff themselves with fish; they are products of ichthyophagia or fish-eating, they are mackerel snatchers. Yet could the poor Abrahams be more besmoked with misery and besmirched with calamity? By your faith, Friar John, do you think Raminagrobis is in the state of salvation? He is shuffling off to thirty thousand basketfulls of devils, damned by God as surely as any serpent. How wicked to slander these worthy, courageous pilfers—I mean pillars—of the church! You may call it the poetic frenzy, so fashionable a doctrine to-day. For my part, I cannot subscribe to it. Raminagrobis is a villainous sinner who blasphemes against true religion; it offends me horribly."

"I don't care a straw!" Friar John replied. "Your friars slander everybody; if everybody returns the compliment, why should I worry? Let's see what Raminagrobis wrote."

Panurge read the kindly old man's verse carefully. Then he declared:

"The poor drunkard is raving! Yet I excuse him, for I know he is at death's door. Let us go write his epitaph. His answer leaves me no wiser than before we turned our hand to this business. Listen, Epistemon, my barrel-bellied bully: don't you agree that Raminagrobis is prejudiced in his answer? By God, he is a born sophister, a sharp wrangler, a caviller; I'll wager he is a renegade Moor, a heathen apostate. By the belly of bull and God, how careful he is to let no mistake creep into his words! He answers in disjunctives, in figures of grammar that involve but the choice between two words; thus he cannot fail to speak the truth, since the truth must lie in one of two alternatives. Oh, what a deceiver! What a prattler, what a Master Pierre Pathelin! By St. James of Compostella, the pilgrim's paradise, by St. James of our little village of Bressuire, here in Poitou, what a despicable race of men Raminagrobis belongs to!"

Epistemon interrupted:

"That is how the famous soothsayer Tiresias proceeded before uttering any prophecy. You remember when Ulysses sought his counsel, he said that what he was about to divulge would happen or, then again, it would not. All wise prophets use such a style."

"Well," Panurge answered, "Juno put out both his eyes, didn't she?"

"True, but out of spite, because he had judged better than she when, in reply to Jupiter's question, he ruled that woman enjoyed the act of copulation nine times more than man could."

"But," Panurge protested, "what devil incites Master Raminagrobis to slander the poor blessed friars, the Dominicans, the Franciscans or the good Minims? And without the slightest cause, reason or preface? I vow, I am deeply offended; I cannot let it go by in silence. He sinned grievously indeed; his soul is doomed to thirty thousand basketfuls of devils."

"I simply cannot make you out!" Epistemon sighed. "I, myself, am deeply offended that you should perversely apply, to the begging friars, what our good poet said about various black, buff and other-colored animals."

To Epistemon, Raminagrobis had not seemed guilty of such fantastic and sophistical allegory. The dying poet had merely referred to the fleas, lice, gnats, flies, moth and other beasts that persecuted him; some were black, others buff, others ashen, others tawny and others dusky and swart; but all were importunate, vexatious and noxious, not only to the sick, but to the healthy and vigorous also. Who knew but he had ascarids, lumbrics and other parasitic worms lodged in his entrails? Who knew but he had been stung in the arm or leg by one of those little speckled dragons the Arabs called *meden*? The Egyptians, and others who dwelled by the Red Sea, quite commonly suffered from this affliction.

To read a different meaning into Raminagrobis' words, as Panurge did, was to err, to wrong the ingenuous poet and to insult the friars by imputation. Man should always interpret the opinions of his fellow in the best possible light.

"Go teach your grandmother to suck eggs!" Panurge replied. "By the power of God, the fellow is a heretic, and when I say heretic, I mean a rooted, scurvy heretic. You haven't forgotten the notorious Clavelle of La Rochelle, who invented a wooden clock, which was consumed at the stake with him, when he sizzled for his Protestant heresies? Well, this Raminagrobis is just such a sixty-minute twenty-four-hour heretic . . . he deserves to sizzle too . . . his soul is headed for thirty thousand basketfuls of devils. . . .

"Would you like to know where?" Panurge exulted. "Why, right under Proserpine's cacking-stool . . . in the selfsame infernal bucket into which she voids her enema-induced fecalities . . . to the left of the giant cauldron of hell . . . three fathoms from the claws of Lucifer . . . very close to the dark chamber of Demigorgon, who dwells in the entrails of Earth, with Chaos and Eternity! . . .

"The wretch, the villain!"

XXIII

HOW PANURGE ADVOCATED RETURNING TO RAMINAGROBIS

"LET us go back," Panurge exhorted them. "Let us go back, for God's sake and in God's name, so we may properly advise poor Raminagrobis concerning his salvation. That were a work of charity; though he lose life and body, his soul, at least, will escape eternal damnation.

"We will make Raminagrobis repent of his sins; we will bring him to a contrite heart; we will persuade him to beg pardon of all the blessed fathers, present or absent, whom he insulted. What's more, we will draw up and witness a document proving his orthodoxy, lest he be posthumously declared a heretic, as was the wife of the Lord Provost of Orléans by the hobgoblin monks."

(Panurge was referring to a notorious scandal. Louise de Moreau, wife of François de St. Mesmin, Provost of Orléans, having been buried in the church of the Cordeliers or Franciscans, the latter, doubtless to obtain money, pretended that her soul returned to haunt them in the midst of their devotions. Investigation revealed that the reproachful ghost was merely an irreproachable novice, hidden in the vault. The monks were given a life sentence, but were eventually let off with banishment.)

"We will invite Raminagrobis to make amends to the holy fathers; he must leave special bequests for extra food, for the singing of masses, for obits and memorials. On the anniversary of his death, they shall, to all eternity, be granted an allowance of food five times as great as usual: and the fattest flagon, filled with the rarest wine, shall canter from table to table; row by row, for the full-fledged priests, the learned clerks, the aged fathers, the ruck of the psalm-droners, the lay brothers, the rawest novices. Thus Raminagrobis shall be assured of divine mercy.

"But no, by God! no! I'm rambling! Satan destroy me, if I go to the old man's house. God preserve us, his bedchamber is full of devils already! Listen to them howl bloody murder, as they vie for the privilege of gobbling up the Raminagrobidic soul! Who will win! Lip strives against lip, mouth fights with mouth; what demon-let will bear Raminagrobis between his teeth to Master Lucifer? Away with you, devils! I'll not go there; the Prince of Darkness slay me if I do! Who knows but these fiends might take a *quid* for a *quo* and, instead of Raminagrobis, snatch up a poor, solvent Panurge? When I was a debt-ridden welsher, they never bothered me. Away with you, devils; I refuse to go. By God, I die of mortal fear; I will not deal with hungry, indefatigable, laboring spirits of Abaddon!

"Away, devils, I cry! I dare wager that never a Jacobin, Cordelier, Carmelite, Capuchin, Theatin or Minim will turn up at Ramina-grobis' funeral. The wiser, they, since he left them nothing in his will. No, no—let the evil one swallow me up if I go there! Let him be damned to his own loss: after all, why did he slander the good re-ligious fathers? What business had he to chase them out of his room when most he needed their help, their devout prayers, their pious admonitions? Harmless folk with nothing but their lives in this world! He should have remembered to leave them money for extra provender, refection and belly timber. Let who will go there, I shan't, by all the unclean spirits of the bottomless pit! Surely, if I did, the devil would capture me! A pox upon you, devils, get you gone!

"Look here, Friar John, do you expect to be lugged away by thirty thousand cartfuls of devils? If so, then do three things for me. First, give me your purse; second, be out of debt; third, go back to your deathly poet. I will expound these three thoughts."

In the first instance, Panurge wished to have the monk surrender his purse. The cross, which figured so conspicuously on all coins, was utterly contrary to charms and divination. Panurge could quote a case in point: that of Jean Dodin, the tax-collector of Coudray, who wished to cross the ford of Vède after the bridge had been broken down by soldiers. The old lecher met Friar Adam Blowprick, an Observantin—the strictest type of Franciscan—from the Abbey of Mirebeau. Dodin promised the friar a new frock if he slung him over his shoulder, as a butcher might a dead goat, and thus bore him across the water. Wasn't the holy man a very colossus?

They struck a bargain. Friar Blowprick bared himself to the scrotum, laid the supplicant publican on his back, and proceeded across the waters. He was a stout little St. Christopher, bearing a Christ child over the flood; he was a jolly Æneas, bearing his father Anchises out of flaming Troy. As they progressed, he sang a tuneful *Ave maris stella, Hail, Star of the Sea*, a nautical and lively hymn! Reaching the middle of the ford, above the mill, Friar Blowprick asked Dodin if he had any money on his person. The tax-collector assured his carrier that he had bagfuls of cash: the promised frock would be forthcoming! But, the friar objected, an explicit rule of his chapter forbade him to carry money on his person. Dodin was truly damned, then, for tempting Blowprick sinfully to infringe this rule. Why hadn't Dodin left his purse with the miller? Undoubtedly, Dodin would be well punished; if ever Blowprick got Dodin within the monastery gates at Mirebeau, Dodin would be soundly whipped from the *Miserere*, that begins the flagellant's psalm, to the *Vitulos*, that closes it with the final thwack. So saying, Friar Blowprick discharged his burden, dropping old Dodin headlong into the water.

Hammering home the first point of his triple argument: "That example should teach you to give me your purse, my sweet friar," said Panurge. "That the devils may carry you off to your greater comfort, you should bear no cross about you. You realize the danger: if you bear money, you bear a cross: obviously then, they will flatten you out on some rock, as eagles toss down turtles to crush their shells. Bald-headed Æschylus, mistaken for such a rock by a myopic eagle, paid for the mistake with his life, but proved my argument. Ay, a fall of the sort would hurt you sorely, and I should be sorry for it. Or, instead of reducing you to dust, those same devils might prefer to let you plunge, like Icarus, into some cold deep sea, God knows where. Therefore, give me your purse!"

In the second instance, Panurge demanded that Friar John be out of debt. Devils adored solvent folk. Panurge could vouch personally for it. Nowadays they never ceased their flirtatious solicitations; whereas, when he was involved and embarrassed, they left him severely alone. The soul of a debtor was feeble, unhealthy, no meat for a fiend.

In the third instance, in that frock and furred cowl, let this rammish groper of a Friar John return to his beloved Raminagrobis. If thirty thousand boatloads of devils did not collar Friar John, Panurge would willingly pay drink and fire at the nearest inn. If Friar John, for greater security, sought some companion on his hellbent journey, let him not seek Panurge, the latter advised.

"Away, devils, get you hence; I shall not go; devil crop me if I do!"

"I wouldn't care as much as I suppose I should, if I had my lusty dagger in my hand," said Friar John.

"You speak like a learned doctor of fiddleosophy, like an erudite master of farts!" Panurge asserted. "When I was a student at the University of Toledo, the home of magic, the reverend father in Satan, Picatrix, rector of the diabolical faculty and author of a compendium of ancient magic, used to tell us that the minions of hell fear the sheen of swords as naturally as they fear the splendor of sunlight."

Why else should they have dreaded Hercules, visiting them in a lionskin, with a club in hand, far less than, later, Æneas, apparelled in shining armor, with a sword scraped of its rust, and polished by the aid and counsel of the Cumæan sibyl? That perhaps was why My Lord Jean-Jacques de Trivulzi, Marquis of Vigevano and Marshal of France, dying at Chartres (now Arpajon), called for his sword. He left this world like a valiant knight, sword in hand, striking on every side of his bed, scattering the devils that lay in ambush for his soul at the passage of his death.

The same principle was recognized by the Massoreths, those learned Hebrew commentators, and by the Cabbalists, interpreters of the holy books the Jews handed down orally. When asked why devils never enter the heavenly paradise—it still exists despite man's fall—they invariably answered that its gates were guarded by a cherub, armed with a flaming sword.

To remain within the strict sense of Toledan demonology, Panurge was forced to confess that devils could not be slain, literally, by swordblows. Yet, according to the doctrine of this science, Panurge maintained that they could and, indeed, did suffer a solution of continuity, just as a flame or smoke could be cut by the swipe of a blade. These demons screamed like the devil, too, when they suffered this devilishly painful solution of continuity.

"Tell me this, Friar John, you ballocktrundler: when you see two armies clash, do you imagine the horrible deafening tumult comes from the shouts of men, the clatter of breastplates, the clang of steel's armor, the thud of axes, the slashing of pikes, the brustle of lances, the screams of the wounded, the roll of drums, the peal of trumpets, the neighing of chargers, the reports of firearms or the salvo of cannons?"

Truth to tell, Panurge must necessarily grant that part of the hubbub was due to these causes. But the main hurlyburly, the most harrowing alarm, came from the agonized howls of devils. These, lying in wait, amid this confusion, for the souls of the luckless wounded, suffered many a swordblow unawares. This caused a solution of continuity in their aerial and invisible substances, just as when Master Greasypig, the cook, rapped some lackey across the knuckles for filching a slice of roast meat on the spit. Thus struck, they whooped and yauped like devils, like Mars, who, as Homer tells, being wounded by Diomedes at the siege of Troy, roared more horrisonously than ten thousand men in chorus.

"But what does this all prove?" Panurge completed. "We were speaking of shining armor, of flashing weapons; those have nothing to do with your offensive instrument, Friar John. For, by discontinuance of work and suspension of labor, it is rustier than the keyhole of an old larder. Therefore, take your choice. Either furbish it back to its original, gallant condition, or, if you keep it begrimed, don't go back to Raminagrobis'. For my part, I'll not go; if I do, devil throttle me!"

XXIV

HOW PANURGE SOUGHT COUNSEL OF EPISTEMON

LEAVING Villeaumaire, they returned to Pantagruel. On the way, Panurge addressed Epistemon.

"Epistemon, you are my comrade and my oldest friend; you see what a muddle I'm in. Knowing so many remedies, can't you come to my rescue?"

Epistemon, taking Panurge at his word, pointed out how Panurge's new disguise was the joke of the countryside. He urged him therefore to take hellebore—the traditional cure for insanity—and purge himself of his peccant humor. Let him resume his ordinary dress.

"Friend Epistemon," Panurge replied, "I am of a mind to marry. But I fear being unhappy and cuckolded in wedlock. I have therefore made a vow to St. Francis the younger, St. Francis of Paula. Why to him and not to St. Francis of Assisi, founder of the Franciscans? Because, at Plessis-les-Tours, whither Louis XI summoned him, St. Francis of Paula is invoked with great zeal by women. (No wonder: he founded the order of Minims or Good Men; women naturally hanker after good, upstanding men!) What did I vow? To wear spectacles in my cap, and to forgo a codpiece on my breeches, until I can solve my problems."

"Truly a noble, splendid vow!" Epistemon mocked. "I am amazed that you do not collect your scattered wits and once again become your true self. You remind me of the shock-headed Argives who, after their defeat by the Lacedæmonians over the question of Thyræa, vowed to shave their pates until their loss of honor and territory were made good. You remind me also of the delightful Miguel Doris, the squire of Aragon, who swore to wear a fragment of thigh-armor on his leg until a Briton accepted his challenge to single combat."

Did this doughty champion deserve to wear the green-and-yellow, hare's ear hood, traditionally consecrated to jesters and fools? Or did that honor fall to Enguerrand de Monstrelet, Governor of Cambrai and continuer of Froissart's *Chronicles*? The former had acted absurdly. But the latter had forgotten what Lucian of Samasota said, in his *On the Method of Writing History*, of the art and technique of reporting battles; he had, on the contrary, been long-winded, detailed and tedious. The reader, beginning Enguerrand's tireless narrative, naturally supposed that it introduced themes of mighty wars and world-shaking revolutions. In the end, he found himself roaring with laughter at the blessed hidalgo, at the Briton who affronted him, and at their historian, Enguerrand, more drivelling than a mustard-pot. Epistemon held his sides for very mirth when he recalled the four challenges duly sent by Doris, the four replies duly filed by the Briton, the eight documents presented by Enguerrand, with, for conclusion: "These letters having been formally exchanged, nothing happened."

Panurge, Doris, Enguerrand, all reminded Epistemon of Horace's mountain, which groaned and strained like a woman in travail. The whole neighborhood turned out at its lamentations, expecting to witness some supernatural, monstrous production. In the end:

Parturiunt montes; nascitur ridiculus mus

The pregnant hills, east, west, south, north
Labor: a mouselet is brought forth.

"Close your mousetrap, mountebank!" Panurge said irritably. "It takes a pot to call a kettle black; the shovel mocks the poker!" He paused a moment; his choler passed. "I shall follow through my vow. How many years ago did you and I swear faith and amity to one another by Jupiter Philios, protector of friends? Give me your counsel: shall I marry or no?"

"It's a thorny point," Epistemon replied. "I myself feel too inexperienced to resolve your problem. Hippocrates of Lango—to give Cos, his birthplace, its modern name—Hippocrates, I say, stated in his *Aphorisms*, edited by François Rabelais in 1532, that judgment is difficult. Certainly it proves difficult in this case. I have various ideas, which may help dispel your doubt; yet they do not satisfy me thoroughly."

Certain Platonists, said Epistemon, asseverated that whosoever could see his own genius, his own tutelary spirit, could learn his destiny. Epistemon neither understood their doctrine, nor advised Panurge to follow it, for there were palpable errors and abuses. Epistemon himself had been furnished with an example by a curious and eager nobleman, in the land of Estangor.

"Estangor?" Panurge asked.

"Ay, the land mentioned in *Lancelot of the Lake*. East Anglia, if you prefer; a land in which is Cambridge, a seat of learning."

"I see."

"So much for the first point," Epistemon went on. "And now for the second."

Was there still authority in the oracles of Jupiter Ammon; of Apollo, in Lebadeia in Bœotia, in Delphi, in Delos, in Cyrrha, in Patara, in Tegyra, in Præneste, in Lycia, in Colophon? Was there still authority in the Castalian fountain, near Antioch, in Syria, between the Branchidians; in Bacchus at Dodena; in Mercury of Pharæ near Patras; in Apis of Egypt, in Serapis of Canopus, in Faunus of Menalia, in Albunea of Tivoli, in Tiresias of Orchomenus, in Mopsus of Cilicia, in Orpheus of Lesbos and in Trophonius of Leucadia? If so, Epistemon would perhaps advise Panurge (and perhaps not!) to journey thither and learn their opinion.

But Panurge must know that all these oracles and prophecies had grown as dumb as fish since the coming of the Saviour King, just as all goblins, vampires, *lemures*, werewolves, imps, and succubi, male or female, vanished before the shining sun. These were now gone; yet even did they exist, Epistemon would think twice before advising Panurge to credit their answers. Too many people had been misled by them. Epistemon recalled how Agrippina blamed the fair Lollia, for having asked the oracle of Apollo Clarius whether she would ever be married to the Emperor Claudius; for which Lollia was first banished, and, later, put to an ignominious death.

"Let us do better, then," Panurge suggested. "You know the Ogygian Islands; Plato tells us, they lie five days' sail west of Great Britain. Well, that is not far from St. Malo; let us journey thither, after consulting our king. On the authority of the most ancient and reliable authors, including Plutarch, I know that the more westerly of the four islands shelters quite a few soothsayers, fortune-tellers, prophets and vaticinators. Saturn lies there, bound with golden chains in the hollow of a golden rock, fed upon ambrosia and divine nectar provided abundantly from heaven by I don't know what sort of birds. (Perhaps the same as fed St. Paul the Anchorite, the first hermit, in the Theban desert.) To all who wish to hear, Saturn clearly foretells their fate, lot and future; for the Fates do not spin, Jupiter does not deliberate, or plan anything, but the good father of the gods knows it, even while he sleeps. It would speed the solution of my perplexities, if we heard him on the subject."

"Thimblerig, humbug and catchpenny coggery!" Epistemon commented. "I'll be damned if I go."

XXV

HOW PANURGE SOUGHT COUNSEL OF HERR TRIPPA

"I'VE an idea!" Epistemon exclaimed. "Before returning to Pantagruel, our sovereign, let us go consult Herr Trippa. He lives near here at l'Ile-Bouchard, in Touraine. You know how he foretells the future through astrology or the study of the stars, geomancy or the study of the figures, chiromancy or hand-reading, metoposcopy or the study of the physiognomy. Learned in all arts of that kidney, he divulges what is to come. Let us consult him."

"I know nothing about all that," said Panurge. "But I *do* know *this*. One day, old Herr Trippa was expatiating to our mighty king upon celestial and transcendental matters. Meanwhile his wife, a comely enough wench, was being taken on the rebound, struck while the iron was hot, excavated and dovetailed, to the high content of the court lackeys, on steps, behind doors and catch-as-catch-could, wherever they might. Herr Trippa could survey, without need of spectacles, all things ethereal and earthly; he could expose past, present and future happenings. But he could not see his wife rambucktifoozling just around the corner, nor was news thereof ever vouchsafed him."

Nevertheless, Panurge was perfectly willing to seek him out; no one could ever learn too much.

On the morrow (Villeaumaire lay four miles distant) they reached Herr Trippa's abode. Panurge gave him a wolfskin coat; a bastard or short, gilded sword, in a velvet scabbard; and fifty gold-pieces, called angels, with St. Michael's effigy upon them. Then he questioned him familiarly upon his problem.

Herr Trippa straightway looked Panurge square in the eye:

"Metoposcopically, or judging by your forehead, and physiognomically, or judging by your face, you look like a cuckold, a notorius, scandalous cuckold."

Then, examining microscopically, the surface of Panurge's right hand, he continued:

"You see the *Mons Jovis*, Jupiter's Mount, that lump just under the root of your index finger; you see the wrinkle beneath it. That wrinkle was never seen in any hand but a cuckold's."

Next, Herr Trippa took up a pen, and hastily plotted a number of random points, which he linked up according to the science of geomancy.

"Truth itself is no truer than this fact: you will be made a cuckold immediately after your wedding."

Next, he asked Panurge for the horoscope of his nativity. When Panurge supplied the data, Herr Trippa combined the signs of the zodiac and the planets, by joining them within a circle, called the circle of generation, and thus formed the "house of heaven." Having considered its position, and examined, in its triple quarters, the "aspects" or lines forming the polygon within the reproductive circle, Herr Trippa heaved a deep sigh:

"Already I had prophesied that you would be inevitably cuckolded. I have just been supplied with additional proof to that effect. Not only will you be very roundly cuckolded, but you will also be beaten and robbed by your wife. The seventh twelfth of the circle of generation is the "house of marriage": yours is of malignant aspect, alive with horned signs like Aries, the ram; Taurus, the bull; Capricorn, the goat. In the fourth portion of the evolutionary circle—the "house of family"—I find a Jupiter declining and a tetragonal aspect of Saturn, associated with Mercury. You will be as soundly rubbed with pepper as any falcon infested with vermin, my dear sir."

"Pox plague you, you old sot, you ill-favored fool, you doddering imbecile. The day the cuckolds of the universe assemble, your name will lead the rest and you shall march, banner in hand, at the head of the procession. But what is this worm, itching here between my fingers?"

So saying, Panurge spread his forefingers like a pair of horns, and, making a fist, thrust his hand close to the astrologer's face. Then, aside to Epistemon:

"This man is the Olus whom Martial ridiculed in his *Epigrams*. Poor Olus spent his life observing and sympathizing with the misfortunes of others, while his wife ran a one-woman brothel. This Herr Trippa is more wretched than Irus, the beggar who tried fisticuffs with Ulysses; yet he acts more insolently, arrogantly and intolerably than seventeen devils. Shall I sum him up in a word? He is a Πτωχαλάζων, as the Greeks very properly name all ragamuffin, vainglorious scum.

"Come along, let us leave this mad, insane, lunatic driveller. He ought to be tied up! Let us leave him rave his bellyful with his own private demons, I am amazed that even the scurviest fiends should hold commerce with such a scoundrel. He is blissfully unaware of the first rudiment of philosophy, to wit, Socrates' dictum: 'Know thyself!' Exultantly he brags of finding a mote in his neighbor's eye, when he cannot discern the enormous beam blocking his own. The fellow is that Polypragmon, the eternal busybody, described by Plutarch; and he's Plutarch's witch, too, that Lamia who abroad, in public, in strangers' houses saw more clearly than any lynx, yet at home proved blinder than a mole. The moment she was by herself, she put away her eyes, as one might a pair of spectacles, hiding them in a wooden shoe hanging on her front door."

Panurge's wrath tapered off into silence; Herr Trippa took up a tamarisk branch.

"Good!" cried Epistemon. "Nicander vaunts the divinatory powers of that shrub!"

Herr Trippa then asked Panurge whether he cared to learn the truth more fully, through pyromancy, or divination by fire? Through aeromancy, or divination by climatic conditions—a science celebrated by Aristophanes in his *Clouds*? Through hydromancy, or divination by water? Through lecanomancy (an Assyrian variation of hydromancy), where gold, silver and precious stones were dipped into liquids? Hermolaus Barbarus of Venice, humanist, translator of Aristotle and commentator of Pliny, had put this method to the test when, consulting the demons on Aristotle's principle of entelechy—or the form-giving cause—he had been answered by a low hissing sound. Herr Trippa was quite willing to let Panurge gaze into a basin of water at his future wife, cuntinnabulalating with a pair of ruffians.

"Remember to remove your spectacles when you gaze up my anus!" said Panurge.

There was also catoptromancy, Herr Trippa continued, a science founded upon divination by means of mirrors. Didius Julianus, Emperor of Rome, foresaw the future by these means. Nor would Panurge require glasses: the looking-glass would reveal his future wife being twatstraddled, quite as surely as the fountain in Minerva's temple, near Patras, revealed the truth. Coscinomancy, or divination by a sieve, also offered possibilities; it was a technique religiously observed by the ancient Romans.

"Take a sieve," said Herr Trippa, "hold it up with a pair of pincers and you shall see devils."

The sage suggested further methods: alphitomancy, or divination by barley meal, indicated by Theocrites in his *Pharmaceutria* . . . aleuromancy, or mixing wheat with flour . . . astragalomancy, the science of divination by small bones or dice. . . . Herr Trippa had the necessary instruments at hand!

"Would you use tyromancy, or divination by cheese? I've a fine Bréhémont cheese here in the larder! Do you know what gyromancy is? It consists in walking around a circle, until you fall from dizziness, the prognostic being drawn from the place of your fall. I'll put you through the paces, but I assure you you will fall to the left every time. . . . Sternomancy might suit you: it interprets marks upon the breast, but, by my faith, you put up a sorry front!"

Herr Trippa suggested libanomancy (he had plenty of incense to burn) . . . gastromancy, or stomachic divination, a practice long cultivated by My Lady Giacoma Rodogina, the ventriloquist prophetess of Ferrara . . . cephalomancy, so often practised by the

Germans, who roasted an ass's head over live coals . . . ceromancy,
or the plunging of melted wax into water, whereby Panurge might
behold the figure of his future wife exercising her gutfiddlers, flue-
pipers, bellydrummers.

"How about capnomancy, or smoke reading? We have but to
strew poppyseed and sesame on the flame. A very pleasant pastime!
. . . How about axinomancy, in its various forms? We can bury
an axe in a stake and gauge its oscillations, or we can burn jet over
its blade? Penelope's suitors to a man failed even to bend Ulysses'
bow; Ulysses, for his part, shot an arrow through twelve axeheads.
Will you not prove as successful as Homer's hero amid Penelope's
lovers?"

If onyomancy interested his client, Herr Trippa could produce
the oil and wax to rub over the revelatory fingernails; botanomancy
only required a few sage leaves which were forthcoming; sycomancy,
a few fig leaves. A divine art at that!

Ichthyomancy, or divination by fishes, was authoritative; Tiresias
and Polydamas had practised and celebrated it, just as the ancient
Lycians, in the ditch of Dina, within Apollo's grove in Lycia, produced water, fish and apparitions that foretold the future. And
choiromancy, or divination by swine? Let them produce a multitude of hogs, and Panurge was welcome to the bladder of any one he
chose.

"If you prefer cleromancy, or divination by Homeric or Virgilian
lot," Herr Trippa said affably, "I can produce an answer just as
surely as the bean appears, when you cut up a cake on Epiphany
Eve. . . . If you fancy anthropomancy, or the study of human
entrails, remember how Heliogabalus, Emperor of Rome, read his
fate in children's. This is not the most pleasant of occupations, but
you will not mind much, since you are destined to be a cuckold. . . .
Does sibylline stichomancy, or an oracle in verse, interest you? Or
divination by names? What is yours, by the way?"

"Chewturd," said Panurge.

Herr Trippa blithely enumerated further ways and means of discovering one's fate. Alectryomancy, for instance: divination by
cock! He had but to describe a definite circle, which he would divide
into twenty-four equal parts, keeping his eyes on Panurge whilst
he did so. In each of these parts, he would write a letter of the al-

phabet and, over each letter, he would place a grain of corn. Then he
would release a fine, virgin cock.

What would happen? Herr Trippa assured Panurge that the
cock would eat only such grains as covered the letters H.O.R.N.S.
This was as fatidically indicated as when the Emperor Valens sought
to know the identity of his successor, and put a vaticinating cock to
the test. The alectryomantic bird ate up only four seeds, those placed
over the letters H. E. O. Δ. or, in our style, T. H. E. O. D. And, as we
all know, Theodosius succeeded Valens!

"Why not try haruspicine?" Herr Trippa proposed. "It consists
in examining the entrails of sacrificed beasts; it is the most ancient
form of divination the Romans knew. Or extispicine, another variety of the same lore? Or augury, based on the flight of birds . . . on
the song of crows, ravens, hoot-owls . . . on the seeds dropped by
sacred fowl . . . ?"

"Foul dung seeds!" Panurge countered.

"Why not try extispicine, the study of animals' bowels?"

"Or crappispicine, the study of mine?" said Panurge.

"Or necromancy?" Herr Trippa persisted. "I can suddenly re-
suscitate some one from the dead. Apollonius of Tyana brought
back a maiden for Achilles' benefit, so Philostratus tells us; the witch
of Endor, too, brought back Samuel at Saul's request. This visitor
will tell you everything you ask of him, no less certainly than a dead
man, called up by Erictho, foretold to Pompey the vicissitudes and
result of the battle of Pharsalus. Of course, if you are afraid of the
dead—as all cuckolds are by nature—I shall not go beyond scio-
mancy, or divination by ghosts."

"To hell with you, madman and fool; go get some Bulgar or Albanian mercenary to backscuttle you. They wear conical hats; that
will make an astrologer of you! Haven't you any other superstitions
up your sleeve? How did you fail to tell me to hold an emerald under
my tongue, or the stones taken from hyenas' eyes. Pliny vouches for
their prophetic value. Why didn't you urge me to provide myself
with hoopoes' tongues (they have erectile crests!), or the hearts of
live frogs? Democritus and Pliny both state that if you place these on
a sleeping woman's breast, she will tell her secrets. You forgot to prescribe a diet of dragon's heart and liver, so that, listening to the song
of swans and other fowl, I might learn my destiny, as the Arabs did

of yore in Mesopotamia. May twice fifteen devils seize you, cuckold that you are, horned wittol, converted Jew, diabolic sorcerer and wizard of Antichrist!

"Come, Epistemon; come, Friar John: let us return to our king. I am convinced he will not be pleased, if ever he hears we came to the lair of this loose-gowned fiend. I regret I did! I would gladly pay one hundred crowns (and fourteen chaplets!)—two hundred sovereigns (and twenty-eight subjects!)—three hundred sterling (and fifty-six starling!)—if the spirit that used to blow in the bottom of my breeches (when I wore breeches!) now arose to cover this rascal's mustachio with its spittle. God's truth, he has suffocated me with vexation and deviltry, with charms and witchcraft! Lucifer seize him! Let us say amen and go drink; I'll be off my feed for two days, if not four!"

XXVI

HOW PANURGE SOUGHT
COUNSEL OF FRIAR JOHN
OF THE FUNNELS

PANURGE, in high dudgeon at Herr Trippa's words, maintained a sullen silence, until they passed the hamlet of Huymes. Then, scratching his left ear, he turned towards Friar John and stammered:

"P-p-please ch-ch-cheer me up a little, old fellow. The claptrap that devilish madman served up to me has befungled and besotted me. Listen, my brangleprick, my sweet and delicate cod!"

Panurge proceeded to invoke Friar John's help and comfort. Naturally, his supplication took the ritual form of a litany. The better to touch and flatter his companion, he lavished all manner of excellent epithets, coupling them with a term of plebeian—not to say generative or urinary—familiarity.

"O dumpy cod, stumpy cod, famous in birth, hamous in girth; O cod, rich in lactary secretions and heavy as lead; O cod, rose-red; O cod, above all things fair, cod covered with hair; O cod, caulked and dawked, veined and ingrained: Hear me, I beseech you!

"O tuck, O cod, O stucco cod; O cod grotesque (what incunabula you scrawl in grottos!) ; cod humoresque, cod arabesque (with styles, devices, mottoes!). O cod, trussed to be cooked; O cod, cooked to be trussed; O antic cod, O frantic cod; O mangled, brangled cod; cod, right as a trivet and sound as a bell; cod, refuge of surety and cod incarnadine, cod switched and thoroughstitched: Hear me, I beseech you!

"O variegated, foliated, hammered cod, gammered cod, cod safely guarded and interlarded; O born cod, sworn cod, cod of the peasant, gamy as pheasant; cod, rich in seed to tempt the hungry bird; cod, glorious word, cod, full of solace as a turd. . . .

"Cod, wrapped in a blanket, blanketed in a crap; O cod, driven mad and tarred over; O cod, covered with a hood, hooded with a cover; O cod in ambush, cod in the jambush; O capped, hatted and behelmeted cod; O cod, tarnished and varnished, thrice-desired; cod lined with ebony, brazilian nutwood, boxwood; O very organized and immaculately Latin cod: Hear me, I beseech you!

"O cod of brave entry, cod who stand sentry; O arrow, O harrow, O crossbow cod, mossblow cod; O small arm, short arm, bilbo, fowling piece; blunderbuss; O cod unbridled, infuriated, wrought-up, all of a heap; O cod of perfect portions and proportions; fat cod, stuffed cod, crammed cod, polished cod; cod, jolly child of folly; O leisure cod, pleasure cod; explosive and erosive, fraught with gunpowder and clamchowder, O Cod: Hear me, I beseech you!

"O cod positive, gerundive, genitive and active; O cod oval, oblong and round as an egg; O cod, gigantic and full of life, masterly and magistral, claustral, monastic, virile and subtle; O cod, lecherous yet never treacherous; O useful for work and play, exertion and repose, relays and halts; O bold, massive and lascivious; O cod, handful of joy, O greedy boy. . . .

"O cod resolute and absolute, upstanding member of society; O cod, growing roundheaded as a cabbage; O cauliflower, jolly flower; O cod, double-studded, the despair of monorchids, or such as boast but a single ballock, O despair of cryptorchids whose treasures remain hidden; O cod Mahometan, automaton; O firking Turk; O fecund, flittering, sizzling, currying, furrying cod; O cod, gentle and urgent, O stallion cod, tatterdemalion cod, meet cod and meaty cod; O cod proper and genteel, O blessed eel: Hear me, I beseech you!

"O fleet, prompt, offhand, impetuous; O fortuned and fortunate; O hangdog dangle-eared cod; O fatted calf of a cod; O very usual cod, and cod, hung with precious tapestries; O cod, requisite and exquisite, comical, astronomical, O arsenal-piercing cod: Hear me, I beseech you!

"O hugger-mugger-bugger cod; O lynx cod, stinks-cod; O Guelph cod, pelf cod, Wolff cod, wolf cod; O cod of the Orsini and Ursins, the Brauns, Browns, Brouns and Bruins; O bear cod, bare cod; O cod that edulcorate, strain, drain, buck and absterge; O patronymic, preened, prinked, pricking, peppery and piquant; O cod, cod of *alidada* (the Arab rule of astronomical alignment), of *algamala* (the mixture of metal with mercury), of algebra: Hear me, I beseech you!

"O cod robust, august and hungry at belly, O cod of jelly; O insuperable, succorable, succulent, agreeable, horrible, borrowable, cod; O cod fearsome and affable; O profitable, memorable, notable, palpable, muscular, bastable, subsidiary. . . .

"O cod tragical and satirical, O musical miracle; O cod transpontine, cod from overseas; O repercussive and digestive, convulsive, incarnative, restorative; O sigillative, riddling the target's centre; O cod masculinizing jigajig; O stallioning, crackflopping, everreviving, fulminant, thundering, sparkling, hammering, ramming, strident, sonorous and spermatazoifugal cod: Hear me, I beseech you!

"O spick-and-span cod, O smart, O smarting cod; O harumscarum snorting cod; O Hannibal, cannibal cod; O cod, wrenching and wenching, happy and sappy; O satrap, rat-trap cod; O cod, whirring and spurring, shooting and booting, cod syndical, abortive, onion-hung, scrounging; O cod twittering, twattering, firing pointblank. O cod arsenic, O Friar John, my friend: Hear me, I beseech you.

"I bear you great reverence and value you: you shall have the choicest morsels of all at my board. But answer me this; should I marry or no?"

Friar John, in high glee, replied:

"Marry, in the devil's name, marry, and let the repercussion of your clapper ring double chimes in her great throbbing bell. Do it as soon as ever you can, too; this very evening you should publish the banns and reënforce your bedstead. God's truth, what are you waiting for. Don't you know the end of the world is at hand? Why, we're three poles and a half-fathom nearer to chaos than we were the day before yesterday. You remember the biblical prophecy: the Antichrist's coming would immediately precede the end of the world? And he would be recognized by his prodigality? Well, the Antichrist is born already, I'm told; but, so far, he has done no more than scratch his nurses, pinch his governesses and display his treasures. He is still a snort, no more. *Crescite, nos qui vivimus, multiplicamini*; be fruitful; we, which live, let us multiply. This is Holy Writ and breviary-timber; its truth will endure just as long as you can buy a sack of corn for a penny, and seventy gallons of wine for twopence! How would you feel on the day of judgment—*dum venerit judicare*, when He cometh to judge—if He found you with genitals filled to the stopcock."

"You are a metropolitan or masterly cod!" Panurge answered. "Your wit is neat, clear, pithy. And you speak to the point. You know how Leander of Abydos, in Egypt, swam across the Hellespont to visit his sweetheart Hero, who lived at Sestos in Europe. As he plowed through the waves, he prayed to Neptune and all the marine gods:

> *O speed my up-stream passage! Coming down,*
> *A wedded man, what matter if I drown.*

"*There* was a man who refused to die with his ballocks filled to capacity!"

And Panurge capped his argument by declaring that, thenceforth, throughout his realm of Salmagundi, no malefactor would be put to death by law, without friggling like a pelican (as lustily as belly can), until his spermatic vessels were drained of the few drops required to trace a Greek Υ, the letter sacred to Priapus. After all, here was a wealth too rich to waste. Your criminal, begetting a male, would die content; forfeiting his life, he would have left the world another.

XXVII

FRIAR JOHN'S MERRY ADVICE TO PANURGE

"By St. Rigomer, a patron of this country, I give you no advice I would not myself follow, were I in your boots. Only put forth a strong arm, put the best of your three legs forward every day, go all lengths in your copulation. Let a long spell pass between brangles, and you are lost, poor soul! what happens to nurses will be your lot. If they desist from giving suck to children, they lose their milk. Similarly, if you do not exercise your pleasure-tool, its milk will dry up, and it will serve you only as a pipe to piss through. As for your cods, they will be of no use save as gamebags. That is my advice, friend; I have seen it happen, often, to men who could not friggle when they wanted, because they hadn't wanted when they could. An ancient maxim of cannon law tells us that nonusage of full privileges makes them forfeit. Be sure to make this base troglodyte scum that inhabit the caves of your trousers labor eternally: never let them live like noblemen, idly, on their revenue."

"Ay, surely, Friar John, you are the apple of the left eye in my scrotum," said Panurge. "I shall take you at your word, for you hit the nail on the head; you do not beat about the bush. How cogently you have dispelled any fear that might have intimidated me! May heaven therefore always grant you the boon of striking home stiffly, and adding spermatic fuel to the oviferous fire. So, then, I shall take your advice and get married; there will be no mishap. I will always have comely chambermaids, when you visit me; you shall be the friend of their bosoms, their buffer and buckler, the patron and visitor of their sisterhood. So much for part one of my sermon!"

"Listen to the bells of Varennes," Friar John suggested. "What do they say?"

(The monk referred to a popular proverb to the effect that the bells say whatever one cares to hear. Jean Raulin, a famous preacher, brought this out in a sermon on widowhood. A widow, advised by her curé to listen to the bells, heard them ringing out clearly the message: "Marry your groom, marry your groom!" No sooner had she done so, than the servant, become master, made a slave of her. Complaining bitterly to the curé, she was again advised to hearken to the bells. This time their chimes spelled out: "Don't wed a groom, don't wed a groom.")

"The closest church bells are at Varennes, very near here, down by the junction of the Loire and Vienne. What do they say?" Friar John asked.

"I hear them clearly," Panurge replied. "In sober truth, by my sacred thirst, their sound is more fatidical than the resounding brass cauldrons hung about Jupiter's sanctuary at Dodona. Listen:

> Marry, marry; do not tarry;
> Marry, marry; take a wife.
> Marry; it will not miscarry;
> Yours will be a happy life:
> Pleasure rife, never strife,
> Marry, marry, marry, marry."

Accordingly, Panurge assured Friar John and Epistemon that he would contract a marriage, since all the elements urged him to do so. Let this decision stand in the monk's memory, as firm and unbreakable as a brazen wall.

"As for the second point, you appear to me to question, indeed to mistrust, the probability of my paternity, as if the erect god of gardens, Priapus, were unfavorable to me. I beg you to believe that he is, on the contrary, at my beck and call, docile, benevolent, obedient to my pleasure. I need but slacken the leash, let go the reins, point out the game and hoicks! yoicks! he foams at the mouth like a hound, the booty is his!"

Even were Panurge's wife as rabid for amatory excitement as ever Messalina, or as the Marchioness of Winchester in London (he knew not which marchioness, but at all events My Lord Bishop of Winchester owned the brothels of London!), he would thank the monk to believe that the Panurgian capacity for content would exceed madame's. Panurge knew Solomon's dictum describing "the barren womb" as being one of the four things on earth that were never satisfied. Solomon spoke as a learned scholar and as an expert in such matters. Aristotle, after him, declared that the female being was insatiable; but Panurge wished the world to know that he could produce tat for tit, Jack to any Jill, a pike for a dike, a ramrod and loader for any muzzle.

Nor need his friends quote, in comparison, certain fabulous fornicators such as Hercules, who made women of fifty virgins in a single night . . . or Proculus, who perforated ten Sarmatian slave-girls in one evening, and the other ninety of the captured hundred within a fortnight . . . or Cæsar . . . or that egregious liar, Mahomet, husband to eleven wives, who boasted, in his *Koran*, that his genitals were as powerful as sixty strapping ruffians. . . . Panurge refused to hear about, or to believe in the Indian, so wonderingly celebrated by Theophrastus, Pliny and Athenæus, that Indian who, thanks to a certain herb, could diddle it seventy times a day.

Panurge begged them to believe—and it was the truth he offered them!—that his own natural parts, his sacred phallus in erection, his Master Inigo Kunnistow, was the stiffest proposition on earth.

"Listen, sweet ballocklet," he told the monk, "have you ever seen the cowl that belonged to the monk of Castres, that Franciscan abbey near Montpellier? In any house where it was laid down, whether in view or hidden, suddenly its horrific stimulus affected with rut all the inhabitants of the place, men and women, beasts, even cats and mice. Well, I swear I have often, in the past, found the same energy, even more highly developed, within my own codpiece.

"I shall not speak to you of house or cottage, of sermon or market. But let me tell you this. At St. Maixent, when they were giving the miracle play of the *Passion*, I entered the pit of the theatre. Suddenly, thanks to the force and occult properties of my codpiece, I saw the whole crowd—audience and actors—fall into such terrific temptation of lust that never angel or man, devil or she-devil but longed to go the whole hog. The prompter forsook his copy; the actor who played St. Michael slid down the pulley used to hoist angels on-stage; those playing the parts of devils emerged from hell, and brangled all the pretty women; Lucifer himself broke free from his chains. In a word, seeing the confusion, I fled from the place, like Cato the censor, who withdrew from the Floral games when the rabble called for the actors to disrobe."

XXVIII

HOW FRIAR JOHN ASSUAGED PANURGE'S DOUBTS CONCERN- ING CUCKOLDRY

"I QUITE understand that," said Friar John, "but time softens every-thing. No marble and porphyry but suffers old age and decay. If you have not at present reached this stage, then a few years hence, I shall hear you confessing that your cods are dragging in the dust, for want of a firmer truss. Already I see your hair growing gray: and, as for your beard—what with its gray, white, tawny and black whis-kers, it looks like a geographical chart. Lo, here is Asia, here Tigris and Euphrates; that is Africa; behold the mountain of the moon; a little further, the marshes of the Nile. On this side lies Europe: can you see the Abbey of Thélème? That white, white tuft there represents the Hyperborean Alps, ranges situated in the extreme north. I' faith and i' thirst, friend, when snow covers the mountains (I mean head and chin), there can be scant heat in the valleys of the codpiece."

Panurge, indignant, cried:

"By the blisters on your heels, Friar John, you don't know the first thing about that section of rhetoric, relating to commonplaces, which we lay scholars call Topics. When snow lies on the mountains, you may be sure the valleys are filled with lightning, in flashes red as pomegranate; with thunder, bursting in terrible bolts; with blasts and white squalls; with tempests, ulcers at the legs, and God knows what devils raging amid the hurricane. If you want to see for your-self, go to Switzerland and have a look at Lake Wunderbar, four miles out of Berne; as you go towards Sion. You hold my gray hairs against me; you fail to realize that, like a leek, I have a white head and a green, straight, vigorous tail."

To be sure, Panurge did recognize one indication of old age, but Friar John must tell no one—it must remain a secret between them.

Nowadays, Panurge found wine much better and tastier than he used to; he dreaded the possibility of encountering inferior tipple; whereas, in the past, he had never given it a thought. Friar John might note that this argued vaguely of dusk and sunset; Panurge's noon was past. But what did that prove, he asked his monkish, ever-gentle companion? Panurge had no grounds for apprehension in this; it was not here the shoe pinched. Where, then, was the rub? Well, Panurge was duty-bound to accompany Pantagruel, their sovereign, even were he to go to the devil; thus, if Pantagruel were absent long, Panurge feared his wife would make him a cuckold. Cuckold: such was the peremptory word. Every single person Panurge had consulted, threatened him with cuckoldry, affirming this fate to be predestined in heaven for him.

"All men, who wish to be, aren't cuckolds," Friar John countered. "If you are to be cuckolded; *ergo* (as we logicians say for *therefore*) your wife will be beautiful; *ergo*, you will be assured good entertainment by her; *ergo*, you will be blessed with the fruition of many friends; *ergo*, having practised the Christian virtues of neighborliness and humility, you will attain salvation. These are what we religious scholars call Topics. You will be all the better for it, O sinner; never before were you so assured of a happy future. You will suffer no loss from it; your property will increase considerably. If the thing is preordained, would you seek rebelliously to oppose your godsent destiny? Listen, O withered cod:

"O mouldy, mildewed, musty cod; O fusty cod; O reasty, rusty cod; cod, frigid and numb, kneaded in ice-cold water; cod, pendent and pendulous, O cod appellant, cod levelled, slack, relaxed and flapping cod: Hear me, I beseech you!

"Cod, innocent of seed in your pod; O cod, weak as water gruel; O cod without fuel: Hear me, I beseech you!

"O cod incongruous; O effete and exhausted, withered, prostrate and prostate cod; O cod beshitten, aswing on loose hinges, somniferous and skimmed of its milk; cod expressed and suppressed, low-hung, wrung and unstrung; cod, O emulsive, repulsive, incommunicative and putative; O cod, food for the worm, good to the germ, cod come to its term, cod infirm, cod, empty of sperm: Hear me, I beseech you!

"Cod semilunar and conchoidal, reniform, lentiform, cod shaped like a weary pear; O dejected and downcast, O ill-shapen, O sallow-complexioned and evil of visage, O hangover cod; O cod, light as cork, flush, floundered and fluked; O cod, diaphanous and brained, drained, chilblained and murrained; cod, cysted and amethysted.

"Cod battered, tattered, shattered and bespattered; O cod, capped with a mitre, cod adangle on a plumbline, cod rancid as ancient butter; O cod, riddled with dimples, hooded with wimples, lined with crimples, studded with pimples; O cod, breakable and fragile as a child's toy, O cod quirked, wrangled, overbrangled and perplexed: O hear me, I beseech you!

"O bedaubed, besmeared and bebungled, O empty and rugous, harassed and how lugubrious! O cod wrung dry, wrenched soft and wrought limber, maggoty and draggletailed: O eunuch-cod, or, in the Greek, cod thlasid; cod thlibid, or, in our tongue, O cod, crushed to testicular atrophy by violent digital pressure; O cod spadonic, or castrated; O cod sphacelous, or rich in gangrene; O cod scalpelled, unhinged, mealy, farinaceous; O cod farcinacious, affected with farcy, cod ripe with glanders, buttons and tumors: Hear me, I beseech you!

"Cod, O herniary, varicose and varicoceleous, septic, festering, carbuncled with imposthume; O cod, mortified and leprous; O cod, crackling with crusts, lame, stripped to the bone and hamstrung between wind and water; O spurious, curious and penurious; O worn to a long stump, to a stretched skeleton, to a beetling shadow, O discolored, O wilted. . . .

"O debased, deflowered, debauched, degraded and depraved; O adulterate, O sophisticated; O livid, fluid, languid, putrid, fetid, arid cod; O bored, O perforated; O sausage, smoked dry; O sheepskin, tinged swart, O home of the wart: Hear me, I beseech you!

"O sesquipedalian, O elongated, O bulbous, O tumid cod; O peduncular, O flagging, swinging ass's prick; O foliated, flaky-puffing, much thumbed-over dick; O pickled, O soused, O marinated, ulcerated, eruptive and corruptive, O extirpated, dissipated, constipated tool; O frostbitten, blight-beshitten, O adulterated, sphacelated, syncopated; O cod, medicated as wine, and dog-eared as a crumpled leaf; O cod, slashed like a pennant, tattered as a thief, slit like the cap of a cavalry lieutenant, of a military chief. . . .

"O cupped for your fever, stripped of your fruit, blown like a pie-crust, scarred, gnarled, chapped and becrapped; O cod, rheumatic, asthmatic, polecatic; O thrice-bestunk, O skunk; O spavined, O lymph-lost; O bitter as tainted wine, tart as of barrel-bottoms, reeking of stale, eructated beer. . . .

"O ire-blooded cod, O lizard's dangle; O touchy cod, punctilious cod, O fistulous cod, O cod, resembling a long pipelike ulcer with narrow mouth; O languid, rankled, cracked, scathed, vitiated, inquinated cod; O tubercular and morbific, abbreviated, diminutive and time-worn cod; O cod mossgrown, fit for the dusthole; O crabbed, crestfallen, clotted and besotted; O object of disgust, corroded with rust, O fly-blown, O feculent: Hear me, I beseech you. . . .

"O antedated, degraded and mephitic cod; O paralytic, O penguin cod; O snake scotched, O unhinged, O spiked gun, O maimed, rotten, palsied and becrippled; O abused, fused, effused, diffused, suffused, circumfused and refused. . . .

"O flittermouse cod, hoot-owl cod, surly dog cod; cod, mouth-trumpeting, anus-fluting, unhelmed, overwhelmed, haled, hauled, beached, grounded, sandfilled and sabulous; O cod, pandiculate, vermiculate, geniculate, carbunculate and emasculate; O decadent, O acescent, O rank, O putrid: Hear me, I beseech you. . . .

"O appellant, O repellent; O supplicating, O replicating; O marred cod, barred cod, charred cod; O dislocated, desiccated cod, O exantlated, excorticated, granulated cod; O enervated, obtunded, benumbed; O nihility, nonentity, O nominal, inane, O null, O zero: Hear me, I beseech you. . . .

"O baked in soggy dough, O sluggard, O lubber's cod; O rumpled cod, O crumpled cod; O cod, occupied, unvisited, unpatronized; O down at heel, O gutted, O absorbed, O hectic, O parched with fever: Hear me, I beseech you. . . .

"Ay, Panurge, my ballocks to the devil! Since you are predestined to cuckoldry, would you reverse the course of the planets? Would you disrupt the celestial spheres? Would you blame the intelligences that move the universe? Would you indict the Fates, blunt their spindles, arraign their clewrings, cite their bobbins, condemn their reels, sentence their yarn, and unravel their threads? A pox on you, dangleballs; you are rasher than the Titans. Look here, wobble-pecker: would you rather be jealous without reason, or cuckold without knowledge of it?"

Panurge heaved a deep sigh:

"I would rather be neither. But if I ever found out for sure, then I would get satisfaction, or all cudgels would have disappeared from this world of ours. I fear I had best not marry, dear Friar John. Listen to the bells; I hear them more distinctly, now we are closer:

> *Pause, deliberate, and tarry:*
> *Do not marry, lest your wife*
> *Beat you, rob you, make you carry*
> *Horns throughout your cuckold life.*
> *If you wish this, welcome strife!*
> *Marry, marry, marry, marry.*

"By God's might, I am beginning to lose my temper. Can't you hooded and cowled intellects find any solution? Has nature so thoroughly destituted mankind that a husband cannot travel the road of life without falling into the quicksands of cuckoldry?"

Friar John came to the rescue:

"I can show you a way," he said. "If you follow my advice, your wife will not make a cuckold of you, without your knowledge and consent."

"O velvety, smooth cod, tell it me, friend, tell it me, I beseech you!"

Friar John then advised Panurge to take Hans Carvel's ring.

"And who is this Hans Carvel?" Panurge demanded.

"The famous jeweller to the King of Melinda," Friar John informed him. "An expert and skilful lapidary, a studious man, reputable, sensible, judicious, debonair, kindly and quite a philosopher. He was ever ready to give alms; he was gay, witty, an excellent friend and capital company, if ever there was. I may add that he was pot-bellied, that his head had a way of wagging beyond his control, and that he was somewhat embarrassed of his person."

"What about his ring?" Panurge asked.

So Friar John told him the story.

In his old age, Hans Carvel married the bailiff Concordat's daughter, a young, attractive, sprightly girl, gay, spirited, cordial—perhaps a trifle too cordial to her neighbors and acquaintances. A few weeks after the wedding, the groom became violently jealous of his bride; suspecting that she went elsewhere to get her buttock-thumping, he raged like a tiger. To prevent this, he would relate all manner of fine tales, illustrating the havoc by adultery; or he would read legends concerning virtuous women; or deliver lengthly sermons on pudicity. Indeed, he presented her with a manuscript, of his own composition, in praise of conjugal fidelity; nor did he fail to excoriate the wickedness of lustful wives. Finally, he gave her a costly necklace of Oriental sapphires. Yet for all his efforts, he still found her on terms somewhat too familiar with her neighbors. His jealousy waxed apace.

One night, as he lay abed with her, tortured by these thoughts, Hans Carvel dreamed he was pouring out his troubles into the devil's ears. To comfort him, Satan slipped a ring on his middle finger.

"I give you this ring," the fiend said. "So long as you wear it on your finger, your wife will never be carnally possessed by another, without your knowing or willing it."

"Gramercy, My Lord Devil," said Hans Carvel. "I renounce Mahomet if ever it come off my finger."

The devil disappeared. Overjoyed, Hans Carvel awoke, to find his middle finger encircled by his wife's what-do-you-call-it.

"I forgot to tell you," Friar John added, "that when his wife felt it, she drew back her buttocks as though to say: 'Oh, no! yes! oh! stop! that's not what you should put there!' But Hans Carvel thought only that some one was trying to steal his ring!"

Was this not infallible insurance against cuckoldry?

"Believe me, Panurge, you should follow his example. Never fail to have your wife's circlet tight about your middle finger."

XXIX

HOW PANTAGRUEL SUMMONED A THEOLOGIAN, A PHYSICIAN, A LAWYER AND A PHILOSOPHER TO CONFER UPON PANURGE'S PERPLEXITY

HAVING reached Pantagruel's palace, they told him of their expedition and showed him Raminagrobis' reply, which Pantagruel read and reread.

"I have never yet beheld answer that pleased me more," said Pantagruel. "Raminagrobis' succinct statement means that each must be judge of his own thoughts, and follow his own counsel, in the matter of marriage. I have always agreed; I said as much to you the first time you consulted me. But I recall you tacitly scorned my advice: *philautia* or self-love blinds you."

Let them do otherwise, Pantagruel suggested, let them consider the following. Whatever we are, whatever we have, consists in three things: soul, body, property. To-day, three sorts of persons are respectively ordained to care for each of this triad: the theologians treat souls; physicians bodies; lawyers property. Pantagruel therefore proposed to invite to dinner, the following Sunday, a divine, a medico and a jurisconsult. They would confer with these experts on Panurge's dilemma.

"By St. Picault, martyr of Nicæa, nothing good will come of it, I can see," Panurge replied. "For you know how ill the world wags. We entrust our souls to theologians, who for the most part are heretics; our bodies to physicians, who, to a man, loathe medicine and refuse to take physics; our property to lawyers, who never sue one another!"

"Spoken like a courtier," Pantagruel objected, "like that courtier described by the Italian philosopher, Castiglione."

Pantagruel flatly denied Panurge's first statement. The principal —indeed, the sole and total—occupation of a good theologian, consisted in extirpating heresy and error by word, deed and writing, and, instead, planting deep in men's hearts, the true, living, Catholic faith.

He commended Panurge's second statement: he had always seen the better physicians use prophylactics and preventives on their persons, thus forestalling all need of therapeutic or curative measures.

In the third instance, he granted Panurge's point, for he had always seen learned advocates so taken up in practising and pleading for others, as to have no time or leisure to bother with their own litigation.

"There," Pantagruel decided, "we shall have with us, next Sunday, our learned Father Hippothadeus for man of God; our eminent Master Rondibilis for physician; our friend Bridlegoose for legist. More, I believe we should remember Plutarch's statement: a foursome or tetrad is the perfect number for the Pythagoreans. Let us, therefore, annex to our council a fourth member, in the person of our faithful friend, the philosopher Trouillogan or Skeinwinder. This is especially important, for your perfect philosopher (Skeinwinder is that!) provides a positive answer to every doubt you submit to him."

Pantagruel then ordered Carpalim to arrange that the quartette be present at dinner the following Sunday.

"I don't think you could have possibly chosen better throughout the whole country," Epistemon said. "I do not say this because each of them is quite perfect in his own calling: this admits of no judgment. I say it especially because Rondibilis wasn't married but is; Hippothadeus wasn't and isn't; Bridlegoose was but isn't; Skeinwinder was and is. I can save Carpalim one chore: if you allow me, I will go invite Bridlegoose myself. He is an old friend of mine. Besides, I have to speak to him about the welfare and progress of a son of his, an honest, industrious fellow, who is now studying at Toulouse under that most learned and exemplary professor, Jean de Boissonné."

"Do as you like," Pantagruel agreed, "and see if I can do anything to further the youth's career or better the dignity of the excellent Boissonné, whom I love and respect as one of the ablest members of his profession. I shall gladly do all I can to this end."

XXX

ADVICE FROM THE THEOLO-GIAN HIPPOTHADEUS ON PAN-URGE'S HYMENEAL UNDER-TAKING

DINNER, the following Sunday, was no sooner ready than three of the guests appeared. But Bridlegoose, deputy-governor of Fonsbeton, between Poitiers and Ligugé, was nowhere to be seen. When the second course had been served, Panurge, bowing deep, spoke as follows:

"Gentlemen, I shall explain my problem in one sentence: shall I marry or no? No lynx or hawk or eagle has sharper eyes than those which singled you out, gleaned you and plucked you, from amid the ruck of humanity, as the great lights of your various professions. Therefore, if *you* cannot solve my problem, then it is as unsolvable as the *Insolubilia de Alliaco*, the scholastic treatise by that learned doctor, Pierre d'Ailly."

At Pantagruel's invitation, Father Hippothadeus rose, bowed to the company, and, with incredible modesty, replied:

"My friend, you are asking our advice, but first you should seek your own. Do you feel the goad of the flesh pricking you importunately?"

"I would not offend you, father, but it stings me sorely," Panurge replied.

"You do not offend me, my son. But amid this torment, have you prayed God to grant you the gift of continence and its special grace?"

"In all good faith, I have not!"

"In that case, I advise you to marry, friend; for, as St. Paul says: 'Better to marry than to burn.'"

"O bravely spoken!" cried Panurge joyously. "Spoken to the point, without circumbilivaginating around the pot. I shall marry without fail, and at the earliest opportunity. I invite you to my wedding. Cock's body, we shall make good cheer! You shall wear My Lord Bridegroom's livery; if we eat goose, it shall not be the imaginary bird Master Pierre Pathelin invited the draper to share with him. Besides, my wife shall not cook my goose. More, I shall beg you to open the ball with the first bridesmaid, if you consent to do me such favor and honor. However, there remains a tiny scruple, a most insignificant consideration. Tell me, father: shall I be a cuckold?"

"Certainly not, my friend, please God."

"Ha!" cried Panurge, "the Lord help us in His might. What recourse are we offered, good folk? This father offers us the dialectic conditional, those precepts of logic that admit of all contradictions and impossibilities. Remember the stock example of the schools? If my transalpine mule had wings, my transalpine mule would fly. Similarly, please God, I shall not be a cuckold; but, please God, I shall!

"Good God," Panurge went on, "were this a condition I could prevent, I would not despair; but your decision dispatches me directly to God's privy council, to the chamber of His little pleasures. How do you Frenchmen find the way there?"

Sarcastically, Panurge suggested that the reverend father had better not come to his wedding. The din and jigjugjaggle of the wedding guests would disturb his thoughts, give him a headache, since what he loved was rest, solitude and silence. No, indeed, Panurge did not believe Father Hippothadeus would attend. Besides, he danced but indifferently, and would be ill-at-ease leading off the first dance. Instead, Panurge would send him some goodies and the bride's favor to his room; and he begged the religious to drink his health.

"My friend," the theologian protested, "please consider what I say in the best light. Did I wrong you when I said 'please God'? Was it ill-spoken? Did I fail to honor the Lord, our Creator, protector and saviour? Did I slight the sole dispenser of all favors? Did I not thereby affirm our total dependence upon Him? Without Him, without the inspiration of His holy grace, we are nothing, we can do nothing, we are worth nothing. Did I not lay down a canonical exception to all our undertakings? Did I not indicate that all we proposed was referred to the disposition of His blessed will, both in heaven and upon earth? Did I not thereby sanctify His sacred will?

"My friend, please God, you will not be a cuckold. To discover His will on that point, you must not despair, as though it were an impenetrable thing, which you could ascertain only by consulting Him in the privy council of His most sanctified pleasures. Our gracious God has befriended us by the clearest, most manifest declarations, revelations and prophecies of the Holy Bible."

The Bible taught Panurge that he would never be cuckold—that is to say, his wife would never be a strumpet—if he chose a woman of gentle birth, instructed in honesty and virtue . . . brought up among respectable people, loving and fearing God . . . seeking to please Him by believing in Him and by following His holy commandments, by dreading to offend Him and thereby forfeit His promised grace . . . by her reluctance to transgress His holy law. . . . For, in this law, adultery was strictly forbidden: a wife was commanded to love, honor and obey, to cherish and to serve her husband, above all beings save God alone.

For his part, in order to uphold this discipline, Panurge should surround his wife with husbandly love, and, in all wisdom and honesty, set her a good example. He should live purely, chastely and virtuously in his household, even as he wished her to live. The best, the most perfect mirror was not that most lavishly gilded and studded with precious stones, but that which truly reflected the object set before it. Similarly, the worthiest woman would not be the richest, most beautiful, most elegant or noblest, but she who strove most assiduously to conform, God helping, to her husband's mode of life.

The moon, for example, borrowed no light from Jupiter, Mars, Mercury or any other star or planet in the spangled firmament. She received all light, and such light only as he gave her, from the sun, her mate. Panurge, Father Hippothadeus hoped, would likewise prove an exemplary husband, and forever implore the grace of God for the protection of himself and his lady.

Panurge tugged at his whiskers:

"So you would have me marry the virtuous woman described by Solomon in his *Proverbs*? She is dead, make no mistake about it. God forgive me, I have never beheld her anywhere to my certain knowledge.

"However, my hearty thanks, father: take this slice of marzipan:

it will help your digestion. Then you shall have a cup of hippocras—claret spiced with cinnamon—it is healthy and good for the stomach's sake.

"Let us proceed."

XXXI

ADVICE FROM THE PHYSICIAN RONDIBILIS

PANURGE turned to Rondibilis.

"After unstoning Friar Fryear, the first thing the gelder of the brownclad Saussignac monks said, was: 'Next!' By the same token, I now say: 'Next!' Come, Master Rondibilis, doctor of medicine: shall I marry or no?"

"By the trot of my mule," Rondibilis answered, "I don't know how to decide on your problem. You have said that you feel the poignant spurs of sensuality. I know by the study of medicine, from opinions founded on rules established by the ancient Platonics, that carnal concupiscence may be quelled in five different ways."

"How?" someone asked.

"First, by wine!"

"I can readily believe it," said Friar John. "When I am thoroughly drunk, I crave only to sleep."

"I mean by wine absorbed in moderation," Rondibilis amended, "for excess of liquor chills the blood, relaxes the nerves, dulls the senses, perverts the movements and dissipates the generative seeds. Thus all desire for the act of copulation vanishes.

"That is why Bacchus, god of drunkards, is painted beardless and clad in woman's clothes, an effeminate and ballockless eunuch. The temperate drinking of liquors acts quite otherwise: the old proverb bears this out when it tells us that Venus takes cold without Ceres and Bacchus. Such was the opinion of the ancients, according to Diodorus the Sicilian; the Lampsacians, too, according to Pausanias, believed that Master Priapus was born of Bacchus and Venus."

The second of Rondibilis' antaphrodisiac measures consisted in the assimilation of certain herbs and drugs, which made man frigid, maleficiated and impotent in the act venereal. This had been often proved by the use of *nymphaea heraclia*, or waterlily; *amerina*, or willow; reed, hempseed and *periclymenos*, or honeysuckle. The ashes of tamarisk, soaked in the piddle of a castrated bull, and absorbed orally by a person would cool off that person's sexual lust . . . mandrake had sheltered Diana and preserved her chastity; it had also served the Athenians, sentenced to continence during the festival of Ceres . . . hemlock, the lesser orchid, the hide of a hippopotamus were also efficient. . . . Both by their elementary virtues and by their medical properties these specifics froze and mortified the seminal germs, or dissipated the spirits appointed by nature to carry them to the proper place, or obstructed the channels and conduits by which they should be expelled. Conversely, there were various remedies which aroused, excited and urged man to coital vigor.

"I need none," said Panurge, "thank God and thank you, my dear doctor! But do not be offended; I say this without the slightest personal bias."

Rondibilis' third method lay in hard work. Toil and labor spent the body: the blood, distributed for the nourishment of each member, found neither time, nor opportunity, nor leisure, to transform itself into the spermatic secretion or into the superfluities of the third stage of digestion.

This stage, Nature was sedulous to reserve unto herself as being more needful for the preservation of the individual than for the propagation of the species. Diana was thus called chaste, because all her labors went into hunting; thus the Latin *castrum*, or camp, was linked with *castum*, or chaste, because here athletes and soldiers were constantly active. Thus, finally, in his book *Of Air, Water and Places*, Hippocrates mentioned certain Scythian tribes, more unready for amative gymnastics than eunuchs, because they were constantly at work and on horseback. Conversely, certain philosophers stated that idleness was the mother of all vice.

When Ovid was asked why Ægisthus became an adulterer, he blamed idleness; banish laziness from the world and all Cupid's arts would perish overnight. Bow, quiver, arrows would be a useless burden; no dart would strike home, because he was not expert enough in archery to wing cranes, as they flew through the air, or to pink deer scudding across the thickets. That feat the Parthians could accomplish, because they strained and struggled, whereas Cupid sought leisurely, quiet victims, seated or stretched out on their backs.

When Theophrastus was asked what sort of beast or object a love affair might be, he replied that it was the passion of idle spirits.

Diogenes also described lechery as the vocation of unoccupied folk. And when Canachus, the Sicyonian sculptor, sought to portray sloth, negligence and inaction as the animators of ribaldry, he moulded a statue of Venus seated, not standing, as all his predecessors had done.

"Humph!" said Panurge.

"Wine, drugs, work," Rondibilis resumed. "I come to my fourth prescription: earnest study."

The latter produced so incredible a tension of the spirit that no strength remained to urge the generative secretion to its proper destination, or to swell the cavernous nerve, whose duty it was to expel it for the propagation of humankind.

Let Panurge consider the attitude of a man engaged in some form of study. All the arteries of his brain stretched like the string of a crossbow, the more skilfully to supply forces necessary to fill the ventricles of common sense, of imagination, of apprehension, of ratiocination, of resolution, of memory, of recordation. These forces, with great agility, ran from ventricle to ventricle, through channels visible to anatomists, to the end of the *plexus mirabilis*, or wondernet. Here all arteries, originating in the left compartment of the heart, were closed up. As for the vital spirits, they refined themselves as they passed through various circuits, until they were turned into animal spirits. Just so, a studious person's natural faculties would be temporarily suspended, his exterior senses would be at a standstill, whilst he was pondering his problem. In brief, he seemed as though living outside of himself, transported by an ecstasy to other realms. Ay, Socrates did not speak improperly when he defined philosophy as naught but a meditation on death.

Perhaps here, too, lay Democritus' reason for putting out his eyes, in the belief that loss of sight was a lesser evil than the diminution of his contemplations, interrupted by the roving eye. For the same reason, Pallas, goddess of wisdom and protectress of the diligent, was represented as a virgin. The Muses, too, were perpetually maiden, and the Graces dwelled in eternal purity.

Rondibilis remembered reading that Venus, Cupid's mother, once inquired of him why he never assaulted the Muses. Because, he replied, they were so beautiful, so fresh, so modest, so simple, so virtuous and so continuously employed: some in the contemplation of the stars, in the supputation of numbers, in the dimension of geometric bodies; others in the invention of rhetoric, the composition of poetry, the disposition of music. Thus, when he approached them, he unstrung his bow, shut his quiver and put out his torch, through shame and fear of harming them. Then, removing the band about his eyes in order to see them more clearly, he would listen to their melodic songs and lyrical odes. Doing so, he experienced the sweetest pleasures he had ever known, and, transported by their beauty and grace, he was charmed to sleep by the harmony. That was as near as ever he came to seeking to assault them or disturb their studies.

Rondibilis now understood what Hippocrates had meant when writing of the Scythians in the book mentioned, and in *Of Reproduction*, also. Men whose parotid arteries—close to the ears—had been severed, were unfit for generation, according to the reasons given earlier, when Rondibilis spoke of the spirits, their spermatic secretion and the spiritual blood of which the arteries were the receptacles. Similarly, Hippocrates maintained that a great part of the generative fluid descended from the brain and from the spinal column.

"Fifth and last," Rondibilis summed up, "you may assuage the sexual stimuli by performing the act of copulation."

"Ha!" said Panurge. "I was waiting for that. Let any one who likes use numbers one to four inclusive: I'm for number five."

"That," Friar John interrupted, "that is what Father Scyllino, Prior of St. Victor near Marseille, calls maceration of the flesh. I agree. So, too, did the hermit of St. Radegonde, a little above Chinon. He believed that the hermits of the Theban desert could not more successfully macerate their bodies, overcome their lecherous sensuality, or still the rebellion of the flesh, than by having their joy-poles wrung twenty-five or thirty times a day."

Rondibilis concluded:

"I see Panurge well proportioned in his limbs, well tempered in his humors, well complexioned in his spirits, of a competent age, in an opportune season, and of a reasonable will to marry. If he meets a woman of like nature, they will produce children worthy of some kingdom across the seas. Does he wish to see these children provided for in his lifetime? Then, the sooner he marries, the better."

"Learned doctor and dear friend," cried Panurge, "married I shall be, don't doubt it, and soon. During your scholarly discourse, that flea I have in my ear tickled me more than ever. I insist on your being present at my wedding: we shall have a time-and-a-half of it, I warrant you. You will bring Madame Rondibilis, if you care to—and of course her neighbors, too, if *she* cares to. And we shall have fair play!"

XXXII

RONDIBILIS ON CUCKOLDRY AS A NATURAL APPENDAGE OF WEDLOCK

"There remains a minor point to settle," said Panurge, continuing his speech. "Doubtless you have seen the legend S.P.Q.R. on Roman banners. It means *Si Peu Que Rien* or *Straw, Pin, Quibble, Rubbish*; in other words a mere trifle!"

"God's haven of safety!" cried Rondibilis. "What do you ask of me? If you shall be a cuckold? My friend, I am married; you will be married too. Therefore take up a pen of steel and inscribe this maxim upon your cerebellum: No husband but is exposed to cuckoldry.

"Cuckoldry is an essential appendage of wedlock; your shadow does not follow you more closely or naturally. When you hear the three words: 'He is married,' add: 'Therefore he is, has been, will or may be cuckolded.' Do this, and no one will ever accuse you of faulty logic."

"By the guts of all the devils, what are you saying?"

"My friend," Rondibilis returned, "let me tell you a story."

"By all means," said Panurge.

So Rondibilis related the following anecdote.

Once Hippocrates went from Lango (or Cos, as the ancients called it) to Polystylo or Abdera, to visit the philosopher Democritus. Accordingly, he wrote to his old friend, Dionysius, begging him in his absence to take Madame Hippocrates to the house of her parents, an honest and reputable couple. For he was unwilling to leave her in her own home, alone. Yet even though she dwelled under the parental roof, Hippocrates besought Dionysius to keep an eye on her: let his friend observe where she went with her mother, and what people visit her at her parents'. Not that he mistrusted her virtue or modesty, Hippocrates wrote; he had already tested and proved these qualities. But she was a woman, a fact which in itself justified such surveillance.

"My friend," Rondibilis went on, "the nature of woman partakes of the moon's in divers ways. Like the moon, she hides, skulks, restrains herself and dissimulates in her husband's presence. But no sooner is he out of the way than forthwith she takes every advantage, gives herself up to pleasure, wanders here, rolls about there, lays aside her hypocrisies and shows herself in true colors. Does not the moon behave similarly in relation to the sun? Though in conjunction with the sun, she never appears on earth or in heaven with him; on the contrary, we see her only in opposition, when she is remotest from him. Then, indeed, she shines in her greatest fullness; then, indeed, we see her at her best. And when is that? At night! Similarly, woman is—just woman!"

When Rondibilis spoke of womankind, he spoke of a frail, variable, capricious, inconstant and imperfect sex. Indeed, with all due honor and respect to Nature, Rondibilis believed that Nature took leave of her senses when she created woman. Surely woman was not fashioned according to the sound principles of common sense, which governed Nature's other creations?

"I have thought of it hundreds and hundreds of times," Rondibilis affirmed. "And I don't know what to believe, save perhaps that, when Nature produced the female, she was far more interested in the sociable delectation of man, and in the propagation of the human species, than in the perfection of individual muliebrity or womanliness."

To be sure, Plato was puzzled as to how he should class women.

Did they belong to the category of rational animals or to that of brute-beasts? Here was the rub: Nature had deposited in a secret, remote coign of their bodies, an animal, an organ, which man did not possess. This tissue or member—which was highly nervous and sensitive—at times engendered certain saltish, brackish, boracic, bitter, biting, lancinating and sharply tickling humors. Their prickling and smart shook up the entire body, ravished the senses, confounded the judgment and unleashed the wildest frenzies. Were it not that Nature suffused woman's brow with a blush of modesty, women would, one and all, pounce insanely upon man's codpiece; they would swoop down upon this prey far more furiously than ever the daughters of Proteus, King of Argos, who went mad and believed themselves to be cows, or than the Mimallonides and Thyades, participants in the orgies celebrated in honor of Bacchus.

This beast or organ of theirs, then, was intimately related with the chief parts of the body; a study of anatomy proved it. When Rondibilis called this tissue an animal, he was merely following the theories of Peripatetic philosophers like Aristotle, and Academic philosophers like Plato. If proper motion were a certain token of animation, as Aristotle claimed, then whatever moved of itself was an animal. Plato, quite rightly, termed this feminine organ an animal, because he recognized in it autonomous movements of suffocation, precipitation, indignation and corrugation or wrinkling. Indeed, these movements were often so violent as to deprive woman of any other sense or action, plunging her into a state of swoon and syncope, into an epileptic and apoplectic faint, into a coma closely resembling death. Moreover, this member threw off an unmistakable odor, the unpleasantness of which women consciously dispelled by the use of perfumes.

Rondibilis was aware that Claudius Galen had striven to prove that the motions of this organ were not spontaneous but accidental. His disciples, furthermore, had sought to demonstrate that it did not itself secrete its own particular effluvium, but rather gave off one of the normal odors figuring in the evolutionary span of all exhalations. Rondibilis invoked Critolaus, the Peripatetic Athenian, who came to Rome in the second century, with his famous theory of body and soul. If the virtues of the soul were weighed on one scale, he said, and if the virtues of the body were weighed on the other, the former would so outweigh the latter as to swamp land and sea. Pondering Critolaus' statement, anyone must be convinced that both Peripatetics and Academics spoke here, as frequently elsewhere, more in a spirit of jest and envy, than in a sincere search for the truth.

Rondibilis would not develop the argument further. Still, he did wish to say that the praise due to virtuous women was not insignificant. Had they not, by living blamelessly and chastely, shown the power of reducing this savage beast to obedience and reason? Here he must add that this beast in woman was pacified (if ever it could be) by the testicular food which nature had created for it in men. To such diet, all female motion tended; in such diet, all female appetite was satisfied; by such diet, all female fury was assuaged. Nevertheless, we must not be astonished to find ourselves in perpetual danger of being made cuckold, since we cannot produce, day-in and day-out, the wherewithal to glut that voracious animal.

"God's fish!" cried Panurge. "Do you mean to tell me the art of medicine knows no preventive for antler-growing?"

"Oh no! we know an excellent one: I often use it myself. A celebrated author recorded it eighteen hundred years ago. Would you like to hear it?"

"By the power of the Almighty," cried Panurge, "you are indeed a righteous man; I love you with all my heart. Have a little of this quince jam: quinces, being astringent, block the orifice of the ventricle and ease the first process of digestion. But Lord! I speak Latin before clerks, I teach my grandmother to suck eggs. Forgive my presumption; let me give you this huge goblet, fit, indeed, for Nestor, god of the sea and bottomless toper. Will you have another draught of mulled hippocras? There's neither quinsy-herb, ginger or cardamon in it: it is pure cinnamon, refined sugar and fine white wine, from the vine set in the slips of the great sorb apple tree planted above the walnut tree at La Devinière."

XXXIII

RONDIBILIS PRESCRIBES A PREVENTIVE FOR CUCKOLDRY

RONDIBILIS went back to the days when Jupiter surveyed the state of his Olympian household and made a calendar of all the gods and goddesses. Each divinity was assigned a day and season for his festival; each was given a place, where he might receive pilgrims and issue oracles; each was allotted sacrifices proper to himself.

Panurge interrupted:

"That was exactly what Tinteville, Bishop of Auxerre, did, if we are to believe legend. Calendar-reform, eh? Our noble prelate loved good wine, as all honest men do; he was especially respectful and solicitous of the great bud of the vine-tree which fathered Bacchus. Now it happened that, after a few years, he saw this bud ruined lamentably by frost, mist, hail, rime, hoar, wind and other calamities ushered in by the feasts of St. George, St. Mark, St. Vital, St. Eutropius, St. Philip, Holy Rood, Ascension, and so forth—days when the sun passes under the sign of Taurus, in late April and early May. Quite logically, My Lord Bishop concluded that these saints were holy frost-senders, hail-shooters, wind-blowers and spoilers of the vines. He therefore transferred their anniversaries from spring to winter, allotting them feasts between Christmas and St. Tiffany's Day (as he called Epiphany, identifying the feast of the Magi with their apocryphal mother). With all respect and honor, he thus allowed them to blast and freeze to their heart's content; for frost, at this season, would cause him no damage, but would actually help the buds. In compensation, he made spring feasts of the days sacred to St. Christopher, St. John the headless Baptist, St. Ann, St. Magdalen, St. Dominick, St. Lawrence, heretofore celebrated in June, July and August. Thus mid-August was to fall in early May. Wise man, this bishop, since that season, far from affording hazards of hail and frost, on the contrary sumptuously rewarded makers of cooling drinks, vendors of junket, owners of shady arbors and re-freshers of wine."

To return to Jupiter, in his calendar-making (Rondibilis went on), he forgot the poor devil Cuckoldry, who happened to be absent at the time.

"Where was he?" Panurge demanded.

Rondibilis explained that Cuckoldry was in Paris, at the law courts, busily engaged in some ballocky case or other for a vassal and tenant of his. Rondibilis did not know how long it was before Cuckoldry learned of the trick played upon him. At any rate, he threw up his litigation, determined to defend his privileged position in the divine commonwealth, and appeared forthwith before the mighty Jupiter. Here he recalled the past aid, favors and services he had rendered Jupiter, earnestly begging the latter not to leave him, and him only, deprived of feast-day, sacrifice or honors.

The sovereign monarch excused himself: all his appointments were made, the list was closed. But, before Master Cuckoldry's importunate insistence, Jupiter finally placed him on the rolls, allowing him due celebration and sacrifice on earth. Because the entire calendar was filled, Cuckoldry had, however, to share celebration and festival jointly with Jealousy. His domination would be exercised over married men, especially over those with beautiful wives; his sacrifices would be husbandly suspicion, mistrust, ill-humor, ambush, trap, investigation, spying. All husbands were strictly commanded to revere and house him, to celebrate his festival twice as solemnly as those of other deities, and to pay him the tributes mentioned above.

Failing to do this, they were threatened with his indifference and wrath; he would never enter their houses or seek their company, however passionately they called upon him. Instead, he would leave them rotting alone eternally with their wives; he would never produce the diversion of a co-rival; he would consider them heretics and miscreants; he would flee them sempiternally. In a word, he would treat them as the other gods treated the renegades of their individual cults, as Bacchus treated disloyal vinedressers, Ceres idle plowmen, Pomona worthless fruitgrowers, Neptune incompetent mariners, Vulcan slack blacksmiths and so forth.

Conversely, rich rewards were promised to his votaries. Let them observe his festival, suspend their own business and lay aside all pursuits save spying upon their wives, locking them up and jealously mistreating them, as the sacrifices ordained. Then, Cuckoldry would favor, love and accompany them; he would haunt their homes night and day; they would never miss his presence by their side.

"That," said Rondibilis, "is my preventive and cure for cuck-oldry!"

"Ha, ha, ha!" Carpalim roared. "There's a specific more efficient than Hans Carvel's ring. Devil take me, if I don't pin my faith upon it. The nature of woman is as you have described it. Lightning strikes and destroys only the harder, more solid and more resistant bodies; it spurns the softer, emptier, more yielding ones. It will shatter a steel sword, without damaging the velvet scabbard sheathing it; it will consume the bones of the body, without affecting the flesh that covers them. Even so, the contentiousness, the subtlety and the contrariness of women's spirit will attack only what they know to be expressly prohibited and forbidden."

Here Hippothadeus, the theologian, interrupted.

"Certainly," he announced, "all our savants agree that the first woman in history—she whom the Hebrews call Eve—would never have been tempted to eat of the fruit of the Tree of Knowledge, unless this had been explicitly forbidden. To prove this, consider how, in the very first words he spoke, the crafty tempter reminded her of the proscription, as who might say: 'This fruit is forbidden; therefore you must eat of it, or you are not truly a woman.'"

XXXIV

HOW WOMEN USUALLY HANKER AFTER FORBIDDEN THINGS

Carpalim addressed the company:

"When I was a whoremaster in Orléans," he said, "the most rhetorical flourish and persuasive argument I could muster, to catch the ladies in my snare and to entice them into adulterous pastimes, was to show them clearly, strikingly and censoriously how jealous their husbands were. This technique was not of my invention. It has been written down; we have laws, examples, reasons and daily experiences to the point.

"Let women once entertain this belief in their noddles, and inevitably they will make their husbands cuckolds. They will do this, by God (I don't mean to swear), even if they must go the lengths of Semiramis, who, Pliny tells us, lay with a horse . . . of Pasiphaë, who conceived the Minotaur by a bull . . . of Egesta, who bore a son to the river-god Crimisius disguised as a bear . . . of the women of Mendes, in Egypt, who, according to Herodotus and Strabo, copulate with goats in honor of Bacchus . . . and of sundry other bitches whom I forbear to mention at the present time. . . ."

"In truth," said Ponocrates, "I have heard tell that Pope John XXII, while visiting the Abbey of Fontevrault, was besought by the abbess and various discreet nuns to grant a curious request. These ladies wished to confess to one another. They declared that nuns often yielded to certain little imperfections, which they were too intolerably ashamed to divulge to male confessors, but which, under the seal of the confessional, they would reveal more freely and familiarly to their own sex."

"What did the Pope answer?" someone asked.

Carpalim told them that the holy father said:

"There is nothing I had rather do for you, but I see one inconvenience: the confessional must be kept secret, and you women would find it difficult to do this."

The same day, the holy father gave them, for safekeeping, a small box with a linnet in it; very mildly, he begged them to lock it up in some secure and secret place. If they stored it away, he promised, on his pope's word, that he would grant their request. However, he strictly forbade them to open it for any reason whatsoever, under pain of ecclesiastical censure and eternal excommunication. This restriction was no sooner uttered, than all of them longed to find out what the box contained; they were beside themselves with impatience and longing for the pope to depart. At last, having given them his benediction, the holy father withdrew to his palace. He was not gone three paces beyond the convent gates before the good ladies crowded about the box.

Next morning, the pope called upon them, intending, they supposed, to grant them the requested indulgence. But before discussing the matter, he bade them bring the box. Opening it up, he found it empty. Immediately, he pointed out to the good nuns how impossible they must find it to respect the secret of the confessional when, within a short span of twelve hours, they had been unable to keep their hands off a box committed so earnestly to their custody.

Pantagruel, turning aside from Carpalim, addressed Rondibilis.

"Ha, my eminent and learned doctor, you are thrice welcome here, and I thank you for your counsel," he said. "I have heartily enjoyed listening to you, and I praise the Lord for all! Why, I had not seen you since you played the morality play of *The Man who Married a Dumb Wife* at Montpellier, with our old friends Antoine Saporta, Guy Bourguier, Balthazar Noyer, Tolet, Jean Quentin, François Robinet, Jean Perdrier and François Rabelais."

"I was there," said Epistemon. "A grand comedy it is, too! The good husband wished his dumb wife to speak. Thanks to the skill of a doctor and surgeon, who operated on an encycliglotta on her tongue, she was able to regain this power. But, at once, she babbled and chattered so furiously that her wretched husband returned to the medico and implored him for some remedy to make her hush. Alas! the physician's science included various specifics to make women talk, but none to silence them; the sole solution he could suggest was to make the husband deaf. By God knows what drugs, the wretch lost his hearing. His wife, realizing that he was deaf as a post, and that her scolding was wasted, went mad.

"Shortly after, the physician visited them to collect his fee. The husband replied that, being deaf, he could not hear what the doctor was saying. The latter threw God knows what other sort of powder over his back; the deaf man lost his reason, on the spot. Whereupon the crazed wife and the lunatic husband fell upon the medico, and trounced him within an inch of his life.

"I never laughed so much in my life as I did at that performance," Epistemon concluded. "It was quite as good as the *Farce of Master Pierre Pathelin*."

" 'Let us return to our sheep,' " said Panurge, quoting the proverbial phrase from *Pathelin*. Then, turning to Rondibilis:

"Your words, translated from technical gibberish into plain speech, mean that I should resolutely get married, without troubling my head about horns. That is about as appropriate as trumping an ace! I very much fear, my dear doctor, that you will be too busy attending your patients to be present at my wedding. I will gladly excuse your absence:

> *Stercus et urina medici sunt prandia prima.*
> *Ex aliis paleas, ex istis collige grana.*

> *Water of urine, bread of excrement,*
> *Such are the medico's chief nourishment;*
> *From this he gleans his chaff, from that his wheat—"*

"One moment, my friend," Rondibilis broke in. "You are misquoting. The first two lines of your poem refer to medicine, to be sure, but your third is a legal, not a medical proverb. The third line reads:

> *To doctors, these are signs; to laymen, meat."*

"Brrr!" said Panurge. "Were my wife ill—"

"Were my wife or your wife ill," Rondibilis interrupted, "I would wish to examine her urine, feel her pulse, grope her hypogaster, and pass my palms over her umbilicary region, as Hippocrates prescribes in his *Aphorisms* (II, 35), before I went any further."

"No, no, that would be useless," Panurge replied. "Such doings are for lawyers like myself. We have, in our *Digest* (xxv, 4), the law *De ventre inspiciendo* or *Of the Right to determine the Pregnancy of Widows*. Bother no more about it, my dear doctor, I will provide an enema—barbed, rhubarbed and barbarous enough. Do not neglect the urgent professional errands that call you elsewhere. I will send you victuals from the wedding table, and always prize your friendship highly."

Going up to the physician, Panurge, without a word, pressed four goldpieces into his palm. Rondibilis accepted them graciously. Then, with a start, as though vexed:

"Heh, sir!" the physician exclaimed. "You need not have given me this. Nevertheless, I thank you. I accept nothing of evil folks; I refuse nothing of goodly folk. I am at your service."

"Provided I pay?" said Panurge.

"Naturally," the physician answered.

XXXV

HOW SKEINWINDER, THE PHILOSOPHER, DISPOSED OF THE DIFFICULTY OF MARRIAGE

PANTAGRUEL then turned to Skeinwinder, the philosopher:

"My faithful friend, the torch, passed from hand to hand, now comes to you. It is your turn to answer. Shall Panurge wed or no?"

"Both," Skeinwinder replied.

"What do you say?"

"What you hear!"

"What did I hear?"

"What I said!"

"Ha, ha! are we come to that pass?" Panurge broke in. "Never mind, dealer: I pass! Now then: should I marry or no?"

"Neither, nor!"

"Devil take me, if I'm not doting; devil fry me, if I understand you. Wait a moment; I'll put my spectacles over my left ear to hear you better."

Just then Pantagruel caught sight of a small dog at the door of the room. It was Gargantua's pup Kyne, named after Tobias' dog in the Bible. Pantagruel cried: "Our king is not far: let us arise!" He had no sooner spoken than Gargantua came in. All rose to bow low before him. Gargantua, saluting them affably, said:

"My good friends, please do me the favor of keeping your seats and continuing your discussion. Bring me a chair, here, at this end of the table, and a glass, ho! that I may drink to the entire company. It is a pleasure to welcome you here, gentlemen. But tell me, what were you discussing?"

Pantagruel then explained that, after the second course, Panurge had posed the problem of his marriage; that Father Hippothadeus and Master Rondibilis had already given their answers; that, just as Gargantua entered, Skeinwinder was beginning to expose his thoughts on the subject. Panurge had put the question: should he marry or no? Skeinwinder had first replied that he should do both, then that he should do neither. Panurge had protested against such contradictory answers, vowing that he could not make head or tail of them.

"I think I understand it quite clearly," said Gargantua. "The answer is much like that given by Aristippus, a philosopher of antiquity. They named a certain woman and asked him whether she were his wife. 'I am master of my mistress,' he answered. 'I have her, yet she hath not me; I possess her, but am not possessed by her or any other devil.' "

Pantagruel suggested that Skeinwinder's reply was not unlike that given by a Spartan servant-girl when asked whether she had ever had commerce with a man. "Never in my life," she retorted, "but men have had commerce aplenty with me."

"Very well," Rondibilis opined, "let us consider the matter to be what we physicians call neuter, as when a body is neither sick nor healthy. Let it be what philosophers call a mean: avoiding either extreme, swinging now toward one pole, now toward the other."

Father Hippothadeus declared that the holy apostle Paul had illustrated the point more clearly when he stated in I *Corinthians*, VII, 29: "They that have wives be as though they had none."

"I interpret having a wife or not having a wife in this manner," Pantagruel volunteered. "Having a wife means having the use of her in the way ordained by nature, namely for company, help and pleasure. Not having a wife means to loll and poltroon it uxoriously, tied to her petticoats. No man should let his wife interfere with the supreme love he owes his God: no man should, for his wife's sake, shirk the duty he owes to country, society and friends. Nor, finally, should he neglect his studies and abandon his business simply to find pleasure at her side. If you interpret the terms 'having a wife' and 'not having a wife' in this sense, I see no contradiction whatever."

XXXVI

OF THE ANSWERS VOUCHSAFED BY THE PHILOSOPHER SKEINWINDER, WHO WAS EPHECTIC (HE SUSPENDED JUDGMENT) AND PYRRHONIC (HE BELIEVED CERTITUDE UNATTAINABLE)

"YOUR words are dulcet and harmonious as organ music," said Panurge, "but I swear I am sunk in that bottomless pit in which, Heraclitus (or was it Democritus?) says, all truth lies hidden. I grope in the dark, I understand nothing, my senses are dulled, I much fear I am bewitched.

"But no—I shall try another mode of attack. Please, please do not move, O faithful friend, O wonderful philosopher. Put nothing in your purse. Instead, we shall change our tune and throw the dice again! But let us not speak in disjunctive or mutually exclusive propositions. These ill-linked members annoy you, I can tell. Therefore, by God, speak out: am I to marry?"

The following dialogue ensued.

PANURGE

Am I to marry?

SKEINWINDER

Conceivably.

PANURGE

And if I do not?

SKEINWINDER

I see no objection.

PANURGE

You see no objection?

SKEINWINDER

None, unless my eyes deceive me.

PANURGE

I can see five hundred.

SKEINWINDER

Count them.

PANURGE

I confess, I spoke loosely: I took a certain number when I meant a vague quantity, I cited the determinate for what was indeterminate. When I say five hundred objections, I mean a large amount of objections.

SKEINWINDER

I am listening to what you have to say.

PANURGE

By all the devils, I cannot do without a wife.

SKEINWINDER

Devils, avaunt! Invoke not the beasts!

PANURGE

Forgive me! I will invoke God! My subjects of Salmagundi have a proverb: "To sleep alone, or without wife, is to live like a beast!" Dido said as much in her lamentations over Æneas' desertion.

SKEINWINDER

I am at your service.

PANURGE

God's body, I'm grateful to you for coming to the point. Shall I marry, then?

SKEINWINDER

Perhaps.

PANURGE

Will marriage prosper me?

SKEINWINDER

That depends upon the circumstances.

PANURGE

If I meet favorable circumstances, shall I be happy?

SKEINWINDER

Happy enough!

PANURGE

Oh, God! Let's go upstream, against the grain! If I meet unfavorable circumstances?

SKEINWINDER

Then do not blame me.

PANURGE

For God's sake, advise me. What must I do?

SKEINWINDER

Whatever you will.

PANURGE

Black and white, yes and no, hocus-pocus, higgledy-piggledy. . . .

SKEINWINDER

Do not invoke Satan, I pray you.

PANURGE

Very well, let me invoke God. I seek nothing but your advice. What do you advise?

SKEINWINDER

Nothing.

PANURGE

Shall I marry?

SKEINWINDER

(*Abandoning the Pyrrhonic philosophy and answering facetiously throughout the rest of the scene.*) I was not present at your wedding.

PANURGE

Well then, I shan't marry?

SKEINWINDER

I cannot help it.

PANURGE

Take me as a husband—

SKEINWINDER

Where shall I take you to?

PANURGE

Take me as a married man—

SKEINWINDER

I'm sorry, I can't "take" you under any circumstances—

PANURGE

Ripe turds in my nostrils! God, if I dared but swear a smart little oath up my sleeve, it would prove a great relief. Patience, Panurge, patience! (To SKEINWINDER) If I marry, shall I be a cuckold?

SKEINWINDER

It is to be supposed.

PANURGE

If my wife is virtuous and chaste, I shall never wear horns.

SKEINWINDER

Your deduction would seem congruous.

PANURGE

Listen to me—

SKEINWINDER

As long as you like.

PANURGE

Will she be chaste and virtuous? That is the only point I care about.

SKEINWINDER

I question it.

PANURGE

Have you ever seen her?

SKEINWINDER

Not that I know of.

PANURGE

Why doubt of a thing you know not?

SKEINWINDER

There are reasons.

PANURGE

And if you knew her?

SKEINWINDER

Even more so.

PANURGE

O page, O my sweet lad, hold my bonnet; it's all yours save for the spectacles, which I need here. Go down to the barnyard and swear in my stead for a full half-hour. I guarantee to do your swearing for you, whenever you call upon me. (To SKEINWINDER) But who will pin the horns on me?

SKEINWINDER

Somebody.

PANURGE

By God's belly, I'll beat that Master Somebody within an inch of his life!

SKEINWINDER

So you say.

PANURGE

May the fiercest of devils, the one with jet eyeballs and a redhot poker for cod, scorch me to death, if I don't clap a Bergamo chastity belt on my wife whenever I leave my seraglio.

SKEINWINDER

Speak more fittingly.

PANURGE

Well cacked, well sung, you and your fitting speeches. Let us come to an understanding.

SKEINWINDER

I am quite willing.

PANURGE

One minute! If I can't draw blood from you here, I'll prick you with my lancet in another vein. Are you a married man or are you not?

SKEINWINDER

Neither one, nor the other, yet both.

PANURGE

God help you, I sweat blood, I'm dropping with fatigue; Christ's death, my digestion is blocked: my *phrenos* or diaphragm, my *metaphrenos* or thorax, my abdomen are taut with suspense, as I wait to pop your answer and elucidation into the gamepouch of my understanding.

SKEINWINDER

I do not worry on that score.

PANURGE

Come, come, my faithful friend: are you married?

SKEINWINDER

So it would seem.

PANURGE

You were married once before too, eh?

SKEINWINDER

Quite possibly.

PANURGE

Were you satisfied the first time?

SKEINWINDER

Possibly.

PANURGE

How about the second time?

SKEINWINDER

According to my lot and fate.

PANURGE

Seriously, man to man: are you satisfied?

SKEINWINDER

Most likely.

PANURGE

Come, come, in God's name! By the burden St. Christopher bore across the water, by the Christchild, it is easier to draw a fart out of a dead mule, than a clear statement of fact from you. This time, I swear I shall catch you! Come, my tried and faithful friend, let us tell the truth and shame the devil. Were you ever cuckolded? When I say *you*, I mean you, Skeinwinder, standing large as life before me, and not some other fellow, swinging a tennis racket in a court, God knows where.

SKEINWINDER

Not unless it was fatally foreordained.

PANURGE

God's flesh, I give up; God's blood, I demur; God's body, I abjure. The fellow eludes my grasp!

Gargantua rose from the table:

"Praise God in all things," he said. "The world has turned into a fine kettle of fish, since I first learned to observe it. What a pass we are come to when, to-day, the most learned and competent philosophers deal in phrontistery or thinkery, professing the doctrines of the Pyrrhonic, Aporrhetic, Ephectic and allied sceptic schools. Praise God, I say, praise God! Henceforth it will prove easier to catch lions by their manes, horses by their napes, wild bulls by their snouts, cattle by their horns, wolves by their tails, goats by their beards, and birds by their feet, than ever philosophers by their words. I bid you good night, my dear friends."

So saying, Gargantua withdrew and, though Pantagruel and the others wished to wait upon him, he would not suffer it. When he had left the hall, Pantagruel turned to the company:

"At the beginning of Plato's assemblies, Timæus used to count the guests; we, on the contrary, will count them at the end of the meeting. One, two, three . . . where is the fourth? Wasn't number four our friend Bridlegoose?"

Epistemon rose to give an account of his errand. He had gone to Bridlegoose's house; the legist was not there. Apparently a messenger from Miralingua, with a summons from the Miralinguan parliament, sitting as a high court of justice, summoned him to appear personally before the senators to vindicate a decision he had handed down. Unwilling to risk being held in contempt of court, he had left the day before posthaste for Miralingua.

"I understand," said Pantagruel. "For over forty years, Bridle-goose has sat as judge at Fonsbeton. During this time, he has pro-nounced over four thousand final sentences. The losers, to a man, ap-pealed to the supreme court of the Miralinguan parliament in Miral-ingua; but that court inevitably confirmed, ratified and upheld Bridlegoose's judgment, dismissing every appeal. If now, in his old age, he is cited to appear, then some disaster has occurred. For, throughout the past, he has ever conducted himself beyond reproach in his appointed office."

Pantagruel declared that he wished to do all he could to help Bridlegoose in all justice.

"I know that, to-day, public malevolence has reached such a point," he concluded, "that poor Bridlegoose will need all my help. I shall examine the question carefully and find a means of warding off all chicanery and pitfalls that menace him."

Dinner done, the tables were removed. Pantagruel gave his three guests several precious and costly gifts—rings, jewels, gold and silver plate—and, thanking them graciously, retired to his private apart-ments.

XXXVII

HOW PANTAGRUEL PERSUADED PANURGE TO SEEK COUNSEL OF A FOOL

On his way to bed, Pantagruel noticed Panurge strolling through a gallery, dreaming and nodding his head.

"You look like a mouse entangled in a snare," he told him. "The more desperately the beast tries to wriggle free, the more hopelessly it is caught. The harder you try to emerge from the gin of perplexity, the more hopelessly you are caught. I know but one remedy."

"And what is that?" Panurge asked dully.

There was, Pantagruel said, a popular saying to the effect that a madman could teach the wisest scholar. Since Panurge had found no true satisfaction in the answers of specialists, why did he not consult some lunatic? Possibly, by doing so, he might find the solution he craved. How many princes, kings and commonwealths had won battles, and settled intricate problems, on the advice and forecast of fools!

"I need not remind you of countless examples," Pantagruel told him. "But you will agree with me in this: What is a wise man?"

"I don't know."

"Well, let us say a man who watches over his private affairs and domestic business . . . who attends to his household . . . who keeps his nose to the particular grindstone he works . . . who loses no chance of amassing wealth and consideration . . . who understands thoroughly how to avoid the pitfalls of poverty. . . . That, according to the world, should constitute a wise man. Yet, in the eyes of the celestial spirits, he may be the most unmitigated ass.

"And whom do these spirits consider wise, then? Ha, that is a horse of another color. For them, a wise man, a man not only sage but able to presage future events by divine inspiration, is one who forgets himself, discards his own personality, rids his senses of all earthly affection, purges his spirit of all human care, neglects everything. All of which qualities are popularly supposed to be symptoms of insanity!"

Thus, Faunus, son of Picus, king of Latium, and a great soothsayer, was called Fatuus by the common herd.

Thus, when the various rôles were distributed among a company of mummers, that of the Fool or Jester invariably went to the most talented and experienced actor.

Thus, mathematicians declared that the same horoscope applied for kings and zanies. Thus, because of his delirium shortly before death, the name of Chorœbus—son of the king Mygdon the Phrygian, betrothed to Cassandra and massacred before Minerva's altar at the siege of Troy—had passed into the language as a common proverb. Moreover, Euphorion, historian, poet and librarian to Antiochus the Great, vouched for Chorœbus' insanity. Well—the horoscopes of Chorœbus and Æneas were identical.

Pantagruel might fittingly quote the comment of John Andrew—Giovanni Andrea, a fifteenth-century glossarist—on a certain papal writ addressed to the mayor and townsmen of La Rochelle. Or he might quote Nicolas Tedesco, the Panormitan, on the subject of the same canon. Or Barbatias, an Italian jurisconsult. Or, more recently, Jason de Maïnus, the Italian scholar, famed for his *Responsa*, concerning Lord John, the celebrated fool of Paris and great-grandfather to Caillette, jester of Louis XII.

"Here is the story, Panurge: it happened in Paris at the cookshop by the Petit Châtelet. A hungry porter was eating his bread in front of a roasting goose; as the meat turned on the spit, he held up the bread to be flavored and perfumed by the vapor emanating from the cooking. The cook did not interfere with him. But when the porter had wolfed down the last mouthful, the cook seized him by the throat, and demanded payment for the smoke of his roast meat. The other replied that he had in no wise damaged his meats, deprived him of anything, or incurred any debt. The smoke in question evaporated and was lost, whether the porter stood by or not. Nor had any one in Paris ever seen or heard of the sale of smoke from roast meats in the city streets.

"The cook replied that he was not compelled to feed porters and like riffraff with the aroma of his goose; he swore that if the porter did not pay him, he would pull his teeth out. The porter drew his cudgel and stood on the defensive. A great altercation ensued; idle Parisians thronged from all sides to witness the debate. Appropriately enough, Lord John the Loony, a citizen of Paris, happened to be there. Seeing him, the cook said to the porter:

" 'Will you abide by our noble Lord John's decision in this matter?'

" 'Ay, by God's blood, so I will,' the porter agreed.

"Lord John listened to their pleas, then ordered the porter to produce a coin from his belt. The porter presented him with a *philip* or sou, a very old coin struck with the effigy of Philip V. Lord John took it and laid it on his own left shoulder as though weighing it. Next, he made it ring on the palm of his left hand as though testing the metal's alloy. Finally, he laid it against his right eye, as though to see if it were well struck. The whole operation was performed amid a deep silence: the loafers watched curiously; the cook confidently; the porter in despair.

"Then Lord John made the coin ring several times over the counter, and, with judicial majesty, holding his jester's wand as he might a sceptre, adorning the marten cap on his head with paper ears ridged like organ-pipes, he cleared his throat deliberately, two or three times, and announced in a loud voice:

" 'The court decrees that the porter who ate his bread by the smoke of the roast has duly and civilly paid the cook with the jingle of his money. Further, the said court orders each to return to his eachery without cost or charges. Case dismissed.'

"This decision handed down by the Paris fool seemed eminently just and admirable to the learned authorities I quoted above. Indeed, they doubted whether a more logical and judicious settlement could have been made by the Parliament of Paris, the Rota of Rome, or the Areopagites in Athens.

"My advice, Panurge, is to consult a fool."

XXXVIII

HOW PANTAGRUEL AND PANURGE PROCLAIMED AND BLAZONED THE MERITS OF TRIBOULET

"By my immortal soul," cried Panurge, "I *will* take a fool. I feel my guts stretching; once upon a time they were taut and constipated. But even as we have chosen the cream of wisdom to question, so let us now consult the flower of folly."

"Triboulet seems to fill the bill," said Pantagruel. "He's the most competent fool I know of."

"And who is Triboulet?"

"The fool to two French monarchs, Louis XII, and later Francis I . . . as wise at thirty as the day he was born . . . ay, a complete fool!"

"An utter and absolute fool," Panurge amended. So they fell to the game of alternate eulogies, vying with one another in qualifying their madman.

"A fool—" said Pantagruel.

"A fool—" said Panurge.

"A fatal fool," said Pantagruel.

"A fool of high tone," said Panurge.

"A natural fool."

"Without sharps or flats," said Panurge. "A fool in C major."

"Celestial," said Pantagruel.

"Worldly," said Panurge.

"A jovial fool, born under the influence of Jupiter."

"A joyous, frolicking fool."

"A fool mercurial," Pantagruel went on, "born under the influence of Mercury, and therefore changeable; under the moon's influence, and therefore lunatic; under the influence of the seven planets, and therefore erratic; under Juno's influence, and therefore ethereal, since she is queen of the upper air; under Septentrio's, and therefore arctic."

"A fool, jaunty and jingling, with pompoms and bells; a fool with tassels on his mortar board—I mean his cap; a fool, laughing, amatory and venereal, being under the influence of Venus, goddess of love. A fool fermented, like all good wine."

"An heroic fool," said Pantagruel.

"Drawn from the mother grape."

"A prime fool!" said Pantagruel.

"Of the first vat."

"Predestined."

"And well-wracked."

"An august fool; a very Cæsar among fools; a fool imperial, royal, patriarchal, original, loyal, ducal, feudal, seignorial, palatine, principal, prætorian and total," said Pantagruel.

Panurge replied:

"A fool original and noble, a very pope among fools; a fool consistorian, conclavist, bullist, synodal, episcopal, doctoral, monachal, fiscal, extravagant, a fool of the first tonsure."

"A genial fool—"

"A penial fool—"

"A fool curial," said Pantagruel, picking up Panurge's papal nomenclature. "A fool primipile, or of the first water, triumphant, vulgar, domestic and exemplary."

"A fool commensal," Panurge came back at him, "a fool graduated at the head of his class; a fool caudatory, or tailgrown; a fool supererogatory, collateral and *a latere,* as the loftiest papal nuncio is termed."

"Aulic," said Pantagruel, "pertaining to a court."

"Migratory . . . here to-day and gone to-morrow," said Panurge.

"Civil, popular, familiar, notable and favorized," Pantagruel continued.

"A bird, following its mother from branch to branch; a haggardhawk, the fiercest of the species; a gentlehawk, bred for the use of noblemen; a nethawk, with wondrous speckling; a very thief."

"A Latin fool—" said Pantagruel.

"A hawk trimmed, plumed, tailed yet ever growing anew in coat, feather, scut!"

"Ordinary, formidable, transcendant, sovereign, special, metaphysical. . . ."

"Wild, rambling, square-jawed; supercocolicantious, or prouder than a cock. A fool corollary. . . ."

"Ecstatic."

"Sublime."

"Categoric."

"Crimson."

"Decuman," said Pantagruel, "large, powerful, fit for the tenth cohort, the pride of the Roman army."

"Decuman? Dyed in grain!"

"Officious."

"A featherduster fool to polish ceilings!"

"Algoristic, mathematical, algebraic, Talmudic, cabbalistic: compendium of Moorish and Jewish science," Pantagruel proposed.

"A fool fit to be caged: I must invoke the vocabulary of Logic to qualify this fool: a modal fool; a fool of second intention. Talmudic, did you say? I find him a *Tacuin,* an Arab maker of almanacs."

"Amalgamized."

"Heteroclite."

"Compendious."

"The sum of all fools," said Panurge.

"He is an abbreviated—"

"An abbreviator!"

"He is a hyperbolic, autonomatic or emphatic fool; a fool allegorical; a fool tropological, who interprets the Bible morally; a fool pleonasmic, or redundant," Pantagruel proclaimed.

"He is a Moorish and Morris dance fool, a well-blown fool, a fool mandatory, behooded and degreed, a titulary fool, if ever I saw one."

"Do you know what a capital fool is?" Pantagruel asked. "Or a fool cerebral, cordial, intestine?"

"Do you know what a skulking fool is?" Panurge replied. "Or a fool crabbed, penicocko-powerful, and clutch-loose, as a weary falcon?"

"Hepatic, or choleric with excess of bile—"

"Well-hung, with excess of ballocks—"

"Splenetic, or hypochondriac, a well-known symptom of folly."

"A sad-faced, sour, scribbledy-dibbledy fool."

"Phlegmatic and full of wind."

"Blown out . . . evaporated!"

"A fool legitimate—"

"A fool culinary, a scullion-cullion fool!"

"An azimuthal fool," said Pantagruel, "that is, a fool fit to be enclosed in the imperfect circles of Arabian astronomy."

"A fool of tall timber."

"An almicantarathian fool, or one fit to be enclosed, by Arab astronomers, in a circle of the heavenly sphere, parallel to the horizon."

"An andiron fool."

"A fool," said Pantagruel, "proportioned, architraved and pedestalled."

"A greasy, kitchen-mopsy fool, a catarrhal and showy fool."

"A paragon fool."

"A twenty-four carat fool."

"Celebrated, sprightly, solemn, annual, festival, recreational, villager, humorous, pleasing, privileged, rustic and ordinary: a fool of all hours and pastimes."

"A fool," Panurge parried, "bizarre, cross-grained and cross-purposed, a fool clad in a martingale, a fool with maggot and bauble, a fool of great price. A vast, trippering, doddering, superannuated fool, a fool of rustic, full-bustic, pompoustic inclinations."

"A diapasonal fool," said Pantagruel, "melodious and full of harmony."

"A caparisonal fool," said Panurge, "malodorous and full of hominy."

"Resolute—"

"Unmovable—"

"Hieroglyphical—"

"A riddle and puzzle fool," said Panurge.

"An authentic, valuable and precious fool."

"A model, hooded and double-brimmed fool; a fool damascened, beswished and bewashed; a fool in Persian satins."

"Fool fanatic," said Pantagruel, "fantastic, lymphatic and panic fool."

"Fool barytoning!"

"Fool far-fetched!"

"Fool farting!"

"Fool, never tedious!"

"Fool, tried and tested," said Panurge.

"Just as the Romans of yore named their Feast of Fools the Quirinales," said Pantagruel, "so we might inaugurate the Tribouletanes in France."

Panurge replied that if all fools wore saddlecruppers, their buttocks would be very sore indeed.

"Were he the god Fatuus, of whom we spoke before, the husband of the goddess Fatua, his father would be Bonadies, or Good Day, his grandmother Bonadea, or Good Goddess!"

"If all fools ambled along," said Panurge, "though Triboulet's legs are twisted, he would win by a good fathom. Let us go to him without delay; I expect great things of him."

Pantagruel objected that he must attend Bridlegoose's trial. But whilst he was across the Loire in Miralingua, he would send Carpalim to Blois, to fetch Triboulet.

Carpalim was immediately dispatched on this errand. Pantagruel, Panurge, Epistemon, Friar John, Gymnastes, Rhizotomos and several others then headed for Miralingua.

XXXIX

HOW PANTAGRUEL ATTENDED THE TRIAL OF JUDGE BRIDLEGOOSE, WHO DECIDED CASES ACCORDING TO THE TURN OF THE DICE

NEXT day, at the appointed hour, Pantagruel reached Miralingua. The president, senators and counsellors invited them to attend the hearing; Judge Bridlegoose was to defend and justify the sentence he had pronounced against Touchcircle, a tax-assessor. To the court of the hundred judges, this decision of Bridlegoose's had not seemed at all equitable. Pantagruel accepted their invitation, and, going in, found Bridlegoose seated in the middle of the enclosure.

As the case progressed, Bridlegoose, for all argument, replied only that he was getting old, and that his sight was failing; he cited, into the bargain, various other vexations and calamities brought on by senescence. As legal proof, Bridlegoose begged to quote: *not. per Archid.* D LXXXVI, *c. tanta.*

(Here he invoked the division of canon law, noted by the Archdeacon Guido Baisius of Reggio. His quotation hinged on the case of a bishop, who had worked in the fields before saying mass, and who was excused by the Pope on the score of old age.)

Unable to read the dice as clearly as in the past, Bridlegoose compared himself to Isaac, who, being old and dimsighted, mistook Jacob for Esau. Thus, having to decide the case in question, he had doubtless taken a four for a five; he begged to assure the learned judges that he had used a very small pair of dice. But, according to the applying of law, the imperfections of nature must not be considered criminal, as is supported by *ff. de re milit., l. qui cum uno; ff. de reg. jur., l. fere; ff. de edil. ed. per totum; ff. de term. mo.; l. Divus Adrianus; resolu. per Lud. Ro. in l.: si vero, ff. solu. matri.*

(Here, I may add, that *ff* stands for the *Digest*, a vast codification of Roman civil law made by Tribonian at the request of the Emperor Justinian in the sixth century; rediscovered in the twelfth, it served as foundation for the teaching of all jurisprudence. The principal part of the *Digest* was the *Pandects*; thus *ff* is perhaps a corruption of the Greek *p* or *π* . . . *l* stands for *lex*, or law . . . *c* for the *Code* of Justinian . . . *d* for the *Decrees* of Gratian.)

This learned argument made use of all manner of authorities: the divine Hadrian's punishment for removing milestones, to be administered with a regard to the delinquent's age . . . the law concerning men born with one testicle . . . the comment of Ludovicus Romanus (Pontanus of Spoleto), a fifteenth-century commentator.

Anyone, therefore, who failed to observe these legal rulings, would not be accusing the man, but rather Nature, as is evident in *l. maximum vitium C. de lib. praeter*, a law establishing a certain equality among male and female heirs.

"Now, my friend," said Trinquamelle, or Blusterer, the Lord High President of the Court, "what dice are you speaking of?"

"The dice of sentences and judgments, or, in Latin, *alea judiciorum*, the hazards of decisions," Bridlegoose explained. "Let me invoke *doct. 26. q. ij. c. Sors; l. nec emptio, ff. de contrah, empt; l. quod debetur, ff. de pecul., et ibi Bartol.*"

(Here Bridlegoose offered laws, together with the comment of Bartolo, professor at Pisa in the fifteenth century.)

"You, too, gentlemen, employ these dice in your sovereign court, as do all other judges when sitting upon a case. Henri Ferrandat of Nevers, in his comments on the *Decretals*, and also *no. gl. in c. fin. de sortil.*, and *l. sed cum ambo, ff. de judi., ubi doct.* state plainly that fate or hazard is a worthy, honest, useful and necessary element in the decision of differences and lawsuits. This is brought out even more clearly in *Bal., Bart.* and *Alex.*, in *C. communia, de l. Si duo.*"

(Here Bridlegoose was quoting Baldus, Bartolo and Alexandro Tartagno, all Italian jurisconsults, and the law recommending the drawing of lots when several co-heirs could not agree.)

"And how do you judge, my friend?" Blusterer inquired.

"I shall answer you briefly," said Bridlegoose, "thus following the instructions of the law *Ampliorem, in refutatoriis, C. de appela* and the *Gl. l. j. ff. quod met, cau*, which enjoin brevity. Ay, gentlemen:

gaudent brevitate moderni, we moderns rejoice in brevity. Well then, gentlemen, I judge just as you yourselves do, according to the custom of the judicatory office, which our law commands us always to observe. Here I invoke, *ut, no. extra. de consuet., c. ex literis, et ibi Innoc.,* a body of rules made by Pope Gregory IX.

"First, I view and review, read and re-read, ponder, weigh, thumb and digest the bills of complaint, subpoenas, appearance by proxy, reports of hearings, investigations, instruments of deposition, petitions, articles of evidence, allegations, rejoinders, rebuttals, requests, inquests, surrejoinders, surrebuttals, confirmation of former testimony, acts, writs, bulls, exceptions taken, grievances, objections, counter-objections . . . confrontation of witnesses and accused; confrontation of the various co-accused . . . certificates, libels and apostoles requesting the judge to refer the case to another court . . . letters of attorney; royal letters; instruments of compulsion, forcing a clerk to produce a document . . . declinatories, questioning the court's competence . . . anticipatories, arguing the opponent's probable plea . . . references to other jurisdictions . . . returns of cases to the judges that had referred them . . . conclusions, accessory contestations, appointments, appeals, confessions, notifications or executions of sentence . . . and all other such spiceries and sweetmeats. . . ."

The last terms referred to the judge's bribes or overcharges, which made law so profitable a pursuit.

"Ay," said Bridlegoose, "I do this as any good judge should, in conformance with *no Spec. de ordinario,* III, *et tit. de offi. om. ju., fi., et de rescriptis praesenta.,* I, as Speculator, or Guillaume Durand, indicates in his repertory of canon law.

"On the end of the table in my chambers, I place all the bags containing the defendant's plea, and I allow him the first hazard of the dice, just as you gentlemen do, according to *et est not., l. Favorabiliores, ff. de reg. jur., et in c. cum sunt eod. tit. lib.* VI, which says: *Cum sunt partium jura obscura, reo favendum est potius quam actori,* when the law is obscure, the defendant is to be favored rather than the plaintiff. This famous maxim from the *Sixte,* added by Pope Boniface VIII to the five books of Gregory IX's *Decretals,* I interpret literally.

"This done—just like yourselves, gentlemen—I place the plaintiff's dossier at the other end of the table, *visum visu,* face to face, for *opposita, juxta se posita, magis elucescunt, ut not. in l. i. videamus, ff. de his qui sunt sui vel alie. juri. et in l. munerum j. mixta ff. de muner. et honor.* Then I throw the dice for the plaintiff, too."

"But, my friend," Blusterer asked, "how do you determine the obscurity of arguments offered by the litigants?"

"Exactly as you, gentlemen," Bridlegoose replied. "When there are many bags on either end of the table, I use my small dice, just as you do, gentlemen, in accordance with the law: *Semper in stipulationibus, ff. de reg. jur,* and the capital, poetical law called *q. eod. tit.* which begins with a hexameter: *Semper in obscuris quod minimum est sequimur,* and which tells us, when in doubt, to take the less consequential course. This rule, moreover, has been adopted by canon law, *in c., in obscuris, eod. tit. lib.* VI.

"Of course I have other large, handsome and most suitable dice, which I use—like you gentlemen—when the matter is more liquid, that is to say, when the bags bearing the pleas are lighter."

"But when you had done all this," Blusterer insisted, "how did you pass sentence, my friend?"

"Just like yourselves, gentlemen," said Bridlegoose. "I decided in favor of the party who won at the judiciary, tribonian and prætorial throw of dice. This is recommended by our laws, *ff. qui po. in pig., l. potior. leg. creditor., C. de consul., l.* I, *et de reg. jur., in* VI: *Qui prior est tempore potior est jure,* the first comer has the best legal case."

XL

BRIDLEGOOSE'S EXPLANATION OF WHY HE EXAMINED THE DOCUMENTS OF CASES HE JUDGED BY DICING

"VERY well, my friend," said Blusterer, "but, since you pass sentence by the throw and hazard of dice, why do you not settle the matter then and there, the very same day and hour the litigants appear before you? Of what use are the papers and writs in the litigants' bags?"

"I find these documents as useful as you, gentlemen, find like documents, in similar instances. They are helpful in three exquisite, requisite and authentic manners: first, for formality; secondly, as physical exercise; thirdly, from considerations of time."

Bridlegoose then went on to explain.

(1) To begin with, form must be observed. If not, whatever a judge decided was valueless, as proved by *Spec. tit. de instr. edi. et tit. de rescrip praesent.* Besides, the gentlemen of the court knew only too well that, in judicial proceedings, formalities destroyed the materiality and substance of the cases. Bridlegoose supported this statement by *forma mutata mutatur substantia, ff. ad exhib., l. Julianus ff. ad leg. falcid., l. Si is qui quadringenta, et extra., de deci., c. ad audientiam, et de celebra. miss., c. in quadam.* In other words: substance, a permanent element, changed in nature with a change of form.

(2) Next, all these documents served Bridlegoose, as they served his honorable judges, here assembled, in the way of honest and healthful exercise. He here quoted the late Master Othoman Vadare, an excellent physician—as the court would say *C. de comit. et archi., lib.* XII, referring to the law, in the twelfth book of Justinian's *Code*, concerning the physicians and surgeons in the pay of the emperor or a municipality. Well, Othoman Vadare had frequently told Bridlegoose that lack of bodily exercise was the sole cause of the unhealthiness and short lives of all judges, including the worshipful court now hearing him, Bridlegoose.

Bartolo noted this admirably in *l. 1. C. de senten. quae pro eo quod*, the very first law in the *Code*. Thus, both his colleagues now trying him, and himself, at the bar, were justified in taking such exercise. *Accessorium natura sequitur principalis, de reg. jur. lib.* VI *et l. cum principalis, et l. nihil dolo., ff. eod. titu.; ff. de fidejusso., l. fidejussor, et extra. de offi. de leg., c. j.* conceded certain honest and recreative sport. Moreover, *ff. de al. lus. et aleat., l. solent, et autent. ut omnes obediant, in princ., coll.* VII. *et ff. de praescript. verb., l. si gratuitam, et l. j. C. de spect., lib.* XI, concurred in this statement. Again, St. Thomas Aquinas *in secunda secundae, quaest.* CLXVIII stated that there is much to be gained from games. And Dom Alberic de Rosata, the fourteenth-century canonist of Bergamo, *fuit magnus practicus,* and a solemn doctor, agreed, on the authority of Barbatia in *prin. consil.* . . . The reason was exposed clearly in *per gl. in proemio ff.* § *ne autem tertii*, which ordered third-year students to keep a holiday celebrating the memory of Papinian.

Interpone tuis interdum guadia curis, was what Dionysius Cassius said, in his *Distichs*, a collection of aphorisms in Latin hexameters. Bridlegoose need not translate for his judges an axiom known by every student in Europe.

Once, indeed, in the year 1489, Bridlegoose had had a financial matter to settle in the High Court of Financial Jurisdiction. By particular, peculiar (and pecuniary!) permission of the usher, he gained access to the Lord High Treasurers. My Lords of Miralingua, Bridlegoose's present judges, knew well that *pecunias obediunt omnia*, money answereth all things, as *Ecclesiastes* puts it. On this score, see *Bald. in l. Singularia, ff. si certum pet., et Salic., in l. recepticia, C. de constit. pecun., et Card., in Cle.* I *de baptis.*, to cite the authority of Salycetus, and of Jean Lemoyne. On entering, Bridlegoose found these lofty judges playing the old game of fly, a schoolboy favorite, in which one person plays the part of the fly, and the others strike at him, as though to drive him off. This salubrious exercise was indulged in before or after dinner.

To be sure, it was altogether indifferent to Bridlegoose at which time they chose to play, *hic not*. (It must here be observed that this game is honest, healthy, time-hallowed and legal.) *A Musco inventore, de quo C., de petit. haered., l. si post motam.* And *Muscarii* (which some take to mean musk-vendors, but others to mean flylayers from *musca*, the Latin for fly) were excusable by law in *l.* I. *C., de excus. artif., lib.* x.

Bridlegoose recalled that Master Tielman Picquet was "it"; he would never forget Picquet's laughter, as the gentlemen of the court ruined their caps, swatting him with them. Amid guffaws of mirth, he told them that this banging of their caps did not excuse them, when they returned home, from satisfying their wives, according to *c.* I. *extra., de praesump., et ibi gl.*

"Now, *resolutorie loquendo*," said Bridlegoose, "I should say, as you gentlemen might, that there is no exercise more fragrant, in this jurisprudential universe, than the emptying of bags, the thumbing of briefs, the consultation of documents, the filling of baskets, and the examination of cases. I cite for confirmation *ex Bart. et Jo.*

de Pra., in l. falsa de condit. et demon. ff., invoking both Bartolo, as before, and Joannes de Prato, the Florentine jurist of the last century."

(3) Bridlegoose's last reason for studying the documents involved a question of time. Like the gentlemen now sitting in judgment upon him, he realized that time brought all things to maturity. Time made everything clear; time was the father of truth, as Aulus Gellius' old poet said: *Gl. in l.* I. *C. de servit., Autent., de restit. et ea quae pa., et Spec. tit. de requis. cons*, merely went to confirm this.

"Accordingly, like yourselves, gentlemen, I put off, delay and postpone my definitive sentence, so that the suit, having been thoroughly sifted, winnowed and thrashed out, may, in process of time, attain its full maturity. Thus, when the fatal throw of the dice takes place, the condemned party will bear its misfortune more cheerfully, according to *no. glo. ff. de excu. tut., l. Tria onera*:

> *Portatur leviter, quod portat quisque libenter.*
>
> *A load borne willingly is light to bear.*"

On the contrary, sentence passed when the suit is crude, unripe, and in its earliest stages, would cause the same discomfort as, according to the physicians, prematurely lancing an abscess, or purging the human body of a peccant humor before its digestion. Was it not written in *Autent., Haec constit. in inno, const., prin.*, and repeated in *gl. in c. Caeterum, extra., de jura. calum*, that:

> *Quod medicamenta morbis exhibent, hoc jura negotiis.*

Further, Nature admonished us to pluck fruits when they were ripe (see *Instit. de re. div. is ad quem, et ff. de act. empt. l. Julianus*) . . . to marry our daughters when they were ripe (see *ff. de donat inter vir. et uxor. l. cum hic status, si quia sponsa, et 27 q.,* I. *c., sicut dict gl.*):

> *Jammatura thoris plenis adoleverat annis Virginitas.*
>
> *Virginity, now ripe in course of years, nuptial and full.* . . .

In conclusion, then, Nature warned us to do nothing save in full maturity, according to XXXIII. *q.* II. *ult. ex* XXXIII *d. c. ult.*

XLI

BRIDLEGOOSE TELLS THE STORY OF THE MAN WHO SETTLED CASES

"IN this connection," Bridlegoose continued, "I recall a man living at Smarve, near Ligugé, in the days I was a law student at Poitiers, under Professor Axiom, *Brocardium juris.* This man was called Perrin Dandin or, as we should say, Tom Noddy. An honorable soul, who worked his land and sang in the church choir; a fellow of credit, about the age of most of yourselves, gentlemen. Well, Tom Noddy used to say that he had seen and known that great, worthy man, Council of Lateran: indeed, Tom Noddy remembered the large red hat Council of Lateran wore. He had also, he said, seen Council of Lateran's wife, the lady Pragmatic Sanction, with her broad blue satin ribbon and her huge jade beads.

"This worthy man used to settle more lawsuits than were ever tried in the court at Poitiers, in the auditory of Montmorillon, with its hundred parishes, and in the town hall at Parthenay-le-Vieux. Every dissension, difference or wrangle in Chauvigny, Nouaillé, Croutelles, Esgne, Ligugé, La Motte, Lusignan, Vivonne, Mezeaulx, Etables, and neighboring hamlets, was settled by Tom Noddy as by a supreme judge—though remember, he was no judge, but simply an honest man! May I draw your attention, on this head, gentlemen, to *Arg. in l. sed si unius, ff. de jureju., et de verb. oblig., l. continuus.*

"No hog killed in the region, but he had some part of the pork chops and sausage; no banquet, feast or wedding, no gossips' reunion or churching of woman, but he was present; no home or tavern but welcomed him. And why? To reconcile two parties at a variance. For Tom Noddy never settled a difference without first making the disputants drink together, as a token of reconciliation, amity and joy to come, *ut no. per doct., ff. de peri. et comm. rei vend. l.* 1, which deals with the selling of wine.

"Tom Noddy had a son, Stephen or Steve. A lusty, roistering lad (so help me God!) who wanted to follow in his father's footsteps and reconcile litigants, for, as you know:

> *Saepe solet similis filius esse patri,*
> *Et sequitur leviter filia matris iter,*
>
> *The son is wont to be more like his father,*
> *The daughter following her mother, rather.*

"*Gl.*, VI. *q.* I *c.: Si quis; g. de cons., d. v. c.* I. *fin.; et est no. per doct., C. de impu. et aliis subst., l. ult. et l. legitimae, ff. de stat. hom., gl. in l. quod si nolit, ff. de edil. ed., l. quis, C. ad le. Jul. majest. Excipio filios a moniali susceptos ex monacho, per gl. in c. Impudicas,* XXVII *q.* I., bears this out, but excepts the sons and daughters of monks and nuns.

"Indeed, Steve Noddy actually dared assume the title of settler-out-of-court.

"Now he was active and vigilant in this business, for *vigilantibus jura subveniunt, ex. l. pupillus, ff. quae in fraud, cred., et idib. l. non enim, et instit. in procœmio,* to quote a law which justifies the watchful and penalizes the negligent. So much so, that he sniffed a difference, as in *ff. si quad. pau. fec., l. Agaso, gl. in verbo olfecit i. nasum ad culum posuit.*"

Here Bridlegoose referred to the law concerning a groom, whose horse sniffed at a mule, in an innyard. The mule kicked out, breaking the groom's leg. Could the groom sue the master of the mule? The law, defining *olfecit*—sniffed—as "placing nose against arse," ruled that he could.)

"Gentlemen," Bridlegoose went on, "Steve Noddy never got wind of a variance or dispute, but he intruded to accommodate the quarrellers. Now it is written in the *Second Epistle of St. Paul to the Thessalonians* that: *Qui non laborat non manducat,* if any would not work, neither should he eat. Further, *gl. ff. de dam. infect., l. quamvis, et currere* at a great pace:

> *Vetulam compellit egestas;*
>
> *Necessity makes the old hag trot.*

Consult, too, *gl. ff. de lib. agnos., l. Si quis pro qua facit; l. si plures,* C. *de cond. incer.* Yet in these undertakings, Steve Noddy was so unfortunate as to prove unable to settle even the most minor argument. Instead of reconciling the parties, he exasperated and antagonized them further. You know Dionysius Cato's distich, gentlemen:

> *Sermo datur cunctis, animi sapientia paucis,*

and you know *gl. ff. de alie. ju. mu. caus. fa. l.* II.

"The innkeepers of Smarve vowed that, in one year of Steve Noddy's régime, they had not sold as much wine of reconciliation (so they called the Ligugé tipple) as in a half-hour under his father's dispensation.

"Now some time later, Stephen happened to complain to his father, attributing the causes of his failure to the perversity of his contemporaries. The son roundly objected that, had the world formerly proved so wayward, refractory, quarrelsome and irreconcilable, Tom Noddy would not have won the honors and title of a perfect peacemaker. In this, Stephen was wrong, since the law forbids children to reproach their fathers: see *gl. et Bar., l.* III, § *Si quis ff. de condi. ob caus., et autene., de nup.,* § *Sed quod sancitum, coll.* IV.

"Tom Noddy then told his son Stephen that he should do otherwise. The old man quoted:

> *'Quand "oportet" vient en place,*
> *Il convient qu'ainsi se face,*
>
> *When Lord Necessity rules you,*
> *This is the course you should pursue'*

and I, Bridlegoose, draw your attention to *gl.* C. *de appell., l. eos etiam.* There lay the rub, gentlemen. Old Noddy reproached Stephen with never making peace. And why? Because Stephen attempted to handle these cases when they were green, raw, indigestible. Why had Tom Noddy always succeeded? Because he assumed responsibility when the variances were waning, coming to a head, pretty well digested. So says *gl.:*

Dulcior est fructus post multa pericula ductus,

The sweetest fruit an orchard bears is one
Which has known trials to bear and risks to run

as you, gentlemen, know from *l. non moriturus, C. de contrah et comit. stip.*

"Did not Stephen know, Tom Noddy asked, the proverb which pronounced the physician happiest, when summoned at the decline of an illness? Such a malady would run its course, and solve its own problem, even were the medico not called in. Old Tom Noddy's cases would have found their own settlement in a last plea, since the litigants' purses were drained; plaintiff and defense would have given over, since there was no cash in hand to prosecute or defend:

Deficiente pecu, deficit omne, nia.

Money lacking, all is lacking.

"The only thing needed then was a paranymph, to act like the best man at a wedding, or like the sponsor of a candidate for a degree. Let such a man but broach the question of an agreement, and each party would be spared the pernicious shame of believing that the other would accuse it of yielding first, of apologizing because it was in the wrong, of coming to terms because it felt the shoe pinching.

"At such a juncture, old Tom Noddy arrived as seasonably as peas with bacon, or as parsley with fish; here lay his advantage and his luck. And he assured his splendid son that, by following the same system, he could establish peace, or at least make a truce, between the great king Louis XII and the Venetians, or between the Emperor and the Swiss, or between the English and the Scots, or between the Pope and the Duke of Ferrara. Need Tom Noddy go further? Ay, he could, with God's help, reconcile the Turkish sultan and the Persian shah, the Muscovite czar and the Tartar chieftains.

"Tom Noddy impressed this fact upon his son: he would approach these powers when both were weary of war; when their treasuries were empty; when their subjects' purses were drained; when their domains were sold; when their property was mortgaged; when their provisions and munitions were exhausted. Then, at this precise moment, by God or by His Mother! they would be forced to take a breathing spell, to curb the fury of their wicked ambition. Such was the doctrine of *gl.* xxxvii *d. c. S. quando:*

> *Odero si potero; si non, invitus amabo.*

> *If hate I can, I will; but otherwise*
> *Reluctant, I shall look with loving eyes.*"

XLII

HOW LAWSUITS ARE SPAWNED AND HOW THEY ATTAIN FULL GROWTH

BRIDLEGOOSE's address continued as follows:

"That, gentlemen, is why, like yourselves, I temporize, awaiting a lawsuit's maturity and its full growth in all its limbs—that is, in its documents and the bags they are kept in. Here I base my stand upon *Arg. in l. si major., C. commu. divi. et de cons., d.* I. *c. Solennitates, et ibi gl.*

"A suit at its birth seems to me—and to you, also, gentlemen— formless and imperfect. A bear, newborn, has neither feet, nor hands, nor skin, nor hair, nor head; by dint of maternal licking, it attains perfection in all its limbs. See *no. doct., ff. ad leg. Aquil., l.* II, *in fi.* Similarly, like yourselves, gentlemen, I attend the birth of a lawsuit. To begin with, it is shapeless, and without distinct limbs. It consists of but one or two documents; it is, in this state, an ugly beast. But heap writ upon writ, pack and pile brief upon brief, and your lawsuit may be termed full-sinewed and well-boned, since *forma dat esse rei, l. Si is qui, ff. ad. leg.* § *Falci. in. c. cum dilecta, extra., de rescrip.; Barbatia, consil. 12., lib. 2,* and before him *Bald. in c. ulti. extra de consue., et l. Julianus, ff. ad exib.,* and *l. Quaesitum, ff. de lega.* III."

(Here Bridlegoose quoted Barbatia and Petrus Baldus, both Italian jurisconsults of the fifteenth and fourteenth century respectively.)

"The manner of this is set down in *gl. p. q.* I. *c. Paulus:*

Debile principium melior fortuna sequetur.

"Just as you yourselves, gentlemen, the sergeants, ushers, summoners, pettifoggers, attorneys, commissioners, advocates, judges of the peace, tabellions or notaries, clerks, scribes and pedestrian judges (I mean the judges of minor courts compelled to walk to and from the tribunal) *de quibus tit, est lib.* III *Cod.*, draw vigorously and continuously upon the purses of the litigants, licking here and there, until they equip the suits with head, feet, claws, beak, teeth, hands, veins, arteries, nerves, muscles and humors. These are, in so many words, the bags containing their writs, as you may read in *gl. de cons. de* IV. *c. accepisti:*

Qualis vestis erit, talia corda gerit.

"*Hic not*, gentlemen, note here that, in this respect, the litigants are happier than the officers of justice, since *beatius est dare quam accipere, ff. comm., l.* III. *et extra. de celebra. miss., c. cum Marthae, et 24 q. j. c. Odi gl.*:

Affectum dantis pensat censura tonantis.

"In this way, then, lawsuits grow to be well rounded, full of charm and fairly fashioned, or, as the canonical gloss expresses it:

Accipe, sume, cape sunt verba placentia Papae,

To take, accept, receive in goodly measure
Are things that give a Pope the greatest pleasure,

which Alberic de Rosata says more pointedly in *Verb. Roma:*

Roma manus rodit; quas rodere non valet, odit;
Dantes custodit; non dantes spernit et odit.

And why, gentlemen? Simply because:

"*Ad praesens ova cras pullis sunt meliora*, to-day's eggs are better than to-morrow's hens, and one bird in hand is worth two in the bush. This we know from *gl. in l. Cum hi, ff. de transac.* The inconvenience of the contrary is set down in *gl. c. de allu., l. F.*:

> *Cum labor in damno est, crescit mortalis egestas.*
>
> *When work is wasted, human need increases.*

"The true meaning of the word *lawsuit* is something that suits the lawyer; legal procedure means something ceded or yielded *pro*, to the benefit of, the judge. We have a glorious quip to celebrate it:

> *Litigando jura crescunt;*
> *Litigando jus acquiritur;*

and, indeed, the body of the law swells as cases are pleaded, just as the bodies of lawyer and judge swell, too. *Item gl. in c. illud, ext. de praesumpt., et C. de prob., l. instrumenta, l. Non nudis;*

> *Et, cum non prosunt singula, multa juvant,*
>
> *Singly, things fail; united they prevail.*"

"Very good, very good," Blusterer interjected. "But, my friend, pray tell the court how you proceed in a criminal case when the guilty party was seized in *flagrante crimine?*"

"Exactly as you, gentlemen," Bridlegoose made answer. "I permit the plaintiff to leave the court; I urge him, as an introductory measure, to take a long sleep. Before reappearing in my presence, he is warned to submit a valid, duly certified statement of his sleep, following *gl. 32 q.* VII, *c. Si quis cum,*

> *Quandoque bonus dormitat Homerus*

or, as Horace says, even Homer nods now and again.

"This mere action brings on some further development, which, in turn, produces still another, just as, link by link, you fashion a coat-of-mail. Gradually, document by document, the suit grows, until, eventually, it is perfectly formed in all its members. I then return to my dice. Nor, indeed, do I intervene at this point without considerable reason or experience."

In confirmation, Bridlegoose told a story about a certain Gascon in camp at Stockholm. Gratianauld, the fellow was called; he hailed from St. Sever. Having gambled away all his pay, he was furious, for, as Bridlegoose's judges knew, *pecunia est alter sanguis*, money is a man's very lifeblood, as is proved by *Anto. de Butrio in c. accedens.*, II, *extra., ut lit. non contest., et Bald. in l. si tuis., C. de op. li. per no., et l. advocati, C. de advo. div. jud.: Pecunia est vita hominis et optimus fidejussor in necessitatibus:* money is man's life, and his best counsellor in an emergency.

The gambling ended, Gratianauld then said loudly in his Gascon dialect:

"*Pao cap de bious, hillotz, que maulx de pipe bous tresbyre; ares que pergudes sont les mies bingt et quouatte baguettes, ta pla donnerien picz, trucz et patactz. Sey degun de bous aulx qui boille truquar ambe iou à belz embiz?*"

This meant:

"God's head, my hearties, may the blindest drunkenness ever distilled in barrel knock you over! Now that I have lost my two dozen coppers, I might as well give you what for, with fist, cuff and kick! Is there one man among you, who will fight me, man to man? By God, I challenge the lot of you!"

Since no one answered him, he passed on to the camp of the hundred-pounders or German lansquenets, repeating the same words, and inviting them to combat. But they merely replied:

"*Der Guascongner thut schich usz mitt eim jedem ze schlagen, aber er ist geneigter zu staelen; darumb, lieben fravven, hend serg zu inuerm hausraut:* the Gascon makes as if to fight everybody, but he is more apt to steal from us; therefore, dear wives, keep an eye on our luggage."

So none of their race offered to take on our Gascon.

Next, he repaired to the camp of the French adventurers, speaking as before, and gaily challenging them, to the accompaniment of various Gasconado gambols. Here, too, no one replied.

At last, at the end of the camp, he lay down, close to the tent of fat Christian, Knight of Crissé. Here he fell fast asleep.

Suddenly, a French freelance, who had lost all his money too, determined to fight with the Gascon.

> *Ploratur lachrymis amissa pecunia veris.*
>
> *With genuine tears, he wept his vanished cash.*

Bridlegoose here cited *glos. de paenitent. dist. 3, c. Sunt plures.*

Having roamed the camp with drawn sword, the Frenchman at last came upon the sleeping Gascon.

"Ho, lad!" he cried, "get up, in the devil's name! I've lost all my money just as you have. Let us fight lustily and have at one another, clapperclaw. Take care my sword isn't longer than your rapier!"

The Gascon, in a daze, replied:

"*Cap de sainct Arnault, quau seys tu, qui me rebeillez? Que mau de taoverne te gyre. Ho, sainct Siobé, cap de Guascoigne, ta pla dormis iou, quand aquoest taquain me bingut estée.*"

Which, being interpreted, meant:

"By St. Arnold's noddle, who are you, waking me up like that? May a drunken rheumatism floor you! Ho, by St. Sever, patron of Gascony, I was sound asleep when the scoundrel woke me up!"

Again, the Frenchman invited him to fight, but the Gascon replied:

"My poor lad, I would make mincemeat of you, now that I have rested. Lie down there and take a nap, as I did. Afterwards, we can fight."

Having forgotten his losses, he had lost all his pugnacity. In conclusion, instead of fighting and probably killing each other, they went off and drank together, each pawning his sword to do so.

"It was sleep," Bridlegoose wound up, "which accomplished this miracle, and pacified the arrant fury of two contentious champions. Here I remind you, gentlemen, of the golden words of Jean André in *c. ult. de sent. et re judic., libro sexto: Sedendo et quiescendo fit anima prudens*, the spirit is made wise by rest and repose."

XLIII

HOW PANTAGRUEL VINDICATED BRIDLEGOOSE'S JUDGMENT BY DICE

WHEN Bridlegoose had stopped talking, Blusterer ordered him to withdraw from the court. This was done. Then Blusterer addressed Pantagruel:

"O most august prince, this parliament, sitting as the highest court of justice, and the marquisate of Miralingua, which it represents, are mightily beholden to you. We are beholden, not only for your generous benefactions, but also for the sound judgment and the admirable learning, with which Almighty God, dispenser of all good things, has endowed you. Reason therefore demands that we ask you for your decision in this extraordinary, paradoxical and unparalleled case. Bridlegoose, in your presence, sight and hearing, has confessed that he passed judgment, according to the turn of the dice. We humbly beseech you to pass whatever sentence you may deem just and equitable."

"Gentlemen," Pantagruel replied, "you know very well that, in my condition, I can scarcely profess to pass judgment in matters of controversy. However, since you are pleased to pay me such honor, instead of acting as judge, allow me to act as suppliant.

"I observe, in the person of Bridlegoose, certain virtues which, on their own account, would seem to merit pardon. In the first place, gentlemen, he is an old man. Secondly, consider his simplicity. Both age and simplicity are, I should say, qualities deserving of pardon and excuse by our own laws. In the third place, I find yet another legal reason that pleads in Bridlegoose's favor. Why not let this one and only error of his be washed out, effaced, and annihilated in the immense sea of the equitable decisions he has handed down in the past? Why not forget it, and remember the forty long years of a career, during which no single reprehensible act has ever been brought up against him? It is as though I were to throw one drop of salt water into the river Loire: no one would feel it, no one would recognize it as salty. I cannot help thinking that God's intervention was manifest, since the whole series of Bridlegoose's decrees, before this last one, was approved and ratified by your venerable and sovereign court. I might add that He often wishes His glory to appear in the dulling of the wise, in the fall of the mighty, in the exalting of the meek and humble.

"You mentioned obligations you owed my family; I do not recognize them. I prefer to invoke the time-hallowed affection you have known us to bear you, on either side of the Loire, in the maintenance of your dignity and office. On that score, and omitting the three legal considerations I established before, I would beg you, for once, to grant Bridlegoose your pardon. Conditionally, I hasten to add; and on the following conditions.

"First, he shall give or promise satisfaction to the party wronged by his sentence. (I will provide for this myself, and amply.) Secondly, I suggest you appoint a young, learned, wise, skilful and honorable attorney, to assist him in his judiciary office. Let this junior officer's deliberation and counsel decide finally, henceforth, all cases brought before the court.

"If, of course, you decide to remove Bridlegoose wholly from the bench, I beg you to make me a free present and gift of him. Within my realm and dominion, I can find room and place to employ him and utilize his services.

"In conclusion, gentlemen, I shall implore Almighty God, our beneficent creator, and the dispenser of all blessings, to maintain you forever in His mercy and grace."

Concluding, Pantagruel bowed to the court and withdrew from the hall. At the door, Panurge, Epistemon, Friar John and the rest were waiting for him; they mounted their horses and returned to Gargantua.

On the way, Pantagruel related the story of Bridlegoose's trial, point by point. Friar John said he had known Tom Noddy in the days when he lived at the Abbey of Fontenay-le-Comte, under the noble Abbot Ardillon. Gymnastes testified that Tom Noddy was in the tent of the fat Christian, Chevalier de Crissé, when the Gascon challenged the French adventurer. Panurge displayed incredulity at the success of Bridlegoose's aleatory justice over so long a period. Epistemon said:

"A similar story is told of a certain Provost of Montlhéry. But what extraordinary luck to continue successfully for so many years! I would not be amazed at one or two chance decisions, especially in ambiguous, equivocal, intricate, perplexing and obscure cases. But forty years . . . !"

XLIV

PANTAGRUEL'S STRANGE TALE OF THE PERPLEXITIES OF HUMAN JUDGMENT

PANTAGRUEL then told them the following story of a controversy debated before Caius Dolabella, proconsul in Asia.

A married woman gave birth to a child named Abeecee. Shortly after her husband's death, she married again, bearing his successor a son, named Eefgee. Now the affection that stepfathers and stepmothers bear children of earlier marriages is proverbial. In this case, it ran true to form. The stepfather and his own son trapped Abeecee in an ambush, and killed him.

Having discovered their treachery and wickedness, the mother determined to punish them; accordingly, she slew both, thus avenging her firstborn. She was at once apprehended and brought before Caius Dolabella. There, unabashed, she faced the issue squarely, confessing her crime, and maintaining that she was logically and legally justified. Such, then, was the crux of the trial.

The proconsul found the problem so thorny that he was at a loss. The woman's crime was, to be sure, a most serious one, since she had killed her second husband and their son. Yet the cause of this double murder seemed to Dolabella to be quite natural, and grounded upon the rights of nations. Had they not premeditated the murder of Abeecee? And why? Not because he had insulted or injured them, but solely to possess his inheritance.

In order to settle the case, Dolabella sent to the Areopagites at Athens, asking them their opinion. This court, for reply, suggested that, in a hundred years, the contestants be personally cited before them, to reply to certain questions which had been left out of the record. It amounted to saying that they were so perplexed at so inextricable a problem, that they were at a loss as to what to say or do.

"Whatever happened," said Pantagruel, "judgment by dice could not have proved wrong. If luck had gone against the wife after all, she deserved to be punished for taking into her hands a vengeance that belonged to the state. If luck had favored her, the decision would have seemed to be based upon the wrong done her, and her mad grief. The only thing that astonishes me is how Bridlegoose was able to remain lucky for so many years."

"I must own, I could not answer your question categorically," said Epistemon. "But, conjecturally, I would attribute Bridlegoose's luck in his decisions to a favorable aspect of the heavens, and to the intervention of spiritual forces. Bridlegoose was kindly and sincere; he mistrusted his knowledge and capacity; he knew the antinomies and contradictions of laws, decrees, statutes and ordinances. He was also aware of the trickery, by which the infernal calumniator transforms himself into an angel of light, through the person of his minions: dishonest lawyers, attorneys, counsellors and other like tools. He knew Satan could turn black into white, make each of two parties believe itself right. Has the most shadowy case ever lacked a lawyer to carry it into court? How else would lawsuits flourish in this, our world? Were it not so, the equitable judge would commend himself humbly to God; he would invoke the help of heavenly grace; he would be governed by the sacrosanct spirit, by chance, by the perplexity of the definitive sentence. By this lot, he would seek counsel of his decree and of his own good pleasure, which we call an unbiased judgment of the court. Ay, and what I called spiritual forces—the motory intelligences—would make the dice fall the way of the upright party in a lawsuit; they would support justice, maintaining the righteous in his cause, as the rabbis have it. In this way, chance would harbor no harm; on the contrary, through dice, the divine spirit would work to dissipate the doubts and anxieties of men."

Epistemon realized that the officials of the Miralinguan parliament of Miralingua were obviously iniquitous and corrupt. Yet he refused to think, say or believe that they could, under any circumstance, consider judgment by hazard worse than such judgment as they themselves, with their bloody hands and perverse hearts, might possibly decree.

What made the abuse even more glaring was that their jurisdiction was ruled by Tribonian, an evil, perfidious barbarian; a man so corrupt, malign and iniquitous as to sell laws, edicts, bills, constitutions and ordinances at public auction, cash down, to the highest bidder. Piece by piece, scrap by scrap, Tribonian had drawn up their mincemeat code, suppressing and abolishing the whole law, the meat and body and spirit of right. For he feared that the latter might remain permanent, like the works of ancient jurisconsults, as immortalized in the Twelves Tables and the Prætorian edicts. This would have exposed to the entire world his dishonesty and baseness.

Therefore, it would often prove better—or less harmful, at any rate—for parties at variance at law, to walk upon caltrops (spikes set on the ground to maim cavalry horses) than to appeal to such courts for rightful redress.

Indeed, Cato, in his time, wished and advised that the law courts be paved with caltrops.

XLV

HOW PANURGE SOUGHT COUNSEL OF TRIBOULET

Six days later, Pantagruel returned. Simultaneously, Triboulet arrived by water from Blois. Panurge presented the fool with a hog's bladder, blown up to capacity, and resonant with the dried peas inside . . . with a wooden sword, lavishly gilt . . . with a small pouch, made of a turtle's shell . . . with a wicker-covered bottle, full of Breton wine, the red stock pressed from the stout grape . . . and with a quarter of Blandureau apples, a sweet, white variety. . . .

"My God!" said Carpalim. "He is mad as a cabbage-apple; a huge head, a slim neck, sure signs of insanity!"

Triboulet girded the sword about him, slung the pouch around his shoulder, ate a few apples, and drained the wine down to the last drop. Gazing curiously at him, Panurge said:

"I've seen ten thousand francsworth of fools, but I never saw one drink more heartily and deeply."

With which, in the most elegant rhetoric, Panurge set forth the object of this interview. But before he had finished, Triboulet dealt him a blow between the shoulders, handed him the empty bottle, flicked him across the nose with the bladder and, for all answer, wagged his head fiercely, saying:

"By God, God, mad fool, crazy fool, beware the monk, Buzançay hornpipe!"

The fool then moved away from the company, and played with the bladder, delighting in the melodious click of the peas inside! Strive as they would, it was impossible to get a word out of him. When Panurge insisted, Triboulet unsheathed his wooden sword, and tried to pink him.

"A pretty number I drew!" said Panurge. "And what a solution to my problem! He's stark mad, there's no doubt of it. But the man who brought him here is madder still. And I'm maddest of all, to have confided in him!"

"Your second point is aimed point-blank at me," said Carpalim.

"Without undue excitement," Pantagruel suggested, "let us consider his words and gestures. As I do so, I cannot but feel they hold portentous mysteries; the more I ponder this, the less I marvel at the Turks, who respect such naturals as devoutly as they do their monks and prophets. Did you notice how he shook and wagged his head before opening his mouth? By the teachings of ancient philosophers, by the lore of magicians, by the comments of legal experts, you can judge that this motion betrayed his seizure and possession by the prophetic spirit. You know well that a small head cannot hold a large brain. Well, this spirit, suddenly entering into a slight substance, caused this commotion. To what do physicians ascribe bodily tremor? On one hand, to the weight and violent impetuosity of the load carried; on the other hand, to the imbecility of the carrying organ."

Pantagruel supported his statement by affirming that a person who had fasted could not hold a great beaker full of wine in his hand without trembling. Similarly, of old, the Pythian prophetess, who, before vouchsafing an oracle, used invariably to shake a branch of her domestic laurel. By the same token, the Emperor Heliogabalus, wishing to earn a reputation as a soothsayer, appeared publicly, at several festivals and among his fanatical eunuchs, shaking his head violently. (Lampridius vouched for the anecdote.)

Plautus, in his *Asinaria*, declared that Saurias walked abroad wagging his head as though distracted and out of his mind. All who met him were terrified. Elsewhere, too, Plautus explained why Charmides shook *his* head.

Catullus told how the Mænads, priestesses and votaries of Bacchus, demented prophetesses bearing ivy-boughs in their hands, used to shake their heads incessantly. Among the Gauls, the gelded priests of Cybele did likewise, as they celebrated their rites; hence her name, for the ancient theologians told us that the word κυβιστᾶν meant to turn, twist or to shake the head, to be wry-necked.

Livy, too, wrote that during the Bacchanals in Rome, both men and women seemed to vaticinate as the result of a certain sudden shaking and convulsion of the body which they affected. For the common voice of philosophers and public opinion agreed that the gift of prediction was never granted by Heaven, unaccompanied by a fury and spasm of the body, a burning and shaking. This occurred not only when the body received this gift, but also later, when it declared and published it.

"Indeed," Pantagruel concluded, "the celebrated jurist Julian—or it might have been Vivian—deserves mention here. They told him of a slave who frequented mad, witless people, and who had been known to prophesy, but without shaking his head. Julian replied that his failing to do so proved the fellow sane.

"Do not schoolmasters and pedagogues to-day shake their disciples' heads, as you might swing a pot by its handles? Ay, they tweak and pull the lads' ears—the Egyptian sages held that the ears were consecrated to the memory—in order to bring them back to their senses. For, very often, the schoolboy's fancy turns to strange topics; disordinate and abhorrent affections make him wild. So the magister must shake him back into sound philosophical grooves. Virgil acknowledged the truth of this in his account of Apollo Cynthius' trepidation."

XLVI

HOW PANTAGRUEL AND PANURGE RESPECTIVELY INTERPRETED TRIBOULET'S WORDS

"HE says you are a fool, and what kind of a fool? A mad fool, who, in his declining years, seeks to bind and enslave himself by wedlock. 'Beware the monk,' said he. By my honor, it is some monk will make you cuckold. I pledged my honor—the most precious thing I own— that this is true; and I would still do so, were I the sole and pacific dictator of Europe, Africa and Asia.

"Note how I rely upon the mad wisdom of our wise madman, our morosoph, our sophomore, Triboulet. The other oracles and responses signified that you would be made cuckold; but none particularized the adulterous auspices under which you would be hornified. An infamous, a flagrantly scandalous cuckolding. Alas, that your conjugal bed should be delivered to incest and contaminated by monkery!

"Further," Pantagruel pursued, "you shall be the hornpipe of Buzançay. In other words, you shall be well horned and hornified, corny and cornuted. I recall the man whose brother deputed him to ask a favor of King Louis XII. Intending to beg for the revenue from the salt-tax at Buzançay, by a slip of the tongue, he kept asking for the Buzançay hornpipe. By the same token, you, my dear Panurge, may believe you are marrying an honorable and virtuous woman, but you will in reality be acquiring a wife devoid of wit, puffed up with the wind of conceit, obstreperous and shrill as a Buzançay hornpipe.

"Consider the fillip he fetched you across the snout with his bladder; consider the thwack he dealt you between the shoulders with his fist. Obvious warnings, these, that she will lead you by the nose; she will beat you; and she will steal from you, just as you stole that self-same bladder from the children of Vaubreton village."

But Panurge would have none of it. Pantagruel was utterly mistaken; the exact contrary of his interpretation was valid. Not that Panurge presumptuously sought to be exempted from his fealty to folly; he was its vassal, and paid due homage. Was not the whole world mad? None of us but was the tool of fate; Panurge wished Pantagruel to remember that, in the land of Lorraine, the village of Fou—or Fool, as we would say—adjoined Toul—or Tool!

Solomon asseverated that the number of madmen was infinite; and nothing could be added to, or subtracted from, infinity. Aristotle had established this. What a mad fool Panurge would be, then, if being a fool, he did not deem himself such!

The legion of maniacs and lunatics was infinite; Avicenna, the Arab philosopher, declared the forms of insanity to be infinite, too. However, to return to Triboulet, Panurge interpreted the rest of the oracle as quite in his favor.

Triboulet had said, "Beware the monk!" This meant simply, "Take heed of the monkey!" What monkey? Some household pet, doubtless, like the sparrow of Catullus' Lesbia. Some pet which, for pastime, would snatch at flies as joyously as ever the Emperor Domitian, the fly-catcher, amused himself by capturing them, and impaling them on a stylus. Or—who knew?—perhaps the monk or monkey mentioned, was that pet concealed behind My Lord Panurge's codpiece?

"As for point three," said Panurge, "the fool meant that my wife will be a gay product of the country, lively and harmonious as a hornpipe from Saulieu in Burgundy, or from Buzançay in Touraine. Truthful Triboulet recognized my natural dispositions and my inward feeling. I assure you I prefer a bright, dishevelled shepherdess, whose bum smells of clover, to your proud lady at court, with her costly toilette, her gum benzoin, her asadulcis. Ay, better the piping of rustic bags than the twanging of lutes . . . . than the harsh squeaking of rebecks, those old, round instruments with pear-shaped body and slender neck . . . than court fiddles and like instruments. . . .

"He gave me a thwack on my back. Well, what about it! Let it pass, for God's sake, as an installment on those I shall receive in Purgatory. It didn't hurt me. The loon thought he was hitting some page: you know how they delight in torturing fools. No, Pantagruel, he is an honest fool, an innocent, I warrant you: whoever thinks ill of him is a hardened sinner. I heartily forgive him!"

"But the fillip he dealt you—?" Pantagruel reminded him.

"A fillip on the nose? It symbolized the little roguish tricks my wife and I will enjoy, like any newly-married couple."

XLVII

HOW PANTAGRUEL AND PANURGE DECIDED TO VISIT THE ORACLE OF THE HOLY BOTTLE

PANURGE pursued his argument:

"There is another point you have not considered, though it is the key to the riddle. He handed me the bottle. How do you interpret that? What does it mean?"

"No doubt it means your wife will be a drunkard."

"On the contrary," Panurge demurred. "The bottle was empty. By the spine of St. Fiacre in Brie, preserved as a relic in the Cathedral of Meaux, I swear that our morosoph sophomore, our wise madman, our anything-but-lunatic Triboulet advises me to commit myself to the bottle. And I hereby renew my earlier vow: I call you to witness that, by the Styx and Acheron, I swear to continue wearing spectacles in my cap, and to leave off a codpiece in my breeches, until I shall have obtained an answer from the Holy Bottle concerning my nuptial undertaking."

Panurge had a friend, a wise, understanding man, who knew the land, realm and place where stood the Holy Bottle's temple and oracle. This friend would certainly lead them thither.

"Let us go together; I implore you not to refuse. I will be an Achates to you, O Damon; I will be your Damis, O Apollonius of Tyana. I will be your shadow throughout the voyage. I know that you have ever enjoyed peregrinations; I know how you delight to see new things, to acquire fresh knowledge. We shall behold wonders, believe me!"

"I am perfectly willing to join you," said Pantagruel. "But, before undertaking a long journey, fraught with hazards and dangers—"

"What dangers?" Panurge broke in. "Why, wherever I go, danger takes to its heels, afraid to come within twenty miles of me. Let me but show myself, and jeopardy retires, just as a deputy resigns his powers before his sovereign, just as shadows dissolve before the sun, just as infirmities vanished before St. Martin's body at Candes."

"St. Martin?"

"Ay, you recall the miracle play, in which two beggars, one blind, the other palsied, were so frightened at the saint's coming, because it would deprive them of their lucrative ailments."

"Incidentally," said Pantagruel, "before we set out, there are certain points we must settle. First, we must send Triboulet back to Blois; secondly, we must ask my royal father's counsel and leave; thirdly, we must find some sibyl to act as interpreter and guide."

(The first point was at once settled: Pantagruel dismissed the fool, but not before presenting him with a gold-embroidered coat.)

"My friend Xenomanes—the name means lover of foreign things! —will do quite well," said Panurge. "What is more, I intend to pass through Lanternland, the home of fond fancies, where we can pick up a wise and learned lamp, to attend us as the Sibyl attended Æneas in his descent to the Elysian Fields."

As Carpalim left to conduct Triboulet homeward, he caught Panurge's last words.

"Ho, Panurge," he cried. "Ho, Master Quit-of-his-debts, ho, Sir Solvent! Take Milord Debty—as the English at Calais call their Lord Deputy—along with you . . . a fell fellow, a felonious fellow, a fallow fellow . . . don't forget *debitoribus*, for the prayer runs *dimitte nobis debita nostra sicut et nos dimittimus debitoribus nostris*, forgive us our debts as we forgive our debtors . . . take the Englishman along with you, to light you with his lantern-jaw!"

"Personally, I do not foresee us engendering melancholy," said Pantagruel. "The future is clearly auspicious. I only regret I cannot speak the language of Lanternland."

"I shall speak it for you," Panurge proposed. "You heard me speak it when we first met. I know it as well as I do my mother tongue: I have spoken it as much as ever French. Listen:

Briszmarg d'algotbric nubstzne zos
Isquebfz prusq; alborlz crinqs zachac.
Misbe dilbarlkz morp nipp stancz bos.
Strombtz Panrge walmap quost grufz bac.

Guess what that means, Epistemon?"

"Those are names of arrant, passant and rampant devils," said Epistemon.

"Your words are true, my fair friend, though those I spoke were in the court language of Lanternland. On our way thither, I will make you a glossary of Lantern words to last you about as long as a pair of new shoes; you will have learned it before you see the next dawn rise. What I told you, translated from the Lantern into French, is:

I was a lovesick bachelor, distressed,
Haunted by grief, dogged by misfortune's spell.
Believe me: married folk are happiest.
Panurge is married and he knows it well.

"Heigh-ho!" said Pantagruel. "There remains but to hear my royal father's will, and to obtain his consent."

XLVIII

HOW GARGANTUA SHOWED THAT CHILDREN MAY NOT LAWFULLY MARRY WITHOUT THE KNOWLEDGE AND CONSENT OF THEIR PARENTS

As they entered the great hall of the castle, Pantagruel met good Gargantua emerging from the Council chamber. He gave his father a brief summary of their adventures, exposed their intention, and begged him to grant them leave to carry it out.

Goodman Gargantua was holding two great bundles of petitions he had granted, and requests under consideration. He handed them to Ulrich Gallet, his trusted chancellor and master of the rolls. Then, with a more jovial expression than usual, he drew Pantagruel aside and said:

"I praise God, my beloved son, that He maintains you constantly inclined to virtuous purposes. I am very pleased that you plan this journey. But, by the same token, I wish you, too, felt the need and desire to marry. It seems to me that you have now reached a suitable age. Panurge has striven heroically to remove such obstacles as lay in his way; speak for yourself, son."

"My dear father," said Pantagruel, "I have never given this business the slightest thought: I refer and submit to your own good will, to your paternal authority. May I lie dead at your feet, because of your displeasure, rather than live, marry and prosper against your pleasure. No law ever I heard of, sacred or profane, justified children in marrying according to their will, without seeking the advice, consent and approval of their immediate parents or near relatives. No court but, denying children this privilege, deposited it in the hands of their parents."

"My beloved son," Gargantua said, "I believe in you. From the bottom of my heart, I thank God that you are inspired with only the most honorable and praiseworthy thoughts. I congratulate you, because the windows of your senses have admitted into the chamber of your spirit nothing save liberal and judicious knowledge."

The aged monarch then told how, in his day, there was, on the continent, a land which allowed its sacerdotal windbags to interfere in matrimonial matters. These priests invariably suggested moles to Gargantua, either because their victims were as blind as moles, or because the priests themselves retired, sleek and solitary, underground. At all events, they remained as aloof personally from the hymeneal act as the eunuch pontiffs of Cybele in Phrygia. Yet they were cocky —ay, cocky as lascivious, salacious cocks are! Imagine their actually daring to lay down the law to man and wife on matters of wedlock! Gargantua felt at a loss which to abominate more: the tyrannical presumption with which these venerated molebillies emerged beyond the gates of their mysterious temples to undertake duties utterly opposed to their condition?—or the witless superstition of married folk, who ratified and obeyed such barbarous, malign laws? These connubial sanctions, ingenuously granted to the religious by wedded folk, were wholly profitable to the august divines, wholly ruinous to bride and groom. Was this not enough to render such sanctions suspicious? To suggest iniquity and fraud on the part of the presbyters? To Gargantua, it seemed clear as the morning star. Yet these church-struck idiots noticed nothing amiss.

Surely, by way of compensation, our laymen might quite as boldly establish laws for the ceremonial and sacrifices of the mysteries of churchdom? Did not the cloth despoil one-tenth of the labor of their hands, of the sweat of their brows? And for what purpose? So the clerics might feed abundantly and lead a life of leisure. Certainly, Gargantua believed that such laws would prove less uncalled for and pernicious than the laws laid down by priests for laymen.

"You spoke to the point, my son," Gargantua went on. "There is no law allowing children to marry without their parents' knowledge, consent and will. Yet, according to the laws of the country I cited, what happens? Take the most arrant ruffian, villain or scoundrel; the most evil-smelling, foul-breathing hangdog; the most scurvy and leprous stinkard; your most vicious footpad or brigand imaginable. Well, such a knave may abduct the most highborn, the richest, the most upright and the chastest maiden in the land; he may snatch her out of her father's house, out of the very embrace of her mother, and far beyond reach of kin and friend. All he needs is a priest to help him, by celebrating a secret marriage, and to share the future spoils."

The cruelty and horror of such an act were, Gargantua thought, comparable only to what the Goths, Scythians and barbarian Massagetæ, east of the Caspian Sea, might do upon capturing an enemy stronghold after a long siege.

Consider, too, the parents' misery. Here they had brought up their beautiful daughters amid health, riches, delicacy and decorum. With love in their hearts, they had schooled them in virtuous discipline, in the ways of honor. They had hoped to unite them, in good time, to the sons of neighbors and friends, lads educated to the same end, with the same care, in the same manner. They had dreamed of unions, consecrating not only the possessions, wealth and inheritance of their houses, but also the hereditary ideals of father and mother. Oh, what a woeful spectacle! Suddenly the basest and most obscure stranger, the veriest barbarian, a putrid and chancre-riddled cur, a wretched, cadaverous, godforsaken bastard arose to snatch away their daughters under their very eyes!

"Do not believe the sufferings of such parents any less profound than the collachrymation, or collective lamentation, of the Roman and confederate nations, when they received tidings that Germanicus Drusus was dead," Gargantua continued. "Do not believe their discomfiture any less harrowing than that of the Lacedæmonians, on learning that the Trojan adulterer had spirited Grecian Helen out of their country. Do not believe their mourning and prostration any less anguished than that of Ceres, when Pluto bore her daughter away to be his bride in hell . . . or of Venus, when Adonis, her beautiful lover, was killed by a boar . . . or of Hercules, when the nymphs carried off his beloved Hylas . . . or of Hecuba, wife to Priam, when her daughter Polyxena was stolen from her, and sacrificed upon Achilles' grave!"

Unfortunately, parents were so filled with fear of devils and like superstition that they dared not object, because the crime had been hallowed by the presence and consent of these sacerdotal molebillies. So they sulked at home, deprived of the company of their beloved children: the father cursing the day and hour of his daughter's marriage, the mother wishing a miscarriage had befallen her, instead of a birth resulting in such ignominy and grief. Thus parents finished their days amid tears and tribulation, instead of amid the joy and tenderness they had reasonably expected.

Others among them, unable to bear such an indignity, aghast with horror and melancholy, went and hanged or drowned themselves in despair. Others, again, proved more heroic. Even as the children of Jacob revenged themselves upon Shechem for the seizure of their sister Dinah, these took matters boldly into their own hands. Finding the seducer and the molebilly plotting, huggermugger, to seduce and prostitute the bride, they forthwith fell upon them, carved up their bodies, and tossed the scraps for pasture to the wolves in the wilderness.

Such manly chivalrous action horrified the molebilly symmists, if I may use a Greek word to qualify these co-initiates in mystic sacraments. The molebillies fretted, fumed and raged; they made hideous protestation; most importunately they appealed to the secular arm, to political justice, as against their ecclesiastical courts. Haughtily and insistently, they implored temporal jurisdiction to step in, to visit an exemplary punishment upon so heinous an offence.

Yet never a clause, paragraph, point or title in the body of natural, international or imperial law prescribed penalty or torture for such an act. Indeed, both reason and Nature opposed legislation of the sort. For no decent man on earth, learning of his daughter's seizure, rape and dishonor, could fail, naturally and reasonably, to consider these misfortunes worse than her death. This constituted the ravisher a plain murderer, guilty of traitorous and wilful homicide upon the daughter's person. Accordingly, the father could, by nature, and should, by reason, slay the culprit on the spot, without thereby making himself liable to arrest.

Could the father find that brute who, at the vile monk's instigation, seduced his daughter and enticed her from her home? Then, though the daughter had consented, he could and should slay the pair shamefully. And he should cast their corpses to the wild beasts, because they were unworthy of receiving that ultimate, sweet, much-desired embrace of great and kindly Mother Earth, which we call burial.

"My beloved son, so long as I live and draw breath, I shall, God helping, avail to keep such laws out of my kingdom. After my death, take care to guard against such abuses. Since you rely upon me to arrange your marriage, I agree and shall provide for you.

"Equip and prepare yourself for Panurge's expedition. Take along with you Epistemon, Friar John, and anyone else you may choose. My treasury is at your disposal: nothing you do could displease me. Go to my arsenal at Thalassa, select any ships, pilots, sailors and interpreters you care to. The first favorable wind you get, put out to sea, in the name, and under guard, of God the Saviour. During your absence, I shall attend to finding a wife for you. And I shall plan, for your wedding-feast, a celebration more sumptuous than ever was known upon earth."

XLIX

OF PANTAGRUEL'S PREPARA-TIONS FOR GOING TO SEA AND OF THE HERB CALLED PANTAGRUELION

PANTAGRUEL took leave of the excellent Gargantua, who prayed for his son's happiness on the voyage. Within a few days, the expedition reached the harbor of Thalassa, near St. Malo, in Brittany. It consisted of Pantagruel, Panurge, Epistemon, Friar John of the Funnels, Abbot of Thélème, and others of the royal house, including Xenomanes. The latter, a great traveller and adventurer over perilous ways, had come at Panurge's request, because he was in some way or other submitted by fee to the jurisdiction of Panurge's domain of Salmagundi.

Reaching Thalassa, Pantagruel gathered a fleet of vessels, equal to that which Ajax of Salamis had gathered to convey the Greeks to Troy. These twelve ships were to transport mariners, pilots, oarsmen, interpreters, artisans, soldiers, provisions, cannon, munitions, equipment, money and other necessities for a long and hazardous journey. Among other things, I saw them load on to the vessels a great deal of the herb called pantagruelion or hemp (both in its raw green state and in its prepared, confected state).

Pantagruelion has a small hard roundish root, which ends in a white obtuse point. There are few filaments to it, and it goes no deeper into earth than a cubit—the length of the forearm, say. From the root, there rises a single, round, umbelliferous, fennel-like stem, green outside, white within, concave like the stem of *smyrnium olus atrum*, of the bean or the gentian. It is ligneous or woody; straight, crisp, jagged, somewhat like a slightly striated column; filled with fibres or threads, which contain the whole virtue of the herb. This is especially true of the middle of the stalk—the part called *mesa*. Hemp from Mylasea, in Asia, is the most prized variety.

In height, pantagruelion usually rises to five or six feet. Sometimes, however, it exceeds the length of a lance, especially if it is grown in a mild, marshy, light, uliginous or muddy, humid and temperate soil, like that of Les Sables d'Olonne, in Poitou, or of Rosea, near Præneste in the Sabine province. This applies especially when rain is plentiful, during the Tiber Fishermen's Holiday in early June, and throughout the summer solstice. Often, then, the herb exceeds, in height, the average tree, thus fitting into the category Theophrastus calls *dendromalache* or tree herb. Yet it is not properly a tree, since it possesses no root, trunk and branches that endure, but, like a plant, it perishes yearly.

Great wide branches issue from the stalk. The leaves are three times as long as they are wide, always green, and slightly rough like boraginaceous plants: the orchanet, bugloss, henna or puccoon. They are tough, jagged as a saw or an alkanet leaf; they end in a point like a Macedonian spear or a surgeon's lancet. In general appearance, they differ little from the leaves of our ash trees; indeed, they so resemble the agrimony and eupatorium species, that various botanists have mistaken *eupatoria domestica* for the wild pantagruelion, and vice versa.

These leaves emerge from the stalk at equal distances, from five to seven in a row. These odd, mystic and divine numbers prove how highly nature favored the plant.

Its odor is strong and scarcely pleasing to fastidious nostrils. Its seed lies towards the top of the stem, somewhat short of the very tip.

It is found as abundantly as any herb known. It may grow oblong or spherical or rhomboid; light black or tawny in color; rude to the touch, covered with a fragile casing. It is much sought after by songbirds: linnets, for instance, finches, larks, yellowhammers and so forth. If man, on the other hand, eats much and frequently of it, it will dry up the spermatic fluid. Of old, the Greeks used to make of it various sorts of fritters, tarts and buns, to top off a meal with, and to enhance the wine's flavor. Yet the plant is nevertheless difficult to digest, it taxes the stomach, produces bad blood and, in its excessive heat, injures the brain, filling the head with offensive and painful vapors.

Like many other plants and trees—laurel, palm, oak, holm or evergreen, asphodel, mandrake, fern, agaric or mushroom, *aristolochia* or birthwort, cypress, turpentine, pennyroyal, peony, etc.—hemp is bisexual, possessing both male and female specimens. The male bears no flower but is rich in seed; the female is rich in small, whitish, and quite useless flowers, but bears no seed of any worth. As in other plants of the same family, the female has a wider and less prickly leaf than the male; nor does it grow to the same height.

Pantagruelion is to be sown at the first coming of the swallows, in early spring; and to be plucked when grasshopper and cicada grow hoarse, in September.

L

HOW TO PREPARE AND APPLY THE FAMED HERB CALLED PANTAGRUELION

THE herb pantagruelion should be prepared in the autumnal equinox in September. How to treat it depends upon its native climate and the disposition of the cultivator.

Pantagruel recommended the following process: (1) Strip leaf and seed from stalk; (2) steep stalk in stagnant water for five days; (3) if water cold and sky overcast, allow to soak nine or ten days; (4) dry stalk in shade; (5) pare and separate fibres or threads from woody or ligneous part to which attached, since fibres contain sole value of plant; (6) use woody part to make bright flame, kindle fire or amuse young, by inserting, for purposes of rattling, in inflated balloon of hog's bladder; (7) though useless, latter part will serve syphonically, as a straw to allow bibbers to suck up new wine from bungs of barrels.

. A minority of modern Pantagruelists shun the manual labor involved in parting the various fibres. Instead, they employ certain cataracting or cleaving instruments, like those choleric Juno wore to bind her fingers together, to prevent Alcmena giving birth to Hercules. Thanks to such tools, these few moderns can discard the chaff and preserve the fibres. Contrary to all accepted opinion and to the *obiter dicta* of every known philosopher, they earn their living by backing-up. (These are the ropemakers, who retreat as they draw, from a bag, the hempthreads they twist into ropes!)

Such Pantagruelists as hold the herb in loftier esteem, indulge in the legendary pastime of the three Parcæ or Fates . . . in the nocturnal pleasure of noble Circe . . . in Penelope's excuse, when wooed by a host of effeminate swains. In other words, they prefer to spin or weave. . . .

The herb pantagruelion is put to admirable use. Short of setting forth its virtues in detail, I can at least expose a few. I will begin with its nomenclature.

I find that all plants come by their names in a variety of ways. First, from the discoverer; second, from the original source; third, in ironic contradiction; fourth, from their effect; fifth, according to their particularities; sixth, by remembrance of their metamorphoses; seventh, by similarity; and eighth, morphologically.

Pliny vouches it.

(1) They may take title from the man who discovered, recognized, distinguished, cultivated, domesticated and applied them to their appropriate uses. Thus mercurial is the plant mercury, named after Mercury, who gave it various names. Elsewhere it is known as Good King Henry for like reasons. (Incidentally, it is used for purgatives!) . . . Thus panacea, or allheal, including valerian and mistletoe, named for Panace, daughter of Æsculapius . . . Thus artemisia, wormwood or mugwort, named for Artemys Diana, or possibly for Artemys, Queen of Caria, wife to Mausolus . . . thus eupatorium, a weed named for King Eupator of Pompus . . . thus telephium, named for Telephus, son of Hercules, wounded and healed by Achilles at the siege of Troy . . . thus euphorbia (which furnish castor oil and croton oil) named for Euphorbus, Greek physician to King Juba of Numidia, in the days of the Cæsars . . . thus clymene or honeysuckle, named for Clymenus, King of Arcady . . . thus alcibiadion, a boraginaceous plant named after Alcibiades—unless, perhaps, it derives its title from Alcibias, the first to employ it against snake-bites, or, thus belonging to another group, from ἀλκή, meaning strength, and βίος, meaning life . . . thus gentian, named after Gentius, King of Slavonia, hard by the Adriatic. . . .

In point of fact, the discoverer's prerogative to impose his name upon the herb he discovered, was so highly esteemed of yore, as to give rise to a struggle between Neptune and Pallas. Each wished to dedicate to himself a land they had found simultaneously and jointly. Since then, the place has been known as Athens, as derived from Athene or Minerva.

Similarly, Lyncus, King of Scythia, a monarch of Asiatic Russia, conspired to do away with young Triptolemus, who had been sent by Ceres to communicate to mankind the discovery of grain. By Triptolemus' death, Lyncus would have gone down to immortality as the inventor of this product, so useful and necessary to human life. Because of his evil plot, Ceres changed Lyncus into a lynx.

Similarly, too, mighty and enduring wars were waged among certain kings in and about Cappadocia. What was the cause of the conflict? Merely the naming of a plant. Because this was so eagerly disputed, the plant has come down to us as polemonia, the warlike. (The genus includes phlox or convolvula.)

(2) Another way of naming plants is after their place of origin. Thus median apples, or lemons, were so named because they came from Media . . . Punic apples, or pomegranates, from the Punic realm or Carthaginia . . . ligusticum, or lovage, from the Ligurian, or Genoese, coast . . . rhubarb, from the barbar river named Rheu, Rea or Volga, according to the testimony of Ammianus Marcellinus, the last Roman historian of importance . . . santonica, or absinthe, from Saintonge, the region about Saintes . . . fenugreek, a veterinary herb, formerly used in medicine, and obviously named for the Grecian fern . . . castanea, or chestnut, from Castanea, a city of Magnesia, in northeastern Greece . . . persicaria, or peaches, from Persia . . . sabine, or oleander, from the Sabine province, north of Rome . . . stœcha, from the Stœchadian Isle or Hyères . . . spica celtica, or nard, from Celtic Gaul . . . and so on and so forth. . . .

(3) Another way of naming plants is by antiphrase, by paradox, by irony. Thus the Greek πίνθιον (pinthion) means grateful to the taste; ἀπίνθιον (apinthion) means unpalatable: hence absinthe. Thus, again, ὁλόστιον or holosteion, meaning bone throughout, is used paradoxically to identify a very soft plant.

(4) Fourthly, plants are named intrinsically, after their force and efficacy. Thus aristolochia, which, from its Greek derivation, means excellent in childbirth . . . thus lichen, a plant botanically blotchy

and, medicinally, a cure for skin diseases . . . thus mallow, which mollifies . . . thus callithrica—water starwort, or stargrass—whose leafstalk suggests hair, and which is a specific against baldness . . . thus alyssum, by philology and application a cure for hydrophobia . . . thus ephemerum, perhaps colchicum (meadow saffron, autumn crocus, which, used pharmaceutically, is narcotic, diuretic, cathartic and excellent for rheumatism) . . . thus bechium or coltsfoot, from Bys or βήξ, a cough, employed in throat ailments . . . thus nasturtium, derived from *nasus torsus* or twisted nose, because its scent causes nasal gymnastics (in France it is called nostrilcress) . . . thus hyoscyama, derived from Greek words meaning swine and bean (wild boars eat it and go into convulsions!) . . . thus henbane, a plant very similar, applying rather to fowl than to swine. . . .

(5) Plants are also named by virtue of their particularities. Thus heliotrope: it follows the sun, like our own sunflower and marigold, spreading as the sun rises, ascending as it mounts, declining as it sinks, and closing shut as it sets . . . thus adiantum (the Greek word means waterproof) or spleenwort, which grows hard by water, may be plunged in water yet resists moisture . . . thus hieracia, from the Greek word for hawk, thanks to which that bird sharpened its sight . . . thus eryngium (or by Hellenic derivation, goat's beard) which includes sea-holly. . . .

(6) Some plants are named after the men and women changed into them. Thus daphne, or laurel, after Daphne, the nymph who escaped Apollo's pursuit by the metamorphosis . . . thus myrtle and myrrh tree after Myrsina or Myrrha, who was so changed because of her incestuous love of Cyniras, King of Cyprus, her father . . . thus pitys, or pine, after the maiden of that name who, preferring Boreas to Pan, was dashed against the rocks by the latter, and transmogrified into a tree by the compassionate gods . . . thus cynara, our artichoke, after Cynara . . . thus narcissus, after him who allowed the nymph Echo to die of unrequited love and, seeing his own reflection in a pool, pined away for love of self until the gods, pitying him, turned him into a river, and fashioned a flower to perpetuate his name . . . thus crocus, after Crocus, a lovesick suitor, and smilax, after the maid he pined for. . . .

(7) Plants are often named after their physical resemblance to other things. Thus hippuris, meaning horsetail, because shavegrass

looks like horses' tails . . . thus alopecuros or foxtail grass . . .
thus psyllium or fleawort . . . thus delphinium, because its nectary
resembles a dolphin . . . thus bugloss or oxtongue, a form of alkanet . . . thus iris, because it is like the rainbow, which was the
scarf worn by Iris, messenger of Juno . . . thus coronopos or crow-
foot, including any plant suggesting a bird's foot. . . .

Reciprocally, just as men have given their names to plants, so they
have taken their names from plants. The Roman Fabii thus derived
their name from *faba*, the bean; the Piso clan from *pisa*, a pea; the
Lentuli from *lentes*, or lentils; the house of Cicero from *cicer* or
chickpea. . . .

Even more striking resemblances are immortalized by plants called
Venus' navel . . . venushair, or maidenhair . . . venuspot, or tea-
zel, with lips agape for rainwater . . . Jupiter's beard, or houseleek,
grown largely on roofs of houses . . . Jupiter's eyes or Jupiter's
flower, called phlox . . . Mars' blood, which gives its name to blood-
wort and other plants of the class *sanguinaris* . . . Mercury's fingers, or *hermodactyla*, likewise specifics for gout. . . .

(8) Finally, plants are named morphologically, according to a
study of their form. Thus trefoil, or clover, because it has *tres folias*,
three leaves . . . thus *pentaphyllum* or cinquefoil, also called five-
finger because its digitate leaves have five leaflets . . . thus *serpil-
lum* (wild thyme) because it creeps like a serpent . . . thus helxine
(pellitory) from the Greek "to cling," because its seeds stick to anyone going near it . . . thus petasite (butterbur), after the Greek
meaning hat or parasol, its leaves resembling a cover for the head
. . . thus myrobalan (a sort of prune, called *ben* by the Arabs),
formed upon the Greek words meaning sweet juice and an acorn. In
point of fact, the fruit is oily as the former, and it looks like the
latter.

LI

OF WHY THE PLANT IS CALLED PANTAGRUELION AND OF ITS WONDROUS POWERS·

IF we except the fabulous manner of naming plants—God forbid that we should quote fable in this truthful and trustworthy chronicle!—pantagruelion gained its name by the methods described above.

Pantagruel discovered it. If not the first to stumble upon it, at least he was the first to use it in a certain way. As such, it has proved more fearful and abhorrent to robbers than doddergrass and chokeweed are to flax . . . than reed is to brake (brake cut with a reed will not grow again, and a preparation of either, ground and applied to the skin, will draw out thorns of the other, embedded in the body) . . . than shavegrass to haymowers, who consider it worthless, and who find that its silicates dull their blades . . . than vetch to chickpeas . . . than darnel to barley . . . than hatchetweed to lentils . . . than atranium, a weed deadly to beans . . . than tares to wheat . . . than ivy to walls . . . than nenuphar, lotus or water lily to lascivious monks . . . than the birch rod to the schoolboy at the Collège de Navarre in Paris . . . than cabbage to vines (did not Lycurgus, King of Thrace, destroy the vines, when suddenly a stalk cast its twigs about him, and when from his tears, shed at Bacchus' vengeance, was born the colewort, a traditional preventive and cure for drunkenness) . . . than garlic to the magnet, whose action is neutralized . . . than onion to the eye . . . than the seeds of ferns to pregnant women . . . than the bark, leaf and seed of willow to your lecherous nun . . . than the shade of the yewtree to such as sleep in it . . . than aconite and wolfsbane to panthers and wolves . . . than the smell of the figtree to mad wolves . . . than hemlock or nettles to goslings . . . than purslane to the teeth . . . than oil to trees. . . .

Thanks to Pantagruel's discovery of this use of pantagruelion, many a bandit has finished his life high and short. Hanging, as a form of demise, appealed particularly to Phyllis, Queen of Thrace, who meditated suicide by that means . . . to Bonosus, Emperor of Rome, a prodigious drinker, who in despair at his defeat by Probus, chose this method of ending it all, earning for epitaph: "There hangs a keg, not a man" . . . to Amata, wife of King Latinus, who, furious at preventing her daughter Lavinia's marriage to Æneas, spitefully selected this mode of suicide . . . to Iphis, dangling in a noose, because Anaxaretus spurned her . . . to Autolyca, on being told wrongly by Nauplius that Ulysses, her son, was dead . . . to Lycambes, the Theban poet, attacked by his rival Archilochus . . . to Arachne, the skilful spinner, who, having challenged Minerva, lost, and had recourse to the rope, Minerva changing her, later, into a spider . . . to Phædra, when spurned by her son Hippolytus . . . to Leda, unless she is wrongly included through some typographical error . . . to Achæus, King of Lydia, strung up by his subjects for overtaxing them . . . to how many hundred others?

One and all were indignant that, without being otherwise sick, they suddenly found pantagruelion obstructing, more villainously than angina or quinsy, the passages through which *bons mots* and bonbons were wont to enter.

Just as Atropos, the merciless of the three Fates, cut the thread of their lives, others have been heard to groan and lament that Pantagruel clutched them by the throat. Alas! this was not Pantagruel, he was never a hangman. No, it was pantagruelion, serving as a halter, and decorating them with a hempen cravat. Besides, they committed a solecism and an impropriety, unless they are to be excused on the grounds of synecdoche—the figure of rhetoric which allows us to use the part for the whole, as, for instance, fifty sail for fifty ships. By this token, they cited the discoverer metaphorically for the discovery, as Ceres is cited for corn, and Bacchus for wine.

By the *bons mots* prisoned within the bottle cooling in that bucket, I hereby swear that noble Pantagruel never seized mortal by the throat—unless the mortal neglected to obviate his impending thirst.

Pantagruelion also derives its name from similarity, since Pantagruel, at birth, was as tall as the herb I speak of. Indeed, it was easy to measure the infant, since he was born at the time of the great drought. This is the season when pantagruelion is culled, and when

Icarus' dog—the constellation Canis Major—by his constant barking at the sun, makes troglodytes, cavedwellers and subterranean tenants of all mankind.

Again, pantagruelion was so termed by virtue of its specific functions. Just as Pantagruel was ever the inspiration and exemplar of all jovial perfection (I doubt if any one dare deny it, O friends and drinkers!) so pantagruelion contains the highest efficacy, energy, competence and force. By dint of these, if pantagruelion had been known when the trees met to elect a king of the forest, undoubtedly pantagruelion would have been chosen, by a majority of votes, to rule and govern them.

(You recall the prophet on the subject—I mean the author of *Judges*, Samuel, Hezekiah or Esdras, who reports Jotham as telling the following parable to the men of Shechem.

The trees assembled to appoint a king: the olive, the fig, the vine and the shrub were successively nominated. The last-named accepted, provided those who would not rest under his shade be devoured by the fire emanating from him.)

Need I go on . . . ? Oxylus, son of Orius, begat by his sister Hamadryas, eight daughters, called Hamadryads. Had pantagruelion resulted from this incestuous copulation, the father had been prouder than ever he was of the eight offspring, to wit: the eldest, his daughter Vine; the next, his son, Figtree and, successively, Walnut-tree, Oak-tree, Sorb-apple tree, Ash, Poplar, to the last, Elm, who, possessing a bark rich with healing virtues, was the greatest physician of his day.

I shall forbear to tell at length how the juice of pantagruelion, poured and distilled in the ears, kills all manner of vermin bred there by putrefaction, and, indeed, any other kind of animal that might have entered the ears. If you place this juice in a bucket of water, its strength is such that the water curdles exactly like milk. This curdled liquid is an excellent remedy for horses afflicted with colic and apt to draw at the flank.

Pantagruelion-root, boiled in water, serves to soften the nerves, distend the joints, alleviate the contractions of gout and rheumatism. If you wish to heal promptly a burn caused by flame or water, apply raw pantagruelion, just as it comes out of the ground, without further preparation or composition. When it begins to curl up over the sore, be sure to remove the dry leaves and make an application of fresh.

Without pantagruelion, your kitchens would be wretched, your board abominable, though they boasted the most delicious viands; your beds would be pleasureless, though gold, silver, amber, ivory and porphyry adorned them abundantly. Without pantagruelion, your millers could not carry their wheat to the mill (for what makes sacks?), or bring back flour. How could the pleas of lawyers be brought to the bar without pantagruelion? How could plaster be conveyed to the worker? How could water be drawn out of wells? How could scribes, copyists, secretaries and writers function? Paper and placards would not exist; we would have no record of official and financial documents. The art of printing would perish from the earth.

How, without pantagruelion, could we ring our churchbells? How cover and protect our windows? From this herb, the priests of Isis and the pastophors, or pontiffs, derive their robes; no human but immediately upon birth is hastily wrapped up in it. Not all the various varieties of laniferous trees, not all the cotton trees of Seres or Tibet, of northern China or India, of Tylos in the Persian Sea, of Arabia, of Malta—not all of these, added together, clothe as many people as that small herb. It covers mighty armies against rain and cold far more efficiently than did the ancient tents of hide. It protects theatres and amphitheatres from the heat of the sun; it surrounds woods and copses for the pleasure of the hunters; it descends into water, both salt and fresh, to the greater profit of the fishermen. It shapes, and makes useful to man, such articles as sandals, shoes, boots, buskins, pumps, slippers, gaiters, leggings and so forth; it stretches the longbow, bends the crossbow, operates the sling. And, as though it were a sacred plant—like vervain, reverenced by the ancient Romans and Gauls—as though it were hallowed by the shades, hobgoblins and phantoms, it is essential to the burial of man.

I shall go even further. Thanks to this herb, the truly invisible substances are stopped, caught, held back, and, so to speak, imprisoned. It serves to hold, to control, to turn huge, unwieldy weights, to the vast profit of humankind. Indeed, I am amazed that the discovery of this use remained so long hidden to the ancient philosophers, considering the inestimable benefit derived from it, and the intolerable labor they had to furnish in their mills.

Pantagruelion can resist the strongest gusts of wind. The mightiest cargo vessels; the heaviest Egyptian passenger-gondolas; the most powerful galleons; chilianders and milianders, equipped to carry a thousand and ten thousand troops, may all, through the virtues of pantagruelion, be unmoored, and put to sea, at their pilot's will.

Nations to all appearances remote, inaccessible, and mysterious to us by nature, have been brought close to us—and we to them. Not even birds, however light their plumage or thorough their equipment for vast migrations, could have spanned such distances as pantagruelion can link together. Thus Taprobrana or Ceylon has been put in touch with Lapland . . . thus Java has beheld the Riphaean Mountains of Scythia, the steppes north of the Black Sea . . . thus Phebol, an island in the Gulf of Arabia, shall behold Thélème . . . thus the Icelanders and Greenlanders shall drink the water of the Euphrates . . . thus Boreas, blowing chill from the north, has visited the realm of Auster, the south wind; thus Eurus, the eastern gust, has visited Zephyrus, the western.

By the same token, those heavenly intelligences we call the gods, both terrestrial and maritime, took fright, when they perceived how, thanks to the blessed herb pantagruelion, the Arctic peoples, under the very eyes of the Antarctic, crossed the Atlantic ocean, passed the twin tropics, pushed through the torrid zone, spanned the zodiac, frolicked beneath the equinox, and held both poles within sight on the horizon.

Faced with such a situation, the gods, terrified, said:

"Pantagruel has, by this mere herb, caused us more worry and labor than ever the Aloides or Giants, Otus and Ephialtes, when they sought to scale Olympus. He will soon marry and beget children by his wife. This is a fate we cannot forestall, for it has been woven by the hands and shuttles of the three fatal sisters, daughters of Necessity. Who knows but Pantagruel's children will discover some herb equally effectual? Who knows but humans may, by its means, visit the source of hail, the springs of the rain, the forge where lightning is produced? Who knows but they will invade the regions of the moon, intrude within the territories of the celestial signs? Some, then, will settle at the sign of the Golden Eagle, others at the Ram, others at the Crown, others at the Harp, others at the Silver Lion. They will sit down at our divine board, take our goddesses to wife, and thereby themselves become divine."

Finally, they decided to call an assembly, and deliberate upon ways of meeting this dire situation.

LII

HOW A CERTAIN KIND OF PANTAGRUELION IS INCOMBUSTIBLE

I HAVE told you great and wonderful things about pantagruelion; but if, short of taxing your credulity, you will believe another divine virtue of this sacred plant's, I will gladly tell it you. To be sure, your faith or scepticism is all one to me; I am satisfied merely to tell the truth, and let it go at that. And tell the truth I shall.

However, to attack properly this thorny and treacherous problem, I must first ask you a question. Let us suppose I put two cupfuls of wine, and one of water, in a bottle, mixed them thoroughly, and presented it to you. How would you unmix them? How would you separate wine from water, in the same quantity as I had blended them?

Or, let us state the question otherwise. Suppose you had ordered a certain number of tuns, puncheons and pipes of wine—Graves, Orléans, Beaune, and Mirevaux in Languedoc—for your household supply. Suppose the carters and bargemen delivering it, drank up one half, and then filled up the containers with water. (The Limousins do this by the barrelful, when they cart wines from Argenton and St. Gaultier in Touraine.) How, I ask you, could you drain the water from the wine? How purify this adulterated product?

Yes, I know: you tell me all you need is an ivy funnel. Examples have been recorded, confirmed and verified. You know all about it. Yet any one who never saw this, or knew about it, would believe it impossible. Let us nevertheless proceed.

Suppose we lived in the age of Sulla, Marius, Cæsar and the Roman emperors, or of our ancient Druids, who used to burn the corpses of their relatives and masters? Suppose you wished to drink the ashes of wife or father in a cup of toothsome white wine?

(Artemisia, widow of Mausolus, King of Caria, drank his ashes in water; and the tomb she built for him—the Mausoleum—was one of the seven wonders of the world!)

Suppose, on the other hand, you preferred to store these ashes in a particular urn or reliquary? How, in God's name, could you separate your loved one's ashes from those of the funeral pyre? Answer *that* question, if you can? By my creed and creel, you will not find it easy.

Well then, I will come to your assistance. Follow my recipe, to wit: (1) take enough of this holy pantagruelion to cover the corpse of the dear departed; (2) close, bind, and sew said corpse in said plant; (3) throw corpse, thus enveloped, on flames as tall and consuming as you will; (4) allow fire to take its course, burning body and bone, reducing them to ashes.

Do this and you will find, not only that the pantagruelion will have lost no atom of the ashes enclosed in it, but also that it will have admitted no atom of the ashes of the pyre. Finally, indeed, it will emerge from the conflagration neater, whiter and cleaner than when you tossed it on the heap. That is why it is called asbestos or incombustible. It is found profusely in Carpasia, in Cyprus; it is obtainable very cheap in the region of Assouan, in Egypt.

O wonder, O marvel! Fire which devours, wastes and consumes everything, on the contrary cleanses, purges and whitens this Carpasian and flameproof pantagruelion. If you doubt it, as the Jews and sceptics did, then demand practical proof.

To obtain such proof, you need but bind this divine pantagruelion about an egg, lay the egg on red-hot coals—the hotter the better—and leave it there a while. Presently, when you decide to draw the egg, you will find it cooked, roasted, stone-hard; but your heavenly pantagruelion will not have been changed, dried or even warmed. The experiment will not cost you fifty-thousand Bordeaux crowns at par—or, for that matter, as many Bordeaux crowns shaved down to the twelfth part of a Poitiers farthing.

Do not come back at me with the argument that the salamander, also, withstands flames. That is an untruth. To be sure, it finds pleasure and strength in a little straw fire. But I guarantee this: like any other animal, the salamander will be soon suffocated, and consumed, by a blaze of any size. This has been proved; Galen, a long time ago, demonstrated and confirmed it; Dioscorides, in his second book, also established it.

Do not invoke feather-alum (sulphate of aluminum in clustered fibres). Do not tell me of the wooden tower of Piræus, which Sulla could not burn, because Archelaus, governor of the city for Mithridates, King of Pontus, had covered it with feather-alum. Do not come forward with the tree Cornelius Alexander calls *eon*—a tree which resembled the oak, because it bore mistletoe, but which was proof against injury and destruction by fire and water. Do not propose the mistletoe, of which the famed ship Argos was built. Search, if you will, for others who will believe it, I beg to be excused.

Do not dare, either, compare to pantagruelion, that very wonderful tree, the larch, found in the upper Alps at Briançon and Embrun. Its trunk provides excellent agaric mushrooms. Its body gives us such perfect rosin, that Galen ventures to compare it to turpentine. In its delicate leaves that sweet honey of heaven, called manna, a sugary white liquid, is deposited for our use. And though both gummy and oily, it is incombustible. It is called *larrix* in Greek and Latin; the Alpine name is *melze* or *mélèze*; the descendants of Antenor, founder of Padua, and the Venetians, call it *larege*. This last word gave the name Larignum to the castle which nonplussed Julius Cæsar on his return from Gaul.

Cæsar had ordered all the yeomen of the Alps, and of Piedmont, to supply stores and provisions, at various designated stages on the military road. All obeyed, except the men of Larignum, who were confident in the natural impregnability of the garrison.

In order to punish them, the emperor led his army directly upon the castle. At the gate stood a tower built of huge rafters of larch, stacked like a pile of timber, and rising so high, that, from the parapet, the defending forces believed they could, with stones and bars, easily beat off an attack.

When Cæsar learned that their chief weapons were so primitive and so ineffectual against his approach, he ordered his troops to pile up faggots, and set them afire. This was done at once. The flames rose so high that they covered the entire castle; the Romans confidently expected the tower to fall, consumed, within a few minutes. But when the flames died down, and the faggots burned out, what was Cæsar's surprise to behold the tower in no wise damaged?

He therefore ordered his men to lay down a circular network of trenches and ditches about the fort, beyond the reach of stones. The men of Larigno thereupon came to terms. From their account, Cæsar learned the admirable virtues of this wood, which produces neither fire nor flame nor coal, and which, by this token, might almost be rated with pantagruelion. The more so, indeed, since Pantagruel used this same timber for the doors, gates, windows, gutters, lining and coping in the Abbey of Thélème, as well as for the covering of the poops, prows, kitchens, decks, gangways and fo'c'sles of the carracks, brigs, galleons, galleys, foists (light galleys propelled by sail and oars), brigantines and other vessels in his arsenal at Thalassa. Yet larch has one defect. Its wood, placed on a blazing pile of other woods, eventually does become corrupted and destroyed like stones in a limekiln.

Whereas this pantagruelion asbestos is renewed and cleansed rather than dissipated and consumed. Accordingly:

> *Sabaean, Indian or Arabian state,*
> *Vaunt not your incense, myrrh and ebony.*
> *France boasts a plant ten thousand times more great:*
> *Visit us, see it, we will give you free*
> *Seeds you may sow in lands across the sea.*
> *If they take root, grant heaven a million thanks,*
> *Cry: "Hail, pantagruelion! Blessed be*
> *Its home, the happy kingdom of the Franks!"*

The Fourth Book

THE DEEDS AND HEROIC SAYINGS OF GOOD

PANTAGRUEL

Set Down by
MASTER FRANÇOIS RABELAIS
Doctor of Medicine

TO THE MOST ILLUSTRIOUS
AND MOST REVEREND LORD
ODET CARDINAL OF CHÂTILLON

You are not unaware, O most illustrious prince, how a number of eminent persons have urged and encouraged me in the past to continue these Pantagruelian fables. To-day, indeed, they still do so, telling me that many languishing, sick, unhappy and disconsolate people cheated their sorrows by reading my books. Ay, these patients discovered a merry pastime, learned new joys and acquired fresh consolation.

Invariably, I reply to such requests that I wrote these tales for my pleasure. I sought neither applause nor glory. My sole concern and intention were to use my pen to afford what little help I might to absent patients, just as I gladly do to present patients, when they avail themselves of my art and service.

Sometimes I tell them at great length how Hippocrates, in several places and particularly in his sixth book, *Of Epidemics,* describes the education of the physician, his disciple. I also quote Soranus the Ephesian, who practised medicine at Alexandria and Rome under the Emperor Trajan; Oribasius, friend of the Emperor Julian; Claudius Galen, friend of Marcus Aurelius; Hali Abbas, a Persian physician of the tenth century, author of the celebrated Arabic *Thesaurus of Medical Art;* and many other equally important authorities. These go into detail, discussing the medico's deportment, gestures, glance, touch, countenance, gracefulness, civility; his clear-cut features; his clothes, beard, hair, mouth and hands. In point of fact, they discuss his very nails, as if he were to play the lover's rôle in some comedy or to enter the lists to fight some powerful enemy. Here I may add that Hippocrates fittingly compares the practice of medicine to a struggle, and also to a farce with three characters: the patient, the physician and the disease.

This passage always reminds me of Julia's words to her father Augustus, as reported by Macrobius in his *Saturnalia.*

One day she appeared before him in a beautiful, loose, lascivious dress. Though much displeased, he did not utter a word. On the morrow, she put on another dress, the modest garb that chaste Roman ladies were wont to wear. As she came into his presence, Augustus, who the day before had not expressed his displeasure at her shamelessness, could not forbear to voice his delight at her welcome change.

"Oh, how much more becoming and commendable this dress is, for the daughter of Augustus!"

Julia, with ready excuse, replied:

"To-day, I dressed to please my father's eye; yesterday, to delight my husband's."

The physician's case is identical. He can disguise himself in looks and dress. He can don that rich, attractive four-sleeved gown, fashionable of yore and called the *philomium*, according to Joannes Alexandrinus, an Italian commentator of Hippocrates' *Of Epidemics*. And, to such as find the metamorphosis surprising, he can reply:

"I have accoutred myself thus, not out of vanity or ostentation, but for my patient's sake. It is my patient and none else that I would wholly please, that I would not offend or dissatisfy!"

There is much further testimony. In a passage in the work quoted, Father Hippocrates causes his readers to sweat, question and dispute. The point at issue is not whether the physician's sullen, morose, surly, frowning, crabbed, dour, dismal and lugubrious looks sadden the patient or whether his happy, open, serene, joyful, pleasing countenance cheers him. This has been solved by experience. No, the point at issue is whether such melancholy or joy is produced by the apprehension of the patient, as he examines these qualities in his doctor. Does the patient draw conclusions about himself, seeing, in his physician's happy mien, a favorable and much-desired recovery from his ailment, and in his physician's mournful mien, a dire and dread catastrophe? Or are such sensations produced in the patient by a transfusion of the serene or gloomy, aerial or terrestrial, joyful or melancholy spirits of the physician into the person of the patient, as Plato and Averroës believe?

Above all else, the authors I have quoted give the physician specific advice about the words, topics, conversation and discussion he must hold with his patient. All these must tend to one aim and purpose: the physician shall cheer his patient without offending God; the physician shall in no wise sadden his patient.

How bitterly Herophilus censures the physician Callianax who, on being asked by a patient "Shall I die?" quoted Achilles' saying to Eycaon, son of Priam, in the *Iliad*:

> *Patroclus, even, had to die,*
> *A mightier man than you or I.*

Another patient, wishing to know his condition, questioned Callianax after the fashion of noble Pathelin in the farce:

> *Doctor, doesn't my urine tell*
> *If I shall perish or get well?*

and he answered foolishly:

"No, it would not tell me even had Latona, mother of those beautiful twins Phœbus and Diana, begotten you!"

Galen, in his fourth book of *Comments on Hippocrates' Sixth Book, Of Epidemics*, roundly censures Quintus, his teacher. A certain Roman nobleman, Quintus' patient, said to him:

"You have breakfasted, learned master; your breath smells of wine!"

"And yours smells of fever!" the medico replied arrogantly. "Which gives off the more delicious aroma: wine or fever?"

Alas! the calumny of certain cannibals (a monstrous African race, with faces like dogs, who bark instead of laughing), misanthropes (haters of mankind like Timon of Athens) and agelasts (enemies of laughter, like that Crassus who, we are told, smiled but once in his life) proved so fierce and unreasonable that it conquered my patience. I resolved to write no jot more. For the least of their detractions was that my works were crammed with various heresies; and this, although they could not show a single example in the slightest passage. What are the sole theme and subject of these books of mine? Comedy and gay fooling, short of offending God and king. Do they contain heresy? Not one word of them does, unless perverse readers misinterpret me against all use of reason and common speech.

Rather than think such thoughts, I would have died a thousand deaths, if it were possible. You write of bread and these scoundrels read stone; you say fish and they interpret serpent; you talk of eggs and they understand scorpions.

I have complained of this in your presence, My Lord Cardinal. And I have said frankly that I considered I was a better Christian than they prove themselves to be. More, if my writings, my words or my very thoughts betrayed one scintilla of heresy, these enemies would not have fallen so detestably into the snares of the spirit of calumny, that Διάβολος who, through their agency, lays such crimes at my door. And I was willing, if proven wrong, to gather dry wood, light a fire and, phœnix-like, to burn myself upon it.

You were then pleased to tell me that the late King François, of blessed memory, being informed of these slanders, had my books read carefully and distinctly to him by the most learned and loyal anagnost, or reader, in the kingdom. I refer to Pierre du Châtel, Bishop of Tulle, and I say "my" books, because several false and infamous volumes have been evilly credited to me. His Majesty, you told me, found no single passage suspicious. Better still, he abhorred a certain serpent-eater and informer, who based a mortal heresy upon an *n* printed instead of an *m* by the carelessness of the printers. (That letter, My Lord Cardinal, made all the difference between the words *asne* or ass and *asme* or soul, in the twenty-second chapter of my Third Book.)

Our most gracious, virtuous and blessed sovereign, King Henri (whom Heaven long preserve!) was as well disposed towards me as his august father had been. He granted you his royal privilege and particular protection for me against slanderers. Since then, you deigned to confirm this happy news when I saw you in Paris, and again, later, when you visited My Lord Cardinal du Bellay. To recuperate from painful and protracted illness, he had retired to St. Maur, that place or, to be more exact, that paradise of health, serenity, convenience, amenity, delight and all sweet country pleasures.

Thus, My Lord Cardinal, being safe from all intimidation, I draw my pen boldly. And I trust that, with your kindly favor, you will still protect me against slanderers, like a second Gallic Hercules in knowledge, wisdom and eloquence, a very Alexicacos, or guardian against evil, in strength, power and authority. For I may say to you, My Lord Cardinal, what Moses, the great Israelitish prophet and captain, said of wise King Solomon, in *Ecclesiasticus*, xlv:

"A man fearing and loving God, who found favor in the sight of all flesh, well beloved both of God and of man, whose memory is blessed. God made him like to the glorious saints and magnified him, so that his enemies stood in fear of him. He made him glorious in the sight of kings, gave him commandment for his people, and by him showed His light. He sanctified him in his faithfulness and meekness, and chose him from among all men. By him, He made us to hear His voice, and caused by him the law of life and knowledge to be given."

In conclusion, I beg to promise that I shall adjure all readers I meet, who commend my merry writing, to give thanks to you alone, to be grateful and to pray Our Lord for the preservation and increase of your greatness. I shall urge them to attribute to me no more than a humble subjection and ready obedience to your worthy commands. For, by your most honorable encouragement, you have endowed me with inspiration and courage; without you, my heart would have failed me and the fountainhead of my animal spirits would have run dry.

May the Lord maintain you in His blessed mercy!
My Lord Cardinal's most humble and devoted servant.

FRANÇ. RABELAIS, physician.

From Paris, the twenty-eighth day of January, MDLII.

THE AUTHOR'S PROLOGUE

GOD save you and preserve you, O men of worth! Where on earth are you; I cannot make you out anywhere? One minute, I beg you: let me put on my spectacles. Ha! there we are, that's better: all our troubles are over. I see you plain as a pikestaff.

Quite a vintage you've gone through, I hear. Bravo! so much the better, for, in the process, you've surely discovered an infallible cure for thirst. Well done, friends, well done! You, your children, your relations, your whole blessed family are in the pink of condition. Just as it should be: excellent, delightful! God be praised, therefore, eternally. And, if so please His sacred will, may you endure healthy for a long time to come.

As for myself, thanks to His favors, I continue in the same state: I thrive by virtue of Pantagruelism. Do you ask what Pantagruelism is? Good heavens, you know as well as I! Pantagruelism is a certain gaiety of spirit produced by a contempt of the incidentals of fate; it is a healthy, cheerful spirit, one ever ready to drink, if it will.

Did someone ask me why? O dearly beloved, I answer positively: because such is the will of the mighty, beneficent and omnipotent Creator, Whom I acknowledge and obey. Whose sacrosanct and auspicious Word I revere. (By Word, I mean Bible.)

Is it not the Bible which derides with excoriating sarcasm the physician who neglects his own health? Does not the Holy Book say: "Physician, heal thyself!"

Claudius Galen had some notion of Scripture and frequented certain of the pious Christians of his age, as is evidenced by Book XI, *De usu partium*, *Of the Use of the Limbs*; by Book II, Chapter 3, *De differentiis pulsuum* and by *Lib. de rerum affectibus*, if the last is indeed his. But it was through no such biblical observance that Galen maintained himself in excellent health. No, Galen did so to avoid the vulgar, satirical reproach:

Ἰατρὸς ἄλλων, αὐτὸς ἕλκεσι βρύων.

495

He can cure others by the score,
Yet he himself is one vast sore.

Ay, Galen grounds his reputation on the proud boast that, between the age of twenty-eight and almost seventy, he lived in the pink of health, save for a few passing attacks of fever, This, though by nature he was not particularly sound, possessing a stomach obviously morbid. As Galen remarks in Book v, *De sanitate tuenda, Of Protecting the Health,* a medico neglectful of himself is scarce calculated to inspire confidence in others.

Asclepiades boasted even more proudly. He had agreed with fate, he said, to be considered a physician only if he never fell ill, from the day he began practising medicine until the day he retired. He lived up to his boast, too, reaching the fulness of age in complete vigor; triumphant, in all his limbs, over fortune. At last, far from suffering the slightest ailment, he passed from life to death by an unlucky fall from the top of a defective, rotting staircase.

Has some disaster befallen Your Lordships, causing health to flee above or below, before or behind, to right or to left, within or without? If so, whether that health be near home or abroad, I pray you catch up with it, through the aid of the blessed Saviour. Should you meet it soon, then seize, appropriate, claim and possess it at once: you are entitled to do so by virtue of the law, by royal privilege and by my personal advice. As you may recall, the legislators of old permitted the master to capture his runaway slave wherever he found him.

Praise God and bless men! Consult the hallowed customs of this noble, ancient, beauteous, wealthy and flourishing realm of France! Do they not warrant, in writing, that the dead seize the quick? On this score, read the testimony of the excellent, learned, wise, humane, courteous and just legist, André Tiraqueau, counsellor to the mighty, victorious and triumphant monarch, Henri, the second of the name. Tiraqueau's words will be found in the proceedings of the most honorable court of parliament in Paris.

Health is our life, as Ariphon the Sicyonian observed sagely in a noble poem he wrote upon the subject. Without health, life is no life, it is unlivable; so spoke Pyrrhus, King of Epirus, when he said ᾿ΑΒΙ´ΟΣ ΒΙ´ΟΣ, ΒΙ´ΟΣ ᾿ΑΒΙ´ΩΤΟΣ, and begged of the gods the single gift of health. Without health, life spells but languor and an image of death. Accordingly, if you are ailing (in other words: dead), then recover your health (in other words: seize the quick, seize life).

I believe God will hear our prayers because our faith is manifest; I believe He will grant our wishes, because they are moderate. The ancients held that moderation was golden, that is to say precious, universally praised and everywhere welcome. Scan the Holy Bible, and invariably you will read that the prayers of those who prayed moderately were never unanswered.

St. Luke gives us an example in the person of little Zacchæus. (The monks at St. Ayl, near Orléans, pride themselves on the possession of his body and relics; they call him St. Sylvan.) Well, little Zacchæus, the publican, wanted but one thing: to behold the blessed Saviour near Jerusalem. A most moderate wish, accessible to anyone. But he was too small; lost in the crowd of spectators, he could not so much as get a glimpse of Him. He wriggled about, stood on tiptoe, trotted this way and that, all in vain. At last he moved away and climbed a sycamore. Whereupon the Lord, knowing his sincerity and moderation, presented Himself to Zacchæus' sight. Not only did the publican see and hear Christ, but he and his family received the Saviour's visit and blessing.

There is also the example of the son of a prophet of Israel. The lad was cutting down wood near the river Jordan, when his axehead fell into the water. He implored God to deign restore it, a most moderate prayer, surely. To prove his trust and confidence, he threw not the hatchet after the helve (as certain slanderous devils wrongly avouch), but the helve after the hatchet (as you yourselves properly have it). Suddenly, a double miracle appeared; the iron, rising to the surface of the water, "did swim" and fit itself back on to the handle. Had this man begged to ride to heaven in a fiery chariot like Elijah, to multiply in seed like Abraham, to be rich as Jacob, strong as Samson or beautiful as Absalom, would he have had his wish? I question it very much.

Speaking of moderate desires in connection with hatchets—remind me when it is time for a drink!—I will tell you what you can read in the apologues of wise Æsop the Frenchman. Did I say Frenchman? Maximus Planudes, the learned Greek monk of the fourteenth

century, calls Æsop a Phrygian and Trojan. But, as you know, the
father of the French race was Francus, son of Trojan Hector, and
our nobles are descended from the royal Phrygian house. Be that
as it may, Ælian writes that Æsop was a Thracian: whilst Agathias
of Myrina, the Byzantine historian of the sixth century, agrees
with Herodotus that Æsop was from Samos. To me, it is all one.

In the days of Æsop, there was a poor villager of Gravot, near
Bourgueil, called Couillatris or Puddingballocks, a woodchopper by
trade, who managed to make a sorry livelihood. One day, he lost
his axe. And who, do you suppose, was infinitely vexed and grieved?

Why, Puddingballocks, of course! Did not his fate and life depend
upon that axe? Did not that axe win him respect and employment
from the prosperous master-woodcutters of the region? Did not
that axe alone stand between him and starvation? Without that
axe, he would have met death six days later, and the grim reaper
would have swept him away with one swift swing of his sickle.

Lost in grief, Puddingballocks began to invoke Jupiter. He cried,
begged, pleaded and, necessity being the mother of invention and
grandmother of eloquence, he hit upon the most convincing prayers
imaginable. He raised his eyes to heaven, fell upon his knees; he bared
his head, reared his arms high, pointed upward in appeal. Over and
over again, he concluded each prayer with the loud, tireless refrain:

"My axe, my axe, Lord Jupiter, all I want is my axe, or money to
buy another. Alas, my poor axe!"

At the time, Jupiter was presiding over a grand council, called to
attend to portentous matters. Aged Cybele, mother of the gods, was
giving her advice—or perhaps, if you prefer, handsome young Phœbus was orating. Nevertheless, Puddingballocks' outcry was so loud
that it reached the divine council and consistory, creating no slight
shock to the assembled members.

"What devil is howling so horribly there below?" Jupiter demanded. "By the power of the Styx, haven't we been plagued enough
in the past with all sorts of puzzling problems? Are we not even now
bothered with the settlement of the weightiest affairs? We have
ended the strife between Presthan, King of Persia (Prester John of
Abyssinia), and Soliman the Magnificent, the Turkish emperor. We
have ironed out the difficulties between the Muscovites of Ivan the
Terrible and the savage Tartars. We have answered the petition sub-

mitted by the Shereef of Morocco. We have even made a zealot of Golgotz Rays, the Ottoman Corsair who pillaged Sicily. Warfare in Parma, Mirandola and Tunisia has been abolished; Magdeburg has been given to Maurice of Saxony; Henri II of France and the Emperor Charles V are no longer enemies. Peace reigns in Africa (that Mediterranean city we call Aphrodisium, and others call Mehedia). Tripoli, negligently defended by the knights of St. John, has found a new master, the Turks; its hour was come.

"Now those renegade Gascons rise up, demanding the restitution of their bells, which once roused them to open revolution against the salt tax. As though an amnesty were not enough! . . . Elsewhere the Saxons, Easterlings of the Hanseatic League, Ostrogoths and Germans, invincible of yore, are being humbled and dominated by a paltry, gout-ridden little fellow. They are, to quote their own lansquenets, *'aberkeids'*—exhausted, whipped by Charles V. So they implore us to grant them succor, help and the renewal of their pristine liberty and good sense.

"What shall we do with that Aristotelian brangler Galland and that platonic champion Ramus, who, with their scullion satellites and vagabond assistants, are turning the whole University of Paris topsy-turvy? I am much perplexed about the whole matter and quite undetermined with whom to side. Except for this wrangle, both seem to me to be lusty enough lads, in their way, and ballocky blades. One is flush with cash (and flushed with gout!); the other aspires to affluence . . . one possesses some culture; the other is no ignoramus . . . one loves decent people; the other is well loved by decent people . . . one is a sly, cunning fox; the other, in word and writing, snarls at the ancient philosophers like an angry cur. . . .

"Let us hear your opinion, Priapus, you great donkeypizzle! Many a time, I have found your counsel opportune and to the point: *Et habet tua mentula mentem,* that rod you wield has a mind to it."

Priapus doffed his hood, discovering a red flaming face:

"King Jupiter," he said, "did you not compare the one to a yelping dog, the other to a wily fox? Well, I advise you to cease cudgelling your brains any further. Deal with them as you did of old with the dog and fox."

"What dog?" Jupiter inquired. "What fox? When? Who were they? I don't seem to remember."

"What a memory!" Priapus gasped. And proceeded to remind his master of the circumstance.

Father Bacchus yonder, clearly discernible by his crimson face, once sought to avenge himself upon the Thebans. Accordingly, he produced a magic fox, uncapturable by any other beast, no matter what harm or damage it did.

Now noble Vulcan had forged a dog of Monesian bronze or copper —a metal later worked by the Monesii of Aquitania. By dint of careful blowing, Vulcan had instilled, into his metallic pet, both life and motion. He gave this dog to mighty Jupiter, who, in turn, presented it to Europa, his sweetheart—who gave it to Minos, judge of the lower regions—who gave it to Procris—who gave it to Cephalus, her husband. (You recall how Procris deserted Cephalus out of jealousy, spied upon him, and was accidentally killed by him in doing so.)

Vulcan's dog, then, was quite as magical as Bacchus' fox. Like a contemporary lawyer, that dog would pounce upon any beast it saw, and would inevitably capture it. One day, dog and fox happened to meet. What was to be done? Dog, by its fatal destiny, was to catch fox; fox, likewise by fatal destiny, was never to be caught.

The case, Priapus reminded Jupiter, was brought before the great god's council. Jupiter refused to go against fate; but here were two contradictory fates, each apparently valid. Yet the authenticity, application and result of both contradictions were declared incompatible in Nature, and poor Jupiter was sweating for very perplexity. (A few drops of the divine sweat, falling on earth, produced what men call cauliflower.) The noble assembly of the gods, lacking a categorical resolution, were seized with a terrific thirst: more than seventy-eight hogsheads of nectar were emptied down so many divine gullets.

Finally, on Priapus' advice—didn't King Jupiter remember now? —he had turned the two beasts to stone. The problem solved, a truce with thirst was declared throughout high Olympus. It was the year of the flabby cods, near Teumessus, between Thebes and Chalcis.

"Remembering this," Priapus urged, "I believe, O King Jupiter, that you should petrify this other pair of irreconcilables, Galland and Ramus, dog and fox. Such a metamorphosis will not be amiss: both bear the name Pierre or Peter, which means stone. Since, to quote a

Limousin proverb, you need three stones to make an oven's mouth, you can add Maître Pierre du Coignet, whom you petrified long ago for the same reason."

(Priapus here referred to a stone marmoset in Notre Dame called Pierre du Coignet; it stood in one corner—*coign*—its nose was used to snuff out candles. It was so named in malice by the Decretalists, or champions of papal secular authority as against the royal cause, upheld by Pierre du Coignet, representing King Philippe VI.)

"These three dead stones may be set in an equilateral triangle inside the vast temple at Paris or in the middle of the porch. As in the game of Fouquet, called also Fucker or Squirrel, their noses will serve to snuff out candles, tapers, torches and firebrands. Would this not be justice since, while alive, these fuckersquirrels used to light fires of faction, schism, ballocking sects and partisanship among the idle schoolboys? I might remind you that before they appeared, since time immemorial, such instances of self-seeking testiculotitillation were scorned rather than condemned by you, O Jupiter.

"I thank you: I have had my say!"

"So far as I can make out," Jupiter answered, "you deal too kindly with them. You are not so indulgent towards everybody, My Lord Priapus. However, since they are so keen on perpetuating their name and memory, let them be turned, after death, into hard marble stone, rather than go back to earth and putrefaction."

This matter settled, Jupiter considered the Tyrrhenian Sea and sundry places close to the Appenines; he exposed the tragic troubles stirred up by certain papal scoundrels. This blazing fury would last its time, like the Limousin oven; then it would cool down, but not so soon! It would yet furnish sport to the gods of Olympus.

However, Jupiter saw one disadvantage. Olympus possessed but a small supply of thunderbolts, since Jupiter's colleagues, by his special permission, had amused themselves by bombarding New Antioch. (Their example, indeed, had been followed on earth by the stout defenders of the fortress of Dingdiddle, who, undertaking to hold it against all comers, wasted their ammunition by firing at sparrows, leaving none for their protection in time of need. So they surrendered bravely to an enemy which was already maddened, desperate and abandoning the siege, having no thought more urgent than a swift retreat and a short-lived humiliation!)

"Attend to this, I pray, Vulcan, my son. Arouse your slumbering Cyclopes, Asteropes, Brontes, Arges, Polyphemus, Sterope, Pyracmon and the rest. Put them to work and let them drink proportionally: men of fire should never want for wine. Now let us attend to this bawling clod below; find out who he is, Mercury, and what he wants."

Mercury looked down the trapdoor of heaven, through which the gods are supposed to keep an eye on earth. It is said to resemble the hatch of a ship, though Icaromenippus, in Lucian, states that it is more like the mouth of a well.

Mercury, having distinguished Puddingballocks and heard his complaint, reported to the council.

"Upon my word," Jupiter grumbled, "the fellow comes opportunely! As though we had nothing to do now but restore lost hatchets. Yet restore it we must; for it is written in the Book of Fate. Do you hear, Mercury? We must as surely restore it as if it were worth the duchy of Milan, which France claims for its value. Is not that hatchet as precious and valuable to him as a kingdom to a king? Let us be done with him; give back the hatchet and let us dismiss him from our thoughts. Come, friends, let us now turn to the variance between the clergy and the Lord High Molebilly of Landerousse or to like enigmas."

Priapus, hugging the fireside, looked up.

"Mighty Jupiter," he said, "in the days when, by your order and special favor, I was keeper of the earthly gardens, I noticed that the word *cognée* or hatchet gave rise to numerous equivokes. Literally, it means a certain instrument used for cutting and splitting wood. But it is also employed figuratively—or used to be in the old days—to designate a female frequently and consentfully tumblerumble-cunneybrangled. No lusty cocksman but called his pleasure-wench 'hatchet.' For with this tool," and Priapus proudly exhibited his duodenal, twelve-inch knocker, "these lads drive in their helves so resolutely and deep that their trollops are utterly exempt of a certain fear epidemic among the female sex. What fear, you ask? The fear lest man's whangdoodle dangle down from mid-belly to his heels for want of such feminine props.

"Well I remember," Priapus went on, "having a long member—I mean a long memory, a beautiful memory, rich enough to fill a tub of butter . . . well I remember how at the Tubilustria—the Roman festival when horns and trumpets were blessed (it was in May, during goodman Vulcan's festival)—I heard a lot of musicians. There were Josquin des Prez, of Hainault, chapelmaster to Pope Sixtus and later in the service of King Louis XII; Ockeghem, also a Fleming, chapelmaster to Charles VII; Hobrecht, Agricola, Brumel, Camelin, Vigoris, de la Fage, Bruyer, Prioris, Seguin, de la Rue, Midy, Moulu, Mouton, Gascogne, Loyset, Compère, Penet, Fevin, Rousée, Richefort, Rousseau or Francesco Roselli, an Italian; Consilion; Constanto Festi, another Italian; Jacquet Bercan, all singing tunefully:

> *Ned Longprick, ere he jounced his bride*
> *(O comely virgin! happy bed!)*
> *Laid down a mallet by his side.*
> *She saw it, stared, wide-eyed, and said:*
> *"What ith thith mallet for, thweet Ned?*
> *Tell me itth uthe before we kith!"—*
> *"To wedge and splice you better with!"—*
> *She smiled: "Thweet huthband, what a farthe!*
> *When Thtout Tham thtrumth my maidenhead,*
> *He only hammerth with hith arthe."*

The gods burst into laughter. But Priapus was not done: "Nine Olympiads and one intercalary or leap year after, I remember—O lovely member! I mean: lovely memory!—yes, I often confound the symbolization and relation of these two words. . . . Well, a long time ago, I recall hearing Adrian Willaert, the Flemish choirmaster of St. Mark's and founder of Venetian music; Gombaert; Jannequin, who composed the *Defeat of the Swiss at Marignano*; Pierre Certon, choirmaster of the Sainte Chapelle in Paris; Manchicourt, Auxin, Villiers, Sandrin, Sohier, Hesdin; Morales, chapelmaster of the Cathedral of Seville; Passereau, Maille, Maillart, Jacotin, Heurteur, Verdelot, Carpentras, Lhéritier, Cadeac, Doublet, Vermont, Bouteiller, Lope, Paignier, Millet, Dumoulin, Alaire, Marault, Morpain, Gendre and many another merry musician, sitting in the shade of a fine tree in a private garden, surrounded by a bulwark of flagons, hams, meat pies—not to mention hooded chickens and like game in skirts—singing daintily:

A hatchet sans handle is useless! Yoo-hoo!
Tools without hafts do no good in themselves.
Let us wedge them together, jam, couple and screw:
Let the ladies be hatchets, the gentlemen helves.

"So," Priapus concluded with a flourish, "the point is to find out just what sort of instrument our friend Puddingballocks is bawling for!"

Hereupon the venerable gods and goddesses burst into fits of laughter, whirling like a microcosm of flies; while Vulcan, despite his limp, broke into a jigstep for the delight of his beloved Venus.

"Enough, enough," Jupiter commanded. "Go to earth, Mercury, and lay three hatchets at Puddingballocks' feet: one made of gold, one of silver, and his own. Take care that all three are of the same size and weight; let him make a choice. If he is content to pick his own, then give him the other two in the bargain; but if he selects either the golden or the silver one, use his own to sever his head from his shoulders. And henceforth, pray employ the same procedure with all such as lose their axes."

With which, Jupiter twisted his head like a monkey swallowing a pill, and assumed so awesome an expression that all Olympus trembled.

With the help of his pointed cap, his hood, the wings at his heels and his wand, Mercury sped through the trapdoor of heaven, cleft the wastes of the air and, a few seconds later, landed upon earth to lay the three hatchets at Puddingballocks' feet.

"You have yelled enough to be dry for a drink," he told the woodcutter. "Jupiter has heard your prayers. Tell me which of these hatchets is yours and take it away with you."

Puddingballocks raised the golden hatchet, examined it, found it too weighty and, turning to Mercury:

"This isn't mine," he said. "I don't want it!"

Next he took up the silver hatchet:

"This isn't mine either. I'll leave this one with you as well."

Finally, he picked up his own old hatchet, studied the wooden helve, and recognized his mark at the end of it. Transported with joy, like a fox who meets a band of runaway hens, he grinned from ear to ear:

"God's turds!" he exclaimed. "That one's mine! If you will only leave it me, I promise you a sacrifice at the next ides—that is May fifteenth! Ay, I'll sacrifice a fine great bowl of milk, covered with the best strawberries in the wood."

"My good man," said Mercury, "I leave you your hatchet; take it. And, by order of Jupiter, because your wish and choice were moderate, you shall have the other two hatchets as well. Henceforth, you have enough to be a rich man. Be honest, too!"

Puddingballocks thanked Mercury civilly, paid tribute to almighty Jupiter, and fastened his old hatchet in his leather girdle, above his buttock, like Martin, the metal figure that strikes the hours on the clock in the belfry of Cambrai. Then, laying the two heavier hatchets on his shoulders, he trudged happily over the fields, cutting a fine figure among his fellow-parishioners and neighbors, and quoting Pathelin's line in the farce:

" 'Am I well provided? Have I got plenty?' "

Next day, he put on a white smock, slung the precious hatchets over his shoulder, and made for Chinon, a most ancient, famous and noble city, ay, the finest city in the world, according to the solemn judgment of the most learned biblical scholars. At Chinon he turned his silver hatchet into fine silver testons and other white money; his golden hatchet into fine angels, new-minted crowns, gleaming royals, full-weight nobles and other goldpieces. With the money he purchased a great many farms, barns, cottages, lodges, outhouses, meadows, vineyards, woods, plowlands, pastures, ponds, mills, gardens, willow groves, oxen, cows, ewes, sheep, goats, sows, porkers, asses, horses, roosters, capons, hens, pullets, geese, ganders, ducks, drakes and other things. In brief, he soon became the richest man in the country, richer even than My Lord of Maulevrier, the limping nobleman.

Puddingballocks' sudden rise in fortune amazed his brother bumpkins and fellow-clods. The sympathy and kindliness they had once felt for him soon turned into envy of his vast and unexpected riches. They bustled about, inquired here and there, put their heads together, pried high and low, seeking to discover the exact circumstances, time, place and motivation of this enormous treasure. When they found out he had acquired it by losing his hatchet: "Ha!" they cried. "If it only means losing a hatchet, we can grow as wealthy as he

is. Easy and cheap enough to do, God knows! So the revolution of the
heavens, the constellation of the firmament and the aspects of the
planets are now such that whoever loses a hatchet gains a fortune, eh?
All right, friend hatchet, lost you shall be, whether you like it or
not!"

Thereupon, to a man, every mother's son among them lost his
hatchet. Never a devil of a hatchet remained, and, for lack of tools,
no wood was felled or split in the forest from that day forward.

Æsop's apologue even goes further. It tells how certain sprigs of
the petty nobility, having learned by what simple means Puddingballocks acquired his wealth, sold him their property, one disposing
of a small meadow, the other of a tiny mill. Still others sold even their
swords to buy hatchets, which they might lose, like the peasants, in
order to gain silver and gold in abundance. They were exactly like
Romebound fanatics, selling their all and borrowing of others, in
order to purchase mountains of indulgences from newly created
popes. And they shouted, and they prayed, and they lamented, and
they invoked Jupiter with cries of "My hatchet!" here, and "My
hatchet!" there, and "My hatchet, Jupiter, O give me back my
hatchet, give me back my hatchet!" The air for miles around rang
with the shouts and imprecations of these hatchet-losers.

Mercury was promptness itself, invariably appearing with three
tools: a silver one, a golden one, and the one lost. Not a man but
chose the golden and offered thanks to its divine donor, mighty Jupiter; but as the fellow bent down to pick it up, Mercury, according to
orders, chopped his head off. The number of severed heads was
exactly equal to the number of lost axes.

The same fate as Puddingballocks' will attend all who entertain
simple and moderate desires. Follow his example, all of you, especially
you greedy, lowland dolts who vow that you would not forego your
wishes for ten thousand francs. From now on, forbear to speak so impudently: do not let me hear you, as I have so often done, saying:

"Would to God that I now had one hundred and seventy-eight
millions in gold. Oh, what I could do with it!"

Poor wretched mules that you are, can you not understand that
king, emperor or pope could not wish for more?

Experience, then, teaches you that when you dream of such extravagant things, all you get is the itch, the scabies and never a

penny in your purse. Indeed, you fare no better than the two beggars, typical Parisians, both.

One wished for as many crowns as had been minted, taken, received and otherwise exchanged in the city, from the day the first foundation had been laid, down to the time of speaking. The sum, incidentally, was to be reckoned in terms of the price, rate and value, current at the peak of the best year during this lapse of time. Do you think this fellow bashful? Was he fastidious? Had he eaten sour plums, peel and all? Were his teeth set on edge?

His colleague's wish was more modest. He longed for the temple of Notre Dame, cram-full of steel needles, from floor to topmost vault. Also, he wished as many golden crowns as could be stuffed into as many bags as might be sewn by all these needles, until the latter were dulled or blunted. What a wish, my friends! What a hope!

The sequel? Well, that evening, both well-wishers had:

> *Ulcerous chilblains on the feet,*
> *Pimples where chin and collar meet,*
> *Lungs wracked by churchyard coughs, a sweet*
> *Catarrh in throat, plus a complete*
> *Series of boils upon the seat*

and devil find a bit of bread for them to pick their teeth with!

No, no, my friends: seek, rather, moderation, and you shall have your wish, and the better, too, if you work hard meanwhile.

"But," say you, "God, being all-powerful, can give me seventy-eight thousand as easily as a thirteenth fraction of one-half. To Him, one million is as little as a copper."

Ha! let me laugh, and once again, Ha, ha, ha! Who, O my unfortunate people, taught you to cite and discuss God's power and predestination? Peace, hush, quiet, and shut up! Humble yourselves before His holy countenance and acknowledge your frailty.

It is on moderation, O my goutstricken friends, it is on moderation I ground my hopes. I am convinced that (please the Lord!) you will obtain good health, since good health is all you ask for at present. Bide your time a while longer, and use an ounce of patience.

Not so the Genoese. In the morning they plan, plot and elect which of their number they can mulct that day; they specify who shall be cheated, swindled, bilked and diddled by their craft. Then they fare forth and, on the Exchange, greet one another saying:

"Health and gain, to you, sir: *sanità e guadagno!*"

Not content with health, they want profit, to boot. They want *guadagno* or gain; they want crowns minted by old Guadagno himself, Tomasso of the name, your Lyons Crœsus. Consequently, they often find neither health nor gain.

So, friends, fetch up a healthy cough, toss off three sound bumpers, prick up your ears and you will hear me tell wonders about the excellent and noble Pantagruel.

I

HOW PANTAGRUEL SET SAIL TO VISIT THE ORACLE OF THE DIVINE BOTTLE, BACBUC

In the month of June, Pantagruel took leave of goodman Gargantua, his father. In keeping with a praiseworthy custom among the early Christian saints, the old man bade Pantagruel and his company godspeed, praying heaven they might make a happy voyage.

Pantagruel set out on the ninth of June, an auspicious day, since it was sacred to the goddess Vesta. It was, likewise, the anniversary of Brutus' conquest of Spain and his humbling of its denizens. That same day, too, miserly Crassus had gone down to defeat at the hands of the Parthians.

They embarked at Thalassa. Besides Pantagruel, there were Panurge, Friar John of the Funnels, Epistemon, Gymnastes, Eusthenes, Rhizotomos and Carpalim, not to mention a host of attendants and servants. Xenomanes, the great traveller and explorer of perilous wildernesses, had arrived some days before, at Panurge's request. For certain excellent reasons. Xenomanes had plotted, on his vast and universal hydrographical chart, the course they were to steer in order to visit the divine Bacbuc, or, to translate a Hebrew phrase, the Holy Bottle. And he had left this diagram with Gargantua.

In the third book, I told the number of Pantagruel's ships. However, they were supplemented by an equal number of triremes, men-of-war and galleons, all equipped, rigged and caulked with plenty of pantagruelion. The officers, interpreters, pilots, captains, mariners, quartermasters and navigators met in Pantagruel's flagship, the *Thalamege*. In the stern, for ensign, this vessel bore a tall fat bottle: one half was silver, very highly polished and very shiny; the other half, gold, enamelled a carnation hue. Thus it was easy to tell that white and red were the colors of the noble travellers, and that they were travelling to ascertain the oracle of the Holy Bottle.

High over the poop of the second ship loomed a lantern, like those the ancients used, fashioned most skilfully of diaphanous stone. This indicated that they were to pass through Lanternland.

The third ship's ensign was a fine deep china bowl; the fourth's, a double-handled jar of gold, much like an ancient urn. The fifth, sixth, seventh, eighth and ninth vessels were respectively distinguished by a [s]permanent emerald . . . a begging-flask, the sort a friar carries on his hip when alms-hunting; it was made of four metals: gold, silver, copper and steel . . . an ebony funnel, embossed and inlaid with gold . . . a very precious ivy goblet with gold scrollwork . . . and a vase with handles of refined gold.

The tenth ship flaunted a huge cup of aromatic agalloch (what you know as aloes), incrusted with Cyprus gold and decorated after the Persian fashion. The eleventh, a gold basket of mosaic work. The twelfth, a wine cask of unpolished gold, covered with masses of Indian pearls grouped to resemble vines.

Accordingly, the saddest, sourest, unluckiest and most melancholy of men would have been filled with a new gladness, and would have smiled at beholding this noble convoy of ships with their brave devices. Even Heraclitus himself, that weepy pessimist, could not have contained his delight. It was impossible to believe that the travellers were not all honest men and gallant topers. It was no less impossible to prophesy with certainty that their journey, both outward and homeward bound, would find them in perfect health and mirthful disposition.

When they were all assembled on board the *Thalamege*, Pantagruel made a short and pious address, based wholly upon appropriate extracts from Scripture, and dealing with navigation. Then, all prayed to God in loud clear voices, their orison audible to the townsmen of Thalassa, who had thronged to the mole to see them off.

Next, they sang the psalm of Holy King David which begins: *When Israel went out of Egypt*. . . . This over, tables were placed on deck, and a banquet speedily served. The Thalassians, who had joined in the psalm, produced many victuals, and quantities of wine. The whole expedition drank to their healths; they returned the compliment. Because of this last fact, none of our voyagers suffered headache or pains at the stomach. Nor could they have avoided seasickness as readily by drinking salt water (pure or mixed with wine) some days previously; or by using quince, lemonpeel, the juice of sourish pomegranates; or by fasting a long time and covering their bellies with paper; or by following other remedies that foolish physicians prescribe for those who go to sea.

After repeated drinking, they returned to their respective ships. Soon they set sail with a fine wind from the southeast behind them; the chief navigator, named Jamet Brayer, shaped his course and turned all the compass needles accordingly. The oracle of Bacbuc, the Holy Bottle, lay in Upper India, close to Cathay or China. But both Jamet Brayer and Xenomanes preferred not to steer upon the usual Portuguese course, which crosses the torrid zone of the equator, skirts the Cape of Good Hope, at the southernmost point of Africa, loses sight and guidance of the arctic pole, and necessitates a lengthy voyage. Instead, they would cling as close as possible to the parallel of India, tacking to the westward of the given pole, so that, progressing under the north, they would be in the same latitude as the harbor of Les Sables d'Olonne. But they would go no further north, for they feared being icebound in the Frozen Sea. According to this canonical turn by the parallel mentioned, they would have to their right and eastward, what, on their departure, had been on their left.

This proved an incredible advantage. For, without shipwreck, danger or loss of men, they sailed serenely (save for one day off the island of the Macreons) all the way to Upper India, in less than four months. The Portuguese, on the other hand, could barely have accomplished the same journey in less than three years, encountering a thousand dangers and innumerable accidents at that.

To my mind, with all due respect to more authoritative judgments, this auspicious course was that steered by the Indians, who sailed to Germany, where they were honorably received by the King of the Swedes (chieftain of the Suevi).

This happened under Quintus Metellus Celer's proconsulship in Gaul; Cornelius Nepos, Pomponius Mela, and Pliny, after them vouch for its truth.

II

HOW PANTAGRUEL BOUGHT MANY SPLENDID THINGS IN THE ISLAND OF MEDAMOTHY, OR NOWHERE

THE first day out, and the two days following, they found no new land or new sight, for they had already sailed that way before. But on the fourth day, they discovered an island called Medamothy, or Nowhere. A most attractive and beautiful place it was, too, with a vast number of lighthouses and high marble towers along its coastline, which is no lesser that that of Canada.

Pantagruel inquired about its ruler. The latter, they told him, was King Philophanes, "he who is eager to see and to be seen." His Majesty, however, was absent at the time, attending the wedding of his brother, Philotheamon (the name means "avid of seeing") to the Infanta of the Kingdom of Engys or "of the peoples near by."

Disembarking while the ships' crews watered and took on supplies, Pantagruel spent some hours examining the various paintings, tapestries, animals, fishes, birds and other exotic merchandise which were along the waterfront and in the markets of the port. It happened to be the third day of the famous fair, which attracts the richest, most renowned merchants of Africa and Asia.

Out of this wealth of goods, Friar John bought himself two rare and valuable paintings. The first represented to perfection the face of a man appealing a case to a higher court. The second showed a varlet looking for his master: it had every requisite of gesture, bearing, look, gait and feature. It was an original by Master Charles Charmois, painter to King Megistus, the same artist who worked at Fontainebleau in France. Friar John paid for these paintings in monkeymoney, that is, with a smile, a bow and a fart of satisfaction.

Panurge bought a large painting copied from the needlework done of yore by Philomela to show her sister that she was not dead. (Tereus had raped her and cut her tongue, lest she tell the shame of it.) I vow by the handle of my cresset that it was a wondrously gallant, a masterly piece of work. Do not imagine, I pray, that it contained the likeness of a male and female playing the double-backed beast. That would have been too silly and too crude. No, it was something quite different and far more intelligent. You can see it at Thélème, on the left side as you enter the high gallery.

Epistemon purchased a painting which recorded, to the life, the ideas of Plato and the atoms of Epicurus, Rhizotomos invested in another, which vividly portrayed the nymph Echo.

Pantagruel had Gymnastes acquire the life and feats of Achilles in seventy-eight pieces of admirable texture, four fathoms long by three wide, all of Phrygian silk, broidered with gold and silver. The work began with the wedding of Peleus and Thetis, then treated successively the birth of Achilles . . . his adolescence, as described by Statius Papinius . . . his warlike prowess and his particular feats, as celebrated by Homer . . . his death and funeral, as reported by Ovid and by Quintus Calaber . . . to end with the apearance of his ghost and Polyxena's sacrifice, as presented by Euripides. . . .

Pantagruel also obtained three fine young unicorns (the male a chestnut, the two females dappled grays) and a tarand, sold him by a Scythian of the Geloni's country, close to the Borysthenes or Dnieper.

A tarand is a beast as big as a bullock, with a head like a stag's, or a whit bigger, bearing two stately horns with large branches. Its feet are cloven, its hair long as a bear's, its hide almost as hard as steel armor. There were few tarands in Scythia, the merchant told

Pantagruel, because the beast varies in color acording to the place where it grazes and dwells. Thus it takes on the hue of tree, shrub, grass, flower, plant and, in general, of whatever it approaches. This quality it shares with the anemone, or sea-polyp; with the thoes, a sort of wolf, in India; with the chameleon, a species of lizard so wonderful that Democritus wrote a whole book upon its form, its anatomy, its powers and its virtues in magic.

I myself have seen this animal change hue, not only at the approach of colored objects, but also of its own accord, under the influence of the fear or other emotion that possessed it. I have certainly seen it turn green on a green carpet; but if it remained there for any length of time, it would turn consecutively yellow, blue, violet, just as you see a turkeycock's comb change color according to its feelings.

What we found strangest in this tarand was that not only its face and skin, but also its hair, assumed the tinge of objects around it. Next to Panurge, in his coarse cloth coat, its hair turned gray. Next to Pantagruel, in his scarlet mantle, its hair and skin turned red. Next to the skipper, clad in white linen, like the priests of Isis in Egypt, its coat turned snow-white. When it was free of fear or strong emotion—in other words, in its normal state—its hair was the color of the asses you see bearing sacks of flour from the mills of Meung-sur-Loire to Orléans.

III

HOW PANTAGRUEL RECEIVED TIDINGS FROM GARGANTUA, HIS FATHER, AND OF A STRANGE WAY OF GETTING SPEEDY NEWS FROM DISTANT LANDS

WHILST Pantagruel was busy purchasing these extraordinary animals, suddenly the salvos of ten guns and culverins rose from the mole. At the same time, loud cheers of joy resounded from every ship in the fleet. Turning to look towards the harbor. Pantagruel beheld the *Chelidonia*, one of his father Gargantua's swift brigantines.

The name, in Greek, means swallow: the ship was so called because its prow bore the figure of a great sea-swallow, carved in Corinthian brass. (A sea-swallow, I may add, is a fish as large as the Loire dace or dart, very fleshy, devoid of scales and equipped with cartilaginous wings like a bat's. These are very long and very broad; I have often seen sea-swallows flying, by means of these wings, a good fathom above water for the distance of a full bowshot. At Marseille, this fish is called the *landole*.) Indeed, Gargantua's ship was light as a swallow, and seemed to fly over the water rather than sail through it.

On board the *Chelidonia*, they found Malicorne, Gargantua's esquire and carver, who had been dispatched expressly to ascertain Pantagruel's health and to bring him credentials. When, after Malicorne's salute, Pantagruel had embraced the messenger, before reading the letters or mentioning any other subject, Pantagruel asked Malicorne:

"Did you bring the *gozal*, the heavenly messenger?"

"Ay, My Lord, he is swaddled up in this basket here!" Malicorne replied.

Gozal is Hebrew for pigeon, and, indeed, it was a pigeon they referred to, which had been taken from Gargantua's dovecote. Its young were just hatched when the *Chelidonia* was sailing. It was to return with tidings of Pantagruel.

If fortune had been unfavorable, they were to fasten to its feet a bit of black ribbon; but since everything had shaped happily so far, Pantagruel, having unswaddled it, tied to its feet a thin band of white taffeta. Then, without further delay, he let it loose.

The pigeon winged away with a whirr, cleaving the air with incredible speed. As you know, no bird can match its flight, especially when it has eggs or young ones awaiting it in its nest; Nature has endowed it with the most dogged concern for the presence and protection of its offspring. Thus, in less than two hours, this pigeon covered a distance which had demanded three days and three nights of a ship at top speed, with oars and sails, and a fair wind behind it. Gargantua's men saw it fly into the dovecote, bound for its nest; the worthy monarch, learning that it bore a white ribbon, was reassured and delighted at his son's welfare.

Such was the custom of great Gargantua and noble Pantagruel whenever they wished for news of something ardently desired or of great concern—the result of some battle, by land or sea; the capture or resistance of some garrison; the settling of some weighty difference; the safe or unhappy delivery of some queen or great lady; the death or recovery of their sick friends or allies, and so on.

They would take the *gozal* and dispatch it, by hand to hand post, to the place they wished to hear news from. The bird bore either a black or white ribbon, according to the circumstances and events; it would fly home with its information, covering, in a single hour through the air, a vaster distance than thirty post messengers could cover on earth in an entire regular day. Was this not redeeming and gaining time? You may well believe that, in all their dovecotes in their farms, they stored large quantities of pigeons hatching eggs and rearing their young.

Having let fly the pigeon, Pantagruel perused his father's message. It read as follows:

My dearest son:
The affection a father naturally bears a beloved son is, in my case, much enhanced by my realization and appreciation of the particular gifts with which Heaven has been pleased to grace you. Thus you have never once, since your departure, been out of my mind. As you know, a sense of fear invariably attends a true, sincere love; and my heart has been filled with fear that some misfortune or trouble may have disturbed your journey.

Hesiod tells us that a good beginning is half the battle won; you know the current proverb "well begun is half done." So to banish all anxiety from my mind, I am expressly dispatching Malicorne to return to me with news of your welfare during the early stages of your voyage. If things are as prosperous, so far, as I hope and wish, then I can easily foresee, prognosticate and judge of the rest.

I have come upon some diverting books which the bearer will de-

*liver to you. You may read them when you seek relaxation from your
more serious studies. The said bearer will also report at length to you
upon what has happened at my court.*

May the peace of the Eternal be with you!

*My greetings to Panurge, Friar John, Epistemon, Xenomanes,
Gymnastes and my good friends, your other followers.*

Your father and friend,

GARGANTUA

Dated at our paternal seat, this thirteenth day of June.

IV

HOW PANTAGRUEL WROTE TO HIS FATHER, GARGANTUA, AND SENT HIM SEVERAL VALUABLE CURIOSITIES

HAVING read his father's letter, Pantagruel engaged Malicorne in
conversation for so long that Panurge interrupted him:

"When are you going to drink, My Lord?" he demanded. "When
are *we* going to drink? When is the excellent esquire going to drink?
Haven't you talked long enough to be dry?"

"Well spoken," said Pantagruel. "Have them prepare us a meal
at the next inn. You know, it's called the Centaur; or at any rate its
sign bears a satyr on horseback."

And while Panurge was carrying out these orders, Pantagruel
wrote the following letter for the equerry to take back to Gargantua:

Most gracious father:

*The unexpected, unforeseen events that occur in this transitory
life come as a more violent shock to our senses and faculties than do
the expected and foreseen. Indeed, sudden surprise may cause death;
often the soul forsakes the body, even when the news received satis-
fies our curiosity and longing.*

The arrival of your esquire Malicorne moved me profoundly, for I had not hoped to see any servant of yours or to hear from you before the conclusion of our journeying. I had had to content myself with the cherished remembrance of your august majesty, a remembrance so deeply engraved upon the hindmost ventricle of my brain that I could conjure up your figure in its true, natural, living form.

You have made me happy beyond hope and expectation by favoring me with your gracious letter; the reports of your esquire upon the health and prosperity of yourself and your household have much heartened me. First, therefore, I must praise the blessed Redeemer, Who, in His divine mercy, keeps you in this long enjoyment of perfect health. Next, I must thank you sempiternally for the fervent, inveterate affection you bear your most humble son and unprofitable servant.

Once upon a time, a Roman named Furnius received from Cæsar Augustus the assurance that his father, who had joined Mark Antony's faction, was forgiven and readmitted to the imperial favor. Furnius said to his master:

"By this noble action, you have reduced me to utter shame. For, being unable during all life and after death to express adequately my gratitude, I must necessarily be deemed an ingrate."

Like Furnius, I may say that the excess of your fatherly love reduces me to anxiety. I, too, shall have to live and die under the opprobrium of ingratitude, unless, perhaps, that crime may be redeemed by the maxim of the Stoics. You recall—do you not?—how they considered a benefit as consisting of three parts. First, the giver's; second, the recipient's; and third, the rewarder's. The recipient proves his gratitude by accepting the favor gladly and by maintaining it in perpetual memory. On the contrary, the most ungrateful man in the world is one who either scorns or forgets a favor.

I am thus overwhelmed by infinite obligations, all of which arise from your vast bounty; and I am wholly unable to make the slightest return. Yet, by never forgetting your generosity, I shall at least hope to escape being taxed with ingratitude. Never shall my tongue cease to proclaim and publish that to return thanks commensurate to my obligations transcends my capacity and power.

For our part, we are confident enough in Our Lord's pity and aid to trust that the sequel of our voyage will continue as auspicious as its beginning. We look forward to returning home as sound and as delighted as we are now.

I shall not fail to set down a complete record of our adventures, which I shall submit to you on our return so that you may know truthfully what has occurred.

I found a Scythian tarand here, a strange, remarkable beast in that its hide and coat take on the color of any object it approaches. I beg you be pleased to accept it; you will find it as manageable and easy to feed as a lamb. I am also sending you three young unicorns, who are milder and better trained than even kittens.

I have explained to your esquire how to look after the beasts. Unicorns do not graze on the ground; the long horn growing from the middle of their foreheads prevents it. Instead, they feed off fruit trees, or from racks nailed within reach, or out of their master's hand. They eat grass, sheaves, apples, pears, barley, wheat, or any root, fruit and vegetable. I am amazed that our ancient writers call unicorns wild, fierce, dangerous, and state that they have never seen them alive. If it please you, you will prove the contrary, and will discover them to be the mildest beasts imaginable, provided they are not maliciously teased.

I also send you the life and feats of Achilles, woven in a rich and beauteous tapestry. And I hasten to add that, please God! I shall bring back to you curiosities of all sorts—beast, plant, bird and gem—that I may happen upon. I pray God to preserve you in His holy grace.

Panurge, Friar John, Epistemon, Xenomanes, Gymnastes, Eusthenes, Rhizotomos and Carpalim humbly kiss your hand and return your salute a hundredfold.

Your humble son and devoted servant,
PANTAGRUEL

From Medamothy, this fifteenth day of June.

Whilst Pantagruel was writing this letter, Malicorne was being welcomed, embraced and fêted on all sides. God knows how he stood their enthusiasm and what messages he promised to deliver.

His letter written, Pantagruel banqueted with the esquire. After, he presented him with a heavy chain of gold weighing eight hundred crowns; in its seven links, disposed in sets of seven, huge diamonds, rubies, emeralds and turquoises were set alternately. To each of the sailors, Pantagruel gave five hundred crowns, gold. To Gargantua, his sire, he sent the tarand, as he had promised (over it he hung a cloth of gold-brocaded satin), the tapestry representing Achilles, and the three unicorns with trappings of frizzed cloth-of-gold.

Then they departed from Medamothy, Malicorne to return to Gargantua, Pantagruel to proceed upon his journey. Once at sea, Pantagruel had Epistemon read the books Gargantua had sent. They proved so lively and jovial that I shall gladly give you an account of them, if you urge me to do so.

V

HOW PANTAGRUEL MET A SHIPLOAD OF TRAVELLERS, RETURNING FROM LANTERNLAND

ON the fifth day, as we began to circle the pole gradually, moving away from the equinoctial line, we discovered a trading ship on our port side. There was great rejoicing both amid our fleet and the passengers of the other vessel: we gave them news of *terra firma* in exchange for news of the sea. Having lain by, we discovered that they were Frenchmen from Saintonge. After some conversation, we learned that they were returning from Lanternland, a fact which pleased us all mightily.

Inquiring about the country and the customs of its inhabitants, we learned that a general council of the chapter of the Lanterns was to convene late in July. If we arrived then, as we easily could, we would behold a large, honorable and happy assemblage of Lanterns. Even now, we heard, they were engaged in great preparations, a proof that they intended lanternizing to the limit. Our informants added that as we passed through the great kingdom of Gebarim (in Hebrew, "the land of mighty warriors") we would be magnificently received and entertained by King Ohabe ("my friend and ally"), their ruler. Like all his subjects, His Majesty spoke the French of Touraine.

As we were listening to this news, Panurge fell out with a sheep-trader of Taillebourg, on the Charente, a fellow named Dingdong. How did the quarrel start? Well, Dingdong noticed that Panurge wore no codpiece; he also saw the spectacles fastened to his cap. Turning to a companion of his:

"Look, friend," cried Dingdong. "Here's a splendid portrait of a cuckold."

Panurge, thanks to his spectacles, could hear much more distinctly than usual. Having caught the trader's comment, he swung round upon him:

"How in the devil's name can I possibly be cuckold," he demanded, "when I am not married—as you are, if I am to judge by your ill-favored snout?"

"Of course, I'm married," Dingdong boasted. "And I wouldn't be unmarried for all the spectacles in Europe, plus all the magnifying glasses of Africa, not to mention the codpieces of Asia and elsewhere. My wife is the comeliest, most thrilling, discreetest and most virtuous spouse in the whole fair land of Saintonge. Indeed, with all due respect to the others, I'm bringing her back a fine present for her Christmas box: it's a hard fat branch of coral eleven inches long. What business is it of yours? What has it to do with you? Who are *you* and where do *you* hail from, O gogglebearer of Antichrist? Answer, if you are of God."

"I'm asking you something important!" Panurge replied. "Suppose all the elements agreed to favor me. Suppose I ramdiddlecuntholebrangled your comeliest, most thrilling, discreetest and most virtuous spouse? Take a look at good Priapus, the stiff god of garden plots, dwelling here in utmost freedom, unhampered by the fetters of a fastened codpiece. Suppose I jammed him so tight into your wife's pleasure-box that he stuck there eternally, unless you pulled him out with your teeth? Would you leave him inside forever? Or would you pluck him out with your gnashers? Answer, O ram of Mahomet, you who belong to the devil's gang."

"I'd strike your gogglebearing ear such a blow with my sword," snarled Dingdong, "that *you* would be the ram—and a dead ram, at that!"

So saying, he sought to draw his blade, but it stuck in its scabbard, for as you know, the excessive nitrous moisture of sea air rusts weapons easily.

Panurge called Pantagruel to his help; Friar John set his hand to his dirk and would have struck Dingdong down. But the skipper and some passengers implored Pantagruel to allow no such outrage on board. Accordingly, the quarrel was patched up. Panurge and the trader shook hands, then drank merrily together in token of perfect reconciliation.

VI

HOW, THE QUARREL SETTLED, PANURGE BARGAINED FOR ONE OF DINGDONG'S SHEEP

THE quarrel appeased, Panurge whispered to Epistemon and Friar John:

"Stand by, friends, and prepare to enjoy a comic interlude. You shall have rare sport or I miss my guess."

Turning to Dingdong, he pledged his health again in a beakerful of Lantern wine; the trader replied affably, all courtesy and briskness. Next, Panurge entreated him to sell him one of his sheep.

"Alas, alas, dear friend, dear neighbor," sighed Dingdong, "what a fellow you are at hoodwinking simple souls. Truly, you seem a rare trader, O my valiant purchaser of sheep! God's faith, you look more like a cutpurse than a buyer of sheep. God's teeth and God's withers, what a delight it would be to carry a purseful of cash on one's paunch with you next to one in the crowd in a tripe shop at thawing-time, when bargains abound and the picking is rare! Humph, humph! you would make a pretty ass of any one who didn't know you! Take a look at him, good people! There's a man whose name will go down in history."

"Patience!" Panurge urged. "But, by the way, as a special favor, won't you sell me one of your sheep? How much do you want for it?"

"Dear friend, dear neighbor, what do you mean?" Dingdong inquired. "These are long-woolled sheep; Jason took his golden fleece from them, and Philip of Burgundy extracted the Knightly Order of that name from their very backs. These are Levantine sheep, oriental sheep, fatted sheep, sheep of high quality."

"Granted," said Panurge, "but please sell me one, that is all I ask. Oriental sheep, you said? I will pay you occidentally, cash down, so many golden suns settled on the counter to the west of you. . . . Fatted sheep? I will give you slim goldpieces! . . . Sheep of high quality? I will give you coins *hors concours*. . . . How much?"

"Dear friend, dear neighbor," Dingdong replied, "listen to what I tell you in your other ear!"

PANURGE

I am at your service.

DINGDONG

You are going to Lanternland, eh?

PANURGE

Ay!

DINGDONG

You are touring to see the world?

PANURGE

Ay, truly, truly.

DINGDONG

And to amuse yourself?

PANURGE

Ay, truly!

DINGDONG

I believe your name is Robin Mutton?

PANURGE

It is your pleasure to call me so, truly!

DINGDONG

You are not offended, I trust?

PANURGE

Not as I understand it, truly.

DINGDONG

You are, I take it, the king's jester. The king's fool?

PANURGE

Ay, truly, truly.

DINGDONG

Shake hands, man, there! Humph! You are touring to see the world, you are the king's fool, your name is Robin Mutton! Have a look at that sheep, there; his name is Robin just like yours. Here, Robin, Robin, Robin. Beeeeh! beeeh! beeeh! A fine voice he has, eh?

PANURGE

A fine, harmonious voice, truly!

DINGDONG

Dear friend, dear neighbor, let us make this bargain. I will fetch a pair of scales. You, Robin Mutton, shall sit upon one scale; Robin Sheep, here, shall sit upon the other. I wager a peck of Arcachon oysters that he will outdo you in weight, price and value. Ay, you'll be left high and dry as the day you die, dangling from a gibbet!

"Patience!" said Panurge, "truly, you would confer a favor upon me and my posterity, were you willing to sell me that sheep or some other inferior one. I beg this of you, noble sir and honored master!"

"Dear friend, dear neighbor," said Dingdong, "out of the shorn fleece of these my sheep, men will make fine Rouen cloth, a product beside which your superfine Leicester wool from England or *limiste* from Segovia, in Spain, is mere fustian. Out of the skinned hides of these my sheep, men will make fine cordovan leather, which will be sold as Turkish morocco or Montélimar or Spanish ware. Out of the disembowelled guts of these my sheep, men will make strings for violins and harps, to be sold as dear as though they came from Munich or Aquilea, in the Abruzzi.

"What have you to say to *that?*"

"Please, please sell me one of them," Panurge implored him, "I shall be eternally grateful to you. Look: here is spot cash!"

So saying, Panurge displayed a purseful of glittering henricuses— a coin newly minted under Henri II, bearing his effigy and four H's in the form of a cross.

VII

CONCLUSION OF PANURGE'S BARGAIN WITH DINGDONG OVER ONE SHEEP OF THE TRADER'S FLOCK

"Dear friend, dear neighbor," Dingdong went on, "these animals are meat for only princes and kings. Their flesh is delicate, savory and luscious as very balm. Why, I brought them out of a country where the hogs, God help us, gorge on myrobalan plums, and where the sows, pregnant—begging the company's pardon—feed upon orange flowers."

"Be that as it may," Panurge declared, "please sell me one; I will pay you royally, on my faith as a Trojan. How much do you want for it?"

"Dear friend, dear neighbor," Dingdong singsonged. "These my sheep are sprung of the race of the golden ram who bore Helle and her brother Phryxus through the air, as they fled from Ino, her tyrannous mother-in-law. Poor Helle fell into the sea, which ever since was called Hellespont."

"Pox and chancres!" cried Panurge, "you are *clericus vel adiscens,* a priest or a novice."

"Ay, I'm a Latin scholar!" the trader replied. "*Ita:* that means a cabbage, and *vere*, a leek. But Rr! Rrr! Rrrrr! . . . Reverend, Reverender, Right Reverend; O Robin, Rev. Robin, Right Reverend Robin! You don't understand such language, do you?"

Panurge did not answer.

"Incidentally," Dingdong resumed, "I want to tell you something else about my sheep. Let them piss anywhere in a field, and corn grows there as though God Himself had watered the place; nor need you till or manure it. Further, from their urine, our chemists extract the choicest saltpetre in the world. As for their turds—begging the company's pardon—their turds provide our physicians with cures for seventy-eight different varieties of disease, including the dropsy dedicated to St. Eutropius of Saintes (from which may God save and deliver us!). Now, what do you say, dear friend, dear neighbor? By God, those sheep cost me a pretty penny!"

"Never mind the cost," said Panurge. "Just sell me a single one: I will pay you handsomely for it."

"Dear friend, dear neighbor," Dingdong made answer, "let me prevail upon you to consider the wonders of Nature compact in these animals of mine, even in a member you might at first sight consider quite useless. See those horns, there? Pound them with an iron pestle or an andiron—I don't care which, take your choice! Then bury them wherever you like, so long as the sun shine down on them. Water them regularly. And, in a few months, you will have the most delicious asparagus in the world, better even than the famed asparagus of Ravenna. Dare you boast, gentlemen, that your cuckold's horns possess virtues or properties as wonderful?"

"Patience!" Panurge said.

"I don't know if you're a scholar or no," Dingdong pursued. "I've seen a heap of scholars, cleric and lay; God's truth, I've seen a heap of great scholars, cuckold for all their wisdom, and no mistake! On this score, if you were a scholar, you would know that, in the most inferior members of my divine animals (that is, the feet!), there is a bone (that is the heel or the astragal, if you prefer), with which the ancient races used to play at the royal game of *tales* or dice. The only other beasts whose heels served thus were the Indian ass and the gazelle of Libya. In one sitting, the Emperor Augustus won fifty thousand crowns at the sport. But cuckolds like your-selves could not hope to win as much."

"Patience," said Panurge, "let us strike a bargain!"

"One minute, dear neighbor, dear friend. Let me but duly praise my animals' internal members, their shoulders, their legs (O legs of mutton!), their saddles, their breasts, their livers, their tripe. Let me sing their bladders, out of which men make footballs. Let me hail their ribs, which serve the warriors of Pygmyland as little crossbows with which to pelt the cranes with cherrystones. Nor shall I ever tire of lauding their heads, which, if you add a touch of sulphur, pro-duce a miraculous decoction to loose the bellies of constipated dogs."

"A dog's turd to you!" growled the skipper of the vessel. "Stop hawking and bargaining. Sell the fellow your sheep, if you care to; if not, don't waste his time."

"For love of you, Captain, I'll sell him my sheep," Dingdong an-swered, "but he shall pay three Tours pounds apiece."

"That is a lot of money," Panurge objected. "Where I live, the same amount would buy me five or even six. A bargain's a bargain, what? You are not the first man I know who, trying to get rich and be successful too quickly, sank back into poverty and even broke his neck in the fall."

"A plague carry you off, blockhead!" Dingdong roared. "By the relic of Christ's circumcision, stored in the Abbey of Charroux in the Vienne, the worst sheep in my flock is four times better than the finest sold of yore, a golden talent apiece, by the Coraxians of Tudi-tania (a land of Spain now called Andalusia). Have you the slightest notion, O spendthrift fool, what one talent of gold was worth?"

"My dear sir," Panurge remonstrated, "you grow hot under the collar, I see and note. Never mind, here is your money!"

Having paid his money, Panurge chose a fine strong ram, and bore it, bleating, away. The flock, hearing its cries, set up one vast, con-certed bleating and stared after their vanishing comrade.

Dingdong turned to his shepherds:

"There's a customer knows how to choose! There's a friggler knows what's what! By God, to think I was keeping that very head for My Lord of Cancale, for well I know what he wants. Ay, My Lord of Cancale is radiant with joy when he can hold a good-sized, juicy shoulder of lamb in his right hand (as you might a left-handed racket!) and, in the other hand, a razor-sharp knife to carve it with. God knows, he's a skilful fencer then!"

VIII

HOW PANURGE DROWNED TRADER AND SHEEP

SUDDENLY, God knows how (it all happened too swiftly for me to consider it), Panurge, without further comment, tossed his bleating purchase into the sea. The rest of the flock, crying and squealing in the same tone, proceeded to follow their leader, tossing themselves overboard. You know that sheep are the silliest and most foolish beasts in the world—Aristotle tells us so in his ninth book *Of the History of Animals*. Their chief natural characteristic is a talent for following the first of the flock. You may therefore imagine how Dingdong's sheep vied with one another in leaping into the sea. It was impossible to restrain them.

Dingdong, appalled at seeing his flock drown and perish under his very eyes, strove manfully to block and restrain them. His efforts proved utterly vain; one after another frisked over the side of the ship to a watery death. At last, on the poop deck, he caught a powerful ram by the fleece, hoping to hold it back and thus check the stampede.

Alas! the ram proved too strong: it dragged its master in its headlong leap to sea, and Dingdong shared its fate. Even so in Homer's *Odyssey*, the sheep of one-eyed Polyphemus, the Cyclops, dragged Ulysses and his companions out of the fatal cavern.

As for the other drovers and shepherds, they, too, sought to stem the ovine tide: some seized their charges by the horns, others by the legs, still others by their fleece. One and all, hurled headlong to seaward, perished miserably.

Panurge, close to the gunwale, oar in hand, worked heroically, not to help the shepherds but, rather, to prevent them from clambering aboard to safety. All the while, he preached as eloquently to them as any fashionable preacher; he reminded one of Friar Olivier Maillard, famous under Louis XI and Louis XII, or of Friar Jean Bourgeois, the popular, bespectacled Franciscan orator of Lyons. With the most flowery rhetoric, he laid bare, for their benefit, the miseries of this world and the felicities of the next, proving in the most convincing terms that, in this vale of tears, the dead were better off than the living. To each martyr he promised to erect, on his return from Lanternland, a stately cenotaph and an honorary tomb on the Alpine summit of Mont Cenis. However, if life among the humans still held attractions, and if they found this death by drowning unseasonable, Panurge wished them good luck. Perhaps they might meet some whale to speed them forth, three days and three nights hence, on to the shore of some fabulous land, like Jonah.

The vessel cleared of Dingdong, drovers and sheep:

"Any other sheepish souls left?" Panurge inquired. "Any followers of Tybalt—shades of the farce *Pathelin!*—or of Robin Ramhorn or Sam Shepherd? Any of the flock asleep while their fellows graze? I'm hanged if I know. It's an old-time trick, obsolete in present warfare. What say you, Friar John?"

"Whatever you do is splendid," the monk assented. "I've nothing to complain of. But you spoke of warfare, and I recall another old trick. The mercenaries, on the day of an engagement, were promised double pay. If they won the battle, there was plenty of booty to defray the expense: if they lost it, they would be ashamed to demand their bonus, as the runaway Swiss did at Cérisoles in Piedmont, where the Duc d'Enghien whipped the Imperialists. You too, Panurge, should have withheld payment: you would now have your cash in your purse."

"Well paid, well cacked," said Panurge. "God's might, have I not had more than fifty thousand francs' worth of amusement? Come, now, let us make off: the wind blows favorable. Listen, Friar John: no man ever afforded me pleasure but I rewarded him or, at least, proved grateful. I never was an ingrate, I am not now, nor ever shall be. By the same token, no man ever caused me grief, without repenting it, in this world or the next. I'm not that fatuous a fool!"

"You are damning yourself like an ancient devil," said Friar John. "It is written: *Mihi vindictam, et cetera*; Vengeance is mine, I will repay. Holy stuff, that, breviary matter!"

IX

HOW PANTAGRUEL REACHED THE ISLAND OF ENNASIN, AND OF THE STRANGE RELATIONSHIPS THERE

WITH a good westerly wind, and the *garbin*, as they call the south-wester in France, behind us, we sailed on for a day without sighting land. On the third day, at the flies' dawn—which, as you know, means noon—we espied ahead of us a triangular island, very much like Sicily in shape and situation. It was called the island of Alliances.

The inhabitants, male and female, were like the red Poitevins of France (Pictavinses, the Romans called them), a people descended from the Picts, who painted their bodies red with the blood of their foes. There was, however, one signal exception: these islanders—man, woman and child—had noses shaped like an ace of clubs. For this reason, the old name of the island was Ennasin, which etymologically derives from a Latin word meaning "to cut off the nose." The islanders were all related to one another and boasted of it. The mayor of the place told us quite frankly:

"You people from elsewhere consider it wonderful that on a certain day—I refer to February 13—through a certain gate—I refer to the Porta Carmentalis formerly situated at the foot of the Capitol, between the Tarpeian rock and the Tiber, and since called the Scelerte—there issued forth to fight against certain enemies of Rome—I refer to the Veientes from Etruria—a host of three hundred and sixty warriors all belonging to the same family—I refer to the Fabii. They had with them five thousand other soldiers—I refer to the vassals of the Fabii. And all of them were killed in a certain place—I refer to a place near where the river Cremera issues from the lake of Baccano.

"My dear friends, this island of Alliances, if need be, can produce more than three hundred thousand men, all relatives and kinsmen!"

Their degrees of consanguinity and alliances were very strange. For, being thus wholly akin and allied, no single one, we found, was any other's father or mother, brother or sister, uncle or aunt, cousin or nephew, son-in-law or daughter-in-law, godfather or godmother. Though I did see this: a tall, snubnosed old man calling a little child of three or four "father," while the girl addressed him as "daughter."

The degrees of this inter-relationship allowed one man to call his wife "sweet minnow" and her to reply: "dear porpoise."

("A devilish fishy stink those two must give off when they've rubbed their bacons together!" Friar John commented.)

One smiled at a buxom baggage who passed by. "Good morrow, sweet currycomb!" he said. "The top of the morning to you, blessed chestnut!" she answered.

("Ho, hum!" Panurge commented. "There's a hot dish of curry! There's a comb often ravels its stallion's hair! There's a fine top, of a morning, and a juicy bottom, of a night!")

One fellow bowed to his sweetheart, saying: "God be with you, dear case!" She greeted him back: "Good day, dear trial!"

("By St. Ninnyhammer, there's a case often comes up for trial!" cried Gymnastes. "Plenty of drumhead sessions in this court, not to mention *subpenal* attachments by the old bumbailiff and tipstaff.")

One attractive lass called her man "my ribbin beast"; he addressed her as "fair chitterling."

("That ribbon's a tape and the beast a worm!" cried Eusthenes. "Here's a tapeworm often thrusts its red head into her quivering guts!")

"Greetings, hatchet!" cried one to his trollop, who made answer, "At your service, good helve!"

("God's belly," cried Carpalim, "that hatchet is well handled, that handle well embedded. Good jamming and dovetailing here! Can this be the gallant blade your Roman harlots prayed for? Is this the haft our Franciscan friars handle so manfully?")

Moving on, I heard a lecher identifying his relative as "my mattress" and she him as "my coverlet, O eiderdown!"

("Humph!" Panurge observed. "There's a coverlet lies snug on its mattress, there's a loverlet lies snug on his mistress. Down, O Ida, down!")

There were further epithets, all of great interest. "Sweet doe" was matched by "rare crust" . . . "O fire" by "O poker" . . . "my slipper" by "my foot" . . . "my boot" by "my stocking". . . .

"My mitten," said one man and "my glove" replied his wench, their relationship being that of glove to mitten; "Hi, bacon!" cried one, and "Hi, rind," his strumpet answered, theirs being that of bacon to rind.

As we roamed through town, we heard such dialogue as this: "Hail, sweet jelly!"

"How nice to meet you, dear egg!" the woman answered.

(They were akin as is a jelly omelet.)

"How now, rooster?"

"How now, salt?"

(We cudgelled our brains to discover the relationship, alliance, affinity or consanguinity that bound this pair, with reference to our own customs. We could find none unless the male were the cock of the roost, the female the salt of the earth, and he pecking at her constantly. At all events, he looked high-wrought and she looked like a crack, a trump, a masterpiece.)

"Hello, sweet shell," said one lad to his doxy.

"Hello, oyster darling!" she replied.

("An edible mollusc," Carpalim interpreted, "that sinks gladly into its bivalve shell to scatter seamen's pearls!")

"Long life to you, pod!"

"The same to you, pea!" the girl simpered.

("Snugly linked as pea to pod!" said Gymnastes.)

A certain repulsive, toothless old man, mounted on a pair of high-heeled wooden shoes, met a squat, strapping, dumpy slut.

"God preserve you, shoe, trumpet, top!"

"God preserve *you*, heel, mouthpiece, whip!" she answered testily.

("Quite right," said Xenomanes. "That heel will not cling to her—ah!—sole . . . that mouthpiece will never fit over her tube . . . that whip will never release and flog a bumming-top like hers!")

A learned doctor, professor in a college, his hair immaculately brushed and curled, conversed for a long while with a lady of high degree. Taking his leave of her:

"Farewell, long knife! precious ship! clear conscience!" the lady said.

"Farewell, skilled cook! snug haven! warm pillow!"

("Perfectly logical," said Pantagruel. "Is it not proverbially true that a cook is known by her knife, a dear ship stands longer in the haven, and a good conscience makes a soft pillow!")

A youth passing a lass cried: "Heh, heh, heh! How long it is since I saw you, bag!"

"True, pipe. Let's get together, I would love it."

("Bring them together," said Panurge, "and blow down their arses. Result: a bagpipe!")

"Hello, sow!"

"Hello, hay!"

(I thought how gladly that sow gobbled up her hay!)

A moment later I noticed a humpbacked gallant, quite close to me, bowing to a relative:

"Good luck, hole!"

"So long, peg!" she replied.

("She's all hole," said Friar John, "and he all peg! Did you hear her say 'So long!' Now it remains to learn if every cranny of that particular hole can be stopped with that particular peg!")

"Greetings, moult," said one.

"How do you do, gosling!" the woman answered.

("That gosling," Ponocrates opined, "is often moulting!")

A rake, talking to a young strumpet, adjured her: "Don't forget, poop!"

"I won't indeed, fart," she replied.

"Do you call these two relatives?" Pantagruel asked the mayor. "I should call them foes rather than kin. Didn't he call her a poop? In our land, you couldn't find a worse insult."

"Good people from abroad," the mayor rejoined, "you have few people in your land as closely allied as this poop and this fart. In one moment, they emerged together, unseen, out of the same hole."

"No doubt the wind *galerne*, as they call the west-northwester in our land, lanterned their mother!"

"What mother are you talking about?" the mayor asked. "Mothers belong to *your* world. Such a relationship is for people from overseas, you affluent, opulent fellows who make ends meet."

Good Pantagruel had stood by, watching and hearing everything. Now he began to lose patience. We then concluded our tour of the island and our survey of Ennasian manners by stopping at an inn to wet our whistles. They happened to be celebrating several weddings according to local customs. Yet their cheer was of the highest.

We were present at one happy marriage. The bride was Pear, a firm, luscious morsel, we thought, though some who had tasted assured us that, on the contrary, she was flabby and overripe. The groom was young Cheese, with downsoft hair and a somewhat reddish complexion. In the past, I had heard of such weddings; I knew that several had been arranged in various places. Indeed, in our own cow-country, there is a proverb:

> *There is no match you could compare*
> *To Master Cheese and Mistress Pear.*

In another room of the inn, we witnessed the wedding of an aged lady, named Boot, to a sprightly young fellow, Buskin. Pantagruel was told that young Buskin was taking old Boot to bed because she boasted a fine hide, was in good shape, well-greased and handy about the house, especially for fishermen who sleep in their boots.

Finally, in a third room, I saw a sprig, Pump, marrying a sexagenarian, Madam Slipper. We were told that he was not wedding her for her beauty, but through greed and avarice. He wanted the money in which she had been rolling.

X

HOW PANTAGRUEL WENT ASHORE ON THE ISLAND OF CHELI, THE ISLE OF PEACE, AND HOW HE MET ITS RULER, KING PANIGON, OR BISCUIT

THE wind was still blowing up astern of us, when we left these unpleasant alliancers, with their ace-of-clubs snouts, and made for the open sea. At sundown, we stopped off at the island of Cheli—which in Hebrew means *peace*—a large, fertile, rich and prosperous island, governed by King Panigon, or Biscuit. The monarch, accompanied by his children and the princes of his court, came down to the harbor to greet Pantagruel and to escort him back to his palace.

Near the gate, stood the queen, with her daughters and court ladies. Panigon insisted that she and all her retinue kiss Pantagruel and his followers, for such was the country's courteous custom. All observed the osculatory rites except Friar John, who stepped aside and ranged himself among King Panigon's officers.

Panigon used every possible means to keep Pantagruel with him that day and the morrow; but Pantagruel begged off, invoking the serene weather and favorable breeze, which voyagers desire more often than they enjoy. Since these were his now, Pantagruel concluded, surely he should make the most of them!

But Panigon would not suffer us to withdraw before every man of us had tossed off twenty-five or thirty bumpers.

On returning to the harbor, Pantagruel, not finding Friar John, asked where he was and why he had left them. Panurge, not knowing how to excuse Friar John, was about to return to Panigon's palace to fetch the monk errant, when the latter came running up, his face beaming.

"God save noble King Panigon," he cried enthusiastically. "By the Lord's belly and my own, he keeps a magnificent kitchen! I've just come from there; everything goes by the dozen and score. I was looking forward to stuffing my paunch and cramming my gut satisfactorily and in true cloister fashion."

"So, my friend!" Pantagruel observed. "Always in the kitchen, eh?"

"By the body gallinaceous," cried Friar John, "I understand better the customs and ceremonies of kitchens than all this crapocum-shittening with these women, *magni magna*, bow to your partner, posture here, salute there, double bow, sweep, reverence, accolade, kiss the lady's hand (kiss mine, lady!), your majesty, your grace, thrice welcome, hinkey-dinkey, fiddle-faddle, and my arse to you, shitter-shatter! No, all that is so much cack and piddle! Lord, I don't say that, making the most of my privileges, I might not press with my right hand, press with my left, and thrust in my great long in-between. But this turdery of bowing and scraping drives me mad, fast as any devil; I mean: as any devil's fast! St. Benedict told no lie on that head!

"You prate of kissing ladies! By the holy and sacred frock I wear, I dodge this chore willingly. For I remember what happened to My Lord of Guercharois, on the Creuse, near Tours."

"What's that?" Pantagruel exclaimed. "I know My Lord of Guercharois: he is one of my best friends."

Friar John then related how My Lord of Guercharois was once invited to a sumptuous, magnificent banquet, given by a kinsman and neighbor of his. All the lords, ladies and damsels of the region were likewise invited. While waiting for him, these ladies dressed the pages in women's clothes, disguising them into so many fair, seductive young women. As the drawbridge rose, these petticoated pages presented themselves before My Lord of Guercharois; he kissed one and all, amid a great show of ceremony and form. At last the real ladies, who had looked on from the gallery, burst out laughing, and signalled to the pages to remove their disguises.

My Lord of Guercharois, in shame and spite, thereupon refused to kiss these true ladies. For, he said, if pages disguised as women had deceived him, then, God's body and blood! how did he know these women here were not footmen and grooms, even more skilfully disguised?

"By God's might," cried Friar John, "*da jurandi*, I mean not to swear! Why do we not transfer our amenities into the noble kitchen of the Lord? Why do we not consider only the swaying of spits, the harmonious click of the jacks that turn them, the position and curtseys of the lardons, the preparations for dessert, the ordering of service and wine? *Beati immaculati in via*, says the psalm, blessed are the undefiled in the way. That is holy timber, breviary matter!"

XI

WHY MONKS LOVE KITCHENS

"Spoken like a true monk," said Epistemon. "Like a monk monkeying, I said, not like a monk bemonked. Truly you remind me of something that happened to me in Florence about twenty years ago. We were a goodly company of studious travellers, fond of visiting the learned men, the ancient monuments and the curiosities of Italy.

"We were curiously contemplating the city of Florence and its wonders; the structure of the Dome, the magnificence of the churches; and the splendor of the palaces. We were vying with one another as to which of us could praise them most eloquently, when suddenly a monk of Amiens, Bernard Lardon by name, burst out, angry and impatient:

" 'I don't know what the devil you find so wonderful here. I too have looked at everything, and I'm no blinder than you. After all: what is there here? Fine houses, to be sure, but nothing else! By God and by My Lord St. Bernard, our good patron, in the length and breadth of this whole city, I've not seen one single pastrycook's shop! Yet I have looked right and left, pried here and poked there, ready to count and number—in every direction, wherever we might come upon them—the various pastrycook establishments in Florence. I have been vigilant as a spy, I have been all eyes, all nose. Lord help us! in Amiens, in one-quarter the distance—nay, in one-fifth the distance we have covered in our tour of inspection—I could show you more than fourteen ancient and aromatic pastrycooks!

" 'I know not what delight you experienced, when you saw their lions, and africans or tigers, near the belfry. I know not what wonder you felt, when you viewed the porcupines and ostriches, in the exotic menagerie, next to the palace of My Lord Philip of Strozzi! By my faith, lads, I had much rather see a fine fat goose, turning on a spit. These porphyries and marbles are beautiful, I will not deny; but our Amiens cheesecakes are more to my taste. These ancient statues are well moulded, but by St. Ferréol of Abbeville, patron of geese, the young wenches of our land are seven thousand times more alluring.' "

"Why is it," Friar John demanded, "you always will find monks in kitchens, but never king, pope or emperor? What does this signify?"

"Is there some latent virtue or some specific property, hidden in kettles and pots, that attracts monks, as a magnet does iron, but proves powerless on emperors, popes and kings?" Rhizotomos asked. "Or is there some inclination, some stimulus, inherent in frock and cowl, that drives the religious into kitchens, whether they will or no?"

"Form follows matter, as Averroës says," Epistemon put in. "That's what Rhizotomos means."

"Right, quite right!" Friar John approved.

"The problem you present is somewhat ticklish: you could hardly touch it without getting pricked," said Pantagruel. "So I will not seek to answer it. But I can tell you this. I remember having read somewhere that Antigonus, King of Macedonia, once entered his kitchens, and there met the poet Antagores, pan in hand, frying a conger-eel.

" 'Ha!' the monarch cried gaily. 'Was Homer frying congers while he wrote of Agamemnon's prowesses?'

" 'Does Your Majesty think,' the poet replied, 'that, while accomplishing these prowesses, Agamemnon made it his business to find out who, in his camp, was frying eels?'

"To the king, it seemed improper that the poet should be messing about in the kitchen. The poet showed his master that it was more indecent for a king to be found in such a place."

"I'll go you all one better," said Panurge. "I'll tell you what Jean Breton, Lord of Villandry and secretary to King François I., once replied to Claude of Lorraine, Duc de Guise. They were discussing some battle waged between their master and the Emperor Charles V. Though armed to the teeth, with heavy plate over every conceivable portion of his anatomy, and though mounted like a very St. George, Breton had nevertheless been seen nowhere on the field of battle.

" 'On my word of honor,' Breton insisted, 'I can easily prove to you that I was in a place where you, My Lord, would not have dared go.'

"The duke, resenting such braggart insolence, began to lose his temper. But Breton appeased him, and sent the company into fits of laughter, as he added:

" 'I was skulking in the rear amid the baggage,' he confessed. 'Was this not a place where you, My Lord, would not dare go, as I did?' "

Thus conversing, they went on board and set sail from the island of Cheli.

XII

HOW PANTAGRUEL PASSED THROUGH THE LAND OF PETTIFOGGING, AND OF THE STRANGE WAY OF LIVING AMONG THE CATCHPOLES

PROCEEDING along our course, next day we visited Pettifogging, a blurred and blotted country. I could not tell what to make of it. We saw some Pettifoggers there, and some Catchpoles. The latter are also known as Bumbailiffs or sheriff's officers; the word "catchpole" comes from two Latin words meaning *chase* and *fowl*. They were men who would stop at nothing.

They did not invite us to drink or eat; they contented themselves, amid endless bowing and scraping, with assuring us that they were wholly at our service—if we paid!

One of our interpreters told Pantagruel of the strange way in which these people earned their livelihood, a way diametrically opposite to that of the denizens of Rome. For whereas the latter support themselves by poisoning, beating and killing people, the Catchpoles do so by being beaten. Thus, if a long time elapsed between beatings, the Catchpoles, their wives and children would die of starvation.

"They are," said Panurge, "like the people Claudius Galen tells us of, who cannot erect their virile member towards the equator, unless they are first whipped. By St. Tybalt! whoever flogged *me* thus would, on the contrary, unsaddle me wholly!"

"This is the way of Catchpoles," said the interpreter. "When a monk, priest, usurer or attorney wishes harm to some country gentleman, he sends a Catchpole to him. The Catchpole proceeds to serve a summons upon My Lord, to insult and outrage him impudently, according to his power and instructions. What is your gentleman's reaction? Well, unless he is weak as watergruel and dull as ditch-water, My Lord will be forced to apply a cudgel, or the flat of his sword, to the rascal's head, or to fetch him a lusty trouncing, or, best, to toss him gently out of the window of his castle.

"Whereupon, Catchpole is as rich, for the next four months, as if cudgellings were his real harvest. For he will obtain from monk, priest, usurer or attorney, a very handsome reward. Poor gentleman! the damages he must fork out are so unreasonably excessive that he loses all he has, and risks perishing miserably in prison, as if he had struck the king."

"I know an excellent remedy to that sort of thing," observed Panurge.

"What?" Pantagruel inquired.

"It is the remedy habitually employed by My Lord of Basché," Panurge said, and proceeded to relate the following anecdote.

My Lord of Basché was, Panurge said, a brave, upright, magnanimous and chivalrous man. He fought in a certain lengthy war in which Alfonso d'Este, Duke of Ferrara, with the help of the French, defended himself valiantly against the furious onslaught of Pope Julius II. On the nobleman's return to France, no day went by but he was served with writs, summonsed and pestered for the sport and delight of the fat prior of St. Louant.

One morning, while breakfasting with his domestics—he was a liberal, easy-going man—he sent for his baker Loire; for Loire's wife; and for Oudart, the vicar of his parish, who also served as butler, according to the custom of the times. In front of his gentlemen and servants, My Lord of Basché addressed them:

"Children," he said affably, "you see how angry these wretched Catchpoles make me every day. I have reached a point where, unless you help me, I am determined to leave the country and go fight for the Sultan, or for the Devil himself, for that matter.

"Here is my plan, if you will work with me. When next the Catchpoles come, I want Loire and his wife to be prepared to appear in the great hall, dressed in wedding robes (as if you were about to be married, and exactly as you *did*, when you *were* married)! Here, take these hundred golden crowns to put your finery in order.

"As for you, Master Oudart, do not fail to appear with your handsomest surplice and finest stole. As for you, Trudon," he turned to his drummer, "you report with pipe and tabor. When

Oudart has read the wedding service, and the bride has been kissed to the roll of the drum, you will all of you exchange light fisti-cuffs in memory of the wedding. When, however, you come to the Catchpole, lay on with a vengeance, thrash him as you would a sheaf of green corn. Thump, swinge, pummel, baste and belabor him! Here, take these steel gauntlets, covered with kid. Lay on, to right and left, without counting the blows: he who wallops most stoutly shall be accounted my best friend. Do not fear to be hailed into court over it; I will bear the full responsibility. Remember, your blows must seem to be dealt in jest, as is customary among us at all weddings."

"But how shall we distinguish the Catchpole?" Oudart asked. "All sorts of people come daily to your castle from everywhere."

"I have arranged that," My Lord of Basché replied. "If you see some fellow, either on foot or mounted on a scurvy nag, with a great broad silver ring around his thumb, he will be your Catchpole. Hav-ing answered the door, the porter will admit him courteously, then toll the great bell. That is when you must be ready to come to hall to play the tragicomedy I have outlined to you."

That very day, God was pleased to bring a fat, red-faced Catch-pole to Basché. He rang at the door; the porter surveyed him. Wide, hulking breeches . . . a wretched mount . . . a canvas bag, filled with documents, strung to his belt . . . especially, a great, broad silver ring around a fat thumb . . . no doubt of it, here was Master Catchpole! The porter introduced him courteously, then tolled the great bell.

At the summons, Loire and his wife swaggered into the great hall in full wedding garb; Oudart emerged from his vestry to meet the Catchpole face to face. At once Oudart invited him in again and, in the little room, they tossed off many a bumper while the crowd donned their steel kid-covered gloves.

"You have come in the nick of time," Oudart told the Catchpole. "Our master is in splendid form. Presently we shall feast and make merry, like so many kings; you will be treated by every one with unsparing hand. For we are celebrating a wedding to-day: here, drink, be welcome and good cheer to you!"

Meanwhile, everything was ready in the great hall: the wedding-guests were assembled and equipped. My Lord of Basché sent for

Oudart, who arrived, bearing the holy water, Catchpole in tow. Bowing and scraping, Catchpole accosted My Lord of Basché and served him with a summons. The nobleman received him with utmost cordiality, gave him a goldpiece and begged him to stay for the wedding. Which the Catchpole did.

The ceremony done, the guests began playfully to tap one another. But when Catchpole's turn came, they whacked with lusty gauntlet, knocking their enemy dizzy . . . bruising his whole frame . . . making one eye look like nothing so much as a poached egg with black-butter sauce . . . smashing eight ribs, staving in his chest, and cleaving his shoulderblades in four . . . breaking his jaw into three separate parts . . . and, accomplishing the whole, amid good-natured laughter. . . . God knows how severely Oudart buffeted him, concealing, under the long sleeve of his surplice, the huge steel gauntlet lined with fur. For the priest was, it must be admitted, a powerful fellow.

Catchpole, striped like a tiger, thus made his way home to l'Ile Bouchard, well-pleased, indeed content, with My Lord of Basché's reception. With the help of the good surgeons of the region, he lived as long as you might hope. Not a word of the business was ever heard; the memory of it died in the tintinnabulation of the bells on the occasion of his funeral.

XIII

HOW, LIKE MASTER FRANÇOIS VILLON, MY LORD OF BASCHÉ PRAISED HIS RETAINERS

LEAVING the castle, our Catchpole clambered on to Blind Sorrel, as he called his one-eyed mare, whilst My Lord of Basché summoned his wife, her ladies and all his retainers into the arbor in his garden. Wine was brought out with pies, ham, fruit and cheese; everyone fell to with gusto. Amid their glee, My Lord of Basché told them the following anecdote concerning Master François Villon.

In his old age, the poet retired to St. Maixent in Poitou, under the patronage of the very honest, kindly abbot of the place. Here, to entertain the citizenry, Villon undertook to produce a passion play in the local manner and dialect. The parts were cast, the actors assembled, the stage prepared: Villon promised the mayor and aldermen that his production of the mystery would be ready about the time the Niort Fair closed. The local officials accordingly set aside that date, and otherwise collaborated.

For the costume of the old peasant playing God the Father, Villon begged Friar Stephen Ticklepecker, sacristan of the Franciscan monastery, to lend him a cope and a stole. Ticklepecker flatly refused. The provincial status of their order, he said, expressly forbade the monks to donate or lend anything whatsoever to the players.

Villon argued that this ruling applied merely to bawdy farces, to mummeries and to dissolute spectacles such as were performed at Brussels and elsewhere. But Ticklepecker, adamant, replied peremptorily that Villon might seek a costume wherever he liked; he need hope for nothing from the monastic wardrobe, for he would get nothing.

Villon, indignant at this abominable attitude, reported to the actors; God, he concluded, would take vengeance upon Ticklepecker, making notorious example of the fellow.

On the following Saturday, Villon heard that Ticklepecker had gone to St. Ligaire, to beg alms in that district. The sacristan was mounted on the monastery filly; he would not be back in St. Maixent before two o'clock that afternoon.

Villon therefore assembled all those playing the parts of devils and paraded with them through the town and market. They all wore the hides of wolves, calves or rams, trimmed with sheep's heads, bulls' horns and huge kitchen hooks; from these, on leather straps, hung heavy cowbells and mulebells that set up a terrific din. Some held black sticks full of squibs and firecrackers. Others bore long lighted brands on which, at every corner, they tossed handfuls of rosin, producing terrible flame and smoke.

The populace was overjoyed at the spectacle, the brats of the town terrified. The parade ended in a banquet at a small house, just outside the city gates, on the road to St. Ligaire. As they arrived, they caught sight of Friar Ticklepecker, returning from his begging tour. Villon burst into macaronic verse:

Hic est de patria, natus de gente scoundrelli
Qui solet antiquo scrappas portare in poucho.

Interpreted in prose, this meant: "Here, from his native heath, comes one of the scoundrelly race which was wont, of old, to bear in their pouches all manner of scraps collected in the name of religion."

"God's death!" cried the devils. "That's the rascal who refused God the Father a wretched cope. Let us give him the fright of his life!"

"A capital idea," Villon agreed. "Let us hide till he rides by. Then, set off your squibs and crackers!"

As Ticklepecker ambled towards them, they leaped up, fell tumultuously upon him, amid a clashing of cymbals, a devilish howling and a rain of fire, falling from all sides upon the wretched monk and his wretched filly.

"Whhhoooo! Whhhooo! Whhooo! Brrrrrr! Grrrrrr! Prrrrr! Are we not proper devils, Friar Stephen?"

The filly, scared out of her wits, started, reared, plunged forward, bucked, galloped, jerked and curvetted, then rushed headlong, her gyrations accompanied by a vast pooping, farting and funking. Very soon (though he clung to saddle with might and main) Ticklepecker lost his seat.

Yet his stirrup straps were so many ropes, binding him to the beast; and his right sandal, caught in the stirrup, as in a vice, prevented his freeing his foot. The filly, meanwhile, charged along the road, shying and then darting, hellbent with terror, through hedge, briar and ditch, with Friar Ticklepecker dragged, peelarse, in her wake. Her progress bashed his head so hard against the road that his brains spurted out somewhere near the Hosanna, that cross by the roadside where the faithful pay homage on Palm Sunday. Both arms and both legs were crushed to a pulp; his intestines were pounded to a jelly; and when the filly reached her monastery stable, the sole trace of Friar Ticklepecker was a right sandal and the stump of a foot inside.

Villon, delighted to see everything fall out as he had expected, addressed his devils:

"You will play your parts well, good friends, I can see that. Ay, you will outdevil the foul fiend, judging by this rehearsal. I defy the most talented actors to hold a candle to you, be they from Saumur, Doué, Montmorillon, Langres, St. Esprit, Angers—and, yes, by God! even from Poitiers, for all their bragging and their town hall to play in! Actors? No, you will *live* your parts!"

His story done, My Lord of Basché pointed out the appropriate moral:

"My friends, I foresee that henceforth you will play our own tragicomedy equally well. Certainly your first appearance in rehearsal was illustrated by a thorough tickling, drubbing and thwacking of Catchpole. As of to-day, I double your wages."

He turned to his wife.

"You, my dear, please do the honors here as you may see fit: my entire treasury lies in your hands to dispose of as you will.

"As for me, first, I drink to you, one and all; drink up, friends, this wine is cool and sweet. You, steward, take this silver basin: I give it to you gladly. Here, equerries, are two silvergilt cups: they are yours, if you promise not to whip my pages for the next ninety days."

There was a burst of cheers, a round of applause.

"Dear heart," My Lord of Basché said to his wife, "give the equerries those fine white plumes of mine with the golden spangles. Master Oudart, butler-vicar, I salute you: here is a silver flagon to remember me by. That other flagon, I give the cooks . . . this silver basket is for my valets . . . this silvergilt bowl to my grooms, with their master's compliments . . . these two plates to the porters . . . ten porringers for ostlers and stablemen . . . you, Trudon, take all these silver spoons, and you, flunkeys, this large saltcellar. . . .

"Serve me well, friends, and I will reward you. Believe me: by God's power, I had rather bear fivescore blows on my helmet, dealt in battle in our good king's defense, than a single summons delivered, for the amusement of a pot-bellied prior, by these rascally Catchpoles."

XIV

HOW THE CATCHPOLES WERE THRASHED AT MY LORD OF BASCHÉ'S (CONTINUATION)

PANURGE proceeded with his story.

Four days after My Lord of Basché's distribution of gifts, another Catchpole appeared to serve him with summons. This time it was a tall, thin, youthful varlet. The porter recognized him at once, and immediately tolled the great bell to warn the whole household of what was afoot. Loire, at the time, was busy kneading his dough . . . his wife was sifting meal . . . and Oudart, butler-chaplain, was holding forth in his pantry . . . the gentlemen were playing patball . . . the ladies, come-seven, come-eleven . . . the officers, too . . . the pages, hothand and smackarse . . . while My Lord and his lady entertained themselves at commerce, connection and all-fours. . . .

Suddenly, all this activity ceased; the word "Catchpole" spread like wildfire. Oudart whisked on his canonicals; Loire and his wife dived into their nuptial paraphernalia; Trudon piped and drummed; one and all laughed merrily as they drew on their gauntlets.

My Lord of Basché went to the outer court. The moment Catchpole caught sight of him, he fell on his knees, entreating this mighty nobleman to do him, a humble man-at-law, no harm. Might he, said man-at-law, herewith serve him, His Lordship, with a writ on behalf of a certain fat prior? Eloquently, the bailiff pointed out that he, said bailiff, was a public servant, a beadsman of monkdom, usher of the abbey mitre. More, he, said bailiff, was ready to do as much for him, My Lord, or for the least of his, My Lord's servants, if the occasion arose. Therefore he, meekest of Catchpoles, begged My Lord to call upon him, Catchpole, whenever he, My Lord, had need of him, Catchpole.

"Come," said My Lord, "you won't serve me with a writ before

you drink some of my good Quinquenais wine, of the Chinon vineyards, and attend the wedding we are about to celebrate? Ho, Master
Oudart, have our friend Catchpole drink and refresh him; then
bring him into the great hall. Welcome to Basché, Master Catchpole!"

The bailiff, having eaten and drunk his fill, appeared with Oudart
before a company of actors, cued and itching to play their parts.
His entrance met with a vast, universal smile; much flattered,
Catchpole grinned back. Oudart breathed the mystic, sacramental
words over the happy pair . . . hand clasped hand . . . the bride
was kissed, and every one besprinkled with holy water. . . .

Presently, wine and refreshments were served, and, according to
the old custom, thumps were exchanged among the guests. With
lusty mirth, Catchpole smacked Oudart on the back several times.
Oudart, confident in the gauntlet concealed under his surplice, bore
it all cheerfully enough. But, suddenly, up came the glove; down it
went, mitten-like over Oudart's hand, and out it shot straight at
Catchpole. This was the signal for other gauntlets to pelt down upon
the bailiff.

"Remember the wedding, the wedding, the wedding," they cried.
"Remember the wedding, the wedding, the wedding."

They laid on so heartily that blood spurted from his mouth, nose,
ears and eyes. Catchpole was beaten to a pulp; his shoulders dislocated; his head, neck, back and breast pounded into mincemeat.
You may take my word for it that Avignon, in carnival time, never
produced youngsters that played more melodiously at thumpsocket
than these vassals of My Lord of Basché's upon the person of Catchpole. The poor devil fell, in a faint, to the ground.

They poured several gallons of wine into his snout; they tied
yellow-and-green ribbons, for favors, to his doublet; and they set
him on his snotty horse.

He returned, thus decorated, to l'Ile Bouchard. I do not know if
he was treated and bandaged by his wife or by the local physicians.
At all events, he was never heard of again.

The same scene was repeated on the morrow, for Catchpole's summons was found intact and unserved, in his bag. A fresh emissary of
the fat prior's arrived at Basché, this time, however, accompanied
by two other bumbailiffs.

The porter tolled the great bell, to the delight of the household, avid for more Catchpole blood. My Lord of Basché was at the table with his wife and gentlemen. My Lord sent for the minions of law, bade Catchpole sit next to him, and placed the bumbailiffs next to the ladies. The company dined copiously and amid much jollity. At dessert, Catchpole rose and, calling his bumbailiffs to witness, served his summons upon My Lord of Basché with the greatest civility. My Lord asked for the document, which was immediately forthcoming; he accepted it and gave the process-servers a bounty of four crowns.

Meanwhile, the actors of the farce were ready to begin. As Trudon beat his drum, My Lord invited the Catchpoles to attend the wedding of one of his officers and to witness the marriage contract. To his invitation, he added a handsome fee. Catchpole, all courtesy, took out his inkhorn, produced paper. His bailiffs stood on either hand. Nuptially, Loire appeared through one door, his wife and her bridesmaids through the other; Oudart, in full pontificals, grasped their hands, asked their intentions and forthwith gave them his blessing, with holy water aplenty. The contract was signed and registered. From one side came wine and spices; from another, maroon-and-white ribbons, the color of the groom's livery, for favors; from a third, very discreetly, the steel, kid-covered gauntlets.

XV

HOW THE CATCHPOLE RE-VIVED AN ANCIENT CUSTOM

CATCHPOLE tossed down a great beaker of wine.

"This is no wedding, My Lord," he protested. "God help us, all the old ways are dying out: you find warrens aplenty, but never a rabbit; people galore, but never a friend. Once upon a time there was a great tippling in churches in honor of the blessed saints. 'O-o-o-o!' they used to sing. 'O *Sapientia*, O *Adonia*, O *radix Jesse*, O *Etcetera!* O Wisdom, O beautiful, O root of Jesse!' To-day this ancient rite has been abolished in certain churches. This world is in its dotage, the end is at hand. I suppose nobody here knows that old refrain: 'Remember the wedding, the wedding, the wedding; remember the wedding, the wedding, the wedding!'"

So saying, Catchpole tapped My Lord, My Lady, the gentlewomen and Oudart. At once the gauntlets rained down upon him to good purpose. Catchpole's head was split in nine different places. The first bailiff's right arm was broken. The second bailiff's upper jaw was dislocated, so that it fell halfway over his chin, baring his uvula, with great prejudice to his molar, masticatory and canine teeth.

Trudon changed the rhythm of his drumming; at once, gauntlets vanished miraculously, and refreshments were served, ever more plentiful. The general merriment increased; friend drank to friend, and the whole company to Catchpole and his bailiffs.

"God damn this wedding!" cried Oudart. "That cursed bailiff there dislocatocrushosnuggered my shoulder."

But, for all his wrath, he drank the fellow's health, punctuating his toasts with the old-fashioned refrain and the old-fashioned thump. The unjawed bailiff joined his hands, as though in prayer, in a pantomime of apology. (He could not speak!)

Loire complained bitterly that the bailiff with dislocated shoulders had, with his leg-of-mutton fist, fetched his elbow such a thwack that he was bruisedblackandcontusedblue down to his very heels.

Trudon protested, as he put his handkerchief over his left eye and pointed to his drum, stove in on one side:

"What harm had I done them? They were not content to maim-anglescotchblemishdisfigurepunch my poor eye, they had to bash in my drum. God knows, tabors are usually beaten and drumskins pierced at weddings but taborers, far from being struck, are royally entertained. Let the devil use my drum for a nightcap!"

"Brother," replied the one-armed Catchpole, "I will present you with a fine, large, old, royal patent I have here in my wallet. You may sell it to repair your drum, and to pray God He forgive us. By our fair Lady of Rivière, I did not mean you any harm!"

One of the equerries hopped and hobbled around the bailiffs. He looked exactly like Jean Châteigner, Lord of La Roche Posay, steward to two kings, who limped from a wound suffered at Pavia. Swinging on the bumbailiff, whose jaw hung down like the beaver of a helmet:

"Are you boomers, bummers or bombers to make ducks and drakes of us?" he demanded. "Weren't you satisfied to griperack-agonizeoppressmaultreatthumppeltkickcalcitrate our upper parts with your great boots? Why did you have to smashendcripplepum-melhamstringbanghavocrucify us by leaving the imprint of your sharply cobbled shoes on our shins? Do you call that innocent fun? By God, there's no fun about it!"

The bailiff wrung his hands, imploring, clicking his tongue like a babe in arms: "Tickl! glick! clook! agickle!"

The bride, weeping for laughter and laughing for tears, complained hysterically. Catchpole had not stopped smiting her, without choice or distinction of members; worse, he had rumpled her hair and, worst of all, he had graspressqueezedrubbangropricknock-neadedandcrumpled her privipudendapeehole.

"Devil take it, Messire Leroy," My Lord of Basché lamented, addressing the Catchpole by name. "You didn't have to smack this good old back of mine so hard, did you? Never mind, I bear you no grudge. These are but gay, nuptial caresses. Does not 'angel' mean 'messenger' in Greek? Are not sergeants of the law courts angels therefore? Well, Messire Leroy summonsed me like an angel and thwacked me like a devil. He's a monk flagellator, or I miss my guess. However, I drink to him gladly and to you, too, his distinguished bailiff."

His wife spoke up.

"What was his grievance? Why did he bash and belabor me with his sledgehammer fist? Devil take me, if I enjoyed it; no, I want none of him. I can say this for him, though: his are the hardest knuckles ever I felt on my shoulders."

The steward appeared with his arm in a sling, as though it had been utterly bashbangdislocodecimated.

"It was Satan himself made me attend this wedding," he grumbled. "As a result, by God's power, my arms are crackcrumblecrush-arrowed. Do you call this a wedding? I call it a shedding—of shit! Yes, by God, I call it the marriage described by Lucian in his *Symposium*. You remember: the philosopher of Samosata tells how the king of the Lapithae celebrated a marriage that ended in war between Lapithae and Centaurs."

Catchpole was now beyond speech. His bailiffs apologized: they had had no evil intent in striking so hard. In God's name, let the company forgive them. With which civilities, they departed.

Reaching l'Ile Bouchard, they declared publicly that they had never before met a nobleman so honest as My Lord of Basché, nor a company more gracious than his household. If trouble had arisen, the culprit was the man who had dealt the first blow.

The bailiffs lived I know not how many days after the incident. But this I *do* know: ever since, Basché's money has been considered more pernicious, pestilential and mortal to Catchpoles and bumbailiffs than the gold of Toulouse or Sejus' horse.

(In the first instance, you recall, *Cæpio*, the Roman consul, sacked Toulouse, and all who shared in the booty perished miserably. In the second, as Aulus Gellius tells us, whoever possessed the animal—which was of the breed of horses captured by Hercules from Diomedes, King of Thrace—suffered misfortune. The victims included Sejus himself, Dolabella, Cassius and Antonius. Both incidents gave rise to Latin proverbs.)

Thenceforth, My Lord of Basché lived in peace, and Basché weddings became a household word.

XVI

HOW FRIAR JOHN TESTED THE NATURE OF THE CATCHPOLES

"A MERRY tale," Pantagruel commented, "were it not that we must constantly hold the fear of God before our eyes!"

"How much better if that hail of glad gauntlets had fallen upon the fat prior!" Epistemon opined. "What did he do with his money? One half, he spent in annoying My Lord of Basché; the other half, in having his Catchpoles roundly beaten. A few cuffs around the prior's shavepate would have proved ample. Consider the extortion practised to-day by the circuit judges of our ecclesiastical or feudal systems, who hold court under the elm trees in the public squares. In comparison, those Catchpoles (poor devils!) were quite innocuous!"

"That reminds me of an ancient Roman gentleman," said Pantagruel. "His name? Lucius Neratius. He was born of a family noble and wealthy in its time; but he had one tyrannous vice. Whenever he strolled through the city, he would have his slaves fill their bags with gold and silver coins. Walking the streets, did he chance to meet some gallant minions or attractive beaux? Without the slightest provocation, indeed out of sheer *joie-de-vivre*, he would punch their faces for them. Did they threaten to prosecute him? At once Neratius pacified and contented them by paying them the damages indicated in the law of the Twelve Tables. Thus he spent his fortune beating people and paying for it!"

"By St. Benedict's holy boot," cried Friar John. "Here and now, I mean to put this to the test!"

Going ashore, he stood on the mole, gathered a crowd about him, thrust his hand in his pocket and extracted twenty shining crowns. Then, to the crowd:

"Is there a man among you willing to be beaten like the devil for twenty crowns, gold?"

"I am!"

"Yes!"

"Certainly!"

"Here, Friar!"

"Beat me!"

"Twenty crowns?"

"You can beat me to a frazzle!"

"It will hurt, but never mind!"

"There's money in it!"

They thronged about him, vying with one another for the privilege of a thrashing. Out of the confusion, Friar John selected a certain red-snouted individual, wearing a great broad silver ring with a heavy rich toadstone set in its bezel. As Friar John made his choice, the crowd protested. I heard a tall thin young Catchpole grumbling. From general rumor, I learned that he was a fine scholar, eloquent counsel and a stalwart in the ecclesiastical courts. He objected because Redsnout carried away all available clients. Were there thirty thrashings to be earned, Redsnout grabbed twenty-eight and one-half every day. But this expostulation and discontent were sheer envy.

Friar John swung his staff manfully, thwacking and cracking Redsnout so lustily on belly and back, on head and legs that, as he fell to earth, a battered pulp, I feared for the Catchpole's death. Then he gave him his twenty crowns. But the churl rose, happy as a king —or a pair of kings, for that matter. His disappointed colleagues addressed the flagellator:

"Master Devil-Friar, please take on some of us for less money. We are all at your disposal, Master Devil, briefcase, document, pens and all."

But Redsnout rose up against them, shouting:

"Corpus Christi!" he growled. "What are you tatterdemalion muckworms up to? Underbidding me to rob me of my bread? Trying to gouge and seduce my customers? Here, here, here: I summon you to appear before the ecclesiastical jurisdiction a week from to-day, folderoldepumpumpum!"

Turning a radiant, glad countenance to Friar John:

"Reverend Father in the devil," he said, "dear sir and dear gentleman, have I given you satisfaction? Would you care to beat me again? If so, I will gladly submit at half the price, and consider it quite fair. Do not spare me, I beseech you. I am your servant, Master Devil, head, lungs, guts and garbage, I promise you!"

But ere he finished, Friar John had walked away.

The other Catchpoles moved over towards Panurge, Epistemon, Gymnastes and the others, earnestly imploring the honor of a beating, at the beater's price. Otherwise, they said, they were in danger of fasting for a long time. But Pantagruel's followers would have none of it.

Later, as we sought fresh water for our crew, we met two Catchpole hags, howling and lamenting in concert. Already Pantagruel had boarded the flagship and sounded retreat. Suspecting these old baggages were related to the Catchpole Friar John had whipped, we asked them why they were so melancholy.

"What wonder?" they exclaimed. "Have not two of our noblest, most respectable Catchpoles just been made to neck it, alas! from a great height."

"My pages," said Gymnastes, "foot it from a great depth. To neck it from a great height means to be hanged at the end of a hempen rope until one strangles."

"Ay, ay," Friar John chimed in. "You speak like Friar John of the 'Pocalypse!"

When we asked the hags why their two paragons had been hung, they replied, in true Poitou fashion, that the lads had appropriated (*read* "stolen") the tools (*read* "ornaments") of the mass and hidden them under the parish handle (*read* "church tower").

"High allegory!" said Epistemon.

XVII

HOW PANTAGRUEL SAILED BY THE ISLANDS OF TOHU (HURLY) AND BOHU (BURLY); AND HOW WIDENOSTRILS, SWALLOWER OF WINDMILLS, DIED A STRANGE DEATH

That day Pantagruel sailed between the twin islands of Hurly and Burly. Here we could find no possibility of frying fish or cooking geese. We were told that Widenostrils, the colossal giant, had swallowed down every pan (stewpan, dripping-pan or saucepan), every skillet, pot, kettle, cauldron and tureen in the whole land. Apparently windmills, his usual fare, were not forthcoming.

Shortly before dawn, about the hour of his digestion, he suffered a certain ventral crudity. The physicians explained that his stomach's power of digestion, accustomed to assimilating windmills, was not able to cope with frying-pans and dripping-pans. (Cauldrons and coppers proved relatively easy to digest.) The medicos swore that this fact was clearly borne out by the sediment and hypostasis found in four tubs of piss, voided at two different times that morning.

To relieve him, they employed various methods prescribed by medical doctrine; but alas! the illness prevailed over the remedies.

Noble Widenostrils died that morning under circumstances so strange that Æschylus' death must henceforth be considered quite usual.

You recall the case of Æschylus? The soothsayers warned him that he would perish, on a given day, as a result of an object falling upon his cranium. The day dawned. Æschylus at once left town . . . roamed far from house, tree or any other object whence something might fall to hurt him . . . settled in the midst of the desert . . . relied upon the wide, open sky to assure his safety. . . . To fulfill the prophecy, he thought, heaven itself must fall upon his head—a phenomenon he deemed impossible.

(Here I may add that larks are terrified lest heaven fall, since, with the fall of heaven, they are necessarily captured, according to the well-known proverb "If the sky falls, we shall catch larks"—a fitting reply to wild and improbable schemes.)

The Gymnosophists of India and the Celts, who once dwelt hard by the Rhine, also feared the heavens' fall. The latter people are our own noble, valiant, chivalrous, warlike and triumphant French. Alexander the Great once asked them what most they dreaded upon earth. He hoped they would say they dreaded him alone, because of his prowess, achievements, victories and conquests. They replied that they were afraid of nothing except the heavens falling down upon their heads. However, they were only too eager to enter into an alliance, league and confederacy with so doughty and magnanimous a monarch. Strabo, in his seventh book, and Arrian, in his first, vouch for this.

Plutarch, in his *Of the Face Appearing on the Body of the Moon,* is as authoritative. Here he tells us of one Pharnaces—Phenaces, Erasmus calls him—who was terrified lest the moon fall upon the earth. What would happen, Pharnaces wondered, to such folk as lived directly under it—the Ethiopians, for example, and the Taprobanians of Ceylon? These wretched peoples had his deepest sympathy.

Indeed, Pharnaces would have been as nervous about heaven and earth, had these not been propped and supported by the Atlas Mountains, which are the shoulders of a titan, condemned to this task by Jupiter. (See Aristotle's Book VI, *Metaphysics.*)

To return to Æschylus, he was killed by a tortoise-shell, which fell

from the claws of an eagle flying overhead. The eagle, taking the
poet's bald pate for a rock, sought to smash the shell upon it.

Deaths no less surprising include those of Anacreon, the poet, who
choked over a grapeseed . . . of Fabius, the Roman prætor, who
suffocated, thanks to a hair in a bowl of goat's milk . . . of that
timid idiot who, fearing to utter a resounding fart in the presence of
Claudius, the Roman emperor, died of excess of wind upon the
stomach . . . of that Roman buried in the cloister of the Augustin-
ian church, in the Via Flaminia, whose epitaph—much commented
upon by travellers—laments his demise, caused by a kitten biting
his little finger . . . of Q. Lecanius Bassus, perishing of a tiny,
barely visible needle-prick on his left thumb . . . of Quenelault,
the Norman physician, deceased at Montpellier as a result of awk-
wardly cutting a fleshworm out of his hand with a penknife. . . .

The death of Philomenes came about curiously. His servant had set
some figs, for first course, on the dinner table; while he went away to
draw his master's wine, a stray, opulently-ballocked donkey walked
into the house, and proceeded earnestly to devour the figs. Philomenes
appeared, saw the sycophage or fig-eater. Entranced with the donkey's sober grace, he told his servant:

"As long as you've served this devout quadruped my figs, you
might as well give him some of this excellent wine you've brought."

So saying, he fell into a fit of uncontrollable laughter, roaring so
raucously, so uninterruptedly, that the strain on his spleen cut short
his breath and killed him off on the spot.

Others, too, went to their deaths strangely. There was Spurius
Saufeius, expiring after swallowing a hard-boiled egg as he stepped
out of his bath . . . the man Boccaccio tells of, who collapsed after
picking his teeth with a sage stalk . . . Philippot Placut, a strong,
brisk man who had never known a day's illness, yet who suddenly
gave up the ghost as he paid off an old debt . . . Zeuxis, the painter,
who died of laughter as he contemplated the face and figure of a hag
he had painted . . . and a thousand others cited by such authors
as Verrius, Pliny the elder, Valerius Maximus, Baptista Fulgosus the
Genoese, Bacabery and Swallowsausage. . . .

Poor Widenostrils (worthy man!) died choking on a lump of
fresh butter at the mouth of a hot oven—a diet prescribed by his
physicians.

Besides all this news of Widenostrils, we learned that the King of Cullan, on the island of Burly, had routed the satraps and governors of the monarch Mechcloth—or King Diseases, to translate his Hebrew name. He had also sacked his fortress of Belima (otherwise Nihil or Nothing).

Leaving Hurly and Burly, we passed by Nargue and Zargue (called Pish and Tush by some); by Teleniabin and Geleniabin (or, to translate the Arabic, Manna and Honey of Roses). These last two islands are beautiful, and amazingly fruitful in material for enemas. We also sailed by the islands of Enig and Evig, which figured in a certain treaty that caused the Landgrave of Hesse some discomfort.

That was in 1547, when the Emperor Charles V substituted the words *ohne ewige Gefängniss* (without eternal imprisonment) for *ohne einige Gefängniss* (without any imprisonment). The difference caused the Landgrave to languish in jail seven long years.

XVIII

HOW PANTAGRUEL CAME THROUGH A VIOLENT STORM

NEXT day, to starboard, we sighted nine vessels, filled with monks of all sorts—Dominicans, Jesuits, Capuchins, Hermits, Augustins, Bernardins, Celestins, Theatins, Egnatins, Amadeans, Cordeliers, Carmelites, Minims and other like holy saints. They were bound for the council of Chesil. (As to this name, it is derived from one of two Hebrew words: *kessil* or madman; *cesil* or star of tempests.) At all events their purpose at this council was to palaver over the articles of faith to be issued against the new heretics.

Seeing these priestridden ships, Panurge was jubilant; he vowed we would have good luck that day, and many more to follow. First, with utmost courtesy he saluted the blessed fathers, commending the salvation of his soul to their fervent prayers and private devotions. Then he had our sailors throw on to their ships seventy-eight dozen hams, caviar—six pots at a time, Bologna sausages by the tens, botargos and other relishes of fish-roe by the hundred containers, plus two thousand fine ringing golden angels to defray the cost of masses for the souls of the departed.

Pantagruel, meanwhile, stood by, pensive and melancholy. Friar John had just finished asking him the reason for this unwonted depression, when the skipper rushed up. The ensign, he said, was fluttering above the poop: this meant a fierce wind and a sudden storm in the offing. Officers, seamen, stewards and even we passengers were ordered to report on deck at once. The sails were lowered: mizzen, spanker, topsails, lug, mainsail and bowsprit, leaving only the yards and shrouds.

Suddenly the sea swelled, roared, rose mountain-high from the depths of an abyss. Huge waves lashed the sides of our vessels. The northwester rose, with, in its train, a terrific hurricane. Black clouds gathered ominously; the gale drove furious gusts whistling through our shrouds. From the heavens above came terrific sheets of lightning, deafening peals of thunder; rain, then hail poured down upon us. All light fled from the sky, which was opaque, dark, obscure, save when the lightning flared and the clouds were rent with flames. Burning hurricanes and whirlwinds blustered and raged about us, taking on a red, hellish hue under the lightning, the fiery vapors and the other aerial explosions overhead. Oh, how grim, how desperate we looked, as we watched the tempest whip up the boiling waters to mountainous heights. You may well believe that we imagined this was exactly like primitive chaos, in which earth, sea, sky, fire and all the elements were lost in rebellious confusion.

Panurge fed the fishes plentifully with the contents of his stomach, a fare these marine dungeaters absorbed with relish. Poor Panurge, hugging the poop deck in misery and affliction, invoked all the blessed saints, male and female, as well as Leda's twin offspring, and the egg that hatched them. He would, he swore, go to confession in opportune time at the most convenient place.

"Steward, ho," he bawled, "friend steward! dear father, dear uncle, please bring me a slice of salted beef. God help us, we shall be drinking all too much as this ship goes down. 'Eat little, drink much' —that is my motto from now on. Would to God, would to the blessed, worthy and sacred Lady, that I were on dry land now, ay, at this very moment, my feet on the ground, and my body at ease.

"Thrice-happy, four times happy, the humble cabbage-planter! O cruel Fates, when you were spinning my destiny, you might have made a cabbage-grower of me! Alas, how scant the company Jupiter so signally favored by making them to tend a cabbage-patch. Lucky, O lucky devils, with one foot forever on dry earth, and the other hard by! Let who will dispute about ultimate felicity and supreme good; for my part, I maintain, here and now, that the happiest mortal on earth is the humble cabbage-grower.

"The philosopher Pyrrho, faced with the same danger as we, once saw a hog on shore eating some scattered oats. From the tossing, frail vessel, Pyrrho declared that hog happy on two counts: first, it enjoyed plenty of oats; second, it stood on *terra firma*.

"Alas! the lordliest, the divinest manor I can imagine, is the cow's floor, or, if you prefer, dry land! God save us, this wave will wash us away! A little vinegar, friends, please: bring me a little vinegar, I implore you. I am bathed in sweat for very agony. O lud, lud, our sails are in tatters, our tackle is smashed, the sides of the ship are cracking, our maintop masthead dives into the sea, our keel is up sky-high, our cables are snapped! O lud, lud, where are our topsails? *Al ist verlooren, bei Gott, kaput, spurloss versenkt*; we are lost, by God, as the German mercenaries say. Our mizzen is floating on the deep! Woe, woe! who shall gather up this wreck of a ship? O dear, O dear, help me find shelter in the sterncastle, good friends! Ho, you there, your lantern fell! Alas and alack! Don't let go the rudder, friend! Hold on to the bowline, you! I hear the pintle crack: is it broken? By God, save the rigging: to hell with the oarlocks. O-o-o-o-o-o-h!"

From then on, Panurge's comments were punctuated by confused sounds expressing hope, terror, encouragement, uncertainty and eructation.

"Look to the needle of your compass, I implore you, dear navigator, good Astrophil, as the Greeks called the friend of the stars. See whence this cursed storm is come? Ughughbubbubughsh! Augkukshw! The game is up, I'm done: I've beshit my breeches in a frenzy of fear. O-o-o-o-h! Bgshwogrbuh! Abubububugh! I sink, I drown, I perish; good folk, I have found a watery death."

XIX

HOW PANURGE AND FRIAR JOHN FACED THE STORM

FIRST, Panurge implored the protection of the great, almighty Preserver; with utmost devotion and fervor he prayed publicly for the salvation of his soul. Then, on the skipper's advice, he clung fast, desperately, to the mast.

Friar John stripped to his doublet to help the seamen; Epistemon, Ponocrates and the rest also lent a hand. But Panurge sat rooted by the arse to the poop deck, blubbering and wailing. Friar John, running back to the quarterdeck, noticed him.

"By God, look at him!" he cried. "Panurge, crying like a calf; Panurge, the coward; Panurge, the whimperer! You'd do better to come and help us than lie there, propped on your ballocks like a barearsed baboon, and bawling like a constipated cow!"

"Bububbububbubu! boo-hoo-hoo-hoo!" Panurge wailed. "Friar John, dear friend, good father in Christ, I sink, I drown, I perish. Dear father spiritual, good friend of my heart, my bolt is shot: not even that mighty broadsword of yours can save me from this end. Woe is me! woe, woe! Look, look, we're above the *Ela*, the highest note in the scale; we're above the high C, we rise, rise. . . . Ubbubbughschwug! Woe is me, woe, woe! Now we're below *gamma ut*, we're at the bottom of the keyboard. We're at the bottom of the sea. I sink, I drown, I perish a watery death.

"Good father, sweet uncle, my friend, my one and all: look, the water has washed down under my collar, it's filling my boots! Ubbubbugshwuplk! Wagh, a-grups-grrshwahw! O-o-o-o-o-o-h! Alas, alas, God help me! I could match your finest tumblers and gymnasts. Look at me: head-down, feet-up, ugh! bubbubbubb! Lud, lud, why am I not in that ship with those splendid, holy men, those worthy council-bound fathers? . . . You remember, good friar, don't you? . . . that fine ship we met this morning, filled with God-fearing passengers, hale, plump, hearty, joyful, pious and eminently comfortable men of God! Ah, welladay, alack, heigh-ho and murder: this devil's wave (*mea culpa, Deus*, forgive me, O Lord!) this wave of God will sink our cursed ship (I mean our blessed ship).

"Alas, alas, Friar John, kind friend, excellent friar and noble father, hear my last confession, I beg you. Am I not down on my knees? *Confiteor*: I would confess my sins. Shrive me and absolve me and give me your holy blessing."

"You come over here, you devil's hangdog," Friar John growled. "You come here and lend a hand. Come on, no nonsense! Will you come, or shall I send thirty thousand legions of devils to fetch you?"

"Don't swear, dear father, please! At least not now," Panurge besought the friar. "To-morrow, you may swear to your heart's content. O dear, dear, dear! Alas and alack, our ship is taking water, I shall drown, I am drowning, I have drowned, ubbubbubbughshw, drowned at the bottom of the ocean. Alas, peace be. . . .

"Friends, I will give eighteen hundred thousand crowns, cash in hand, to the man who lands me on shore, all bepissed and beshitten as I am now. Was there ever a fellow-countryman of mine in such a mess! *Confiteor*, shrive me! Alas, just one word of my will and testament, one word of codicil, at least."

"May a thousand devils seize this cuckold's ordurous body!" Friar John roared. "God help us, here you talk blithely about your will and testament, while we are in extreme peril and need every ounce of energy we can muster!"

Panurge whimpered.

"Are you coming, devil!" Friar John threatened.

Then, turning to the business in hand:

"This way, friend . . . right, thanks! . . . here, you, petty-officer in charge of the galleys . . . bravo! . . . the gallows birds have a sporting chief . . . ho, Gymnastes, up, here, on the poop deck . . . by God's power, this time we're a goner! . . . there goes our light! . . . we're rushing headlong towards a million expectant devils. . . ."

"Alas, alas, alas," Panurge moaned, "bubbubughshwtzrkagh! Was it written in heaven that we perish here? Good people, I sink, I drown, I perish: *Consummatum est*, it is finished! I have lived!"

"Magna, gna, gna," said Friar John. "Ugh! what an ugly, beshitten whimperer it is! . . . Ho, boy, hold on, by all the devils, hold fast to the galley door! . . . Are you hurt? . . . God's might, hold on to a timberhead! Here, here, by all the devils! . . . Good lad, that's the stuff. . . ."

"O-o-o-o-h! Friar John, good father spiritual, sweet friend, let us not swear, I beg you. You must not sin, dear friar! Alas, alas! ub-bubbubbugh! bobobobobo! bubububuss! I sink, I drown, I perish, friends. God knows I forgive you all. *In manus*, into Thy hands, O Lord, I commit my spirit. Ubbubbughsh! Grrrshwappughbrdub! Farewell, farewell! St. Michel d'Aure in the Pyrenées, St. Nicholas of Montsoreau, it is now or never! I hereby vow to you, and to our Saviour, that if you help me this one time, if you set me safe on dry land, I will build you the finest, great, little chapel—nay, two, I swear it!—

> *Between Montsoreau's limits and Candé's,*
> *Where never cow or calf can graze."*

(Panurge certainly risked little, since the houses of the two towns are adjoining.)

"Alas, alas," Panurge's threnody continued, "that time, more than eighteen pailfuls or two of that water poured down my gullet. Bubububbugh! boo-hoo-hoo! How bitter it is, how salty!"

"By the belly and blood, by the head and flesh of God Almighty," Friar John roared, "if I hear you bawling again, you devil's cuckold, I'll thrash you within an inch of your life, I'll beat you like a seadog! Good God, let's toss the idiot to the bottom of the sea! . . . Here, you, oarsmen! . . . That's right, my lad, good! Hold on, there, hold fast above! . . . Did you see that lightning? Did you hear that thunder? I swear that all the devils of hell are loose to-night! Or else Proserpine's pregnant! Ay, the devils are dancing a jig!"

XX

HOW PILOTS ABANDON THEIR SHIPS AT THE HEIGHT OF THE STORM

"Oh, you are committing a sin, Friar John, dear former friend," Panurge moaned. "I say 'former friend' because at this moment, I am no more, you are no more!"

Friar John spat angrily.

"I hate to tell you this," Panurge pursued, "because I think it does your spleen a world of good, when you can utter a round, mouth-filling oath. You get the same relief as a woodchopper, when at every blow of his axe, a bystander grunts. You feel as pleased as a bowler, who throws wide of the alley, and looks up to see some intelligent fellow in the crowd turning head and body to follow the path the bowl should have taken to spill the pins. Nevertheless, O gentle friend, when you swear, you are committing a grievous sin!

"Suppose we ate some cabirotadoes or rashers of goatsmeat? Do you think that would secure us from this dreadful storm? You know the gods Cabiri, mysterious Phrygian deities, are supposed to protect men in peril on the sea; their worshippers are never afraid and never in danger. As you know, Orpheus, Apollonius, Pherecydes, Strabo, Pausanias and Herodotus have celebrated their powers."

"The poor devil's delirious," Friar John grunted. "A hundred, a thousand, a million, a hundred thousand million devils take this horny cuckold to hell! Come, help us, you godforsaken, lecherous sodombugger! Are you coming or no? Here, on the port side! God's head cramfull of relics, what monkey's paternoster is he muttering between his teeth? This devil of a seacalf caused the whole storm, and he alone won't help the crew. By God, let me get up on the poop and I'll lambast you like a Cabirian storm-devil! . . .

"Ay, ay, sailor, I'm there, lad: hold fast till I make a double knot. . . . Good lad, well done! . . . Would to God you were the Abbot

of Talemouze, and the present abbot were in charge of the Franciscans at Croulay near Chinon. . . . Ponocrates, friend, you'll get
hurt there . . . Epistemon, look out, old fellow . . . stand clear
of that hatchway, I saw lightning strike there. . . . Heave-ho!
hoist."

"Right: hoist!"

"Hoist, hoist, hoist!"

"Steer, man; bring her round! So!"

"Hoist, man, hoist!"

"By God, what's that? Her head is smashed to bits! Turn her,
man, ho! Now thunder, devils, fart, belch and shit your guts out!
Shit for the sea, shit for the ocean, shit for the ballocky blue!"

"God's might, I was almost washed overboard that time. I swear
that every one of the million devils are holding their provincial
assembly here, or canvassing for the election of a new university
rector."

"Larboard! port! bring her round to port!"

"Good, that's the stuff! Watch your noddle, there, lad! Ho, boy!
Midship, ho! look out, God damn it! Port, port!"

"Ubbubbubbugh! Grrwh! Upchksvomitchbg!" Panurge maun-
dered. "O-o-o-o-o-o-h! I sink, I drown, I perish. Where is heaven? I
cannot see it. Where earth? Ugh! the only elements left us are fire
and water. . . . Ububbubgrshlouwhftrz! Would that, by God's
mighty will, I were now in the abbey close at Seuilly! Would that,
by divine mercy, I were now standing in front of Innocent's, the
pastrycook, over by the winecellars at Chinon! Yes, I would strip
to the doublet and bake the cakes myself, could I but see the place
again!"

The wind howled ever more horribly, whipping up fierce whirl-
pools of water that drove huge sheets of ice across the vessel's bow.
The sky thundered, crackled.

"O-o-o-o-o-oh! Help, friends! Is there one of you can toss me
ashore? I've heard you were all expert mariners! If you can, I will
deed over to you all of Salmagundi, plus my vast variable revenue
of cockchafers and snailshells. They are yours, if, by your industry,
I can but touch *terra firma*. . . .

"Alas, alack, ah! Wellaway and woe! I sink, I drown, I perish
utterly. For God's sake, dear comrades, since we cannot make port

safely, let us come to anchor in some roadstead, anywhere you like, please, please! Lower all your anchors; let us keep clear of all danger, I beg you. Come, good sailorman, man the chains, heave the lead, if you please! Let us find how many fathom we are in. Take soundings, friend. In God's name, let us find out if we can drink here without stooping. I daresay we might!"

"Helm to leeward, ho!" cried the master. "Helm a-lee! A hand on the halyard: hoist, up she goes! Bring her about, so, back! Helm a-lee! Stand off there . . . firetack . . . maintack . . . ho! helm a-lee and let her drive!"

"Have we sunk to this?" Panurge groaned. "May our good Saviour come to our aid!"

"Let her ride," cried Jamet Brayer, the skipper. "So, let her ride! To your prayers, men. Let each and all of you look to his soul and prepare himself for Eternity. Only a miracle from Heaven can save us now."

"Let us make some worthy, pious vow," Panurge whined. "Alas, alas, alas! Ubbubbububugh! ugg! ugg! Alas, alack and woe! Let us vow to go upon a pilgrimage, ay: let each and every one of us contribute his share. Out with your purses, lads!"

"This way, hey, by all the devils," Friar John bawled. "Here, for God's sake, let her drive! Never mind the rudder! Ho, there, pull, man! Come, a drink! Do you hear, steward, I called for a drink: the best and most ventrally exhilarating you have. Come, man, serve up the liquor: don't you know we are headed for the land of the million devils? Boy, my drawer, here?"

"Your drawer, Friar?"

"Yes, my drawer."

"I don't understand!"

"Do you know what a drawer is in falconry?"

"Ay, sir: a ball of feathers given the bird to make it vomit and give it an appetite."

"Right," said Friar John. "Do you know what a breviary is?"

"Ay, sir!"

"Well, do you see that breviary there?"

"Ay, sir."

"Bring it to me, then."

The boy brought Friar John's flask, shaped and leather-covered like a psalter.

"Wait, friend, stay. Draw . . . draw . . . God's power, there's a fine stinging hail . . . there's a sonorous thunderclap! Hold fast, above, there! It ought to be All Saints' Day soon; to-night's the Feast of All Million Devils."

"Alas," Panurge lamented, "Friar John is certainly damning himself with a vengeance! Oh, what a good friend I lose! Alas, alas, now things are worse than ever: we go from the Charybdis of desolation to the Scylla of despair! Alas, I sink, I drown, I perish! *Confiteor!* Shrive me! One word of my last will and testament, Friar John, good father, sweet Master Abstractor, old comrade, my Achates, my Xenomanes, my all! Alas, I drown: two words of my last will and testament. Here, now, here, father, beside this hatch!"

XXI

THE STORM (CONTINUATION), TOGETHER WITH A BRIEF COMMENTARY ON THE MAKING OF WILLS AT SEA

"To talk about making a will now," said Epistemon, "when we should bend every effort to help the crew save this ship, seems about as idle and inappropriate as the behavior of Cæsar's officers and henchmen when they invaded Gaul. They wasted their time drawing up their wills, with elaborate codicils; they bewailed their ill-fortune; they deplored the absence of their wives, of their Roman friends. And what should they have been doing meanwhile? Why, rushing to arms, fighting tooth and nail against their enemy, Ariovistus.

"To talk about a will at this moment is to be foolish as the carter in the well-known story. His wagon was stuck fast in a plowed field; instead of goading his oxen and putting a hand to the wheel, he fell on his knees and implored the aid of Hercules!

"Of what use would it be to draw up our wills here? Either we survive this peril or we drown. If we survive, our wills are useless, since no will is valid unless the testator is deceased. If we drown, surely our wills will go down with us. For who should bear them to our executors?"

"A wave," said Panurge, "would cast my will ashore, just as it bore Ulysses safe out of the deep. Some king's daughter, playing on the beach, would find and execute it. And she would have a magnificent cenotaph erected on the shore to my memory, just as Dido did, for her husband Sychæus . . . as Æneas did, for Deiphobus, on the Trojan shore, hard by Rhæte . . . as Andromache did, in the city of Buthrotum, for her husband Hector . . . as the Athenians did, for the poet Euripides . . . as Aristotle did, for Hermias and Eubulus . . . as the Romans did, in Germany, for Drusus, and in Gaul, for the Emperor Alexander Severus . . . as Argentarius did, for Callaïschrus . . . as Xenocrates did, for Lysidice . . . as Timarus did, for his son Theleutagoros . . . as Eupolis and Aristodice did, for their son Theotimus . . . as Onestes did, for Timocles . . . as Callimachus did, for Sopolis . . . as Statius did, for his father . . . as Catullus did, for his brother . . . as Germain de Brie did for Hervé, the Breton sailor. . . ."

"Are you mad?" asked Friar John. "Come help us here, by five thousand millions of cartloads of devils, help, help! May a chancre decorate your whiskers with rot; may three rows of cauliflower-blossoms and gangrenous passion-flowers cover you like breeches and codpiece. Is our ship sunk yet?"

"By God, she is almost! How shall we clear her? Hello, hello! here are all the devils of mishaps at sea! We shall never escape, or I deed my soul to Lucifer!"

Just then, Pantagruel's piteous exclamation was heard by all:

"O Lord my God, save us, for we perish. Yet not as we would wish it, but Thy holy will be done!"

"God save us, Our Lady help us, alas, alack, woe is me! I sink, I drown, I perish. Ubbubbubbugh! Boo-hoo-hoo! *In manus*, into Thy hands. . . . O very God, send me some fish to transport me to shore like Arion, the Greek poet, who was cast into the sea and carried to Tænaros on the back of a dolphin. I shall strum the lyre—or play the harp!—if there be strings to twang!"

"My immortal soul to all the devils!" cried Friar John.

"God be with us!" Panurge muttered between clenched teeth. "Holy Virgin, help us!"

"Just let me get over to you, you horned, cuckolded wittol! and I'll prove that your stones dangle from the arse of an impotent calf! Gua-a-a-h! Guaa-a-a-h! Come, help us, you great bawling son of a cow! or let thirty million devils gripe your body! Are you coming, seacalf? Faugh, the ugly beast, the milksop blubberer!"

"You keep on saying the same thing over and over," Panurge objected.

"Here, falcon-drawer, let me stroke your feather; here, breviary drinking-flask, let me peruse you. *Beatus vir qui non abiit*, blessed is the man that walketh not in the counsel . . . I know it all by heart!"

Interrupting himself in the midst of his quotation of the psalm, Friar John turned his attention to his good master, St. Nicholas, patron of sailors in peril on the sea.

Speaking of tempests, Friar John quoted:

Horrida tempestas montem turbavit acutum

the initial line of a poem composed by the scholars of the Collège de Montaigu against Pierre Tempeste, their principal, a harsh disciplinarian. Literally, the line read: "The awful tempest racked the mountain peaks!" The scholars' reading was: "The awful Tempeste was a great flogger of boys at Montaigu (*montem acutum*)."

"If pedagogues are damned for whipping poor little innocent wretches, then, by my honor, he is now on Ixion's wheel of fire, lashing the bobtailed cur that sets it going. If pedagogues are saved for whipping defenseless children, he must be high above the—"

XXII

THE STORM
(CONCLUSION)

"LAND, land!" cried Pantagruel. "I see land. Pluck up your courage, lads, we're almost there. A louse's guts, and you're safe in the haven! Look, the sky is clearing. Look to the southeast!"

"Courage, lads," cried the skipper. "The swell is spent, the sea smoother. Up, maintop! Mizzen . . . topsail . . . hoist, hoist! . . . haul your bowlines, after-mizzen . . . haul, there, haul . . . capstan, ho, slack! . . . about, man, about, ho! . . . Your main tack about . . . clear your sheets, clear your bowlines. . . . Port, ho, port! . . . slack, slack, to starboard, you son of a bitch!"

"My worthy friend," Friar John turned to a sailor beside him, "you must be delighted to hear news of your mother from the skipper."

"Luff, luff, luff the helm."

"Done, done!" said the sailors.

"Keep her up . . . bring her round . . . so, ho, high! . . . hoist, haul!"

"Golden words!" Friar John commented. "Hoist, hoist; haul, haul! A little elbow grease, your guts into it, lads, and we've done the trick! Luff, luff. Starboard . . . helm. . . ."

"The storm is almost spent; a little longer, my hearties! Praise God, our devils are slinging their hooks! Out with your sails!"

"Larboard! Larboard!"

"Let her go!"

"Slack, man, give her slack. . . ."

"Right! right!"

"Slack, luff!"

"Here, by God, here, old Ponocrates! You're a lusty fornicator: it's only boys you will breed. . . . No, Eusthenes, stout brangler, pop up the fore-topsail!"

"Hoist sail, hoist sail."

"Well said: hoist, by God, hoist:

> *Away with fear, away!*
> *This is a holiday!*
> *Hurrah! Hurrah! Hurrah!*"

"A fine song of cheer!" said Epistemon. "I can feel the holiday spirit in the air!"

"Hoist, hoist. Wooh! there!"

"Cheer up!" cried Epistemon. "Cheer up! All's for the best! Look at Castor, there, to starboard!"

"St. Elmo's fire!"

"Hoist, hoist away!"

"Ubbubbu! brghsh!" Panurge moaned. "You say you see Castor —and Pollux, ballocks! What if it's that bitch Helen . . . a single flame, a portent of evil!"

"As a matter of fact," Epistemon replied, "it is Mixarchagetas, if you want the original name the Argives gave Castor. Hurrah, hurrah, hurrah! I see land, land! Land ahoy! I see the shore . . . the harbor . . . crowds of people on it . . . and an obelyscholychny —what you would call a lighthouse!"

"Hurrah, hurrah," the skipper echoed. "Double that point . . . watch the shallows . . . soundings. . . ."

"Done . . . done already," the sailors answered.

"Good, she's clear!" cried the skipper. "So are the other ships!"

"By St. John," cried Panurge, "that's music to my ears! Say it again, Captain!"

"Mmm! that's good tipple!" said Friar John. "If you, whoreson coward of a cuckold, ever sniff a drop of this liquor, then let Satan snatch me, you devilish ballocker! . . . Here, sailor, here's a potful for you: well done, lad, drink up! Drinking-mugs, Gymnastes! Ho, bring them on! And that ham too, whether porcine, swinish, suiform or *sui generis*! Take care you don't spill any wine, man!"

"Cheer up, lads, cheer up!" Pantagruel encouraged. "Pluck up your spirits and rejoice. Look at all those ships quite near! I can make out two skiffs, three sloops, five brigs, eight schooners, four clippers and six frigates. The good islanders must have sent them from yonder to our aid."

Then, hearing Panurge:

"Who is this useless loafer here, lamenting and despairing? Who is this idle Ucalegon, stepped out of the pages of Homer's Troy? What is he moaning about? Wasn't I holding the mast firmly in both my hands? Didn't I keep it straighter than cables could?"

"It's that poor devil, Panurge," Friar John enlightened him. "The churl is troubled with calf's fever. He's got a bellyful and he's chattering with fear."

"To have been apprehensive during that horrible storm, under the stress of that terrific hurricane, was quite natural. Had Panurge helped us in spite of his fright, I would have retained my respect for him. Of course, dread of every emergency is the sign of a base and cowardly heart. Because Agamemnon was ever fearful, Achilles reproached him ignominiously for his dog's eyes and his stag's heart. On the contrary, not to be afraid, when there is quite obviously cause for alarm, is the sign of scant common sense or none at all.

"What is most to be dreaded in life? The danger of offending God. Beyond this, I shall not discuss, as Socrates and the Academics did, whether death be evil or fearful in itself. Nor shall I treat of the Pythagorean theory, which, considering the soul as a fiery substance, holds that a man dying by water (the element contrary to fire) necessarily suffers the destruction of his soul. But, with Homer, I *do* say *this*: death by shipwreck is an unnatural, grievous and abhorrent thing.

"Do you remember Æneas, caught in a storm near Sicily, regretting that he had not perished at the hands of valiant Diomedes, the Grecian hero? Thrice-blessed, four times happy, he said, are those who gave up the ghost in the Trojan fires. Thank God, I say, no one of us has lost his life: may God our protector be eternally praised therefore.

"To be sure our ship is badly damaged; we shall have to make all sorts of repairs. . . . Take care not to run her aground, Skipper!"

XXIII

HOW PANURGE PROVED HIM-SELF THE BEST OF FELLOWS, AFTER THE STORM WAS OVER

"Ho, hum, and all's for the best!" said Panurge.

"The storm is over, my hearties: please be kind enough to let me be the first ashore: I really must attend to my own business, now. Do you need any more help? Let me give you a hand with that rope: it needs winding. No, no, I'm not in the least afraid, I swear. Pass me that rope, my hearty! *No*, I said, I'm not afraid of anything. I must confess that wave—the tenth wave, the crack regiment of the army of waves—swung us around pretty fiercely and made my pulse beat somewhat faster! But still—"

"Down with your sails!"

"Well said, Skipper!" Panurge beamed. "Ho, Friar John, you're idling! This is no time to be drinking. How do you know that St. Martin's footman isn't shadowing him, to tempt or to vex him? In other words, how can you tell that the Devil isn't hatching another storm for us? . . . Do you need my help over there? Hold fast: I'm coming. . . . It's a trifle late, I know, but by God's might! I swear I'm sorry I didn't follow the sound philosophical concept that says: to stroll by the sea or to sail by the shore is as safe and agreeable sport as to walk beside a horse, bridle in hand. . . .

"Ha, ha, ha! by God, everything is tophole, now. . . . Want any help, friend? . . . Ho, there, good man, give me a chance: I'll do it for you, or the devil's against me!"

Epistemon, nursing a bleeding, raw palm, heard Panurge's words:

"I was just as frightened as Panurge, My Lord," he said, "but God save us! I didn't grudge my help: I clung to those ropes until my hand was mangled. I believe that if we die—as, fatally and inevi-tably, we must—we do so at an hour, and under circumstances, ap-pointed partly by God's holy will, and partly by our own efforts.

Thus we must not stop at unceasingly invoking, imploring, supplicating, beseeching and worshipping Him; we must also work ourselves. As the holy Apostle says: 'We are laborers together with God!'
If what I say goes against the *Decretals* and their theological champions, I pray they forgive me!"

Epistemon then amplified his argument by quotations from history. What, for example, did Caius Flaminius, the Roman consul,
say when Hannibal cornered him by Lake Trasymene?

"Lads," he told his soldiers, "vows and prayers will not get you
out of this corner! If we are to go safe, see to it you hack out a path,
at the point of the sword, through the thick of the enemy!"

Sallust illustrated the same idea when he quoted M. Porcius Cato's
dictum, to the effect that the divine aid was not to be obtained by idle
vows and womanish lamentation. No: if we watched, worked and
strove, we could bring all things to the desired end. Let a lazy, idle
and enfeebled man implore the gods in time of need, it was in vain.
It served but to antagonize and rile them.

Friar John roared:

"Devil take me—"

"I'll go halfway with you on that," Panurge interrupted.

"Devil take me," Friar John resumed, "devil take me, what would
have happened at Seuilly, if I had been content to sing: *Contra hostes
insidias*, which is breviary timber? I'll tell you: the whole abbey close
would have been despoiled of its last grape and utterly destroyed by
Picrochole's bastards. God help us! Wasn't that what all the other
devil monks were doing, instead of joining me in laying on to the
Lerné bandits with the staff of the cross?"

"Let her sink or swim," cried Panurge. "Black or white, good, bad
or indifferent, Friar John does nothing! Friar John Doolittle, they
call him, the loafer monk! Look at him watching me moiling and
toiling to help this worthy sailor here, first of the name. . . . Ho,
friend, ho: a word with you, and please don't be angry! How thick
do you think the planks of this ship are?"

"Some two good inches!" the skipper assured him. "There's no
cause for alarm!"

"God Almighty!" Panurge cried. "Are we always to be within
two inches of death and damnation? Is this one of the fifteen joys of
marriage so highly vaunted in our literature? Ay, Skipper, you are

right in measuring danger by the yardstick of fear. For my part, I am without fear: William the Fearless, they call me, Bill Dreadnought, the terror of the company.

"And when I speak of bravery, I don't mean sheep's pluck or goat's heart: I mean a lion's daring, a wolf's ferocity, a murderer's sangfroid."

Panurge paused, drew a deep breath:

"I fear nothing but danger," he concluded.

XXIV

HOW FRIAR JOHN PROVED THAT PANURGE'S TERROR DURING THE STORM WAS UNREASONABLE

"GOOD day to you, gentlemen, good day, good day!" said Panurge briskly. "You are all well, I see, thanks to God's grace and your own efforts. Welcome, welcome, I am delighted to see you, you are most welcome!

"Shall we go ashore? Ho, Coxswain, draw up to that skiff; out with the gangplank! . . . Shall I give you a hand there, too? I don't mind: I've the strength of a wolf and the power of a lion. Let me help you: I'll sweat like a steer."

Panurge looked to shore:

"A fine place, this, friends, and splendid folk, too. . . . What? you need my help again? Certainly, certainly: don't spare me, for God's sake, I'll sweat blood to be of service. Adam, and all of us, were born to labor and toil, just as the birds were made to fly. God wills— never forget!—that we eat our bread by the sweat of our brows."

"Breviary matter," Friar John grunted.

". . . by the sweat of our brows," Panurge went on, "and not by loafing, like Friar John, who stands there, with a bellyful of wine to give him Dutch courage against his mortal fear."

It was, Panurge declared, a fine day: the climate was most temperate. He recalled that noble philosopher Anacharsis who, being asked what ship was safest, replied that the safest ships were those in harbor.

"That wasn't Anacharsis' best remark," Pantagruel put in. "Somebody asked him which were most numerous: the living or the dead? For answer, he asked among what class to number those who sailed the seas. Were they not constantly in danger of destruction, living amid death and dying amid life?

"I, too, will quote M. Porcius Cato. He said that life held but three things to repent of. First, sharing a secret with a woman; second, wasting a day idly; third, travelling by sea to a place accessible by land."

Friar John spoke up:

"By the worthy frock I wear, friend Panurge, you had no cause or reason to fear during the storm. Your fatal destiny is not to perish by water, but either to dangle at the end of a rope or to fry over a bonfire like our church fathers."

Did My Lord Pantagruel wish a coat to protect him against the rain? Then let him dismiss wolfskin and badger's hide; let him flay Panurge, use his skin for covering.

"Take care not to go near the fire, My Lord," Friar John advised, "and keep clear of a blacksmith's forge, in God's name. One instant's exposure to heat would reduce your proud garment to ashes; whilst all the rain, snow and hail in the world could not impair it. By God, toss it into the seas, let it sink to the bottom, it will still be waterproof. Make boots of Panurge's hide, they will not admit moisture; make balloons of it to teach the young to swim, they will learn with impunity."

"Panurge's skin is like maidenhair," said Pantagruel, "it is never damp or wet. Keep it under water, it remains dry. That is why the ancients called it *adiantos*."

"Panurge, my friend," Friar John entreated. "Never fear water: you will eventually be consumed by a contrary element!"

Panurge allowed the monk's meaning. But he objected that the devil's kitchen staff were often absent-minded, and thus bungled their jobs. Choice game, intended for roasting, they set to boil, exactly as our modern cooks.

"What do you mean?" someone asked.

"I mean," Panurge said, "that our modern cooks often lard partridges, pigeons and doves as though to roast them. Do they roast them? No—the partridges end up in a pot, boiled with cabbage; the pigeons stew in the company of leeks; the doves simmer amid watery turnips. . . .

"No, my friends, I call the noble company to witness: I made a vow, I know! I promised to Messire St. Nicholas a chapel between Candé and Montsoreau. Well, he shall have his chapel, a watery chapel, yes, but of rose water and toilet water. How could cow or calf graze there, when I intend to throw the chapel to the bottom of the sea?"

"Splendid!" Epistemon approved. "There's a rogue, if ever I saw one: there's the proper thief set to catch a thief! Panurge proves the perfect illustration of the Italian proverb:

> *Passato el periclo gabato el santo,*

which may be translated,

> *Danger past, the saint is cheated*

or

> *Danger past, God forgot.*"

XXV

HOW, THE STORM PAST, PANTAGRUEL VISITED THE ISLANDS OF MACREONS, WHERE DWELT THE LONG-LIVED HEROES OF OLD

WE nosed into the harbor and landed on one of a group of islands called the islands of the Macreons.

The inhabitants received us handsomely. An old Macrobius—such is the title they give their senior aldermen—was bent upon taking

Pantagruel to the city hall to allow him to rest, eat and drink. But Pantagruel refused to leave the dock until all his men had landed.

Having called the roll, he ordered the men to change their clothes, to bring ashore the stores on board, and to give the crew a banquet. His orders—executed immediately, God knows!—had the sailors drinking and feasting heartily in good time. The natives of the island contributed provisions in abundance; the Pantagruelists gave them measure for measure, though, truth to tell, their wares were somewhat damaged by the storm.

The meal done, Pantagruel asked everybody to fall to and repair the damage done to the ships. They did so gladly, the more so since the islanders were all, like the Venetians, carpenters and artisans.

Only the largest of the group of islands was inhabited, and that sparsely: the whole population resided in the three harbor towns and ten parishes. The rest of the place consisted of tall woods and wasteland, much like the forest of the Ardennes.

At our request, the old Macrobius showed us what was particularly noteworthy in the island. In the shady, deserted forest, we discovered several old ruined temples, obelisks, pyramids, monuments and ancient tombs, with various inscriptions and epitaphs, some in hieroglyphics, others in Ionic, in Arabic, in Hagarene or Moorish, in Slavonic, and in still other tongues. Epistemon carefully copied them.

While waiting for him to finish, Panurge engaged in conversation with Friar John:

"As you know, this is the island of the Macreons. In Greek, *macreon* means 'burdened with years.'"

"Who cares?" Friar John answered. "Do you expect me to change the name? I wasn't present when they baptized the island."

"As a matter of fact," said Panurge, "I think the French word for 'procuress'—*maquerette* or mackerel—must be derived from this source. Isn't pimping as natural to the old as thigh-squeezing to the young? Therefore, I really think this is Mackerel Island, the origin and prototype of Mackerel Island in Paris, home of bawd, pimp, ponce and procuress. Shall we go and dig for cockle-oysters? Shall we open up some clammy shells?"

Speaking in the Ionic tongue, old Macrobius asked Pantagruel under what circumstances, and by what skill, they had managed to land here that day, considering the terrible weather and the frightful storm at sea. Pantagruel answered that the Saviour in His might had looked mercifully upon the simplicity, sincerity and affection of their party, since they travelled without thought of gain or profit. One aim alone had sent them upon their travels: a keen desire to visit, to contemplate, to know, to understand the oracle of Bacbuc, and to receive the Bottle's judgment concerning certain problems posed by one of the company. Nevertheless, though saved, they had suffered considerable hardships and come very close to being shipwrecked.

Pantagruel then asked old Macrobius his opinion of such a terrible tempest. Were seas in these latitudes subject to frequent storms, he wondered? Was their weather as inclement as that found in the ocean, off St. Mathieu, in Brittany, for instance . . . or off Maumusson, in the Saintonge, near the island of Oléron . . . or in the Mediterranean . . . in the gulf of Sataly or Adalia . . . by Montargentan or Telamone in Tuscany . . . off Piombino opposite Elba . . . off Cape Malea in southern Laconia . . . off the Straits of Gibraltar or those of Messina? . . .

XXVI

HOW GOOD MACROBIUS TOLD PANTAGRUEL WHAT OCCURRED AT THE DEATH OF HEROES

"My dear friends and travellers," good Macrobius replied, "this island is one of the Sporades—not your Sporades, which lie in the sea of the Archipelago and include the isles called Carpathian by the Greeks, but the Sporades of the ocean, in British waters. Once they were much frequented, wealthy and populous, a centre of trade under the British crown. In the course of time, with the world's decadence, they became as poor and as desolate as you see.

"That dark forest yonder—it is over seventy-eight thousand square parasangs, or Persian leagues—houses the souls of heroes who have grown old. Since the comet, which we saw shining three whole days, is no longer visible, we believe that some one of these heroes must have died yesterday. The horrible storm you encountered arose, no doubt, at this hero's death.

"Whilst they live, prosperity and happiness reign here and in the islands near by: the sea is calm, the weather wholly serene. Let one of them die, and a vast, tumultuous lamentation rings through the forest; pestilence, tempests and affliction visit the land; the air is filled with mists and darkness; the sea knows hurricanes and storms."

"What you say seems likely enough," said Pantagruel. "A torch or candle, so long as it has life and flame, shines forth, offering its service and brilliance, delighting all who look upon it, harming no man on earth. The moment it goes out, its smoke and stench infest the air, annoy the company and prove generally objectionable.

"So it is with noble and remarkable men. While they inhabit their bodies, peace and pleasure and profit and honor reign where they abide. But when their souls forsake their bodies, the continents and islands usually suffer commotions in the air, darkness, thunder and hail; on earth, quakes, tremors and disasters occur; at sea, storms and hurricanes arise. Everywhere, the people are reduced to misery, racked by religious dissension, upset by changes of government, undermined by the fall of commonwealths."

"We had an instance of this lately," said Epistemon, "in the death of the valiant and learned knight, Guillaume du Bellay. During his lifetime, France enjoyed such prosperity and happiness that all Europe envied her, sought her friendship, and held her in high respect. For a long time now, since his death, she has been the object of universal contempt."

Pantagruel cited the terrific storm which harrowed Æneas when Anchises died at Trepani in Sicily. Perhaps, he added, the consideration of such factors urged Herod, the cruel and tyrannical king of Judæa, to act as he did. He was on the verge of a horrible death— indeed, he perished of *phthyriasis* or *pediculosis*, devoured by lice and worms, an affliction that had previously killed Lucius Sulla, Pherecydes the Syrian (Pythagoras' teacher), the Greek poet Alcman and various others.

Herod realized that the Jews would light bonfires to celebrate his passing. So he summoned all the nobles and magistrates from city, township and castle; he had, he pretended fraudulently, various matters of import to discuss concerning the rule and administration of the province. When they arrived, he shut them up in the Seraglio hippodrome. Then he said to his sister, Salome, and to her husband, Alexander:

"I know the Jews will rejoice over my demise. But if you will hear and carry out what I am about to tell you, then my funeral will be an honorable ceremony, marked by a period of general mourning. I have given my archers special instructions. The moment I am dead, I want you to have them put to death every nobleman and magistrate shut up in the hippodrome. Thus all jewry will, in spite of themselves, mourn and lament, and the foreigners, observing this, will credit it to grief over my end, as if some heroic soul were dead."

Pantagruel further cited a desperate tyrant who declared:

"At my death, let earth and fire mingle!" which amounted to stating, "Let the whole world perish!" This dictum the scoundrelly Nero amended to "During my lifetime . . . ," Suetonius tells us. A detestable saying—mentioned by Cicero in *De Finibus* or *Of Deaths*, Book III, and by Seneca, Book II, *De Clementia* or *Of Mercy* —and ascribed to the Emperor Tiberius by Dion Nicæus and Suidas.

XXVII

PANTAGRUEL'S DISCOURSE ON THE DEATHS OF HEROIC SOULS AND ON THE HORRIBLE PRODIGIES PRECEDING THE DEMISE OF GUILLAUME DU BELLAY, LORD OF LANGEY

"It was worth going through the trials and tribulations of the storm to hear what Macrobius had to tell us," said Pantagruel. "I am quite prepared to believe what he said about a comet that appears in the sky some days before the death of a hero. Are not certain souls so noble, so precious and so illustrious that heaven gives us notice of their departure and demise some days previous?

"The prudent physician, judging from his patient's system that death is at hand, warns that patient's wife, children, relatives and friends of his condition. The medico does this so that, in the short span of time left the patient to live, his loved ones may exhort him to put his house in order, to instruct and bless his children, to recommend his wife in her widowhood to his friends, to make necessary provision for his orphans, to draw up his will, to compose his soul, and to apprise his friends before death surprises him.

"Even so, the kindly heavens, as though happy at the arrival of these blessed souls, appear to set off fireworks—comets and other meteors—to advise humans distinctly and infallibly that the venerable souls of certain heroes will, within a few days, abandon their bodies and this terrestrial globe.

"Much the same sort of thing existed formerly in Athens. The judges of the Areopagus, deciding what sentence to pass upon criminal prisoners, used certain notes according to the particular judgment. Thus θ or TH signified *thanatos* or condemnation to death; T stood for freedom or absolution; A meant ampliation or further study of the case. These signs, publicly posted, eased the prisoners' relatives, friends and such as sought news of the sentence passed."

Comets, Pantagruel went on, provided, as it were, ethereal signs through which the heavens communicated with humanity.

"O mortal men," they seemed to say, "would you hear, ascertain, learn or know anything these blessed souls can tell you concerning the public good or your private affairs? If so, hasten to visit them and get your answer, for the end and catastrophe of the comedy approach. Once past, your regrets will be vain."

The heavens, Pantagruel concluded, did even more. To show earth and its inhabitants how unworthy they were of the presence, company and enjoyment of such mighty souls, they alarmed and frightened us by prodigies, monsters and other supernatural phenomena. This was evident several days before the decease of the heroic soul belonging to Guillaume du Bellay, Lord of Langey, that doughty and scholarly knight Epistemon had mentioned.

"How well I remember it!" Epistemon sighed. "My heart leaps to my mouth and I shudder, as I recall the many dreadful prodigies we saw clearly five or six days before his death. Among those present were François de Genouillac, Lord of Assier . . . François Errault, Lord of Chemant and president of the parliamentary court of Turin . . . one-eyed Mailly, the commissary of artillery . . . Etienne Lorens, Lord of St. Ayl, captain of the garrison of Turin . . . Jacques l'Aunay, Lord of Villeneuve le Guiart, the nephew of the moribund . . . Gabriel Taphenon, the physician in attendance, from Savigliano in Piedmont . . . François Rabelais, and Cahuau . . . Claude Massuau, Lord of La Belle Croix . . . and Majorici; Bullou Cercu, *alias* Bourgmaistre; François Proust; Ferron; Charles Girard; François Bourré . . . and many other friends and servants. . . ."

Dismayed, they looked blankly at each other without uttering a word; their thoughts were filled with the impending tragedy. Alas! how clearly they foresaw France's loss of a perfect knight, essential to its welfare, and heaven's reclaiming its natural due!

"By the tip of my cowl," said Friar John, "I'll end up as a scholar yet! You must confess my brainpan is no mean organ. By God, I ask you authoritatively (as a king asks his equerry) and coaxingly (as a queen asks her child): can these heroes and demigods you talked of really die? By Our Holy Lady, God forgive me! I thought they were immortal as so many splendid angels, until our reverend father Macrobius, here, assured us they die at long last."

"Not all die so," Pantagruel objected. "The Stoics maintained that all beings were mortal save One who alone is immortal, impassible and invisible."

Pantagruel quoted Pindar as stating plainly that the Destinies and hard-hearted Fates strung and spun no more thread (in other words, life) for the Hamadryads or tree-goddesses than they did for the trees they protected—which were the oaks that gave them birth, according to Callimachus, to Pausanias in *Phoci*, and to Martin Capella, the fifth-century Latin grammarian. As for demigods, fauns, satyrs, woodsprites, ægipans, hobgoblins, nymphs, heroes and demons, several authorities have—from the total sum of the diverse ages calculated by Hesiod—estimated their lives as lasting 9,720 years. The number was obtained by taking the first four numbers, adding them together and multiplying them by four; then multiplying this sum by solid triangles five times. Put otherwise: $1 + 2 + 3 + 4 = 10$; $10 \times 4 = 40$; 40×3^5 (or 243) $= 9720$.

Plutarch's work *On the Cessation of Oracles* was important in this connection.

"That is not breviary matter!" Friar John grumbled. "I believe only so much of it as you would have me believe!"

"All intellectual souls, I think, are exempt from the scissors of the cruel Fate, Atropos," Pantagruel commented. "They are all immortal, be they angelic, demonic or human. But I will tell you a tale on this subject—a strange tale, yet written down and affirmed by several well-informed and learned historians."

XXVIII

PANTAGRUEL'S PITIFUL TALE ABOUT THE DEATH OF HEROES

PANTAGRUEL then related the following story:

Epitherses, the Chæronese (a grammarian, father of Æmilianus the Rhetorician and teacher of Plutarch), was once travelling from Greece to Italy on a vessel bearing an assorted cargo and various passengers. Towards evening, the wind failed them near the Echinades Islands, between Morea and Tunis; their ship was driven close to Paxos, off the coast of Epirus, south of Corfu. Here they lay over for a spell.

Now while some of the passengers were asleep and others, awake, supped and drank, suddenly a voice was heard coming from the island of Paxos and crying aloud: "Thamous!"

They were startled, terrified. What could it mean? (Only a few passengers knew that Thamous was the name of their skipper, an Egyptian by birth.)

A second time, the voice cried "Thamous!" in fearsome tone. No one dared answer: they stood there, silent, quaking in their boots.

A third time, the voice resounded, more dreadful than before. Thamous therefore replied:

"Here am I: what wouldst thou of me? What shall I do?"

The voice, in accents ever louder, bade him publish, when he reached the port of Paloda in Epirus, that the great god Pan was dead.

According to Epitherses, when passengers and sailors heard these words, they were amazed and frightened. Should they conceal the news, they wondered? Or should they publish it, as had been enjoined? Together they took counsel. Finally Thamous declared that, since they had the wind behind them, they should sail on without breathing a word; if they were becalmed at sea, then he would proclaim the tidings he had been ordered to spread.

As they neared Paloda, the wind subsided and they were in no current. Thamous then climbed to the top of the forecastle, gazed at the shore, and, according to orders, shouted:

"The great god Pan is dead!"

The words were hardly out of his mouth when, from the land, came cavernous groans, grievous lamentation and shrieks of terror —not of one person but the vast chorus of many mourners.

As there were many witnesses to the scene, the news soon reached Rome. Tiberius Cæsar, then emperor, sent for Thamous at once and, having heard his report, gave it full credit. Next, having inquired of the numerous learned men, at his court and in the city, as to the identity of this Pan, he learned that Pan was the son of Mercury and Penelope, as Herodotus and Cicero, in Book III, *Of the Nature of the Gods*, had stated.

"For my part," Pantagruel observed, "I consider the Pan in question to have been the mighty Saviour of the faithful, Who was shamefully put to death in Judæa by the envy and iniquity of the doctors, pontiffs, priests and monks of the Mosaic law. I really think this interpretation is in no wise shocking. For, after all, God may perfectly well be called, in the Greek tongue, *Pan*, which means 'All.' All that we are, all that we live, all that we hope is Himself, in Him, from Him and by Him. He is the good Pan, the supreme Shepherd. As the loving shepherd Corydon attests, in Virgil, he bears not only his flock, but also their shepherds, the deepest affection and tenderness. At Christ's death, just such groans, cries, lamentation and mourning rent the fabric of the universe in earth, sea, sky and hell. Finally, the element of time bears out my interpretation, since this most mighty, all-merciful Pan, our one and only Saviour, died near Jerusalem, in the reign of Tiberius Cæsar."

His story told, Pantagruel relapsed into profound silence, lost in his own thoughts. Shortly after, we noticed tears dropping from his eyes, tears fat as ostrich eggs.

God drag me hence at once if every syllable of what I tell you is not gospel truth.

XXIX

HOW PANTAGRUEL SAILED BY SNEAKS ISLAND WHERE KING LENT REIGNED

OUR jocund fleet was repaired and refitted, new stores were taken aboard, the Macreons were overjoyed at Pantagruel's expenditures in their island, and our party was happier than ever. Setting sail gleefully on the morrow, we had a fresh, favorable wind at our backs.

Towards noon, Xenomanes pointed out a distant island, Tapinois or Sneaks Island, over which reigned King Shrovetide or Lent. Pantagruel had heard of the monarch and would have been happy to meet him personally, but Xenomanes advised him against it. To land there, they must go far out of their course; worse, the cheer at King Lent's court and, indeed, in the whole island, was of the leanest.

"All you can see there for your money is King Lent. A huge greedy-guts, a glutton for peas, a crookfingered splitter of herring-barrels, a mackerelsnatcher, an overgrown molecatcher, a great nest-featherer. Shall I describe the fellow further?" Xenomanes paused a moment. "He is a fernchinned demi-giant with a double tonsure to his crown; of Lantern breed, he is in the light business, and ready to sell candles on the slightest provocation. He is the standard bearer of the fisheaters, the dictator of Mustardland, a flogger of small children and a calciner of ashes. Shall I go on? Well, he is father and foster-father to physicians; he swarms with pardons, indulgences, stations; an honest man, withal, a good Catholic, and devout as can be. Three-fourths of the day, he spends weeping; nor does he ever

attend a wedding. But (to give the devil his due) he is the most industrious maker of lardingsticks and skillets in forty kingdoms!"

Xenomanes then told how he happened to be passing through
Sneaks Island some six years before and picked up a large skewer,
which he subsequently presented to the butchers of Candé. The latter, quite properly, valued the gift highly. Xenomanes promised
that on their return home, he would show the company two such
skillets, framing the portal of the church at Candé, though some
might declare they were not skillets but architectural designs.

This fellow King Lent, Xenomanes added, fed upon pickled coats-
of-mail, salted sallets or helmets, and devilled headpieces. Such fare
occasionally gave him hotpiddle or clap.

King Lent's clothing was merry indeed, in color and cut: gray and
cold, nothing fore and nothing aft, with sleeves to match!

"Thank you, Xenomanes," said Panurge, "you have described his
clothing, his diet, his behavior, his pastimes. I would be gratful for
information concerning the shape and configuration of his bodily
parts."

"Please, please, little ballock of my heart, tell us about it!" Friar
John piped up. "I have found King Lent in my breviary. He figures
after the movable holy days."

"I shall be delighted," Xenomanes assured them. "We shall probably hear more of Lent as we land at Savage Island, the land of the
squat Chitterlings and fat Tripe. They are his hereditary enemies and
wage mortal, sempiternal warfare against him. Were it not for the
help of noble Carnival, their protector and good neighbor, that cockroach bastard of a Lent would long ago have exterminated them and
razed their homes."

"Who are these Chitterlings?" Friar John inquired. "Are they male
or female, angels or mortals, women or virgins?"

"They are female in sex, and mortal in condition," Xenomanes answered. "Some are virgins, some are not."

"My soul is the devil's if I am not all for them!" Friar John vowed.
"How unnatural, how perverse to make war upon women! Let us go
back and wipe up the floor with that cowardly villain's carcass!"

"What? Fight against Lent?" Pantagruel sighed. "By all the devils,
I'm not that mad and I'm not that bold! *Quid juris*, what decision

of law, if we found ourselves caught between the Chitterlings and King Lent? between hammer and anvil.

"Pox and chancres, away with you, let us press on! Farewell to you, King Lent: I recommend the Chitterlings to you—and don't forget the Sausages!"

XXX

XENOMANES' ANATOMICAL DESCRIPTION OF KING LENT

"As for Lent's internal parts," said Xenomanes, "his brain boasts— at least it *did* in *my* time—the dimensions, color, substance and strength of an itchworm's left ball. The ventricles of his mighty brain are like that lovely tool for boring holes in wood, known technically as an auger . . . its wormlike excrescences are like a flat-headed mallet . . . its membranes like a monk's cowl . . . its funnel like a mason's mortar . . . its *fornix*, or, more simply, the arch or vault of the cranium, like a woodnook . . . its *conarium* or pineal gland, like a bagpipe."

Xenomanes ranged further afield: King Lent's *rete admirabile* was like the armor that protected a horse's head . . . his mammillary appendices like old shoes . . . his tympanums like windmills or coffee-grinders . . . the bones at the temples like feather-dusters . . . the nape of his neck like a paper lantern. . . .

His nerves were so many faucets. . . .

"Do you know what an uvula is?" Xenomanes asked. "The pendent, fleshy part of soft palate?—the similar part of the cerebellum? —Well, King Lent's uvula is the nearest thing known to a peashooter, short of a peashooter.

"His palate is like a mitten and also like a disease of the skin . . . his spittle resembles a shuttle, his tonsils are like monocles, his isthmus (the narrow portion of the brain) is like a hod, his gullet like a grapebasket, his noble stomach like a belt. . . .

"His *pylorus*—for the profane I interpret: the opening from stomach into duodenum—his pylorus, I say, is like a pitchfork . . . his windpipe is like a sickle, his throat like a ball of wool, his lungs like an amice, his heart like a chasuble, his mediastinum (the space between the pleural sacs) like a goblet. . . .

"Oh, those arteries of his, like bérets, that diaphragm like a beribboned bonnet, that mattocklike liver, those veins like window sashes, that spleen like a decoy for quails, those guts like fishing nets, that gall bladder like a paring knife!

"If you see them, you can recognize an abbot's mitre, a filtre for spiced wines, a breastplate, a drinking-cup, a monk's leather bottle, a trowel, a padlock and a pothook. Well, these objects resemble respectively King Lent's mesentery, his hungergut, his blindgut, his colon, his bumgut, his kidneys and his loins.

"You can differentiate between a pair of syringes, a creampuff, an inkpot, a small bow, a bellclapper and a high-crowned hat, such as the Albanian mercenaries wear? Well, these objects are indistinguishable from King Lent's ureters, as they transfer his urine from kidney to bladder; from his emulgent veins; from his spermatic vessels; from his prostate gland; from his bladder; from its neck, and from his *mirac* or abdomen. . . .

"Can you tell an armlet from a bellows, a hawking-glove from a tinker's bag? Then you can tell his *siphac* or peritoneum from his muscles, his tendons from his ligaments.

"Do you know what a jawbreaker is? It is a biscuit. King Lent's bones are like jawbreakers.

"His marrow is like a pouch, his cartilages like heath tortoises or moles, the glands of his neck like billhooks; his animal spirits like fisticuffs, his vital spirits like fillips on the nose, hard and repeatedly. O that blood, that boiling blood of his, that reminds one of nothing so much as of a series of punches. O his urine, it is like a popefig, like one who scorns His Holiness the Pope. And his sperm! If you have ever seen a hundred cobbler's nails, then you know what his sperm is like. In fact, his nurse told me that when he married La Micarême or Mid-Lent, he begot only a number of local adverbs and certain double fasts. The local adverbs were in answer to questions about where to obtain indulgences between Lent and Easter.

"His memory reminds you of a scarf, his common sense of a great bell's chime, his imagination of a carillon. His thoughts suggest a flight of starlings; his conscience an unnestling of young herons; his deliberation a sack of barley, the grains rattling at the slightest shift. . . .

"His repentance is like the carriage of a double cannon, his undertakings like the ballast on a galleon, his understanding like a dogeared breviary, his notions like snails crawling out of strawberries. . . .

"Further, his will is three nuts in a bowl, rattling; his desire, six trusses of hay, changing shape at the slightest pressure; his judgment a slipper, altering according to the foot it contains; his discretion, soft and empty as a mitten; his reason hollow as a drum. . . ."

XXXI

ANATOMICAL DESCRIPTION OF KING LENT (CONTINUATION)

XENOMANES pursued his catalogue of King Lent's members, citing the external parts. In this respect, Lent was better favored than the average man, for he boasted seven ribs more.

"His toes suggest the keyboard of a spinet, his nails gimlets, his feet guitars, his heels clubs, his soles crucibles, his legs bird snares, his knees stools, his thighs cross-bowstring-winders.

"His hips are like augers; his potbelly is buttoned in the old style with a girdle over the chest; his bellybutton is like a fiddle; the hairy places of his body like creamcakes; his member like a slipper, his ballocks like leather flasks, his genitals like carpenters' planes, his testicle muscles like tennis rackets, his perineum like a mouth organ, his arsehole like a crystal mirror, his buttocks like harrows, his loins like butterpots, his *alkatim* or scrotum like a billiard table.

"Oh, let me sing his back, his *spondyls* or vertebræ, his ribs, his chest, his shoulderblades, his breast, his paps, his armpits, his shoulders, his arms, his fingers, the bones of his wrists and of his forearms, his elbows, his hands, his neck and his throat. Let me compare them respectively to a huge crossbow that can be strung only by a machine, to bagpipes, to spinning wheels, to a canopy, to mortars, to organ pipes, to cowherds' horns, to chessboards, to wheelbarrows, to great hoods, to andirons, to stilts, to sickles, to mousetraps, to currycombs, to beakers and to the filtres used for straining spiced wines.

"His Adam's apple is like a barrel: from it hang two bronze goitres, beautiful, harmonious and shaped like hourglasses; his beard is like a lantern, his chin like a mushroom, his ears like mittens, his nose like a buskin embroidered with shields, his nostrils like hoods, his eyebrows like dripping-pans. Under the left eyebrow, he has a birthmark of the shape and size of a urinal.

"No doubt you can discriminate between a rebeck (that early form of fiddle), a combcase, a tinderbox, a drinking-cup, a watering pot, a pair of wooden shoes and a goblet? Then, certainly, you can tell apart his pupils, his eyes, his optic nerves, his forehead, his temples, his cheeks and his jaws.

"Oh, those teeth of his, like so many stout staves. You will find a first-tooth like his at Coulonges-les-Royaux, near Fontenay in Poitou, and two at La Brousse, near St. Jean d'Angély. They are affixed to the cellar door.

"His tongue," Xenomanes concluded, "is like a harp, his mouth like a horsecloth, his face is embroidered like a mule's packsaddle, his head is fashioned like a still, his skull like a gamepouch; the sutures or seams of the latter resemble the Fisher's signet, *i. e.* the signet-ring worn by His Holiness the Pope.

"Ay, friends, if you saw his skin you would liken it to a gaberdine jacket, his epidermis to a sieve, and his hair to a scrubbing brush. As for his whiskers, I have already mentioned them!"

XXXIV

KING LENT'S ANATOMY
(CONTINUATION)

"To hear and see King Lent," Xenomanes pursued, "is one of the wonders of Nature. When he spits, it is whole baskets full of goldfinches; when he blows his nose, it is pickled eels; when he weeps, it is ducks with onion sauce; when he trembles, it is large venison pies; when he sweats, it is kingfish with butter sauce.

"Does he belch, it is oysters on the half-shell. Does he sneeze, it is whole tubs full of mustard. Does he cough, it is boxes of quince marmalade. Does he sob, it is watercress; does he yawn, it is pots full of purée of peas; does he sigh, it is dried oxtongues; does he whistle, it is hods full of green peas; does he snore, it is pans full of fried beans; does he frown, it is larded hog's feet.

"When he speaks, it is coarse, brown, Auvergne cloth. You can imagine nothing further removed from his talk than the crimson silk with which, in Plutarch, Parysatis desired to compare the words spoken by her son Cyrus, King of Persia."

Let King Lent blow, wink, growl, nod, pout, mutter, stamp his feet, shuffle backward, slobber or clear his throat, the operations were successively boxes to collect indulgences, cakes and wafers, March cats or martens, ironbound wagons, broken staves, plays performed by the Clercs de la Basoche (dramatic companies recruited in the law courts), letters of adjournment and writs of postponement, seadungchaferflies, communal ovens and figures of a Moorish dance.

Oh, those farts, those poops, those scratchings and those songs of his! They were a dun cow's legcloths, cordovan boots, new ordinances and peas in the pod. Did he cack, it was pumpkins and nightshades; did he puff, it was cabbages cooked in oil; did he hold forth, it was of the snows of yesteryear; did he worry, it was about cock and bull; did he give nothing, so much for the recipient; did he woolgather, it was of gnats and camels; did he doze, it was of leases and mortgages he meditated.

Xenomanes pointed out even stranger pursuits of King Lent's. While working, he did nothing, and, doing nothing, worked; he slept, carousing, and, carousing, slept with eyes open, like the hares in Champagne, who fear a sudden descent of the Chitterlings, their hereditary foes. Biting, he laughed, and, laughing, bit; when he fasted, he ate nothing, and, eating nothing, fasted; he nibbled at the merest nothing and drank through the imagination; he bathed over the tops of high steeples, dried himself in rivers and ponds, fished in the sky, catching decuman lobsters. He hunted at the bottom of the sea where he bagged ibises, wild goats and chamois. If he stole up on a crow and captured it, he inevitably put out its eyes; he feared nothing but his own shadow and the cries of fat kids; he always stirred his stumps, plowed his way and, on holidays, rang bells, both on belfries and on monks. Finally, he made a mallet of his fist and was used to writing on his hairy parchment, with his huge pencase, all manner of prognostications and astronomical data.

"That's the rascal," cried Friar John. "That's my man. I'm out after him: I shall challenge him at once."

"A strange, monstrously fashioned man, if man you can call him," Pantagruel commented. "You remind me of the form and aspect of the figures in Logic called *Amodunt, sine modo* (formlessness) and *Dissonantia* (confusion)."

"What figures? What shapes?" Friar John inquired. "God forgive me, I have never heard of them."

"Let me tell you what I read of them in the ancient apologue of the Renaissance scholar, Cælius Calcagninus, a humanist of Ferrara, who published his *Gigantes* at Basle some years ago."

Physis, or Nature, said Pantagruel, bore, in her first litter, Beauty and Harmony; she begat these without carnal copulation, being, in her own person, most fecund and prolific. Antiphysis, who, by name and function, was Nature's contrary, was immediately jealous of such beautiful and noble offspring. In opposition, she copulated with Tellumon, the productive god, and begat Amodunt and Dissonance. Their heads were round and spherical like footballs; their heads, further, lacked the gradual flattening, on either side, like most humans'. Their ears stood high, pricked up like the ears of asses; their eyes bulged fixedly out of their heads, on the end of bones such as we have at our heels. Their feet were round as tennis balls; their arms and hands turned backwards toward their shoulders; they walked on their skulls, constantly revolving, arse over head, their heels upside down.

Just as apes consider their young the handsomest in the world, so Antiphysis extolled her children. Their shapes, she said, were fairer and more beauteous than those of Physis' children: to boast of spherical heads and feet, to walk wheeling circularly, were so many signs of perfect form. Amodunt and Dissonance, Antiphysis declared, partook of the divine power which moulds the heavens and all eternal things in its image. Were their feet uppermost, their heads below them? It was in imitation of the Creator of the universe, who gave men hair for roots and legs for branches; after all, were not trees more easily planted by their roots than by their branches?

This thesis, then, confirmed Antiphysis' opinion that her children resembled a standing tree whereas Physis', on the contrary, were like a tree upside down. As for the arms and hands, she maintained that it was more natural to have these turned towards the shoulders, because a person's back should not remain defenseless. Did not his teeth already protect man in front? They were useful for chewing without the help of hands; but surely they could also serve as defense against noxious attacks?

Thus, following the example and testimony of brute beasts, Antiphysis brought all the numbskulls and crackpates over to her opinion, and became the subject of the admiration of a host of brainless idiots. Since then she has begotten the hypocritical dissemblers . . . the snivelling sham-Abrahams and popemongers . . . the maniac bigots and blowhards . . . the demoniacal and Calvinist impostors of Geneva . . . the insane acolytes of Gabriel de Puy-Herbault, that monk-bigot of Fontevrault, who cries scandal at honest books . . . the gormandizing beggar-priests . . . the dunces of the cowl . . . the Pharisee shufflers, the hooded pinchbecks and all manner of other formless ill-favored monsters, fashioned in spite of Nature. . . .

XXXIII

HOW PANTAGRUEL DISCOVERED A MONSTROUS WHALE OFF WILD ISLAND

TOWARD noon, as we neared Wild Island, Pantagruel spied a monstrous, great *physeter* (Greek for "blower") or whale. It was still far off, but was heading straight toward us. It was snorting, spurting, swelling and rising above the waves, high over our maintops; it spouted water aloft in front of it. It looked like a great river flowing down a mountainside.

Pantagruel pointed it out to Xenomanes and to the skipper; the latter had the buglers of the *Thalamege* sound a general alarm to warn the fleet. Immediately the ships, galleons, frigates and brigantines drew up, according to naval discipline, in a formation shaped like the Greek *upsilon* or Y, Pythagoras' letter, for Y corresponds to the number 400, and the number four was considered sacred by the philosopher's disciples. They were disposed like cranes in flight, forming an acute angle, with, as cone and basis, the *Thalamege*, ready to fight gallantly.

Friar John climbed briskly on to the forecastle and consulted with the *bombardiers*. Panurge began to howl and lament more forlornly than ever.

"Ubbubbughshw!" he moaned. "This is worse than anything that's happened before. Let us flee, I beg you. God's death, this is Leviathan, as described by the noble prophet Moses in the life of holy Job. That whale will swallow us up like so many pillules: ships, crew and all the rest of it. We will hold no more space in his infernal, great gullet than a sugarplum in an ass's snout. Look, look, he's on top of us already. Flee, flee, make for land, men, speed! I vow it is the sea monster sent by Neptune to devour Andromeda because her mother boasted that she was lovelier than the Nereids. We are lost, every one of us! Ah, would there were some valiant Perseus here, to deliver us as he delivered Andromeda."

"I'll give him Perseus," Pantagruel cried. "Never fear!"

"God's strength," said Panurge, "put us beyond fear, then, my Lord Pantagruel. When, in God's name, should a man be frightened, if not in the face of danger?"

"If your fatal destiny is that described by Friar John some time ago, then you have cause to fear Pyrœis, Eöus, Æthon and Phlegon, the flame-snorting horses of the sun. But certainly you need take no fright at whales that expel merely water from snout and ear. You will never be in danger of death by water; on the contrary, water is an element that will preserve and guard rather than harm or molest you."

"Splendid, splendid!" said Panurge. "At that, I would rather die by hanging than face this present danger. God's fish, haven't I explained the transmutation of elements to you? Haven't I told you often enough of the scant difference between roasting and boiling? Haven't I emphasized the possible confusion between boiling and roasting?

. . . Here comes the dreadful monster; I shall go hide below, we are dead men, every mortal soul among us! Look at the hag Atropos on the maintop, with her newly sharpened scissors ready to snip our life-threads. Look out, here's the monster! O horrible, O abominable: how many good men have you drowned before us, poor lads who never had a chance to brag of it? God! If only the beast spouted a good, toothsome red or white wine, instead of this bitter, salt, stinking water, the situation might be tolerable.

"We might then follow the example of a certain British lord who, being sentenced for his crimes, was allowed to choose the form of death he preferred. My Lord elected to be drowned in a butt of malmsey.

"Lord God! here comes that monster, that devil, that Leviathan! I cannot bear to look at it, it is too hideous, too abominable. Go to the bar, beast, to the law courts, to the pettifoggers!"

XXXIV

HOW PANTAGRUEL SLEW THE MONSTROUS WHALE

THE whale swam between the ships and galleons, spouting whole tuns of water upon them, like the cataracts of the Ethiopian Nile. Arrows, darts, javelins, spears, lances and harpoons rained down on the beast. Friar John did yeoman work; Panurge was half-dead of fright. The guns boomed and thundered; a devilish din arose. Piece after piece roared out in great earnest but to no purpose: the heavy iron and bronze shot struck the whale's body, pierced its skin and apparently melted like tiles in the sun. That was when Pantagruel, aware of the desperate emergency of the moment, stretched out his arms and showed what he could do.

You may quote, from the written record, the skill of Commodus, Emperor of Rome, who could plant an arrow between the parted fingers of children without ever touching them. . . . You may vaunt the Indian archer who, when Alexander the Great conquered India, was such a crack shot that he drove his arrows through a ring, though they were three cubits long, large and weighty enough to pierce steel cutlasses, thick shields, reënforced breastplates and, indeed, anything else, no matter how hard, firm, resistant and solid. . . . You may retail the wonders told of the ancient Franks, those masters of shooting, when they hunted black or dun beasts; they would steep their iron arrowheads in hellebore, because it made the flesh of game they killed more tender, delicate, wholesome and pleasing. (Naturally, they cut out the actual portion where the arrow struck.)

You may cite the Parthians, who, shooting backwards as they retreated, could inflict greater casualties than other warriors facing the enemy.

You may even celebrate the dexterity of the Scythians.

(One day, they sent an ambassador to Darius, King of Persia, bearing a bird, a frog, a mouse, five arrows and no explanation whatever as to their use. Darius questioned the envoy, who declared that no message had been given him. The Persian monarch was amazed and puzzled, until Gobryas, one of the seven captains who killed the Magi, said:

"These gifts and offerings of the Scythians are tantamount to saying that unless the Persians fly like birds through the heavens, skulk like mice in the bowels of earth, retreat like frogs to the bottoms of ponds and marshes, the arrows of the Scythians will send them to their doom."

Roman, Indian, Frank, Parthian, Scythian notwithstanding to the contrary, noble Pantagruel was peerless and beyond compare in the bowman's art. In length, width, weight and ironwork, his fearsome darts and javelins were like nothing so much as the huge beams that support the bridges at Nantes, at Saumur, at Bergerac, and, in Paris, the Pont-au-Change, where the money-changers work, and the Pont-aux-Meuniers, where the millers hold forth.

At a mile's distance, Pantagruel could open an oyster without nicking either shell, trim a candle without extinguishing it, hit a magpie square in the eye, unsole shoes without damaging the uppers, sever its lining from a hood with no damage to either, and turn page after page of Friar John's breviary without tearing a single one.

Taking one of these darts (he had plenty aboard), Pantagruel scored a mark with his first shot. It hit the whale downward in the forehead, piercing both jaws and tongue so clean that the beast could not open its mouth to suck up or expel water. With his second shot, Pantagruel put out the monster's right eye; with his third, its left eye. No man but exulted as he saw the whale's brow adorned with a trio of horns meeting in an equilateral triangle. The whale veered and whirled, now to the right, now to the left, staggering and swaying like one dazed, blinded and about to die.

Not satisfied with this, Pantagruel shot another dart at its tail; this, too, caught it at an angle. Three more shots struck it in the back, at equal intervals of distance, forming a perpendicular line. Then, nonchalantly, Pantagruel gave it fifty shots on the left and fifty on the right, so that the wretched monster looked like the hulk of a three-masted galleon, abristle with spars and tackle. It was a fine sight! Tipping back, belly-up, as all dead fish do, with Pantagruel's darts upside down in the sea, the whale looked like so many *scolopendra* or centipedes, as described by Nicander, the ancient Greek sage.

XXXV

HOW PANTAGRUEL VISITED WILD ISLAND, THE ANCESTRAL HABITAT OF THE CHITTER-LINGS

THE crew of the *Lantern*, the second ship of the fleet, roped the dead whale and towed it ashore, near by, to Wild Island. Here it was duly dissected, and the oil and grease drawn from its kidneys to provide a useful and necessary remedy for a certain distemper known as "lack of money." As for Pantagruel, he remained blithely indifferent to the disposal of the whale: in French waters, he had seen many like it or, in fact, even larger ones.

But he did condescend to put in at a small deserted harbor in the southern part of the island, for he wished his men to dry their clothing and refresh themselves after the whale's drenching. Towards noon, they landed close to a high thick pleasant wood, with a cool clear silvery brook rippling through it. They pitched their tents smartly, set up their kitchens, lighted double fires, changed their clothes, comfortably. Then Friar John rang the bell, tables were promptly set up, and a meal was served.

Suddenly, as the second course was brought on, Pantagruel, who was cheerfully dining with his men, noticed certain diminutive Chitterlings, busy as beavers and quiet as mice, climbing a very tall tree near the camp pantry.

"What sort of animals are they?" he asked. "Squirrels? Weasels? Martens? Ermines?"

"Chitterlings!" Xenomanes answered. "This isle is the Wild Island I was telling you about this morning. For many years, the Chitterlings have waged fierce war against King Lent, their bitter, hereditary foe. I wouldn't be at all surprised if they had heard our gunners firing at the whale. If so, they were naturally suspicious and frightened, probably imagining that Lent had come with his forces to surprise them and ravage their land. As a matter of fact, he has done exactly that, several times in the past. But he came off poorly: the Chitterlings are wary and vigilant. In this respect, they are like Dido: you remember her telling Æneas' companions, when they sought to land at Carthage without her permission or knowledge, that she was obliged constantly to guard and watch her lands, because of her enemy's malice and the proximity of his lands."

"Heaven help us, dear friend!" Pantagruel said. "If you can think of some honest means by which we could end this war and reconcile these enemies, let me know, I beg you. I will do my best, gladly, I promise; I will spare no pains to temper and accommodate the differences between them."

"For the moment, it is impossible!" Xenomanes replied. "I was passing through this land about four years ago, and I did my utmost to encourage peace, or at least a long truce, between them. It would have made good friends and good neighbors of them. But neither party would yield on a single point. On one hand, King Lent indignantly refused to include in the treaty the wild Bloodsausages and the mountain Bolognas, their old cronies and confederates. On the other hand, the Chitterlings insisted that the stronghold of Cacques—Fort Herringbarrel, a Lenten citadel—be under their jurisdiction, as is Château Sallouoir or Castle Salting Tub, where the meats are preserved. I forget who the occupants of Fort Herringbarrel were; at any rate, the Chitterlings called them evil stinking brigands and murderers, and wanted them dispossessed. These conditions seemed grossly unfair to both parties.

"Thus, no agreement could be reached. This must be granted, though: for a time, their enmity became less fierce, less furious than before. Alas! just as the Council of Trent pronounced in favor of fasting, against the Protestant and moderate Catholic protest, so the national Council of Chesil cited, insulted and manhandled the Chitterlings. Worse, they declared King Lent a putrid, desiccated, beshitten codfish if he made so much as one move towards agreement and reconciliation with them. Obviously, then, their hostility had been embittered, heightened and made inveterate.

"As well make peace between cats and mice," Xenomanes concluded, "or leash hound and hare together."

XXXVI

HOW THE WILD CHITTERLINGS LAY IN AMBUSH FOR PANTAGRUEL

As Xenomanes spoke, Friar John spied some twenty-five or thirty slender young Chitterlings, speeding away from the port to their capital, citadel, castle and fort of Chimney.

"There's trouble in store, if I know what's what," the monk confided to Pantagruel. "You look nothing like King Lent, God knows; yet these worshipful Chitterlings might easily have taken you for him. Let us cut short this meal, My Lord, and prepare to resist them."

"Not a bad idea," Xenomanes agreed. "Chitterlings are Chitterlings, ever doubledealers and traitors!"

Pantagruel rose to look over the wood, whirled back suddenly, and told us that our fears were justified. To the left, he had sighted a force of fat Chitterlings in ambush. To the right, a half-league away, a vast body of mighty, giantlike Chitterlings were marching resolutely towards us along the side of a little hill; they were progressing in battle formation to the tune of bagpipes, sheep's bladders, paunchskins, merry fifes and drums, bugles and trumpets. From the seventy-eight standards he could count, Pantagruel judged them to be forty-two thousand strong.

Their array, their proud bearing and confident mien proved to us that here were no tyro sausagemeat, no paltry links but, rather, fierce storm-troops recruited among the veteran Chitterling and Forcemeat warriors. From the front ranks to the colors, they were all well equipped with pikes that seemed small from afar, yet were undoubtedly very sharp and stout. The wings of the approaching host were supported by numerous Wieners, stout Frankfurters, woodsy Salamis and mounted Bolognas, all of them tall, upstanding islanders, brigands and bandits.

Pantagruel, not without reason, was much disturbed. Epistemon sought to reassure him. Might it not be the custom and habit of Chitterlingdom to turn out in full battle array to welcome distinguished foreign visitors? In France, the noble monarchs, immediately after their coronation and succession to the throne, were greeted and honored in just that fashion by the chief cities of the kingdom.

"After all," Epistemon observed, "this may be the Queen's ordinary guard. The young Chitterlings you saw on watch in the treetop probably told her of the arrival of your great, pompous fleet. She concluded that a rich and powerful prince had come to visit her; she is on her way to welcome you in person."

This explanation, however, did not satisfy Pantagruel. He called a council and asked for the various opinions of its members in this dubious and sinister dilemma. In a few words, he reminded them how often such armed demonstrations of welcome, under guise of friendship and affection, proved prejudicial, and even fatal, to the visitor.

"By the same stratagem, Antoninus Caracalla, Emperor of Rome, once slew the citizens of Alexandria and, on another occasion, massacred the troops of Artabanus, King of Persia. (In the second instance, he pretended to be seeking the Persian's daughter in marriage. Anyhow, he was well punished for it: soon after, he went blind!)

"The children of Jacob employed the same tactics to destroy the city of the Shechemites, in revenge for the rape of their sister Dinah. With like treachery, Gallienus, the Roman emperor, put to death the fighting men of Constantinople. Again, under cover of friendship, Antonius drew Artavastes, King of Armenia, into an ambush, cast him into chains and ultimately murdered him.

"History supplies thousands of like instances. Who can blame King Charles VI for what was but intelligent caution? Returning, fresh from victories over the Ghenters and other Flemings, to his good city of Paris, he learned, at Le Bourget, that the citizens had marched out to greet him twenty thousand strong, armed with mallets.

"That is why the Parisian burghers have since been known as Maillotins or malleteers.

"King Charles refused to enter the city until his faithful subjects put down their arms, and returned home, despite their protestations that they had assumed these arms only to welcome him the more honorably."

(Epistemon remembered how the townsmen had rebelled against taxation, killed the collectors and conspired with the foreign Flemings. The malleteers returned to Paris mildly; and King Charles clapped down the taxes the more strongly upon them.)

XXXVII

HOW PANTAGRUEL SENT FOR COLONELS CRUSHCHITTERLING AND SLICESAUSAGE AND HOW A NOTEWORTHY COMMENTARY RESULTED, UPON THE NAMES OF PLACES AND PERSONS

PANTAGRUEL'S counsellors decided that, whatever befell, they should stand on their guard. Pantagruel therefore ordered Carpalim and Gymnastes to summon the troops at present on board his ninth vessel, the *Cup* (Colonel Crushchitterling, Officer Commanding) and his twelfth, the *Wine Cask* (Colonel Slicesausage, O. C.).

"Let me help!" Panurge urged. "I'll relieve Gymnastes: you need him here anyhow!"

"By the holy frock I wear," said Friar John, "I know you're trying to dodge the fight, you ballocking poltroon! By God, if ever we let you go, you'll make yourself scarce. Small loss, at that: he would do nothing but whimper, weep, lament and dishearten our stout soldiers."

"No, no, Friar John, I swear I will come back," Panurge protested. "I swear I will come back soon, too, dear father spiritual. But please take care these cursed Chitterlings do not climb aboard our vessels. While you are fighting, I shall pray God for your victory, just as valiant Captain Moses, leader of the Israelites, prayed for his people."

(Friar John recalled that Joshua battled against the Amalekites while Moses, supported by Aaron and Hur, held his arms raised to the heavens until the sun sank, thus assuring his people's victory.)

Epistemon observed that the colonels' names, Crushchitterling and Slicesausage, augured well for safety, victory and success, if ever the Chitterlings set upon them.

"You are right, Epistemon!" Pantagruel answered. "I am happy to hear you foretell and prognosticate our victory by our commanders' names. This form of prophecy is by no means new: already the Pythagoreans hailed and observed it solemnly. Not a few great lords and emperors made use of it."

Pantagruel then cited examples. There was Octavius Augustus, Roman ruler, who once met a peasant called Euthyche (the word means "lucky") leading an ass called Nikon (the word means "victorious"). The name of both ass and driver so inspired him that he felt assured of prosperity, victory and eternal happiness. Subsequently, indeed, he erected a temple to them on the very spot where he had first encountered them.

Then there was Vespasian, another Roman emperor, who was praying one day in the temple of Serapis. Suddenly a servant of his, who had been left behind because sick, appeared. The fellow's name was Basilides ("son of kings"). Vespasian at once knew that he would mount the throne.

By the same token, Regilian was appointed to the purple by his soldiers simply and solely because of his name. Divine Plato said as much in his *Cratylus* which treated of the arbitrary or natural designation of names.

"By my thirst for faith and faith in thirst," Rhizotomos declared, "I must read Plato. How often I hear you quote him, My Lord Pantagruel!"

Pantagruel pursued his argument. Did not the Pythagoreans conclude, through the study of names and numbers, that Hector undoubtedly slew Patroclus, that Achilles killed Hector, that Paris dispatched Achilles, and Philoctetes, Paris? Whenever Pantagruel considered Pythagoras' extraordinary findings, he was lost in wonder. Imagine taking the odd or even number of syllables in any proper name, and deducing therefrom on which side a man was lame, humpbacked, blind, gouty, paralytic, pleuritic or otherwise slighted by Nature! Well, Pythagoras assigned the even numbers to the left, the odd to the right.

"For my part," said Epistemon, "I saw the same system worked out at Saintes during a general procession. That noble, virtuous, learned and equitable Briand Vallée, Lord of Douhet, then chief magistrate of the district, was present. As a man or woman, lame, one-eyed or humpbacked, passed by, a clerk told My Lord the name of the unfortunate. If the syllables of the name were odd, without looking at the person, My Lord said that he or she was lame, one-eyed or humpbacked on the right side. Conversely, even-syllabled names assigned the affliction of their owners to the left. And, so help me God if I lie: he proved right every time!"

Pantagruel showed how this study of syllables had confirmed learned scholars in various historical statements. Achilles, kneeling, was struck by Paris' arrow in the right heel, because Achilles had an imparisyllabic name. (It might here be added that the ancients, kneeling, were accustomed to bend the right foot.)

Venus, whose Greek name Ἀφροδίτη was even-syllabled, was wounded in the left hand by Diomedes before Troy . . . Vulcan, by the same process, was lame of the left foot . . . conversely, Philippus, King of Macedon, and Hannibal the Carthaginian, were blind in the right eye. (Here Pantagruel suggested that sciaticas, hernias and *hemicrania* or one-sided headaches, could be accounted for by the same reasoning.)

To return to names, it was interesting to note how Alexander the

Great, son of King Philippus, mentioned above, attained his ends through the mere interpretation of one name. He was laying siege to Tyre, at the time, and had had a hard time of it for some weeks. In vain: engines and battleworks proved unavailing. He had decided to raise the siege and was melancholy, since his retreat meant a signal loss of prestige.

Baffled and grieving, he fell asleep, and dreamed that a satyr was leaping and dancing on his goat's legs in the imperial tent. Alexander strove to seize him, but the satyr ever eluded his grasp. Finally, Alexander cornered him and caught him.

At this point in his dream, Alexander awoke.

Shortly after, he related it to the philosophers and scholars of his court; their interpretation was that the gods promised him victory and Tyre would be taken soon. For the word *satyros,* divided, read *Sa Tyros* or *Tyre is his.* In effect, the next attack he made resulted in the storming of the town and the subjugation, by a complete victory, of a rebellious people.

Conversely, Pompey was driven to despair by the sense of a single word. Defeated by Cæsar at Pharsalus, his sole way of escape lay in flight. He took to his ships and soon reached the island of Cyprus. Ashore, near Paphos, stood a great sumptuous palace. The pilot informed him it was called Κακοβασιλέα, which in Greek meant *evil king.* This struck such terror and abomination in Pompey's heart that Pompey fell into despair: he was sure he could not escape; he would die soon. The passengers and sailors heard his cries, groans and lamentations. What happened? A few days later, a certain Achillas, an unknown peasant, cut off his head.

L. Paulus Æmilius was another case in point. The Roman Senate elected him imperator or commander-in-chief of the army sent against Perseus, King of Macedon. That very evening, at home preparing for the expedition, kissing his little daughter Tratia, he noticed that she looked sad.

"What is the matter?" he asked. "Why are you so crestfallen and sad?"

"Persa is dead," she told him.

Hearing the word Persa (her dog's name), L. Paulus Æmilius at once thought of Perseus, the foe he had been sent to defeat. Here was an omen: L. Paulus Æmilius felt certain of victory.

Did time permit, Pantagruel asserted his willingness to illustrate the same point in sacred Hebrew writ; one hundred notable passages proved beyond question how religiously this people observed names and their significance.

As Pantagruel finished, the two colonels, Crushchitterling and Slicesausage, appeared at the head of their well-equipped and resolute detachments. Pantagruel made a short address, urging them to be brave in battle, if they were attacked. He still believed, however, that the Chitterlings could not possibly be treacherous enough to turn upon them. So he forbade them to give the Chitterlings offence; and he appointed the imparisyllabic word *Mardigras* or *Carnival* for watchword.

XXXVIII

HOW MEN HAVE NO REASON TO DESPISE CHITTERLINGS

Do you rail, drinkers? Do you doubt my word? Do you think I speak nonsense? If you do, I cannot help it; it's your business. Believe what you will; if not, go see for yourselves. All I know is that I saw it distinctly.

It happened in Wild Island . . . I name names! . . . And I beg you to recall the ancient giants who sought to pile the mighty mountain Pelion on top of Ossa . . . to topple the latter over Olympus . . . to annihilate the gods, and drive them out of heaven. . . . Theirs was no mean or usual strength, was it? Well, to tell the whole truth, those giants were no more than sausages or Chitterlings (or serpents) from the waist down. (Do not the Latin poets call these giants *anguipedes* or snakefooted?)

Speaking of serpents, the specimen of serpentdom that tempted Mother Eve was a Chitterling; he nevertheless went down into history as the smoothest, subtlest beast of the field. And succeeding Chitterlings live up to his reputation. To this very day, certain university teachers hold that the serpent who tempted Eve was the Chitterling called in Greek, Ithyphallus; in Latin, Penis Erectus; and, in English, Upjohn. It is believed, too, that Messire Priapus, god of gardens, transformed himself into this same Chitterling—that fine lusty Priapus, tempter of women in paradise or, to translate from the Greek, in pleasure gardens.

How do we know that the Swiss, to-day a bold warlike people, were not once Chitterlings? Certainly, I would not put my hand in the fire to prove the contrary. Then there are the Himantopodes, a celebrated Ethiopian tribe, undoubtedly Chitterlings, according to Pliny, who describes their walk as serpentlike, because of their long limber feet.

Do my statements satisfy your lordships? Are you still incredulous? Well then, presently—but drink with me first, I beg you—go visit Lusignan, Parthenay, Vouvant, Mervant, and Pouzauges in Poitou. Here you will find reputable time-hallowed witnesses of the stoutest credibility to swear to you by the knucklebone of St. Rigomer—a relic revered in the region—that Melusine, who built these castles, was a woman down to the cockpit but, below, a snake Chitterling or a Chitterling snake.

(Having enclosed her father in a high mountain for offending her mother, she was condemned to become every Saturday a serpent from the waist down. She married Raymond, Count of Toulouse, and made her husband vow never to visit her on a Saturday; but he hid himself on one of the forbidden days and viewed her transformation. So she was obliged to quit him and destined to wander as a spectre until the day of doom.)

Chitterling-serpent she was, but she had a brave, noble gait for all that—and to-day the Breton dancers, when they do their country-dances, imitate her movements.

Why do you suppose Erichthonius first invented coaches, litters and chariots? Shall I tell you? It was because Vulcan begat Erichthonius with sausage-legs; to hide his deformity, the latter preferred to ride in a litter rather than on horseback. (Chitterlings were not yet highly esteemed in his day!)

Ora, the Scythian nymph, was also half-woman, half-Chitterling. Yet she seemed so beautiful to Jupiter that he bedded with her and produced a fine son named Colaxes.

Therefore, I urge you to cease railing at my statements and believe that nothing is truer save the gospel.

XXXIX

HOW FRIAR JOHN JOINED THE COOKS IN AN OFFENSIVE AGAINST CHITTERLINGS AND SAUSAGES

As these furious Chitterlings marched boldly forward, Friar John warned Pantagruel:

"I foresee a sham battle, a mock fight, mere child's play!" he roared. "What signal honor, what magnificent praise will attend our victory? I wish you would board your vessel and watch me and my men settle this fight."

"What men?" Pantagruel asked.

"I quote from Holy Writ," the monk replied. "You remember Potiphar, My Lord? He was chef of chefs in Pharaoh's kitchens, and he bought Joseph, who would have cuckolded Pharaoh, had he not been a juggins. Well, how did Potiphar rise to be Master of Horse (Captain of the Guard, biblically speaking)? How did the celebrated glutton Nabuzardan, head cook to King Nebuchadnezzar, manage to be chosen from among all other captains to besiege and destroy Jerusalem?"

"Go on," said Pantagruel.

"By the chasm of the Holy Virgin," Friar John asseverated, "I dare wager that these scullions rose to such heights because they had previously fought Chitterlings or men of no greater worth. To strike down, rout, conquer and annihilate such foes, cooks prove incomparably superior to all the men-at-arms, Balkan mercenaries, German lansquenets and footsoldiers of the world."

"That reminds me of what I read in the gay and facetious sayings of Cicero," said Pantagruel, and told the following story:

During the Roman civil wars that pitted Pompey against Cæsar, Cicero was naturally more inclined towards the former, despite the latter's overtures and marked favors. One day, hearing that Pompey's party had suffered serious losses in an engagement, Cicero determined to visit their camp. Here he perceived scant strength, less courage and much disorder. Foreseeing that failure and destruction lay in store for them (as eventually happened), Cicero began to mock and banter now one, then another, in that bitter invective style of which he was master. Some of Pompey's captains, to prove their assurance and determination, played the good fellows and, referring to the Romans' standards in time of war, answered:

"Don't you see how many eagles we still have?"

"They might be useful and appropriate if you were fighting magpies," Cicero replied.

Similarly, Pantagruel concluded, if they were to fight Chitterlings, Friar John considered the war to be culinary, and, therefore, wished to join the cooks. The monk might do as he pleased; for his part Pantagruel would stay on the spot, awaiting the issue of the battle.

Friar John at once went into the kitchen tents and told the cooks with great courtesy and gaiety:

"My lads, I wish to see every one of you cover himself with honor and victory to-day. You shall accomplish feats of arms as never yet were accomplished within the memory of man. God's belly, man's belly, beast's belly, shall no one take store of valiant cooks? Let us go fight these frigging Chitterlings. I will be your captain. So, drink up, lads, there! And be of good courage."

"Well spoken, Captain," the cooks replied. "We are at your noble service; we will live and die under your leadership."

"Live, live, by all means!" Friar John shouted. "But die: no! That is the Chitterlings' fate. Come, then, let us get ready. *Nabuzardan* is the password, in honor of Nebuchadnezzar's chef of chefs, a lusty gourmand."

XL

HOW FRIAR JOHN BROUGHT THE SOW INTO ACTION AND WHAT VALIANT COOKS MANNED IT

THEN, at Friar John's orders, the engineers fitted up the great sow or siege-engine that was stored in the sixth ship—the ship whose poop bore a beggar-monk's flask, and which was called the *Leather Bottle*. This sow was a wonderful machine so built that, out of great engines set in a row all around it, it shot forth great stone cannon balls and long steel-tipped bolts. Within, more than two hundred men could easily find shelter and space to fight from.

It was modelled after the sow of Réole, thanks to which the French recaptured Bergerac from the English in the reign of young King Charles VI.

Here are the names of the noble and valiant cooks who went into the sow, even as the Greeks went into the Trojan horse:

Soursauce, Sweetmeat, Filthychops, Luggardspit, Pigballock, Saltslop, Hogshand, Breadlost, Dogweary, Pocketspoon, Herringwine, Curlycut, Master Stinker, Fatguts, Stealmortar, Lapwine, Hotchpotch, Goatroast or Cabirotado, Grillmeat, Hasletpluck, Potroast, Liverbroach, Sliceface and Gallimaufry. The coats-of-arms of all these lordly cooks bore, in a field *gules* (crimson), a larding-pin *vert* (green).

There were also Bacon and Baconlard, Nibblebacon, Filchbacon, Fatlard, Sparebacon, Toplard, Antibacon, Curlbacon, Lacebacon, Scrapelard, Chewbacon, and a native of the Rambouillet country called Gaylardon. This last culinary doctor's name was formed by process of syncopation, as you say "idolatrous" for "idololatrous" and "Gloster" for "Gloucester." Originally he was called Gaylardidardilardon.

We must add to the list Stiffbacon, Astolard, Sweetlard, Crunch-bacon, Snapbacon, Bastelard, Guybacon, Snuffbacon, Fairbacon, Freshlard, Bitterbacon, Logbacon, Oglebacon, Weighlard, Scanbacon, Watchlard. None of these names was known among the Marranos (Christianized Jews or Moors) or among the Jews proper, who, of course, forgo pork.

The list further includes Ballocky, Washsalad, Cresspicker, Scratchturnip, Cunneycunt, Rabbitskin, Pareapple, Pastycock, Flatbacon, Freepudding, Mustarder, Hotsauce, Snailflavor, Clearbroth, Soupsnuffle, Winebraggle, Pottagepiss, Wastecrust, Simplestew, Verjuice, Raspskewer, Guzzlehash, Potroast, Roastpot, Crackpot, Potscrape, Dishdiddle, Spinescrapple, Gravysuck, Macaroon and Blowskillet.

Then there was Stagpecker. Subsequently he was taken from the kitchen and appointed to the chamber-service of My Lord Cardinal Jean Le Veneur-Carrouge, late Bishop of Lisieux. This was particularly appropriate as Le Veneur means the hunter.

The muster included: Rotroast, Dishwasher, Fritterpuff, Firefeeder, Cocksup, Longprick, Tailpusher, Prettytool, Newdingus, Crackpusher, Victorpole, Hairpoker, Quickmutton or Rashcalf, Sirloinsteak, Muttonshoulder, Burncake, Jointstealer, Swellgut, Thirstysoil, Grizzlepizzle, Girdlecrack, Crocodilemaw, Buttercutler, Slashsnout and Crapface. Also Mondam, as the Scots Archers mispronounce the name of the inventor of *Sauce Madame*.

Still others swelled the roll: Toothclick, Lubberjaws, Wondertong, Gulliguts, Potswabber, Swillspiller, Grimyhands, Birdinpaunch, Cakeswallow, Saffronsauce, Stuffsphincter, Horsarse de Watercress, Parsnipballs, Beetmanroot, Puddingstones and Hogg.

Special mention must be accorded to Robert, inventor of the sauce that bears his name. (What a masterpiece, I may add. It is a brown sauce, made by boiling meat; flavoring vegetables and spices in beef broth to a glaze; thickening it with brown roux, flour and melted butter; then adding onions, mustard and vinegar. It is indispensable and delicious in the accommodation of roasted rabbit, duck, fresh pork, poached eggs, salted mackerel and a myriad like dishes.)

Finally, the siege-engine captained by Friar John and manned by master-chefs contained: Coldeel, Redsnapper, Devilfish, Morselmaw, Saltingtub, Fuckfood, Turkeyroast, Salmagundifry, Stonebroiler, Sourherring, Creampuff, Bigsnout, Lapscrap, Fritterbag,

Frogscuttle, Pepperstew, Redmullet, Frydaddle, Pantrysleep, Cunt-botch, Friggletwatt, Shitbreeches, Squaregallon, Sturdevant or Turdy, Hidedingus, Porkswallow, Wheelfucker, Dodocock, Hide-brangle, Badelory or Widestaff, Wantawench and Codpizzini.

All these highborn cooks entered the sow, merry, brisk, in fine fettle and longing to fight. The last to enter was Friar John, broadsword in hand. The doors closed and were locked from the inside.

XLI

HOW PANTAGRUEL BROKE THE CHITTERLINGS AND SAUSAGES AT THE KNEES

THERE is a French saying: to break the chitterlings at the knee. It means to woo success by unusual methods. Now you shall read how My Lord Pantagruel accomplished a feat of genual and genuine sausage-breaking.

The Chitterlings came so close to Pantagruel that he could observe them quite clearly, stretching out their arms and lowering their lances. He therefore sent Gymnastes forward to find out what they purposed, and what grievance moved them to attack their traditional allies, without slander or malfeasance on the latters' part.

Gymnastes advanced toward the vanguard, made a deep sweeping bow, and shouted at the top of his voice:

"Yours, yours, yours, we are wholly yours; we are at your orders; we are all for Mardigras or Carnival, your ancient ally."

Certain authorities state that he cried "Gradimars" instead of "Mardigras" or "Cavernal" instead of "Carnival," so that the French-speaking Sausages believed he referred to March and Lent, and the English-speaking Chitterlings expected to be prisoned in caves. Be that as it may, Gymnastes was no sooner done than a huge, fat, furious Brainsausage (called Cervelas in French, Saveloy in English) strode out at the head of his forces, bent on wringing Gymnastes' neck.

"By God!" said Gymnastes. "If you ever reach me, it will be in scraps, for you're far too fat to be swallowed whole."

With which, Gymnastes seized his great sword in both hands—it was called Kissarse—and sliced the Brainsausage in half. God's truth, was it a stout sausage! (It reminded me of the Swiss they called the bull of Berne, a huge lout who sounded the attack on a bull's horn; poor lad was killed at Marignano in 1515, when the French whipped the Swiss. He tried to spike a cannon and was blown up!) To return to Gymnastes' victim, the latter must have had four good inches of lard over his belly at the very least.

The Brainsausage brained, the Chitterlings bore down upon Gymnastes and would have villainously felled him, when Pantagruel hurried up with his men to succor him. A fast and furious hand-to-hand combat ensued, helter-skelter, higgledy-piggledy, pell-mell. Colonel Slicesausage sliced the enemy Sausages manfully; Pantagruel, for his part, broke them at the knee. Meanwhile, Friar John lay low in his sow, surveying the battle and awaiting the decisive moment. Suddenly the ambushed Bolognas charged out upon Pantagruel.

Friar John witnessed the tumult and disarray. Opening the doors of his sow, he emerged with his crack troops at his heels. Some bore iron spits, others long andirons, others cogged spitbars. Still others sported frying-pans, skillets, cauldrons, grills, pokers, pincers, dripping-pans, brooms, saucepans, mortars, pestles, all in battle array, like so many housebreakers and bandits, howling and shrieking at once.

"*Nabuzardan!*" they shouted "*Nabuzardan! Nabuzardan!*"

Raising the devil's din, they swooped down upon the Chitterlings, Sausages, Bolognas and kindred tribes. Before these reënforcements, the foe fled at the gallop, as if a million fiends were after them. Friar John sent a rain of cannon balls down on them, flattening them down like flies against a wall; his soldiers spared none. It was a piteous sight: the field was strewn with dead or wounded Chitterlings. History relates that had not God provided otherwise, the entire Chitterling race would have been wiped off the face of the earth. But a miracle occurred—a miracle which you may believe or not, as you like.

Out of the north, suddenly, flew a huge, great, fat, gray swine, with wings as long and wide as the arms of a windmill. His plumage was crimson as the phenicoptera's or flamingo's, to use the word current in Languedoc. His eyes were fiery red as carbuncles; his ears were green as leek green emeralds or chrysoprase; his teeth were yellow as topaz; his tongue very long and black as jet; his feet white, diaphanous and transparent as diamonds, and splayed, as formerly Queen Pedauque's were, at Toulouse. Around his neck hung a golden necklace, bearing a vague legend of which I could distinguish only the characters: ῾ΥΣ᾽ΑΘΗΝΑΝ or *Hog teaching Minerva.*

So far, we had had fine clear weather. The moment this monstrous, flying hog appeared across the heavens, there was such loud thundering to the left that we were astounded. The Chitterlings, aghast, threw aside their weapons and fell on their knees, raising joined hands in supplication, wordlessly, as if in adoration.

Meanwhile Friar John and his men kept felling and spitting the Chitterlings: but, upon orders from Pantagruel, retreat was sounded and fighting ceased.

The monster then whirled and wheeled about several times between the armies, tossing down more than twenty-seven pipes of mustard. Then it disappeared, winging its way through the air, shouting:

"Mardigras! Carnival! Mardigras! Carnival!"

XLII

HOW PANTAGRUEL SIGNED A TREATY WITH NIPHLESETH, QUEEN OF THE CHITTERLINGS

THE monster having disappeared, the armies stood facing one another in silence. Pantagruel then asked whether he might parley with Niphleseth, Queen of the Chitterlings. (In Hebrew, the word means *penis.*) As Her Majesty was in her royal carriage, near the ensigns, the matter was easily arranged.

Descending, Queen Niphleseth greeted Pantagruel courteously

and expressed her pleasure at seeing him. The slight misunderstanding that had occurred, she said, was due to faulty intelligence on the part of her staff. Her spies and observers had reported that King Lent, her hereditary enemy, had landed, and was passing the time examining whale's urine—that is, seeing what stuff they were made of.

Would not Pantagruel overlook the offence? Would he not remember that there was more shit than gall in Chitterlings? Herself and all her people would hold the whole island realm in obeisance, faith and homage to him; they would do his bidding at all times and in all places, befriending his friends and opposing his enemies; in recognition of such fealty, each and every year she would deliver seventy-eight thousand royal Chitterlings as hors d'oeuvre for his meals six times a year. She lived up to her word: the very next morning, she sent Gargantua six great brigantines, with just that number of royal Chitterlings, in charge of young Niphleseth, the Infanta.

Good Gargantua, when they reached him, made a present of them to the mighty King of Paris. Doubtless because of a change of temperature (or lack of mustard, the natural balm and traditional restorative of Chitterlings), almost all of them perished. The mighty Parisian monarch graciously granted that they be buried in heaps, in a certain spot which has been known, ever since, as the Rue Pavée d'Andouilles—Sausage Paved Lane.

At the request of the ladies of his court, the King of Paris preserved young Niphleseth, dealt with her fairly, and, eventually, she married happily and richly. In time she produced several fine children, praise God!

Pantagruel thanked Queen Niphleseth graciously, refused to acknowledge any offence committed, told her he could not accept her tribute, and presented her with one of those small knives they manufacture in the Perche district—of the sort that Jacques Cartier distributed so lavishly among the natives of the New World. Then, very curious, he questioned her upon the apparition of the monstrous flying hog. It was, she told him, the Ideal, the supracelestial embodiment of Carnival, their tutelary War God, the first and original founder of the Chitterlingsausagic race. Were not Chitterlings and Sausages derived from pork? Why, then, was Pantagruel surprised at a flying hog?

Pantagruel then inquired why the beast had shed so much mustard. Had it a curative value? Her Majesty replied that that mustard was, to the Chitterlings, what the Holy Grail, or the blood of Jesus itself, or holy balsam, was to other peoples. One drop of it applied to a fallen Chitterling healed his wound (if wounded) and brought him back to life (if killed in action).

Pantagruel's conversation with Queen Niphleseth went no further. He retired to his ship, as did his followers, with their armaments and sow.

XLIII

HOW PANTAGRUEL LANDED AT RUACH, OR WINDY ISLAND

Two days later, we reached the Isle of Ruach or, to translate the Hebrew, Windy Island. I swear by the Pleiades that I found the local way of living so strange and wonderful that I cannot possibly do it justice.

The inhabitants lived entirely on wind; they ate and drank nothing but wind; they had no houses but weathercocks. In their gardens, they sowed three kinds of windflowers; rue and other like specifics for flatulence, they plucked most carefully. Eating these plants, they broke wind to good purpose. For nourishment, the common people made use of fans of feathers, paper or linen, according to their means and capacity. The opulent relied upon windmills for their existence. When they had cause to celebrate or feast, they would set tables under a windmill or two, indulge themselves gaily as you might at a wedding, and, during the meal, discuss the body, fragrance, tang, odor, bouquet, ripeness, warmth and salubrity of winds as you, happy drinkers, discuss wines. One vaunted the merits of the *sirocco* or southeast wind; a second declared the *libecchio* or southwest wind supreme; a third favored the *barbino*, also a southwester; a fourth championed the *bise* or north wind; a fifth, the *zephyr* or west wind; a sixth, the *galerne* or northwester; and so forth. As for lovers, dandies and ladies' men, they liked the gentle poop that rustled under their sweethearts' skirts. Finally, the sick were treated with draughts, just as your own sick are given draughts of medicine.

"Oh!" said a little puffbelly, "where could I get a good bladderful of that fine Languedoc wind, that west-northwester called Circius by the ancients? The famous physician Jean Esquiron of Montpellier, or Schyron (how like his name is to the Greek wind Scyron!) was once travelling through Windy Island, and told us that that Languedoc wind could overturn a loaded wagon. Oh, what great good it would do my œdipodic leg!"

The classical reference to Œdipus the seer, whose leg was bloated —his name means "swollen foot"—was not lost on his hearers.

"Ay," the swellbelly sighed. "The biggest are not necessarily the best."

"For my part," said Panurge, "I would like a large butt of that good Languedoc wine that grows at Mirevaux, Canteperdrix and Frontignan."

I saw a quite fine-looking man, dropsical in appearance, who was greatly enraged at a big fat servant and a little page. He was kicking them in the arse with the devil's own boot. Not knowing the cause of his anger, I supposed he was following his physician's advice: it is a healthy thing for masters to lose their tempers and thrash their domestics, just as it is a healthy thing for these same domestics to be thrashed. But, a moment later, I heard him heaping reproaches upon them, because they had stolen more than one-half of a leather bagful of excellent southwesterly wind, which he had stored preciously, as a rare specific against the cold season.

If they do not spit, piddle or cack in this island, in compensation, they belch, poop and fart prodigiously. They suffer every sort and kind of illness, all of which spring and develop from ventosity or flatulence, as Hippocrates shows in his *Lib. de Flatibus, Of Gas*. Their worst epidemic is wind-colic. As a remedy, they use large *ventouses* or dry-cupping vessels, into which they blow veritable gales of wind. They all die of dropsy and tympanites (swelling of the abdomen caused by air in the intestine). The men perish, farting; the women, pooping. Their immortal souls make their exit from between their buttocks.

Later, while strolling about the island, we met three great, giddy windguts, who were off to amuse themselves by watching plovers.

(These birds abound in the island and, as you know, live on wind.)
I noticed that just as we drinkers, strolling in the country, carry
flasks, bottles and flagons, so each of them carried at his belt a fine,
small pair of bellows. Should the wind fail, they could thus produce
fresh wind for themselves by working these bellows in attraction and
reciprocal expulsion. As again you know, wind, essentially defined,
is nothing but fluctuating and agitated air.

Just then we received warning, by the king's orders, not to take a
single man or woman of the island on our ships for three hours. This
was because somebody had robbed His Majesty of a bag containing a
rousing full-bodied fart of the very wind that goodman, Æolus, god
of winds, a rumbling snorer, had granted Ulysses to push his ship
when unexpected calm should befall him. The King of Windy Island
kept this fart religiously, like another Holy Grail. Already, several
times, he had used it to cure critical maladies, by merely letting loose
and distributing to the patients a quantity sufficient to compound
a virginal fart—which is what our Sanctimonials or nuns call "ringing the back doorbell."

XLIV

HOW SMALL RAINS LAY
HIGH WINDS

PANTAGRUEL praised their form of government and their mode of
life. To their hypenemian mayor (to use the Greek for "windy") he
declared that, if Epicurus was correct in defining the supreme good
as easy, painless pleasure, then the islanders were happy, indeed.
What was their existence based on? Wind. What was their food?
Wind. What did it cost them? Little or nothing: all they had to do
was blow!

"Ay, My Lord," the mayor answered. "But alas! nothing is perfect
here below. Very often, we may be seated about the table, feasting
upon some great blessed wind of God, as upon so much heavenly
manna. We are happy as kings, gay as church fathers. What happens?

Suddenly down comes a small rain to still our wind and steal our food. Thus many a meal is lost for want of nourishment."

"Ho!" Panurge broke in. "That reminds me of Jenin de Quinquenais, old Johnny Blowgut. One day he was with his wife Quelot. A most noisome wind was blowing out of her postern, as out of some colossal *æolipyle*."

"What on earth is an *æolipyle*?" somebody interrupted.

Pantagruel explained. The word meant "gate of Æolus." An *æolipyle* was a bronze, closed instrument with a small hole in it. If you filled the vessel with water and set it near the fire, you would notice the wind issuing continually from it. The winds in the air were produced in just that fashion; so were the ventosities in human bodies. In the latter instance, it was a question of heatings and concoctions, begun but not completed, as Galen showed. Pantagruel further referred the questioner to the comments of his great friend and lord, M. Philander, on the first book of Vitruvius. This authority, of course, was Guillaume Philandrier, philologist, architect and scholar of the day.)

"Well," Panurge went on, "as I told you, Quelot was expelling malodorous winds from her bummery, as from some gigantic *æolipyle*. What does husband Johnny do but piddle on the windbox and lay the ill-fumed wind? I wrote a pretty poem to celebrate the occasion:

> *John, having spent all day testing his wine,*
> *   (A wine as yet too heady and too strong)*
> *Bade his wife cook some turnips: he would dine!*
> *She, nothing loath, obeyed her John. Ere long*
> *The happy pair feasted, with jest and song,*
> *Retired to bed, and, having friggled, tried*
> *Vainly to sleep: the good wife at John's side*
> *Blew endless bumblasts, trumpeted and dinned.*
> *In self-defense, John pissed on her and cried:*
> *'Behold! a small rain lays the highest wind.'* "

"We are also troubled by a great and fearsome calamity every year," the mayor continued. "I refer to Widenostrils, the giant. He lives on the island of Hurly. Every spring, by advice of his physicians, he comes here to purge himself, swallowing a great number of our windmills as you would a pill. He also devours numberless bellows, a dish he finds most appetizing. This is a source of deep misery to us: we fast for it three or four lents every year, not to mention the various particular rogations and orisons we offer up."

"Can you do nothing about it?" Pantagruel asked.

"On the advice of our *mezarims* or stomach specialists," the mayor replied, "at about the time he usually comes, we placed many roosters and hens in our windmills. The first time he swallowed them, he almost died. They crowed inside him and fluttered across his belly; as a result of which he suffered a *lipothymy* or collapse and a weakening of the heart, amid dreadfully dangerous convulsions, as if some serpent had crept into his mouth, slid down his windpipe and begun to frisk inside his stomach."

"That," Friar John commented, "is an inappropriate and incongruous comparison. I have often heard it said that a snake can crawl into a man's belly without causing him the slightest discomfort. What's more, it can be driven out if you hang the patient by the feet, laying a bowl of warm milk near his mouth."

"You heard it said, ay," Pantagruel acknowledged. "So did those who told you. But you never saw it or read it in any authority. Hippocrates in his *lib. v. Epidem, Of Epidemics*, states that in his time a snake did enter a man's belly, but the poor patient died amid spasmodic convulsions."

The mayor of Windy Island continued his story. Things had gone from bad to worse. All the foxes of the land had chased the fowl down Widenostrils' gullet, until the giant was about to die at any moment. A jocular enchanter advised him to flay the fox or vomit, whenever these paroxysms came on, as antidote and counterpoison. Since then, he had had better advice. His present treatment consisted in taking an enema made of a decoction of wheat and millet (which attracted the poultry), and gooseliver (which drew the foxes). He also swallowed hounds and terriers.

"You can imagine how unhappy we are!" the mayor concluded.

"Never fear any more, good people!" Pantagruel told them. "For great Widenostrils, the swallower of windmills, is dead, I assure you. He choked to death while eating, by order of his physicians, a lump of fresh butter at the mouth of a hot oven."

XLV

HOW PANTAGRUEL LANDED ON THE ISLAND OF POPEFIGGERY

NEXT morning we reached the island of the Popefiggers. Once this people had been wealthy and free; they were then known as the Goodfellows. Now, alas, they were poor, unhappy, and submitted to the tyranny of the Papimaniacs. Here is how their misfortune came about:

On a certain yearly holiday, when crosses and banners were brought out, the mayor, the aldermen and the big rabbis of Goodfellowland happened to visit the neighboring island of Papimania, to watch the local holiday processions. Following the laudable tradition of major festivals in Papimania, the pope's image was publicly displayed. One of the Goodfellows, seeing it, gave it the sign of the fig—a derisive gesture made by thrusting the thumb between index and middle finger, a gesture not unlike thumbing the nose.

To avenge this affront, the Papimaniacs, without the least warning, took up arms a few days later, descended upon Goodfellowland, surprised the inhabitants, sacked and ravaged the entire island. They carved up every man above the age of puberty, sparing only women and children—and these only on the conditions which Emperor Frederick Barbarossa imposed upon the inhabitants of Milan.

(It was in the twelfth century. The Milanese had rebelled against him in his absence. They had driven the Empress ignominiously from the town, mounted on a mule called Thacor—which in Hebrew means "a fig in the bumgut." Worse, Her Majesty had ridden arsey-turvy, that is, with her seat close to the mule's head, her face to its crupper. On his return, Frederick defeated and dominated them. Then he went to the pains of recovering the celebrated mule Thacor. In the middle of the Broglio—the main square of Milan— at the Emperor's order, the hangman placed a fig in the mule's tindercrack. In the presence of the subjugated townsmen, the Emperor's heralds proclaimed, to the sound of trumpets, that whoever wished to save his life, must publicly pull out the fig with his teeth. Then, without using his hands, he must put it back into the very crevice from which he had extracted it. Any man refusing to submit to this ordeal would be incontinently hanged.

Some of them were shamed and horrified by the abominable penance; they considered it worse than death, and dangled from the gallows for their conviction. Others proved less punctilious. Having pulled out the fig with tooth if not with nail, they showed it plainly to the hangman, saying: "*Ecco lo fico!* Behold the fig!")

In just this humiliating way, the remnants of the wretched, disconsolate Goodfellows were allowed to save their lives, to become slaves and bondsmen to the Papimaniacs, and to bear the name of Popefiggers, because they had given the pope's image the sign of the fig. Ever since, that unhappy people has fallen upon evil days. Every year they are visited by hail, storms, plagues, famines and all manner of woes, as an everlasting punishment for the sin of their ancestors and kin.

Perceiving their misery and calamity, we did not care to visit the country further; we wished only to commend ourselves to God and to sprinkle ourselves with holy water. So we entered a little chapel near the harbor. It proved as dilapidated, roofless and ruined as the basilica of St. Peter at Rome, which gapes to the open sky. As we went in and dipped our fingers, we spied, in the middle of the font, a man swaddled in stoles. He was deep under water, with only the tips of his nostrils emerging; he was like a diving duck. About him stood three bald, shaveling priests, reading the mystic conjuring screed and invoking devils.

Pantagruel, amazed, asked what game they were playing at. They replied that, for the past three years, the plague had raged so fiercely that over one-half the island was abandoned and tenantless. When at last its ravages were over, a terrible adventure had befallen the Popefigger now lying under water in the font.

This man, who owned a large fertile field, was sowing Lammas wheat. On that very day, at that very hour, a devilkin—who had not yet learned to thunder or hail, except parsely and cauliflower, and who could not yet read or write—was interviewing Lucifer. This shaver of a fiend implored his master to allow him to visit the island of Popefiggery, where the devils, on very familiar terms with men and women, often sought entertainment.

Reaching Popefiggery, the devilkin asked the farmer what he was doing. The wretched man answered that he was sowing Lammas wheat to support him next year.

"Perhaps!" said the devil. "But this field isn't yours. It's mine; *I* own it! Since the time you mocked the pope, this whole country has been made over, deeded and abandoned to us. Never mind, though: sowing wheat is not my business. Therefore, I will leave you the field, but we must share the profits."

"Very well," said the farmer.

"We will divide the land's yield in two parts," the devil proposed. "First: what grows above the ground; second, what lies below. I have the right to choose, being a devil born of ancient and honorable race, whereas you are but a churl. Well then, I choose for my portion what lies underground; you may have everything above earth's surface. When do you expect to reap?"

"Come August," said the farmer.

"Good!" cried the devil. "I shall not fail you. Meanwhile, do your duty: work away, churl, work away. I'm off to tempt the august nuns of Dryfart to the sprightly sin of fornication. There are a few bigots and cowled hypocrites I must provide for these ladies; but that job is easier, the fathers are for me already! Then, touch and go, give and take, higgledy-piggledy, flippety-flop!"

XLVI

HOW THE DEVILKIN WAS FOOLED BY A POPEFIGGER FARMER

THE devilkin appeared promptly on the first of August, with, in his wake, a squadron of devil's choristers. Appearing before the farmer:

"Here I am, Master Churl," he announced. "Have you been well since last I saw you? What about my share of our yield?"

"Fair enough, Master Devil."

The farmer, with his farmhands, cut the wheat and reaped it; the devilkin and his cohorts pulled up the stubble. The farmer threshed, winnowed, packed and transported his crop to market; the devilkin's minions did as much. The farmer took his stand in the marketplace; the devils, theirs, next to him. The farmer sold his wheat at a profit and filled half an old buskin, that hung at his girdle, with the gold coin he earned. The devilkins sold nothing. In point of fact, the peasants laughed in their faces.

Market done, the devilkin turned on the farmer:

"Very well, clod, you have fooled me, for once! Next time, you will sing a different tune!"

"How could I fool you, Master Devil? Did you not have the privilege of choice? The truth of the matter is that *you* thought to fool *me*. You hoped that nothing would grow on my land; then you would find underground all the seeds I had sown. With these, you would tempt the impoverished, the sleezy and the skinflints to fall into your nets. Pooh! you're a beginner, a shaver, a pup! The seed you saw me sow is dead and rotten; its blight produced the wheat you saw me sell. I pity you: you chose badly. The 'chooser is choused,' saith the Bible."

"Never mind, never mind," said the devilkin. "What will you sow in our field next year?"

The farmer scratched his head.

"Well," he said, "to get anything out of it, we ought to sow beets."

"You're an honest serf," the devilkin said. "I'll take your word. Come on: sow beets aplenty; I will protect them from storms and never hail on them, come what may. But remember: I insist on taking for my share whatever grows above ground: you may have what lies below. Work away, churl, work away. I'm off to tempt the heretics; their souls are very toothsome when fried over charcoal. My Lord Lucifer is laid up with colic; they will prove a tasty mouthful for him."

When it was time to harvest the beets, our devilkin was on the spot with a squadron of devilkins-in-waiting. He appeared before the farmer and farmhands, and, without further ado, cut and gathered all the leaves on the plot. When he was done, the farmer and his men dug, spaded and gathered the fat beets, and put them into their bags. Devils and Popefiggers then proceeded to market. The farmer sold his beets handsomely; the devilkin not only sold nothing, but was insulted by the customers.

"Ho, ho!" cried the devil. "I see you have fooled me again. I want to settle matters between us, once and for all. Let us agree to clapper-claw one another; the first of us who surrenders shall give up his part of the field. To the victor, the spoils. I appoint a week from to-day as the day of trial. Meanwhile, work away, churl, work away blithely! I'm off to tempt those frigging Catchpoles, lawyers, attorneys, pettifoggers, counterfeiters and double-dealing clerks. Not that it's hard work: already they sent me word, by some vague hireling, that they are mine. Lucifer is vastly troubled as to their souls; to prove it, he sends them down to his kitchen-scullions unless they are highly seasoned!"

The devilkin then quoted the saying that there was no breakfast like the student's, no luncheon like the lawyer's, no snack like the vintner's, no supper like the tradesman's, no late repast like the chambermaid's, and no meal whatsoever like every single meal those fat, hooded hobgoblins sit down to in monasteries. The devilkin acknowledged the truth of this saying. Indeed, My Lord Lucifer had monks served to him as hors d'oeuvre at every meal; and he used very often to lunch on students. But alas! in the last few years, by a piece of bad luck, they had added the Holy Bible to their studies; Satan's minions now found it impossible to bring in a single scholar. Unless the priestly hypocrites helped the devils by employing threats, abuse, violence and the stake to remove their St. Paul from these biblecrazed students, then the hordes of hell would have few to nibble at. Lucifer usually dined off pettifogging lawyers, despoilers of the poor; these were plentiful, of course, but the same dish proved somewhat monotonous in the long run.

A few days before, at a meeting of the full chapter of Hades, Lucifer declared that he would gladly eat the soul of any claptrap sham-Abraham preacher who forgot, in his sermon, to recommend himself to the charity of his congregation. Lucifer promised double pay and a handsome pension to any fiend who could bring him such a soul, piping-hot. His minions all set out to search for such a *rara avis*; they found none. Every preacher they heard advised all good women to remember their monasteries.

As for his afternoon snacks, Lucifer had given them up since his recent colic, brought on by the dastardly treatment given his sutlers, grocers, butchers, chefs and pastrycooks in the northern countries.

He supped satisfactorily on tradesmen, usurers, apothecaries, forgers, counterfeiters, adulterators of wares. Occasionally, when in a jovial mood, he made a midnight snack of waitresses, who, having drunk their master's good wine, filled the barrel up with stinking water.

"Work away, churl, work away," urged the devilkin. "I'm off to tempt the students of Trebizond to abandon their fathers and mothers, to abjure their regular mode of life, to free themselves from their sovereign's edicts, to live in liberty, to scorn everybody, to laugh at mankind and, donning the fine, jocund hood of poetic licence, to become so many charming hobgoblins."

XLVII

HOW AN OLD WOMAN OF POPEFIGGERY FOOLED THE DEVIL

THE farmer trudged homeward, pensive and sad. His wife, observing his dismal mood, thought he had been robbed at market. When she heard the cause of his unhappiness, and saw his purse full of coin, she comforted him gently. No harm whatever would come to him from this scratching-bout with the devil, she assured him. Let him but leave things to her and think no more about them: she had already found a way to save them.

"If the worst comes to the worst," said the farmer, "I shall get but one scratch, for I'll surrender at the first stroke, and leave him the field."

"Nonsense, nonsense," said his old wife. "Let be; rely on me; I know what to do. You say it's just a petty devil, eh? Pooh, I'll make him yield, and the field will be yours. Were it a big devil, we might have cause to worry."

The day we landed in Popefiggery happened to be the day of the combat. Early in the morning, like a good Catholic, the farmer had made confession and received the Eucharist. Then, by advice of the curé, he had hidden himself in the font, just as we found him.

While they were telling us this story, we were informed that the old woman had fooled the devil and gained the field. This is how she managed it.

The devilkin turned up at the farmer's door, rang the bell, crying: "Ho, churl, ho! Come out with the sharpest claws you have!"

Then, going briskly and confidently into the house, he found no farmer, but only the wife, lying on the ground, weeping and lamenting.

"What is this?" the devilkin asked. "Where is he? What is he up to?"

"Alas!" moaned the wife. "I wish I knew where that rascal, that scoundrel, that hangdog robber is! He ravished me, I am lost, I die of the harm he did me!"

"How was that?" the devil asked. "What is the matter with you? I'll flay him for you presently."

"Oh!" the old woman lamented, "he is a cutthroat, a tyrant, a devilripper. He told me he had an appointment to claw with you to-day. While testing his claws, he merely touched me here, between the legs, with his little finger. Alas! I am completely ruined by it. I shall not live through it, I shall never get well. Just look at the wound!"

The devilkin did.

"Even worse," she went on, "he has gone to the blacksmith to have his nails sharpened and pointed. You are a dead man, Master Devil, my friend. Run away, if you can, for he will stop at nothing. Please, please, take to your heels."

So saying, she uncovered herself to the chin, as the Persian mothers were accustomed to do when they met their sons who were fleeing from battle. ("Where are you running to?" they would shout. "Don't you know you cannot hide in our wombs again?") The old woman, then, exposed her thingummijig to the devilkin. Beholding the enormous solution of continuity in all its dimensions, the devil was aghast.

"Mahomet! Demiurge! Megæra! Alecto! Persephone!" he screamed. "That farmer shall not touch me! I'm off at top speed. What a gash! Pah, he can have the field, I leave it to him."

Having heard the dénouement of the story, we retired to our ships. We did not prolong our stay in Popefiggery. Pantagruel gave the church-building fund eighteen thousand gold royals, in pity at the poverty of the people and the calamity of the place.

XLVIII

HOW PANTAGRUEL LANDED ON THE ISLAND OF PAPIMANIA

LEAVING desolate Popefiggery behind us, we sailed serenely and happily for a day, before reaching the blessed island of Papimania, inhabited by the Papimaniacs or idolaters of papacy.

We had dropped anchor in the road, but not yet fastened our moorings, when a skiff rowed up towards us. We could distinguish four men in different costumes on board.

One was befrocked, bedraggled, booted and beshitten like a monk. The second was clad like a falconer, with a lure and a bird-glove in hand. The third wore a lawyer's garb, with a huge bag, full of summonses, subpoenas, briefs, chicanery, pettifoggery and post-ponements. The fourth looked much like an Orléans vintner, with trim canvas leggings, a large basket on his shoulders and a pruning-knife at his girdle.

No sooner had they boarded our vessel, than they all cried in one voice:

"Have you seen him, good passengers, have you seen him?"

"Seen whom?" Pantagruel demanded.

"You know him we mean!" they answered.

"And who may he be?" Friar John inquired. Then, thinking they were looking for some robber, murderer or church-thief: "God's death, I'll trounce the bastard for you!"

"Wonderful, wonderful! Do you mean to tell us, O foreign travellers, that you do not know the One and Only?"

"My Lord," said Epistemon, "we do not understand these terms. I beg you please to explain to us who it is you mean, and we will answer you quite frankly."

"We mean: he that is. Have you never seen him?"

"According to our theological doctrine, He that is, is God," said Pantagruel. "Did He not tell Moses: 'I am that I am.' We never yet saw Him—for He is not visible to mortal eyes."

"We do not refer to the supreme God Who rules in heaven," they replied. "We mean the god who rules on earth. Have you never seen *him?*"

Carpalim came to the rescue:

"Upon my honor, I swear they mean the pope."

"Ay, ay," said Panurge, "truly, gentlemen, I have seen three of them: Clement VII, Paul III and Julius III. Yet I am none the better off for the sight."

"What!" they protested. "Our sacred *Decretals* proclaim that there is never more than one living."

"I meant that I had beheld them successively, one after the other," Panurge replied. "Strictly speaking, I saw only one at a time."

"O happy, thrice-happy people!" they cried. "You are welcome, and doubly welcome here!"

They kneeled down before us and wished to kiss our feet, but we would not allow it. We remonstrated that if His Holiness the Pope were to come in person, they could find no greater homage to pay him.

"Oh, but yes, we could," they objected. "We have already decided how we could honor him. We would kiss his bare arse without baulking at it, and his stones, sans figleaf, too. For the holy father has a pair of knockers; our fair *Decretals* tell us so. Otherwise he could not be pope, since a physical examination must precede his enthronement. This has been the rule ever since the scandal of Pope Joan. Thus, according to our subtle decretaline philosophy, the pope has genitals; let genitals perish from the earth and earth would have no more popes."

While they talked, Pantagruel inquired of one of the skiff's crew who these people were. The sailor told him that they were the Four

Estates of the realm; he added that we would be honorably received and handsomely treated because we had beheld the pope.

Panurge, informed of this by Pantagruel, whispered in his master's ear:

"I swear to God that must be so! All things come to him who waits. We never derived the least profit from beholding the pope; here and now, by all the devils, it will serve us to great advantage."

We then went ashore. The whole population, men, women and children, advanced processionally to meet us. Our Four Estates cried loudly:

"They have beheld him! they have beheld him! they have beheld him!"

At this proclamation, the people kneeled down before us, raised their hands towards heaven, and shouted:

"O happy folk! O blessed, fortunate folk!"

Their ovation lasted a full quarter-hour.

The local schoolmaster came running up with all his pedagogues, pupils and abecedarians. He proceeded to deal them a magisterial flogging, as used to be done in our country, when a criminal was hanged and the schoolboys must be made to remember it. Pantagruel was offended.

"Gentlemen," he cried, "unless you stop whipping these unfortunate lads, I shall leave the island."

The people heard his stentorian voice with amazement. A little humpback with very long fingers asked the headmaster:

"By the virtues of the *Extravagantes*, that supplement to the *Decretals*, do all those who behold the pope grow as tall as that giant now threatening us? Ah, how I long to see his holiness, that I may grow as mighty as this visitor!"

We were acclaimed so enthusiastically that Homenais or Stoutmoron, as they called their bishop, hastened to meet us. He rode an unbridled mule with green trappings; he was attended by those he called his *apposts* (that is, his vassals, who resided within the church fiefs), and by his *supposts* or officers, who bore crosses, banners, standards, canopies, torches and vessels filled with holy water.

He, too, craved to kiss our feet, just as good Christian Valfinier had kissed Pope Clement's. He quoted the writings of one of their *hypothetes* or scavengers. This scourer and commentator of their holy *Decretals* had written that, just as the Jews, having long awaited the Messiah, were at length rewarded by His coming, so these islanders of Papimania would one day behold the pope. Until such blessed time, should any one land here who had seen the pope at Rome or elsewhere, that traveller was assured of a reverential welcome and royal feasting.

However, we courteously begged to be excused.

XLIX

HOW STOUTMORON, BISHOP OF PAPIMANIA, SHOWED US THE URANOPET, OR HEAVENSENT, DECRETALS

STOUTMORON told us:

"Our holy *Decretals* command and require that we visit the churches first and the taverns after. Let us therefore observe this noble decree and repair to church. Later, we will go banquet."

"Lead the way, man of God!" said Friar John, "we shall follow you. You spoke in season and like a good Christian; it's a long time since we saw a proper church! I am delighted, my spirit rejoices: truly, I believe I shall feed but the better for previous devotions. A fine thing it is to meet a God-fearing man!"

As we reached the church gate, we saw a fat, gilt book, studded with highly precious stones, such as rubies, emeralds, diamonds and pearls, quite as valuable, if not more so, than the jewels Augustus consecrated to Jupiter Capitolinus. This book hung in the air, suspended, by two thick golden chains, from the *zoophore* of the church porch—that is, the sculptured frieze between architrave and cornice, where animals, monsters and various other figures were presented.

We gazed admiringly at it: Pantagruel, who could easily reach it, turned it over in his hands and enjoyed examining it. He told us that the mere action of touching it brought such a tingling to his fingertips, and such a thrill to his arms, that he was violently tempted to beat a bailiff or two, provided they were not of the cloth.

"Of old," Stoutmoron told us, "the law, as handed down to the Jews by Moses, was written by the very hand of God. . . . At Delphi, before the portal of Apollo's temple, the Greeks found this legend written by the divine hand: ΓΝΩΘΙ ΣΕΑΥΤΟΝ, KNOW THYSELF. . . . Some time later, the legend ΕΙ, THOU ART, also appeared, divinely written, and transmitted from heaven. . . .

"The image of Cybele, goddess of earth and mother of Jupiter, was transported to Phrygia and set in a field called Pessinus . . . that of Diana was brought to Tauris, if we are to believe Euripides . . . the *oriflamme*, or standard of St. Denis, was conveyed from heaven to the noble Christian kings of France, to guide them against the infidel. . . .

"In the reign of Numa Pompilius, second king of Rome, the famous copper buckler called *Ancile* was seen descending from the clouds . . . Minerva's statue fell from the empyrean dome into the Acropolis at Athens. . . .

"Here in Papimania, you now witness a similar miracle. This book contains the sacred *Decretals*, penned by a cherub. Possibly you foreign folk will find this difficult to believe."

"It is indeed difficult!" said Panurge.

"This book has come down to us miraculously from the heaven of heavens. You recall Homer, father of all philosophy (excepting, of course, the holy *Decretals*). You recall how he names the river Nile 'Diipites' or 'sent by Jupiter.' Well, our *Decretals* are Uranopet, sent by heaven.

"Because you have beheld the pope—their evangelist and everlasting protector—you shall be allowed to look into this book and to kiss its pages, if you desire. But, ere you do so, you must fast three days and you must make official confession, mustering and retailing your sins so studiously and severely that not a single one fall by the board. Such are the divine directions of the holy *Decretals* you see here. I may add that this will require some time."

"O man of God," said Panurge. "We have descried excretals and exscrotals—I mean *Decretals*—in vast quantities. We have seen them on paper, on parchment thick as lantern paper, on vellum; we have seen *Decretals* written by hand, and others, printed. You need not take the trouble to show us these. We thank you for the kind attention and beg to be excused."

"God's truth!" cried Stoutmoron, "I swear you never saw any *Decretals* penned by angels. Those of your land are but transcripts of ours; one of our ancient decretaline scholars vouches for this. Besides, I beg you to consider it no trouble on my part. Simply tell me if you are willing to fast and to confess for only three little days of God."

"We are perfectly willing to confess," Panurge declared. "But the idea of fasting scarcely appeals to us. For we have so overfasted at sea that the spiders have spun cobwebs over our teeth. Just look at good Friar John of the Funnels, here—"

Stoutmoron put one arm courteously about his neck.

"Look at Friar John! He has a lining of moss growing over his throat for want of exercising his jaws and working his chops."

"True, true," Friar John agreed. "I've fasted so much that I'm almost round shouldered."

"Come, let us go to church," Stoutmoron suggested. "You will forgive us if we do not just now sing you God's fine, high mass. It is past noon; our holy *Decretals* forbid us to sing mass—I mean high and lawful mass—after midday. But I will say a low, dry mass—one without communion!"

"I would prefer one moistened with a fine Anjou wine!" cried Panurge. "Set to, then, say your low mass, and look sharp!"

"God's belly!" Friar John roared. "I bitterly resent having an empty stomach at this hour of the day. Had I eaten a copious breakfast and fed according to monkish habit, I could have handled matters. If Stoutmoron then chanced to sing us the *Requiem*, I would have brought him bread and wine for 'those which have gone before.' I don't mean the dead, either, I mean the bread and wine I buried in my belly in the past. But patience! Fall to, lay on, dispatch, heave away, but make it short and sweet, please. Pull up its skirts lest they draggle in dung! And for various other reasons, too."

L

HOW STOUTMORON PRODUCED THE PROTOTYPE OF A POPE

Mass done, Stoutmoron went up to the master altar and, out of a chest near by, drew a huge bundle of keys. Thirty-two of them, he put into as many keyholes; fourteen others fitted into fourteen padlocks. At last, a large, barred window above the altar swung open. With a great show of mystery, Stoutmoron covered himself with wet sackcloth, drew a crimson satin curtain, and revealed to us what was, in my opinion, a somewhat inferior image. Grazing it with a longish staff, he made us kiss the tip of the staff where it had touched the image.

"What do you think of it?" he asked us.

"It is undoubtedly the likeness of some pope," said Pantagruel. "I can recognize it by the tiara (or triple crown), the amice (or shoulder-piece), the rochet (or surplice), and the slipper (which needs no elucidation)."

"Quite right!" said Stoutmoron. "It is the idea, the archtype, the prototype of that same god of earth whose coming we await so devoutly. Ay, some day we shall see him in this country. O happy, O blessed, O long-expected day! O happy you, O thrice-happy, whom the stars have favored so signally! Happy, you, to have seen that god of earth, face to face, to have known his reality. We, alas! have but seen his image; yet, at the mere sight, we gain not only complete remission of all our remembered sins, but also one-third of all the sins we have overlooked, plus eighteen times forty for good measure. To be sure, we view it only on annual high festivals."

Pantagruel observed that Dædalus had invented the art of sculpture, of rendering living things in dead clay. The representation might be faulty and botched, yet there lay within, hidden and perhaps inaccessible, some godlike energy.

"Just like at Seuilly," Friar John commented.

And he told of an evening at Seuilly, when the beggars gathered in the infirmary of the monastery to celebrate the end of a holy day. One boasted of the farthings he had collected, another of the pence, a third of his caroli, a fourth of his shillings. A fifth fat rascal bragged of having taken in a whole crown.

"Easy enough," his colleagues jeered. "After all, you have the leg of God!"

"As though there were some divine power concealed in a leg gangrenous and rotten," Friar John commented.

(Certain sceptics might have explained that the cankered leg was called "leg of God" because the beggar, so afflicted, recovered miraculously at night, as he counted his alms.)

"When you tell us such nauseous tales," said Pantagruel, "please provide a basin, for I swear I feel like throwing up. To use God's holy name in a connection so ordurous and horrible! Faugh! how disgusting! If such abuse of words is usual in your monastery, then pray leave it there; let it lie within your cloisters."

Epistemon suggested:

"Physicians have always attributed to human ailments a certain divine participation. Thus Nero extolled mushrooms, and, coining a Greek phrase, called them divine food, because he had used them to poison the Emperor Claudius, his predecessor on the Roman throne."

Panurge contributed his quota to the discussion:

"*I* think this statue is not much like our late popes. I never saw them wear amices, but rather war helmets. These same helmets, I may add, resembled the tops of Persian turbans. The entire Commonwealth of Christendom enjoyed peace and quiet; those popes alone were waging cruel, truculent warfare."

"If they fought," Stoutmoron rose to the defense, "if they fought, it was to punish such rebel, heretic, protestant villains as refuse to abide by the holy program of god on earth. Not only is His Holiness the Pope authorized and entitled to do this; he is commended for it by the sacred *Decretals*. If emperor, king, duke, prince or commonwealth transgress one iota of his commands, he is bound to put them to fire or sword, to strip them of their realms, to proscribe and excommunicate them. Worse, he must not only destroy their own bodies, but also those of their children and relations. He must, finally, damn their souls to the bottom of hell's deepest cauldron."

"By all the devils," said Panurge, "these people are no heretics like Raminagrobis, or the Germans, or the English. You Papimaniacs are the choicest, finest, crackest Christians ever I saw."

"Ay, by God's power, so we are," said Stoutmoron. "For which, we shall all find salvation. Let us go bless ourselves with holy water, then adjourn to dinner."

LI

TABLETALK IN PRAISE OF THE DECRETALS

I BEG you to note, tosspots, that while Stoutmoron was wheezing his dry mass, three of his assistants proceeded through the church, basin in hand, crying:

"Remember the happy folk! Forget not the thrice-blessed, who have viewed him face to face."

As we left church, they brought Stoutmoron their basin overflowing with Papimaniac coin. Stoutmoron explained that the purpose of this voluntary contribution by the faithful was twofold conviviality: one part was earmarked for good drinking; the other for good eating. This was in accordance with a wondrous subparagraph concealed in some corner of their holy *Decretals*.

We obeyed the law and presently found ourselves in a tavern not unlike Guillot's—Guillaume Artus'—*Sign of the Silver Dolphin* in Amiens.

Need I tell you that we fed abundantly and drank in proportion? Two facts struck me particularly. In the first place, no meat was brought on without a rich complement of stuffing, whether kid, capon, pork (swine are plentiful in Papimania), pigeon, rabbit, hare or turkey. In the second place, every course, from soup to nuts, was served by a bevy of highly attractive, marriageable young wenches. Slender and alluring, blond, shapely and soft, clad in long flowing robes fastened twice by the merest of ribbons, they offered the most pleasant spectacle to be imagined. Their heads were bare; their hair was intertwined with narrow chaplets and fillets of rose, carnation, marjoram, daffodil and other flowers. Most opportunely, the lowered goblet met with an engaging curtsey, a pouring of liquor and a smile. Friar John leered at them like a cur ogling a capon.

The first course served, they sang a melodious canticle of praise in honor of the sacred *Decretals*. The second course served, Stoutmoron, infectiously gay, turned to a pulchritudinous handmaiden:

"Light, acolyte," he murmured, as a priest might order during mass. "Light!"

At these words, one of the wenches brought him an extravagant gobletful of wine. Extravagant? Yes, for it was of the *Extravagantes* or supplement to the *Decretals*; and it was also overflowing. Stoutmoron held it in his palm and, heaving a deep sigh, addressed the company:

"My Lord Pantagruel," he said, "and you, good friends, I drink your health! I bid you welcome and thrice welcome here!"

He drained the cup, returned it to the smiling wench, and added ponderously:

"O divine *Decretals*! God be praised that you sanctify the drinking of wine!"

"That is the cream of the jest," said Panurge.

"Ay," said Pantagruel, "but how much better if those *Decretals* could turn bad wine into good."

Stoutmoron, meanwhile, was embarking upon a *Decretal* rhapsody, praising each successive addendum to the bibliography of papal decrees: the *Sextum* of Pope Boniface, the *Clementinæ* of Pope Clement, the *Extravagantes* of Pope John:

"O seraphic *Sextum*! How essential you are to the salvation of wretched humanity!" Stoutmoron cried: "O cherubic *Clementinæ*! How aptly you define and outline the functions of the perfect Christian! O angelical *Extravagantes*! How graciously you guard such wretched souls as wander in mortal shape through this vale of tears. Alas! when shall humanity receive, as a special gift of divine favor, the ability to abandon all other studies and pursuits? When shall men rise to that ecstatic state where they may read, learn, know, use, apply, practise, incorporate and sanctify you alone? When shall they concentrate you within the ventricles of their cerebella, within the interior marrow of their bones, within the intricate labyrinths of their arteries? Oh, then, and then only, then and not otherwise will they know happiness."

At these words, Epistemon arose, and said frankly to Panurge:

"For want of a cacking stool, I'm forced to retire. This stuff has loosened my bumgut. I shan't be gone long."

"Oh, if ever we attain that blissful state," Stoutmoron sang on, "there will be no hail, no hoar, no frost, no ice, no climatic calamities! Instead, oh what abundance of earthly goods man would enjoy! Think, my dear friends, oh think of the endless, unbroken peace that would reign in the universe! Wars would cease; pillage, plunder, brigandage, vexation and murder would disappear—save as applied against heretics and cursed rebels. Gaiety, joy, happiness, merriment, amusement, delight in all human nature would become the order of the day. O great doctrine, O inestimable wisdom, O eternal precepts established in the divine chapters of these eternal *Decretals*! What a fire of divine love a single one of these sacrosanct tenets kindles within! They teach you charity towards your neighbors (exclusive of heretics); they enjoin a lofty contempt of all worldly and fortuitous things; they bring you content amid your passions; they elevate your spirits to the ecstasies of the third, supreme heaven!"

LII

OF THE MIRACLES ACCOMPLISHED BY THE DECRETALS (CONTINUATION)

"Spoken like an organ: melody and air!" said Panurge. "Spoken like an oracle! Those words are nuggets of—gold? Still, I believe it as little as possible. Let me tell you what happened to me at Poitiers, at the house of that most decretalipotent Scotch doctor, Robert Ireland, of the University Law Faculty. I chanced to read a chapter of those *Decretals*, and devil take me if this did not constipate me so severely that, for four or five days, I couldn't cack more than a single mangy turdlet. And what a turd! Do you wish to hear what it was like? Well,

I swear to you, it was like those Catullus ascribes to his neighbor Furius:

> *Nec toto decies cacas in anno,*
> *Atque id durius est faba, et lapillis:*
> *Quod tu si manibus teras, fricesque,*
> *Non unquam digitum inquinare possis.*

> *Ten turdlets, hard as bean or stone, are all*
> *The yearly quota that his tail lets fall.*
> *Take them in hand, roll, press, push and exert,*
> *You will not find one particle of dirt."*

"Ha, ha!" Stoutmoron warned. "Ha, ha, my friend, you were probably in a state of mortal sin."

"That is a horse of another color!" cried Panurge. "And wine out of another vat."

Friar John observed that, one day at Seuilly, he had happened to swab his swabbable parts with a page torn out of the *Clementinæ*, which the monastery assessor, Jean Guimard or John Pusspudding, had tossed out into the cloister meadow. Friar John hereby called all the devils of hell to witness that piles and hemorrhoids resulted. Indeed, the wretched nozzle of his brownbetty was completely lacerated.

"Hi, hah! hi, hah!" Stoutmoron brayed derisively. "That was divine punishment: God avenged the sin you committed in arsenalling the holy page you should have kissed and adored. You were assoiled for it, His vengeance done. I may add that you should have adored that page not only with *dulia* (the honor due a saint), but with *hyperdulia*, which is one degree higher, if not with *latria* (which is due God alone). Our good Nicolo Tedesco, Bishop of Palermo (Panormus) and therefore called the Panormitan, one of the greatest commentators of the *Decretals*, never lied on that score."

Ponocrates intervened:

"At Montpellier," he said, "John Upcock once bought, from the St. Clary monks, a fine collection of *Decretals* written on excellent parchment from Lamballe in Brittany, a place famed for the product. Between the leaves, he would beat out his gold. By a strange misfortune, no piece he struck ever turned out properly. One and all were chipped or broken."

"That was the punishment and vengeance visited upon him by God," said Homenais.

"At Le Mans," said Carpalim, "François Cornu, the apothecary, used a dog-eared set of *Extravagantes* for paper bags. I deny Satan if everything wrapped up in those bags was not immediately spoiled, rotten and poisoned. Incense, pepper, cloves, cinnamon, saffron, wax, spices, cassia, rhubarb, tamarind—all his drugs and purges and medicament—were lost!"

"Heavenly vengeance! Divine punishment!" Stoutmoron cried. "Imagine putting sacred writ to such profane use!"

"In Paris," Carpalim piped up, "Stitchsnout, the tailor, used an old set of *Clementinæ* to make patterns and measures. O wonder of wonders! Every garment cut out on these patterns was irremediably spoiled: gowns, hoods, cloaks, tunics, skirts, jackets, capes, doublets, petticoats, wraps, farthingales, not one turned out properly. Instead of cutting a hood, Stitchsnout found he had shaped a codpiece; intending to make a tunic, he produced a hat with high crown; designing a tunic, he ended up with an amice; he followed the pattern of a doublet and the result was an overcoat. His prentices sewed it up, then slashed it at the bottom and the thing looked like a pan to fry chestnuts in. Instead of a cape, he made a buskin; instead of a farthingale, one of those huge hoods, covering the whole head; instead of a cloak, the drumshaped cap of a Swiss mercenary. Eventually, poor Stitchsnout found himself condemned to repay his customers for the material he had ruined, and he went to the wall!"

"Divine vengeance!" said Stoutmoron. "God's punishment, and nothing else!"

"At Cahuzac in Gascony," said Gymnastes, "an archery match was arranged between My Lord Louis of Estissac and the Vicomte de Lauzun. Perotou or Peterkin ripped up a half-set of *Decretals* written on fine, strong, canonical parchment, and made a target out of the pages. I lend, I sell, I present my body to the hosts of hell if a single archer in the land (Guyenne is proverbial for its marksmen!) could lodge an arrow in the bull's-eye. Not one nick was made on the holy scribble; the *Decretals* remained virgin and intact. Sansornin the elder—Garniarnaut de Buade, Lord of St. Sernon—swore on his strongest oath ('By the figs of God!') that he had clearly, patently and manifestly seen Carquelin's shot move over the white target towards the bull's-eye . . . pause, a fraction of a second before it would normally have scored a hit . . . then shift, instead . . . and go shy about seven feet, over towards the bakehouse. . . ."

"O miracle!" cried Stoutmoron, "miracle of miracles! Light, acolyte! Your health all round: you seem to me to be true Christians!"

As he said this, the girls began to snicker and giggle. Friar John neighed through his snout, ready to cover, to stallion, to lay these fillies and to go riding hellbent, like a beggar on horseback.

"I think a man would have been safer near the target," Gymnastes mentioned, "than Diogenes was years ago."

"What's that?" Stoutmoron asked. "What did you say? Was he a decretalist?"

Epistemon, returning from his defecatory errand, approved:

"Well said, My Lord Pantagruel!" he cried. "What a reëntry in spades, partner! That ought to win us the rubber!"

Pantagruel then told how once Diogenes visited the archers for his amusement. One of them was so unskilful, clumsy and inaccurate that, when he took his stand, the spectators retreated, terrified lest he hit them. A shot of his fell a whole perch wide of the mark; before his second shot, the people scattered far off, left and right of the target. Diogenes, however, stood right up against it, convinced that this guaranteed the maximum of safety: the lout's arrows would land anywhere except there.

Gymnastes finished off his story:

"Chamouillac, one of My Lord of Estissac's pages, discovered the spell cast by the *Decretals*. Instead of the holy target, he fashioned one made up of documents used in the famous lawsuit at Pouillac in the Charente. Immediately, each marksman hit the bull's-eye."

Next, Rhizotomos contributed his tale to the *Decretal* anthology:

At Landerousse, he told the company, at Jean Delif's wedding, there was a fine banquet, with sumptuous festivities and much ado, as usual in these parts at the time. After supper, farces, comedies, and burlesques were enacted; Morris dances were enjoyed to the sound of bells and tabors; various masques and mummeries were performed. Rhizotomos and his schoolfellows were bent on doing honor to the festival. That morning, they had been given handsome violet-and-white liveries; now, for the merry masquerade they organized, they attached to these liveries various shells (brought back from pilgrimages at St. Michel in Normandy), snailshells, etc. Since they had no wide leaves (such as arum, burdock and elephant's ear), and no paper to make masks of, they used an old *Sextum* that had been laid aside there, cutting out holes for eyes, nose and mouth. O marvel of marvels! Their childish antics and jokes done, when they stripped off their masks, their faces were more hideous and fearsome than those of the devils in the famous miracle play at Doué, in Touraine. Wherever the *Sextum* had touched their skin, the latter had broken out. One suffered smallpox, another sheeprot, a third measles, a fourth ulcers, a fifth boils; in a word, the least seriously hurt was the man who lost all his teeth.

"O miracle, miracle!" Stoutmoron clamored.

"Steady!" Rhizotomos warned. "I haven't yet given the cue for laughter. My sisters, Catherine and Renée, had used this splendid *Sextum* as a press, for it was bound between great boards held down by heavy metal clasps. Into it, they had slipped the ruffles, cuffs and collars they had just washed and starched. Well, by God's might—"

"Hold, hold!" Stoutmoron interrupted. "What god do you mean?"

"There is but one God!" Rhizotomos answered.

"Ay, there is but one God in heaven," Stoutmoron agreed. "But we have another god here on earth!"

"True, true!" Rhizotomos conceded, "but by my soul! I swear I had forgotten him. Forgive me; I amend my phrase. Well then—by the virtue of God the Pope, my sisters' guimpes, ruffles, collars, coifs and other linen turned as black as a charcoal-burner's sack!"

"O miracle, miracle!" Stoutmoron cried. "Light, acolyte! Listen to these amazing stories, sweet wench!"

"How then," asked Friar John, "do people say:

> *The day* Decretals *came to be a duty*
> *And soldiers lugged huge trunks to store their booty,*
> *And monks began to fill both paunch and purse,*
> *Our poor world started going from bad to worse.*"

"I see what you mean!" said Stoutmoron. "You are quoting a satiric verse by some newfangled heretic."

LIII

HOW GOLD IS ARTFULLY DRAWN FROM FRANCE TO ROME BY VIRTUE OF THE DECRETALS

"I WOULD gladly pay for a pint of the best tripe that ever filled human guts," Epistemon vowed, "if we could have compared some of the horrible chapters of the *Decretals* with the original.

"Immediately I think of the chapter *Execrabilis, Execrable is He*, in the *Extravagantes*, where Pope John XXII damns the multiplicity of benefices accruing to a single priest, and orders the reversion of all but one benefice to the Holy See . . . of the chapter *De multa, Concerning Plural Benefices*, where Pope Gregory IX does the same thing . . . of the chapter *Si plures, If several*, in the *Clementinæ*, which, again, treats the same subject . . . of the chapter *De annatis per totum, Of the First year's Tax*, which forces the new incumbent of a benefice to pay an *annatis*, or annual tax equivalent to one year's revenue, into the papal treasury . . . of the chapter *Nisi essent, Unless they were*, in the *Decretals* of Pope Gregory IX, which deals with two candidates simultaneously appointed to the same office . . . of the chapter *Cum ad monasterum, When the Monk comes to the Monastery*, which regulates the life, discipline, dress, fare and recreation of the religious . . . of the chapter *Quod dilectio, Because Love*, which suffers young people related in the sixth degree to crown their love by marriage—at a specified price! . . . of the chapter *Mandatum, It is ordained*, which grants exemption of canonical rights. . . .

"These chapters, and certain others I shall not mention," Epistemon concluded with a flourish, "draw yearly from France to Rome four hundred thousand ducats or more."

"That's no small sum," Stoutmoron agreed. "Still, it isn't large, when you stop to consider that the most Christian realm of France is the only nurse that suckles the See of Rome. Besides, scour the whole world and find me a single book—of philosophy or medicine or law or mathematics or humane letters or, indeed, by my God, of Holy Writ!—that can draw as much money Romeward as my *Decretals*. Pooh! pish! tush! there *is* no such book; you can spend a lifetime without coming upon a volume so compact with aurifluous energy, I promise you!"

Stoutmoron then turned his attention to the devilish heretics who refused to learn and apply the *Decretals*.

"Squeeze them between red-hot pincers, hold them over the flame, hack them to pieces, hang, draw and quarter them—it does no good. Pierce their breasts with spits, their conduits with rapiers; make mincemeat of them; fry, grill or broil them; split them in half; grind them to powder—it is labor lost. Pluck out their entrails; crush, pound, bash and smash them; snap their legs and arms off, roast them to ashes—you are no better off than when you started. These evil heretics remain decretalifuge (they run away from our *Decretals*), and decretalicide (they slay our canons!). Far worse, they are, than murderers, far worse than parricides. They are decretalictones (they assassinate the *Decretals!*). They are very devils of hell!

"As for you, good people, if you would be accounted true Christians, I implore you on bended knees to think, believe, say, undertake or accomplish nothing which does not figure in the sacred *Decretals* or their corollaries, that noble *Sextum*, those splendid *Clementinæ* and those superb *Extravagantes*."

By obeying these deific tomes, Stoutmoron's friends would enjoy glory, honor, exaltation, riches, dignity and preferment upon earth; they would be respected and revered by all mankind; they would be chosen and elected above all other human beings. For, under the wide cope of heaven, no class of men proved so fit to handle and to accomplish anything as did those men who, by divine prescience and eternal predestination, applied themselves to the study of the holy *Decretals*.

"Do you seek a valiant emperor, a talented captain, a true chief and commander of armies in wartime? A man who can foresee emergencies, avoid danger, lead his men joyfully to storm a city or to fight a battle? A man who risks nothing, who proves always victorious without large losses of life, who knows how to turn his victory to advantage? Then choose a decretist . . . no, no, that was a slip of the tongue! Choose a decretalist, my friends!"

"That slip was no error," Epistemon whispered. "A decretist follows the *Decrees* of Gratian, which are good, sound canon law; a decretalist, the *Decretals*, which are spurious tools for papal ambition."

"Do you seek a man capable of governing a commonwealth, a realm, an empire or a monarchy in times of peace? A wise man who can maintain church, nobility, senate and people in riches, harmony, friendship, obedience, virtue and honesty? Choose a decretalist, my friends!

"Do you seek a man who, by his exemplary life, eloquence and saintly admonitions, can, in a short time, without bloodshed, conquer the Holy Land and bring over to the Holy Church those miscreant Turks, Jews, Tartars, Muscovites, Mamelukes, and even those corrupt Egyptian monks called Sarrabovites? Choose a decretalist, my friends.

"What, in many lands, makes the people rebellious and perverse, the pages greedy and malicious, the schoolboys idle and fatheaded? Merely this: their guardians, esquires and tutors were not decretalists.

"What power determinedly founded, strengthened and protected those fine monasteries and convents, which everywhere adorn, grace and honor Christendom, as the bright stars do the lofty firmament? It was the divine *Decretals*.

"What power established, propped up and consolidated, what power now maintains, feeds and nourishes the devout monks and nuns in monasteries, convents and abbeys? What power gave us these holy folk to pray daily, nightly, unceasingly for us, and thus save the world from falling back into its primitive chaos? It was the holy *Decretals*.

"What power created the famous and celebrated patrimony of St. Peter? What power increases every day that patrimony's abundance of temporal, corporal and spiritual blessings? It is the sacred *Decretals*.

"What power has made the Holy Apostolic See of Rome dreaded and respected throughout the universe in past ages and to-day? What power made His Holiness the Pope so mighty that, willy-nilly, all the kings, emperors, potentates and lords of earth depend on him, hold their office by his favor, are crowned, confirmed and given authority by him, go to Rome to prostrate themselves before him, to do him honor and to kiss his wondrous slipper—a picture of which you just saw? It is the noble *Decretals* of God.

"I shall reveal a great secret to you, my friends. The universities in your world usually have, in their arms and crests, a book, either open or shut. What book do you suppose it is?"

"I really don't know," said Pantagruel. "I've never read it."

"That book," said Stoutmoron, "is the *Decretals,* without which the privileges of every university would very soon perish. You must grant me that one! Ha, ha, ha, ha, ha, ha!"

Here Stoutmoron began to belch, to break wind, to laugh, to slobber and to sweat. Taking off his great, greasy, four-cornered cap, he handed it to one of the girls; she placed it on her comely head with great joy, having first kissed it lovingly, as a certain token that she would be the first to marry.

"Vivat!" cried Epistemon. "Huzzah! Hurrah! Bravo! O apocalyptic secret!"

"Light, acolyte," cried Stoutmoron. "Light, here, with double lanterns. Bring on the fruit, virgins!"

As they were doing so, Stoutmoron summed up his argument.

"I was saying that, by devoting yourselves to the sole study of these sainted *Decretals,* you will become wealthy and honored in this world. I add that, consequently, in the next, you will infallibly be saved to enjoy the blessed kingdom of heaven, the keys of which are given to our good god on earth and Decretaliarch.

"O my good god, whom I adore yet never saw, do thou, by thy special grace, open up to us, at least at the point of death, the most sacred treasure of our holy mother church. Art thou not, indeed, its protector, preserver, steward, administrator and governor? Do thou then take care lest these precious works of supererogation, these goodly pardons, fail us not in our time of need. Do thou grant us such help lest the devils rend, with their teeth, our miserable souls, and lest the dreadful jaws of hell swallow us utterly. If we must pass through purgatory, thy will be done. It lies within thy power and will to deliver us from there whenever it please thee."

Here Stoutmoron began to shed huge, scalding tears, to beat his breast, to cross his thumbs and kiss them fervently.

LIV

HOW STOUTMORON GAVE PANTAGRUEL SOME GOOD-CHRISTIAN PEARS

OBSERVING this doleful conclusion to Stoutmoron's tabletalk, Epistemon, Friar John and Panurge hid their mouths behind their napkins, howled "Meeow! meeow! meeow!" and wiped away imaginary tears from their eyes. The girls bustled about, bringing the guests huge beakers of Clemintine wine and sweetmeats aplenty. Thus the banqueting was resumed joyfully.

The meal done, Stoutmoron gave us quantities of large juicy pears.

"Here, my friends," he told us, "take these, I beg you. They are a singular variety; you will not find them elsewhere. No soil bears everything, you know: black ebony grows only in India, good incense comes but from Saba in southern Arabia, the red earth used by painters and apothecaries all originates in the Greek island of Lemnos. Similarly, this island is the only place to produce these fine pears. You may, if you care to, use the kernels in your nurseries at home."

"Have they a special name?" Pantagruel asked. "I find them excellent, their flavor is delicious. If you sliced them and put them to cook with a little wine and sugar, I'm sure they would prove to be most healthy fare, for sick and healthy alike."

"They have no other name than you have heard," said Stoutmoron. "We are the plain, downright people it pleased God to make us: we call figs, figs; plums, plums; and pears, pears."

"Upon my word," said Pantagruel, "when I reach home—which, please God! will be soon!—I shall set and graft some of them in my Touraine garden by the banks of the Loire. And they shall be known as Good-Christian pears, for I never beheld better Christians than you excellent Papimaniacs."

"I would consider it just as gracious of him," said Friar John, "if he gave us two or three cartloads of pretty wenches!"

"What would you do with them?" Stoutmoron inquired.

"They are a fruit I would stick and bleed, midway between the two big toes, with a certain sharp prodding-tool that works wonders. By this operation, we would graft upon them Good-Christian children. That breed would multiply in our country, where, unfortunately, we've none too many good Christians!"

"God's truth," cried Stoutmoron. "We will not do this: you would back them to the wall, fill their calyx tubes, crack their pipkins and, like as not, blight them. I know what a nose like yours means; at first sight, I can tell what sort of man you are. Alas, alas! my poor erring brother! Would you damn your soul? Our *Decretals* forbid it: I wish you knew them properly!"

"Patience!" said Friar John. "But, *si tu non vis dare, præsta quæsumus*, if Thou wilt not give, we beseech Thee to lend. . . . That is breviary matter. On that subject, I fear no mother's son in cap and gown, were he a crystalline—I mean a decretaline—doctor, with triple hood and supreme honors."

Dinner over, we took our leave of Stoutmoron and his good Papimaniacs, humbly thanking them for their hospitality. In return for their generosity, we promised them that, when we reached Rome, we would press their cause so effectually that the holy father would certainly visit them in person very soon.

We then boarded our ships. Pantagruel, as a mark of generosity and an acknowledgment of the sight of the pope's image, gave Stoutmoron nine bolts of double-frizzed cloth-of-gold, to be hung before the barred windows. The collection-box assigned for church repairs and upkeep, he filled with double crowns. To each of the girls who had waited upon us at the banquet, he presented nine hundred and fourteen angels (money under Charles VI and depicting the Annunciation), so that they might find husbands when the time were ripe.

LV

HOW PANTAGRUEL AT SEA HEARD VARIOUS THAWED WORDS

OUT at sea, we were banqueting, feasting, chatting, telling stories and passing the time away in pleasant discussions. Suddenly, Pantagruel rose to his feet, looked all around him, and said to us:

"Do you hear anything, friends? It seems to me I can hear men talking in the air. Yet I can see nobody. Listen!"

We strained our ears, sucking in the air as you would a fine oyster out of its shell; if there were voices or any other sounds, we must certainly hear them. Determined to miss nothing, some of us held our hands to our ears, as Antoninus Caracalla, Emperor of Rome and employer of spies. Nevertheless, we assured Pantagruel that we distinguished no voice. He insisted he could hear various voices, male and female. Presently, we also believed we, too, could make them out—or our ears were ringing. The more assiduously we listened, the better we discerned these voices. Now we could perceive the actual sounds of words. This frightened us greatly, and not without cause. It was terrible to see nothing, yet to hear voices of men, women, children and horses.

Panurge cried:

"God's belly, is this a devil's joke? We are lost! Let us flee! Our foes lie in ambush for us. Friar John, are you there, my friend; stay by me, I beg you. Have you your sword handy—that fine, fighting-tool of yours? Make sure it does not stick in the scabbard; you never polish it enough. We are lost! Listen: by God, those are guns, firing! Let us flee, let us flee! (I don't mean to flee by hand not afoot, as Brutus said after the battle of Pharsalus; I'll not flee by cowardly suicide.) Let us flee, I say, by sail and oar. Come, let us withdraw. I seem to lose all courage at sea; in cellars and elsewhere I have enough and to spare! I always say that, like the Militiaman of Bagnolet in the famous farce:

Danger is the sole thing I fear on earth.

No, friends, let us run no chance of getting our heads cracked. Let us take to our heels! About face, tack about, you whoreson! Would to God I were now in Quinquenais, even though I forfeited all chance of getting married. Let us flee! We are no match for them; they're ten to our one, I promise you. What's more, they are on their own dunghill; we don't know the lie of the country. They will surely kill us. Let us flee: we will not lose our honor. Demosthenes says that

He who fights and runs away
Shall live to fight another day.

At least, let us withdraw. Helm-a-lea, bring the main tack about, starboard, haul the bowlines! We're dead men now, unless we flee. Flee, by all the devils, flee!"

Pantagruel, hearing Panurge's outcry, asked:

"Who is that chicken-hearted blubberer? Who mentioned flight? Let us first find out who these people are: they may be friends, for all we know. I can discover no one yet, though I can see a hundred thousand miles around. Let us listen and wait."

Pantagruel then said he had read of a Pythagorean philosopher, named Petron, who believed that there were many worlds, contiguous and together forming an equilateral triangle: sixty on each of the three sides and one at each angle, making one hundred and eighty-three in all. In the centre was the dwelling of Truth, where dwelled words, ideas, copies and likenesses of all things past and future. Around them was the age then being lived. In certain years, at very great intervals, parts of these words, ideas, copies and likenesses would fall upon humankind like vapors, or like the dew falling upon Gideon's fleece. Thus they would be preserved for the future until the age was fulfilled.

Pantagruel also recalled that Aristotle had described Homer's words as fluttering, flying, moving and therefore living. Again, Antiphanes compared Plato's philosophy to words spoken in some arctic country, during a hard winter: no sooner spoken, they froze up and congealed in the chill air, without ever being heard. Indeed, his young lads could scarcely understand what Plato taught them, even when they were become old men.

"Now we must philosophize and search whether this might not chance to be the place where such words are thawed. How extraordinary if these sounds came from the head and lyre of Orpheus! After the Thracian women tore him to pieces, they tossed his head and lyre into the river Hebrus; these flowed down with the stream into the Pontian Sea, and floated together to the island of Lesbos. Out of his head, there came incessantly a lugubrious dirge, as though lamenting Orpheus' death. From the lyre, as the wind blew its strings, came a harmonious accompaniment to the dirge. Let us see if we cannot find them hereabouts!"

LVI

HOW AMONG THE THAWED WORDS PANTAGRUEL FOUND SOME THAT WERE GHOUL'S AND OTHERS GULES, BUT ALL OF THEM VERY STRANGE

"My Lord need have no fear," said the skipper. "We are on the edge of the Frozen Sea. Here, early last winter, was a great and bloody fight between the Arimaspians—the one-eyed race of the far north, mentioned by Herodotus—and the Nephelibates or cloud-walkers. The shouts of the warriors, the shrieks of the women, the thud of battleaxes, the clangor of armor and mail, the neighing of horses, and the whole tumult of battle froze in the air. Now that winter is over, with the warmth and serenity of the air, this din melts and becomes audible."

"By God, I believe it!" cried Panurge. "But why can we see nothing? I remember having read that, on the edge of the mountain where Moses received the Judaic law, the people actually saw voices."

"Hark, hark!" cried Pantagruel. "Here are some more that have not yet thawed out."

So saying, he threw on to the deck whole handfuls of frozen words. They looked like sugarplums of various colors. Some were *gules* or red, others *sinople* or green, others *azure* or blue, others *sable* or black, others *or* or gold. As we warmed them between our hands, they melted like snow; we could hear them clearly, but we did not understand them, for they were in barbaric idiom. A somewhat large one, warmed between Friar John's hands, popped like unslit chestnuts thrown on to a fire. We shuddered in alarm.

"Don't worry," the monk told us, "that was the report of a cannon!"

Panurge asked Pantagruel for more words; Pantagruel quoted Ovid's "*Verba dat omnis amans*, All lovers give words," which means that lovers are deceivers.

"Well then, sell me some, My Lord," Panurge begged.

"To sell words is a lawyer's job," Pantagruel replied. "I would rather sell you silence, at a higher price, just as Demosthenes sold it with his *argentangina*."

"What is an *argentangina*?" somebody asked.

Pantagruel explained how Demosthenes, bribed by the Milesians not to speak against them, appeared in the senate with muffled throat, explaining that he had *angina* or quinsy. Somebody shouted: "That's *argentangina* or money-quinsy."

Nevertheless, Pantagruel threw three or four fistfuls of words on deck. I saw some very cutting ones and some quite bloody. The skipper informed us that the latter sometimes returned to their place of origin, but found the throat that had uttered them was slit. There were also horrible words and others, most unpleasant to behold; when they melted we heard:

"Hink, hink, hink, hink, ticketty tock, briddety broddety, froofroo-froo, bubbub boo, boobeddy-bood, boo-boo-boo-boo-boo; track-track tracketty-track, trr, trr, trr, trrrrrrr! Haw-haw-haw-wheeeeee! gog-atty-gog, gog, gog, magog!"

There were many other barbaric sounds which, the skipper told us, represented the uproar made by the clash of arms and the neighing of horses. Other loud words, thawing, rang like bugles and trumpets, whistled like fifes, rolled like drums. They afforded us much entertainment.

I would have been glad to preserve some of the ghouls' gules words in oil, as ice and snow are stored, and between clean straw. But Pantagruel would not allow it. It was folly, he argued, to hoard a commodity we were never short of; all good, jovial Pantagruelists always had plenty of gullmaking words in their gullets.

Panurge annoyed Friar John somewhat and had the monk sulking, for he took him at his word, when Friar John was in a brown study. Friar John threatened to make Panurge repent as Guillaume Jousseaume did in the farce of *Maître Pierre Pathelin*. (You remember, Jousseaume the draper took the merry Pathelin at his word—that is, on credit—sold him some cloth and was sorry ever after.) More, if Panurge ever married, Friar John vowed he would take him by the horns like a bull (or a calf!) because Panurge had taken him, Friar John, at his word like a man. The monk quoted:

Verba ligant homines, taurorum cornua funes.

Words bind men, ropes bind the horns of bulls.

Panurge clicked his tongue derisively, then:

"Would to God I had the word of the Holy Bottle here and now," he said, "so we would not have to continue our travels."

LVII

HOW PANTAGRUEL VISITED THE ABODE OF MASTER GASTER, OTHERWISE BELLY, THE FIRST MASTER OF ARTS IN THE WORLD

THAT day, Pantagruel went ashore on an island which, for its situation and its governor, may be called peerless. On all sides, the approach was rocky, steep, barren, dangerous of access, unpleasant to the eye, harsh to the feet.

It was almost as forbidding as the Mont-Aiguille or Needle Peak in Dauphiné, which resembles a toadstool, and which no one, in the memory of man, ever scaled—except Jean Doyac, who led the artillery of Charles VIII over the Alps into Italy. This engineer, reaching the top thanks to his marvellous engines, found an old goat there. He wondered how it had managed to get up: somebody suggested that an eagle or a huge horn owl had carried it up when it was but a kid, that it had got away from the bird of prey and hidden in the bushes.

Having landed, we had a difficult time of it surmounting the obstacles at the entrance; straining and sweating, eventually we came to the mountain-top. I found it so fertile, healthy and pleasant that I thought I must be in the true garden of Eden or earthly paradise, about the exact location of which our good theologians labor and dispute. Pantagruel, however, assured us, subject to contradiction by men of sounder judgment, that here was the dwelling of Arete or Virtue, as described by Hesiod.

The ruler of the place was Master Gaster or Belly, the first Master of Arts in the world. Do you believe, as Cicero writes, that fire is the great Master of Arts, i. e. the source of everything? If so, you are utterly wrong; Cicero himself never believed it; he was merely quoting Heraclitus. Do you consider, with the ancient Druids (according to Pliny, Cicero and Cæsar), that Mercury was the earliest discoverer of the arts? If so, you are committing a gross error. The sentence of the satirist Persius, which affirms Master Gaster to be master of all arts, is unimpeachable truth.

With him, old lady Penia, or Poverty, resided peacefully; she was the mother of the nine muses. Of yore, by Porus, Lord of Plenty, she begat Love, that noble child, the mediator of heaven and earth; Plato, in his *Symposium*, relates the circumstance at length.

We had all to pay homage, swear allegiance and do honor to this mighty sovereign, for he is imperious, severe, blunt, hard, difficult and inflexible. He cannot be made to believe anything he will not. Persuasion and remonstrance are unavailing; he will not listen. The Egyptians were wont to say that Harpocrates, son of Isis and Osiris and god of silence (the Greeks called him Sigalion), was astomous or mouthless. So Gaster was created earless, like Jupiter's image in Candia or Crete.

He only speaks by signs. But let him make them, and everyone observes them more rapidly than the edicts of prætors or the decrees of kings; he does not admit of the slightest delay or postponement in the execution of his orders. When the lion roars, every beast within earshot, for miles around, shudders. I have seen it written; it is true; I have beheld it, I assure you that, at Master Gaster's command, all heaven trembles and all earth quakes. His orders are: do this or die.

The skipper told us of a rebellion fomented against Gaster by the whole kingdom of the Somates or Body-members, much as, in Æsop's fable, the various members rebelled against the belly. They plotted and conspired to throw off his yoke. But they very soon found out their mistake, repented and humbly returned to his service. Otherwise they would have died of starvation.

In whatever company he is, none dare dispute Gaster's superiority and precedence. He walks first, before kings, emperors and even the pope. At the council of Basle, an eighteen-year meeting notorious for squabbles about precedence, Gaster was unquestionably the leader. None but labors to serve him, none but bustles to do him reverence. As a reward, he confers as a benefit upon mankind the invention of all arts, machines, trades, engines and crafts. To the very brute beasts, he teaches manners contrary to their nature. Out of jays, parrots and starlings, he makes poets; out of magpies, he makes bards; he teaches birds to utter human language, to speak and to sing. And all for the sake of their guts. Ay, hunger is the best teacher in the world!

Eagles, falcons, gerfalcons, sakers, lanners, goshawks, sparhawks, haggards, merlins, peregrines, hobbies, luggers—all manner of wild and predatory birds—he tames and trains. He may abandon to them the freedom of the skies, if he sees fit; he may let them fly high as they wish, keeping them suspended, floating, planing, straying, hovering about him, courting him aloft above the clouds. Then, suddenly, he makes them swoop down from the firmament—and all for the sake of their guts.

The elephant, the lion, the rhinoceros, the bear, the horse, the dog —these he teaches to dance, prance, vault, fight, swim, hide, fetch and carry. And all for the sake of their guts.

Saltwater and freshwater fish, whales and monsters of the main, he brings forth out of the unfathomable deep; he drives wolves out of the woods, bears out from the rocks, foxes out of their holes, snakes out of the ground. All for the sake of their guts.

In a word, his fury is so extreme that he devours man and beast.

This was proved by the Vascones or Basques, at Calagurris on the Ebro, when Sertorius repulsed Q. Metellus . . . it was proved when Hannibal besieged Saguntum . . . it was proved when the Romans starved out the Jews . . . it was proved by six hundred other examples I forbear to cite. . . .

And all for the sake of their guts!

When Penia, or Poverty, Gaster's regent, sets out anywhere, no matter where she goes, senates adjourn, statutes are repealed, laws go by the board. She is subject to no ordinance, she is exempt from all decrees. Everywhere, people shun her, preferring to risk the dangers of sea, fire, mountain or abyss, than seizure by this dread goddess.

LVIII

HOW PANTAGRUEL MET THE DETESTABLE ENGASTRI-MYTHES, OR VENTRILOQUISTS, AND GASTROLATERS, OR STOMACH-WORSHIPPERS, AT THE COURT OF GASTER, MASTER OF ARTS

At the court of that great master of ingenuity, Pantagruel noticed two kinds of troublesome and officious servants: the Engastrimythes or ventriloquists, and the Gastrolaters or stomach-worshippers. Both, he detested cordially.

The Engastrimythes claimed descent from the ancient race of Eurycles; they based their claim on Aristophanes' comedy, *The Wasps*. (Perhaps you recall how Aristophanes tells that, by anonymously helping fellow-authors, he was comparable to Eurycles, the famous Athenian ventriloquent soothsayer, who placed many a jest on another's lips.) Thus the Engastrimythes were called Euryclians, as Plato observed in his *Sophist* and Plutarch in his *Of the Cessation of Oracles*. In the holy *Decrees*, drawn up by Gratian in the twelfth century, and ever since the basis of canon law, they were referred to as "ventriloqui." Hippocrates, in his fifth book, *Of Epidemics*, describes them in the Ionic idiom as "men who speak from the belly." Sophocles calls them "sternomantes" or soothsayers who practice through the chest. They were prophets, enchanters and swindlers of the common people, as, artfully they appeared to answer questions from the belly, rather than from the mouth.

A typical Engastrimythe came to light in the year of our Lord 1513. Her name was Jacoba Rodogina; she was an Italian of mean extraction. Many a prince and lord this side of the Alps, his curiosity aroused, summoned her to perform for him; innumerable citizens of Ferrara, and elsewhere, including ourselves, heard her often. From her belly issued the voice of the evil spirit. It was pitched very low, to be sure; it was weak, slight and tremulous. But it was clearly articulated, distinct and intelligible. In order to remove all doubt and establish the authenticity of her performance, her consultants used to strip her naked, and stop up her mouth and her nose. The fiend who used her as medium was called Cincinnatulo or Curlpate; delighted, when called by name, he never failed to respond. If questioned on things past or present, he replied so pertinently that his audience was dumbfounded. Did somebody ask him about the future? Invariably reality seemed to escape him; he told untruths, he flatly confessed his ignorance. In lieu of a reply, he would utter a rousing fart or mutter some unintelligible barbarous gibberish.

So much for the first class of servant that riled Pantagruel. The second class consisted of Gastrolaters or bellyworshippers. They kept their own company in groups and cliques. Some were gay, wanton, downy milksops. Others were solemn, stern, grim, dour; utterly idle, working at nothing, they formed a useless weight and burden on earth, to quote Hesiod. In so far as we could judge, what they most feared was to offend or reduce their bellies. They wore disguises and clothing so odd as to amuse anyone who saw them.

You know well that not a few ancient philosophers and sages declare that the skill of Nature is wonderful. She appears to have taken special delight in moulding seashells of a form, color and design inimitable in art. I swear that in the vestments of these holy bellyworshippers, with their shell-shaped hoods and conchlike frocks, we saw no less differentiation and diversity. Gaster, they had as their supreme god; they adored him like God; they sacrificed to him as to a god omnipotent; they had no other gods but him; they served and loved him above all other things; they honored him.

The holy apostle Paul said, in his *Epistle to the Philippians*, III: "For many walk, of whom I have told you often, and now tell you even weeping, that they are the enemies of the cross of Christ: whose end is destruction, whose God is their belly." His words fit these Gastrolaters like so many gloves.

Pantagruel compared them to the Cyclops Polyphemus, who is made to say by Euripides:

"I sacrifice to myself alone, not to the gods. This, my belly, is the greatest of all gods."

LIX

OF THE ABSURD STATUE CALLED MANDUCUS AND OF THE SACRIFICES OFFERED UP BY THE GASTROLATERS TO THEIR VENTRIPOTENT GOD

WE were observing the faces and gestures of those craven, great-gullied Gastrolaters when, to our amazement, we heard a carillon. At once, they drew up in rank and file, each according to his office, degree and seniority. In this formation, they advanced towards Master Gaster. Their leader was a fat, potbellied youth; he wore a long, richly gilt staff, with, at its end, an ill-carved, roughly bedaubed statue. Plautus, Juvenal and Pompeius Festus have described it; at Lyons, in Carnival time, it is called Gnawcrust. The Gastrolaters called it Manducus.

A monstrous, hideous, ridiculous figure it was, too, calculated to terrify children, equipped with eyes larger than its belly, topped by a head larger than the rest of its body. Its jaws wide, broad, and alarming, were lined with teeth which, by means of a small wire within the hollow gold staff, were made to rattle together as dreadfully as those of St. Clement's dragon in the processions at Metz on Rogation days.

Drawing close to the Gastrolaters, I noticed that they were followed by cohorts of fat varlets, bearing baskets, hampers, dishes, bags, pots and kettles. Manducus in the lead, they advanced, singing God knows what *dithyrambics* (wild songs), *cræpalcomes* (chants of drunken revelry) and *epœnons* (canticles of praise). Opening their baskets and pots, they offered up to their god all manner of gifts, as listed below.

White hippocras or spiced wine, with toasts and sippets . . . plain white bread and bread of the snowiest dough . . . *carbonados* or grilled meats of six different varieties . . . *Couscous*, an Arabian stew . . . haslets, pluck and fry . . . fricassées of nine sorts . . . bread and dripping, bread and cheese . . . gravy soup, hotchpotch and potroast . . . shortbread and household loaf . . . *cabirotado* or grilled viands . . . cold loins of veal, spiced with ginger, meat pies and broths flavored with bay leaves . . . marrowbones of beef with cabbage . . . salmagundi, which is a mixed dish of chopped meat and pickled herring, with oil, vinegar, pepper and onions.

(Drink after drink, eternally, it seemed, provided the transition from course to course. First came a brisk, tartish white wine; next claret; then a dry red wine, iced to polar temperature and served in great silver cups.)

Next came sausages, caparisoned with choice mustard, chitterlings, smoked oxtongue, salted meats of various sorts, pork's back with peas, pig's haslets, blood sausages, brain sausages, Bolognas, hams, boars' heads, dried venison with turnips, chicken livers on the spit, olives-in-oil.

(These dishes were accompanied by sempiternal bibbage.)

Next, they poured into his maw the following fare: shoulder of mutton with garlic, meat pies with hot sauce, pork chops with onion sauce, roast capons basted in their own dripping, spring capons . . . goose, kid, fawn and deer, hare and leveret, partridge and choice young partridges, pheasant and delicate young pheasants, peacock and toothsome young peacocks . . . stork and storklet, woodcock, snipe, ortolan, turkey; gobbler, hen and pullet . . . ringdove, wood pigeon, pork with wine sauce, duck with onion sauce, blackbird, rail, heron and excellent young herons, bustard and wild turkey, fig-

pecker or *beccafico*, an Italian warbler fed on sweet fruits . . .
young guinea hen, plover, goose and gosling, rockdove, wild duck,
mavis and flamingo. . . .

(To these dishes were added vast quantities of vinegar.)

Then, they fed Gaster pies and pasties of venison, lark, dormouse,
roebuck, pigeon, chamois, capon and bacon . . . hogsfeet in lard,
fried piecrust, stuffed capons, cheese and juicy peaches . . . artichoke, sea grouse, crier, crane, egret, teal, diver and loon, bittern
and stakedriver, curlew, wood duck, waterhen with leeks, hedgehog,
kid, shoulder of mutton with caper sauce . . . beef royal, breast of
veal, boiled chicken and stuffed capon with blancmange, pullet and
pullen, rabbit and cony, waterfowl, cormorant, francolin, ringdove,
cottontail, porcupine, rail. . . .

Next, they filled him with pastries, including cream tarts, fruit
squares, sweet biscuits, sugar plums, fritters, tarts of sixteen varieties,
waffles, pancakes, quince rolls, curds and cream, whipped cream, preserved myrobalans or prunes, and jellies.

(With, of course, red and pale hippocras to wash them down.)

And, finally, seventy-eight species of dry and liquid preserves and
jams, sweetmeats of one hundred different colors, cream cakes and
light confections.

(Vinegar followed, for fear of quinsy, and toasts, to scour the
teeth.)

LX

HOW, ON THE FAST DAYS IN-
TERLARDED IN THE CALEN-
DAR, THE GASTROLATERS
SACRIFICED TO THEIR GOD

PANTAGRUEL was vexed at this rabble of kitchen-sacrificiants and
their abundant offerings. He would have left, had not Epistemon
begged him to wait for the end of the farce.

"What," Pantagruel demanded, "do these scoundrels offer their
ventripotent deity on days of fasting?"

"I will tell you, My Lord," the skipper volunteered. And he proceeded to enumerate their menu.

For the first course, this god received caviar, *botargos* (relish of salted mullet roes), fresh butter, pea soup, spinach, fresh roe herring, dried herring, sardines, anchovy, tuna fish, cauliflower in olive oil, salted beans. Also one hundred kinds of salad, including cress, barley, and bishop's ballocks or celandine . . . Judas ear or Jew's ear, an edible fungus growing at the foot of old elders . . . asparagus, woodbine and a host of others. . . . Also smoked salmon, pickled eel, and oysters on the half-shell.

(At this point Gaster must needs drink or the devil would carry him off. His servants did not fail to supply the need.)

Drinking over, Gaster received lamprey with sweet wine sauce, barbel and barbelfry, sturgeon, whale, mackerel, maidenfish or shad, plaice, raw oysters, cockles, lobsters, smelt, gurnard, trout, whitefish, goby, octopus, dab, flounder, cuttlefish, bream and gudgeon . . . brill, turbot, carp, pike, jack, dogfish, searobin, seaurchin and seapoacher . . . lordfish, which fattens without moving from its place . . . *imperator* or swordfish; angelfish, a kind of shark . . . lamprey, sturgeon, pickerel, morays, tortoise, turtle and serpent, *i.e.* forest-eel. . . .

Also cutlass fish, sea goose or dolphin, sole, flatfish, mussels, lobster, shrimps, dace, ablet, tench, grayling, haddock, cuttlefish . . . red charr, tuna, gudgeon, bleak, crawfish, brill, halibut, devilfish, garpike, congers . . . seabass, barfish, salmon, bream, cod, hake, darb, eels, perch, sterlet, crabfish, crawlabottoms, snails and frogs. . . .

(This food devoured, Gaster found himself face to face with death, unless something was done. His followers did the needful.)

Then, they sacrificed to him salted forkbeards, stockfish . . . eggs fried, poached, boiled, *en cocotte*, broiled, steamed, tossed in the chimney and tarred-and-feathered . . . more cod . . . ray, skate, squid and hausen, a variety of Caspian sturgeon, at least one yard long. . . .

(In order to speed and favor the digestion of these dishes, Gaster was provided with ample belly-soaking.)

The meal ended with rice pudding, millet shape, gruel porridge, corn pudding, butterball trifle, pistachio fool (etymologically, *fistacii* or small nuts), figs, raisins, edible seaweed, prunes, dates, walnuts and hazelnuts, parsnips and artichokes. . . .

(This fare was topped off with a perpetuity of tipple.)

"Believe me," the skipper came to a climax, "this god of theirs, Gaster, is more fittingly, abundantly and honorably served in his sacrifices than was the idol Heliogabalus set up of himself, or even the image of Bel and the Dragon—which, in Babylon under King Balthazar, received twelve measures of fine flour, forty sheep and six vessels of wine. Yet Gaster insists that he is no god, but rather a poor, base, miserable creature!"

The skipper then cited King Antigonus, first of the name. One Hermodotus, a poet, called His Majesty a sunborn divinity.

"My *lasanophore* would not agree," the monarch replied.

(Which is not strange, considering that *lasanon* means a bedpan, and *lasanophore*, the officer charged to administer it.)

Thus Gaster sent his mad votaries to his stool to see, examine, meditate upon, discuss and ponder the divinity to be extracted from his excretocrapturdivasation.

LXI

HOW GASTER INVENTED MISCELLANEOUS MEANS OF ACQUIRING AND PRESERVING GRAIN

When those gastrolatrous devils withdrew, Pantagruel carefully studied the system of the famous Gaster, our first Master of Arts. By natural law, as you well know, bread and its corollaries were assigned him for food and nourishment. Besides this heavenly blessing, he was so favored as never to lack means of acquiring and preserving bread.

First, Gaster invented the arts of the blacksmith and farmer, to cultivate earth and grow grain in it . . . next, weapons and the science of warfare, to defend that grain . . . next medicine, astronomy and mathematics, to safeguard that grain for several centuries against the wrath of the elements, the spoliation of beasts, the robbery of brigands. . . . He invented windmills, watermills, handmills, and a thousand other mechanical devices to crush his grain and reduce it to flour . . . leaven to make the dough ferment . . . salt to lend it savor (for he realized that nothing on earth bred more diseases in man than the use of heavy, unleavened bread) . . . fire to bake it . . . dials and clocks to time its baking. . . .

Was grain wanting in a certain region? Gaster at once discovered ways and means of transporting it from one country to another. By a stroke of genius, he bred two animals of different species, the ass and the mare, thus producing a third, the mule; faced with the most gruelling labor, this new beast proved more powerful, more resistant and longer lived than its sire or dam. To convey his grain with greater ease, he devised carts and wagons. Did river or sea stand in his way? To the amazement of the elements, he fashioned boats, galleys and ships, to bear and deliver grain across oceans, lakes and streams from remote, barbarous, untravelled and far distant lands.

In certain years, after he had tilled his land, his crop was an utter loss; it perished underground, because there had been no rain in due season. Other years, there had been too much rain, and his grain rotted. Still other years, it might be spoiled by hail, beaten down by the wind or destroyed by storms. Yet long before our coming upon earth, Gaster discovered a way to bring down rain from heaven: it consisted merely in cutting a certain grass, quite common in the fields, yet known to but few people. He showed us several stalks. I took it to be the plant described by Pausanias.

(The latter tells us that in time of drought, a priest of Jupiter had but to dip a single branch into the Agnonian fount, on Mount Lycæus in Arcadian Greece, and vapors rose up, which gathered into thick clouds, which dissolved into rain, which moistened the whole countryside!)

Gaster also founded a mode of arresting rainfall in mid-air, keeping it suspended there, then diverting it into the sea; of annihilating hail; of suppressing the winds, and of checking storms, as the Methanians of Trœzenia, in Greece, were wont to do. (They used to carry a white rooster around their vines, then bury it, as a charm against winds.)

Further misfortunes arose. Brigands and thieves pilfered grain and bread from his fields; accordingly, Gaster evolved the science of building cities, forts and castles to store and preserve his grain securely. Presently, none was to be found in the fields: it was all hoarded in cities, forts and castles, with the inhabitants watching and guarding it more carefully than ever the three sisters and the dragon Ladon protected the golden apples of the Hesperides. So Gaster hit upon a means of storming and demolishing stronghold or citadel by war-machines and battle-engines, including battering-rams, *ballistas* that hurled great stones, and catapults. The plans of these he showed us: they were none too clearly grasped by engineers, builders and disciples of M. Vitruvius Pollio, the celebrated Roman architect. Master Philibert de l'Orme, superintendent of architecture for King Megistus ("the very great") confessed as much to us.

More recently, since the subtle cunning or cunning subtlety of the fortifiers rendered these armaments unavailing, Gaster invented cannons, serpentines, culverins, mortars, basilisks, weighing more than huge anvils. These belched forth balls of iron, lead and bronze, thanks to a horrific powder, which nonplussed Nature herself, and forced her to recognize the supremacy of Art.

Philostratus tells us of a people called the Oxydraces, who dwelled between the Hyphasis or Bea (a river rising in the Himalayas) and the Ganges. Protected by thunder, lightning, hail and storm, they could slay and vanquish their enemies in the field. But Gaster's latest inventions made these instruments of destruction obsolete and childish. A single shot from a modern cannon proves more dreadful, more horrible, more diabolical than a hundred thunderbolts; it can maim, shatter and kill more men than do a hundred thunderbolts; it can cause greater consternation and inflict destruction direr than do a hundred thunderbolts.

LXII

HOW GASTER FOUND A MEANS TO AVOID BEING WOUNDED OR TOUCHED BY CANNON BALLS

HAVING retired with his grain inside strongholds, Gaster was frequently attacked by his enemies; those thrice-evil and infernal machines razed his fortresses; titanic ruffians seized his grain, and snatched the bread out of his mouth. So he hit upon a scheme that maintained his walls, bastions, ramparts and battlements from such cannonades. The shots never struck; they remained suspended in air, short of their mark; or, if they hit, they did no damage to the besieged or to their bulwarks. Long ago, he perfected his defense against this particular hazard; he gave us a demonstration of it. Later Fronton—Julius Sextus Frontinus, contemporary of Domitian and author of the *Stratagematica*—followed these principles of Gaster's. To-day, their application is a common pastime and harmless sport among the Thélèmites.

I shall tell you how he managed it. And I shall ask you, in the future, to be less sceptical about the experiment Plutarch vouches for. You remember it? Suppose a herd of goats to be rushing off at top speed; you need but place a sprig of *eryngium* or sea holly in the mouth of the hindmost, and the whole herd will come to a stop. (Need I add that *eryngium* is a powerful aphrodisiac?)

As for Gaster, he had a bronze cannon loaded with the right amount of gunpowder, which was carefully compounded, purged of its sulphur and mixed, in given proportions, with superfine camphor. Over it, he put into the cannon a well-turned ball, with twenty-four iron pellets, some round, some pear-shaped, some oval. Ordering a page of his to stand sixty paces away, Gaster took careful aim at the fellow, as if to hit him in the belly. Halfway between the cannon and the page, in a straight line, Gaster hung a rope to a wooden gallows; this rope held suspended a very large siderite or ironlike stone. (Such stones, also known as herculeans, were found of old on Mount Ida, in Phrygia, by one Magnes, so Nicander tells us. We commonly call them loadstones or magnets.)

Gaster put a flame to the touch-hole, thus setting fire to the powder. This at once exploded, projecting the ball and pellets with incredible force out of the cannon's muzzle, so that air might penetrate into its chamber. Had this not occurred, the cannon's chamber would have been a vacuum. Now nature will not tolerate a vacuum: the machine of the universe—earth, sea, sky and air—would return to primitive chaos, before it admitted the slightest void. The ball and pellets, thus violently discharged, seemed to spell the page's doom. But their celerity waned as they neared the loadstone; they remained suspended, hovering and floating around it. Not one, however fiercely propelled, passed beyond it to reach the page.

Such was not the limit of Gaster's ingenuity. By a system he discovered, bullets were made to fly backwards, recoiling upon their senders with their original fury, danger and range.

In point of fact, why should this feat be difficult for Gaster? Does not the herb *ethiopis*, according to Pliny, open any lock whatever? Does not the fish *echineis* (*remora* or sucking fish), though the wind blow to a gale, stop, in their course, the most powerful ships that sail the seas? Does not its flesh, preserved in salt, draw gold out of the deepest well you could ever sound? Do not Democritus and Theophrastus cite an herb which need but touch the most deeply imbedded wedge, to extract it from the hardest wood obtainable? This same herb is used by Pliny's *pici martii* (we call them woodpeckers) to break through the iron wedges we use to stop up the holes they have so industriously bored and dug into the trunks of sturdy trees.

Stags and hinds may be grievously wounded by dart, arrow and bolt. What happens if they come upon the herb called dittany, so common in Candia, or Crete? Doubtless you recall how Juturna, sister of Turnus, wounded Æneas in the left thigh and how Venus cured her well-beloved son? Let your stags and hinds eat a little dittany, and at once, the arrows fall off their bodies, the wounds heal miraculously.

Does lightning ever strike laurels, figtrees, sea calves or seals? No—because one breath of air emerging out of them can still thunderbolts!

Mad elephants are restored to sanity if they but sight a ram . . . wild, raving bulls suddenly stop dead, as though cramped, growing quite docile if they draw near a *caprificus* or wild figtree . . . the venomous rage of vipers collapses if you touch them with a bough of birch. . . .

Does not Euphorian tell us that, before Juno's temple was built in the island of Samos, he saw beasts there called *neades*, at whose mere voices earth sank into chasms and abysses? Do not the ancient sages, as reported by Theophrastus, declare that elders, growing where no cock crows, prove better and more sonorous material for the making of flutes? It is as if chanticleer's song dulled, deadened and ruined elderwood. Yet that same song is said to startle and daze the lion, a most powerful and tenacious animal.

To be sure, certain critics assign this reference to the wild elder, which grows out of earshot of the loudest cock in town or village. Certainly, as timber for flutes and musical instruments, the wild elder is preferable to the domestic variety you find by cottage and farmhouse.

Others, however, have given the passage a higher sense; they take it not literally, but allegorically. When we wish to define a solitary, unfrequented place, do we not say that no cock was ever heard to crow there? Accordingly, the nobler interpretation is that wise, studious men should not stoop to trivial and vulgar music, but rather to music that is celestial, divine, abstract, borne from more distant regions, where the crowing of cocks is unknown.

The Pythagoreans held that Mercury's statue should not be made at random from any sort of wood, because God must be worshipped not vulgarly, but in a chosen, devout form.

LXIII

HOW PANTAGRUEL FELL ASLEEP NEAR THE ISLE OF CHANEPH, OR HYPOCRISY ISLAND, AND HOW HE WAS SET VARIOUS PROBLEMS WHEN HE AWAKENED

ON the following day, as we pursued our route amid various discussions, we sailed close to the island of Chaneph (in Hebrew "Hypocrisy"). Pantagruel's vessel could not reach it, because the wind failed us and we were becalmed. We tacked about from starboard to port and port to starboard; we could make no headway, though we added studding sails on extra yards and booms. We simply hung about deck, moping, oppressed, bored and metagrobolized, none breathing a word to the other.

Pantagruel lay slumbering on a stool, close to the upper cabin, a copy of Heliodorus in his hand. Our old pedagogues used to say that a lesson learned by book was better than a person learned by heart; Pantagruel invariably slept better by book than by heart.

Epistemon was studying his astrolabe to find out what latitude we were in . . . Friar John had adjourned to the cookhouse, there to discover, by the ascendant of the spits and the horoscope of the stews, what time of day it might be . . . Panurge, a stalk of pantagruelion or hemp between his lips, was blowing bubbles and making a potful of water seethe and foam . . . Gymnastes was cutting himself toothpicks out of lentisk or mastic wood . . . Ponocrates napped and daydreamed, scratching his head with one finger, and tickling himself to make himself laugh . . . Carpalim, out of the shell of a walnut, was making a small, dainty, beautifully proportioned windmill, cutting the arms out of an elder board . . . Eusthenes, astride a huge cannon, was strumming on it with his fingers, as on a spinet . . . Rhizotomos was fashioning a velvet purse out of the shell of a moor-tortoise or mole . . . Xenomanes was repairing an old lantern with the leather straps used on hawks in falconry . . . the skipper was pulling crows out of his crew's nostrils, which is a crude old expression for getting the truth out of someone. . . .

Emerging at last from the forecastle, Friar John noticed that Pantagruel was awake. Breathing the oppressive silence, the monk, in a loud voice and with much cheer, asked Pantagruel how to raise fair weather—a phrase which means to feast heartily . . . Panurge seconded the motion, demanding a cure for ennui . . . Epistemon suported them, craving to be told how to bepiddle himself with merriment, when he had no wish to be merry or water to make . . . Gymnastes, rising to his feet, requested a remedy for dizziness . . . Ponocrates, rubbing his forehead and wagging his ears, begged to be informed how to avoid dogsleep. . . .

"Hold on, there!" cried Pantagruel. "The wise Peripatetic philosophers ruled and taught us that all questions, doubts and problems proposed for solution should be stated clearly and intelligently. You say 'dogsleep,' Ponocrates. What do you mean?"

"Dogsleep," Ponocrates defined, "is to sleep with empty belly in the noonday sun—just like dogs!"

Rhizotomos, huddled on the poop deck, raised his head and, yawning cavernously, set every one else, by natural sympathy, doing likewise.

"What specific can you suggest against gaping and yawning?" he begged.

Xenomanes, limp as a lump of lamprey after his lamp lumpering, interrogated Pantagruel on how to balance and poise the bagpipe of the stomach in such a way that it would not incline to either side . . . Carpalim, twirling his diminutive windmill, sought to know how many motions must be felt in Nature before a person might be properly termed hungry . . . Eusthenes, hearing their talk, came to the poop and, from the capstan, called out:

"Why is a hungry man bitten by a hungry snake, in greater danger of death than a well-fed man, bitten by a gorged snake? (Aristotle is my authority.) Again, why is a hungry man's spittle poisonous to serpents and vipers? (Pliny vouches it!)"

Pantagruel sighed.

"Gentlemen," he said, "a single solution will serve to settle all the doubts and questions you have propounded; a single medicine will cure all the symptoms and phenomena you have exposed. My answer will be brief: I shall not weary you with pedantic oratory or long-winded periphrase. The hungry belly has no ears to hear, runs the rune; fair words make no meal. You shall be satisfied, your doubts resolved and your minds at ease through signs, gestures and facts."

Pantagruel quoted, in illustration, from Livy's account of Tarquin the Proud, the last king of Rome, who communicated with his son, Sextus Tarquinius, by means of such signs. Sextus was among the Gabini; he has sent to his father, asking how he should subjugate that people and reduce it to perfect obedience. Tarquin, suspecting the messenger's loyalty, made no answer. But he took the fellow into his private garden and, in his presence, under his very eyes, lopped off the heads of the tallest poppies with his sword. The messenger returned to Sextus with no oral answer; he could but tell his master what he had seen Tarquin do. Sextus readily understood his father's signs: he must behead the leading citizens, in order to keep the rest of the population dutiful and obedient.

"So I shall solve your problems by a sign," Pantagruel concluded.

A short silence followed. Then Pantagruel pulled the string of a small bell. Friar John dashed off to the kitchen.

LXIV

HOW PANTAGRUEL GAVE NO ANSWER TO THE PROBLEMS PROPOUNDED

"What kind of people live in that island of bitches?" Pantagruel asked. Xenomanes replied:

"They are all hypocrites, unholywaterswallowers and paternoster-maunderers . . . smoothcats, chapletjugglers and sham-Abrahams

. . . wretched rogues who, like the anchorite of Lormont, between Blaye, on the Gironde, and Bordeaux, live wholly on the alms given them by passers-by. . . ."

"I cannot see myself there, I swear," said Panurge. "If you catch me landing, let the devil blow up my cackpipe. Hypocrites, eremites, pussyfooters, holier-than-thous, away with you, by Satan and all his legions! I have not forgotten those sleek pilgrims bound for the council of Chesil. (Chesil means star of tempests in Hebrew; you remember the storm we encountered when we left them. Oh, that Beelzebub and Ashtaroth had sent them to a council presided by Proserpine in hell! We would have suffered less devilish hurricanes!) Listen to me, friend dear as my belly, dear Corporal Xenomanes, tell me, please: are these dissemblers, humbugs and shufflers virgin or married? Do they exist in the feminine gender? Could a man scour, with pounder and holystone, the hole in the holy of holies of these wholly holier-than-thou females?"

"Upon my word, that's a pointed, fine question!" observed Pantagruel.

"Ay, certainly," Xenomanes answered. "You will find plenty of beautiful, hardworking, happy hypocritesses, smoothpussies, hermitesses and women of deep piety. They reproduce in their own image, too, all manner of humbuglets, sham-Abrahamkins, hermiticules and minor cockatrices."

"To hell with them," bawled Friar John. "You know the proverb: A young whore, an old saint. Well, it's no less authentic to say: A young hermit, an old devil."

"True, true," said Xenomanes. "Without such multiplication of progeny, Hypocrisy Island had long ago been deserted and desolate."

Pantagruel dispatched the pinnace ashore, with Gymnastes and a gift of seventy-eight thousand fine half-crowns, minted of imaginary gold by nonexistent coiners in Nevernever Land. Then:

"What time is it?" he asked.

"Past nine," Epistemon told him.

"That is the best time for dinner," said Pantagruel. "The sacred line, so celebrated by Aristophanes in his comedy the *Ecclesiazusœ* or *Women in Parliament*, is at hand: now the shadow is decempedal or falling on the tenth point of the dial!"

He told how of yore, among the Persians, only the kings were forced to dine at a certain hour; all others might use their bellies and appetites for clocks.

So, in Platus, a certain parasite complained bitterly of his hatred for the inventors of hourglasses and dials: they were, he said, notoriously less reliable than the human stomach.

Diogenes, too, might be cited in this instance. When asked at what time a man should eat, he replied:

"The rich man, when he is hungry; the poor, when he has food."

Physicians gauged the canonical hour more accurately:

> *Get up at five, have lunch at nine,*
> *Supper at five, retire at nine.*
> *And you will live to ninety-nine!*

There was even a famous astrologer to the Egyptian king, who affirmed that any one following his régime could live to one hundred and twenty-four years of age. His name was Petosirus. But—

At this point, Pantagruel was interrupted by the entrance of his belly-officers, who set up tables and sideboards; laid fresh, white, sweet-smelling cloths; put down napkins, plates, saltcellars, tankards, flagons, cups, goblets, bowls and large vessels. Friar John, with, in his wake, the stewards, footmen, butlers, cupbearers, carvers, servers, caterers and minor flunkies, brought on four tremendous ham pies, that looked for all the world like the four bastions of the city of Turin.

God's truth, how the company fell to and made merry!

They had not reached the dessert, when a northwester began to swell their mainsail, mizzen and foresail—for which they sang canticles of praise to the Almighty in heaven.

When dessert was served, Pantagruel asked:

"Now friends, tell me, are your doubts fully settled or not?"

"I've stopped yawning, praise God!" said Rhizotomos.

"My dogsleep is over!" Ponocrates chimed in.

"I'm not in the least dizzy now," Gymnastes attested.

"I'm not hungry," said Eusthenes. "Thus, for the whole span of this blessed day, my spittle will in no wise endanger asps . . . *amphisbæna* (those fabulous serpents with heads at either end) . . .

anerudutes, abedessimons, alhartafs, ammobates, apimaos, alhatra-bans, aractes . . . *asteria* (the starfish family) . . . *alcharates* . . . *argas* (those venomous worms that attack beast and man) . . . *aracnida* (the genus spider) . . . *ascalabes, attelabes* and *æmerrhoïdes* (which some spell with an *h*).

"For twenty-four hours my saliva cannot injure *belletesictides* . . . *boidæ* (which include boa and python) . . . *buprestes* or beetles, and basilisks.

"I may sputter all day long with impunity to *cantharides* (which you call Spanish fly) . . . to caterpillars, to crocodiles, to crap-toads, to *catoblepes*, to *cerastes* (those Egyptian snakes with horns over their eyes) . . . to cockmares (so called because they induce evil dreams or *cauchemars* at night) . . . to *canes furiosi* (or mad dogs) . . . to *colotes*, to *cychriodes*, to *cafezates*, to *cauhares*, to *coleoptera* (which include weevils) . . . to *cuharsves*, to *chel-hydres*, to *croniocolaptes*, to *chersydres*, to *cenchrynes* (which have milletlike protuberances on the skin) . . . and to cockatrices (which some hold to be merely water serpents, while others vow that they are hatched from cocks' eggs).

"No dribble of mine until this time to-morrow could harm *dip-sades* (those reptiles whose bite produces intense thirst) . . . *dom-eses, dryinades* and dragons.

"Until to-morrow's sun sets, my slobber is powerless against *elopes* (including tarpons) . . . *ennydrides* (including otters and bea-vers) . . . *fanuises* . . . *galeodes* (those hairy, scorpionlike spi-ders) . . . *harmenes* and *handons* . . . *ichneumones* (called Phar-aoh's mouseflies and believed by the Egyptians to devour crocodile eggs) . . . *icles* and *iarraries* . . . *kesudures* . . . *lepores marini* (also known as sea horses and sea hares).

"Within twenty-four times one hour, I would sneeze to no avail upon *myopes* (those notoriously shortsighted reptiles) or upon *man-ticores* (those fabulous monsters with men's heads, lions' bodies and scorpions' tails) . . . upon *molures, myagres, muscardinidæ, miliares* and *megalaunes* . . . upon *pytades* and *porphyres* or purplesnakes (so called for their color) . . . upon *pareades* and *phalangia* (a sort of spider) . . . upon *penphredones, pityocampes* and pitvipers (the deadliest of the lot, including rattlers and copperheads).

"For one day, my sputum is but harmless water to *ruteles* (and kindred *scarabeids* and goldsmith beetles) . . . to *rimoires* . . . to *rhagia* (venomous spiders whose bite makes the blood flow) and to *rhaganes* (reptiles whose skin gives their name to the excoriations of syphilis) . . . to salamanders, *scytales* and *stellions* (*agamoid* lizards) . . . to scorpions, *stuphes, sabtins, sangles, sepedons, scolopendres* (centipedes) . . . to *selsirs* (thousand leggers), to *scalavotins* (a type of lizard), to *solpugida* (hairy spiders), to stinkfish, to scab-serpents and to *surdes* or slow-worms . . . to *sanguivora* (bloodsuckers) . . . to *salfuges* (leeches, because salt is noxious to them) . . . to *solifuges* (dangerous ants that fear the sunlight) . . . to *sepes* (a sort of cuttlefish) and to *stinces* (or crocodiles).

"For one day, it will not matter to them if I expectorate upon tarantulas and *typholopes* (or blindworms) . . . upon *tetragnaties* (four-jawed spiders) . . . upon *teristales* and upon vipers."

LXV

HOW PANTAGRUEL DRANK AWAY THE TIME WITH HIS DOMESTICS

FRIAR JOHN piped up:

"In what class, in this venomous hierarchy, do you place Panurge's future wife?"

"How dare you speak ill of women?" cried Panurge. "Why, you're nothing but a scurvy, shavepate, shagarse monk."

"By the bladder and guts of the Cœnomani, whose name suggests *cœnae* or feasts, and who first settled in Maine, in France," said Epistemon, "let me tell you this, Euripides has his character Andromache say that man's industry, under guidance of the gods, discovered excellent remedies against all poisonous creatures; but none has ever been found against a bad wife!"

Panurge took exception:

"That braggart Euripides was forever slandering women. Therefore, heaven took vengeance by having him devoured by dogs, as Aristophanes tells us. Let us continue our discussion: who wants to speak now?"

"I could piss now like a cart horse," said Epistemon.

"I am full to bursting," Xenomanes said. "I am so ballasted as to incline in neither direction."

"A truce with thirst, an armistice with hunger," exclaimed Carpalim. "I couldn't face wine or food now for a while."

"My doldrums have vanished," said Panurge, "thanks to God and yourselves. I feel merry as a cricket, brisk as a beet, happy as a lark, and jolly as a sandboy. Your Euripides can sometimes make sense, as for instance when he has Silenus, a toper of blessed memory, declaring:

> A mad man, he, who, drinking, feels
> Melancholy and down at heels.

"We must not fail to magnify our blessed God, our creator and preserver, for giving us such excellent food and such cool, delicious wine to clear our bellies and minds of their ills. (Not to mention the pleasure we experience in eating and drinking!)"

Then turning to Pantagruel, Panurge continued:

"But, My Lord Pantagruel, you have not answered the question our holy and venerable Friar John put to you. Don't you remember: he asked how to raise fair weather?"

(This phrase, you recall, means to banquet and make merry.)

Since all they sought was the answer to a question as easy as that, Pantagruel promised to satisfy them, postponing to some future time and elsewhere, the discussion of further problems they had set.

"Well, then, Friar John asked how to raise fair weather. Have we not admirably done this? Look up and see our topsails! Hark how the wind whistles through the shrouds! Observe our taut ropes, cables and hawsers! While we were raising our cups and goblets to our lips, banqueting and making merry, the elements, by a secret sympathy, were raising fair weather over sea and sky. Thus Atlas and Hercules raised the burden of the world, if you believe the ancient mythologists. But they raised it a half inch too high. For the titan Atlas wished to entertain his collaborator Hercules more joyously. And Hercules wished to slake the thirst he had acquired while crossing the deserts of Libya, having come to Atlas all the way from Caucasus, where he had delivered Prometheus."

"God's truth!" said Friar John, interrupting him, "I have heard from several reverend theologians that Tirelupin, butler to your noble father Gargantua, sets aside more than eighteen hundred pipes of wine yearly to make servants and visitors drink before they are thirsty!"

"True," said Pantagruel. "But to return to Hercules. He did what the camels and dromedaries of a caravan do when they drink to slake past, present and future thirst. So when Atlas and Hercules raised the earth somewhat too high, they gave the sky a new convulsive, pitching movement, which has caused wrangling and controversy among our crackpate astrologers ever since."

"There," said Panurge, "is the origin of the old proverb:

> *Whilst round a ham we drink with might and main,*
> *The storm goes by, fair weather comes again."*

"We have not only raised fair weather," said Pantagruel, "but we have also greatly lightened the ship's burden. Nor did we do this according to the principle by which Æsop, when his master travelled, invariably chose to carry the basket containing the provisions, since, though heaviest, it was soonest emptied. It is not by easing the vessel of its provisions that we lightened it, but by breaking our fasts. Just as a dead body weighs more than a live one, so a hungry man is heavier and more terrestrial than one who has eaten and drunk. They speak to the point who, having eaten and drunk before setting off on a journey, say: 'Now our horses will gallop the better.'"

Pantagruel climaxed his argument with an example from history. The Amyclæans worshipped noble Father Bacchus above all other gods, and very properly named him Psila, which, in the Doric, means wings. For, as birds, thanks to their wings, rose in easy flight through the air, so, thanks to Bacchus (*i. e.* helpful, delicious wine) the spirits of humans rose . . . their bodies were lightened . . . what was terrestrial and pedestrian in them became delightfully pliant and supple. . . .

LXVI

HOW, BY PANTAGRUEL'S ORDER, THE MUSES WERE SALUTED NEAR GANABIM, THE ISLE OF THE ROBBERS

THE wind continued fair, the conversation brisk. Suddenly, far ahead, Pantagruel spied a mountainous land, which he pointed out to Xenomanes:

"Do you see that high rock to port, with two tops to it, much like Mount Parnassus in Phocis?"

"Quite distinctly, My Lord: it is Ganabim or Robbers Island. Do you care to go ashore?"

"No, I do not."

"You are very wise," Xenomanes commented, "there's nothing worth seeing in the place. The people are all robbers and thieves. Yet, over by the right peak, there is the finest fountain in the world, surrounded by a vast forest. Your fleet might take on wood and water there."

"My Lord Pantagruel spoke words of gold," said Panurge. "Good God, let us not land in an island of brigands and thieves. Take my word for it, this place is just like others I saw years ago: Sark and Herm, Channel Islands between Brittany and Britain, the resort of pirates and scavengers of wreckage. Such too was Poneropolis, 'the city of the wicked,' in Thrace, in the days of Philip. These are islands of thieves, robbers, bandits, brigands, murderers and assassins, islands peopled by the vilest scum of our prisons. Let us not land, I implore you. If you will not believe me, at least follow our kindly, wise Xenomanes' advice. God's death, I vow they are fiercer than cannibals; they would certainly devour us alive. Do not put to shore, I implore you; better, indeed, journey to Avernus, descend into the jaws of hell. Listen! By God, I hear a most frightening tocsin: they are tolling the alarm, as the Gascons about Bordeaux used to do, when the revenue officers were in those parts to collect the *gabelle* or salt-tax. I hear the din plainly or my ears tingle. Let us sheer off, let us sail afoul of these islands."

"Let us land," Friar John insisted. "Let us land. Come along, come along, let's sail on. We will land, carve them up to pieces, and get a night's free lodging! Land, say I."

"The devil take you!" cried Panurge. "This fiend of a monk, this foul fiend of a crazy monk fears nothing. He is rash as all the minions of hell, without ever a thought for other people. He must think everyone else is a monk just like himself."

"Pooh, you milklivered coward!" roared the monk. "May all the millions of devils dissect your brain and make mincemeat of it! That devil's madman is so cowardly and terrified that he beshits himself every minute for sheer terror. If you're so overcome with unreasonable fear, don't land, stay on board, here, with the baggage. Or else cross hell with its million devils and go hide under Proserpine's petticoat."

At these words, Panurge slunk away from the company and hid below, in the storeroom, amid breadcrusts, biscuit crumbs and scraps.

"Friends," said Pantagruel, "I feel an urgent retraction in my soul: something like a distant, small voice that advises me not to land here. Whenever I have felt such a motion within me, I have been right and well favored in avoiding what it bade me avoid. Conversely, I have never had cause to repent of doing what it bade me do."

"It is like Socrates' dæmon, so famous among the Academics," said Epistemon.

Friar John spoke up:

"Well then, My Lord, let us not land. But while the crews take on water, let us have some sport. Panurge is lurking below somewhere, like a snake in the grass. Let us fire off that cannon over the roundhouse, on the poop. It will serve to salute the muses of this Mount Antiparnassus. Besides, the powder in this piece is merely rotting away."

"Right!" said Pantagruel. "Send me the master-gunner."

The gunner appeared at once: Pantagruel ordered him to fire the gun, then charge it with fresh powder against all eventualities. This was straightway done. The gunners of the other vessels, galleys, fri-

The second example is furnished us by King Edward V of England. Messire François Villon, banished from France, had retired to the English court; the king granted the poet his complete favor; nothing of the most intimate household affairs, even, was spared him. One day, His Majesty was sitting up, doing as much as in him lay. Swinging around on his cacking-stool:

"See, Villon, what respect I bear your French kings! Their arms are nowhere in this palace save in this closet, beside my close-stool."

"God's life," Villon retorted, "Your Majesty is extremely wise, prudent, careful and solicitous as to your royal health. And Your Majesty's learned physician, Thomas Linacre, looks after you admirably. He realizes that you are growing old, and therefore apt to be rather constipated. He knows that an apothecary—I mean a suppository, clyster or enema—should daily enter the royal bum, if there is to be a royal movement. What does he do, then? Very sagely, fitly and opportunely, he has the French royal arms painted here, in your privies, and nowhere else. Why, the mere sight of them puts your Majesty into such horrible terror and funk that you immediately let fly as much as eighteen *bonassusi* of Pæonia. (I might explain to Your Majesty that the *bonassus* resembles the bison: it is as large as a bull but more thickset. When chased, it opens the rear sluice and evacuates to a distance of four paces or more. Thus it escapes, burning the skin of the pursuing hounds with its excrement.)

"If the French arms were painted elsewhere in Your Majesty's palace—in your bedroom or hall or chapel or galleries—by God! you would pollute your breeches instanter! Worse, had you here a picture of the great oriflamme of France, one look at it would bring your bowels spurting out of your belly through your fundament. But ho, ho, ho! *atque iterum* and once more, ho!

> *Né suys je badault de Paris.*
> *De Paris, diz-je, auprès Pontoise*
> *Et d'une chorde d'une toise*
> *Scaura mon coul que mon cul poise.*

> *A Paris dolt, I, born (not far away*
> *From Pontoise) in a town called Paris!*
>   *Lo,*

My neck, strung to six feet of rope shall know
Exactly what my precious buttocks weigh.

"What a dolt, ay, what a shortsighted, ill-advised and rash dolt I am! When I came here with you, I wondered why Your Majesty undid his breeches in the royal bedroom. Naturally, I thought that Your Majesty's close-stool stood behind the tapestry, or beside your bed. Otherwise, it seemed to me very odd that you should prepare your clothing so far from the scene of defecatory operation. Wasn't that a fool's fancy? By God, Your Majesty acted thus for a far more mysterious reason; and very rightly, too, ay, you could not have done better. Be sure to prepare long beforehand, at a great distance, and with much care. For if ever you entered here without such preparation, these arms—by God! mark my words!—would turn Your Majesty's breeches into a bedpan, cackpot, privy, hopper, commode and close-stool."

Friar John, stopping up his nose with his left hand, pointed his right finger at Panurge's shirttail and winked at Pantagruel. The latter saw what a stew Panurge was in, appalled, shivering without cause, beturded and scratched by the razorsharp claws of the celebrated feline Rodilardus or Gnawbacon. And, beholding, Pantagruel could not check his laughter.

"What on earth are you doing with that cat?" he asked Panurge.

"With that cat?" Panurge echoed. "Devil take me if I didn't think it was a downy-coated devilkin that I stole upon unawares . . . that I snatched up in my stocking as in a vise . . . and that I brought out of that great trough of hell where I have been wallowing! The devil with this devil! He has slashed my skin until it looks like a lobster's whiskers."

With which he tossed his cat away.

"Go, go, for God's sake," Pantagruel advised. "Wash and clean yourself, calm your fears, put on a clean white shirt, and then dress."

"My fears!" Panurge cried indignantly. "Why, I'm not in the least afraid. God's might, I'm bolder than if I had swallowed as many flies as are put into pudding paste in Paris, from St. John's Day in June, to All Saint's Day in November. As you know, a man becomes as reckless as the fly he swallows."

"Humph!" said Pantagruel.

"Oh, ho, ho, ho, ho! What the devil is this?" Panurge shouted. "Do you call this ordure, ejection, excrement, evacuation, *dejecta*, fecal matter, *egesta*, *copros*, *scatos*, dung, crap, turds? Not at all, not at all: it is but the fruit of the shittim tree.

"Selah! Let us drink!"

The Fifth and Last Book

THE HEROIC SAYINGS AND DEEDS OF THE EXCELLENT

PANTAGRUEL

Set Down by
MASTER FRANÇOIS RABELAIS
Doctor of Medicine

CONTAINING
THE VISIT TO THE ORACLE OF HOLY BACBUC
—AND THE BOTTLE'S ANSWER
THE OBJECT OF THE LENGTHY QUEST

THE AUTHOR'S PROLOGUE

O INDEFATIGABLE topers, and you, thrice-precious poxbitten hearties, I see you enjoy leisure aplenty. I, too, have nothing more weighty in hand. Therefore, allow me to ask, by way of asking, a certain question.

You know the saying *Le monde n'est plus fat*; men are not such sawnies nowadays! It has become a common proverb. Why?

(*Fat* is a Languedoc word: in the southern dialect, it means savorless, insipid, dull, and hence, metaphorically speaking, it designates a fatuous, shallow-brained, blunt-witted jobbernowl. By a not very different process, *sawny* came to signify the same thing. Derived from *sandy*, and applied to Scotsmen, it at first characterized all that is Caledonian, flat, monotonous, dry, and hence, metaphorically, came to identify any silly blatant, inept doodle.)

Here is my question, then. Would you maintain, by perfectly logical inference, that the world was formerly muddle-headed, but has now acquired wisdom? How many and precisely what conditions made men simpletons; how many and what circumstances developed men into sages? Why were men ever idiots; how should men now be intelligent? What indicates their quondam folly; what betokens their contemporary reason? Who in the devil made them silly; who, in God's name, made them wise? Which are more numerous; those who once loved man in his imbecility or those who now love man in his discernment? How long did he continue bewildered; how long will he remain enlightened? Whence came this pristine giddiness; whence comes this present equilibrium? Why did hallowed ignorance cease abruptly to-day, and not a century hence; why did modern authority begin to-day, and not ages ago? What evils have we reaped from man's former witlessness, what benefits from his later penetration? How was primordial hebetude abolished, how was current perspicacity established?

You may answer, if you care to. I shall not insist, My Lords, for fear of annoying your holy and paternal worships. No false shame, now; out with the truth, confound Mynheer van Teufel, shame the foul fiend, archfoe of Paradise and suppressor of veracity.

Be of good cheer, lad! Are you one of my lot? Very well, then: toss off three, five or seven bumpers of the best, to celebrate the first part of my sermon. But, the bumpers drained, answer my question. (If you belong to the other party, *avalisque Satanas*, Satan avaunt!)

By St. Curly-Hurlyburly, I swear that, unless you help me solve this problem, I repent having ever proposed it. Yes, I shall be as perplexed and grieved as a man who, hanging on a wolf's ears, bawls for help and knows it is in vain.

What's that? Carneades, here? Carneades, the Greek sceptic, who denied the existence of truth? Hence, devils; no, no, you are wrong, things will not go your way. God help us! years ago, Lucilius and Neptune tried that game, and the gods were nonplussed.

Oh, I see: you've decided to give me no answers! By my whiskers, I'll not answer either. But I *will* quote the prophecy of a venerable, highly sapient doctor of philosophy, author of a work called *The Prelate's Bagpipe*. What do you suppose the old lecher said? Listen, donkey-pizzles, and you shall hear this oracle's vaticination:

> *Twice fifteen jubilees were past: then, one*
> *Shaved every foolish mother's foolish son.*
> *O base irreverence, what do you here?*
> *They only seemed fools. Should they persevere,*
> *They shall quash greed and folly; resolute,*
> *They shall be shelling that plant's tender fruit,*
> *What flower they dared not touch this time last year.*

Now you have heard it, what do you make of it? The prophet is ancient, the style laconic, the thoughts obscure as those of Duns Scotus. A splendid performance, though the author treated of matters in themselves profound and difficult. The ablest commentators of this good father interpret the thirty jubilees as the calendar years up to 1550—a date which would thus mark the thirty-first jubilee of the Christian era. None shall fear the flowers of that fair year 1550; the world will no longer be deemed stupid once that spring has dawned. The infinite number of fools Solomon refers to—*Stultorum infinitus est numerus*—will perish deliriously; the innumerable varieties of folly cited by Avicenna—*maniæ infinitæ sunt species*—will disappear.

Folly, which had been driven back to the centre of earth during the rigors of winter, now appears on the surface. Like a tree, it puts forth its buds. You see this happen, you know it is true, experience bears it out. Many years ago, that great good man Hippocrates discovered it for himself in his *Aphorisms: Vere etenim maniæ, etc.*

The world thus grown wiser, men will no longer dread the flower and blossoms of beans in spring. Glass in hand, tears in your eyes, you may pitifully realize that this means the lenten season! In other words, men will no longer dread whole cartloads of books, which appeared florescent, flourishing and beflowered, gay as so many butterflies, but which, in reality, were boresome and dull . . . mischievous, arid and unprofitable . . . ungrateful and dark as the words of Heraclitus . . . swathed in obscurities like Pythagoras' numbers. . . .

(Incidentally I might add that Horace in his *Satires*, Book II, 6, dubs Pythagoras King of the Bean, for he calls the bean Pythagoric.)

These books shall perish; no hand shall lift them; no eye shall see, let alone read them. Such was their destiny; to such an end were they predestined.

In their stead, we now have beans in the seed pod, *i. e.* jocund and fructifying books, born under the star of Pantagruelism. These are reputed to-day to be selling like hot cakes; they will continue to do so until the next jubilee period comes around. Countless men are devoting themselves to studying these books; that is why the world is now reputed to be wise!

So, now, your problem is solved and settled. Clear your throats lustily, fetch up a cough or two, then toss off nine bumpers—bottoms up and no heel-taps, since the vintage is good and the money-lenders are hanging themselves for lack of business. Those usurers will cost us plenty in rope if the fair weather holds out. For I vow to furnish them with any amount of it, liberally and free of cost, whenever they care to hang themselves. At that, I shall be saving the hangman's fee.

Tell me, friends: do you long to shake off the ancient folly? Would you share in the new wisdom? If so, erase from your scrolls the instructions of the old philosopher with the golden thigh—I refer to

Pythagoras—who forbids you to eat beans. We believe it a truth established and valid among all lovers of good food that Pythagoras proscribed the use of beans just as that freshwater physician, the late Amer, nephew to the lawyer, My Lord of Camelotière, forbade his patients to eat a partridge's wings, a chicken rump, or a pigeon's neck. "*Ala mala, cropium dubium, collum bonum pelle remota,*" he used to say. "The wings are bad, the rump doubtful, the neck good only if the meat is removed." So he ate them himself, leaving his patients the bare bones to pick at.

Next, after Pythagoras, to place an embargo upon beans—*i. e.* volumes of Pantagruelism—came the cowl-bearing, monkeyshine bigots of religious brotherhoods. They much resembled Philoxenus and Gnatho the Sicilian, the inaugurators of their monastic and stomachic joy. In the midst of a banquet, when the best cuts were served, these ancient thinkers used to spit on the meat in order that their fellow-guests, disgusted, would not choose them. So this hideous, snotty, mucous, worm-eaten rabble of hypocrites detest in public and abhor in private the toothsome volumes I have referred to. Impudently, they spit their villainy upon them.

To-day, we have at hand many works of great excellence, both in prose and verse, couched in the Gallic vernacular; indeed, the cant and sham of the Gothic age may be said to have practically disappeared. Nevertheless, I have decided to warble and hiss like a goose among these lyric swans, to quote the old saw. For I would resent being deemed mute among so many delicate poets and eloquent orators. Truly, I would prefer to play the rôle of country bumpkin beside the many gifted actors in this noble performance, than to pass for one of the army of shadows and ciphers, who gape at passing flies . . . who, like Arcadian asses, wiggle their ears as if they understood this lovely chorus . . . who mime in silence their appreciation of this harmony. . . .

Having made up my mind and chosen accordingly, I considered I was not acting unworthily in moving my Diogenic tub; you could scarcely accuse me of doing so without authoritative example.

I contemplate a vast array of French poets, led by Colinet or Colin d'Auxerre, secretary to François I . . . by Clément Marot, that sterling writer of madrigals and rondeaux . . . by Antoine Herroët the Platonist and author of *The Perfect Mistress* . . . by

Drouet . . . by the graceful Mellin de Saint-Gelais . . . by Hugues Salel, the famed translator of the *Iliad*, who wrote a dizain for the Second Book of these joyous *Chronicles* . . . by Claude Massuan. . . . I see hundreds of French authors who, in both prose and verse, preferred the use of French to Latin. Ay, they have for a long time been masters at Apollo's academy on Mount Parnassus; they have drunk many a beaker from the caballine fountain with the merry Muses. To the frame of vulgar idiom, they bring pure marble of Paros, alabaster, porphyry, and fine royal cement. They treat solely of heroic feats, of noble undertakings, of arduous, grave and difficult matters; and they treat of them in a style as smooth and luminous as satin, as rich and colorful as crimson velvet. Their writings are divine nectar, a rare, fragrant, sparkling, delicate, toothsome and muscadine wine.

Nor is the honor of this invested in our sex alone: the ladies, too, have a share in its glory. Among them is a daughter of the royal blood of France, the sister of a king, herself a queen. To speak her name here would be utter profanation. She has amazed our age by the transcendent imagination in her writing, by her magnificent mastery of our native tongue, by the peerless graces of her style. Copy her, if you can; for my part, I am unable to. It is not allowed to all men to go to Corinth; many are called but few are chosen.

When Solomon built the temple, every citizen could not offer gold by the handful, but one and all contributed something. The poorest, even, gave a half shekel. Since it lies not within my power to match the lofty edifice reared by the writers I have mentioned, I am determined to do as Renaud de Montauban. For penance, in his old age, Renaud had to help the masons who were building the Cathedral of Cologne. Well, I too, then, will help the masons, setting the water to boiling for them. Put otherwise, since I may not be the peer of these authors, I shall be the indefatigable auditor of their celestial writings.

Ha! envious rivals, ha! carping critics. You were worse than Zoïlus, the fourth-century grammarian of Amphipolis, whose acrimonious critiques of Homer were proverbial. Go hang yourselves, I say; go choose your own trees to hang from. (Rope will be forthcoming aplenty.)

I hereby make the following protestation on my own Mount Helicon in the presence of the divine Muses. Am I to be granted a span of hale and healthy life, equal to the sum of years lived by a dog and three crows? May I expect to live as long as the Holy Jewish leader Moses, who died at the age of one hundred and twenty, according to *Deuteronomy* . . . as Xenophilus the musician, who lived to one hundred and five, Pliny tells us . . . as Demonax, the first-century philosopher who, Lucian tells us, reached the century mark . . . ? If so, I promise to appear before your cuckoos, your eternal re-hashers of subjects settled ages ago, your scatologizing boobies, your refurbishers of old Latin claptrap, your secondhand retailers of mouldy, dubious words, current in Rome fifteen hundred years ago. I shall proclaim in their very teeth that our own idiom is neither so common nor inept, nor wanting nor contemptible as they make out.

Of yore, Phœbus distributed all the treasures of literature to his favorite poets; to wretched Æsop fell only the perquisites and office of a maker of apologues. By the same token, I humbly implore the powers of letters to allow me the same rôle. I aspire to no loftier station: let them not disdain to accept me as a petty *rhyparographer* or painter of low subjects, like Pyræicus, who depicted such stuff as barbers' shops, vegetable stands, asses and curs. The powers of letters will do so, I dare swear, for they are supremely gracious, generous, humane and debonair.

For this reason all worthy tipplers, and all good goutridden poxi-crats, insist upon enjoying, to the last drop, the tonic wine of joyous books. Quoting from them when they foregather, discussing the high mysteries treated in them, our bibbers and scrabbies acquire as singular a mastery as Alexander the Great, when he studied Aris-totle's capital works of philosophy.

God help us, belly to belly, what swilling reprobates, what lecher rapscallions!

Therefore, fellow-topers, let me give you a piece of timely advice. Get in a large supply of such books, whenever you come upon them in a bookshop. Do not content yourselves with merely shelling these beans in their pods; toss them down as you would an opiate cordial. Incorporate them within yourselves. You will soon discover the advantages they reserve for all good shellers of beans.

Here, then, I offer you an attractive basketful of them, culled in the same garden as those that went before. And I implore you, rev-

erend sirs, to accept them, in the hope of a better crop when next the
swallows visit us.

I

HOW PANTAGRUEL REACHED RINGING ISLAND, AND OF THE NOISE WE HEARD THERE

PURSUING our way, we sailed along three days without discovering
anything. On the fourth day, we sighted land, which, the skipper
told us, must be Ringing Island. From afar, we heard a tumultuous
and repeated din; it sounded like a simultaneous ringing of large,
middling and tiny bells, as is customary on high holidays at Paris,
Tours, Jargeau near Orléans, Nantes and elsewhere. The closer we
sailed to land, the more loudly we heard this pealing of bells.

Some of us imagined it was Jupiter's brazen oracle at Dodona, the
holy kettles clashing; some suspected it might be the portal of Olym-
pia, called Heptaphona, because it re-uttered seven echoes. Others
proposed the eternal din of the colossus erected over Memnon's tomb
in the temple of Therapis, at Thebes in Egypt; every morning, this
statue was known to make a particular noise when the sun struck it.
Still others inclined to the belief that here was the hub-bub formerly
heard over a tomb at Lipara, one of the Æolian Isles, northwest of
Sicily. To suport their opinion, they reminded us that the ancient
poets located Vulcan's forge in Lipara. But these beliefs flew in the
face of chorography.

"I think probably some swarms of bees have taken to flight," Pantagruel ventured, "and, to call them back, the people of the region
are setting up this hullabaloo of pans, kettles, basins and corybantic
cymbals of Cybele, mighty mother of the gods. Let us listen carefully."

Coming closer, we heard, under the perpetual resonance of bells,
what we believed to be the tireless chanting of the inhabitants. Pantagruel, therefore, decided not to land at once, but rather to go in

the pinnace to a rock, near which we spied a hermitage and a small garden.

Here we found a hermit, who was called Bragibus or Codfriggle, and who was born at Glennay, near Parthenay. This diminutive old man cleared the mystery of the bells' clang; he also offered us the most extraordinary hospitality. We had to fast four whole days in succession; otherwise, we would be refused access to Ringing Island. When we asked why, Codfriggle explained that this was one of the four fasting periods.

"Fasting periods!" Panurge groaned. "Farting periods, I call them; I can make tail but not head of them. If we fast, are we not crammed with wind?"

Codfriggle made plain that the four fasting periods were the Ember Days in the religious calendar.

"Member days, you mean," Panurge expostulated. "Days when the tongue (unruly member!) is penalized! Legal holy days that prove wholly lethal days! Slim fare, say I; we can do without so many 'fastivals'!"

Friar John spoke up.

"In my grammar," he said, quoting Donatus, the fourth-century authority of medieval scholarship, "I find but three periods or tenses: past, present and future. I daresay they throw in the fourth for luck!"

"That period or tense they throw in," the learned Epistemon commented, "is the Aorist, a tense derived from the preterimperfect of the Greeks and Latins. It is admitted in variable and uncertain times. It denotes past occurrence without limitations as to continuance. An unlimited period in the past: thus, in future, you will remember having gone unlimitably hungry for an indefinite period. But patience! as the lepers say. Patience is not only a moral virtue; it is another name for sorrel, which cures leprosy!"

"As I told you," the hermit interrupted, "to oppose this rule is fatal. Whoever does so is heretic; to be burned at the stake is all too good for him!"

"No doubt about it, Father," Panurge agreed. "When I'm at sea, I'm much more frightened of a ducking than a burning, of drowning than sizzling. Never mind, let us fast, by God, though I've fasted so long that I'm pared clean to the bone. Alas, I much fear that the battlements of my body will finally collapse. Nor is that my only anxiety. What if I offend you, fast as I fast? I know very little about it, apparently; several people have told me so, and I will take their word for it. Temperamentally, I must confess I have never lost sleep over the question: fasting is a feat so easy to accomplish, so readily at hand! I'm more concerned about avoiding the future necessity of fasting. To do that, a man must have cloth to make clothing of, and grain to take to the mill. By God, let us fast fastidiously, since fasts are now fastened upon us. It's many a day since I had troubled my head about them."

"If we must do it, we can lump it," Pantagruel remarked. "We will follow the régime as we would a thorny path—in hopes of turning to an easier one as soon as possible. Meanwhile, I shall study my charts to learn if marine science is as good as terrestrial. Plato, seeking to describe a certain stupid, ignorant, incompetent lout, compared him to a man brought up on shipboard—much as we talk of a man brought up in a barrel, who never saw anything save through the bunghole."

Our fasting proved a fearsome and terrible ordeal. The first day, we fasted piecemeal; the second, wholesale; third, we went the whole hog; the fourth, we did things up brown!

Such were the orders of the fairies.

II

HOW RINGING ISLAND WAS ONCE INHABITED BY THE SITICINES, WHO BECAME BIRDS

OUR fast accomplished, the hermit gave us a letter of recommendation to a certain Abihen Camar. In Hebrew, the name means pagan priest. He was the Master Ædituus or Master Sexton of Ringing Island. Panurge, however, bowing ceremoniously, called him "Master Antitus"—the stock name in comedy for the fool. The sexton was a small old man, bald of head, with a shining snout and a rubicund face. Knowing by the hermit's recommendation that we had fasted, as I have told, he received us cordially.

After we had eaten plentifully, he cited the remarkable features of the island. It had originally been inhabited by the Siticines, who, as the name indicates, sang and played over graves. In other words, they were mourning musicians. Later, since all things are subject to change, these people became birds.

Besides the Siticines, I heard about the Sicinnists, dancers who performed a dance named for its inventor, Sikinnos. I learned all that had been said of them by Ateius Capito, the jurist of the Augustan age . . . by Julius Pollux, the grammarian appointed professor of rhetoric at Athens by Commodus because he had a lovely voice, and the author of a vast dictionary of Greek institutions . . . by Marcellus . . . by Aulus Gellius, author of the *Attic Nights* . . . by Athenæus, of Naucratis in Egypt, author of an invaluable compendium on banquets and everything pertaining thereto . . . by Suidas, the tenth-century Greek lexicographer, a veritable treasure-house of quotations . . . by Ammonius the grammarian, and by various other writers. . . .

Nor did I find it difficult to credit various transformations I recalled, of people into birds. There was Nyctimene, who conceived an incestuous passion for her father, Epopæus, King of Lesbos, and was metamorphosed into an owl. . . . There was Antigone, daughter of Laomedon and sister of Priam, who, for boasting that her beauty was greater than Juno's was changed into a stork. . . . There were Halcoyne and her husband Ceyx; he drowned and, in pity of her grief when she found his body, the gods made them kingfishers. . . . There was the terrible story of Tereus, who, having ravished his sister-in-law Philomela, cut out her tongue, whereat Procne, his wife, slew her own son Itys, and served him up to her husband in a dish of meat. All of them were transmogrified into birds: Tereus became the hawk, Procne the swallow, Philomela the nightingale, and Itys the pigeon. . . .

I remembered, too, how the children of Matabrune were changed into swans. There were seven of them, six lads and one girl, born during their father's absence, and protected by the talisman of a golden chain around their necks. A spiteful mother-in-law exposed them in a wood, stole their chains and had them all changed into swans, save the girl. Subsequently the latter won back the chains, placed them on the swans' necks and these birds straightway became men again. . . .

There was also the case of the men of Pallene, in Thrace, who, by bathing in the Tritonic lake nine times, were also made into birds.

After this information of the sexton's, we could get no word from him save of cages and birds.

The cages he showed us were large, costly, luxurious, and sumptuously built; the birds were tall, handsome and proportionally sleek. They reminded me of my compatriots. They ate and drank like men; they digested their food, pooped their zephyrs, evacuated their dung, slept their sleep and friggled their females, just as men do. Seeing them face to face, you would have sworn they *were* men. Master Sexton, however, assured us that they were anything but men, insisting that they had nothing secular, or lay, about them.

To tell the truth, their plumage set us to wondering about them. Some were wholly white, others entirely black, others completely gray; some were black-and-white, others red all over, still others part blue, part white. They were a fair sight, indeed.

Master Sexton called the males Clergyhawks, Monkhawks, Priesthawks, Abbothawks, Bishophawks, Cardinalhawks and Popehawks, the last-named being unique. He called the females Clergykites, Nunkites, Priesteskites, Abbesskites, Bishopkites, Cardinalkites and Popekites.

"Take the bees, for instance," Master Sexton suggested, "among them, you find plenty of drones, who do nothing but buzz, consume food, and ravage everything. Similarly, for the last three hundred years, these happy Monkbirds, here, have been put upon (I don't know how) by a swarm of Bigotbirds. It happens every fifth moon. The Bigotbirds befoul and arsefruit the island from end to end; they are so monstrous ugly as to drive every bird of ours away. Their necks are wry and twisted . . . their feet are hairy . . . their claws and bellies are like those of harpies . . . their bums are like the bums of stymphalides, birds afflicted with a loathsome diarrhœa. . . . We cannot cope with the Bigotbirds: kill one, and twenty-four appear in its stead."

I wished Master Sexton a second Hercules, to rid him of this pest, just as the first of that name had, in his sixth labor, shot down the evil birds by Lake Stymphalon. Friar John, beholding the lovely birds, was so disturbed about it that he all but ran amuck. As for Pantagruel, his condition was that of My Lord Priapus, who, contemplating the Virgin Vesta asleep during the sacrifices to Ceres, was seized by a lewd desire.

III

HOW THERE WAS ONLY ONE POPEHAWK ON RINGING ISLAND

We then asked Master Sexton why there was but one Popehawk among the countless varieties of venerable birds on the island. He replied that it was so in the beginning; such was the fatal destiny decreed by the stars. The Clergyhawks, without carnal copulation, gave birth to Priesthawks and Monkhawks, just as, of yore, a young bull, accoutred ceremoniously in honor of the pastoral god Aristæus, gave birth to a swarm of bees.

The Priesthawks engendered the Bishophawks, who, in turn, produced the stately Cardinalhawks. If the last-named lived long enough, they finally achieved the position of Popehawk. As I said before, there was usually only one Popehawk, just as you find only one king to a beehive, and one sun in the firmament. At his death, another Popehawk was born of the Cardinalhawks, again, of course, without fleshly copulation. Thus this species enjoyed individual unity, with perpetuity of succession, like the Arabian phœnix.

It must be admitted that about two thousand seven hundred and sixty moons ago nature produced the extraordinary phenomenon of two Popehawks. This proved to be the direst calamity ever visited upon the island.

"For," Master Sexton went on, "all these birds robbed and trounced one another so lustily that the whole island population was seriously menaced with extinction. One faction supported and defended one Popehawk; another, struck dumb as fishes, refused to sing. Some of our bells here, as though they had lost their tongues, did not utter a sound. During these unruly times, the various factions summoned, to their help, the emperors, kings, dukes, marquises, counts, barons and commonwealths from their homes on the continent. This schism and sedition ended only when one of the two Popehawks departed this life, thus reducing the duality of Popehawkdom to unity."

What impelled these birds to sing so tirelessly, we asked.

"The bells hanging over their cages," Sexton replied. "Do you see those Monkhawks there, becowled and behooded with what look like winestrainers? Shall I make them sing like woodlarks for you?"

"Please do," we urged him.

He rang six peals on a bell; the Monkhawks came running up, and burst into song.

"Do you see those Monkhawks there, with plumage the color of red herring?" Panurge piped up. "If *I* struck that bell, would they sing for us?"

"Certainly, just like the others!"

Panurge did so. Immediately these smoked birds came fluttering up to lift their voices in song. A harsh, unpleasant sound; Sexton ascribed it to the fact that, like the herons and cormorants of the world, they fed solely upon fish. They formed, he added, a fifth species of Monkbird, newly issued. Soon, a sixth species was due to arrive; Sexton had been warned of this by Robert Valbringue. (Roberval, associate of Jacques Cartier, appointed, by François I, Viceroy of Canada. Valbringue had passed through Ringing Island on his way home from Africa.) This sixth species was the Capuchinhawks; they were more dismal, more monklubberly and fouler than any variety known locally.

"Africa is proverbial for producing strange and wonderful things," Pantagruel commented.

IV

HOW THE BIRDS OF RINGING ISLAND WERE BIRDS OF PASSAGE

"You told us that the Popehawk was born of Cardinalhawks," said Pantagruel, "Cardinalhawks of Bishophawks, Bishophawks of Priesthawks, and Priesthawks of Clergyhawks. What *I* should like to know is: who gives birth to Clergyhawks?"

"They are all birds of passage," Sexton answered. "They come to us from the other world: some from a remarkably vast country called Nobreadland, others from a westerly realm called Alltoomany. Every year, the Clergyhawks arrive here in quantities, having left their fathers, mothers, relatives and friends at home."

Sexton ascribed the supply of Clergyhawks to overpopulation in Alltoomany. A noble family might have so large a progeny, male and female, as to make it impossible to do as reason required, Nature directed, and God enjoined. They could not divide the paternal estate equally without reducing each share to practically nothing. So the parents packed their young off to Ringing Island, even if these children were subjects of Isle Bossard.

"You mean Isle Bouchard, in the Vienne, near Chinon?" Panurge asked.

"Not at all. I mean Isle Bossard or Warp Island," Sexton corrected. "You see, these children are usually humpbacked, or blind, or club-footed, or short an arm, or lame with gout—at any rate, in some respect misshapen, deformed, a useless burden upon earth."

"This way of doing things is the exact opposite of the custom observed, of old, by the Vestal Virgins," Pantagruel remarked. "Antistius Labeo, the Roman jurisconsult of Augustus' day, tells us that any girl was rigorously debarred from the dignity of Vestal sisterhood, if she possessed a moral flaw or a bodily defect, were it the tiniest and most secret blemish!"

Sexton expressed his surprise that the mothers of Alltoomany actually bore their children in their wombs for nine months, when they could not bear them in their homes for nine or even seven years. Of old, in Egypt, the priests of Isis were appointed only after submitting to depilation and to the imposition of a white surplice of some sort. Similarly, to-day, the children of Alltoomany were given a white robe to put over their clothes . . . suffered God knows how many hairs to be shaved off their heads . . . heard and uttered certain vague apostrophes and expiatory formulas . . . and, visibly, overtly, manifestly, by Pythagorical metempsychosis, without hurt or wound, were magically transformed into the birds we had before our eyes. . . .

Another thing puzzled Sexton, he told his good friends. Why didn't the females called Clergykites, Nunkites and Abbesskites, carol joyful hymns and pleasurable anthems, as the followers of Zarathustra did in honor of Ormażd, lord of light and goodness? Why, instead, did they wail dismal and deadly dirges, like those to Ahriman, lord of the evil spirits dwelling in darkness? This held true of both young and old: they were forever offering up devotions for the parents and relatives who had changed them into birds.

Thousands of these birds came from Nobreadland, which was an extremely large country, inhabited by the Assaphi, a word from the Hebrew, meaning either "those that are called" or "people of low condition." Did these folk lack food? Were they in danger of starvation? Could they find no honest task or profession to work at? Was no decent family available to take them in its service? Were they crossed in their love? Were they foiled in some undertaking? Were they desperate? Had they committed some evil crime, and were they being sought so they might be ignominiously put to death? What did they do? Why, one and all promptly flew off to Ringing Island, where they found a certain livelihood. Some, who had come lean as rails, grew fat as hogs. Ringing Island offered them perfect freedom, security and indemnity.

"But," Pantagruel asked, "don't these birds ever go back to the land where they were hatched?"

"Some do," Sexton admitted. "In the early days, very few did— very rarely and very regretfully. However, since certain eclipses, revolutions and reformations, by virtue of the celestial constellations, a large crowd has fled back into the world. We are in no wise sorry; it leaves all the more for those who remain. All those who fly away leave their feathers here—in other words, they cast off their frocks among the nettles and briars, and so are unfrocked."

Indeed, we actually found a few. Searching for them, we chanced to meet a cat that had been let out of the bag.

V

OF THE DUMB KNIGHTHAWKS ON RINGING ISLAND

SEXTON had barely finished talking, when twenty-five or thirty odd birds flew towards us. Their plumage and hue were unlike anything we had seen so far. Their feathers changed color as variably as the skin of the chameleon and as the petals of the *tripolion* or *tencrion*, a sort of aster. Under the left wing, each bore a mark that resembled two diameters bisecting a circle, or, say, a perpendicular line crossing a straight line. The marks were almost all the same in shape, but their color differed. Some bore white crosses (just as Knights of Malta); others green (like Knights of St. Lazarus); others red (like Knights of St. James); others purple, and still others blue (like Knights of St. Anthony).

"What are those birds?" Panurge asked. "What do you call them?"

"They are mongrels," Sexton elucidated. "We call them Knighthawks; they are Gourmander or Commander birds. They enjoy a large number of fat commanderies, or livings, in your part of the world."

"Please make them sing a little," I begged. "We should love to hear their voices."

"They never sing," Sexton returned. "But they make up for this by eating double rations."

"What are the females?"

"There are no females."

"What!" Panurge gasped. "How is that? What about those scabs and crusts and sores on their faces? Why, they're riddled with pox."

"Quite so: this class of bird is subject to such discommodity, because they haunt the brine. Why? Because they are forever launching forth overseas on warlike expeditions. And so they have to soak in the salting-tub—or sweatbox—for the treatment of their malady!"

Sexton then elucidated what had brought these Knighthawks flying up to us. Apparently, they wished to find out whether we had in our party a certain sort of monk, a virulent bird of prey, which could never be brought to the falconers' lure or made to perch on his glove. The Knighthawks af Ringing Island declared that this horrible species came from our world. Some of them were said to wear, around the knee, a rare, precious band bearing the legend *Honi soit qui mal y pense*, which, freely translated, meant that whoever thought ill of it was doomed to soak in dung. These birds somewhat resembled the Knights of the Most Noble Order of the Garter. Others were said to have an effigy of the Evil One stamped upon the plumage at their breast, much as the Knights of the Order of St. Michael display an emblem of the archangel overcoming the devil. Others, again, were said to boast the reproduction of a ramskin, much as the Knights of the Order of the Golden Fleece have a golden sheepskin for a badge.

"Possibly we may have some such birds among us," said Panurge, "but I'm sure we are not aware of it."

"We have chattered enough," said Sexton, "let us go drink."

"And eat!"

"Ay, friend, eat and drink: eat with the stomach of an ostrich, drink with the gills of a fish! The most important and precious thing is time; let us apply it to good works."

Nevertheless, Sexton wished first to take us to bathe in the beautifully and luxuriously appointed baths of the Cardinalhawks, then to have us massaged and anointed with precious balm by the rubbers. Pantagruel, however, protested that he could drink only too well without this ceremony. Accordingly, Sexton led us to a spacious and stately banquet hall.

"I know Codfriggle the hermit made you fast four whole days," he said. "Here you shall do the exact contrary: for four whole days, you shall eat and drink!"

"What about sleeping?" Panurge demanded.

"Suit yourself!" Sexton made answer. "You know the proverb: *Drink deep, sleep well!*"

God's truth, how well we fared! Oh, what an excellent man Master Sexton was!

VI

HOW THE BIRDS ON RINGING ISLAND FED

PANTAGRUEL looked glum; he seemed none too pleased with the four-day banquet Sexton imposed upon us. Sexton, noticing this, asked:

"Don't you know, My Lord, that, a week before and a week after the winter solstice, there is no storm at sea? The elements grant this lull to the halcyons or kingfishers, a race sacred to Thetis, chief of the Nereids or sea-nymphs. Kingfishers make the most of it to lay and hatch their eggs close to shore. In these parts, the sea seeks compensation for so long a calm by treating us to a terrific tempest whenever travellers land hereabouts. We fancy it does so because, during the dirty weather, our guests are forced to tarry here and be feasted on the revenue we collect from our bell-ringing. We dare hope you do not feel it is time wasted. You must stay, willy-nilly, unless you intend to declare war upon Juno (perhaps you recall how she raised a storm against Æneas?) . . . upon Neptune whose trident could crack your ships up in less than no time . . . upon gray-eyed Doris, mother of the fifty Nereids . . . upon Æolus, god of the dread winds . . . in a word, upon all the malevolent, anti-Jovian deities. . . . Therefore, My Lord, be of good cheer and fall to, lustily!"

After wolfing down the first gigantic rations, Friar John turned to his host:

"This island, Master Sexton, seems to contain only caged birds. They do not till or cultivate the soil; for sole occupation, they hum, twitter and sing. From where do you get the horn of plenty and abundance that provides such copious, delicious fare?"

"From everywhere in the other world, except certain northern countries which have lately stirred tempests in cesspools! But

They will be sorry, hey-diddle-diddle,
Ay, they shall rue it, tarra-ra-diddle!

Never mind; let us drink up!"

They did.

"What land are you from?" Sexton questioned.

"From Touraine."

"Well, well!" Sexton beamed. "You were hatched of no ill-omened bird; your nests were never fouled! So you come from blessed Touraine, eh? My friends, you have no idea of the vast store of benefits we derive every year from that region. Recently, some fellow-countrymen of yours happened to touch at this island. Do you know they told us that your present duke's income did not allow him to eat his bellyful of beans and bacon? Can you tell why? Because of his predecessor's great liberality towards these holy birds of ours on Ringing Island. Why, he used to stuff us cram-ful of pheasants, partridges, pullets, turkeys, fat capons of the Loudun region, venison and game of every kind."

Sexton urged the company to drink up. Then:

"Do you see those birds there, perched in line on a stick! How fat and plump they look! They acquired that sleekness from the contributions we receive from lands in your world; nor do those birds fail to acknowledge it by singing in the contributor's behalf. You never heard the golden-throated nightingales of Arcady twitter more harmoniously than these birds when they catch sight of a dish, or of these two golden staffs!"

"Staves!" Friar John bawled. "Don't you make your living by music!"

"You should hear them chant when I ring the heavy bells over their cages. Drink up, ho! drinking is a pastime, a pleasure, a necessity: drink up, then! For my own part, I pledge your healths heartily. You are welcome, thrice welcome to our banquet!

"Never fear: food and drink are not lacking here. Though the heaven that is over thy head were brass, and the earth that is under thee were iron—to speak biblically—still, we should not be wanting food for seven or even eight years longer than the famine of Egypt. Drink up, then: let us pledge our respective healths in friendship and good will."

"Devil take it," Panurge objected. "You do yourselves well in this world!"

"We do ourselves even better in the next," said Sexton. "The Elysian Fields will not fail to supply us! Drink up, friends: your health, there!"

"I admire the earliest settlers on your island, those Siticines who sang over graves," I told Sexton. "They managed, by divine inspiration and wordly sense, to bequeath you such means as all men seek but few obtain. I congratulate you on achieving Paradise, both in this world and the next. O happy, by all odds; O very demigods! would to God I were lucky as you!"

VII

HOW PANURGE TOLD THE SEXTON OF RINGING ISLAND ABOUT A HORSE AND AN ASS

WE had eaten aplenty, we had drunk, to boot. Sexton thereupon took us into a handsomely furnished, richly tapestried and finely gilt chamber, where he ordered myrobalans, catechu and candied ginger, with hippocras and light wine. By these antidotes, sweeter than the waters of Lethe, he invited us to forget our hardships and travail on the sea. He also had abundant provisions loaded on to our ships. We then retired to rest, but I could not sleep because of the everlasting jangle of the bells.

At midnight, Sexton awakened us for an interlude of drinking; himself set the example, saying:

"You people from the outer world declare that ignorance is the mother of all evil. You are right. Yet do you banish it from your minds? Not at all: you live in ignorance, for ignorance and by ignorance. That is why such mischief afflicts you day by day. You keep complaining and lamenting; nothing is ever good enough for you. I can see that clearly at the present moment. Alas, ignorance chains you supine on your beds just as Vulcan chained Mars. Can't you realize that you should forgo sleep in order to enjoy to the full the advantages of this celebrated island? Why, you should have polished off three meals already! Believe me: to feed on the fare of Ringing Island a man must rise betimes. Consume our provender and it multiplies; be sparing, it diminishes."

He advised us to make hay while the sun shone. Did we mow a field in due season, the grass grew again, thicker and better; did we fail to do so, a few years would smother it under moss. We, Sexton's friends, must therefore imbibe.

"Come, let us drink up, one and all!" he concluded. "The leanest of our birds are now singing in our honor; let us pledge them a toast, if you please, in return. Drain the cup, friends, I beg you: you will hawk and spit all the better for it later. Let us toss off one, two, three, nine bumpers. *Non zelus sed charitas*, said Erasmus, let us not employ the zeal of those who mortify their bodies, but rather the charity of those who wish their fellows the greatest corporal enjoyment."

At dawn, Sexton awakened us again to taste an early, monastic brew. From then on, our stay on the island was literally one protracted meal, call it lunch, dinner, supper, as you will. At intervals, to take our minds off the business of banqueting, we strolled about, listening to the singing of the sacred birds.

That evening, Panurge offered to relate to Sexton a blithesome tale of life in the Châtellerault region twenty-three moons ago. Sexton agreeable, Panurge told the following story.

One April morning, a certain groom was exercising his master's horses in the fields. Suddenly, he came upon a lusty wench, who

> *Watched the white flock she had to keep:*
> *She was a shepherdess of sheep . . .*

not to mention one donkey and a few goats.

Having engaged her in conversation, he persuaded her to straddle his horse behind him, inspect his stable and indulge in a piece of rustic fun. While groom and herdess conversed, the beau's horse talked to the belle's ass. (That year, in various parts of the world, beasts spoke to one another.)

"Poor, weakly jackass," the horse whispered into the other's long ear, "I pity you so! I can tell how strenuously you toil every day; compassionately I scan the marks of wear and tear on your rump. You do well to labor, since God created you to serve mankind: ay, you are an excellent jackass. Yet it seems harsh and unreasonable that you are never rubbed down, currycombed, caparisoned and well fed. How rough your coat is! How coarse your hair! Poor, skinny, undernourished jackass, with only thorns, briars and thistles for food. I'll tell you what, donkey: I'll invite you to my stable. Just jog along behind me, and I'll show you the treatment and nourishment given to such creatures as Nature designed for purposes of war. You shall have a chance to see how I fare every day."

"Oh, Master horse, you are too kind: I shall be delighted to come."

"Call me My Lord Stallion, Jackass," the horse sniffed.

"I beg your pardon, My Lord Stallion: we rustic boobies are crude, we express ourselves grossly. Indeed, I will gladly obey you. Since you are pleased to grant me this honor and privilege I am humbly grateful. But I will follow you at some little distance, for I would not court a drubbing. (My skin is one mass of stripes; I look like a zebra!)"

The shepherdess climbed on horseback behind the groom; the donkey brought up the rear, licking his chops as he looked forward to the lush banquet. Reaching the manor, the groom perceived the donkey. Forthwith, he ordered the stable boys to welcome the beast with pitchforks and speed it with cudgels. The donkey, hearing the groom's orders, commended his asinine soul to the god Neptune—creator of the horse and therefore patron of all quadrupeds—and beat a hasty retreat.

"That groom was right," Master Jackass thought, as he bolted off. "I've no business to be consorting with mighty lords; Nature created me to be useful to humble folk. Æsop warned me of this in the fable about the ass who caressed his master. Alas, I have been all too presumptuous. The only expedient left me is to whisk off tantivyteararse."

Which he proceeded to do in a succession of leaps, bounds, springs, curvets, trots and gallops, with a rousing salvo of poops and a furious rectal barrage.

The shepherdess, seeing her charge scamper off, protested to the groom. Didn't he know that ass was hers? She implored him to deal kindly with that ass; otherwise she would not come on. And how should he, the groom, come off, then?

The groom, rising to the occasion, told the stable boys to deprive his master's horse of oats for a week, rather than let his mistress's ass go short of them. The great problem, however, was to recapture the beast. In vain the stable boys coaxed and wheedled:

"Here, donkey! Psst, ass! Whisht! Come here!"

"I can't see my way to it," the fugitive replied. "I'm bashful!"

The more civilly they pleaded, the more briskly he pursued his impetuous and explosive progress. Indeed, they would be chasing him still, had not the shepherdess advised them to pelt him with oats. Of a sudden, Master Jackass wheeled about, faced them, and:

"*Avenia*, oats!" he brayed. "*Adveniat*, Thy Kingdom come! Oats? Oh, 't's too wonderful! But no pitchfork and no drubbing! On that basis, I consent to arbitrate!"

Whereupon he advanced towards his pursuers, uttering most melodious music the while. No doubt my readers know what tuneful effects these Arcadian beasts can achieve.

Master Jackass was duly led to a stall next to My Lord Stallion; amid much ceremony, he was rubbed down, mopped off, currycombed. Fresh straw was tossed bellyhigh into his stall; his rack was stuffed with hay, his manger with oats. As the stable boys sifted the latter, he wagged his ears, signifying that he could eat it all too well without sifting. Such honor, he added, was excessive. Was he not humble?

When both Master Jackass and My Lord Stallion had eaten their fill, the latter questioned his guest.

"Well, poor Jackass, how do you do? What do you think of our diet? Silly of you not to want to come, wasn't it? Tell me what you think of life among us?"

"By the fig an ancestor of mine ate, thus causing Philemon to die of laughter at the sight," Master Jackass declared, "so far, My Lord Stallion, this is balm of Gilead. Yet it is but half-fare. Are My

Lords Stallions never up to donkey-shines? Is there no dam to damage, no assaying to essay, no astatic assentation to puzzle my pizzle?"

"What assimilation do you asseverate, Ass? Your kernels are
swelling in the shell. Do I look like an ass?"

"Ha!" said the donkey, "I find it somewhat hard to learn the
courtly idiom of horses. I simply asked whether My Lords Stallions
stallionize. Is there no horseplay here? Do horses ride bareback or is
this a mare's nest?"

"Hush, Ass!" growled the horse. "If the stable boys hear you,
they'll lay on to you with pitchforks so fiercely that you'll lose all
aspiration to prodpizzle. Why, we daren't even prick up our ears
here; if ever we stiffened so much as to stale, we would be thrashed
roundly. Otherwise, of course, we live happy as kings."

"By the alblike frame of my packsaddle," said the ass, "I am done
with you. Fie for your straw, a horselaugh for your hay, and my
donkey's tail to your oats! Give me the thistles of the fields, where
an ass may ride-a-cockhorse! Less food and more friggling: fru-
gality and fructifying, that's my motto! In this connection—bless
it!—we asses go all lengths, coming off in the ascendancy, thanks
very much! Ah, My Lord Stallion, dear friend, could you but see us
at a country fair, when we hold a meeting of our provincial chapter!
Our human mistresses are busy selling their geese and pullets in the
market; meanwhile we branglefriggle our bestial mistresses, leaving
no stone unturned to drive home our points."

Whereupon, they parted.

"*Dixi!*" Panurge finished. "I have had my say."

Pantagruel would have liked him to go further, but he kept
mum, refusing to be drawn out.

"A word to the wise . . ." Sexton broke in. "I know what you
infer by this equo-asinine apologue. You ought to be ashamed of
yourself. I warn you: here you will find no fire to thrust your iron
into. Pray let us dismiss the subject.

"And yet," Panurge demurred, "a moment ago, I saw a white-
plumed Abbesskite that I had rather straddle than perch on my
wrist. There's a bird better to be had in the bush than in the hand.
Surely she is shapely and comely enough to warrant a sin or two on
my part."

Sexton frowned.

VIII

HOW WITH MUCH DIFFICULTY WE WERE SHOWN POPEHAWK

LIKE the two previous days, the third was spent in feasting and banqueting. It was then that Pantagruel asked insistently to be allowed to see Popehawk. But Sexton replied that Popehawk did not suffer people to see him so easily.

"What?" Pantagruel gasped. "Has he Pluto's helmet on his head, or the ring of Gyges around his finger, or a chameleon in his breast, to make himself invisible to the world?"

"No, no; but he *is*, by nature, somewhat difficult of access. I shall arrange for you to see him, if it can possibly be done."

Leaving us at our food, he disappeared for a quarter of an hour. When he returned, it was with tidings that Popehawk was at present visible. Quietly, on tiptoe, he led us straight to the cage in which Popehawk squatted, amid a brace of diminutive Cardinalhawks and six fat lusty Bishophawks. Panurge carefully examined Popehawk's form, gestures and bearing. Then:

"A pox on the bird," he said in a loud voice. "With that tuft, he looks like a hoopoe!"

"Hush, hush!" Sexton warned. "God help us, Popehawk has a pair of ears, as certain prelates have sagely reported."

"I insist; he's only a hoopoe! Look at his tuft, man!"

"You just let him hear you blaspheming like that," said Sexton, "and you are lost, good people. Do you see a basin in his cage? Well, that basin holds thunder, lightning and the devil's own blasts, which, in the twinkling of an eye, can cast you one hundred feet underground."

"Better to drink and to banquet!" Friar John suggested.

Panurge remained lost in profound contemplation of Popehawk and his suite. Suddenly, above the cage, he caught sight of a screech owl.

"God's might, we're being sniggled, bubbled and diddled!" he roared. "Take a look at that madge owl! Answer me: aren't madge owls used in catching bigger and better birds? I tell you we're being bamboozled, by God!"

"Not so loud, for heaven's sake," Sexton pleaded. "That is no madge owl or female bird. It's a noble male, a Prelatebird, the guardian of Popehawk's treasures."

"Can't we hear Popehawk sing?" Pantagruel interrupted. "We should enjoy his harmonious warbling."

"Popehawk only sings when he likes, and eats when he pleases."

"Not like me!" said Panurge. "All hours are mine. Since you insist, let us go eat and drink."

"Now you are making sense," Sexton declared. "Speak like that, and you'll never be taken for a heretic. Come along, I agree with you thoroughly."

As we returned to our drinking, we noticed a group of birds huddled together: there were an aged, green-headed Bishophawk, his Suffraganhawk and a trio of Protonotaryhawks, gay birds all, snoring under an arbor. A pulchritudinous Abbesskite sang merrily near by. We derived such pleasure from her music that we wished our body were covered with ears, so we might listen to her without anything to distract us.

"That lovely Abbesskite is singing her head off," said Panurge, "while that fat scoundrel of a Bishophawk lies snoring. By all the devils of hell, I'll make him sing presently."

Panurge reached over to ring a bell which hung above the cage; but the louder Panurge rang, the louder the Bishophawk snored. Not one note of song could be got out of him.

"God's truth, you old buzzard," growled Panurge, "I'll find a way to make you sing."

Seizing a large stone, he was about to hurl it at the Bishophawk, when Sexton protested:

"My excellent friend, you may attack, wound, poison or kill all the kings and princes of this earth, by treachery or by any other means you wish. You may dislodge the angels from the heavens. Whatever else you do, Popehawk will forgive you. But if you value your life, prosperity and happiness—not to mention those of your kin, dead, alive, or to be born in future generations—do not touch these sacrosanct birds! Look at this basin carefully!"

"Better to drink and banquet, eh?" said Panurge.

"Panurge is right, Master Sexton," Friar John put in. "We look at these devilish birds and do nothing but blaspheme; when we're draining our cups and flagons, we do nothing but praise God. Let us go drink, then. A fine phrase!"

The fourth day, after copious potations, of course, Sexton dismissed us. We gave him a fine little Norman knife, such as Jacques Cartier distributed among the natives of Canada. He liked it better than the glass of cold water a peasant offered Artaxerxes. (You recall how a rustic cupped his hands, drew up water from the river and offered it to the mighty Persian king, receiving in return a golden cup and a large sum of money.)

Sexton thanked us graciously and stocked our vessels with provisions, wishing us godspeed, a prosperous voyage and success in our undertakings. He made us promise and swear by the stone of Pope Jupiter Peter that we would visit him on our return. Finally:

"My friends," he said, "doubtless you have noticed that the world contains more stones than men, and ballocks than boys. Do not forget it."

IX

HOW WE LANDED AT TOOL ISLAND

WE ballasted our stomachs well, and sailed on, the wind at our stern; with our main mizzen aloft, we reached Tool Island in less than two days. It was deserted land with a vast number of trees bearing hoes, mattocks, pickaxes, scythes, sickles, spades, trowels, hatchets, pruning bills, saws, shears, adzes, scissors, pincers, shovels, augers and wimbles. Others bore daggers, poniards, dirks, knives, scimitars, broadblades, cutlasses, rippers, knives and arrows.

Did you wish a tool or weapon, you had but to shake the tree: it fell at your feet like a plum. What is more, it fell snugly to earth to meet a hollow stalk of scabbard-grass which enclosed it like a sheath. You had to take care it did not land on your head, on your foot or on any other part of your body, since, to be sheathed properly, it fell point downward. It might thus seriously wound any one who was not spry.

Below another kind of tree—I don't know its name—I saw various species of tall grasses that looked like pikestaves, lancehilts, spear-shafts, halberdshafts, partisan hafts, handles and stakes. These grew all the way up to the trees, where heads, steels, points, helves, blades and hafts met; the trees furnishing the appropriate blade for each wooden utensil, as carefully as fond mothers provide coats for infants ere they grow out of swaddling clothes.

In order to convince you that Plato, Anaxagoras and Democritus (no mean philosophers!) were right when they assigned intellect and feeling to plants, I must add that these trees were in reality animals, if you will. How did they differ from beasts? They had skin, flesh, tissues, veins, arteries, ligaments, nerves, cartilages, glands, bones, marrow, humors, matrices, brains and articulation. These were not immediately apparent, as in the case of animals, but existed and functioned none the less, as Theophrastus proved in his *Treatise on Plants*. These trees differed from animals merely in that their heads (*i. e.* trunks) grew downwards, their hair (*i. e.* roots) was invisible, their feet (*i. e.* branches) kicked out into the air. These trees, in other words, looked like a man or beast standing on his head.

From leagues hence, and weeks aforetime, you, O my beloved venereals, feel, in your sciatic legs and rheumatic shoulders, the coming of rain, wind and calm. Your very bones presage a change of weather. So these trees, through root, stock, sap and gum, sensed the kind of staff growing beneath them, and prepared a blade to suit it.

To be sure, all things, God excepted, are subject to error: even Nature is not exempt, since Nature, too, produces deformities and monstrosities. Occasionally, these trees wrought amiss. A pikestaff, growing high aloft the earth, rose to meet a tool-bearing tree, and found itself accidentally fastened, not to a metal head, but to a broom. (What matter? That grotesque implement would serve the better to scour the chimney.) A spearshaft, pushing up from the ground, might meet a pair of garden shears? (Very good: it would serve to trim trees and rid the garden of caterpillars!) The haft of a halberd found itself joined to the blade of a scythe, with results I can describe only as hermaphroditic in appearance. (Why worry? It would do yeoman service in the mowing season.)

Verily, to put one's trust in the Lord is a noble thing!

We returned to the ships. On our way, I glimpsed, behind God knows what bushes, God knows what people, doing God knows what, and God knows how. They were sharpening God knows what blades, which they held in God knows what place, and wielded to God knows what advantages. . . .

X

HOW PANTAGRUEL VISITED SHARPERS ISLAND

SAILING away from Tool Island, we reached Sharpers Island on the morrow. The place was a perfect reproduction of Fontainebleau, a sandy, stony place. The land is so lean here that its bones (*i. e.* rocks) stick out of its skin. A gravelled, barren and unprofitable place.

The navigator and pilot of our expedition (his name was Jamet Brayer, you recall) pointed out two small cubic blocks of rock, so dazzling white that I thought they were made either of alabaster or covered with snow. Not at all; he assured us they were made of bone.

("Dice, surely!" said Panurge.)

In these rocks, on six different landings, were the apartments of twenty devils of chance or hazard—devils much feared in our own country. They would accouple themselves in various combinations, the largest called Double Six, the smallest Aces; others *cinques* or fives, *quatres* (a pair of fours), treys and deuces. There were further combinations such as a six-and-five, six-and-four, six-and-trey, six-and-deuce, six-and-ace; five-and-four, five-and-three, etc.

It occurred to me, as I gazed at these cubic rocks, that few dicers and gamblers in the world failed to invoke the devil. Get two gamblers over a board, and, no sooner at their devotions, than they begin crying: "Double Six, Big Dozen!" (Which is the name of the largest devil dwelling on Sharpers Island.) Or they invoke the smallest devil, crying: "Come, Baby, come Aces, a pair of Aces!" Or they address various other devils by their particular names: "Come, Nona: a six and a three!" or "O Octo, O Otto! twice four, five and three, or six and two!" No devil but possesses name and surname; the dicers not only invoke them, but boast of being their friends and familiars.

To be sure, these devils do not appear forthwith at their votaries' summons. But herein they are excusable, for they are engaged elsewhere by prior invocation and call. Let no one accuse them of lacking ears to hear or eyes to see; on the contrary, their senses are highly developed.

Our navigator informed us that these cube-shaped, white rocks had caused more shipwrecks, entailing a greater loss of life and property, than the Syrtes, off the coast of Tripoli, or Scylla and Charybdis off the coast of Sicily, or the Sirens, or the Strophades in the Ionian Sea, where resided the Harpies, or all the other gulfs in the world. I could well believe this, as I recalled that the wise Egyptians of old hieroglyphically represented Apollo by the ace, Diana by the deuce, Minerva by the seven, and so on.

We also learned that Sharpers Island possessed a phial of sangreal or liquid of the Holy Grail, a divine property, little known of men. Panurge so civilly entreated the aldermen of the place, that they consented to show it to us. They did it with thrice the pomp and solemnity that attend the viewing of Justinian's *Pandects* at Florence, or, at Rome, of the Holy Veronica (the kerchief lent to Christ, on his way to Calvary, by the saint of that name). I never saw so many torches, candles, tapers, relics and holy objects in my life. This elaborate pother ended in our being vouchsafed a glance at a face that looked like a roasted rabbit's.

The only other memorable things we saw were Master Cheergrin, husband to Dame Jinx (you recall the proverb about being a game loser!) and two shells. The latter came from the eggs dropped and hatched centuries ago by Leda, when she produced Castor and Pollux, brothers of fair Helen of Troy. The aldermen gave us a fragment of them for a bit of bread.

Before leaving, we bought a box of hats and caps manufactured on Sharpers Island; I much doubt if we can ever sell them off to advantage. Nor will their ultimate purchasers find it possible to wear them to advantage, either.

XI

HOW WE PASSED THROUGH THE WICKET INHABITED BY GRASPALL, ARCHDUKE OF THE FURRY LAWCATS

SEVERAL days later, having almost suffered shipwreck various times, we sailed past Condemnation, another wholly deserted island, and so came to the Wicket. Pantagruel refused to land here, and wisely, for those of us who did were arrested and clapped into jail by Graspall, Archduke of the Furry Lawcats. Our misadventure arose from the sale of a Sharpers Island hat by one of our party to a local Catchpole; summons had been served on the vendor, who blithely disregarded them and thrashed their server.

The Furry Lawcats were dreadful, horrible beasts; they fed upon marble slabs such as you see in law courts, and they devoured little children. (Should they not have had their snouts slit, O friends and topers?)

The hair of their hides did not grow outward as ours, but inward. Every single Furry Lawcat had, for crest and device, an open pouch; but they did not all expose it in the same way. Some wore it dangling from the neck, others over the shoulder, others over the rump or on the paunch or at one side. There were mystical causes and practical reasons for this variety of custom.

Their claws were extraordinarily long, strong and sharp; let them get something between their clutches and nothing would make them let go. Sometimes they bedizened their heads with mortar boards, four-cornered caps such as our French high judges wear;

sometimes, with mortuary boards, which they removed on passing the sentence of death; sometimes with skullcaps; and sometimes with brimmed hoods.

As we went into their lair, a ragamuffin to whom we gave a penny, told us:

"Good people, God grant you come forth again safe and sound. Look carefully at the faces of these stout props and pillars of rapacious, catch-coin justice! Will you last six olympiads, plus the life-span of a pair of dogs—or fifty years in all, say? If so, remember I foretold how you would live to see these Furry Lawcats become lords and masters of all Europe, peacefully enjoying its entire domains and possessions. Unless, of course, God punishes them by depriving their heirs of such ill-gotten gains and income. Take this from an honest beggar!"

The fellow then informed us that while the alchemists regarded the fifth essence as the highest attainable refinement of analysis, the lawyers knew a sixth essence. By its means, they gobbled up anything worth gobbling, and bedaubed all earth with their defecation. Without the slightest consideration of right or wrong, they would destroy whoever stood in their way; right and left, they imprisoned, ruined, ravaged, assassinated, burned, hanged, drew, bequartered, beheaded and beshitted all who stood in their path. Among them, vice was deemed virtue; evil passed for good; treachery was termed loyalty; and robbery, justice. Plunder was their motto, and behold! all humankind approved of this organized loot, except a parcel of heretics! These Furry Lawcats pillaged and sacked the universe; they enjoyed sovereign and unimpeachable authority.

To bear out the truth of his prophecy, the beggar bade us notice that their mangers (which were much like the benches of judges in France) were above their racks (which resembled the recorder's desk in one of our courts). Thus they were always well provided for, just as our judges, who have but to bend down to take their provender of legal documents.

"Some day you will remember this!" he continued. "For if ever plague, famine, war, fire, quake, cataclysm, cyclone or other misfortunes rock the universe, do not attribute them to the conjunctions of malevolent planets, to the abuses of the Papal Court, or to the tyranny of secular kings and princes. Do not blame the imposture of hooded zealots, the heresy of apostates, the extravagances of false prophets, the villainy of usurers, the knavery of counterfeiters, the depravity of coin-trimmers. Do not impugn the ignorance of physicians, the imprudence of surgeons, the impudence of apothecaries; do not assail the lewdness of adulteresses, the depravity of poisoners, the fury of infanticides! No, my good friends: ascribe every disaster to the ineffable, incredible and inestimable infamy which is continually hatched and developed in the den of these Furry Lawcats."

Yet their wickedness, being no more generally known to the world than the Cabbala of the Jews, was not abominated, chastised and punished as it should have been. Oh, if but their crimes were presented and exposed to the public! Oh, then never orator, past, present or future, could, by the art of eloquence, save these Furry Lawcats from destruction . . . then never law, rigorous and Draconian though it were, could, by the power of fear, preserve them from due punishment . . . then never magistrate could, by the strength of influence, prevent their being mercilessly burned alive in their lairs! Their own children, the Furry Lawkittens, and all the Lawfeline kin, would hold them in abomination and horror.

"Now you know, friends," the beggar concluded, "why I stand here. Hannibal was solemnly and religiously sworn by Hamilcar, his father, to pursue the Romans so long as he drew breath. I was likewise begged by my late father to remain here until the thunderbolts of heaven reduce these Lawcats to ashes, as it did the other Titans, profane villains and enemies of God. For alas! men are too thoroughly inured to the past, present and future oppression of Furry Lawcats to remember or feel or foresee such affliction. Or if they *do* feel it, then they either dare not, will not or cannot exterminate this pestilence!"

"Is this true, man!" Panurge cried. "Ah, no, no: I'll not go in there, by God! Let us turn back, I say; let us retrace our steps, by God!

> *This noble beggar stirs more fear and wonder,*
> *Within my breast, than wild autumnal thunder."*

We wheeled around and sought to get out, but were faced with closed doors. Like Avernus, the entrance to Hell, this place was easy enough to get into; the whole difficulty lay in getting out. We were informed that no man could possibly emerge without a pass and discharge from the bench. This for no other reason than because Macedon was different from Monmouth, because the prisoner's dock was not the free man's daisy, and because the dust could not be so easily shaken from our feet.

Our worst trouble was when we went through the Wicket, for, to obtain our pass and discharge, we had to appear before the most hideous monster that pen has ever described. His name was Graspall. How can I hope to portray him? The best I can do is to compare him to the Chimæra, a monster with a goat's body, a lion's head and a dragon's tail . . . to the Sphinx . . . to Cerberus . . . or to the Egyptian image of Osiris, around whose three heads—the first a roaring lion's, the second a fawning cur's, the third a howling wolf's —a dragon coiled, biting its tail, and blinding rays shot forth tongues of flame. . . .

Graspall's hands were red with gore, his claws like those of the Harpies, his snout like a crow's bill or a ripping-iron, his tusks like a wild boar's. Flames shot from his eyes as from the mouth of Hell on the stages of our mystery plays. His body was covered with mortars and interlaced with pestles, through which only the claws appeared.

Graspall's seat, as that of his collaterals, the Warren-scourers or Wildcats, was a long, brand-new rack, above which, as the beggar had warned us, were some handsome, capacious mangers, installed upside down.

Over the chief seat hung the picture of an old woman, with an empty scabbard in her left hand, a pair of scales in her right, and spectacles on her nose. The cups or dishes of the scales were velvet purses: one, full of bullion, over-poised its mate, which was empty, long, and looming far above the middle of the beam. I took this to be a faithful portraiture of Justice, as practised by Graspall and the Furry Lawcats. How horribly different this was from the ancient Theban custom of symbolizing Justice! I recalled how at Thebes, after a dicast's or judge's death, the people erected, to his memory, a statue of gold or silver or marble, according to his merits. The likeness was perfect, save in one respect: the figure lacked hands. The Thebans could not conceive of a judge entertaining the notion of accepting a bribe.

As we appeared before Graspall, certain odd-looking men (God knows what they were!) ran up to us. They were clad in costumes made up of bags, pouches, purses and pockets. They pushed us violently on to low stools; we were prisoners at the dock.

"Ha, my rascally friends!" Panurge protested. "I would prefer to remain standing. This prisoner's stool is much too low for a man like myself, wearing new breeches and a short doublet."

"Sit down, sit down!" Graspall growled, "and don't make the Court repeat the injunction. What's more, if you fail to reply truthfully and with due respect, the earth will open up and bury you alive!"

XII

HOW GRASPALL SET US A RIDDLE

WHEN we were seated, Graspall, from the midst of his Furry Cats, called to us in a hoarse angry voice:

"Here: give me—give me—give me—"

"Give me a drink!" said Panurge between clenched teeth.

"Here, give me—your attention," said Graspall. "Here, give me—your ears!"

And he proceeded to recite the following lines:

> *A youthful, comely, fair-complexioned wench*
> *Conceived a baby, fatherless and black,*
> *Born of her womb, yet with a painless wrench*
> *Though, viper-like, it gnawed away a crack*
> *To issue through her tissue. . . . Then, alack,*
> *The negro bastard took French leave. He fled,*
> *Walking the ground with swift but certain tread,*
> *Up-hill, down-dale, flying, birdlike, through the air.*
> *Then wisdom's lover, filled with wonder, said:*
> *"Here is an animal, I do declare!"*

"Here," Graspall urged, "give me—give me your answer to this riddle."

"By the golden-mouthed, as they called eloquent St. Chrysostem," I replied, "I wish to God that, like Verres, one of your forerunners, I had Sphinxes to give away. Then I could answer your riddle."

(Here I referred to a story about Verres, the venial governor of Sicily, prosecuted by Cicero, and defended by Hortensius. The latter objected to some of Cicero's innuendoes, insisting that he was no Sphinx, no hand at answering riddles. Cicero retorted that, on the contrary, Hortensius had a Sphinx close at hand, at his home. Cicero was alluding to a golden statue of the Sphinx given to Hortensius by his corrupt client.)

"Give me—" cried Graspall.

"Give me—a chance to answer, My Lord," I asked the Court. "If I had such a Sphinx, by the golden-tongued, as they called St. Peter of Ravenna, I could solve the riddle you set. But give me—a chance, My Lord. I was not there, was I? And, not all the gold of Eldorado could make me say I was. I protest: I am innocent!"

"Here give me—no impudence!" Graspall growled. "By the Stygian darkness of hell, I'll not be paid in such coin. Give me—any more nonsense, and I'll make you give—in! I'll show you that you would have done better to fall into Lucifer's clutches than into ours. Do you understand, rascal? By all the devils, I'll not have you out of hand to no purpose! You allege your innocence, as though that should deliver you from our racks and tortures? Give me—the satisfaction of believing that our laws are like cobwebs: mean, paltry insects and petty butterflies are caught in their toil, while the more powerful miscreants, giant oxflies and small birds, break through ruthlessly. (Give me—any reason why this should not be!) Just so, we do not spread our nets for great robber barons and tyrants. They are harsh fare to digest; besides, they would gobble us up. No: give me—leave to tell you that we like to make innocents of you innocents, and to let the prince of devils sing a mass over your corpses!"

Friar John, impatient at Graspall's harangue, broke in:

"Ho, great begowned and bewigged Master Devil, by the golden age of innocence, how do you expect that man to answer a question he knows nothing about? Isn't the plain unvarnished truth enough for you? Or must it be gilt!"

"Give me—air!" Graspall sputtered. "I never heard the like of this! O for the gift—of patience! Never yet in my reign has a man dared open his mouth without being bidden by the Court to speak. Give me—an explanation of how this lunatic was set loose among us."

"You're a dirty, lying villain," Friar John muttered, without moving his lips.

"Give me—this man when his turn comes," growled Graspall, "and he'll have plenty of business on his empty hands, the scoundrel!"

"Dirty liar!" Friar John said, under his breath.

"Do you imagine," Graspall pursued, "that you are in the jungle of your university, flanked by a rabble of idle seekers and hunters after truth? Give—another guess, fool! We have other goldfish to fry here. Give—heed! Here, men give—categorical answers to what is asked of them . . . here, men offer—information on things they know nothing about . . . here, men confess to actions they never committed . . . here, men claim authority upon matters they never learned . . . here, men achieve patience by dint of frothing at the mouth . . . here, geese are plucked without a cackle. . . .

"You, rascal," Graspall brought his speech to a dramatic climax, "you speak without brief, I plainly see: not even the four-day fever deputed you to defend the pox, which God grant you will wed!"

"O devils, archdevils, protodevils and pantodevils," Friar John shouted, "the man wants to marry me! Pox would wed a monk. Ho, ho, ho, ho! The poxman is a rank heretic!"

XIII

HOW PANURGE SOLVED GRASPALL'S RIDDLE

PRETENDING not to hear Friar John, Graspall pointedly addressed his remarks to Panurge:

"Be careful to give the Court—no offence, clown!" he admonished. "Hand me—no flapdoodle. What have you to say for yourself?"

"Holy Father in the Devil," Panurge replied, "by the Pope's golden bull, I plainly see that the pox is abroad among us. And how not, by that foul fiend yonder, when innocence is not safe here, and the Evil One sings mass among you? So, by the golden ointment, I'll pay for that mass, in all our names, by that demon yonder, and let us go freely about our business. I can't hold—out any longer; I can't hold—*in*, any longer, by all the unclean spirits!"

"Go freely about your business!" Graspall gasped. "Give me—pause to recover from my amazement! Why, not one solitary soul, within three hundred years, has gone away from here, without leaving something behind him. (Most often, a tuft of hair or a pound of flesh!) Were you to do so, you would be giving—rise to all manner of gossip; people would accuse the Court of arraigning you arbitrarily, of dealing with you unfairly. Give me—the lie, wretch, if you can! Your hands are not tied, are they? Give—your thoughts free rein! You're in bad odor now, but you'll be in worse, presently, if you don't answer my riddle. By the Golden Horn, give me—an explanation of its meaning."

Panurge replied (by the gelded devil yonder!) that he would solve it, hands down.

"By the devils of the Pope's golden rose," he cried, "the answer is: a weevil . . . the larva of a black weevil, born in a white bean . . . boring and gnawing a hole through which to emerge (by all the boring and gnawing devils at hand!) . . . developing from insect into beetle (by all the beetle-brained devils of hell and hereabouts!) . . . and so sometimes walking on the ground and sometimes flying through the air. . . .

"To continue! Pythagoras, the first philosopher (the word in its original Greek form means lover of wisdom), Pythagoras, I say, held certain theories about the weevil. Its birth in such a place (devil take it!) argued for a metempsychosis or for the transmigration of a human soul into the insect's body.

"By the same token (devil rot your guts!), were you people real men, after the evil death of you, your souls would inhabit the bodies of weevils. Such by the parasites of Beelzebub, is the opinion of Pythagoras. And why? Because throughout this life, you gnaw, bore and nibble away at anything within reach. So in the next world (by the foul demon's cloven foot!) you vipers:

Will gnaw beyond your earthly tomb,
Will gnaw your mother's very womb,
Will gnaw until the day of doom."

("God's mighty body!" Friar John swore. "When I die, may my rear flue become a bean for these bean lice to batten upon!")

Having delivered himself of these thoughts, Panurge tossed a fat leather purse, stuffed with golden crowns, into the middle of the room. The jingle of the coins had not subsided before the Furry Law-cats were clawing away, like a rabble of fiddlers going mad over a *pizzicato* passage. They yelled at the top of their lungs:

"Fees and bounties, considerations, compensations, bonuses! A remunerative, sumptuary, numismatical trial! God bless these worthy people."

"I give you—gold," said Panurge, "pure gold!"

"By the golden mean, by the golden rule, by the golden fleece," Graspall proclaimed, "the Court has heard you!"

". . . has heard our gold!" said Panurge.

"Give me—a pen, clerk, so; give me—sand, to dry my signature. So. The Court pronounces you discharged—without costs! You are good as gold, my friends; so, be on your way. We are not such devils, gentlemen, as you imagine, even though we wear a black livery!"

Clearing the Wicket, we were afforded an escort of barrisinister clawyers to see us to the harbor. Ere we embarked, they advised us not to set off without first making the usual tributary offering to My Lady Graspall and to all her Furry Lawpussies; otherwise our escort must lead us back to the Wicket.

"Good, good," said Friar John. "We'll shake up the bottom of our bags and raise a handsome testicumonial for the ladies!"

"Remember us poor devils," they begged. "Leave us something to drink your health!"

"Devils' wine is never forgotten!" said Friar John. "Red or white, it comes out yellow. In all lands and climes, it is poured out liberally!"

XIV

HOW THE FURRY LAWCATS LIVED BY CORRUPTION

THE words were scarcely out of Friar John's mouth when sixty-eight galleys and frigates came sailing into port. He ran to meet them, curious as to their cargo and its destination. Investigating for himself, he discovered that the cargo consisted of venison, hares, capons, pigeons, pigs, kids, plovers, hens, ducks, teals, goslings, wild fowl of all sorts, together with bales of velvet, satin and damask, all destined for Graspall and his Furry Lawcats.

"What is all this stuff?" he asked.

"Corruption," they told him.

"So those Furry Lawcats live on corruption, eh? Very good; they shall die in generation, saith the apostle. God's might, I see it all, now. Listen!"

Friar John then explained. The good gentlemen of the nobility used to go hunting and hawking in order to inure themselves to toil, and train themselves for battle. Was not hunting a miniature reproduction of warfare? Xenophon was wholly right when he maintained that hunting brought forth as many warrior-leaders as ever the Trojan horse. Friar John begged to observe that he was no scholar: he had simply been told this, and he believed it implicitly.

Well, these brave, hunting gentlemen had been devoured by the fathers of the Furry Lawcats. Their souls, after this hideous death, had, according to Graspall's riddle, entered the bodies of wild boars, stags, bucks, herons, partridges and such beasts as they had, throughout their lifetime, loved and pursued. To-day, the Furry Lawcats, having devoured and destroyed the lords' castles, lands, domains, possessions, income and revenue, continued grasping for their blood and souls in after life. What an honest fellow that ragamuffin, who had called our attention to the Sign of the Manger over the Rack!

"True, Friar John," Panurge chimed in. Then, to the travellers who had brought this cargo of corruption: "It seems to me, gentlemen, that our lofty sovereign issued a royal decree which strictly forbade the killing of stags, does, wild boars and roebucks, on pain of hanging."

"That is indeed so," a spokesman replied for them. "But you must remember that His Majesty is very kind and gracious. These Furry Lawcats, on the other hand, are insane with thirst and rage for Christian blood. Naturally, then, we are less afraid of offending our good monarch than anxious to preserve our lives by maintaining these Furry Lawcats through bribery and corruption. Further, you must know that to-morrow Graspall is marrying off a Furry Lawpuss of his to a fat Attorneytomcat. In the old days we used to call that species Haygnawers, but alas! they have long since ceased to gnaw. Now they gobble, crunch, chew, bolt, gulp, champ, grind and wolf, so we call them Haregobblers, Partridgecrunchers, Woodcockchewers, Pheasantbolters, Pulletgulpers, Buckchampers, Rabbitgrinders and Porkwolvers. No other meat will do them!"

"Shit! shit!" Friar John bawled. "Next year, you'll be calling them Shitgobblers, Dungcrunchers and Turdchewers!"

They hung their heads in shame.

"Will you take my advice?" Friar John suddenly demanded.

"Ay, ay!"

"Well then, let us do two things. First, we will seize all this game here; I'm sick to death of salted meat, it overheats my bile. But we must pay for the game, mind you!"

"Ay, ay!"

"In the second place, let us go back to the Wicket and stamp out those devilish Furry Lawcats."

"Excuse me," Panurge interrupted. "I'm most certainly not going, for I am somewhat timid by nature."

XV

HOW FRIAR JOHN PLOTTED THE DESTRUCTION OF THE FURRY LAWCATS

"By the virtues of my holy frock," Friar John demanded, "what kind of a journey is this? A dungvoyage, a shitcruise, I call it: all we do is fozzle, fart and piddle away our time to no advantage. By God, I'm not born nor naturally suited to that sort of business; unless I'm doing something heroic, I can't sleep nights. Did you take me along to say mass and hear confession? By the Easter sun, the first man that comes to be shriven will do proper penance: I'll make the rascally poltroon dive headfirst into the deep blue sea, and I'll chalk it up against his future pains in purgatory!

"What was it," Friar John asked, "made Hercules a hero of sempiternal memory and fame? Merely the fact that, wherever he chanced to wander, he made it his business to deliver the people from tyranny, error, danger and vexation. Robbers, ministers, venomous serpents and maleficent beasts—he slew them all! He destroyed the Stymphalides, those cannibal birds of the foulest lake ever known . . . he discomfited the nine-headed Hydra of the Lernean marshes . . . he strangled the flame-belching giant Cacus, who had stolen four pairs of sheep from him while he slept . . . he lifted Antæus, Neptune's son, from the ground, and choked him to death . . . he put the Centaurs to the sword. . . .

"I'm no scholar," Friar John pursued. "The scholars tell me this and I believe it. I therefore suggest we follow the example of Hercules and free all the countries through which we pass. Let us massacre those Furry Lawcats, let us rid this fair land of these rapacious vultures of the devil. I deny Mahomet, the devil's lieutenant, if, being as powerful as he, I were to ask your advice and aid. Come, are we off on this punitive expedition, or are we not? I vow we will blot them out easily and I doubt if they will object, seeing that they have already swallowed more insults than ten hogs rooting up slop on an all-day shift. Forward!"

As no one moved, Friar John developed his theme. Furry Lawcats, he pointed out, were serenely unaware of the vilest insults and most abject dishonor, so but they had coins in their purses, even were that coin coated with dung, or those purses choke-full of midden. Friar John and his friends could easily annihilate these Furry Lawcats; unfortunately, no lord was present to impose such labors upon them as the twelve labors Eurysthenes piled upon Hercules. Friar John prayed that Jupiter might even now be walking among the Furry Lawcats, for two short hours, in the form he chose when he visited his mistress Semele, goodman Bacchus' mother—*i. e.* scattering his thunderbolts right and left.

"No!" Panurge replied. "God has done us the signal mercy of letting us escape from their clutches. I, for one, refuse to go back. Good Lord, man, I'm still weak and giddy from the gruelling labor of it. Here I may tell you that I was horribly vexed for three excellent reasons. One: I was horribly vexed; two: I was horribly vexed; three: I was horribly vexed. Put your right ear close to my left stone, Friar John: so! Do you hear two great peas rattling in a peapod? Those are my convictions making themselves clear.

"Listen! If, as and when you wish to appear before the tribunal of Minos, Æacus and Rhadamanthus, the three judges of Hell, I am ready to accompany you . . . to cross the rivers of the Acheron, Styx and Cocytus, if so you wish . . . to drink bucketfuls of Lethe water . . . to pay the ferryman Charon your fare and mine. . . . But return to the Wicket, if you want me to return? No, no—find some other companion; I refuse to go back. No wall of brass could prove firmer and more impenetrable than my determination. Unless I am violently and forcibly dragged there, I shall not go within ten miles of the Wicket, so long as I draw breath. Ere ever I do, you will find Calpe coming over to Abila, making the twin pillars of Hercules one. Did Ulysses go back to the cave of the Cyclops to recover his sword? The answer is in the negative, is it not? Well, I left nothing at the Wicket; why should I go back?"

"Ho, brave heart!" cried Friar John. "Ho, stout comrade with the palsied arms! But let us speak about the shot—ay, by the Scot, Duns Scotus, that most subtle and obscure philosopher! What about your paying the shot at the Wicket? Why did you toss the Furry Lawcats a whole purseful of crowns? Have we money to burn? Weren't a few mangy, clipped pieces of silver enough?"

"I gave him golden crowns because, at every point, Graspall said 'Give me!' so earnestly, that I did not imagine it possible to beg with such insistence for silver. And whenever the word *gold* was mentioned, he opened his velvet pouch so wide! I therefore concluded that we could escape by speaking golden words and mentioning devils of all sorts. You mentioned Scotus; did we not get off almost scot-free? Remember that Graspall's velvet pouch is no reliquary to which the faithful contribute silver and small change; it is a repository for goldpieces—and don't forget it, my beloved monklet bastard. When you have been larded, basted and roasted as I was, you will sing another tune! Anyhow, we must be off; that's what our Clawyercat escort told us!"

The mangy rascals were still waiting for us on the docks, hoping for a few pennies. Seeing that we were about to set sail, they rushed up to Friar John.

"Stay, stay!" they begged. "Don't forget your bounty to the Clawyers! You said you would give us something to drink your health! You owe it us for your discharge!"

"Corruption and chaos! Are you still here, you Clawyercats and Scrawlercats of hell!" the monk bawled. "Haven't I been annoyed enough here without you fly-catchers bothering me further? God's body, look!" He drew his great sword. "My discharge, eh? Here's a tool will produce the wine you ask for, you slabberdegullions!"

And he rushed ashore, bent on murder; but the sight of his naked blade sent them scurrying away.

Do you think our troubles were over? Not at all: further complications arose to challenge us.

While Graspall was trying us, some of our sailors, granted shore leave by Pantagruel, had gone to an inn for refreshment and relaxation. Whether they paid the reckoning or not, I do not know. In any case, the aged landlady, meeting Friar John at the docks, complained bitterly to him. She had with her as witnesses a sergeant (the son-in-law of one of the Furry Lawcats) and a brace of bumbailiffs.

Friar John, riled by their molestation, cried:

"Look here, my money-grubbing, scoundrelly friends, do you

mean to say our sailors are not honest men? I maintain they are, and I'll prove it by the justice of this sharp sword in my hand."

Whereupon, he waved and brandished it in the air.

The churls scampered off, terrified; only the old hag remained, to protest that these sailors were really honest as the day. Her only grievance, indeed, was that they had neglected to pay for the bed they had slept in after dinner. The price of that bed, she added, was five Touraine pence.

"Dirt-cheap at the price!" said Friar John. "Those sailors are ungrateful wretches; they won't find such bargains every day. Oh well, *I'll* pay you the money, and gladly. But I should first like to see the bed!"

The landlady at once led him to the inn, showed him the bed, praised all its points, and vowed that fivepence was not excessive. Friar John handed her fivepence. Then, drawing his broadsword, he ripped up the mattress and bolster, tossing the feathers out of the window. While the old hag rushed out, crying "Help! Murder!" and chasing the windblown feathers every which way, Friar John marched off blithely with blanket, quilt and sheets. He managed to get them on board undiscovered, for the docks were as dark now with feathers, as in winter, sometimes, with snow.

He gave this booty to the sailors. Then he informed Pantagruel that beds were much cheaper here than in the region of Chinon, even though the latter boasted the famous geese of Pontille. The old hag here had charged him only fivepence; the same bed, anywhere near Chinon, would have cost at least twelve francs.

As soon as Friar John and the rest were on board, Pantagruel set sail. But a southeast wind rose up suddenly and blew them off their course, and, so it seemed, back towards the land of the Furry Law-cats. Plowing through the heavy seas, they rode into a huge whirl-pool; the waters surged incredibly high, the lad atop the mast crying out that he once more sighted Graspall's habitat.

Panurge, beside himself with terror, shrieked:

"Dear Skipper, sweet friend, in spite of wind and wave, for God's sake, turn about! Friend, comrade, let us never go back to that cursed land where I left my purse!"

So the wind bore us close to an island, where, at first, we dared not touch. We did so about a mile further along, close to some large rocks.

XVI

OF THE ISLE OF THE APEDEFTS (IGNORAMUS ISLAND), OF ITS NATIVES WHO HAD LONG CLAWS AND CROOKED PAWS, AND OF THE TERRIBLE ADVENTURES AND MONSTERS THERE

We cast anchor, moored the ship, and put the pinnace over the side. On deck, good Pantagruel held public prayers of thanksgiving to God for saving us from this great peril. Then, with his suite, he boarded the pinnace and made for shore—no hard task, since the wind had fallen and the sea was calm.

Epistemon, examining the spot, and studying the curious formation of the rocks, suddenly caught sight of some natives. The first he accosted wore a three-quarter length coat of royal purple; a doublet of a rough, hairy material with chamois sleeves and satin cuffs; a heavy hat with many ribbons. His appearance was imposing.

Later, we learned his name was Doublefee.

What, Epistemon asked, did they call these strange rocks and hollows? Doublefee replied that these rocks were a colony settled by natives of Attorneyland; they were called the Rocks of Appeal. A little further along lay the Isle of the Apedefts or Ignoramus Island.

"By the sacred virtues of the *Extravagantes* and other *Decretals*!" cried Friar John, "what do you good folk live on? Can we not crack a bottle together? The trouble is I can't see anything here except pens, inkhorns and scrolls of parchment."

"These are our only fare," Doublefee assured him. "You see, anybody with business on Ignoramus Island must first pass through my hands."

"The Rocks of Appeal, eh?" said Panurge. "We have to pass

through you yet to get to Ignoramus Island, eh? Just as in France, you have to pass through the Court of Appeals to get to the Court of Accounts, eh?"

"Anybody with business on Ignoramus Island must first pass through my hands," Doublefee repeated.

"Why?" Panurge asked. "Are you a barber? Do you trim your clients?"

"I am no barber," said Doublefee, "but I trim them. My business is with their purses."

"By God, you shall have not one penny, not one groat out of me!" Panurge stormed. Then, more gently: "Nevertheless, my honorable friend, pray lead us to the land of the Ignoramuses, for we hail from the land of the Learned. Not that we ever learned much there!"

And so, conversing the while, we reached Ignoramus Island, which lay just beyond a neck of land.

The first thing that struck Pantagruel was the amazing shape and structure of the native buildings. For the Ignoramuses lived in a vast winepress, looking down from the eminence of a stairway of fifty steps. Before entering this main winepress—there were presses of all dimensions and sizes, from minor, through middle-high, to superior —we had to pass through a peristyle. From within these rows of sur-rounding columns, we looked out upon a vast landscape of ruins, with everywhere gallows, gibbets, stakes and racks. We were terri-fied. Doublefee, observing Pantagruel's rapt air, urged him to press forward:

"Let us go further, My Lord, this is nothing," he said.

"Nothing?" Friar John protested. "You call this nothing? By the soul of my white-hot codpiece, I swear Panurge and I are quaking for very hunger, faintness and cold—but not fear! I would prefer a stiff drink to another look at these ruins."

"Follow me, if you please, this way!" Doublefee urged.

And he led us into a small winepress, lying to the rear of the main edifice, and out of sight. In this respect, it resembled the drinking-bar of the Chamber of Accounts in Paris. This attractive room was known in the local idiom as the *Pithies*, which, in Greek, means wine jar. Need I add that Friar John and Panurge did full justice to it? No; I need but state that there were Bologna sausages, turkeys, capons, bustards and malmsey in profusion, with other meats and delicacies of all sorts, dressed and seasoned to perfection. A small potboy, seeing the loving glances Father John kept lavishing on a flagon on the sideboard, at some distance from the arsenal of bottles, whispered to Pantagruel:

"I beg pardon, My Lord, but I see one of your men ogling that flagon. I humbly implore you to allow no one to touch it. It is reserved for their honorable lordships of the winepress."

"So!" Panurge exclaimed. "You have privileged characters here, eh? I dare say there's plenty of vintaging done in this place, judging by appearances!"

Doublefee led us up a private stairway into a small room, whence, through a loophole, we could gaze upon My Lords of the Winepress, without being seen ourselves. We were informed that none was allowed further, without special leave of My Lords.

We looked through the vent into a huge winepress, where some twenty or twenty-five gallowbirds were standing around a green-baized counter, facing one another. Their hands were long cranes' feet, their claws twenty-four inches from cuticle to tip. My Lords being strictly forbidden to pare or clip them, they had grown crooked as billhooks or scythes.

A huge bunch of grapes was brought in to them—of the local variety called Extraordinary, which often grows on trellises. At once, they ran it through the press. Not one grapeseed but crunched, yielded oil-of-gold, for the cluster was put through again and again, until never a bubble of juice or substance remained.

That particular growth, Doublefee told us, was not often brought before My Lords. But there were always plenty of other varieties forthcoming.

"Tell me, friend," Panurge asked, "are there many different growths and varieties?"

"Certainly," said Doublefee. "Look: do you see that small bunch about to go through the press? That is the Tithegrowth or Clergy-grape; the other day My Lords ground out its very heart's blood. But the juice had an aroma of the clerical chest and My Lords of the Press found little yield in it."

"Why are they putting it through again?" Pantagruel asked.

"To make sure there's no juice left in the mash."

"God in heaven!" Friar John gasped. "You dare call them Ignoramuses? What in the devil's name do you mean? Why, those officials could skin flints or draw blood out of stones."

"That's exactly what they do. Very often we run castles, estates, forests through our press to draw out all the *aurum potabile* they contain."

"And what is *aurum potabile*?" some one asked.

"Liquid gold. Physicians have pronounced it a cure for all ills. *Potabile* means liquid, or drinkable."

"*Aurum portabile*, you mean," Friar John corrected. "Portable or negotiable gold!"

"Potable, I said, liquid, or drinkable. Many a tall bottle more they drink than they should. They get innumerable growths and varieties of grapes to crush. Come over here. Look at this garden. Here you see one thousand different growths, waiting to be crushed. So much for the public growth. Over there, lie the private variety, raised from restricted levies and taxes: fortification, gift, forfeiture, crownlands, privy purse, post office, donation and royal household."

"What is that fat kind, with all those small ones around it?"

"That is the plump treasury growth," Doublefee told us. "It is the choicest in the land. When we squeeze that bunch, My Lords of the Press have juice enough for six months long."

When My Lords rose, Pantagruel entreated Doublefee to take us into the winepress. He consented freely. Once inside, Epistemon, who understood practically every known language, pointed out the various mottoes engraved around the huge, imposing press. The latter, Doublefee assured us, was made of the true wood of the Cross.

Each part of the press bore its proper name in the language of the country. Thus the spindle of the press bore the legend *receipts*; the conduits, *expenses*; the mainscrew, *state*; the shank, *credited but not paid*; the vats, *pending redemption*; the branches, *excused*; the side beams, *to be collected*; the tubs, *above par value*; the double baskets, *rolls*; the treading place, *receipt in full*; the panniers, *validation*; the holders, *registered decrees*; the pails, *potential revenue* and the funnel, *liquidated*.

"By the Queen of the Chitterlings," said Panurge, "all the hieroglyphics of Egypt do not hold a candle to this. These words are as like as docks and daisies, chalk and geese, guns and goatdung. But explain this to me, Doublefee, good friend and companion: why are the folk here called Ignoramuses?"

"Because here they are not, and should not, in any way, be intelligent or educated. Ignorance is the rule and principle; nothing is transacted here for any reason other than 'My Lords decree that . . . ,' 'The Court orders that . . . ,' 'It is the pleasure of My Lords of the Court that . . .'"

"By God, with all those grapes to wring," cried Panurge, "they must toil like bell-ringers on a high holiday!"

"Every day's a high holiday here," Doublefee answered, "and there's juice aplenty three hundred and sixty-five days in the year. If the grapes they wring may be compared to bells, I dare say they ring like gold!"

From this great winepress, Doublefee promised to take us to see a thousand smaller presses. As we emerged from the main one, we noticed another small drinking-bar, around which stood four or five filthy Ignoramuses, furious as donkeys with firecrackers tied to their tails. They were very busy over a little press, crushing out the lees and dregs of the grapes left by the others. In the language of the country, these were known as Auditors, Revisers or Correctors.

"Here is the most villainous scum of humanity I ever laid eyes on!" said Friar John.

Thence we went past an infinite number of minor presses, all full of vintagers raking over the grapes with instruments called bills of charge or writs of account. Finally, we reached a large hall, where we saw a huge two-headed mastiff, with a wolf's belly and claws long as the Lamballe parchment claws made for the devils in mystery plays. The cur lived on fine milk and almonds—fines, mulcts and amends! My Lords of the Winepress ordered him to be treated with the utmost consideration; none among them but deemed this monster worth the annual income My Lords derived from the best farmlands. In the idiom of the Ignoramuses, the beast was named Doublefine. His dam—a bitch of similar hair and form, differing from him only in that she had four heads, two male and two female—was known as Quadruplefine. The most ferocious and dangerous beast in the land, except for her grandam, whom we saw behind the bars of a dungeon. Grandam's name was Neglect-of-Receipts.

Friar John, who was ever ready with twenty yards of empty gut when it came to gobbling a fricassée of lawyers, began to fret. He reminded Pantagruel that we had given our dinner no thought. Should we not bring Doublefee along with us and eat at once? So, leaving by a rear gate, we came upon an old man in chains. He was half-wise, half-ignoramus, like some hermaphrodite of the devil; he was as richly covered with spectacles as a tortoise with shells. His diet was a meat which, in their gibberish, they called Appeals or Revision-of-Accounts.

Pantagruel asked Doublefee what breed this protonotary or clerk belonged to. What was his name? Doublefee informed us that he had been chained here, time out of mind, much to the regret of My Lords, who practically starved him. His name was Review or Protest or Appeal.

"By the Pope's holy scrotumstones, no wonder My Lords Ignoramuses set store by that fawning hypocrite!" cried Friar John. "God's truth, friend Panurge, if you observe him closely, you'll find he looks like Graspall. Ignorant as these fellows are, they can still hold their own against others. Were I in their shoes, I would have sent him packing, with the bastard's back bastinadoed red as a sunset."

"By my oriental goggles, by my fine Arabian spectacles," Panurge agreed, "you are right! As I look at this clod Review's ill-favored snout, I find him even more ignorant and mischievous than these poor Ignoramuses here. At least, they grapple and claw without tedious, long lawsuits. With two or three words, they clear the vineyard, blissfully unaware of interlocutory and interpoxutory procedure."

XVII

HOW WE SAILED ON TO FORWARDLAND AND HOW PANURGE NARROWLY ESCAPED DEATH

WE put to sea at once, sailing towards Forwardland; en route, we told Pantagruel about our terrible adventures at the Wicket. (You recall, he had refused to accompany us ashore.) He sympathized so heartily with us that he wrote several elegies to pass the time away.

Safe in port, we refreshed ourselves and took on water, wood and provisions. The natives looked like jovial, gay folk. They were prominent in front, taut as wineskins, potbellied, and fairly farting with fat.

Here we noticed a thing we had never before seen in land or clime. The Forwarders actually slashed their skin to let the fat ooze out, much as the shitabreeks at home slit their breeches to allow the taffeta facing to flare out. They claimed they did so not through vanity but through necessity: their skin simply could not hold in their guts. Thanks to this surgical operation, they expanded, like the trees whose bark our gardeners slash in order to make them grow.

Close to the harbor, we found a fine, luxurious inn. A great number of Forwarders, male and female, of all ages and condition, were congregating there. We supposed they were holding some notable feast or banquet. But we were quite wrong. The mob consisted of various friends and relatives invited by the landlord of the inn to witness his bust or bursting.

Not understanding the native jargon, we imagined that a bust meant festivities such as we hold in France, on the occasion of the betrothal of our lads and girls, the wedding of our men and women, the churching of our mothers, the shearing of our sheep and the harvesting of our crops. We soon learned differently.

In his day, mine host had been a rollicking blade, a two-fisted eater, a glutton for rich stews, prepared as they do at Lyons. He was as

celebrated for his talent in contemplating the clock from his permanent seat at an eternal dinner, as the landlord of the inn at Rouillac,
near Angoulême, on the Bordeaux road. Consequently, for the last
ten years, he had pooped out so much fat that he had now reached
bursting point. In keeping with local tradition, he was ending his
days by going the way of all flesh. Alas! the lining of his abdomen
and outer skin had been jagged and hacked so many years, that it
could no longer encompass his guts. These were spurting their way
out, like wine from a split barrel.

"Eh, but good people, is there no way to tie up the fellow's belly
with stout girths or sorb-apple hoops or iron rods, if you must? Bind
him up like that, and he would be less likely to spill his guts and
burst."

Panurge had not finished when we heard a sharp report, like the
crack of a giant oak splitting in half.

Panurge fell as though he had been shot.

But the bystanders told us that mine host's bust was no more; the
thud we had heard was the death-fart.

This reminded me of that venerable Cistercian, the Abbot of
Châtellières, who would not frigglephuck his chambermaids save
in his pontifical vestments. Pestered in his old age by his relatives,
who wished him to resign his abbey, he protested that he would not
divest himself of anything before going to bed. His last poop, his
paternal reverence vowed, would be an abbot's!

XVIII

HOW OUR SHIP RAN AGROUND
AND HOW WE WERE RESCUED
BY SUBJECTS OF
QUINTESSENCE

WE set sail with a good westerly breeze behind us. But some two
hundred and twenty-two miles out, the winds rose from various
points, raising a veritable whirlwind. With mizzen and jugsail, we

lay by and drifted, rather than attempt to go through. Herein we obeyed our skipper, who bade us neither dread a disaster nor hope for a miracle. Considering the mildness of these winds, their leisurely contention, the air's serenity and the smooth current, we should apply Epictetus' maxim, *Sustine et abstine*, bear and forbear, temporize.

But the whirlwind lasted so long and we so plagued him, that the skipper decided to break through and follow his original course. Indeed, he raised the great mizzen, and, the compass pointing favorably, he righted his helm. Thanks to a sudden, furious gust, we rode through the whirlwind.

Alas! our manœuvre proved as successful as if we had avoided the frying-pan of Scylla, only to fall into the fire of Charybdis. No more than two miles on, we ran aground, stranded on a sandbank as high as that off Cape St. Mathieu in Brittany.

Our crew was dismayed. The wind whistled through our sails. But Friar John refused to lose heart. Undaunted he ran here, encouraging this man . . . darted there, comforting that with cheerful words . . . assured a third that heaven's aid would be forthcoming . . . swore to a fourth that he had seen St. Elmo's fire at the yardarm. . . .

Panurge, however, sang a different tune:

"Oh, would to God I were on land now: that is all I ask, nothing more! Would to God all of you, who love the sea so, had two thousand crowns apiece; it might encourage you to do your best and get us safe on land. Meanwhile, I would roast a fatted calf and cool one hundred bottles of wine against your early return. Ah, Lord, so be it; I am doomed not to marry. Thy Will be done. Only get me ashore. Give me a horse to ride home on. (I can dispense with the groom: I want no jack or knave at my stirrups or in my cards!)

"Plautus did not lie when he said that the number of our crosses (I mean trials and tribulations) corresponds exactly to the number of our servants. This is true even of tongueless servants. Nor need I tell you that the tongue is the most dangerous and pernicious organ a servant possesses. Thumbscrew, rack and torture were invented solely to treat servants' tongues and draw confession from them. To be sure, in our day, certain foreign legists have other theories on this subject—theories I can only call unreasonable and illogical."

Just then a vessel came sailing straight towards us. As it drew up, I could see it was loaded with drums and, among those on the passenger deck, I recognized Henri Cotiral, also known as Cornelius Agrippa or Herr Trippa. An old friend and a hearty fellow! At his belt, he wore a donkeypizzle, dangling like a rosary from a woman's girdle; in his left hand, he held a large, greasy, threadbare cap, such as your scurvies and scabscalps affect; in his right, a huge cabbage stump.

Seeing me:

"God bless you!" he shouted joyously. Then:

"Look, friend, am I a lucky man? Have I prospered? Here—" he pointed to the ass's pizzle, "here is the *algamana*, the true compound of mercury. And here—" he held up his headgear, "this doctor's cap is our true elixir. And here—" he held up the cabbage stump, "here is *lunaria major* or moonwort, that cruciferous plant beloved of alchemists. Ha! the moment we get home, I shall set to work to compound the philosopher's stone!"

"Where have you come from?" I asked. "Where are you going? What cargo do you carry? Have you sniffed the sea?"

"We come from Quintessence; we're bound for Touraine, and we're up to our arses in a cargo of alchemy."

"Who are those people on deck?"

"Alchemists, astrologers, diviners, fortune tellers, mathematicians, watchmakers, singers and poets," he told us. "All of them come from Quintessence; they have letters patent to prove it."

Panurge, highly vexed, interrupted:

"Ho, you wise men, who can make anything including fair weather and little children, why not get busy? Why don't you tow us into the current instead of leaving us here, high and dry?"

"That's just what I intend to do," said Henri Cotiral affably. "Just a moment, now, and we will clear you!"

He then had seven million five hundred and thirty-two thousand eight hundred and ten drums unheaded on one side, and set that side facing our pennant. Then, fastening them to stout tackles, and bringing our prow astern of their vessel, with cables attached to the broadest part of their bow, he towed us easily and pleasantly off the sands with one pull. The rattling of the drums, the crunching of the sand and the cheers of the sailors produced a harmony only a little less beautiful than the music of the whirling spheres, which Plato said he sometimes heard in his sleep.

Loath to appear ungrateful for such a service, we gladly gave them some of our chitterlings, filling their drums with sausage meat of all sorts. We were just hoisting sixty-two hogsheads of wine out of the hold, when suddenly two huge physeters or whales swooped furiously through the waves towards them, spouting more water than you can find in the river Vienne, from Saumur to Chinon. Their drums were filled to the top, their sails were soaked, they themselves sodden, as the water poured down their necks into their breeches.

Panurge, delighted, held his sides for very laughter and shook his spleen so violently that it gave him the colic for two hours.

"I wanted to serve them wine," he exploded, "but they got water instead. They never cared for fresh water, save to wash their hands in; this fine salt water will afford them nitre, borax and sal ammoniac in their alchemists' kitchen!"

We could converse no further with them because the whirlwind had put our rudder out of commission. The skipper advised us to let our ship run adrift, following the current; we need not bother about anything, save filling our bellies with food and wine. We must trust to the whirlwind and current to bring us safely to the Kingdom of Quintessence.

XIX

HOW WE CAME TO ENTELECHY OR PERFECTION, THE KING-DOM OF QUINTESSENCE

HAVING cautiously skirted the whirlwind for half a day, we sailed forward uneventfully for two days. The third day, the air seemed somewhat clearer. We rode, safe and sound, into the port of Mateo-techny or Vainscience, a short distance from the palace of Quintessence.

As we went ashore, we were met by a great number of bowmen

and other soldiers of the arsenal garrison. They made us somewhat
nervous, at first, by ordering us to lay down our arms. Their captain
challenged us in loud, haughty tones:

"What land do you come from, men?"

"My friend," Panurge answered, "we are citizens of Touraine; we
come from France. Our purpose is to pay homage to My Lady of
Quintessence and to visit this very celebrated realm of Entelechy."

"What's that you say, man: Entelechy or Endelechy?"

(His query reminded me of the tremendous war that raged, not
only among the ancients, but among our present philosophers over
the two Greek words ἐνδελέχεια duration, and ἐντελέχεια continuance
of being.)

"My friend," Panurge replied, "we are but simple, idiotic people.
Forgive the crudity of our speech; we are honest and loyal, for all
our lack of polish."

"We questioned you upon this point for a very good reason," the
captain explained. "A great many folk from your land of Touraine
have passed through here; they seemed to be decent fellows and
pleasant of speech. But from other realms, God knows what conceited and overbearing folk we have seen. The Scots, for instance.
Immediately upon landing, they insisted on arguing and wrangling
with us. We gave them a good dusting down, even though they did
have grim hatchet-faces."

They then asked whether we had so much time on our hands, in
our world, that we could employ it solely in impudent discussions,
debates and writings concerning the Queen of Quintessence. What
earthly necessity made Cicero abandon his *Republic* and busy himself about Her Majesty? How did their ruler concern Diogenes
Laertius . . . Theodore Gaza, the Greek priest and translator . . .
Agyropoulos, the philosopher from Constantinople who taught at
Florence . . . Bessarion, the Greek of Trebizond, patriarch of
Constantinople, then cardinal in Italy . . . Politian, the Italian of
the last century . . . and Guillaume Budé, the eminent Frenchman
. . . and Janus Lascaris, the Greek, librarian to François I. . . .

As though all these devilish wiseacres were not enough, their number had been recently swelled by such as Julius Cæsar Scaliger, the
physician of Agen . . . Guillaume Bigot, the professor of philosophy at Tübingen . . . Joachim Chambrier, Cicero's commentator

. . . Fleury, the Italian . . . and the Lord alone knows what other young blown dungchafers! The quinsy swell their epiglottis till they choke! Devil take them—

"They flatter the Devil here and prettify his name," Panurge growled between clenched teeth.

"You have not come here to uphold their folly, you have no authority to speak for them," the captain went on. "Therefore let us dismiss them from our minds. Aristotle, the first of men and the model of all philosophy, was our Queen's godfather: he very properly baptized her Entelechia. Entelechia, then, is her true name. Let all who would call her otherwise go and smother in their own midden! You, friends, by heaven! you would not err so grossly as to mar her name; therefore you are heartily welcome among us!"

They embraced us; we were delighted at their cordiality. Panurge whispered in my ear.

"Weren't you a whit frightened at first?"

"Frankly, yes!"

"I was more frightened than the Ephraimites, when the Gileadites slew and drowned them for saying *sibboleth* instead of *shibboleth*. Truth to tell, there's not a farmer in the whole land of Beauce who couldn't have stopped up my bumnozzle with a cartload of hay."

In silence and with great ceremony, the captain then led us to the Queen's palace. Pantagruel wished to converse with him. The wretched captain, looking up at the giant towering above him, longed for a pair of very tall stilts or a ladder.

"Never mind!" he said. "If our sovereign lady wished it, we could be as tall as you are. When she *does* wish it, we *shall* be!"

Entering the palace, in the first galleries we met a multitude of sick people, grouped according to their respective maladies. The leprous were isolated. Poison cases stood on one side, the pestiferous on the other. The venereals were in the van; the rest, ranged accordingly.

XX

HOW QUEEN QUINTESSENCE CURED THE SICK WITH A TUNE

In the second gallery, the captain showed us the Queen. Though at least eighteen hundred years of age—was not Aristotle her godfather three hundred years before the birth of Christ?—she looked youthful and comely. Clad in beauteous raiment, standing before her lords and ladies, she looked every inch a queen.

"You must not address Her Majesty yet," the captain warned. "Just watch her carefully. In your land, there are kings who fantastically, by a mere laying-on of hands, can cure certain ailments: scrofula, for instance . . . scabies or the king's evil . . . four-day fevers and the rest. . . . But our Queen can cure every known ailment without touching the patient. She has but to play a tune appropriate to the nature of the disease."

He pointed out the organ which she played to effect her wonderful cures. It was of curious manufacture: the pipes of cassia, the bellows of guaiacum or holy-wood, the keys of rhubarb, the pedals of turbith or jalap, the keyboard of scammony—all drastic purgatives.

While we examined this amazing, new species of organ, the lepers were ushered in by Her Majesty's specialists. These included abstractors, who drew off the material, the concrete, the tangible . . . spodizators, who burned the metal to ashes . . . masticators or chewers . . . prægustics or foretasters. . . . After them, followed the hierarchy of Quintessence's servants, all bearing Hebrew names used as titles of honor by the learned rabbis. There were tabachins or cooks, chachanins or savants, neemanins or faithful, rabrebans or illustrious, nereins or inspired, rozuins or princes, nedebins or aristocrats, nearins or servitors, segamins or satraps, perazons or leaders, chesinins or stalwarts, sarins or mighty lords, sotrins or scribes, aboths or barons, enilins or lieges, aharchdarpentins or governors, mebins or teachers, giborins or giants, and other Quintessential officers.

Her Majesty sat at the organ and proceeded to play a tune. I cannot remember it, nor do I know its name. But this I can tell you: when she was finished, the lepers were healed.

The poison cases followed. Again Her Majesty played on the organ —a different melody, this time—and at the last bars, they were on their feet. Blind, deaf, dumb and apoplectic followed in due order and were duly healed.

We were awed and terrified at these miracles. Was there not cause for our amazement? With one accord, we fell to earth, prostrate, rapt in ecstatic contemplation of Her Majesty's divine gifts. Had our lives depended upon it, we could not have uttered a word.

I do not know how long we lay there, prone. I only know that the Queen stood above Pantagruel and touched him with the bouquet of white roses she carried. Perhaps hers were not the white silken tones that Parysatis wished his followers to employ when addressing her son Cyrus, King of Persia. But they were at least of crimson taffeta, as she said:

"The probity I observe scintillating upon the surface of your persons inspires me with the certitude that the loftiest virtues are latent in the penetralia of your intellects. As I consider the mellifluous suavity of Your Gracious Honors' bearing, I naturally incline to predicate that your hearts harbor no vice, no deficiency or privation of liberal knowledge or magnanimous science. Rather, you abound in exotic and recondite sapience such as, in this advanced day and forward age, is more frequently desired than encountered, confronted as we are by the vulgarity of the learned. For this reason, and by the agency of their motivation, I who have heretofore subjugated my private affections, can no longer withhold my desideration to pronounce the utterly trivial and plebeian phrase 'You are welcome and more than welcome.'"

"I'm no good at making speeches," Panurge whispered to me. "Answer her, if you can!"

I did not. Nor did Pantagruel. None spoke a word. Her Majesty continued:

"From your taciturnity, I hypothecate two things. First, you are disciples of the Pythagorean school, whence, in successive generations, my ancient race is sprung. Second, I apprehend also that, retrograding over multitudinous revolutions of the moon, you were in Egypt, that celebrated nursery of sacred wisdom; there you meditated long, biting your nails and scratching your heads.

"In the school of Pythagoras, taciturnity was a symbol of superlative sagacity. Mutism, among the Egyptians, signified divine worship; thus at Hieropolis, the high priests sacrificed without a sound, much less a word. It is not my intent forcibly to impenetrate gratuitously into your intellects; rather, by courteous ceremony, I would communicate to you, through excentrication, the warmth of my thoughts."

Turning to her officers:

"Tabachins," she said, "a panacea!"

These officers then begged us to excuse Her Majesty for not dining with us. The Queen followed a diet of categories . . . abstractions, or, to give the dish its Hebrew name, sechabets . . . eminins or truths . . . dimions or images . . . harborins or concepts . . . chelimins or dream-pictures . . . caradoths or hallucinations . . . antitheses, metempsychoses and transcendental prolepses or anticipations of thought.

As for us, we were taken to a small room decorated with trumpets, where we fed on the fat of the land. Ah, God, how we fared!

Jupiter is said to inscribe, on the hide of the Amalthæan goat that suckled him in Crete, all that happens on earth. (He used this hide as a shield against the Titans, thus gaining the cognomen Ægiochus or Shield-bearer.)

By my thirst, dear friends and deep topers, I should need eighteen goatskins to describe the bountiful and exquisite dishes served up to us. And, even at that, I should have to write in characters as small as those Cicero saw in an *Iliad* which fitted into a nutshell. Had I one hundred tongues, one hundred mouths, a voice of brass and the mellifluous cornucopia of Plato's style, I could not begin to cite one-third of one-half of our magnificent fare.

Pantagruel suggested that when Her Majesty cried "Panacea," she quoted their native symbol for divine cheer. So Lucullus used to say "To Apollo," when he wished to regale some friend of his—though sometimes they took him unawares, as Cicero, for example, and Hortensius.

XXI

HOW THE QUEEN SPENT HER TIME AFTER DINNER

AFTER dinner, a servant led us to the Queen's hall. Here we saw how Her Majesty and the ladies of her Court were accustomed to sift, riddle, bolt and pass time through a fine, large, blue-and-white silk strainer.

Reviving the pastimes of antiquity, they practised such dances as the Cordax, the Emmelia and the Sicinnia, all three of the theatre; the first a wild lascivious step, the second tragic, and the third satiric . . . the Iambica, the Persica, the Phrygica and the Thracia . . . the Calabrism, a frenzied measure . . . the Molossia and the Cornophorum, a dance of the Corybantes . . . the Mongas and the Thermanstry, both frantic . . . the Florula, the Pyrrhic and a thousand others. . . .

Her Majesty having arranged for us to tour the palace, we were treated to such a series of singular, curious and weird sights that to-day, as I recall them, I am staggered. Nothing, however, struck our imagination so forcibly as the feats performed by the gentlemen of her household: abstractors; perazons or leaders, nedebins or aristocrats; spodizators or metal-melters, and the rest. They told us quite frankly that Her Majesty did the impossible, cured the incurable, whereas they, her officers, merely attended to ordinary cases.

I saw a young perazon alchemist curing case after case of syphilis, the genuine article such as may be picked up only on the docks at Rouen. How so? By merely striking the dentiform member thrice with the tip of a wooden shoe. A little further on, patients suffering from the dropsy were being restored to health by nine strokes of a double-edged axe on the belly, without the slightest scratch on the surface of the skin.

Another alchemist cured instanter all manner of fevers, by hanging a foxtail on the left side of the patient's girdle . . . another banished toothache by washing the root of the aching tooth with elder vinegar, and putting it out to dry a half-hour in the sun . . . another stopped gout of all kinds—hot, cold, natural or accidental— by bidding the patient shut his mouth and open his eyes. . . .

I saw another alchemist, in the space of a few hours, rescue nine good gentlemen from the ravages of St. Francis' il!, or poverty. He removed all their debts by clapping around their necks a rope, at whose end dangled a purse of ten thousand golden crowns.

One alchemist operated a wonderful machine that turned a house inside out, thus clearing it of infection. Another, without prescribing baths, milk, depilatory, pitch or any other medicament, banished all manner of fevers, whether hectic, tabid or emaciated. How? By turning the good consumptives into monks for a period of three months. If they failed to grow fat on monastic life, he said, they were utterly incurable, either by science or nature.

I saw another alchemist hemmed in by a vast regiment of women. Of its two battalions, one consisted of fresh, youthful, comely, pulchritudinous lasses; the other of toothless, blear-eyed, wrinkled, weatherbeaten and cadaverous old hags. Pantagruel learned that our alchemist recast and rejuvenated women. The battalion of hags on the right, there, would soon be transformed into creatures as youthful as those on the left. Indeed, the latter had been treated that very morning. The hags would recover the bright eye, the shapely figure, the proud bearing, the vivacity and the grace they had possessed at the age of fifteen. There was one flaw: their heels would be somewhat shorter than in their salad days. This was all to the good, though, since it permitted them to fall back more readily when they confronted a man. The ancients, waiting their turn at the alchemist's oven, stamped, pushed, fretted and stormed; it was a horrible ordeal, they said, to inhabit an unlovely frame, with so highly ticklish a scut, withal.

The alchemist practised his art continuously with considerable profit, as you may suppose. Pantagruel asked whether, by a like process, old men could be turned into striplings; the alchemist replied in the negative. But he did admit that a sexagenarian could obtain a new lease on life by cohabiting with a rejuvenated female. By doing so, he would obtain a fifth species of pox called *pellade*, in Greek *ophiasis*. This enabled him to cast off skin and hair, as snakes do, and recover his youth, like the Arabian phœnix. Quintessence held the secret of the true Fountain of Youth, by means of which the old and decrepit became young, eager, lusty. So, according to Euripides, Iolaus, nephew and collaborator of Hercules, regained his youth through the agency of Aurora . . . and Phaon, Sappho's lover, through that of Venus . . . and Æson, through that of Medea . . . and Jason himself, through that of the same Medea, if you credit Pherecides and Simonides, who assert that Medea, by her magic, kept him forever by her side . . . and the nurses of goodman Bacchus, and their husbands, into the bargain, if Æschylus speaks true.

XXII

HOW HER MAJESTY'S OFFICERS LABORED AND HOW WE WERE RETAINED IN THE QUALITY OF ROYAL ABSTRACTORS

NEXT, I saw a great number of Her Majesty's officers following in their lady sovereign's footsteps.

Some washed blackamoors white, in a few hours, by merely rubbing their bellies with the bottom of a basket . . . others, with three pairs of foxes under one yoke, plowed a sandy shore without losing their seed . . . others washed tiles, making their colors fade . . . others extracted water from pumice stone, by pounding the latter in a marble mortar, and changing its substance . . . others sheared asses and obtained the finest fleece . . . others plucked grapes from thorns, and gathered figs from thistles.

Among their divers occupations were: milking he-goats into sieves, with much profit to the household . . . beating the air, lashing the waves and holding farthing candles to illumine the sun, all to immense advantage . . . setting nets to catch the wind and bagging great lobsters . . . artificially drawing farts out of a dead donkey, and selling the same at fivepence an ell . . . and putrefying beetles. (O luscious food!)

Poor Panurge was violently sick at the sight of an officer of Quintessence distilling human urine, in a huge tubful of horsedung and Christian shit. Ugh, faugh, the dirty villain! Yet that same dirty villain informed us that this sacred distillation, sprinkled upon the person of kings and lofty princes, lengthened their lives by a fathom or two.

Various of them were busy breaking chitterlings at the knee . . . making silk purses out of sow's ears . . . flaying eels at the tail, without those eels crying before they were hurt, as those of Melun do . . . extracting milk from cucumbers and turning it back into cucumbers again . . . cutting blocks with a razor, cleaving flame with a blade, and gathering up water in a bucket from an empty well . . . making lanterns of bladders, chalk of cheese, and honey out of a dog's turd. . . .

About a dozen alchemists sat under an arbor, banqueting. Out of handsome, great jugs, they drank the health of one and all in four kinds of cool, delicious wines. We were told they were passing the time as local custom demanded, just as Hercules and Atlas passed the time, when they held earth up and drank the moon down.

Others made a virtue of necessity (I must say their handicraft seemed excellent and appropriate) . . . made alchemy with their teeth, supped with Democritus and dined with Duke Humphrey (the three processes are identical). . . .

Others carefully measured the progress of fleas hopping down a long lawn. These statistics, they told us, were indispensable for the ruling of kingdoms, the conduct of warfare and the administration of commonwealths. They assured us that Socrates, who first brought philosophy on earth from heaven, thus turning an idle, trifling pastime into a useful, profitable vocation, spent half his time measuring the leaps of fleas. Their authority on this score was Aristophanes, that master of Quintessence.

I saw two colossal stalwarts mounting guard on the top of a tower; later, I learned they were guarding the moon from wolves and baying dogs.

A few moments later, I met four more alchemists, in one corner of the garden. They were quarrelling fiercely; they had been at it for four days.

"What is it all about?" I insisted.

"We are arguing about three lofty super-metaphysical propositions. If we can solve them, they will bring us mountains of gold. The first concerns the shadow of a ballocky, well-hung ass . . . number two, the smoke of a lantern . . . number three, the problem: is goat's hair wool or is it not?"

Obviously, their logic embraced the flattest contradictions in mode, form, figure and time. I reflected how, rather than confess as much, the sophist pedagogues of the Sorbonne would have renounced baptism and forfeited heaven.

We were busy observing these supernatural operations, when Her Majesty arrived with her courtiers in tow. Already, bright Hesperus, the evening star, glittered in the sky. Perceiving our admiration at her officials' versatility, Her Majesty remarked:

"The stimulation and causation, thanks to which human cogitation wends its discursive way through labyrinths of stupefaction, are not motivated by the projaculation or puissance of natural phenomena, seconded by the dexterity of pantological artisans. No—stupefaction proceeds rather from privation of inurement, from the shock of surprise to intellect and senses, which had failed to foresee and predicate, meditate and adjudicate the excessive simplicity and facility of these phenomenal operations."

("She means," Panurge whispered, "that nothing is new under the sun!")

"Nevertheless," Her Majesty pursued, "pray fasciculate your diffused and disseminated powers; divellicate your stupefaction at the performance of my officers."

("In other words," said Panurge, "she wants us to take her and her works for granted.")

"My domain," Her Majesty pursued, "together with its perquisites and appurtenances, is yours. It offers a multitudinarious field of observation. Gradually, by dint of concentrated intellectualization, you will achieve a psychotherapohyperanimatic emancipation from vulgar ignorance. Such is my very sincere wish. Therefore, considering your transcalent propensity towards veritable sapience, by virtue of that same studious, physical manifestation of prominence,

I hereby appoint you as abstractors-royal to my person. Geber, the famous Arabian mathematician, who serves as my tabachin-in-chief, will register you as you depart."

Humbly and in silence, we thanked Her Majesty, accepting with much pleasure the honors she conferred upon us.

XXIII

HOW THE QUEEN WAS SERVED AT DINNER AND HOW SHE ATE

Her Majesty turned to her lords-in-waiting:

"My stomachic orifice, ambassador-in-ordinary for the alimentation of all my members, superior or inferior, importunes me to restore to them, by ingurgitation of idoneous aliments, that which they dissipated by a continuous calefactory action of nature upon my radical humidity."

("She means she's hungry!" Panurge whispered.)

"Therefore, O spodizators (good smelters!), O chesinins (men of brawn!), O neemanins (tried and faithful!), we merely wait for you to set up our tables and make them to pullulate with all delicious species of nutritive aliments. You, O noble prægustors or foretasters, and you, O gentle masticators, I need not command you: your ordinary industry and coördinative diligence, so often tried and tested, absolve me from ordaining order in your kitchens. Nor shall I bid you be on the watch. I have but to suggest you continue to operate as heretofore."

Her Majesty then retired with some of her handmaidens—to bathe, we were told. This practice was as popular among the ancients as our own preprandial manual ablutions among us.

Tables, promptly set up, were at once covered with snow-white napery. Her Majesty's rarefied menu consisted of celestial ambrosia, washed down with heavenly nectar. We, grosser folk, together with the members of the royal household, were served such rare and delicious dishes as Apicius, the noted Roman gourmet, never dreamed of.

After the meal was done, they set a hotchpotch on the table, in case we had not effectively declared an armistice with hunger. This dish was so enormous that even the golden plane tree, which Pythius Althius gave King Darius, could not have covered it. It consisted of various sorts of stews . . . vegetables and salads, devilled, moulded, mashed, curried and mixed *en macédoine* . . . fricassées . . . delicious meats, roasted, grilled, broiled, braised and sautéd . . . great slices of smoked beef . . . huge hams, cured in the old way . . . countless fried foods . . . heavenly salted dishes . . . cakes, and tarts . . . curds and whey, prepared in the Moorish fashion . . . cheese, junkets, jellies and fruits of all sorts. . . .

This hotchpotch appeared to me to be succulent and delicate, but I did not taste it, for I was satisfied and replete. I must add, though, that I saw a rare thing indeed: pasties in paste; and these pasties in paste were pasties in the pot. At the bottom of the pot, I saw dice, cards, chips, counters, chessmen and checkers; with many bowls full of golden crowns, for such as wished to gamble.

Under all this, I saw a quantity of mules, covered with rich trappings and velvet cloths, and of ambling hackneys, all provided for the use of the ladies and gentlemen. I don't know how many velvet-lined litters and coaches of Ferrara manufacture there were, to accommodate those who cared to take the air.

Most extraordinary of all, I found Her Majesty's mode of eating. She chewed nothing. Not that her teeth were anything but fine and strong; not that her food did not require mastication. No—it simply happened to be a habit of hers never to chew. Meats, previously tasted by her prægustors, were chewed for her by her masticators, who had gullets lined with crimson satin, with small ridges and golden purling, and teeth of choice white ivory. Having chewed Her Majesty's food, they poured it down a funnel of fine gold into her throat.

By the same token, we heard that she never evacuated, either, except by proxy.

XXIV

OF A COURT BALL, IN THE FORM OF A TOURNAMENT, HELD IN HER MAJESTY'S PRESENCE

AFTER dinner, a ball was given in Her Majesty's presence. It took the form of a contest or tournament; it proved to be a spectacular and memorable event.

First, the floor of the hall was covered with a long piece of velvet tapestry; its design was chequered, the white and yellow squares being three spans by three in area.

Thirty-two young people entered the hall, in two groups of six-teen; one group clad in cloth-of-gold, the other group in cloth-of-silver. Each group consisted of eight youthful nymphs, such as the ancients describe in Diana's train . . . a king . . . a queen . . . two archers of the palace, with headgear like bishops' mitres . . . two knights . . . and two wardens of the castle. . . .

They took their places on the tapestry as follows: the kings in the fourth square of the rear rank, the gold king on a white square, the silver on a yellow . . . each queen beside her king, the golden on a yellow square, the silver on a white . . . the mitred archers, on either side, to guard their respective kings and queens . . . the knights . . . and, on either flank of the line, the castle-wardens. . . . The front rank was filled by the eight nymphs, with one square vacant between each.

Each host had its own musicians, clad in appropriate livery; the golden army's band in orange damask, the silver's in white. Each orchestra consisted of eight different pieces. They proceeded to play tunefully and harmoniously on divers instruments of the most ingenious manufacture, varying the tone and measure according to the figure of the dance they accompanied. I was entranced by the infinite variety of steps, advances, retreats, leaps, vaults, turns, returns, flights, traps, ambushes, moves and double moves.

Even more astounding, I thought, was the ability of the dancers to recognize, in each measure of music, the cue for a particular move forward or back; the band had not finished ere they stood in their appointed places, though these were different each time.

The nymphs, in the first row, as though spoiling to begin the fight, marched straight against their enemies, square by square, save that for their first move, they were allowed to go forward two squares. They alone of all the dancers were forbidden to retreat. If a nymph succeeded in reaching the enemy king's line, she was crowned queen to her own king, and, thenceforward, enjoyed the same privileges as any other queen. Short of such coronation, a nymph could capture a foeman only forwards and obliquely, in a diagonal line. The nymphs, and all other participants, were not supposed to capture enemy pieces if, in so doing, they left their king uncovered and in danger.

The kings advanced to take their enemies, but rectangularly; they could proceed only from white to yellow square and conversely. For his first move, however, should a king's line lack any officers save wardens, these were allowed to set His Majesty in their place and to retire beside him.

Queens were given greater liberties than any other dancers. They might move to and fro in a straight line as far as they cared to, in all directions, provided no space in the line was occupied by one of their own host. They might also move diagonally, if the diagonal line were of the same color as the square upon which they stood.

Archers had leave to proceed forward and back, far and near, but must keep to the original color on which they stood.

Knights moved to seize their enemies in a lineal manner; they could step scot-free over one square, though friend or foe occupied it. Their second step might be made to right or left, on to a square of different color. This proved dangerous indeed for the enemy; knights bore much watching, since they never effected seizures in a direct onslaught, but rather stole up unawares.

Wardens moved to capture right and left, forwards and back, resembling kings in this respect. They could advance as far as they wished over unoccupied squares, a liberty even kings did not take.

Martial law, observed by both armies, decreed that, at the end of the battle, the kings of both armies should be besieged and shut up, without possibility of escape in any direction. When His Majesty had been bottled up, beyond hope of flight or succor by his men, he had lost the day. The battle was over.

To spare him such disgrace, not one subject, male or female, but would gladly have laid down his life. Fiercely, they vied with one another in capturing a foeman, wherever the music allowed. As soon as some champion seized an enemy, he bowed deep, tapped him on the right hand, sent him off the field, and took his place.

If one of the kings stood in danger of capture, the opponents were not allowed to lay hands on him. The most the attacker could do was to salute him courteously and offer warning, with a:

"God preserve Your Majesty!"

This gave the menaced king an opportunity to seek protection and succor among his followers, or, if this were unhappily impossible, to take up his stand elsewhere.

Nor was His Majesty ever taken without a ceremonious bow from the captor, who cried "Good Morrow!" as he bent the left knee.

The king taken, the tournament came to an end.

XXV

HOW THE THIRTY-TWO DANCERS FOUGHT AT THE BALL

THE rival hosts having taken their places, their bands blared martial music. A harsh, fearsome blast. . . .

Either host trembled all along the line, but soon regained courage, awaiting the signal for the charge.

Suddenly the music ceased. There was a pause. Then the golden host's band broke into an air, thus warning us their army was on the attack.

It was at once forthcoming. One more tune for the onslaught, and we beheld the nymph in front of the queen, moving. She made a complete turn to the left, towards her king, as though to ask his leave to fight. Next, she bowed to the company. Then, proceeding with modesty and decorum into the second square ahead, she favored her antagonist with a sweeping curtsey. The golden band then ceased playing, and the silver began.

I must not neglect to mention that, when the nymph bowed to her king and his company, they returned her greeting with a full turn to the left, except the queen, who turned right to pay homage to her royal consort. Throughout the ball, this salutation was observed on both sides by all the participants.

Now the argentine orchestra played, it was the silver nymph directly before her queen, who turned, made obeisance to her sovereign, then honored the company, which at once returned the tribute. The entire procedure was as before, save that all the silverites turned to the right, and their queen to the left. The silver nymph in question advanced to the second square in front of her. Gold and silver nymphs now stood face to face, as though ready to have at one another. But they could not try conclusions, since nymphs may only capture obliquely.

The comrades of each then followed them, attempting to intervene, creating a mêlée in the midst of which the first golden nymph swerved to the left, tapped the silver nymph on the hand, put her hors-de-combat, and took her place.

But soon, as the musicians played another measure, the conqueror nymph of gold was herself conquered by the silver archer, who was at once chased off by another golden nymph. This brought the silver knight out of the line, at which the golden queen took her stand in front of her royal husband.

The silver king, terrified at the golden queen's ferocity, shifted into the place occupied by his right-hand warden, a well-guarded and safe position.

On the western front, the left-flank knights, gold and silver, now pressed forward, overhauling many a goodly nymph whose escape was blocked. The golden knight wrought signal havoc.

The silver knight, however, was not bested: he resorted to a strategical movement that proved even more telling. He could easily have snapped up a golden nymph but, instead, allowed her to forge ahead so far, that suddenly he found himself in a position to draw up to his foe, salute the golden king and:

"God preserve Your Majesty," he cried.

The golden host, seeing their monarch's pressing need, trembled all along the battle line. Not that they could not rescue him; but if they did, it would mean the loss of their wardens and no gain in compensation. The golden king therefore retired leftward, and the silver knight seized the golden warden, to the great discomfiture of the aureate army.

Bent upon vengeance, the golden troops then hemmed in the silver knight on all sides. Desperately, he strove to flee, now right, now left, here, there and everywhere. But in vain. Though his followers resorted to every possible ruse, in the end, the silver knight bit the dust, captive to Her aureate Majesty.

The golden army, deprived of one of its stoutest champions, fought tooth and nail, thirsting for vengeance, and, in its rash, headlong advance, inflicting great damage to the enemy ranks. The silver host bided its time, coolly sacrificing one of its nymphs as bait, destined to draw the golden queen into a trap. When the golden queen took the silver nymph, she came within a hair's breadth of being herself caught by the golden archer.

His ally, the knight, then challenged the silver king and queen, bidding them good morrow with the utmost civility. The silver archer stepped into the breach, only to be seized by a golden nymph, who, in turn, succumbed to a silver nymph. The battle waxed even fiercer, the wardens rushing into the fray. A terrible scrimmage ensued.

The silver host moved up within a few inches of the golden king's tent, but they were speedily repulsed. In another quarter of the field, the golden queen wrought miracles, laying out the enemy archer in one move, and, glancing sidewise in the next, felled a silver warden. Her silver Majesty, perceiving the damage, fell with such savage force upon the foe that she accounted for the last golden warden and a trail of golden nymphs.

A fast and vicious duel now took place between the two queens. Each lunged and feinted at the other, now striking boldly, now stealing back, determined at once to escape and to guard themselves against the enemy king. Eventually, the golden queen captured her silver rival.

At this point, the golden king had only three nymphs, an archer and a warden; the silver king only three nymphs and the knight on his right. The fighting therefore became slower, more deliberate and wary.

The two kings, heartbroken at the loss of their beloved queens, made every effort to win this dignity for one of their nymphs. They were ready to marry and cherish forever the one who could break through to the enemy's rearguard.

The golden nymphs seemed more alert; it was from their ranks that a nymph was crowned and invested with the regalia.

This new queen, proud of her golden crown, proposed to display her ardent prowess. Meanwhile, the silver knight bagged the golden warden as the latter patrolled the limits of his camp. This led to a second coronation, a silver nymph being raised to royal rank. She, too, now sought to prove her valor, as discord and strife waxed apace. A myriad skirmishes, attacks, stands, routs and sallies were enacted, until presently the silver queen stole into the tent of her archenemy, and:

"God preserve Your Majesty," she cried.

His luckless Majesty, who could be rescued only by his newly wed queen, was now in parlous straits. As she ran to his aid, the silver knight, ranging across the field, moved to his queen's side. This placed the golden king in such a critical situation that, for his own safety, he agreed to forfeit his consort; still, he managed to hew down the silver knight. The survivors in the silver camp—one archer and two nymphs—defended their liege with might and main, only to succumb, after a last stand, and be placed hors-de-combat. Now the golden king stood alone, without a single soldier to command.

The entire silver host made genuflection and obeisance to His golden Majesty, bidding him good morrow, thus indicating that to their monarch, King Silver, went the victory.

The two bands then intoned a victorious tune, and the first dance ended amid such enthusiastic appreciation, such courtly gestures and such rare grace that we remained rapt and ecstatic. Not without cause, we fancied we had been spirited away to Olympus, and were even now savoring its supreme delights and felicity.

The first tournament done, the two groups resumed their initial positions and prepared to wage war anew. This time the music was one-half beat faster than before; the strategy of the combat, too, was different.

I saw the golden queen, resentful at the rout of her army, sally forth at the call of her orange orchestra, an archer and a knight in tow. Almost, she caught the enemy king napping in his tent with his officers about him.

Then, realizing that they saw through her game, she skirmished briskly among the ruck of the enemy, sowing destruction amid nymphs and henchmen. That golden queen was a very Amazon; she was Penthesileia, Queen of the Amazons, scattering destruction in the Greek camp.

This havoc was short-lived. The silver host, furious at their casualties, yet carrying on calmly, laid an ambush for Her Majesty in a distant corner of the field. Her Majesty promptly fell into it, was seized by the lurking archer, and led away by a knight errant. Her followers were speedily vanquished.

(Next time Her Majesty would be better advised. She would cling to her husband's side, or, if she must make a sortie, she would do so in better company than a knight and an archer.)

Once again, the silver host won.

In the third and last figure of the ball, the two armies took their stand as before. It seemed to me they looked livelier and more determined than ever. The tempo of the music was one-fifth quicker, the tune as violent, Phrygian and rousing as that composed by Marsyas, the prince of flutists, when, in their musical bout, he was unjustly beaten by Apollo, the mellifluous lyricist.

The participants began to press forward, turning and swirling so nimbly, with the appropriate salutes and obeisance I described above, that they covered four steps to one bar of music, in a series of leaps, tumbles and curvets that recalled dancers on the tight-rope. Or, better, as they gyrated upon one foot, they reminded us of tops, spinning under the whips of children, so rapidly that their motion seems to be rest, and they "sleeping," to quote the brats' phrase. The colored dot upon them then appears not in its true likeness, but rather as a continuous line—a fact which Nicholas de Cusa, the erudite Franciscan prophet, sagely noted in discussing questions of high divinity.

On either side, we heard loud handclapping and cheers, as one champion captured an enemy. The music played in incredibly swift time. The dancers raced at breakneck speed in five hundred combinations of ways. These battlers and queens and nymphs swayed, jumped, vaulted, skipped, capered and whirred with such agility as never to jostle one another. And as I contemplated this extraordinary exhibition of gymnastic skill, I wagered that they would have drawn smiles of appreciation from Crassus, the old sobersides who was never known to laugh in his lifetime . . . from Timon, the celebrated Athenian misanthrope . . . from even Heraclitus, who so bitterly despised man's most natural inclination to laugh. . . .

The fewer combatants remained, the more the audience enjoyed watching the extraordinary ruses and subtle stratagems they employed, as the music urged them on.

I must say this, and I have done. If this delightful spectacle swept us off our feet, dazzling our sight and thrilling our senses, the effect of the music upon our hearts proved overwhelming. It rendered wholly credible the story of Ismenias who, by merely playing the flute, so excited Alexander that the conqueror leaped from the dinner-table to take up arms.

From this, the third and last bout, King Gold emerged victor.

During these last dances, Quintessence disappeared: we did not see her again. Geber's tourist-pilgrim guides, tried alchemists all, led us to him, and had us registered as alchemists-extraordinary to Her Majesty.

Returning to Mateotechny or Vainscience Harbor, we boarded our ships at once, for we had a fair wind we were determined to make the most of.

Not in three-quarters of a waning moon could we have found such favorable conditions for our departure.

XXVI

HOW WE VISITED ISLE OF ODES WHERE THE ROADS WENT UP AND DOWN

AFTER two days' sailing, we sighted Isle of Odes, where we were to see an extraordinary thing. Here the roads were animals, if Aristotle is right when he defines animals as all such things as move of themselves.

In Odes, then, the roads, like animals, went up and down; the ways went to places; the paths led on to destinations; the walks rambled over hill and dale. Some, like planets, strayed through realms unknown; others were highroads and by-roads, highways and crossways, footpaths, short cuts and so forth.

Did a traveller or a native ask: "Where does this way lead to?" or "Where does that path go?" the reply would be: "From noon to the city," or "From five o'clock to the parish," or "From seven o'clock to the river."

Whereupon the questioner at once followed the right path, and, without further effort or fatigue, found himself at his destination. It was as direct, easy and inevitable as travelling by water from Lyons to Avignon or to Arles.

But, as you well know, nothing here below is perfect, nor is all life a bed of roses. We were warned that Isle of Odes was infested with a species of humanity called highwaymen, footpads and road-prowlers. The luckless ways and roads feared them and avoided them as you would robbers, since these waylaid them, as you trap wolves, or snare woodcocks.

I saw one of them taken in by the police because wrongly, and *invita Minerva*, against nature and reason, he had taken the way to school, which was the longest of all ways. Another boasted of having fairly and rightfully taken the shortest, thus reaching the end of his quest first.

By the same token, one day Carpalim met Epistemon, piddle-bracket in hand, irrigating a wall.

"Now I know why you are always first at Pantagruel's levee," he said. "You hold to the shortest and least used."

Among these various roads I recognized the Bourges highway: it proceeded at the steady, deliberate gait of an abbot. Presently, alas! I saw it sink at the approach of some wagoners, who threatened to trample it under their horses' hooves, and to run their carts murderously over it, as ambitious Tullia, daughter of Servius Tullius, sixth king of Rome, ran her chariot over her father.

I also recognized the old road from Péronne to St. Quentin, very personable and attractive in appearance.

Among the rocks, I discovered the good old white-capped road leading to La Ferrate in Savoy. This road went upon a huge mountain bear, and, seen from afar, suggested a painting of St. Jerome. To be sure St. Jerome is traditionally represented with a lion in tow, whereas the road in question straddled a mountain bear. Still, the La Ferrate road was mortified . . . it boasted a long, hoary, flowing, unkempt beard, that suggested a cluster of icicles . . . it bore a string of fat chaplets, coarsely fashioned of wild pine . . . it neither stood up nor lay back, but appeared to kneel . . . it smote its breast with round huge stones . . . it both frightened and stirred our pity. . . .

As we examined it, a runner, who looked like a minor professor in a university, drew us aside. Pointing out a smooth white way, covered with straw:

"From now on, gentlemen," he said, "do not scoff at Thales the Milesian, who assures us that water was the beginning of all things . . . do not dismiss Homer, who assures us that all things are born of the sea. . . . The road you see was born of water and to water it shall return. Two months ago, proud vessels sailed over it; to-day, it is a trail for carts and wagons to travel."

(He seemed very pleased with his frozen river!)

"God's truth!" cried Pantagruel, "you set no Thames afire and freeze no Danube. In our part of the world, we can see five hundred or more such artificial roads, any week in winter."

As we watched these roads winding ahead, moving forward, leading on and going to places, our erudite runner-professor kept up his running professorial comment.

He quoted many a philosopher who had meditated here in Isle of Odes, including Philolaus of Crotona, the great Pythagorean . . . Aristarchus of Samos, astronomer, teacher and commentator of Homer . . . and Seleucus, the famed mathematician. . . . One and all held that earth turns about the poles, and not heaven about a stationary earth, despite all appearances to the contrary. In this connection, he pointed out that when we sailed down the river Loire, it seemed to us that tree and shore moved; but it was really we and our boat moving.

On our way to the harbor we saw the local hangmen breaking three waylayers on the wheel. They had been caught lurking in ambush by the crossroads.

We also saw a great fornicator roasting to death under a lingering fire: he had beaten a path and broken a way. The way, we heard, was that which followed the banks of the Nile in Egypt.

XXVII

OF SANDAL ISLAND AND THE ORDER OF DEMISEMIQUAVER FRIARS

WE sailed on to Sandal Island, where the natives wore monks' sandals and subsisted solely on mackerel. Nevertheless, we were handsomely entertained by the local potentate, King Benius, third of the name. Having banqueted us handsomely, he took us to visit a new monastery, founded, endowed and built at his instigation for the Holy Order of Demisemiquaver Friars.

Why were these monks called so? Because in the world we inhabited, there were already many brotherhoods.

First, the *Servi Sanctæ Mariæ* or Servitors of Holy Mary, sometimes known as Augustinians, or Austin Friars.

Next, the noble and glorious Friars Minor or Minorites, sometimes known as Franciscans, in honor of their founder, St. Francis of Assisi. These, by virtue of their name, were a species of half-men—semibreves, musically speaking, and semi brief or semibrevet, in so far as the Pope's chancelry ordained.

There were also the Minim Friars, founded by St. Francis of Paula. These wore coarse, black, woolen stuff, fastened by a girdle, which they never put off at night. These were gluttons for dried herring.

There were the Semi-Minim Friars, called Crochets, because they were musically half-a-minim and personally *crochetés* or crooked, both in the claws they stretched out as they begged, and in their morals.

King Benius, then, could abbreviate no further musically or pontifically: he therefore shaved the name of his order down to Demisemiquaver.

According to the statutes and bull obtained from Quintessence, their good mentor and ally, they wore the tatterdemalion garb of your highway ruffians in Touraine, and, as bricklayers and masons elsewhere have pads on the knee, so these friars had reënforced bellies. Bellypadders were in high repute among them.

The codpieces of their breeches were shaped like your average monk's sandal or slipper. But they wore two, one before, and one behind. They believed that this trouserflied duplication housed some mystical and dreadful wonder.

Their shoes were round as basins, like those worn by Arabs who dwell beside quicksands. They were clean shaven; they were iron shod, like mules or like our elegants who wear metal on their foot-gear.

To illustrate their contempt of Fortune, from crown to shoulder-blade, they shaved the back of their heads, clean as a bird's arse, a monkey's rectum or a swallow's lungs. Their frontal hair grew rich and long, *ad lib*. Thus they turned their backs upon Fortune, dis-daining to consider the goods of this world. And, like Opportunity, their hair grew only in front, for Time must be taken by the fore-lock.

In further proof of their contempt of Fortune (which had honey in the mouth and a dirk at the girdle), the Demisemiquaver Friar wore a razor dangling from his belt like a rosary. He honed that razor twice daily, and stropped it twice nightly. . . .

Fortune is said to walk very steadily, but with ball-bearing soles, which expose her to rotatory hazards. In contempt of Fortune, the Demisemiquaver fathers wore balls on their shoetops. Likewise, the tips of their cowls pointed not fore but aft; this hid their faces, enabling them to fly, laughing, in the face of Fortune—and Fortune's minions. They were much like our ladies when they wear a mask to disguise—what? Some call it a neckerchief—others something else. Let us call it Charity; God knows! it covers a multitude of sins!

The back of their heads, as naked as our own faces, gave them free rein to work arse-upward or belly-down.

(Had you seen them arsing downward, you would have sworn it was their natural gait, because of their ball-bearing soles, their fore codpiece and the back of their heads, upon which was painted crudely two eyes and a mouth, as on coconuts at a country fair. Had you seen them fronting or counter-arsing, you would have sworn they were playing blindman's buff.

The Demisemiquaver Friars lived according to a definite regimen.

When the owls went to bed, as Lucifer rose in the morning sky, they put on boot and spur, and, for sweet charity's sake, booted and spurred one another. Thus, bebooted and bespurred, they slept, snoring like tops, besicle-barnackles over the bridge of their noses, not to speak of other spectacles or goggles.

We thought this a curious way of living; but they objected that humanity would have time aplenty to rest and sleep on the Day of Judgment. And, to demonstrate their will to appear in good time—a thing about which Fortune's minions were most reluctant—they made a point of being booted, spurred and ready to climb on horseback at Gabriel's first blast.

The clock struck noon. (Here I must point out that both chapel and refectory bells were made according to Pontanian specifications: the mouth lined with finest down, the clapper a fox tail. What are Pontanian specifications? The dream of an Italian savant Pontanus, who loathed the peal of bells.

At the twelfth stroke of the bell, the Demisemiquavers rose and took off their boots. Those who wanted to then piddled, cacked or sneezed; but, in obedience to a very strict statute, all of them had willy-nilly to yawn. They therefore yawned vastly, copiously: this was their breakfast. It provided a pleasant sight.

Having laid their boots and spurs on a rack, they went to the cloisters, where they washed their hands and rinsed out their mouths carefully. Then, sitting down on a long bench, they picked their teeth, until the provost gave the signal by whistling through his fingers. At once, each Demisemiquaver Friar stretched his jaws as far as he could, for a half-hour, more or less, according to the prior's determination to fit this breakfast to a particular feast day.

Next, they formed a stately procession with two banners in the van: the first, a portrait of Fortune; the second, a portrait of Virtue.

The Demisemiquaver in the lead bore the banner of Fortune; the next in line marched with that of Virtue. This friar also held a holy-water sprinkler. It was filled with the holy mercurial water Ovid describes in his *Fastes*: the lustral water from Mercury's fountain with which dishonest tradesmen annually besprinkle themselves to obtain the blessing of the god of thieves. With this sprinkler, the second Demisemiquaver kept banging the leader, as regularly as if he were ringing a bell.

"Their order," Pantagruel commented, "contradicts the prescription of Cicero and the Academics, who believed that Virtue should go before, Fortune follow after."

The Demisemiquavers protested that they preferred to do it their own way, since it was their intent to belabor Fortune.

During the procession, they trilled and quavered most melodiously, through their teeth, God knows what anthems. (I do not, for I am not privy to the jargon.) Observing them closely, I perceived that they sang only with their ears. But what fair harmony, and how well tuned to the peal of their bells, with never the least jar or discord! Pantagruel made a noteworthy comment upon their procession.

"Have you noticed," he asked, "how subtle these Demisemiquavers are? They marched out of one door of the church, and went in at the other. Most intelligent animals do not trust to one passage only; these friars took care not to enter at the exit."

"Upon my honor," said Panurge, "they are wise as March hares, subtle as leaden daggers, intelligent as buzzards!"

"Their subtlety," Friar John opined, "is derived from occult philosophy. Devil take me if I can make head or tail of it."

"It is the more to be feared," said Pantagruel, "because it is incomprehensible. Subtlety suspected, grasped and understood, loses the essence and name of subtlety; it becomes what we call dullness. Make no mistake: those fellows know a trick or two!"

The healthy processional stroll done, the friars retired to the refectory, where they kneeled under the tables, resting their breasts and bellies against lanterns. While they were in this position, a tall Sandal entered, pitchfork in hand, and proceeded to belabor them with it. They began their meal with cheese, ending it with mustard and lettuce, as Martial tells us the ancients did. As each received a dishful of mustard after dinner, they made good the old proverb:

> *Mustard after dinner*
> *Is good for saint and sinner.*

Their diet was as follows: Sunday, chitterlings, link sausage, Bolognas, forcemeat, fricandeaux, chicken livers on skewers, and quail, with always cheese before and mustard after . . . Monday, a fine dish of peas and bacon with a rare comment of sauce and interlineary glosses of gravy . . . Tuesday, vast quantities of holy bread, cakes, buns, pastry, crullers and biscuits . . . Wednesday, country-fare, *i. e.* fine heads of sheep, mutton and calves, which are very plentiful in this region . . . Thursday, seven different sorts of hotchpotch, with the eternal mustard . . . Friday, nothing but sorb apples, and none too ripe, if I may judge by their color . . . Saturday, bones. . . . Not one among them went hungry; all were handsomely provided with a fine fat belly, first and foremost. Their drink was antifortunal wine, to cite the name with which they grace God knows what local tipple.

Whenever they wished to eat or drink, they would turn the flaps of their cowls forward; these then served as bibs. Dinner done, they would pray to God in quavers, semiquavers and, especially, in demi-semiquavers. In expectation of the Day of Judgment, they spent the rest of the day performing acts of charity. Thus Sunday, they would beat one another . . . Monday, flick and fillip each other on the nose . . . Tuesday, claw and scratch each other's faces . . .

Wednesday, unsnot one another . . . Thursday, pump one another . . . Friday, indulge in mutual tickling . . . Saturday, pummel and fustigate, with might and main.

Such was their schedule when residing in the monastery. When ordered by the prior to go abroad into the world, they were severely forbidden (with terrible penalties for the disobedient) to touch or eat any fish whatever, if they were travelling over sea or river, or any meat whatever, if they ranged over the land. This was done as proof to all men that, though they enjoyed the object, they denied themselves the power and desire, standing firm as the Marpessus rock in Paros.

Whatever they did was accompanied by antiphonal chanting, always uttered through the ears, as I mentioned before.

When the sun sank in the western sea, they booted and spurred one another, clapped on their spectacles, and composed themselves for sleep. At midnight, the great Sandal entered. All rose to their feet, honed and sharpened their razors, marched in procession, settled under tables and took their nourishment as previously described.

Friar John of the Funnels, having carefully watched these jovial Demisemiquavers, and having learned full particulars of their statutes, lost all countenance.

"Ho, the fat table rat, ho, what a swindle! God's mercy, for every one of them you squash, two more arise. Oh, if but Priapus were here, as when he witnessed the nocturnal incantations of Canidia, the sorceress, and scared her off by salvos of the bum. How he would poop and counterpoop his gutful in quavers, semiquavers and demisemiquavers of rectal harmony. Now I realize we are in an antipodean land. In Germany, they pull down monasteries and unfrock monks; here they raise them awry and athwart."

XXVIII

HOW PANURGE, QUESTIONING A DEMISEMIQUAVER, ELICITED ONLY MONOSYLLABIC REPLIES

FROM the moment we entered, Panurge did nothing but stare at these royal Demisemiquavers. Suddenly he plucked one of them—a gaunt, cadaverous fellow, thin as a pickled herring—by the sleeve.

"Friar Quaver, good Friar Semiquaver, good Friar Demisemiquaver, where is the wench, the trollop, the bitch, the doxy?"

"There," said the monk, pointing downwards. And the following dialogue ensued:

PANURGE

Would you mind very much telling me whether you have many harlots hereabouts?

THE FRIAR

Few.

PANURGE

Without wishing to be indiscreet, I should like to ask you how many score harlots you have?

THE FRIAR

One.

PANURGE

Thank you. And how many score would a good Demisemiquaver Friar wish to have?

THE FRIAR

Five.

PANURGE

Hm! (*clearing his throat*) Where do you keep them hidden?

THE FRIAR

There.

PANURGE

I presume these sweet frails vary in age. But in corsage? What of their figures?

THE FRIAR

Slim.

PANURGE

Good: a slim, straight figure under a tight corsage is much to be admired. What of their complexion?

THE FRIAR

Clear.

PANURGE

Their hair? You know, a woman's crowning glory is her—

THE FRIAR

Hair.

PANURGE

What of their eyes? Are they—

THE FRIAR

Black.

PANURGE

Ah, ha! (*rubbing his hands together*) And their bubbies?

THE FRIAR

Round.

PANURGE

Thank you, Friar; I feel I am learning a great deal. What about their faces? Would you describe them as—

THE FRIAR

Soft.

PANURGE

They sound most attractive. I'm sure their graces would qualify as—

THE FRIAR

Ripe.

PANURGE

An apt description: thank you, good Friar Demisemiquaver. How would you qualify their expression, the glance in those black eyes you just—

THE FRIAR

Bold.

PANURGE

These gladsome hoydens naturally move from place to place, and, to do so, must tread upon feet which, good Friar, are presumably—

THE FRIAR

Flat.

PANURGE

And on these flat feet, the heels—

THE FRIAR

Short.

PANURGE

Very good! Hm! (*scratching his ear; then, quickly*) What of their lower parts, eh, Friar, their lower parts?

THE FRIAR

Hot.

PANURGE

A woman's arms add much to her beauty. Pray what are theirs like?

THE FRIAR

Long.

PANURGE

And their hands? Do they wear anything on them?

THE FRIAR

Gloves.

PANURGE

Needless to say they wear rings on their fingers. What sort of rings?

THE FRIAR

Gold.

PANURGE

Much obliged, friend, for the information. Perhaps you will tell us what kind of costumes they wear? Are their gowns of—

THE FRIAR

Cloth.

PANURGE

Yes, yes, but what sort of cloth?

THE FRIAR

New.

PANURGE

To be sure: you would scarcely attire them in rags. I mean: cloth of what color?

THE FRIAR

Blue.

PANURGE

And over these blue gowns, they wear coifs and headdresses and veils of what color?

THE FRIAR

Bice.

PANURGE

Doubtless their stockings are also blue, smalt or azure?

THE FRIAR

Buff.

PANURGE

Tell me something about the materials for all these garments. Would you be prepared to state that these materials are—

THE FRIAR

Fine.

PANURGE

We spoke of their feet a short while ago; you defined them as flat. Will you kindly say something about their shoes, which, I am certain, are of—

THE FRIAR

Hide.

PANURGE

How do they usually look?

THE FRIAR

Foul.

PANURGE

You mean they are covered with—

THE FRIAR

Mud.

PANURGE

These level feet then, shod in superfine leather, move about frequently, I wager. Where do your harlots go to, for the most part?

THE FRIAR

Out.

PANURGE

How do these comely *filles-de-joie* walk? The gait of a pulchritudinous woman is—

THE FRIAR

Fast.

PANURGE

So far, so good: let us now talk of the kitchen—I mean your trollops' kitchens. Let us not go hand over head, dive off the deep end, or plunge *in media res*; let us proceed step by step. What is there in their kitchens?

THE FRIAR

Fire.

PANURGE

What fuel do you use to keep that fire going?

THE FRIAR

Logs.

PANURGE

Wood, eh? But what sort of wood, pray?

THE FRIAR

Dry.

PANURGE

Dry wood; I see. But what kind of wood is it?

THE FRIAR

Yew.

PANURGE

Thank *you*: that settles the main question. Still, you must need faggots and brushes for kindling. I suppose you employ various varieties of—

THE FRIAR

Holm.

PANURGE

In your own chambers, you burn—

THE FRIAR

Pine.

PANURGE

Exclusively? Or do you sometimes light fires of—

THE FRIAR

Lime.

PANURGE

Let us go back to the trulls. (I'm sorry we left them: I'll meet you halfway on that score!) How do they feed them?

THE FRIAR

Well.

PANURGE

What fare do you supply?

THE FRIAR

Bread.

PANURGE

Yes, but what kind of bread?

THE FRIAR

Black.

PANURGE

Black bread, ah! we're getting along famously. Still, you surely give them something else?

THE FRIAR

Meat.

PANURGE

Ha, meat! May I ask in what form—

THE FRIAR

Roast.

PANURGE

Do the darlings never get hotchpotches or stews?

THE FRIAR

None.

PANURGE

Meat pies? Rich crusts covering the roasted meat of—

THE FRIAR

Lots.

PANURGE

Well, I'm with you there; I fancy meat pies myself. But let me ask you something else. Do your drabs get fish?

THE FRIAR

Tons.

PANURGE

Lucky girls! But don't they get anything else?

THE FRIAR

Eggs.

PANURGE

And how do they like their eggs prepared?

THE FRIAR

Hot.

PANURGE

Yes, certainly. But do they like their eggs shirred or poached or *en cocotte*?

THE FRIAR

Boiled.

PANURGE

Boiled! Boiled! (*wearily*) But boiled—

THE FRIAR

Hard.

PANURGE

Is that all they eat?

THE FRIAR

No.

PANURGE

What more? What else? Let me—

THE FRIAR

Beef.

PANURGE

Anything else?

THE FRIAR

Pork.

PANURGE

Besides pork?

THE FRIAR

Goose.

PANURGE

They fare well, by God. Besides beef, pork and goose, I imagine you also give them—

THE FRIAR

Duck.

PANURGE

Ah, wellaway! What else?

THE FRIAR

Cock.

PANURGE

I suppose they season all these meats with—

THE FRIAR

Sauce.

PANURGE

. . . flavored no doubt with mustard, probably the kind of mustard known as—

THE FRIAR

French.

PANURGE

(*affably*) Now if I am not trying your patience too much, possibly you will inform me how these strumpets finish their meal off? Do you offer them—

THE FRIAR

Rice.

PANURGE

What else?

THE FRIAR

Milk.

PANURGE

Nothing more than rice and milk?

THE FRIAR

Peas.

PANURGE

But what sort of peas?

THE FRIAR

Green.

PANURGE

With what do you boil these excellent green peas?

THE FRIAR

Pork.

PANURGE

No doubt their desserts usually consist of fruit. May I ask what fruits?

THE FRIAR

Good.

PANURGE

What's that you say?

THE FRIAR

Raw.

PANURGE

And after this, is there—

THE FRIAR

Nuts.

PANURGE

Nuts? Oh yes, yes, yes, yes! (*affably*) We have not touched the subject of drinking. Do they drink—

THE FRIAR

Neat!

PANURGE

What do they drink—

THE FRIAR

Wine.

PANURGE

What kind of wine?

THE FRIAR

White.

PANURGE

In the wintertime, it is—

THE FRIAR

Strong.

PANURGE

True, true. And the wine in the spring is of course—

THE FRIAR

Tart.

PANURGE

In summer?

THE FRIAR

Cool.

PANURGE

In autumn, in the sweet vintage time—

THE FRIAR

Sweet.

"By the potbellies of the guzzling monks," Friar John broke in. "These Semiquaver trollops must swell fat as sows. With all that food under their belts, they must jog, frisk and prance under their riders!"

"Wait," Panurge cautioned him, "let me finish."

And he continued his catechism:

PANURGE

What time do they go to bed?

THE FRIAR

Night.

PANURGE

When do they get up?

THE FRIAR

Late.

"God help us, this is the finest little Demisemiquaver I've ridden in a year," said Panurge. "Would to God, would to blessed St. Semiquaver, would to the great and holy virgin, blessed St. Demisemiquaverina, that this lad here were Chief Justice of Paris! God's truth, friend, with what dispatch he settles cases, with what immediacy he speeds suits, with what rapidity he quells arguments, with what activity he runs through briefs, with what expedition he peruses documents. Oh, what a Registrar of Deeds he would make!"

The notion left Panurge breathless. There was a brief silence. Then:

PANURGE

Let us go back to the choice game we were discussing, good Friar Demisemiquaver. Let us treat coolly and collectedly, part by part and member by member, of the further virtues of your sweet sisters of charity. What of holy sliturgy, what of the snatchblatch?

THE FRIAR

Rough.

PANURGE

The entrance is—

THE FRIAR

Lush.

PANURGE

And once within, you find it—

THE FRIAR

Deep.

PANURGE

That's not what I meant. I wished to know if the climate, there, was—

THE FRIAR

Hot.

PANURGE

Around the floodgate, I suppose, they have—

THE FRIAR

Tufts.

PANURGE

What sort of tufts?

THE FRIAR

Red.

PANURGE

But the oldest?

THE FRIAR

Gray.

PANURGE

What of their yield, good Friar?

THE FRIAR

Prompt.

PANURGE

Their buttocks: the motive power must be—

THE FRIAR

Quick.

PANURGE

Is every single one a vaulter and crack shot?

THE FRIAR

All.

PANURGE

What kind of gear do you use? Are your tools—

THE FRIAR

Long.

PANURGE

And their helves?

THE FRIAR

Round.

PANURGE

What color are they at the tip?

THE FRIAR

Red.

PANURGE

When these instruments have served their purpose, how are they?

THE FRIAR

Shrunk.

PANURGE

And the tool kit? Is it always heavy, or does it vary? What, for instance, would an average bag weigh?

THE FRIAR

Stones!

PANURGE

What's that?

THE FRIAR

Pounds.

PANURGE

How do you carry them?

THE FRIAR

High!

PANURGE

After they too have done their duty, what are they like?

THE FRIAR

Lank.

PANURGE

Now by your friar's oath, Friar, tell me this: when you feel the urge to cunnyscrunch these baggages, do you throw them—

THE FRIAR

Flat.

PANURGE

What do they say while you discharge your duty, friggle-trundling?

THE FRIAR

Mmmmmmmmm!

PANURGE

They may not speak, but I vow they tickle your fancy and warm the cockles of your hearts. They say no word, because their minds are riveted to mystic thoughts: but they come to the point, I daresay.

THE FRIAR

True.

PANURGE

Do they bear you children?

THE FRIAR

None.

PANURGE

How do you lie together?

THE FRIAR

Nude.

PANURGE

Remember your monastic oath, Friar, and tell me honestly how many times a day you ride the monk's mare?

THE FRIAR

Six.

PANURGE

And how many performances at night?

THE FRIAR

Ten.

"Good God!" bawled Friar John. "The lecher stops at sixteen: he's bashful, poor lad. Shame on him!"

"Hah!" Panurge retorted. "Would you do as well, Friar John? Could you by any stretch of the imagination come up to him? Why, he's a fornicator of the first water, and in hot water all the time, the leper lecher!"

PANURGE

Tell me, good Friar, do your fellows keep pace with you?

THE FRIAR

All.

PANURGE

Who among you is cock of the walk?

THE FRIAR

I.

PANURGE

Are you never out of gear? Never a flash in the pan or a jammed trigger?

THE FRIAR

None.

PANURGE

I'm completely bowled over! Do you actually mean to tell me that you can drain your spermatic demijohns dry one day, and on the morrow find them—

THE FRIAR

Full.

PANURGE

Either I'm dreaming or these Demisemiquavers possess the Indian aphrodisiac herb cited by Theophrastus! Look here, Friar, suppose some impediment legitimately or otherwise caused a decrease in your membership, how would it go with you?

THE FRIAR

Ill.

PANURGE

What would your wenches do?

THE FRIAR

Curse.

PANURGE

Suppose you let one day pass without scouring the snatchblatch, how would things be then?

THE FRIAR

Worse.

PANURGE

What would you give them, then?

THE FRIAR

Thwacks.

PANURGE

When you beat them, how do they respond? I imagine they—

THE FRIAR

Shit!

PANURGE

What's that you say?

THE FRIAR

Poop!

PANURGE

Poops of what *timbre*?

THE FRIAR

Low.

PANURGE

How do you chastise them?

THE FRIAR

Hard.

PANURGE

What is the upshot?

THE FRIAR

Blood.

PANURGE

What is their complexion then?

THE FRIAR

Red.

PANURGE

. . . which could please you no better, even if they used—

THE FRIAR

Paint.

PANURGE

Consequently, they always regard you with much—

THE FRIAR

Fear.

PANURGE

And, after the thrashing, they look at you as—

THE FRIAR

Saints.

PANURGE

By your holy oath, tell me what time of year you rest on your oars. Is it June, the sixth month, or is it the—

THE FRIAR

Eighth.

PANURGE

August, you mean?

THE FRIAR

Right.

PANURGE

When do you ply the long arm most vigorously?

THE FRIAR

March.

PANURGE

And the rest of the year, how is your performance?

THE FRIAR

Stout.

Panurge smiled then:

"There's a poor Demisemiquaver for you! Did you hear how set, how summary, how compendious his answers were? I verily think he would make three bites of a cherry."

"God's body," said Friar John, "he never talks like that to his trollops; then, he's polysyllabic enough, I'll warrant. You said something about making three bites of a cherry. By St. Ninnyhammer, I vow the lecher would make two bites of a shoulder of mutton, and one gulp of a gallon of wine. Look at him: cadaverous, shagged-out, down at the mouth—"

"These monks are a putrid crew!" Epistemon observed. "The world over, they think of nothing but their guts, and then prate to us of how they forgo the pleasures of this life for those of the next. They have here below, they tell us, nothing, nothing at all, merely food and raiment. Good Lord! What more have kings and princes?"

XXIX

HOW THE CUSTOM OF LENT ANNOYED EPISTEMON

"Did you hear this foul, evil Demisemiquaver quote March as the best month for caterwauling?"

"Ay," said Pantagruel, "but March is always in Lent, remember that. Lent was instituted for the maceration of the flesh, the mortification of sensual appetites, the control of amorous passions."

"In this respect," said Epistemon, "judge of the lofty intelligence of the pope who first inaugurated the custom. This ordurous Sandal of a Demisemiquaver, himself, confesses that he is never deeper bedunged in lechery than in Lent. Moreover, the best and most experienced physicians offer conclusive proof that in no other season of the year do men eat more aphrodisiac foods than in Lent. Think of all the white beans, kidney beans, peas, chick peas, onions, nuts, oysters, herring and salted food we consume! Think of the garum, a sauce of fermented fish! Think of the countless salads made up wholly of venereal herbs and fruits, such as rocket or colewort, nosesmart or peppergrass, tarragon, root of ginseng, rampion or bellflower, poppyseed, hopbuds, figs, raisins and rice!"

Pantagruel remarked that they would be much surprised if some one gave a valid explanation of that good pope's purpose in instituting the custom of Holy Lent. Doubtless the pontiff realized that this season marked the period when man's natural heat rose from the centre of the body, where it had been dammed up during the winter cold. Rising, it diffused itself through the circumference of the

members, just as sap does in trees. Hence, to foster the propagation
of humankind, the pope prescribed the diet Epistemon had mentioned. Pantagruel was convinced of this, because the register of
christenings at Thouars in Poitou shows that more children were
born in October and November than in the other ten months of the
year. Reckoning backward, he realized that these children were all
made, conceived and begotten in Lent.

"I am all ears to hear you!" cried Friar John, "and I enjoyed every
word you said. But François Rabelais, the curé of St. Christophe de
Jambet, attributed this copious fertility of women not to Lenten
fare, but to those little humpshouldered friars mendicant, those little
booted preachers, those draggletailed little confessors who, during
their Lenten reign, damn all married lechers three fathoms below
Lucifer's underclaws. Being fairly terrorized, these wretched husbands dare not tarrawangdiddle their chambermaids, so they go back
to their wives. I have spoken."

"You may interpret the custom of Lent as you please," said Epistemon, "none of you will agree. But our physicians, to a man, will
oppose the suppression of Lent, which I believe to be forthcoming,
either because of the new liberalism, or by decision of the Council
of Trent. I know this for a fact; I have heard the medicos say as
much. For, without Lent, medical art would be useless and they
would not earn a penny, for no one would be ill. All diseases are sown
in Lent; Lent is the true nursery, the native bed, the natural dispenser of all illness. Remember, too, that Lent not only rots the
body, but maddens the soul. Then, it is, the devils do their worst;
then, canting monks emerge from their lairs; then, becowled hypocrites hold holiday and high tumult with their sessions, stations, pardons, confessions, whippings and anathematizations. I do not infer
that the Arimaspians, that ancient one-eyed race in the far north,
are any the better than we for not knowing Lent. But I speak to the
purpose."

"Well," said Panurge to the Demisemiquaver Friar, "what do *you*
think of this? Tell me, my ballocking, scutwiggling, demisemiquav-
ering cod, what kind of a heretic would you call this fellow?"

THE FRIAR

Rank.

PANURGE

Ought he not be burned at the stake?

THE FRIAR

Yes.

PANURGE

And at the earliest possible moment?

THE FRIAR

Now.

PANURGE

Shouldn't we first have him scalded?

THE FRIAR

No.

PANURGE

How then should he be burned?

THE FRIAR

Live.

PANURGE

Till, in the end, he be—

THE FRIAR

Dead.

PANURGE

Because, after all, he *has* offended you.

THE FRIAR

Much.

PANURGE

What do you take him to be?

THE FRIAR

Mad.

PANURGE

How would you have him treated?

THE FRIAR

Burnt.

PANURGE

Have others been burnt here?

THE FRIAR

Lots.

PANURGE

Were they as grossly heretical as this fellow?

THE FRIAR

Less.

PANURGE

Will many more be burnt?

THE FRIAR

Crowds.

PANURGE

Will you save or redeem any of them?

THE FRIAR

None.

PANURGE

Should not every single one of them be burnt?

THE FRIAR

All.

"I cannot imagine," Epistemon put in, "what pleasure you derive from arguing with this foul tatterdemalion of a monk. If I did not know you well, I swear my opinion of you would be very low!"

"By God, let us go, then," said Panurge. "But I swear I would dearly love to take this Demisemiquaver Friar home to Gargantua. I'm delighted with him. When I'm finally married, he can serve as my wife's fool."

"And, by way of interjection, serve to make a fool of *you*!" said Epistemon.

"You got what you bargained for, poor Panurge," said Friar John. "You'll never fail to wade arse-deep in cuckoldry."

XXX

HOW WE VISITED THE LAND OF SATIN

HAPPY at having been afforded an opportunity of seeing the new Order of Holy Demisemiquaver Friars, we sailed on for two days. On the third day, our skipper landed in the most beautiful and delightful island we had yet seen. It was called Isle of Frieze, for all the roads were of woolen cloth.

On this island lay the land of Satin, famed among pages at court. The trees and high grasses, which were of figured velvet and damask, never shed their leaves or flowers.

The beasts and birds were all of tapestry work. We had occasion to examine not a few beasts, birds and trees, which in shape, size and color, resembled ours at home. But they ate nothing, sang not at all and did not bite as ours do. We also viewed many sorts of creatures we had never seen before, especially elephants.

There were several of these in various postures: among them, I recognized the six males and six females exhibited by their trainer in the arena at Rome in the days of Germanicus, nephew to the Emperor Tiberius. Some of them were learned elephants, others musicians, others philosophers or dancers or conjurors or players; all sat at table, in orderly fashion, eating and drinking, in silence, like so many fat fathers in a refectory. Their snouts—which we call probosces or trunks—were two cubits long; they used them not only to drink or to pick up palm leaves, plums and all manner of food, but also for purposes of attack and defense, as we use our fists. In a fight, these beasts could toss men high into the air, and, as they fell, make them split their sides with laughter.

They had joints in their legs and possessed the power of articulation, just as human beings; any writer testifying to the contrary can never have seen elephants save in drawings or paintings. Between their teeth, they had two large horns.

(At least that is what Juba, King of Mauretania and son-in-law of Cæsar, called them; so did Pausanias, the second-century author of the *Periegesis*. Philostratus, however, insists that they are teeth, not horns. It is all one to me so long as you recognize these tusks to be real ivory.)

They were two or three cubits long, and grew out of the upper, not the lower, jawbone. Believe any testimony to the contrary, and you will find you have the wrong sow by the ear, especially if you credit Ælian, arch-purveyor of falsehood, who claims they are teeth.

It was here in Satinland, and nowhere else, that Pliny watched elephants dance on tight ropes with bells and stride over banquet tables without touching the toping topers.

I saw a rhinoceros in every way similar to the one I was once shown by Henri Cleberg, the charitable Nuremberger of Lyons, knighted by King François I. It was not unlike a boar I once saw at Limoges, except for a horn on its snout. This horn, one cubit long and very sharp, allowed the rhinoceros to try conclusions with an elephant; piercing the great beast with it under the belly—the elephant's most sensitive part—the rhinoceros laid his rival flat, often killing him.

I saw thirty-two unicorns. These were extraordinarily vicious beasts, in every respect like thoroughbred horses, except that their heads were like a stag's, their feet like an elephant's, their tails like a boar's, and, out of their foreheads, grew a sharp black horn, six or seven feet long. The latter usually dangled down like a turkey-cock's crest, but when the unicorn meant to fight or to use it for any other purpose, she thrust it out, straight and hard as an arrow. I watched one unicorn leading a throng of wild animals to a fountain, which she proceeded to purify, by dipping her horn into the water.

Panurge assured me that he, too, possessed a horn, growing out, not from the middle of his forehead, but somewhat lower down. It was comparable to the unicorn's, if not in length, at least in its virtues and properties. Hers cleaned the waters of marshes and fountains of all ordure and poison, enabling animals to drink there in safety. So, too, Panurge with his nervous horn, scoured out foul sewers and mephitic sumpholes, allowing others to slosh about after him, without risk of chancre, pox, clap, scaldstale, ulcer or gangrenous sores.

"When you're married, we'll try this out on your wife," cried Friar John. "This for mere charity's sake, since you are gracious enough to give us such instructions."

"You try it," said Panurge, "and I'll feed you a pill that will bring you face to face with your Maker . . . a pill known as Cæsarian, because it did for Julius of that name . . . a pill compounded of twenty-two stabs of the dagger."

"Thanks," said Friar John, "but I would prefer a draught of cool wine!"

I beheld other marvels in Satinland.

There was, for instance, the Golden Fleece conquered by Jason. Whoever states that Jason's spoil was a golden apple, not a fleece, arguing that the Greek μῆλον means both apple and sheep, is utterly mistaken, and must have visited Satinland with his eyes closed.

There was a chameleon, such as Aristotle describes, and such as Charles Marais, a famous physician in the noble city of Lyons on the Rhône, once showed me years ago. It lived exclusively on air, like the other.

There were three hydras—a sort of seven-headed snake—such as I had seen elsewhere in the past.

There were fourteen phœnixes. Now I have read in many authors that there was but one phœnix in the wide world in every century. In my humble opinion, these authors had never beheld a phœnix, save those woven in tapestries that hung on palace walls. This holds true of Firmianus Lactantius, the third-century rhetorician, too, even though he was known as the Christian Cicero.

There was the skin of Apuleius' Golden Ass. I recalled the satiric romance concerning the adventures of Lucian, who, while sojourn-

ing in Thessaly, was accidentally metamorphosed into an ass. I recalled how he fell into the hands of robbers, eunuchs, magistrates and
others who treated him scurvily. I recalled how eventually he regained human form.

There were three hundred and nine pelicans. And six thousand
six hundred seleucides. (The birds Jupiter sent to devour the locusts
that were ravaging Mount Cesius.) This is exactly what they were
doing to Satinland locusts, as they marched forward, row upon
orderly row, across the fields.

What else did I see? Well, I saw cinnamologi, strange Arab birds
. . . argathyles . . . caprimulgi or goatsuckers, a sort of raven
that flies into goatsheds and milks the goats . . . tinnunculi, who
defend pigeons against hawks . . . stymphalides, the cannibal
birds slain by Hercules in his sixth labor . . . protonotaries! no,
these are prelates: I mean onocrotaries or bitterns . . . harpies,
winged monsters with the heads and breasts of women, fierce, starved
and grasping creatures living in an atmosphere of filth and stench
. . . panthers, so little known in France that some doubt their existence . . . dorcades or gazelles . . . cemades or fawns . . . cy-
nocephali, great apes with heads like dogs . . . satyrs, with hind-
legs, horns and ears like a goat's . . . cartasons or Indian unicorns
. . . tarands, which resemble reindeer . . . uri or aurochs, wild
oxen . . . monopodes or bonassi, which are like bison . . . pep-
hages, cepes and neares . . . stera, a sort of snake . . . cercopitheca
or long-tailed monkeys . . . bugles or young bulls . . . musimons
or Sardinian sheep . . . byturi, insects that devour the vines . . .
ophyri, a deadly sort of serpent . . . stryges or screech dragons
. . . and griffins, who had an eagle's head and wings on a lion's
body. . . .

I saw Mid-Lent on horseback, with Mid-August and Mid-March
holding the stirrups. And I saw werewolves, centaurs, tigers, leopards, hyenas, camelopards or giraffes, and oryges, a variety of Egyptian unicorn with certain features of the antelope.

I saw a remora, a small fish named *echeinis* by the Greeks. Before
it stood a tall ship, unable to budge an inch, despite a full complement of sails, a high wind and a strong current. I am convinced it
was the vessel of Periander, the tyrant of Corinth, which, according
to Pliny, was stopped by a denizen of the deep, despite wind and tide.

Mutianus, Pliny's authority, beheld it in Satinland, and not else-where.

Friar John remarked that two kinds of fish used formerly to reign in the law courts, rotting the bodies and racking the souls of all plaintiffs, whether noble or base, rich or poor, exalted or humble. The first were April fish or mackerel. (Did not mackerel abound in April? Were not pimps called mackerel? Well, then, you found plenty of mackerel to bear false witness in court!) The second were remora, which, with their perpetual litigation, stayed the course of Justice.

I saw sphinxes, a sort of ape . . . raffes, a kind of jackal . . . ounces or lynxes . . . cephi, with forelegs like man's hands and hind-legs like man's legs . . . crocutas, half-hyena, half-lioness . . . eali, large as the hippopotamus, with a tail like an elephant's, jaws like a wild boar's, and horns as pliant as an ass'. . . .

There were also cucrocutes, very swift beasts about the size of our donkeys in Mirebelais, with neck, tail and chest like a lion's, legs like a stag's, snout split to the ears, and only two teeth, one upper and one lower. They spoke with human voice, but when I examined them, they were sulking in silence.

You have probably never seen an aerie of saker falcons. Let me hereby assure you that I saw no less than a dozen.

I saw some left-handed halberds, the first I had ever beheld.

I saw some manthicores, a strange sort of beast: the body a lion's, the coat red, face and ears like a man's, and three rows of teeth closed together, like joined hands with fingers interlocked. Their tails secreted a sting like a scorpion's; their voices were very melodious.

I saw some catoblepes, reptiles diminutive of body and huge of head, the latter so unwieldy as to be difficult to lift off the ground. So venomous were their eyes that, as with the basilisk, to face their glance spelled certain death.

I saw some two-backed beasts, marvellously happy and extraordinarily prolific at arseclicking; their dual rumps wagged more riotously than ever the most tail-wagging wagtail.

I also saw crawfish being milked, after which they paraded home in drill formation. You, too, would have watched them with delight.

XXXI

HOW WE SAW HEARSAY IN SATINLAND, WHERE HE CONDUCTED A SCHOOL OF TESTIMONY

PUSHING through Tapestryland, we saw the Mediterranean Sea opening up and airing its bed, much as the Red Sea rose up out of the Arabian Gulf, to make a way for the Jews when they fled Egypt.

I spied Triton, son of Neptune, blowing through his great shell to make the roaring of the ocean . . . Glaucus, the fish-monger of Bœotia, who became a sea-god endowed with the gifts of prophecy . . . Proteus, Neptune's herdsman, counting his sea-calves at noon before going to sleep . . . Nereus, father of the Nereids and tutelary god of the Ægean . . . and countless others. . . .

We observed an infinite number of different fishes dancing, flying, vaulting, fighting, feeding, breathing . . . bolting and sifting away their time and their consorts, as they milted and spawned . . . hunting, setting traps, lying in ambush, making truces, bargaining, swearing and raising merry liquid hell in their sport. . . .

In one corner, we descried Aristotle holding a lantern. He looked for all the world like the hermit whom painters represent holding a light for St. Christopher, as the latter crossed the river with the infant Jesus on his back.

Behind him, like so many bumbailiffs behind their chief, stood a host of philosophers among whom we could distinguish Appian, that impartial Roman historian of Trajan's day, who furnished such admirable information on the peoples conquered by his nation . . . Heliodorus, author of the *Ethiopica* . . . Athenæus, the great grammarian and rhetorician of Alexandria, whose *Deipnosophistes* or *Philosophers' Banquet* contains such encyclopedic information . . . Porphyrius of Tyre . . . Pancrates the Arcadian, who celebrated the art of fishing . . . Numenius, commentator of Plato and master of Plotinus . . . Posidonius of Corinth, another authority on angling . . . Ovid . . . Oppianus, author of the *Halieutica*, a poem on fishing, dedicated to Marcus Aurelius, and of a work on swans . . . Olympius or Aurelius Nemesianus, the Carthaginian critic of hunting on land and sea . . . Seleucus of Emesa, another piscatorial writer . . . Leonides of Byzantium and Agathocles of Thessaly . . . Demostratus, the Roman senator and student of fishing . . . Mutianus . . . Nymphodorus, the historian of Syracuse . . . Ælian the Sophist, high priest of the gods, student of Pausanias, denouncer of Heliogabalus, author of the *History of Animals*. . . .

Five hundred such stood by, with nothing to do and time hanging heavy on their hands. There was Chrysippus, the Stoic, physician, naturalist and reformer of Zeno's doctrine . . . there was Lycon's disciple Aristomachus of Soli, who for fifty-eight years did nothing but observe the habits of bees . . . there was Pierre Gilles of Albi, the zoologist, armed with a urinal, and lost in rapt contemplation of piscicultural piss. . . .

After a prolonged survey of the land of Satin, Pantagruel decided:

"I've feasted my eyes to the point of repletion, but my belly is clamoring for very hunger."

"Let us feed, let us feed!" I urged. "Let us try some of these anacampserotes hanging there, over our heads."

"And what are anacampserotes?" somebody asked.

"A plant that revives dead love and reconciles lovers."

"Ugh!" said someone else who had tasted them. "They're perfectly horrible!"

I picked some myrobalan plums from the tapestry on which they hung, but could not chew, let alone swallow them. Had you tasted them, you would have sworn they were so much twisted silk, with no savor whatever. You recall how Heliogabalus used to entertain those whom he had caused to fast a long time? He promised them an abundant, sumptuous and imperial banquet, then served them up painted foods of wax, marble and pottery, upon figured tablecloths. Well, you would have sworn that Heliogabalus followed the idea of these tapestry myrobalans, as exactly and faithfully as the transcript of a papal bull follows the original.

As we searched all about us for some substantial food, we heard a harsh, strident tumult, like that of washerwomen beating their dirty linen with paddles, or like the churning of the Bazacle mill at Toulouse. Immediately, we rushed to the spot whence came the noise, to find a tiny, misshapen, humpbacked, monstrously ugly old man. His name was Hearsay. His snout was slit to the ears: inside he had seven tongues, each of which was cleft into seven parts. With all seven at once, he was chattering away on various subjects in various languages. His head and body bore as many ears as, of yore, that of Argus bore eyes. He was blind as a bat and paralyzed below the waist.

Around him I saw an innumerable host of men and women, listening attentively. Among these, I noticed several, strutting up and down very importantly. One, in particular, caught my attention. The fellow held up a map of the world and, by dint of terse aphorisms, gave a compendious explanation of any subject on earth. Topic after prodigious topic passed glibly over his tongue. The auditors, memorizing his epigrams, grew wise and learned, became specialists and authorities in less time than it takes to tell. They could discourse most cogently and fluently on a stupendous diversity of subjects, one-hundredth part of which would require a lifetime's study of the most serious scholar. Among these subjects, I may cite the Pyramids, the Nile and Babylon . . . the Troglodytes or Cave-dwellers . . . the Himantopodes, with long, limber, thonglike feet, that permit them to walk like snakes . . . the Blemmyæ, who, lacking heads, have eye, nose and mouth in the middle of their chests . . . the Pygmies, those Ethiopian dwarfs . . . the Cannibals . . . the Hyperboreans, that happy people who resided beyond the north wind, thus enjoying perpetual warmth and sunshine, amid extreme virtue, double harvests and perpetual spring . . . the Ægipans, semi-goat, semi-man . . . the devil and the rest of it! . . .

All this (I repeat) through Hearsay.

Allowing for mistaken identity, I fancy I recognized quite a few familiar faces in the crowd. There were Herodotus, the vast traveller and father of history . . . Pliny . . . Caius Julius Solinus, third-century author of the *Polyhistor,* a work of ethnography and natural history . . . Berosus, the Babylonian astrologer . . . Philostratus . . . Pomponius Mela, author of *De Situ Orbis,* that celebrated work . . . Strabo, the great geographer . . . and God knows how many other antiquarians.

There were Albertus Magnus, the celebrated Jacobin friar . . . Pierre Témoin or Peter Martyr, the Milanese scholar and councillor of Ferdinand and Isabella . . . Pope Pius the second, the cosmographer . . . Volterranus or Raphael Maffei of Volterra, translator of Xenophon and chronicler of Rome. . . .

There were Paulus Jovius or Paolo Giovio the Valorous, an annalist of the fifteenth century . . . Jacques Cartier, the explorer of Canada . . . Chayton the Armenian, who wrote of his travels in the East . . . Marco Polo, the Venetian . . . Louis de Vertema, another traveller in the Orient, who proudly claimed Roman citizenship and called himself Ludovico Romano . . . Pedro Alvarez, the discoverer of Brazil. . . .

There were God knows how many other modern historians, hidden behind a piece of tapestry. These were all secretly scribbling down page after page of information—all from Hearsay!

Behind another tapestry, this one of mint-leaf design, I caught sight of a throng of young men from the Loire provinces of Perche and Maine—a region notorious for its liars and bearers of false witness. They crowded about Hearsay, brilliant students at the feet of the master.

I inquired about their course of study and learned that, from their tenderest youth, they were taught to supply testimony, affidavit and evidence. Hearsay drilled them so thoroughly in this art that they became highly proficient. Returning to their native habitat, they earned a comfortable living, by testifying on anything under the sun, in favor of whoever paid the highest daily wage. All this, of course, through Hearsay.

Think what you will of it. I, for my part, assure you that they gave us crumbs of their cake and drops of their wine-casks. It proved imperial fare and kingly tipple.

Then, cordially, they advised us to be as sparing of truth as was humanly possible, if we ever hoped to obtain preferment in court.

XXXII

HOW WE SIGHTED LANTERN-LAND

HAVING been poorly received and sorrily banqueted in the land of Satin, we sailed on, for three days. Early the fourth day, we sighted Lanternland. As we drew closer to the coast, we saw little hovering lights on the sea.

I did not believe they were lights. They seemed more like lantern-fishes, darting flaming tongues out of the water, or like lampyrides (cicindelæ or glow-worms) shining, as they do in France, to warn the farmer that his barley is ripe.

But the skipper insisted that they were the Lanterns of the Watch, or lighthouses, set up around the island to make it clearly visible. They served as guides and beacons for other lights and illuminati who, like good Franciscan and Jacobin friars, were on their way to a meeting of the provincial chapter.

Some of us feared that these lights foreboded a storm. Our skipper, however, convinced us that we were wrong.

XXXIII

HOW WE LANDED AT PORT LYCHNOBII, THE HARBOR OF SUCH AS BURN THE MIDNIGHT OIL, AND HOW WE VISITED LANTERNLAND

SOON we sailed into the Port of Lanternland. Here, on a high tower, Pantagruel discovered the light of La Rochelle, which guides mariners safely along the Atlantic coast. Other lights of famed lighthouses were there, too: that of the island of Pharos, guarding the harbor of Alexandria, built by Ptolemy . . . that of Nauplia, guarding the harbor of Argos, built by Nauplius, father of Pala-mides . . . that of the Acropolis at Athens, built by Callimachus and sacred to Pallas. . . .

Near the harbor was a village inhabited by the Lychnobii, a folk who live by lamplight, as assiduously as in our land the members of a certain order of friars live off the nuns they beg for.

These Lychnobii were a worthy, studious lot; Demosthenes had burned the midnight oil here and perfumed his speeches with the fragrance of the lamp.

We applied to a trio of Obeliscolychnii or Lighthousers, the coast-guards of the land. They wore tall, rounded hats, like those of the Albanian mercenaries we see in France. We explained the reason and aim of our visit: we wished to obtain, from Her Majesty of Lanternland, a Lantern to illumine and conduct us to the Oracle of the Holy Bottle. They promised to help us, adding that we could not have come more opportunely, because they were even then hold-ing their provincial chapter. We had but to choose our Lantern.

Reaching the royal palace, we were received by Her Majesty of Lanternland. Our sponsors were two great lights: the Lantern of Cleanthes, the Stoic, and that of Aristophanes of Byzantium, the grammarian. Panurge, speaking Lantern, briefly acquainted Her Majesty with the purpose of our journey. The Queen welcomed us and commanded us to attend her at supper, so that we might choose the Lantern we wished to guide us. Delighted, we kept our eyes open, observing the dress, movement and deportment of Her Maj-esty's subjects. We were particularly interested in discovering how they served their royal mistress.

The Queen wore a gown of virgin crystal, with inlay and damas-cene work, and large diamonds inset. Princes of the blood, or Lan-terns Royal, were clad in imitation diamonds, diaphanous stones, paste or glass. Courtiers wore horn, paper and oilskin. The Oil-lights and Cresset-lights took precedence according to seniority, though I noticed one earthenware luminary, that looked like a thundermug, walking among the proudest. When I expressed my astonishment, I was told it was that of Epictetus, a Lantern valued at three thousand drachmæ. And why? Because the philosopher had refused to sell it to a Greek, who offered this sum in hope of acquiring both material light and spiritual enlightenment.

I admired the shape and mechanism of Martial's polymyx or many-spouted Lantern, which, as a reader of Martial, you know he used as title to one of his satires. I marvelled at the icosymix or Lantern of twenty wicks, consecrated of yore to Canope, daughter of Tysias. I was awed by the hanging Lanterns—such as that dedicated to Apollo, and, at the sack of the temple at Thebes, brought to Cyme by Alexander the Great.

Another arrested my attention because of the red glow emanating from its dome. It burned like the crimson tassel on the hood of a Doctor of Law. I was told it belonged to the Italian jurisconsult Bartolus, called "the beacon of civil law."

Two other Lanterns struck me as particularly noteworthy, because of the enema-bags hanging from their belts. I learned that these were *Luminare Majus* and *Lumen Apothecariorum*, lights designed to guide the apothecary and pharmacist through the maze of their science.

When it was suppertime, Her Majesty took her place first; then the others sat down according to their rank and dignity. For the first course, they were all served large moulded candles. There were, however, certain exceptions. The Queen, for instance, was served a large, stiff, white, wax taper, somewhat reddened at its flaming tip. The Lanterns of the Royal Family and the provincial Lantern of Mirebalais, were served nut lights—candles made of crushed nuts, with a hemp wick. And the provincial Lantern of Lower Poitou received a candle adorned with armorial bearings.

After this, heaven knows what splendid luminosity they shed with their wicks, save for a number of junior Lanterns under the government of a mighty Lantern. These did not shine like the others, but seemed to flicker lazily.

After supper, we retired to rest. Next day the Queen bade us choose a Lantern among the most illustrious of the land, to guide us on our quest.

And so we took our leave.

XXXIV

HOW WE CAME TO THE ORACLE OF THE HOLY BOTTLE

OUR noble Lantern lighting and directing us merrily forward, we came to the much longed-for island where was the Oracle of the Bottle. Landing, Panurge gaily cut a caper on one leg, for very joy.

"We have reached our destination!" he exulted. "This is the place we sought with such toil and labor!"

Then we paid our Lantern a compliment, to which she replied graciously, warning us to be of good cheer and to allow nothing to daunt us, no matter what we might see.

To reach the temple of the Holy Bottle, we had to pass through a large vineyard in which were vines of all sorts: Falernian, whose wine the poet Horace celebrated . . . Malevoisie or Malmsey, a sweet Greek variety . . . Muscadine, which gives delicious Muscatel . . . Tabbia, an excellent Genoese growth . . . Beaune, balm of blessed Burgundy . . . Mireval, from the Montpellier country . . . Orléans . . . Picardan, a product of Languedoc . . . Arbois, from the Jura, and Coussey, from the Vosges . . . Anjou, Graves and Corsican varieties . . . Véron, from Touraine, and Nérac, from the Garonne region, to mention only a few.

This vineyard was planted by good Bacchus, and blessed so bountifully that it yielded leaf, flower and fruit all the year round, like the orange trees in the royal gardens of Suresne, or those growing at San Remo. Our magnificent Lantern ordered us to eat three grapes per man, to put vine-leaves in our shoes, and take up a vine-branch in our left hand.

At the end of the vineyard, we filed out under an arch built in the style of the ancients. The trophies of a toper were delicately carved over its surface.

On one side, there were long lines of flagons, leather bottles, flasks, carafes, pots, firkins, crocks, stoups, noggins, decanters, pitchers, and old-fashioned demijohns, hanging on a shady arbor. On another side, a profusion of garlic, onions, shallots, hams, botargos (relish of salted mullet roes), smoked oxtongues, round cheeses, old sharp cheeses and like provisions, interwoven with vine-leaves and most cleverly packed together with vine stocks. On a third side, were hundreds of drinking glasses, tumblers, cups, bowls, mugs, tankards, goblets, jorums and such other Bacchic artillery.

On the frontispiece of the triumphal arch, below the *zoophore* or sculptured frieze, the inscription read:

> *Before you pass beneath this noble arch,*
> *Find a good Lantern to direct your march.*

"We were careful to provide for that!" said Pantagruel. "In all the length and breadth of Lanternland, we could not have found a better or more heavenly Lantern than ours."

This arch ended in a fine round arbor, covered with vine-branches and adorned with clusters of grapes, golden, tawny, blue, azure, black, green, purple, streaked with combinations of hues and, in all, offering five hundred different shadings to the enchanted eye. More, these clusters of grapes, thanks to the ingenuity of horticulture, grew in five hundred different shapes: long, circular, triangular, codlike, crownshaped, fat as cabbages, luxuriant as a beard, and lush as a fair lawn. Old ivy trees, verdant and laden with rings, stood at the end of the arbor.

Our most illustrious Lantern now ordered us to pick ivy leaves and to make tall, high-crowned hats of them. We did so at once, and, under this towering headgear, looked like Albanian mercenaries.

Pantagruel observed that Jupiter's priestess would not have walked under this arbor.

"For a particular and mystical reason," our perspicacious Lantern replied. "Had she stepped here, the wine—or the grapes over her head—would have seemed to top, master and dominate her. Of course, all priests and contemplators of divine mysteries must maintain their spirits in a state of calm, avoiding anything that might disturb their senses. And, of all known passions, drunkenness exerts the most disrupting influence."

Our sagacious Lantern went on to state that we ourselves might not come into the Holy Bottle's presence, after passing under this arch, unless the noble priestess Bacbuc found our shoes full of vine-leaves. The act of placing them there was diametrically opposite to the hypothetical stroll of Jupiter's priestess under the arbor; it signified that we despised, mastered and trampled down wine.

"I am no scholar, much to my sorrow," said Friar John. "Yet on consulting my breviary, I find that, in *Revelation*, a woman was seen with the moon underfoot. A wonderful sight, truly! My old friend Bigot—Guillaume Bigot, the philosopher of Tübingen and Nîmes—explained all this to me. He said it meant that she was not of the race and nature of other women, who have the moon at their heads and whose brains are therefore lunatic. Which convinces me that all you have said is true, sweet Madame Lantern!"

XXXV

HOW WE WENT UNDERGROUND TO ENTER THE TEMPLE OF THE HOLY BOTTLE, AND HOW CHINON IS THE OLDEST CITY IN THE WORLD

WE descended underground through a plastered vault, decorated by a coarsely daubed painting. It represented women and satyrs dancing attendance upon old Silenus, grinning atop his ass.

"This entrance reminds me of the painted caverns in the world's oldest city," I said to Pantagruel.

"Where's that? What *is* the world's oldest city?"

"Chinon, in Touraine, My Lord," I told him, "Caïno, Gregory of Tours calls it. It has just such paintings, in caverns just as cool as this!"

"I know where Chinon is," Pantagruel asserted. "And I know its cavern or painted wine cellar. It is hewn out of the cliff against which the city is built; I have drunk many a glass of cool wine there. No doubt Chinon is a very ancient city. Its coat-of-arms bears this out, with a legend that repeats 'Chinon' twice or thrice, and the lines:

> *Chinon, small town*
> *Of great renown,*
> *Cut into good*
> *Old rock; a wood*
> *Above; and then,*
> *Below, the Vienne,*
> *Stream, loved of men.*

Nevertheless, how can Chinon be the oldest city in the world? Where do you find it in writing? What proof can you give?"

"I found it in Holy Writ," I told him. "Cain was the first man to build; he named Caïno after himself. Ever since, in imitation, founders of cities have imposed their names upon their creations. Thus Athens is named for Athene, the Greek name of Minerva . . . Alexandria for Alexander the Great . . . Constantinople for Constantine . . . Pompeiopolis in Asia Minor for Pompey . . . Adrianople for Hadrian . . . Canaan for the Canaanites . . . Saba for Seba, son of Cush . . . Assyria for Asshur, god of heaven . . . thus, finally, Ptolemais Cæsarea, Tiberiopolis in Phrygia and Herodium in Judæa. . . ."

While we were discussing this, the Grand Flask—our Lantern called him philosopher—appeared. He was the governor of the Holy Bottle. Behind him came the Temple Guard, consisting wholly of small French half-bottles. Grand Flask saw our ivy-crowned branches and recognized our illustrious Lantern. So he commanded us to be admitted directly into the presence of Bacbuc, lady-in-waiting to the Holy Bottle and pontiff of all the mysteries. This was done forthwith.

XXXVI

HOW WE DESCENDED THE TETRADIC STEPS—SACRED TO THE NUMBER FOUR—AND HOW PANURGE WAS TERRIFIED

WE then descended a marble stair leading underground, where there was a landing. Bearing to the left, we went down two more stairs to another landing; then three more to a side passage, with a similar landing; then four more, with a landing again.

"Is this it?" Panurge asked.

"How many stairs have you counted?" our magnificent Lantern challenged.

"One, two, three, four," Pantagruel answered.

"How many are there?" she asked.

"Ten," said Pantagruel.

"Multiply what you have counted by four—the Pythagorean tetrad," she advised him.

"Ten . . . twenty . . . thirty . . . forty . . . " said Pantagruel.

"Which makes how many in all?"

"One hundred."

"Add the first cube," our Lantern said, "which makes eight. After that fatal number, we shall find the temple gate. Note carefully that this is in accord with the true psychogeny or genesis of the mind, as discovered by Plato, as esteemed by the Academics, and yet little understood by men. The half of it consists of unity (1), of the two first whole numbers (2 and 3), their squares (4 and 9) and their cubes (8 and 27)."

As we went down these subterranean steps, we had good need of our legs, without which we would have rolled like barrels into a cellar. Our dear Lantern, too, proved invaluable; except for her, we had as much light as you find in St. Patrick's Hole in Ireland (one

of the entrances to Hell) or in the cave in Bœotia, where Trophonius,
son of Apollo, utters his oracles.

When we had taken about seventy-eight steps into the bowels of
the earth, Panurge called to our gleaming Lantern:

"O wondrous lady, I beg you, with contrite heart, to go back.
God's death, I'm dying of sheer fright. I promise I will never marry
if we but retrace our steps. You have gone to a great deal of trouble,
you have endured much fatigue for my sake; God will reward you
in Paradise. For my own part, the moment I emerge from this cave
of troglodytes, I shall not prove ungrateful. For pity's sake, let us go
back! I would swear this is Tænarum, the gateway to Hell, the dread
cave through which Hercules dragged up Cerberus. By God, I can
hear Cerberus barking: listen! Either it's Cerberus or my ears play
me false. Confound it! I never fancied the cur; no toothache is worse
than that when a dog has you by the calf. If this is the cave of Trophonius, then the *lemures* or ghouls and the goblins will eat us alive.
Never forget how they devoured one of Demetrius' followers who
dared enter without the ritual honey cakes.

"Are you there, Friar John? Please keep near me, friend of my
belly, cock of my walk. Have you got your great blade handy? I
am without arms, either offensive or defensive. Let us go back!"

"All right, all right, here I am!" the monk cried. "Don't worry; I
have you by the collar. Eighteen devils couldn't get you out of my
clutches, unarmed though I am. A stout heart, strong muscles and a
man need never worry about weapons. God help us, heaven would
rain down weapons, before it consented to leave a courageous and
resourceful soul without defense. That happened once in Provence,
in the fields by the river Crau. The firmament poured down stones
to supply Hercules with ammunition to attack Neptune's sons. You
can see those rocks there to-day, near Mariane, where Marius had
his soldiers dig a canal."

Panurge whimpered.

"What's happening?" Friar John grumbled. "Are we bound for
the *limbus infantium*, that limbo where little children suffer torment
without sorrow? Good God! They'll make diapers of us! Or are we
bound for the real limbo, for Hell itself, home of all the devils? If
so, I'll give them a drubbing, now that I've vine-leaves in my boots.
Watch me lay on, lads! Where *is* Hell, where are they? All I fear is

their horns. But the thought of the twin horns our bridegroom Panurge is fated to wear will save me! Ho! already, in a prophetic vision, I see him clearly, a latter-day Actæon."

"Why Actæon?" some one asked.

"Actæon," Pantagruel said, "was a huntsman who surprised Diana bathing. She changed him into a stag, and had him torn to pieces by his own hounds. Stags have horns and are therefore symbolic of—"

"A latter-day Actæon," Friar John concluded with a flourish. "Actæon, the horn-merchant, horning in on people's enjoyment, blowing his own horn labially and sphincterially, horn-mad and horn-swoggled!"

"Take care, Father," Panurge counselled. "Until priests are allowed to wed, take care you don't marry a sweet dispenser of quartan poxfever. Shall I ever emerge safe and sound from this *hypogæum*, as the Greeks call an underground hold? If so, take care I don't cunny-fructify her for the sole pleasure of making you a hornbearing, double hornblowing cuckold! Whatever the other circumstances, I hold the poxfever for a scurvy wedding-gift. I recall how Graspall, the great legist, threatened to marry you to just such a baggage; but you got out of it by calling him a heretic!"

The discussion was interrupted by our splendent Lantern. She informed us that we should be silent; here, out of respect, words must be suppressed and tongues stilled. Moreover, we could not hope to go back without permission from the Holy Bottle, since our boots were lined with vine-leaves.

"Let us push on, then," said Panurge, "let us face all the devils there are: we can die but once. I was preserving my life for some lofty battle, but never mind! Come along, forward, march! I've aplenty and to spare! To be sure I'm shaking a little—but that's because this cave is so cold and damp. I've no fever and I'm not afraid. Pish, pish, push on, man! Paddle ahead, piddle ahoy! Pass on, piss up! William the Fearless, they call me, Bill Dreadnought, the terror of the company."

XXXVII

HOW THE TEMPLE GATES
OPENED MIRACULOUSLY
BY THEMSELVES

At the bottom of the flight of stairs, we came upon a gate built
entirely of the finest jasper, in the Doric style. Across its front ran
an inscription in Ionic letters of purest gold, ΕΝ ΌΙΝΩ ΆΛΗΘΕΙΑ,
which corresponds to the Latin *in vino veritas*, in wine, truth.

The gates were of solid Corinthian bronze, with small plates,
countersunk and enamelled as daintily as the modelling required.
They were joined together and fitted in their mortise without lock,
padlock or any other connection whatever. Over them hung an
Indian diamond about the size of an Egyptian bean, set in pure gold,
with two points of hexagonal shape opposite each other. On either
side, towards the wall, hung bunches of garlic.

Our noble Lantern now begged us to excuse her if she accompanied
us no further. From now on, we had but to obey the pontiff Bacbuc's
instructions. Lantern herself was not allowed to enter the temple,
for certain reasons which were better hidden than known of mortals.
At any rate, we must keep up our spirits, banish fear, and trust to
her to get out.

Pulling out the diamond hanging at the junction of the two gates,
she cast it to the right, into a silver casket placed there for that purpose. From the threshold of each gate, she drew an eighteen-foot
cord of crimson silk, from which hung the garlic. Fastening it to two
golden rings suspended at either side for that purpose, she withdrew.

Suddenly, the two gates opened, of their own accord, without any
one touching them. As they did so, instead of the horrible creaking
that heavy bronze gates usually make, we heard a soft, pleasant murmur resounding beneath the temple vault. Pantagruel understood
what had caused this murmur, for he caught sight of a small roller,
fastened to the bottom of each gate. As the gates turned back toward

the wall, they rolled over a hard piece of serpentine, polished with use; this, it was, produced the agreeable light sound we had heard.

I was astounded that the gates should open without human impulsion. As soon as we were all within, I looked carefully at the space between the gates and the wall. What mechanism or device had shut these gates? I must confess I suspected our kindly Lantern of having inserted between them the herb *æthiopis*, which opens anything that is closed. But in an interior mortise, I noticed a tongue of pure steel, wedged into the Corinthian bronze.

I also noticed two tablets of Indian lodestone—the most powerful magnets known. They were about half a span wide and thick, blue in color, very smooth and highly polished. The entire thickness of these tablets was set in the temple wall, where the fully opened doors met the wall.

What happened was this. The tongues of steel, drawn by the lodestone, caused this movement by a wonderful, hidden process of Nature; this set the gates in motion and drew them forward steadily. Yet the operation did not succeed inevitably: first, the lodestone must be removed so as to release the steel from its attraction; second, the two bunches of garlic must be taken away. For garlic nullifies the lodestone, robbing it of its power of attraction. By pulling the crimson cord, our gladsome Lantern had displaced and suspended the garlic outside its range of influence.

The tablet on the right bore the Latin line

> *Ducunt volentem fata, nolentem trahunt*
> *Fate leads the willing, drags the unwilling man*

exquisitely engraved in ancient Roman script.

On the lodestone to the right ran a decoratively chiselled sentence in capitals:

ALL THINGS MOVE ON TO THEIR APPOINTED END.

XXXVIII

OF THE WONDROUS DESIGNS AND ALLEGORIES IN THE TEMPLE PAVEMENT

HAVING read these inscriptions, I gazed about the magnificent temple, admiring especially the extraordinary disposition of its pavement. No workmanship under the cope of heaven can be compared to it. Neither the temple erected to Fortune at Præneste, under Sulla, nor the Greek pavement called *asarotum*, laid by Sosistrates at Pergamon, is to be mentioned in the same breath.

Imagine a mosaic of small blocks of precious stones, polished in their natural colors: one of red jasper, beautifully mottled . . . another of ophites or serpentine . . . another of porphyry . . . another of lycophthalmy or wolf's eye, a gem of four colors, powdered with flecks of gold as small as atoms . . . another of agate, streaked with milky waves . . . another of the most precious chalcedony or onyx . . . another of green jasper, crossed by a network of red and yellow veins. . . . These stones were arranged in diagonal lines.

At the portico, I saw a design, made of small inserted stones, each in its natural color outlining the pattern. It was as though branches and leaves of vine had been aimlessly strewed over the pavement: here they seemed widely scattered, there piled in thick tufts. This remarkable incrustation of leaves was everywhere about. In the dim, mysterious light, you would have sworn you saw snails climbing over the grapes, and small lizards scurrying across the vine-branches. And the grapes! Green, ripening, half-ripe and luscious in their full growth, they were so deftly outlined and so skilfully composed by the architect, as to deceive starlings and other little birds as readily as those drawn by Zeuxis of Heraclis, the Greek painter.

And realistic enough to deceive us, too. Where we saw vine-stock heavily planted, we leaped and bounded as though over rough stony ground.

I glanced up at the vaults and walls of the temple, studded with marble and porphyry mosaic of wondrous design. Glancing from left to right, I first saw a portrayal, unbelievably rich, of the wars in which Bacchus bested the Indians.

A description follows.

XXXIX

BACCHUS' ADVANCE AGAINST THE INDIANS, AS PORTRAYED IN MOSAIC IN THE TEMPLE

FIRST, there were fields, woods, villages, forts and citadels, devoured by flames. Crazed, furious women were carving up live calves, sheep and lambs, devouring their flesh apace. This represented Bacchus invading India, levelling everything by fire and sword.

The Indians despised him so cordially that they suffered him to advance unchecked. Had not their spies informed them that Bacchus' army boasted no warriors worthy of the name? A small, fat, effeminate old man, an aged drunkard . . . flanked by a rabble of youthful rustics, with tails and horns like young rams', stark naked and forever leaping and dancing . . . with a host of crapulous camp-followers in their wake. . . . Such, the scouts reported, were Bacchus' forces.

The men of Ind therefore decided to let him pass with impunity through their land; to be victorious over such scum would have spelled shame and disgrace, rather than honor and glory.

Thanks to their indifference, Bacchus kept pushing forward, consolidating his gains, and burning everything in his path. Was not fire his native element, his paternal birthright?

(When Semele, his mother, rashly demanded that Jove, his father, appear in all his splendor before her, the great god did so. His flaming presence was enough to set her and her house afire. But Jove rescued the embryo Bacchus from the same sizzling plight, by plucking him from Semele's womb and carrying him in his thigh.)

Truly, fire was Bacchus' native element. And blood was his portion. It was as natural to him to shed blood in warfare as to rouse it in times of peace. Proof of this is furnished by the fields of Panæma (the word means blood-drenched) in the island of Samos; they are so called because Bacchus here killed by phlebotomy, or bleeding, the Amazons, as they fled from the land of the Ephesians.

There was an old proverb, once current, to the effect that mint should not be planted or eaten in time of war. Aristotle, in his *Problems*, explains it by saying that mint freezes the body and impairs the reproductive powers, thus affecting a man's courage. From what I have told you, you will understand that, on the contrary, mint thins the blood. As, in wartime, blows are indiscriminately exchanged, it is difficult, if not impossible, to staunch the wound of a man who has handled or eaten mint.

The next scene on the temple walls pictured Bacchus advancing into battle. He stood on a magnificent chariot, drawn by six young leopards, harnessed two by two. He looked like a young child, cherubically rosy; his chin was innocent of the slightest suspicion of a beard. Sharp horns, springing from his head, bore a splendid wreath of vine-leaves and grapes, topped by a crimson velure mitre. He was shod with golden buskins.

Not a single man followed in his train; his bodyguard and, indeed, his entire forces, consisted of Bassarides, Evantes, Euhyades, Edonides, Trieterides, Ogygiae, Mimallonides, Mænads, Thyades and other types of Bacchantes—wild, furious, frenzied women, girdled with dragons and live serpents, their streaming hair bound with vines. They were clothed in deer- and goatskin; they bore small axes, thyrsi, hooks and halberds shaped like pine cones, and peculiar little light shields that rang and clashed if you touched them. These, in time of need, they used for drums and tabors. These women numbered seventy-nine thousand, two hundred and twenty-seven.

Silenus, who enjoyed Bacchus' full confidence, because he had in many instances proven his courage, wisdom and competence, led the vanguard. A small, aged, tremulous man, bent almost double over a bursting potbelly; an old man with long, erectile and pointed ears, with a sharp, aquiline nose, with eyebrows rough and crude as the furrow a plow leaves behind it. Mounted on a fat, well-hung ass, he held a staff in hand, to lay gallantly about him in a fight, if he should have to dismount. He wore a woman's yellow gown.

His troop was made up of young rustics, horned like goats and fierce as tigers; completely naked, they kept continually leaping and prancing in *cordaces* or lascivious dances. These Tytyrs (to use the Doric name), or Satyrs, were eighty-five thousand, six hundred and thirteen strong.

Pan led the rearguard—a terrifying and monstrous creature. Below the waist, he resembled a he-goat: his thighs were very furry. He had a long trailing beard, a crimson, inflamed face, and a pair of perpendicular horns pointing to the dome of heaven. A brave, bold, desperate fellow, easily angered. In his left hand he held a flute; in his right, a crooked stick. His soldiers, too, consisted of Satyrs, Hemipans, Ægipans, Sylvans, Fauns, Fatues, Lemurs, Lares, Elves, Hobgoblins and Poltergeists, numbering seventy-eight thousand, one hundred and fourteen.

The password common to all the host was EVOE.

XL

BACCHUS' ATTACK UPON THE INDIANS, AS PORTRAYED IN MOSAIC IN THE TEMPLE

FURTHER along, Bacchus' battle against the Indians was depicted. Silenus, the leader of the vanguard, with sweat streaming over his forehead, vigorously belabored his ass. The luckless beast kept gaping horribly, driving the flies off, prancing and cavorting about, as if a hornet were caught in its arsehole.

The Satyrs—captains, sergeant-majors, squadleaders and corporals —blew martial, orgiastic airs upon their cow-horns, darted furiously round and round the army, encouraged their comrades to fight valiantly to the accompaniment of reels, prances, leaps, kicks, a flying-out at heels and a sustained bumbardment from the rear. "Evoe!" cried the entire mosaic army. "Evoe!"

The Mænads led the assault upon the Indians, shouting horrendously and setting up an ear-splitting din, as they beat upon their bucklers and tabors. The artist in his design depicted most realistically the air resounding with the clamor of the Bacchantes. His work surpassed the art of Apelles, of Aristides the Theban, and of countless other specialists, in the depiction of lightning, thunder, thunderbolts, winds, words, hobgoblins, spirits and other subjects that defy portraiture.

The next scene showed the Indians, at last aware of the havoc wrought by Bacchus, putting an army into the field: an infinite number of soldiers filed by, in the wake of a battalion of elephants, bearing vast castles on their backs. Very soon, though, the Indian army was in headlong flight, hard-pressed by their own elephants, crazed and panic-stricken by the Bacchantes' horrisonous din.

Silenus was shown viciously spurring on his ass, and fencing with his staff in the classical French style, which is far sounder than the newfangled Italian manner. Master Ass, jaws agape—you would have sworn you heard his braying!—most martially sounded the charge, as he galloped after the elephants. The beast's courage and lung-power were as magnificent as on a famed occasion, during the Bacchanals, when it roused the nymph Lotis, whom Priapus, full of Priapism, sought to Priapize in her innocent sleep.

Pan was pictured frisking about, with his legs twisted around a Mænad or two, exciting them with rustic flute to virtuosities of sword-fleshing, trigger-drawing, exchanging blows at close quarters and contending bravely hand to hand. There were a youthful satyr taking seventeen kings prisoner . . . a Bacchante using her serpents to strike down forty-two captains . . . a small faun bearing away twelve standards captured from the enemy . . . and goodman Bacchus himself, atop his chariot, rambling safely around the battlefield, roaring with laughter, rejoicing and drinking impartially to one and all.

The last part of the design in the temple illustrated the triumph of Bacchus and the spoils of victory.

His triumphal chariot was smothered under ivy—an extreme

rarity—picked on Mount Meros, the only spot in India where it grows. (Much later, Alexander, in his Indian triumph, followed Bacchus' example in this respect.)

Bacchus' chariot was drawn by four elephants harnessed together. (A spectacle subsequently imitated by Pompey the Great in Rome on the occasion of his African triumph.)

Seated in his chariot, Bacchus drank out of a colossal urn. (Many years after, Caius Marius, celebrating his defeat of the Cimbri near Aix-en-Provence, did likewise.)

Bacchus' entire host was crowned with laurel. Their thyrsi, shields, and drums were hidden under it; the lowest denominator, down to Silenus' ass, was lavishly festooned with it.

Beside the chariot walked the captured kings of Ind, fettered with massive gold chains. The whole procession moved forward amid heavenly pomp, ineffable joy and supreme exaltation; warrior after warrior paraded by, bearing trophies and spoils, playing and singing pæans of victory, boisterous rustic songs, and sonorous dithyrambs.

The last scene depicted in the temple presented the land of Egypt with the Nile and its crocodiles . . . its cercopitheci or long-tailed monkeys, its ibises and its baboons . . . its trochili or wrens, standing sentinel over the crocodile to pick its teeth . . . its ichneumons or Pharaoh's mice, which gnaw the crocodile's belly and so cause it to die . . . its hippopotami, and all other animals indigenous to the country. . . .

Bacchus stalked forward, bound for this land, two bulls preceding him. Each bore a word stamped on his hide in golden letters: the first *Apis*, the second *Osiris*.

Indeed, history tells us that Bacchus introduced ox and cow into Egypt from India. In the course of time, they became national deities.

XLI

OF THE WONDERFUL LAMP
THAT LIGHTED THE TEMPLE

BEFORE proceeding to describe the Holy Bottle, I must tell of the wonderful lamp that lighted the temple. It shed such a lavish light about it that, though we were underground, we could see as clearly as when the sun shines, bright and serene, on earth at high noon.

A golden ring, large as a closed fist, was affixed to the centre of the vault. From it hung three slightly smaller chains, beautifully wrought; they were two and one-half feet long, and, to the triangle they formed, held a round disk of fine gold over two and a half cubits in diameter.

This disk was pierced by four holes or orifices. A ball, hollow and open on top, like a lamp, was firmly fastened into each of the holes. These balls, about two spans in circumference, were made of precious stones: one amethyst, another Libyan carbuncle, the third opal, the fourth anthracite. Each was filled with a firewater, which some call *aquavitæ*, others *eau-de-vie*, and still others brandy. This liquid had been distilled five times in a spiral still. It was as incombustible as that oil which Callimachus, the Greek librarian, polygrapher and poet, poured into Pallas' golden lamp, in the Acropolis, in Athens; it would suffice a whole year. In each ball was a flaming wick, partly asbestos fibre, partly flax from Carpasium, in Cyprus. The asbestine flax was like that used of old in the temple of Jupiter Ammon, according to the report of Cleombrotus, that most studious philosopher; like the Carpasian, it was revived rather than consumed by fire.

Some two and one-half feet below this lamp, the chains passed through three handles, projecting from a round lamp of purest crystal, one and one-half cubits in diameter. The open top of this lamp was about two spans wide. In the middle of this opening was a vessel of like crystal, shaped like a pumpkin or a pisspot. Reaching to the bottom of the main lamp, it held so much burning liquid that the flame of the asbestos flax rose to the centre of the main lamp. Thus the whole spherical body of the latter seemed to glow and burn because the flame was at its exact centre.

It is difficult to stare fixedly at the disk of the sun; it was no less so to gaze steadily at this lamp. For its marvellously limpid material and subtle, diaphanous workmanship were obscured by the reflection of the different colors natural to the precious stones of the four small lamps above it. Their glitter flickered variably all over the temple. As this uncertain light flashed upon the polished marble surface of the temple walls, the latter reflected all the colors appearing in the rainbow, when the sun darts its rays upon the rain-drenched clouds.

Admirable as was the lamp's design in general, I considered more admirable still the decoration around its crystal body. In cataglyphic or engraved work, the sculptor had chiselled a group of little naked boys, waging gay and sprightly battle. Mounted upon little hobby-horses, they had whirligigs for lances, and armor cunningly contrived of bunches of grapes, interlaced with vine-leaves.

Art here rendered their childish efforts and naïve gestures so cleverly as to defy nature to do better. Thanks to the bright and changing light within the lamp, these figures did not seem to be engraved in the material, but rather to stand out in relief like grotesques.

XLII

HOW THE PRIESTESS BACBUC SHOWED US A FANTASTIC FOUNTAIN IN THE TEMPLE

As we gazed in ecstasy upon this wondrous lamp and the stupendous structure of the temple, the venerable priestess Bacbuc appeared before us, followed by her attendants. Her face was wreathed in smiles. Seeing us equipped as I described—vine-leaves in our shoes, hats of ivy-leaves on our heads, vine-branches in hand—she led us without further ado to the middle of the temple. Here, under the great lamp, stood the beautiful, fantastic fountain, of material and workmanship rarer than anything Dædalus, or Pluto in his limbo, ever dreamed of.

Its base was of purest, transparent alabaster; it stood somewhat over three spans high. The outside of the fountain was, in shape, a regular heptagon; it was decorated with stylobates (bases bearing columns), arulets (ornaments that looked like little altars), cimasules (mouldings imitating waves), and Doric undulations. The inside of the fountain was exactly round. Midway from each angle-edge rose an orbicular pillar, like an ivory or alabaster cylinder. There were seven in all, one for each angle of the heptagon.

The length of each pillar, from base to architrave, was some seven handbreadths or a little less: in other words, the exact length of a diameter of the interior of the orb passing through the centre. If we glanced behind any one of these concave pillars to see the opposite pillars, we discovered that the pyramidal cone of our line of vision ended at the said centre. There, with the two pillars opposite, we formed the apex of an equilateral triangle: two sides of which equally divided the pillar we wished to measure, then passing on both sides of two pillars that were clear, found, in the first third of the interval between, the base, fundamental line, which, by a test line drawn to the universal centre, equally divided, exactly bisected the distance of the seven pillars. Nor was it possible, starting at the obtuse angle of the edge, to draw a straight line to another pillar opposite; for, as you know, in every odd-sided angular figure, one angle is always inserted between two others.

From this, we understood that seven semidiameters are, in geometrical proportion, compass and distance, somewhat less than the circumference of a circle from which they are extracted—that is, three whole parts with one eighth-and-one-half more, or one seventh-and-one-half less, according to the ancient teachings of Euclid, Aristotle, Archimedes and others.

The first pillar we saw—that which faced the entrance to the temple—was of azure, celestial sapphire.

The second was of hyacinth, a precious stone reproducing not only the color, but also the design of the flower hyacinth. As you may remember, the latter derives its name from the Greek letters A and I, standing for Ajax, whose blood, at his death, was transformed into hyacinths.

The third pillar was of anachite, a diamond, bright and glittering as lightning.

The fourth was of balas ruby, a male stone and therefore more brilliant than the female. It was of the amethyst variety in that its flame and lustre ended in violet and purple.

The fifth pillar was of emerald, five hundred times more magnificent than that of Therapis, the Egyptian sun god—a stone which stood nine cubits high. It was more radiant and scintillating than the jewels placed in the head of the marble lion that stood guard over the tomb of King Hermias (the tyrant of Atarneus and protector of Aristotle) at Cyprus.

The sixth pillar was of agate, more richly veined and dazzling of color than that which Pyrrhus, King of Epirus, valued so highly. Remember, too, that Pyrrhus' stone bore the image of Apollo and the nine Muses playing on the lyre, with the stone's veins reproducing the insignia of each Muse.

The seventh pillar was of transparent syenite or moonstone, white as beryl and clear of hue as the sweetest honey of Hyblan or Hymettan bees. Within it appeared the moon as it looks in the sky, full, invisible, waxing and waning.

The seven stones of which these pillars were fashioned are attributed, by the ancient Chaldeans and magicians, to the seven heavenly planets. This was so illustrated in the temple that the rudest intelligence must have grasped the artist's intent. For each pillar, on a central, perpendicular line to its chapter, bore the appropriate effigy.

The sapphire pillar held a statue of Saturn, moulded of most costly elutian lead, representing the God of Time, scythe in hand, with, at his feet, a gold crane, enamelled in the colors natural to this saturnine bird.

Leftward, the second pillar—that of hyacinth—showed Jupiter in Jupiterial brass or tin, since white was the color sacred to him. On his breast perched a gold eagle, enamelled to the life.

The diamond pillar bore the effigy of Phœbus in purely refined gold, a white chanticleer in his right hand.

The fourth pillar, of ruby balas, held the image of Mars, fashioned of Corinthian brass, with, at his feet, a lion.

The emerald pillar was topped by a statue of Venus in copper. It was of this metal that Aristonides made his celebrated statue of Athamas, when, by means of an amalgam of copper and iron, he was able to portray so realistically Athamas' consternation as he gazed at the son he had killed.

The sixth or agate pillar showed Mercury in hydrargyrum or quicksilver made, fixed, malleable and unmovable. At his feet lay a stork.

The seventh or moonstone pillar presented the moon in silver with a greyhound at her feet.

These statues were all rather more than one-third the size of the pillars they stood on. They were wrought in such admirable, mathematical proportion as to surpass the canon of Polycletus—that statue he made as a model from which his students might learn the essentials of their craft.

The bases of the pillars, the chapters, the architraves, the *zoophores* or sculptured friezes, and cornices were Phrygian work of massive gold, purer and finer than any to be found in the river Lez near Montpellier, in the Ganges in India, in the Po in Italy, in the Hebrus in Thrace, in the Tagus in Spain or in the Pactolus in Lydia. The small arches between the pillars were of the same precious stone as the pillars next to them. Thus a sapphire arch reached over to the hyacinth pillar, a hyacinth to the diamond, and so forth.

Above the arches and chapters of the pillars, on the inward side, surrounded by the planetary statues, rose a crystal cupola to cover the fountain. It was heptagonal at the bottom, spherical at the top. Its crystal was so pure, so diaphanous, so highly polished, so very even and uniform, so perfectly free of vein, cloud, flaw or streak, that even Xenocrates himself, the famous authority on crystals, can never have seen its like.

Within it, in their proper order, were the twelve signs of the zodiac, the twelve months of the year with their properties, the two solstices, the two equinoxes, the ecliptic line, with some of the most noteworthy fixed stars about the Antarctic pole and elsewhere. Their representation was so exquisitely engraved, so artfully and strikingly designed, that I would have sworn here was the work of some king of Egypt: Nekhipso, say, the wizard and astrologer, or Petosiris, the great mathematician.

On top of the cupola, plumb above the centre of the fountain, were three wondrous pearls, all of the same size and all shaped like pears or tears; they were linked together in the form of a lily. So big were they that the flower was larger than a palm branch. From its calyx, rose a carbuncle, fat as an ostrich egg. It was cut heptagonally (seven is a number much beloved of nature) and so prodigiously sparkling that it all but blinded us when we looked up. The blazing sun and the crackling lightning are not more dazzling and unbearably bright.

To tell the truth, were some expert appraisers to value this fountain and lamp, they would undoubtedly maintain that it exceeded all the riches, singularities and treasures of Asia, Africa and Europe put together. The carbuncle alone would have easily darkened the pantharb (that famed fiery-red magnetic jewel of Iarchas, the Indian magician), dimming it as certainly as the sun dims the stars with his noonday rays.

(Queen Cleopatra of Egypt proudly dangled her invaluable pearls from her ear-lobes. In the presence of Mark Antony, the triumvir, she took one, which was worth hundreds of thousands of sesterces, and dissolved it in vinegar. . . . Pompeia Plautina proudly exhibited a dress, covered all over with alternate rows of emeralds and pearls, to the stupefaction of all Rome. She was actually dubbed the storehouse and grave pit of all the conquering robbers of the universe. . . . But Cleopatra and Pompeia paled into insignificance before the incalculable riches in the temple of the Holy Bottle.)

The flow and fall of the fountain's water was assured by three tubes and spouts of genuine pearl, placed in the three equilateral angles already mentioned, and extending over the margin. The tubes were in the form of a bisected snail-like or spiral line.

Having examined them carefully, we were looking in the other direction, when Bacbuc bade us watch the water. Suddenly, we heard a most wonderfully harmonious sound, occasionally muffled or interrupted, as though coming from a great distance or from under the earth. This only made it the more delightful than if we had heard it clearly and near by. Thus our minds were enchanted by the lovely objects we contemplated through the windows of our eyes, and bewitched by the heavenly music wafted through the doorways of our ears.

Bacbuc then addressed us.

"Your philosophers," she said, "deny that all motion is generated by the power of figures. Here you see the contrary. Observe the snail-like or spiral line traced by these tubes which are bisected, as you see. Also remember there is a fivefold infoliature moving at every inward meeting. By this means, the water of this sacred fountain flows into the *vena cava*, rather than into the right ventricle of the heart. This creates such a harmonious music that it ascends as high as the ocean of your world."

XLIII

HOW THE WATER OF THE FANTASTIC FOUNTAIN TASTED LIKE WINE, ACCORDING TO THE IMAGINATION OF THE DRINKERS

THEN Bacbuc directed that we be given an opportunity to drink. Cups, goblets and tumblers of gold, silver, porcelain and crystal were produced, and we were invited to drink the water of this fountain. We did so willingly.

For, if the truth must be told, we are scarcely comparable to sparrows, that must be tapped on the tail before they eat. Nor are we of the same calibre as your droves of fat-headed calves, that must be roundly thrashed with a club before they fall to. We have never refused a courteous invitation to drink.

When we had imbibed, Bacbuc asked us what we thought of the tipple. We replied that it was fine, cool, clear, spring water, more silvery and limpid than the water flowing from Argyrontes in Ætolia . . . from Peneus in Thessaly . . . from Axius in Macedonia . . . or from Cydnus in Cilicia, a brook whose freshness in midsummer so tempted Alexander the Great that, though he foresaw the nefarious consequences attendant upon his rash action, he could not deny himself the transitory pleasure of bathing in it. . . .

"Ha!" cried Bacbuc, "that is what comes of not considering or understanding the motions of the muscular tongue, as the drink glides through, on its way to the stomach. Tell me, noble travellers, are your throats lined, paved and enamelled as was the throat of Pithyllus? (You recall, doubtless, how this gourmand covered his tongue with a mucous matter in order to retain the taste of his food and then cleared it off with a fish.)"

Unless our tongues had been thus previously coated, Bacbuc could not conceive how we had missed the flavor and bouquet of this divine liquid.

"Here," she said, turning to her maids, "bring my scrubbing brushes (you know which!). I'll scrape, rake and cleanse their palates for them."

At once, they brought fine, fat, groaning hams, oxtongues, salt meats aplenty, delicious Bologna sausages, botargos and other roe appetizers, venison and other gullet-sweepers. At Bacbuc's command, we stuffed ourselves until we confessed that our stomachs were successfully scoured, but that we were grievously plagued by thirst.

"Years ago," said Bacbuc, "a very learned and valiant Jewish chieftain was leading his starving people through the wilderness. By dint of prayer he obtained manna from heaven. The people, eating it gratefully, found—by imagination—that it tasted like meat —a taste they had known before in reality. By the same token, drink of this marvellous water and you will find its taste like that of any wine you care to think of. So—use your imaginations! Drink up!"

Which we proceeded to do.

"By God!" Panurge cried, "this is real Beaune! Oh, what wine; it's the best Burgundy ever I drank or may ninety-six devils feed upon my soul. Oh, to keep its taste longer on my tongue, I wish I had a neck three cubits long, as Philoxenus desired, or at least as long as a crane's, which was Melanthius' modest wish!"

"On my faith as a true Lanterner," cried Friar John, "this is real Graves, real, gallant, joyous Bordeaux. For the love of heaven, sweet friend, tell me how you make it?"

"It tastes to me like Mireval, for I thought of Mireval before drinking," said Pantagruel. "The only trouble I find with it is that it's so confoundedly cold. It's colder than ice . . . colder than the waters of Nonacris in Bœotia or Dirce near Thebes . . . colder than the Contoporian spring at Corinth, which froze up the belly and nutritive organs of such as drank of it."

"Drink, once, twice, thrice more," Bacbuc exhorted him. "Change your imagination, every time you drink. You'll find this water's bouquet and body exactly that of the wine you thought of. Then, never again say that anything is impossible to God."

"No one of us ever dreamed of saying so," I replied. "On the contrary, we hold that He is omnipotent."

XLIV

HOW BACBUC EQUIPPED PANURGE SO THAT HE MIGHT HEAR THE WORD OF THE HOLY BOTTLE

Our chat and tippling done, Bacbuc inquired:

"Which one of you would have the Word of the Holy Bottle?"

"I," said Panurge, "I, your most humble servant and your meek little funnel."

"My friend," she said, "I have but one thing to tell you: when you come before the Oracle, make sure that you listen to the word and hear it with one ear only."

"Ho!" said Friar John. "In at one ear and out at the other. Can the Holy Bottle make a silk purse out of Panurge's ear?"

Bacbuc bundled Panurge up in a gabardine cloak . . . clapped a fine white hood over his head . . . crowned him with a felt funnel such as hippocras wine is filtered through . . . at the bottom, instead of a cowl, she hung three skewers . . . invested him with a brace of old-style codpieces in lieu of gloves . . . girded him about with three bagpipes, tied together . . . doused his face three times

in the fountain . . . threw a handful of meal in his eyes . . .
affixed three cock-feathers on the right of his Hippocratic felt headgear . . . ordered him to walk nine times around the fountain, to
give three little leaps in the air and to bump his arse seven times
against the ground. . . .

All the while, she was repeating God only knows what sort of
conjurations in the Etruscan tongue, or reading out of a book of
ritual, which a mystagogue, or priestess of hers, carried after her.

For my part, I firmly believe that neither Numa Pompilius, second
king of Rome, the institutor of Roman religious rites, nor the Cærites
of Etruria, custodians of the Etruscan religion, nor the old Hebrew
captain Moses, ever instituted as many ceremonies as I saw enacted
there. And I am certain that the soothsayers of Memphis, in Egypt,
praying to Apis, their sacred bull; and the Eubœans at Rhamnus in
Attica, invoking Nemesis; and their respective votaries calling upon
Jupiter Ammon and Feronia, his consort, in Italy, never employed
one-half the religious forms I heard.

Having thus accoutred Panurge, Bacbuc led him from us, and,
taking him by the right hand, conducted him out of the temple
through a golden gate. They disappeared into a round chapel made
of sphingitides, stone of Cappadocia, hard as marble, white and
transparent. There were no doors or windows within: the light shone
straight through the rock, dispersing itself throughout the greater
temple so clearly and fully that the sun seemed to be shining out of
the temple rather than into it.

The workmanship was no less admirable than in Apollo's ancient
temple at Ravenna or on the floating island of Chemnis in Egypt.
I must add that the work in this round chapel was so symmetrically
contrived that its diameter was just the height of the vault.

In the middle of it stood a heptagonal fountain of costly alabaster,
with engravings and incrustations of a leaf-pattern all around it. It
was full of water so clear and limpid as to pass for an element in
its very purity.

And, half-submerged in this pool . . . clad in noble crystal
. . . oval in shape save for its muzzle, which was somewhat wider
than consistent with that figure . . . there stood the Holy Bottle.

XLV

HOW THE HIGH PRIESTESS BACBUC USHERED PANURGE INTO THE PRESENCE OF THE HOLY BOTTLE

THERE the noble priestess made Panurge stoop and kiss the brink of the fountain, then rise and perform three ithymbi, or Bacchic dances. This done, she commanded him to sit between two stools, set there for that purpose, his arse on the ground.

Next, opening her book of ritual, and whispering in his left ear, she made him chant the following epileny or vintage song:

> *O Bottle, great*
> *With mysteries,*
> *I am come here*
> *To learn the fate,*
> *Which it shall please*
> *Thee to make clear:*
> *Speak but one word into my ear*
> *To fall like manna on my soul.*

> *Thy twinkling liquor holds the whole*
> *Of truth, which India's conqueror*
> *Lord Bacchus gave thee to control,*
> *And which all honest men adore.*

> *The lies we loathe, the falsehood we deplore*
> *Are not in thee, O wine, deific wine!*
> *Let Noah's sons nail down the ark's trapdoor*
> *And celebrate thy glories, O divine!*

> *Speak to me from thy lofty shrine*
> *That one word which will bring me cheer,*

Let no red drop or white we squeeze
Be wasted while we celebrate.

O Bottle, great
With mysteries,
I am come here
To learn the fate,
Which it shall please
Thee to make clear.

This chant completed, Bacbuc threw something (I don't know what) into the fountain. Suddenly its waters began to boil fiercely like the great monastic pot in the Benedictine abbey of Bourgueil, on high holidays, when cross and banner are brought to it. Panurge, silent, strained one ear towards the Holy Bottle; Bacbuc kneeled by his side.

Presently from the Holy Bottle issued a rumble not unlike the buzz of bees bred in the belly of a young bull, killed and dressed as Aristæus, discoverer and god of apiculture, recommends. Or perhaps the sound might better be compared to the whirr when a bolt flies out of a crossbow, or to a suddenly heavy midsummer shower.

Immediately after, came the single word: *Trinc.*

"God's truth, that Holy Bottle is broken, or—to be truthful—at least cracked. That's how the crystal bottles in our land speak when they burst near the fire!"

Bacbuc rose, pressed Panurge gently under the arm, and:

"My friend," she said, "give thanks to heaven, as reason requires you to, for you have been vouchsafed the Word of the Holy Bottle. And what a word! The most gracious, godliest, most certain word of answer I have ever heard her give since I have officiated here at her most sacred oracle. Rise, friend; let us try the chapter in whose glass this noble word is explained."

"Ay, let us be off," Panurge agreed. "By God, I'm none the wiser than I was. Pray, shed some light on all this. Where's the book? Turn it over: where's that chapter? Let me see your merry gloss."

XLVI

HOW BACBUC INTERPRETED THE WORD OF THE HOLY BOTTLE

BACBUC again threw something into the fountain and immediately the water ceased to boil. Then she led Panurge back to the centre of the greater temple, where stood the fantastic fountain.

Here she produced a large, unwieldy silver book, shaped like one-quarter of a four-volume work of erudite philosophy or, if you prefer, like a half-hogshead of learning. Having dipped it in the fountain, she announced:

"The philosophers, preachers and learned doctors of your world feed you up with fine words, cramming their cant down your ears. Here, on the contrary, we really incorporate our precepts at the mouth. Therefore I shall not tell you to read this chapter or consult that gloss; I prefer to suggest that you taste this succulent chapter or swallow this rare gloss."

We looked at her in amazement.

"In olden days," Bacbuc pursued, "at the Lord's bidding, an ancient prophet of the Jewish race, Ezekiel, ate a book and became scholarly to the back teeth. I now tell you to drink a book to become learned to your very liver. Come, open your jaws!"

Panurge was gaping wide as his jaws would stretch. Bacbuc picked up the silver book—and we watched, spellbound. For we believed it to be a real book, because of its shape: it looked like a breviary. And a breviary it was, too: a tome-shaped flask filled with Falernian wine, every drop of which she made Panurge swallow.

"A notable chapter! A most authentic gloss!" Panurge declared. "Is this all the trismegistian or thrice-mighty Bottle's word meant? I'm very grateful, of course. . . ."

"Exactly that and nothing more," Bacbuc explained. "For *Trinc* is a panomphæan word, that is a word employed, understood and celebrated among all nations. It means simply: *Drink!*

"We in our world," Bacbuc continued, "declared that the word sack was common to all languages and justly admitted in the same sense by all nations. Æsop's fable brought this out, when it showed how all men were born with a sack at the neck, naturally indigent and begging of one another. No king under the arch of heaven, were he ever so powerful, could do without his fellow men; no pauper, were he arrogance personified, could dispense with the rich. Not even the philosopher Hippias, who boasted he could do everything, was able to eliminate his fellow men from his existence."

Well, then—here came the point of Bacbuc's argument—man could not do without a sack. But how much less could he do without a drink!

"That is why," Bacbuc concluded, "we folk here hold drinking, not laughter, to be the essence of mankind. Mind you, I do not mean drinking in the simple and absolute sense in which any beast may be said to drink. No—I mean the drinking of cool, delicious wines. Remember, friends, that by the vine we grow divine: no argument could be surer, no divination less hazardous. Why, your own Academics say as much, when they give the etymology of wine—*vinum* in Latin, ὄινος in Greek—as being connected with *vis*, which means strength and power. Has not wine the power to fill the soul with all truth, wisdom and philosophy?

"So, if you observed what was inscribed in Ionian characters on the temple gate, you understood that truth lurks hidden in wine. Our goddess, the Holy Bottle, therefore directs you to that divine liquor; she bids you to interpret and expound the meaning of your undertaking yourself."

"It is impossible to speak more cogently than this excellent priestess," Pantagruel told Panurge. "I said as much to you when first you spoke to me about it all. *Trinc*, then. What says your heart, elevated as it is by Bacchic enthusiasm?"

"I say this," cried Panurge:

"Trinc! Drink up, by goodman Bacchus!
Let no ponderous problem rack us!
All our quest was one long farce.

I foresee a jogging arse,
Gaining vast momentum under
Good Panurge's wedding thunder.
From my arsenal, I draw
My gigantic pleasure-saw,
Working it in the soft wood
Of Milady's maidenhood.
Trinc! I know I shall be wed.
How my wife will love her bed!
The pot snaps shut, the stout eel wriggles,
Lord! What juicy framblefriggles!
Marriage? Marriage is my oyster!
Harder, deeper, lower, moister,
Toss them down and drain them dry.
Hail, the hymeneal urge
Of the perfect groom, Panurge!
Sing Io pæan! Victory!
Hail, to Bacchus! Hail, to me!
Hail, to marital relations!
Hail, to joyous copulations!
Friar John, I swear that Bottle
Spoke the truth; and I will throttle
Any oaf who dares deny
I'll be married, by and by."

XLVII

HOW PANURGE AND THE REST RHYMED WITH POETIC FRENZY

"HAVE you suddenly gone mad, or are you bewitched?" said Friar John. "Look at the lout foaming at the mouth! Listen to him rhyming! In the name of all the devils of hell, what has he eaten? His eyes are rolling in his fat head like a dying goat's. Is he going to friggle off, or stay here unloading his ripe, poetic dung on us? Give

him some dog's-burr to help him get it off his belly. Or stick your
arm down his gullet to the elbow; that's what the monks do when
they want to scour their paunches. Is he going to take a hair of the
dog that bit him?"

Pantagruel rebuked Friar John, saying:

> *"Believe me, friend, this must be noble Bacchus—*
> *His mad, poetic frenzy will attack us*
> *Through his sweet wine, and grant the gift of song.*

> > *His mind and soul*
> > *Cheered by the bowl*
> > *Sing and extol*
> > *Bacchus; his whole*
> > *Being proclaims*
> > *The wine-god's names.*
> > *Poetic art*
> > *Makes of his heart*
> > *Its home, and uses*
> > *Him like the Muses*
> > *Lyric, rhetoric,*
> > *Rapt, allegoric,*
> > *By hell and Tophet,*
> > *A major prophet*

> *Speaks through his voice; and that man is a stinker*
> *Who dares poke fun at such a noble drinker."*

"What!" Friar John gasped. "You, too, go in for rhyming? God's
truth, we're all properly peppered and poxed. Would to heaven Gargantua could see us in this state. I don't for the life of me know
whether I shan't rhyme like you or not. The whole place is grimy
with rhyme. Yes, by St. John, I *will* poetize, like the rest of you. I can
feel it coming. But forgive me, I beg you, if my rhymes are not of
the quality of crimson silk."

Then, scratching his head, he recited:

> *"Heavenly Father, let a man turn*
> *Prayerfully to you, Whose labor*

Made the water into wine.
Hear this humble prayer of mine:
Change my tail into a lantern,
To shed light upon my neighbor."

Panurge then continued:

"The Pythian tripod, by my soul!
A very noble three-legged bowl,
Never rendered, through its chapter,
Oracle more terse or apter
Than this admirable fount.
I would swear, to good account,
It has been transported here
From far Delphos. Had its clear
Waters been beheld by great
Plutarch, he could then relate,
According to his savant wish,
Why oracles were mute as fish
In the Delphic temple. . . . I
Can explain the reason why:
Fate's great tripod does not stand
Elsewhere; it is here at hand,
Ever ready to relate
All men's destiny and fate.
The tripod is this Holy Flask
Filled with wine. You need but ask
And you shall be straightway told
Thoughts of silver, words of gold.
Friar John, while we are here,
Test the Bottle without fear,
Ask of its thrice-mighty voice
(Which has made my soul rejoice)
Whether there be any reason
Why you should not wed in season.
Take these objects, leap and prance
In a whirling-dervish dance,
Throw some flour upon the pool,

Ask the Bottle, monkish fool,
While we linger here and tarry;
Ask her: will you ever marry?"

Friar John, furious, replied:

"Marry? By the giant boot
On the huge and saintly foot
Of St. Benedict, you prater!
By the good man's holy gaiter,
All who know my heart will vouch
That I'll fill no wedding-couch.
Better drain a cup of shame
Than to play the wedding-game,
Better wallow in the mud
Than spill hymeneal blood.
Never shall a wife rob me
Of my treasured liberty,
Whom earth's loftiest commander,
Pompey, Cæsar, Alexander
Would not find apt to behave
Like a bondsman and a slave."

Panurge, pulling off his fantastic costume and mystic accoutrement, replied:

"You shall rot, you dirty beast,
Damned to hell; while I shall feast
Like a king in Paradise
And, if that should not suffice,
I shall drench—hey-diddle-diddle!—
Your foul soul with my fair piddle. . . .
When you dwell in Satan's arms,
Should his wife prefer your charms,
Taking it into her noodle
To enjoy your great whangdoodle
And accept a few fell stitches
From the awl inside your breeches,

> *Pluto surely will not wrangle*
> *While you and his lady brangle.*
> *So, live happy and fare well*
> *In your marriage bed in hell."*

"Devil gripe you, you cursed fool!" cried Friar John. "I can rhyme no more; the rheum grips my gullet. Let us pay the score here, and be off."

XLVIII

HOW WE TOOK LEAVE OF BACBUC AND DEPARTED FROM THE ORACLE OF THE HOLY BOTTLE

"Do not worry about the score here," Bacbuc replied. "So long as you are satisfied, we ourselves are. Here below, in these circumcentral regions, we do not place sovereign good in taking and receiving, but in bestowing and giving. We find no happiness in gain and profit (as possibly the teachers of the sects in your world do) but vast happiness in charity and help. All I ask of you is to leave a record of your names and native cities, in this book of ritual, here."

She opened a fine large book and we dictated the desired information to one of her mystagogues who, with a gold stylus, traced some fine lines. She looked as if she were writing, yet when she had finished there was no sign of any characters.

Bacbuc then filled three small leather flasks with fantastic water and thrust them in our hands, saying:

"Go, my good friends; may you depart under the protection of that intellectual sphere, whose centre is everywhere, whose circumference is nowhere, and whom we call God. When you return to your world, bear witness to your fellow men that the greatest treasures and most wonderful things lie hidden underground—and not without reason.

"Of yore, Ceres was worshipped by the entire universe, because she taught mankind the art of husbandry and, by the use of corn, which she invented, put an end to their brutish diet of acorns. Bitterly Ceres lamented when her daughter, Proserpine, was banished to Hades to dwell with Pluto. For Ceres was jealous; she foresaw that her daughter would find more delights and blessings underground than ever she, Ceres, above.

"Your wise Prometheus discovered the art of bringing down thunder and celestial fire on to earth, for the use of men. What have you done with it? Surely, you have lost it; it is nowhere on your hemisphere. Yet, here below, we possess it. How often you marvel, without cause, when you see whole cities struck by lightning and destroyed by ethereal fire. You are at a loss to know who visited such catastrophes upon you, by whom they were brought down and to what end. But to ourselves, they are familiar and useful.

"Your philosophers who complain that the ancients have left them nothing to write about or invent, are obviously very much mistaken. The phenomena you see in the sky, the wonders earth, sea and river offer you are not to be compared to what is hidden in the womb of earth.

"For this reason, the subterranean ruler is in almost every language accorded the epithet of rich—Pluto, Dis and countless others. Your philosophers must learn to apply their energies and to direct their studies towards the search for eternal truth. They must pray for the assistance of the sovereign God, Whom the Egyptians of old used to call, in their language, the Hidden, the Concealed, the Absconce . . . Whom they used to invoke by that name . . . Whom they used to implore to reveal and manifest Himself unto them. . . .

"When your philosophers have done this, God will discover and make Himself known unto them; He will not only teach them to know His creatures, but Himself also. Thus they will be guided by good Lanterns.

"For all the philosophers and sages of antiquity have deemed two things essential in order to pursue safely and pleasantly the search for wisdom and the road to God: first, God's guidance; then, man's aid.

"So, among the philosophers, Zoroaster took Arimaspes as a companion on his travels; Æsculapius, Mercury; Orpheus, Musæus;

Pythagoras, Aglaophamus. Thus, among princes and warriors, Hercules, in his most difficult undertakings, was aided by his bosom friend, Theseus; thus Ulysses had Diomedes; and Æneas, Achates. Thus, you too came here under the guidance of your illustrious Dame Lantern.

"Now depart, in the name of God, and may He guide you ever."